Shelby Lies

ANGELA S. MOORE

Copyright © 2024 Angela S. Moore
All rights reserved
First Edition

PAGE PUBLISHING
Conneaut Lake, PA

First originally published by Page Publishing 2024

ISBN 978-1-64350-107-9 (pbk)
ISBN 978-1-64350-108-6 (digital)

Printed in the United States of America

"Oh my gosh, I didn't realize what time it is," Ailese said to herself as she was proofreading her presentation that she had been working on for weeks. Ailese wanted her speech to be perfect; it had to be. She was going to be presenting her presentation in two days in front of very important people, friends, colleagues, and most of all, vice presidents and lawyers from top law firms. People who were very important would be there. Ailese was a role model to a lot of people. She changed a lot of people's lives. They looked up to her, and she came from a long way. Just a few years ago she was a secretary, working in the very same office, running errands, getting coffee, and making copies—pleasing everyone. She worked hard to get where she is now, the President of Lindell & Co., which she helped build from the ground up, and she believed in her multibillion-dollar company and was very proud of it!

Ailese was a very beautiful woman. She had the darkest brown eyes that they looked black, she would receive so many compliments on her eyes. She was very ladylike, carried herself very well, dressed well, and made sure 100 percent of the time that nothing was out of place, not her hair, not her clothes—everything matched perfectly. Even though Ailese wasn't a size 2, and never was and never wanted to be, she was a beautiful woman with curves in all the right places who attracted a lot of men—young, old, white, black,

Hispanic, you name it. And she was "doing something right," her friends would say to her. Ailese wasn't good at taking compliments because she was a bit insecure, but you would never know it; she would hide it a lot. Ailese was the type of woman that didn't have a conceited bone in her body. She just carried herself well, and it was how she was raised.

Her skin was brown and flawless. Her hair changed like the weather. Ailese always had a new hairstyle; she never kept a hairstyle for more than a week. She even had her own trademark. If she would wear her hair down, she would wear a silk scarf around the crown of her head. Her friends used to tease her when they were younger because of the way she carried herself. They would joke and say, If you needed lotion, you could always count on Ailese having some in her purse Ailese would carry her makeup, mirror, hairbrush, and whatever she was wearing, perfume or lotion that she was wearing that day would be in her purse.

Ailese had an okay life. Her mother, Alonda, was the oldest of her siblings, she was the only girl. She had two brothers that lived in another state. Her first husband died when Ailese was very young. She had a stepfather named Don Zell. Everyone called him Don for short. Ailese loved him like he was her real father. She loved him unconditionally, especially because Don loved her mom unconditionally. He made her mom so happy, and that mattered a lot to Ailese. Ailese's mother had been through a lot of bad relationships before Don came into their lives. Ailese only had a younger brother, named Allen, who lived in Sabella Hills, California. He was married with no kids. He was three years younger than Ailese. They would visit one another whenever they could. Allen had his own booming business and traveled a lot. Ailese was so proud of her brother. They were proud of one another's accomplishments.

Ailese would tell anyone that her mother always instilled in her brother and her that education was very important. "Be strong, you can do anything," her mom would say to her children, and those words of her mother always stuck in both their heads. Her mother had given her children things that she didn't have growing up, and one of them was determination. She was determined to see both of her children graduate and walk across that stage. Dropping out of school was not an option! Alonda made sure that her children did well in school and made goals for themselves. "Finish what you started, and there is no such word as *can't*," she would tell Allen and Ailese.

"I have got to get going if I want to pick up my surprise dinner for Mikell, smiling to herself. She put all her papers neatly in her folder, and tucked the folder in to her briefcase and made sure she had everything before she turned off all the lights. Ailese and Mikell met each other through a mutual friend, named D'Andra. D'Andra and Ailese had been friends since they were in kindergarten. They're practically sisters. They met while living in the same apartment complex. They stirred up a conversation and just hit it off. They've been inseparable ever since. D'Andra owned her own business as well. She owned a magazine company, which was doing great. She's had her magazine company for over five years now D'Andra was the only child. She was a very smart, beautiful woman. She turned heads when she would walk into a room. She wooed men with her flawless caramel skin and her light green eyes. D'Andra was Caucasian and Asian. Her green almond-shaped eyes came from her mother. Her hair, was wavy and curly, which went down past her shoulders. When D'Andra would get tired of it being curly and wavy, she would straighten her hair; it would be silky smooth. D'Andra would wear eyeliner and lip gloss and sometimes foundation or eye shadow on special occasions.

D'Andra was short and slim. She would never gain weight. She hated working out, and Ailese would jokingly say that she hated her because she had that high metabolism that she would kill for. D'Andra looked up to Ailese as her mentor. She thought that Ailese was the strongest, most beautiful woman she'd ever met in her life. D'Andra cherished their sisterly relationship. They both always had each other's back no matter what, and they never ever judged each other.

As time went by, Mikell and Ailese realized that they shared some of the same friends and were at the same gatherings but never spoke to one another. It's a small world," they would say to each other.

As Ailese pushed the down button on the elevator, she called home to check in with the kids. Her oldest answered the phone. "Hi, Mom!" She was very excited. "Aunt D is on her way to pick us up to take us to the movies. She's taking us to see—"

Ailese cut her off. "Honey, I'm sorry to cut you off, but I need you to do me favor, okay?"

"Okay, Mom, what do you need me to do?"

"I need you to go in my room and look in my top drawer, and you'll see a red velvet bag. Could you please give that to Aunt D, please. It's very important that she gets that. Okay, hun?"

"I got it, Mom, no problem. I'll make sure that Aunt D gets the bag."

"Thanks. Okay, I've got to go, and I'm sure whatever movie Aunt D takes you to see, you guys will have fun. Love you. I will see you tomorrow, sweetie. Bye."

"Bye, Mom."

As Ailese hung up her cell phone, the elevator door opened. She was the only one on the elevator. Even though it was getting dark, she knew that she was safe. Ruben the security guard would be waiting on the second floor to walk her to her car and make sure that she gets out of the parking garage safely.

"Hi, Ruben, how are you this evening?"

"I'm good, Mrs. LaShay," said Ruben with a smile on his face. Ruben was a very handsome, husky, dark man, well groomed and very respectful.

"I hear congrats is in order. I heard that you are expecting your first child, must be very exciting, huh?"

Ruben looked at Ailese and gave her a huge smile. "Yes, it is, yes, it is. I can't wait. I am counting the days, Mrs. LaShay."

"I am sooo happy for you and your wife. I don't care what anyone else say, kids are a joy."

"I agree, and they grow up sooo fast. I still remember when my niece was born. She's five years old now. I'm like, where did the time go, you know?"

"I hear you, so that's why you take dozens and dozens of pictures," Ailese said as she laughed. As the conversation went on, time went by fast, and before they knew it, they were at Ailese's car.

"Well, here we are," said Ruben. He made sure that Ailese was situated in her car before waving good-bye.

As Ailese went on to the main street, she thought about how much fun she knew that the girls were having with their aunt D'Andra and how much she's been there for the kids and for her no matter what. D'Andra was there and had always been since day one, even when Ailese was in labor, worked late, or even in a midlife crisis. One time when Ashanee was three years old, she had spiked a fever, and Ailese panicked because her fever was high but her body temperature wasn't. Ailese thought that the thermometer was broken. She called D'Andra, luckily, she lived only five minutes away. Ailese just felt so safe when D'Andra was around. D'Andra told Ailese that they should just take Ashanee to the emergency room, just to be safe. When they arrived at the hospital, Ashanee was seen right away, and she did have a fever, but she wasn't in jeopardy. The doctor explained that there was a virus going around, and he gave instructions on how to get rid of the virus. D'Andra stayed at Ailese's house until Ashanee got better.

Ailese thought about the look on her husband's face when she surprised him with his favorite dinner, his gifts, some grown folks' time and conversation, and Mikell had no idea. She loved surprising him. She loved seeing the look on his face, the joy in his eyes, the extra kisses he'd give her. Mikell was a very affectionate man, a gentleman, very loving. He was the type of man that didn't care who was around or where they were; he would kiss Ailese very passionately. Mikell had a very unique face, long eyelashes, thick eyebrows, and chubby cheeks. He kept his hair well groomed. He was a husky, good-looking tall African American man. He was five feet eleven, even though people would tell Mikell that he looked six feet. He was the eldest of two brothers and one sister. Mikell had a brother named William and Brandon, his sisters name was Aileyah. Mikell loved Ailese unconditionally; a lot of women would love to have a man like Mikell.

Mikell's mom and dad, Verneil and Johnnie, were still alive. They traveled a lot. They had been to Paris, France, Hawaii, and even Africa. Mikell talked his mom and dad into retiring early when Mikell was financially able to take care of his mom and dad. They agreed to retire early. His mom and dad did a lot of volunteer and charity work to pass the time. Ailese had always gotten along with her in-laws. She loved her in-laws and felt that she was lucky. A lot of people despised their in-laws. They all treated each other with respect, so everyone got along. Mikell's parents lived about forty minutes away and would visit from time to time; they loved their grandchildren, always spoiling them whenever they got the chance. They actually had six grandchildren. Mikell's brother William was openly gay. No one loved him any less, and they all accepted him with open arms. When Ailese met Mikell's family, they quickly welcomed her and Armont with open arms and treated them as their own.

As Ailese pulled up to her driveway, she was relieved that Mikell wasn't home yet and that she had more time to get things ready. Ailese wanted everything to be perfect. Ailese went into the house and threw her keys on the table that was by the door and kicked off her shoes and headed straight for the kitchen. As she went to the refrigerator, she saw a note from her son stating that he would be at his father's until Sunday. Ailese and Mikell's home was very simple but beautiful. It was a one-story house. Ailese always wanted a house that was a bit unique. The house looked like a one-story house from the outside, but it was actually a three-story house. Ailese and Mikell had their house built in a unique style. There were a few stairs that led to rooms; for example, there were stairs that led to Mikell and Ailese's room, then you would keep walking, and a few stairs led to another room and so on. The house complemented Ailese and Mikell's taste. They didn't hire any fancy decorators; they both worked hard on decorating the house, but one thing Ailese did have a hand in, and only hers, was the kitchen. It had everything from

Sub-Zeros, Fisher and Paykel, to Viking. She had always told herself that when she was able to afford them, she wanted her whole kitchen to be decorated in only the finest.

The house was a six-bedroom home. The only stairs that were in the house led to the den, in which Mikell would spend some of his time, writing songs or watching some television.

Ailese's children were very responsible when it came to communication. Mikell and Ailese had two children together, two daughters, Ashanee and Adrieana. Ashanee was eleven years old, and Adrieana was twelve years old. The oldest was Armont, he was sixteen years old. Armont was born before Ailese and Mikell were together. Mikell treated Armont like he was his own. Mikell was in Armont's life when he was very young.

Even though Armont's biological father was still in his life, Armont called Mikell Dad and looked up to him. Mikell had always been there for Armont; they always had a great relationship.

Ailese started to prepare dinner. Her cell phone rang. "Man!" she said to herself. It was her husband, the love of her life, her everything. "Hey, you, I miss you so much. Are you on your way home?"

"Yes, sweetie, I am. I just wanted to tell that I'm stuck in traffic, and I didn't want you to worry, honey."

"Well, thank you for calling to tell me that. Was there an accident or something?"

"No, it's just Friday traffic, it looks like it's getting a little better. So how was your day today, babe?"

"Oh, busy as usual, you know we're getting ready for our presentations for next week so we can pitch some new ideas before the New Year gets in."

"I know how that is. Well, babe, have you finished your presentations?"

"Yes, we did. I think we have a lot of strong points."

"Well, that sounds good, hun. Only my baby can hold down that company with her eyes closed and her hands tied behind her back."

Ailese chuckled.

"It's true. Okay, well, I will be there shortly. Is there anything you need me to pick up for you? Are you craving anything?"

"No, babe, I just want you home."

"Okay, hun, I will see you later, and I love you and miss you so much."

"Bye, bye, babe." Ailese hung up the phone.

When Ailese was done preparing Mikell's surprise, she lit beautiful vanilla-scented candles, which were their favorites. She made sure nothing was out of place. She looked in the mirror probably over ten times to make sure her outfit was perfect for the occasion. Just as she sat down with a glass of sweet tea, she heard Mikell's keys going in to the lock. She met him at the door, in a beautiful leopard-print silk dress. "Hey, sexy! Surprise!" Mikell hugged Ailese tight and kissed her passionately. Mikell put his keys on the table by the door and dropped everything else neatly by the door. Ailese took his hand and led him into the kitchen. "Baby, I'm the luckiest man in the whole wide world! Oh my gosh, you have all my favorite food from my favorite restaurant! Thanks, baby!"

Mikell pulled out a chair for his wife and catered to her needs. He fixed her plate before he fixed his. "Wow, hun, this looks so good, thanks again, and did I mention how beautiful you look, as always."

"Thanks, hun. So how was your day today? Did you get through all of your meetings?"

"Surprisingly we did, we signed the new artist that we saw at Jeremy's club last week, remember her?"

"Oh yes, I do, she was really, really good."

"Baby, I wish you would reconsider what we talked about. I want you to sing on a few songs and write some songs for some of the artists, you're so talented."

Ailese loved to sing. Music was her first love, and she dreamed of having someone sing her songs that she had written; she even dreamed of being in the studio and making a full-length album. Ailese's voice was beautiful. Her mom put her in a choir at a young age. Her family was very gifted, and the majority of her family had beautiful voices.

Ailese was offered a lot of deals. One time she was asked to sing some songs for a local producer from her hometown. He heard her sing when Ailese was in the studio, singing backup for her friend. He really thought highly of Ailese and told her point-blank that she was way too good to be a backup singer, but she was just doing her friend a favor. He hounded and hounded her, but she turned him down because her oldest son was very young. This was before Ailese had met Mikell. Ailese was a very dedicated mother, sometimes she would think about what would have happened if she had said yes, especially when she was homeless once.

Ailese was very dedicated to her business and her work. She was sort of a perfectionist, or you can say if it weren't a certain way, there would be an issue. Ailese would dream about what she would wear to work, church, or even an outing, how her hair would look; it would be in her head, and when she would wear the outfit, have her hair a certain way even her jewelry! She was always this way. Some of her friends would tease her, and they would say to her, you are the girliest girl I have ever met.

SHELBY LIES

Her nickname was Laydee, but Ailese added Mrs. Laydee. She loved that name a lot; it described her to a tee.

"Mik, you know that I have a lot to focus on, and I know that you guys are looking for something fresh and new, but I just can't right now. I mean I do appreciate you thinking of me, but I can't right now, I'm sorry."

"Yes, I know. I'm sorry that I brought it up. We need to enjoy ourselves this weekend. I love you so much, Lee."

"I love you too, Mik," said Ailese.

They enjoyed the meal and the great conversation. Mikell commented on the evening; he wanted to make sure that Ailese knew he appreciated everything.

"Close your eyes, hun. I will be right back. I have a surprise for you, okay?"

"Okay." Ailese excitedly closed her eyes and waited patiently. Mikell got up from the table and went to his car. He opened the passenger door and pulled out two big boxes and one huge bag, and hurried inside. "Open your eyes," he said as he walked back to the kitchen table. Ailese opened her eyes and saw Mikell standing there with the gifts. "Oh my gosh, hun, it's not my birthday."

"I know," said Mikell. These are I just love you gifts." She kissed him and took the gifts. She opened the first box, it was four outfits from her favorite clothing store. The second box was a beautiful coat. She then opened the bag; it was filled with her favorite lotions and sprays and perfume from Victoria's Secret and Bath and Body Works and Macy's. "Thank you so much. You knew that I needed all of this."

"Baby, look in the bag again. I think you missed something." She looked in the bag again and pulled out a beautiful purple box. She opened it and gasped. "Oh my gosh, how did you remember that I wanted this? We were looking at these last week." She pulled out a set of gold and silver rings with necklaces to match. Ailese loved jewelry so much she could never have enough. "I went back the next day and bought it." She hugged Mikell and started to tear up. "Baby, you're so good to me all the time. Thank you so much!"

"Don't cry, I hope those are tears of joy, right?"

"Yes, there are. Mikell, can I ask you to do me a favor?"

"Sure whatever you need."

"Could you go into the room and get my favorite blanket, I'm a little chilly."

"Sure, hun."

As Mikell went into the bedroom, Mikell saw a huge card with his name on it, which read, "Open me." The card told him to open the box that was on the bed. He gasped. "Oh my gosh!" He came out of the room with a new laptop and a new laptop case. "Baby, I don't know what to say!" He was so excited. Lee, you knew how much I wanted and needed one of these for the studio, but never really had the time to look for one."

"Well, you don't have to look any further."

As time passed, Mikell and Ailese were praising one another and looking at their gifts. The telephone rang. "Hello." It was their daughter, Ashanee, on the other end. "Hey, Mom. I just wanted to say good night to you and Dad. Is Dad up?"

"Yes, he is. You want to talk to him?"

"Yes please, I love you, Mom. Good night," said Ashanee.

"Good night and I love you so much and I miss you, Ash." Ailese called her by that name for short. Ailese handed the phone to Mikell.

"Hey, baby, I miss you guys. Hey, where is your sister?"

"She's already asleep. She said to tell you that she loves you guys. You know how Adrieana gets when she's worn out, Dad."

Mikell chuckled. "Give your sister a kiss for us, okay?"

"Okay, Dad. Dad, Uncle Chris wants to talk to you."

"Okay, hun, put him on before you go. Is there anything else?"

"No, just that I love you. Here is Uncle Chris. Bye, Dad."

"Bye, hun," Mikell said as he looked at Ailese to make sure it was okay to talk to Chris.

"Hey, buddy, what's going on? I won't hold you too long, I was just wondering if we could keep the girls until Sunday afternoon?"

"Okay, that will be fine with me. Let me just check with Lee, hold on."

Babe, Chris wanted to know if he could keep the girls until Sunday afternoon. Would that be okay?"

"Yes that's fine, let me talk to him when you're done, okay?"

"Yeah, that would be cool, are you guys sure?" Aunt D'Andra took the phone from Chris.

"Hey, guys, I wanted to spend more time with the girls, that's all. You know how much we enjoy them. I wanted to take them shopping—girl stuff, you know."

"Okay," Mikell said. "Okay," Ailese said as well. "So it's settled, we will drop the girls off around 3:30? Is that okay?"

"Okay, see ya then." Mikell hung up the phone.

"Well, I guess we can extend our plans for the weekend. I wanted to take you up to Romanville and stay at the suite we stayed in for our honeymoon. Do you want to go there with me and leave in an hour?"

"Mik, yes! Oh my gosh, what made you want to go there?"

"Well, I have been wanting to take you there for awhile. We both have been so busy with work, life, and the kids, and we deserve it. I just want to spoil you every chance I get."

"Aw, hun, I love you so much with all my heart. You work so hard, how do you find the time to think and plan?"

"Well, to be honest, Lee, only when I am asleep." Mikell chuckled.

Mikell and Ailese went into their room to start packing. They made sure that they had everything. Mikell cleaned up the kitchen and tidied up the house as Ailese was finishing packing her things. Mikell went back into the bedroom to grab their luggage. "Babe, I'm going to load the car, okay?"

"Okay, hun," Ailese shouted to Mikell as she was changing in the restroom.

When Mikell finished loading the car, he looked up, and there was Ailese, with her hands on her hips. "Hun, you have a phone call, it's a female by the name of Cara Cabbs?"

"Oh, thank you, thank you, hun. I love you! I will be right back, and I will explain to you why this phone call is very important, okay?" He kissed her on the lips and quickly ran into the house. Ailese double-checked to make sure all the luggage was in the car. She took the keys out of the ignition and locked the car and set the alarm.

Ailese walked back into the house. She didn't see Mikell as she entered the house. He may be out in the back, she thought to herself. She went back into the bedroom and picked up her cell phone, keys, and sunglasses and grabbed some bottled water out of the refrigerator, and headed out to the car.

While she waited for her husband to come out, she called her voice mail to check her messages that she had been ignoring while spending time with Mikell earlier. She had thirteen new messages. Ailese sighed. "Man, what's up with that, and on a Friday night too?" She took her pen and pad out of her purse, which she carried everywhere with her. Even though she was smart, she could be a bit forgetful, so she had to write all info on paper so she wouldn't forget.

Ailese wrote down all of the messages, a few of them were from some colleagues and people who were just touching base with her. Ailese called them back so she wouldn't have to when she had got back on Sunday. When she was done with her last call, Mikell eased in on the driver's side. "Sorry, babe, I had to take that call, I have been waiting for that call all week. Well, let me tell you what the call was about. We have a new artist that wants out of their contract, and we had to wait for his attorney to touch base with us so that we could release him from his contract because he's really good and a good performer. We just wanted to get through all the red tape. Sorry if I took too long."

"Mik, you know that I don't mind. I know that you like to take care of business. I knew that the day we met, I just wanted to get on the road, that's all, and I thought that your colleagues were going back on their word when they promised us that you wouldn't have to go into the office no matter what, that's all. Is everything okay?"

"Yes, it's great. Now let's talk about something else. Don't get me started talking about work, you know I'll never shut up." Mik laughed.

Mikell was very proud of his accomplishments; he was very lucky that he got to do what he was good at—actually, not only good, but perfect! His work was perfection; all the producers could only wish to be as perfect as Mikell was.

Mikell was always asked, what was his secret? Mikell would say, "There is no secret, just hard work."

As they pulled into the hotel's parking garage, Mikell was very eager and excited because Ailese had no idea that there were more surprises waiting for her in the hotel room. Mikell even checked on their reservations when he was finished with his phone call earlier to make sure that everything was in place like he requested with the front desk; everything was going as planned.

The hotel was called The Marble. It was a beautiful hotel and was well known for their beautiful marble structures and statues. The staff there were very nice and catered to your every need. There was nothing that they could not do to make you feel comfortable. The hotel had ten floors and enormous windows. The view was so beautiful; it was Ailese's favorite view—purple lilies surrounded by a park. When you were on the tenth floor, the people in the park looked very small. Mikell and Ailese would walk the park whenever they would stay there.

"Ailese, let me take your bags, okay? They are a bit too heavy for you to carry."

"Babe, you have too much to carry. Okay, let me take the small ones. I can do that at least."

Mikell gave her the two small bags and smiled at her. Mikell made sure he got off the elevator first so that Ailese didn't see his surprise on the bed. As Mikell slid the hotel key and opened the door, he put down the bags and requested that Ailese close her eyes. When she opened them, she gasped!

"Mikell, oh my word!" There were four bags from Ailese's favorite clothing stores. "Open them, sweetie," said Mikell. Ailese opened the purple bag. She pulled out a beautiful elegant purple satin dress, a cocktail dress. Mikell knew that she would love it! "Mikell, what is all this for? You spoil me too, too much!"

"Well, we have reservations tomorrow at 7:00 p.m. at one of your favorite restaurants, and that dress will look great on you, but you will have to see which one tomorrow."

"Okay," said Ailese as she opened the rest of the bags. Mikell really went all out. He sometimes felt bad that he worked so much, and he sometimes didn't see Ailese for days, missing breakfasts, lunches, and dinners with her, not to mention with the kids too. He didn't mind spending the money on her; she deserved it, and it wasn't their anniversary or birthday. It was because he loved her so much!

After unpacking and hanging up their clothes, Ailese asked Mikell if he wanted to go to the coffeehouse downstairs, because she was so excited that she couldn't sleep. Mikell gave her a look. "Hun, are you sure that's all?"

"Yes, that's all." They went to the coffeehouse that was on the first floor of the hotel and talked for a bit. Ailese had a hard time sleeping sometimes, her mind never stopped working, Ailese had a bit of anxiety, she gets over whelmed very easily and wouldn't sleep. Sometimes Ailese would have nightmares of her past. As a child Ailese felt as though she was never good enough and that is why she is somewhat of a perfectionist, even though Ailese never would see it that way, she saw it being thorough and neat. Ailese had one bad relationship in her life; the man mentally and physically abused her badly, before Ailese even knew what was happening the damage had been done.

Ailese had to have weekly sessions, at first she was a bit embarrassed that she had to see a shrink, but as time passed she felt that she was making progress. Sometimes she would have nightmares of him abusing her like he did, he would make her feel low, unwanted. Ailese's mother confronted her about the man and asked her if something was going on, Ailese instantly started crying and wept for hours, her mother took her in her arms and held her, reassured her that everything would be alright. The next day Alonda took Ailese back to her home and confronted the man that had been mentally, physically and emotionally abusing her daughter for quite some time now, Alonda had a huge heart but when it came to her children she was like a lion protecting their cubs.

Alonda told the man that he needed to leave at once and to never show his face again! Even though she knew that her children could fight their own battles, Alonda was fighting this one. The man packed his things and left, and was never seen again. Ailese moved to Shelby and closed that chapter of her life.

"Are you ready for bed, Lee?" Ailese yawned. "Yes I am even though I thought the coffee would keep me up for a while longer, let's go up to bed."

Ailese slept like a baby so did Mikell. Mikell was up before Ailese. He kissed her on the lips until she woke up. "Hey, you do you want to grab a shower with me?"

"Okay, yawned Ailese. Why not." They both got ready and both agreed to go out to breakfast and look at some shops, Ailese loved long walks, she saw it as exercising too, she didn't exercise to get skinny she exercised for herself and she didn't want to gain extra weight. Ailese was the last one to get ready of course. I'm ready babe, do we have everything we need?"

"I'm going to double check right now, looks like we do." Ailese came out to where Mikell was, he looked at her and told her that she looked so beautiful, she had worn one of the outfits he bought for her, it was a long flowing dress, with beautiful butterflies, the butterflies looked like they were flying on the dress, it was perfect for Ailese, her shape was beautiful he thought to himself. "Thanks, Mik."

Well let me check to make sure I have everything too, looks like we're ready to go." Mikell swiped the hotel key and made sure it was locked. They went to breakfast at a small café, Mikell and Ailese both ordered omelets and coffee, with toast. They enjoyed their meal and planned out their day. Ailese excused herself to wash her hands and touch up her lip gloss, when she was done, she looked up and a woman was having a conversation with her husband. Ailese wasn't the jealous type, her motto was; if they're happy with you they won't stray, if they stray they're not happy, to put it plain and simple, Ailese was a lover not a fighter, no man was worth fighting over, not even her husband.

Ailese trusted her husband, she walked over to her seat, "Hello," Ailese said to the woman. Mikell immediately introduced Ailese to the woman, "Sharon this is my beautiful wife, Ailese." "Hello, I've heard so much about you it's so good to finally meet you." "Thank you." "Sharon and I have been working together with one of her artist that she's promoting, we wrote a few songs together."

"Oh wow! How exciting." "I hear that you have a beautiful voice, Ailese, I would love to hear you sing sometime."

I know that Mikell has been wanting you to sing some songs that we have written, he talks about how beautiful your voice is." "Well thank you, I write songs as well, even though that is my passion I do have a business that depends on me and that needs my undivided attention."

"I do understand that Sharon said, with a smile on her face.

"Well, I better get going. You two have a great day, okay, bye." Mikell and Ailese said bye at the same time Sharon exited the door.

"So, she's nice, but I don't recall you ever mentioning her." "I have, I'm sure I have," said Mikell with a puzzled look on his face. Ailese smiled at him.

"Are you ready to go?" "Yes, I am! Let's go shopping! Ailese and Mikell grabbed their belongings and headed to the car. Ailese saw a jewelry store, she told Mikell to pull over. Ailese loved handmade jewelry; from time to time she made some herself and was very good at it. They got out of the car and entered the shop. A woman dressed in African attire greeted them.

"Mikell, look at all the fascinating things that they have here. Let's pick out something for your mom and the girls, oh, and D too, okay?" "Okay, Mikell said as he walked to the other side of the store. Ailese picked out turquoise, amber, silver, and gold jewelry. She also picked out some unique one-of-a-kind pieces as well. Mikell came over to Ailese with what he had picked out. They both admired their choices. They went to the cash register to pay for the jewelry. The woman in the African attire asked if they found everything that they needed, Ailese and Mikell told the woman they were satisfied, and praised her shop. The woman put the jewelry in individual satin sacks in different beautiful colors.

Ailese was very pleased with the purchases. "So, let's go to a shop that you will like, babe." As they walked down the street, Mikell stopped at a music store that had records, record players, etcetera. They both went in and looked around. "Wow! Mikell said, they have a lot of cool stuff in here. I'm going to look around. We can meet back up here in the front of the store, is that okay?"

"Yes, okay." Ailese kissed Mikell on the lips. "I love you," "I love you too," said Mikell. They parted ways.

If there was one thing that Mikell loved more than his family, it was music. He knew his music like the back of his hand. Mikell loved all kinds of music- R&B, Jazz, Alternative, Rap, even Country—yes, country. He opened his mind to different music—he always has. He was always open to listening to all kinds of music. When Mikell was younger, his friends from high school used to have a group called the Men of Kings, which consisted of four guys: two rappers, a singer, and a hype man. They did talent shows here and there for a couple of years. The Men of Kings were very popular in Mikell's hometown; they were very talented young men. The group stayed together throughout high school. After high school, everyone wanted different things, including Mikell, who decided that he wanted more in life and moved to another city.

As Ailese and Mikell went to more shops and enjoyed one another, they were a bit burned out and headed back to the hotel. "Are you hungry?" Ailese had just woken up from a nap. "Yes, I can eat a horse, Ailese grinned. Mikell kissed her on her cheek and told her that it was 5:00 p.m. and she needed to get ready because he knew how Ailese felt about her appearance.

Ailese was getting ready when Mikell's cell phone rang, it was D'Andra. "Hey you, what's up?" "Oh, nothing, said D'Andra. We're just having a blast. I don't mean to interrupt your time alone, but I had a question, or more like I need permission from you guys about something."

Mikell looked puzzled. "Okay, shoot." D'Andra went on to speak to Mikell. She hesitated, and Mikell waited patiently. "Well, both girls wanted to get their ears pierced. I explained to them that I needed permission from you guys. Is that okay with you and sis?" "Hold on, let me get Lee, okay?" "Hey, sis, the girls wanted to know if they could get their ears pierced? I told the girls that I needed your permission first."

"You know what, why not? They have been bugging me and my schedules been crazy, so it's okay, sis."

"Are you sure, sis?"

"Yes, just make sure that they get studs or something simple other than that, I'm fine with it. Mikell?" "Hey, I'm fine with it too."

Mikell went to the passenger side of the car and opened the door for Ailese. "Thanks, Hubby, she said with a smile on her face. This was one of her favorite restaurants! Her husband surprised her; she loved surprises, especially romantic ones. Ailese wore the dress that Mikell picked out for her. She looked very beautiful, perfect as usual, her hair was up in a French roll with diamond clips. It suited her.

"You look so handsome. You're so sexy, Ailese said with a smile. "Why, thank you, hun. You don't look bad yourself." Mikell grinned and smiled at her. She got in front of him and gave him a kiss.

A waiter that looked very young walked over to their table to take their orders. The restaurant looked as though you were in Italy but without the people and the accents. The lights were dimmed. The waiters and waitresses wore white long- sleeve- button down shirts with a black vest with red and green stripes. The men wore slacks that looked like they were finely pressed to a tee. The women wore long black skirts with ruffles and gold lining at the ends of their skirts. Everyone was very pleasant and thorough.

"May I start you off with something to drink?" "Yes, may I have a Midori Sour." Ailese thought she would treat herself tonight even though she rarely enjoyed alcohol, but she was in the mood tonight. Mikell ordered an orange Italian soda; he was to be the designated driver tonight. When the waiter came back with the drinks, he asked Mikell and Ailese if they were ready to order their meals. Mikell told the waiter that they needed a few minutes. When their meals arrived, Ailese and Mikell's eyes widened. "Wow this looks good," Mikell said.

Ailese and Mikell enjoyed their meals and conversation. They talked about music and the shops and what they needed to do when they got home tomorrow.

"Did you want dessert?" "No, Ailese said to Mikell, I would like to go to the workout room at the hotel. Ailese started laughing and looked at Mikell with a look that said she was kidding. "Babe, if you want to go, I'll gladly go with you."

"Um, I'm so stuffed, you're going to have to roll me out to the car, she laughed. "Come on, let's go, beautiful."

As they got ready for bed, Mikell sat beside his wife. Mikell started kissing Ailese on her neck and made his way to her lips. Ailese kissed Mikell back. "Hun, we better get some rest." "Resting is the last thing on my mind right now. I just want you so bad." Ailese asked Mikell to hold her, he held her as tight as he could, and then they became one.

The next morning, Ailese and Mikell got up and ate breakfast. They wanted to start early like the day before. They headed out to meet some friends and stop by Ailese's grandmother's house. Ailese always made it a point to visit her grandmother when she was in Romanville. Her grandmother and her had so much in common, especially antique jewelry. Ailese called her grandmother to make sure that she knew that she'd be there at noon. Ailese called her grandmother Mommie. She was like her second mom, and they had a special relationship ever since she was a little girl. Ailese would always stay with her Mommie. She loved it because she would teach her how to cook different recipes. This was how Ailese learned how to cook, and Mommie was the reason why Ailese was known to "put her foot" in her potato salad that everyone loved!

They arrived right on time. Ailese and Mikell were greeted at the door by a four- foot -eleven woman with caramel skin who didn't look her age at all. Her hair was long and curly, and she had the face of an angel. "Hello, you two," Mommie said, smiling from ear to ear, as she hugged Mikell and Ailese. Mommie's house was decorated from a magazine that Mommie loved. The magazine originated in the South, and when she saw a home that was decorated "just for her", she wanted her home to look exactly like the house she had seen in the magazine, so she asked Ailese to help her decorate her house just as it was in the magazine. The house was filled with cow skin furniture and ceramics from cows to horses. There were beautiful and elegant ceramics in the shapes of roosters, fruits, and sunflowers.

They had tea and cookies and talked about what had been going on in each other's lives. "Mommie, I have something for you. Close your eyes. Mommie closed her eyes with excitement she knew that Ailese's surprises were big surprises. "Open your eyes, Mommie." When she opened her eyes, she put her hands over her mouth and took a deep breath." This is so gorgeous. You remembered that I was looking for this type of jewelry, you sneaky thing you. You didn't have to go through that much trouble."

"I didn't, and if I did, you're worth it, Mommie." "Thank you so much. I am going to add this to my collection right now. Mommie went to her room to add the pieces to her jewelry box.

"Mommie really loved the jewelry a lot! I just love to see that smile on her face. It's priceless." Ailese said, she was pleased with herself. "Yes, Mommie was, "Mikell said with a smile on his face. Ailese went into Mommie's room

SHELBY LIES

to make sure that she didn't need any help. "Let me help you Mommie." She put the jewelry right where it belonged. Mommie sat on the bed and asked Ailese to come and join her. She had something in her hands. "I want to give you something. I've been meaning to give this to you." She took Ailese's hand and put a beautiful brooch in her hands. It had purple and turquoise crystals in a shape of a heart. "I can't take this Mommie. This is too beautiful!"

"No, I want you to have it, because it would mean a lot to me if you wore it close to your heart, and when we miss each other, just look at this brooch. I look at the jewelry and your pictures when I miss you." Ailese hugged her Mommie very tight.

When Ailese and Mikell arrived home, they unpacked and Ailese started some chores around the house. She tidied up the rooms and unloaded the dishwasher. Ailese smiled as she looked at the time. She knew the kids would be home soon. Oh, how she missed them.

Ailese sat down on the couch to read a book, but just as she attempted to read the book, her eyes were getting heavy. She told herself that she didn't want to go to sleep, so she went into the kitchen to make some coffee and went back to the sofa. "Mikell, where are you, hun?" Mikell came to the living room. "Oh, I was just getting our laundry started, are you okay?"

"Can you keep me company until the kids get home?"

"Sure, you look tired." He kissed her on her forehead.

"I am. I'll relax later."

There were voices coming from the front door, and Mikell approached it to be greeted by the girls, D'Andra, and Uncle Chris. Mikell gave the girls huge, long hugs and said, "Oh how I missed you guys." D'Andra and Ailese had already disappeared into the spare bedroom to talk; it wasn't unusual.

"Dad, we want to show you and mom what Auntie and Uncle got us please," said Ashanee. "Okay, hun, in just a minute, okay?" Uncle Chris and Mikell talked among themselves until D'Andra and Ailese came into the living room. D'Andra showed everyone the gifts that she had gotten from Mikell and Ailese. "Oh, here Chris," D'Andra gave Uncle Chris a shopping bag. He opened the bag and pulled out a bunch of t-shirts of different colors and designs. "Wow, thanks guys, these are really nice. I was just kidding when I told you guys to buy me some cool shirts." Uncle Chris smiled, and everyone laughed.

Uncle Chris was a t-shirt and jeans type of person. He hated wearing suits, and he would only wear them on special occasions. Uncle Chris had his own business, and he didn't have to wear a suit; that was so cool to him. If he had it his way, he would have worn jeans and a t-shirt on his wedding day, but D'Andra didn't let him.

"Okay, girls, it's time to wake up and start getting ready for school." Ailese stood in the hallway where their rooms were. She poked her head into Ashanee's room. "Hey, pumpkin, you up?" "Yes Mom. Mom, are you driving us to school or, is dad?" "I am pumpkin, so don't make mom late, okay?" Ailese went into Adrieana's room, and before Ailese said anything, she didn't see Adrieana in her bed, so she called for her. "I'm in the restroom, mom, Adrieana shouted.

Mikell was already downstairs eating breakfast. He's always up before anyone, and his day starts before anyone's.

Mikell kissed everyone good-bye and asked Ailese where Armont was. Ailese had forgotten to tell Mikell that Armont called when they were shopping and asked if he could go to school from his dad's, and Ailese gave him permission and said that he would be home today. It wasn't unusual for Armont to stay at his dad's an extra day. It happened often.

When Ailese dropped the girls off, she called Armont to make sure that his weekend went okay with his dad. "It went good mom, the deep voice said over the phone. Dad took me to the new mall that was just built. We had a blast, and mom, guess what? Dad took me clothes shopping he even brought me some cool shoes." "That's great, Armont. Sounds like you had lots of fun. I just wanted to make sure you knew to come straight home after school. I want to see my handsome young guy, okay?" "Yes, Mom I will. Have a good day, mom." "I will, hun, and you too." They both hung up, and Ailese started to think about how time flies and that it just seemed like yesterday that she gave birth to her only son; he's a young man now.

Ailese sat at her desk going over some paperwork when her assistant buzzed her on the phone to let her know that someone named Jonathan Baxter was here to see her. "I don't know that name, Ell." "He says that he was here on behalf of a Mr. Tollen." "Oh yes, send him in. Thanks Ell." Ailese met Mr. Baxter at the door and shook his hand. "Hello, Mrs. LaShae, I do apologize that Mr. Tollen couldn't be here today. He sends his apology; he had an emergency to attend to." "No problem. Have a seat Mr. Baxter. Would you like anything to drink?" "Oh, no thanks, I've already had my two cups of coffee this morning."

Mr. Baxter was a very tall, thin man with a receding hairline and ocean blue eyes. He had a wrinkly face, he looked older that he was. He was a very kind man.

Mr. Baxter and Ailese went over contracts and figures and agreed to meet again with Mr. Tollen. Ailese showed Mr.

Baxter out and went back to her desk. She was very busy the rest of the day. She had meetings back- to back.

Ailese didn't get home until 6:30, just in time to make a quick dinner. She went into Armont's room. She knocked on the door. She found Armont doing homework with his headphones on. Ailese walked over to him and hugged him. He took off his headphones to hug his mother. "I missed you so much, handsome, how was school?" "Good, mom, good." Armont was a senior at Grandell Christian Academy and an honor student. Ailese was very proud of all her children. They work hard to keep up their grades, they know how important it is to get into good colleges. Ailese always instilled that in her children.

"Dinner's ready guys, wash your hands please," Ailese shouted to her family which stirred around in different directions to wash their hands. Ailese had made a quick but luscious dinner: baked lemon pepper chicken, corn, and stuffing.

"Wow, it smells great mom, said Ashanee. I love your cooking mom." Ailese smiled. The family talked about school and upcoming events as they enjoyed their meal.

After everyone pitched in to clean the kitchen, the kids asked if they could watch TV in the game room. Ailese told them that they could if all their homework was done, and all the kids headed to the game room. "No fighting over the remote, guys." "Okay, Mom, we won't." The house was quiet.

Ailese sat down next to Mikell, who was writing in his book. "What are you working on, babe?" "Mmmm, nothing really, I just have some ideas for the new artist that we signed, and I don't want to forget them." Mikell yawned and continued to write. Ailese decided to read a book she had been trying to finish.

The kids came into the living room to say good night to their mom and dad. Ailese and Mikell told the kids good night. Mikell looked at the time, and it was almost midnight. "Hun, we better get to bed."

Ailese screamed so loudly that she woke up the entire house.

"Baby, are you okay?" Mikell held her in his arms as she wept. The kids knocked on the door. Mikell told the kids that their mom was okay and to go back to bed he didn't want to let Ailese out of his arms. Don't worry, baby. It was it was only a dream. I'm right here." Ailese was sobbing with her eyes closed tightly; she was afraid to open them because she would see the man standing in front of her.

Mikell gave Ailese the bottled water that he kept by his bedside and held it to Ailese's mouth. "Come on, hun, drink some water, okay?" Ailese felt better after she drank the water. It took her awhile to get back to sleep, but Mikell held her until she fell asleep. Mikell went to check on all the kids. They were asleep except for Armont. Mikell told him that his mom was okay and that he calmed her down and that his mom was asleep.

The next morning, Ailese felt a bit groggy, but she knew that she had to make it through the day. She got up, showered, and dressed. Mikell was already making breakfast in the kitchen, and the kids were getting ready as well.

"Thanks for making breakfast. I had a late start this morning."

"No problemo, hun. Are you hungry?" "Yes, I am." Mikell gave his wife a look of concern.

"Sit down, Lee. I want to talk to you before the kids come down. Ailese sat down in the chair, and Mikell made her a plate with bacon, eggs, and toast and sat it in front of her. Are you sure you're okay? You haven't had one of those attacks in a while. Are you working too hard? Did something happen? Please tell me. I'm here for you and you know that you can tell me anything."

"Mikell I'm fine, and no, I'm not working too hard, and nothing happened to trigger an episode." "I worry about you." Mikell loved his wife unconditionally and cared about her; she is his best friend; he was very concerned.

"I think you should take it easy today. I'm sure they could make do with one day without you. I think you should call Dr. Salvino", he handed Ailese the phone. Ailese didn't take the phone. She assured Mikell that she was fine.

Mikell accepted that his wife was fine; they both agreed that she would call Dr. Salvino before the end of the day.

Mikell called his wife on her cell to check on her. He told her that he would pick up the kids at 5:30 from study hall. All the kids went to study hall every day so that they wouldn't be home alone, so much being that both parents' schedules were a bit crazy. Mikell told his wife to go straight home and relax and he would pick up something for dinner. This made Ailese happy. She thanked Mikell and told him that she loved him.

There was a knock at the door, and she knew that knock anywhere. "Come in," she said with excitement. It was Uncle Chris. Ailese gave him a huge hug. "Hey, you, how are you? This is a surprise, brother." "I hope you don't mind me showing up like this, but I was in the neighborhood and wanted to take my sister to lunch."

"Aw that is so sweet. You know that I don't mind you stopping by; you know that. Okay, let me get my coat."

Ailese told her assistant that she was going out for lunch and to call her cell if she needed anything.

It wasn't unusual for Uncle Chris to stop by to take Ailese out to lunch every now and again or even hang out at the office with her; he adored her too.

They would talk about everything from family to politics. Ailese enjoyed their conversations; she treasured them.

The two ended up at a Greek restaurant that had just opened. They were both pleased with the service and the food. "So you know that project that we were bidding on?" "Oh, the one that's on 5th Street, the one that wanted to expand?"

"You're a good listener, that's it, we've got it!" "That's great, Chris. Well, this lunch is our celebration, and it's on me." "No, Ailese, put your wallet away. I got it," he said with a smiled. Do you have time for me to show you something?" "Yes, sure." They got into the car and drove down Cannon Street. They pulled up to a huge house that was for sale; it looked like something out of a million- dollar home magazine. Chris went over to the passenger side to let Ailese out of the car. "Well, this is what I am thinking about buying. What do you think?"

"Oh, wow are you serious? D'Andra will love this! "That makes me happy that you mentioned that I wanted to make sure D'Andra would like this house before buying it and surprising her." "You've made my day!

Ailese had a great deal of work to do. She was swamped with clients and deadlines. She couldn't stop thinking about Chris's surprise for her best friend in the whole world and the look on her face when she saw the house. It looked like they were getting ready to start a family of their own, and Ailese would be there every step of the way.

Ailese was able to meet all the deadlines. She even had time to go over her presentation that was scheduled for Friday, because she wanted to make sure it was perfect!

As she was leaving, she noticed Mr. Salamar speaking to Ruben, which she thought was unusual because she had hardly seen Mr. Salamar really talk to anyone. He was a slender man with flawless brown skin and a well-cared-for beard. He had cat-shaped eyes and spoke with a lisp. Ailese and Mr. Salamar didn't speak too much to one another, except when they were in the same room.

As Ailese came closer to them, Ruben made eye contact with her. "I will be right with you, Mrs. LaShae. It will only be a minute." Ailese nodded and continued to walk slowly to her car. Her cell phone rang as she was looking in her purse for a piece of gum. "Hello." It was Dr. Salvino on the other end. She was returning Ailese's call from earlier. "I do apologize for not getting back to you sooner; it's been one hectic day." "Oh, I do understand. How are you, Dr. Salvino? It's been awhile. Ailese put up one finger to Ruben to let him know that she'd only be a minute. Ruben gave her privacy and made sure that he wasn't out of sight. I'm on my way home, but I wanted to see if you could squeeze me in for a session. I really need to discuss some issues with you as soon as possible." "Well, you're in luck. I had a cancellation for tomorrow at 5:00 p.m. Would that work for you?" Ailese took out her work phone and looked at her calendar. It was full but nothing was filled for 5:00 p.m. "That's perfect, Dr. Salvino. See you then, thanks so much." "Okay, see you then, Mrs. LaShae. I penciled you in, see you tomorrow."

Ruben looked a bit upset. Ailese asked if he was okay, and he told Ailese that Mr. Salamar was complaining to Ruben as usual about the same thing. He said that Mr. Salamar wanted Ruben to carry all his belongings to his car. Ruben explained to Ailese that he was not obligated to carry all his belongings to his car, and it wasn't in his job description. Ailese told Ruben to make a complaint to Human Resources if the situation gets any worse and that Mr. Salamar was never happy about anything and not to take it personally.

Ailese told Ruben that sometimes people would take your kindness and use it to their advantage.

Mikell was already making dinner when Ailese arrived home. She kissed him on the cheek and hugged him as he was stirring something in the pot. Ailese went into the bedroom to get comfortable. She checked on the kids, who were playing a game and behaving themselves, which made her happy.

Ailese was very tired. Her body felt like a huge truck had hit it. She knew that she was working too hard, but there were deadlines to meet, and she didn't like to procrastinate on the important things because if she did, it would stress her out even more. Ailese thought about her presentation and her appointment with Dr. Salvino. She knew that it was going to be hard talking about her past; it was something that she always dreaded. She sometimes, didn't like to talk about her bad dreams to anyone, not even her husband. She kept some things to herself. She was very private in some ways. Ailese didn't like to burden anyone with her problems; she knew that they had their own problems to deal with, even though she had understanding friends who would never judge her.

Mikell and Ailese talked about Uncle Chris and D'Andra's new home and how they wanted to plan a housewarming party for them soon. They agreed that they would surprise them, and before Ailese knew it, she was fast asleep.

Mikell kissed her on her forehead and watched her sleep until he himself fell asleep.

When Ailese arrived at work, Ell was waiting for Ailese; the look on her slender face wasn't a good one. Ell was a well-dressed woman with a short feathery haircut that suited her.

She was a bit of a shoe freak, and she knew the exact date and day that all the name- brand shoes would arrive. You would think that Ell squandered her money all on clothes and shoes, but she was very smart, thanks to Ailese, who told her to save money for a rainy day, Ell would give Ailese a report on how much money she's saving for that rainy day. Ailese thought that Ell was sharing too much information. She didn't have to know about her finances, but Ell meant well, and Ailese eventually got used to it.

"Ailese, Mr. Saxx is in your office. I didn't know he was coming, so I pushed back all the meetings, okay?"

"Thanks, you're one of a kind; what will I do without ya? Hello, Mr. Saxx, how are you this morning?" Mr. Saxx was a tall, chubby man who wore the finest suits and smoked the finest cigars, but he wouldn't smoke them in Ailese's presents because he knew the cigars, bothered her allergies and just bothered her in general. Mr. Saxx was a proud man and a proud father. He had been divorced for some time now. Surprisingly he was a catch to a lot of women; they were attracted to him, and not just because of his money. He was seeing a model from Korea named Lin. She was in every magazine you picked up. Lin appeared in perfume and lingerie advertisements. Ailese met her on several occasions and found her very nice. Mr. Saxx had a bottle of water in his hand and sat it down on the small table that was beside him. He shook Ailese's hand. "Hello, my love, I thought you could show me some of your presentation before we present it to the Marlow Corporation. I know that this is very important and that I have no doubts that the presentation is great. I'm just so excited to see what you have come up with". "Oh sure, let's go over to the conference room for privacy. I will have Ell bring us some water. Was there anything else you needed her to bring you?" "Oh, I'm fine thanks. I do have a meeting soon."

Ailese asked Ell to bring some bottled waters to the conference room, which was on the third floor. Ell came into the conference room with two bottled waters. She sat them down and left the room. Ailese opened her laptop, turned off all the lights, and set up the projector so that Mr. Saxx could see her presentation in a bigger version than on the laptop. Ailese showed Mr. Saxx her presentation. He was very pleased and told her that the Marlow Corporation would be very pleased, he just knew it. Mr. Saxx said he wanted a full report from her as soon as the meeting was over.

"Next time I'm here, I need to take you and Ell out for lunch, okay?"

"That sounds great. Talk to you soon Mr. Saxx. Mr. Saxx walked into the elevator and waved to Ailese as the doors closed.

Ailese was so happy: she was proud of herself and she loved what she did. Her job helped so many people who needed it, and the people that she helps did not have to worry about someone taking them for granted just because their finances are in jeopardy. Ailese's job was to fix the problem, figure out where they went wrong, and she saved them. She loved seeing the smiles on their faces and receiving thank you- cards, gifts from new clients that were referred to her and when her plan for them worked!

It was the big day Ailese had made sure that she had gotten plenty of sleep she did not want anything to go wrong. All her clients meant a lot to her. She gave them her undivided attention.

The meeting was started on time. Mr. and Mrs. Marlow were punctual, as was everyone else, even Ailese's assistants. There were a few questions from Mr. and Mrs. Marlow and

Ailese answered their questions thoroughly. Everyone paid close attention to Ailese and her presentation. Ailese spoke about why they should move their location to a place downtown that had just been remodeled, and the office building will be visible so people can see their business. She went on to explain the reasons why their current location wasn't working for them and that the new location that was suggested would work for them, and so on. Ailese explained the finances and showed them figures etcetera. The Marlows agreed and was very pleased with Ailese and her staff. Before they knew it, the Marlows were signing on the dotted line and wanted to get started right away. Ailese thanked the Marlows and walked them to the elevator, telling them to call her if they needed anything.

Ailese wanted to thank all her employees for doing such a wonderful job, so she decided to take everyone out to lunch, besides, everyone deserved it. Ailese told everyone to enjoy themselves and there was no rush to get back to the office. Ailese took care of the check and went back to the office to call Mr. Saxx. She told Mr. Saxx all the details of her presentation. After hearing the good news, Mr. Saxx told Ailese that the Marlows had already called him an hour before she did. The Marlows praised Ailese and her team.

There was a knock on Ailese's door. She asked who it was. A man's voice said he had a delivery for her. "Hello, I'm sorry there was no one at the front desk. I asked someone where I could find you, and they said you were here. I have a delivery for you Mrs. LaShae." The man was holding a huge basket that was bigger than him. "Come in. Let me get my purse." She told the man to sit the huge basket down on the large purple marble table. Ailese got her purse and took a ten-dollar bill out of her wallet and handed it to the delivery man. He gave her a clipboard and asked her to sign the receipt. She signed the receipt and thanked him and walked him to the door.

The basket was filled with fruit, candies, and gift cards from spas to eateries, there was even lotions and sprays in the basket. It was so huge Ailese wondered if it would fit in her car, and she giggled to herself. She read the card, and it read, "We just wanted to give you a huge thank you. What would we do without you! The Marlows. P.S. We hope you love the gift basket. Thanks again." Ailese smiled. She called them to thank them, but she had gotten their voice mail, so she left a short message.

Ailese dreaded driving 45 minutes to Dr. Salvino's office, but she knew she had to do this no matter how she felt about it. Her cell phone rang. It was Mikell. He wanted to tell her he was thinking about her. Mikell told her he would be home before she arrived home. He told her he loved her.

Ailese knew that she would hit traffic, so she left early so she could still arrive at Dr. Salvino's on time. Ailese was 10 minutes early, so she decided to pick up a cup of coffee from a deli that was across the street from Dr. Salvino's office and headed to the second floor. "Your earrings are gorgeous!" Ailese looked up and there was a woman in the elevator. She didn't pay attention to who was on the elevator with her. She touched her purple and gold earrings; she forgot which ones she was wearing. "Oh, thank you."

"May I ask where did you get them from?" "Oh, I made these some time ago." The woman explained to Ailese that she didn't want to be to straight forward but her mother's birthday was in a month and her mom has been wanting some earrings like Ailese's, but she could never find anything that came close to what Ailese had. "How much would you charge to make those for me?" "Are you serious? I was just bored one day and thought that I would just making jewelry, being that I am a jewelry freak, "Ailese smiled. "No, I am serious. "I wouldn't charge you anything. Mothers are priceless. Why don't we exchange numbers, and we can talk. Do you live here or in Romanville?" "I live in Romanville. I work here though. My name is Karen. What's yours?" "My name is Ailese." Their words collided together, and they laughed. They exchanged numbers, spoke for a few minutes, and went their separate ways.

Ailese thought that Karen was a very nice person. They seemed to have a lot in common. She reasoned that she could stop by the crafts store on her way home to get the supplies that she needed to make the earrings, knowing how important the earrings were to Karen and how happy she would be to finally have the gift her mother had always wanted. Ailese told herself that she would make sure she put extra love into making the earrings.

Ailese walked into Dr. Salvino's office. An elderly woman was waiting in the large waiting room. The room smelled like peaches and raspberries. Ailese loved that smell, and it reminded her of her Mommie. "Hello, I have a 5:00 appointment with Dr. Salvino. My name is Ailese LaShae." The receptionist looked at her clipboard and smiled at Ailese, telling her that Dr. Salvino was a bit behind schedule, and that she would be with her in a few minutes.

Ailese sat down and pulled out her book from her purse. She waited for fifteen minutes, until she was called into Dr. Salvino's office.

Dr. Salvino was a plus-size beautiful Latina woman and was a very well-known therapist. She even worked with famous people, and her credentials spoke for themselves. Dr. Salvino had long black curly hair, her eyes were sky blue, her skin was an almond tone and well taken care of. Her nails were always groomed very well. Her nail polish would be wacky colors like pink with yellow tips or black with orange tips. The colors were different and beautiful at the same time.

"Hi, Dr. Salvino, how are you?" "I am good, and yourself?" "I've been keeping busy. I see that you have redecorated your office it looks great," Ailese said as she looked around the newly refurbished office and was very impressed.

"So let's get started." Dr. Salvino had gotten her pen and pad and sat them on her lap. "Ailese I just want you to relax and take deep breaths. Whatever we speak about does not leave this room, and you know that I take client confidentiality very seriously." Ailese closed her eyes, and took a couple of deep breaths, and made eye contact with Dr. Salvino to let her know that she was ready. Ailese knew that she could always trust her.

Ailese told Dr. Salvino that she had been having the dreams again and that she was having them more often than before. Dr. Salvino explained to her that sometimes things could trigger them. She asked Ailese a series of questions to see if she could pinpoint why Ailese was having the dreams again. Ailese explained to Dr. Salvino that her dreams seemed real at times. The session went on for an hour, and having the session did Ailese some good, like Mikell said it would. Ailese made another appointment with the receptionist for next week.

As Ailese was driving home, she felt that the session went well and was looking forward to another session next week. Ailese was hoping that Mikell was home so she could tell him about her day. Ailese stopped at the crafts store to pick up the supplies since she had decided to work on Karen's gift for her mother. Ailese had bumped into D'Andra at the craft store. They had spoken for a bit because they both needed to get home, they did agree to call each other to plan a girls' day out. Ailese congratulated D on her new home. D'Andra told Ailese that Chris and she would be moving into the new house in a few weeks, and she was very excited.

"Hey babe, I saw D'Andra at the craft store. She is so excited about moving into their house. Did I tell you that Chris showed me the house before he put his John Hancock on the dotted line?" Mikell kissed his wife and gave her a huge hug. "No, you didn't. That must have been cool. I knew you wanted to tell D, huh?" "You know me, don't you? But I was good at keeping my lips sealed."

"Sit down, hun. Tell me about your day, baby."

"Well, hun, I would, but I need to get dinner started. Mikell interrupted his wife and reminded her that he had already told her that he oversaw dinner tonight, and that everyone had already eaten dinner. Mikell already had a plate for her in the oven. Mikell took her hand and led her into the kitchen. He catered to her and whatever she needed. "Now tell me about your day." Before Ailese could say anything, Adrieana entered the room and hugged and kissed her on the cheek.

"Well, thank you sweetie." I missed you mom, she yelled to the others to let them know that Ailese was home, they all gave her hugs. "Let mom eat dinner, guys," Armont said to his sisters as they all went into their rooms.

"So, the funniest thing happened to me today. I was going to Dr. Salvino's office, which by the way I will get to after I tell you this story. I know how anxious you are to know how our session went. So anyway, this woman was on the elevator with me, and so she asks me where I bought these earrings from. Ailese touched her ears and said I told her that I made them, so guess what she asks me to make them for her mom. Her mom has been wanting something different, and my earrings are what her mom would want for her birthday. I was very pleased when she told me that she wanted me to make the earrings for her. She even asked me how much I would charge her to make them. So, her name is Karen, she works in the same building as Dr. Salvino, and she is a very nice person. So, I went to the crafts store and picked up the supplies. Karen's mother's birthday is in a month. I mean, we exchanged numbers and everything." Ailese took a drink of her raspberry iced tea and looked at her husband. "Well, that is great, hun. I told you that you were talented at everything that you do.

So please tell me how the session went with Dr. Salvino?" "Okay, it went great. I'm glad that you told me to call her. I feel like having the session with her will do me some good and help me get through this. Mikell took her hand in his and kissed her hands. "This is so good; you know how much I love your spaghetti; it's delicious. I am so stuffed." "Hey, do you want to work out with me later?" "Okay, hun, that sounds good." "I'm going to get some work done before we work out. I will be in the den if you need me, okay?" "Okay, I'm going to check on the kids to see if they need anything."

Ailese went into Ashanee's room. She was reading a book, Ailese sat on her bed, and Ashanee didn't even look up. She was so into her book. "Hey, you," Ailese tapped her on her head. Ashanee looked up. "Oh hi, Mom, we have to read this book for my English class. It's a really good book." Ailese took the book out of her daughter's hands and looked at the title on the front of the book. It read, Tim's Old Coat. Ashanee explained to her mom that the book was about a lucky coat that belonged to Tim, who thought that the coat was a lucky charm. Tim loses the coat, so he goes on this journey to find his coat.

Ashanee gave her mom a few things that needed to be signed for school. "Is that everything kitten?" "Yes, thank you, Mom."

Ailese went into Armont's room, where he was fast asleep. Thinking to herself that he must have had a long day. She put a blanket over him and turned off his light and computer. Adrieana was getting ready for bed. She said that she was going to turn in early and that she had a long day. "Mom, don't forget about the school dance next Friday." "Okay, honey I won't, and we will need to make sure that you have everything before the dance, okay." "Okay, love you, mom, good night."

Ailese went into the den to find Mikell working hard. He had his headphones on and was listening to music. Ailese looked at the clock and it was already 9:00 at night. She thought that she would be sleepy, but she was wide awake. She was trying to decide if she wanted to watch television or work on the earrings, so she decided to do both.

"Wow, that looks great, babe," Mikell said as he sat on the bed. "Thanks, I thought so myself," Ailese smiled. Mikell laid down next to Ailese and watched television with her. Mikell gave Ailese a foot and back massage before they went to bed. He told her that he thought that she was working too hard and needed to take it easy. Ailese told Mikell about the Marlows and how her presentation went, how much people depended on her, and that she wasn't working too hard.

Mikell knew that her job meant a lot to her. Sometimes he was a bit jealous because her commitment to her work was getting in the way of her writing songs and recording them in his studio, but he would shrug it off. Mikell felt that his wife's talent should be shown to the world. Mikell described her voice as beautiful as an angel singing. He only hoped that Ailese would one day lend her voice to him and to his colleagues. Ailese would sing in the shower and around the house. She would also occasionally do Karaoke, which the kids and Mikell enjoyed. She would put on a long black

SHELBY LIES

straight wig, red lipstick, and one of her shiny ball gowns and put on a show for them.

Mikell was awakened by his cell phone that was by his bed. He knew that it had to be late, as he reached sleepily for his phone and answered it. "Hello, this is him. What can I help you with?" Ailese woke up and leaned on Mikell to see what was going on. "Oh no, I will be right there. Thank you. Yes, sir."

Mikell hung up his cell and turned to his wife. "Someone broke into the studio. I have to go down there to speak with the police." "Oh no, are you serious? Well, I am coming with you, babe." "No, stay here, hun. I may be there for a while." Mikell put on his clothes and kissed Ailese. Lee, don't worry, I will call you as soon as I know more information, okay?" Mikell kissed her forehead and told her not to worry, promising that he would call her as soon as he knew something. Ailese told him to be careful and gave him a hug. Mikell thought about the look that was in Ailese's eyes, the look that she has when she's worried, and he knew that she wasn't going to sleep until he returned home safely.

Mikell saw police lights and cars parked in front of the building. Mikell was greeted by a police officer. "Mr. La Shae?" "Yes, I'm Mr. LaShae." "I'm Officer Brown, Daniel Brown. The two men broke into the building. They got as far as breaking into the recording studio, we will need to know if anything is missing. I guess they got frightened when the alarm went off. We do have them on video. I do apologize for calling you so late, but we wanted to get right on this case and lock the bad guys away. I also wanted to add that our officers tried their best to catch these guys, but they lost them. We are combing the area and asking people questions and looking into anything that looks suspicious, Mr. LaShae."

"Thank you, Officer Brown. I am happy to help in any way I can." Mikell started to think of who would want to break into the studio and steal the things that he and his colleagues worked so hard for. Who? Why? This was a good neighborhood, but it didn't matter where you lived, there's bound to be someone who's itching to break the law and doesn't care about how hard a person works or how a person puts their blood, sweat, and tears into their hard work.

Some of the items in the studio were irreplaceable. How could he replace the demos, the finished ones, and the not-so-finished ones? Mikell told himself that he had better keep it together.

Mikell and Officer Brown reached the elevator and entered the studio. Mikell was relieved that it wasn't trashed, but he knew right away that there were items missing. "Is anything missing, Mr. LaShae?" "Yes, Mikell said, looking around the studio. Would you like for me to call my assistant so she could give you the itemized documents?" "That would be very helpful. Could you get that info for me as early as today? You know when your assistant is available. I'm sure she is asleep; I don't want to disturb anyone else." "Okay, that will be fine. Could you excuse me for just a moment? I have to make a very important phone call." Mikell walked out of the studio into the hallway while Officer Brown waited inside the studio. "Hun, it's me. I just wanted to let you know that everything is getting taken care of. It's not as bad as I thought, but I do have to look at some video footage with the officer." "Okay, I'm just glad no one was hurt or anything. I'll wait up for you, okay?" "Ailese, you need your rest. I will wake you up when I get home. Get some rest, baby. I love you."

Mikell didn't recognize the two men on the video that Officer Brown showed him, but he was assured that they would catch these guys and charge them with theft and breaking and entering. Officer Brown gave Mikell his card and told him to keep in touch. Mikell told him that his assistant would call him first thing in the morning with the info that was needed. Officer Brown insisted that Mikell and his colleagues not show up for work because a crime was committed, and that he would notify them when they could return.

The building employed a lot of people, being that it had six floors, three of which were studios, and the rest were business offices for executives, receptionists' etcetera.

Mikell thought to himself that he needed to stay up so he could call his assistant first thing when the sun came up and that he also needed to make some calls. "We've never had to close—ever! He said to himself that he began to get angry. His eyes were boiling, and he just couldn't believe this! Mikell began to feel more anxious to catch these assholes! So he could picture himself whipping their asses! Mikell took a deep breath. He didn't want Ailese to see him this upset.

"Hey I'm home," Mikell whispered in Ailese's ear. "Okay, did you need me to stay up with you? I could make us some tea?" "Well, I do, but Lee, you need your rest." Mikell looked at his watch, it was late. Ailese sat up and reached for her robe, leading Mikell to the kitchen. Mikell did need someone to talk to; he needed his wife's company. As they went into the kitchen, Ailese looked at the stove and saw that it was 4:30 a.m. She didn't mind not getting her rest; she could feel that Mikell needed her as much as she needed her rest.

Ailese looked at Mikell, he was looking down at his cup that she had sat on the table. "Talk to me, Mik. I'm here."

Mikell was silent for a moment, and then he began to speak. "Why is it that people like to rob and steal things that are not theirs? I can't comprehend it because I was taught not to steal or hurt people. I know you understand how much I put into the studio- my blood, sweat, and tears, -I mean,

I would sleep there sometimes and work long, exhausting hours. It was difficult to be away from you and the kids, but you understood, babe. These guys don't understand that! Mikell got out his cell phone. He needed to call Gabe, Jaden, and Emmanuel to let them know what had happened at the studio. He knew eventually he had to tell his partner. Ailese touched Mikell's hand before he made the call. "Can you wait? I just wanted to tell you that I'm so proud of you. You're holding up well," Ailese said with a smile.

All his colleagues were a bit upset and wanted these guys found as much as Mikell. They all told Mikell that if there was anything he needed to let them know and that they understood why they couldn't show up for work. They discussed calling the officer to let them look at the videotape; they may be of help. Mikell had decided to call Emmanuel even though he knew it was late, but he needed to know. Just as he started to dial the number, his cell started to ring, and he saw that it was Emmanuel. "Hello, yes, I was just about to call you." "I got a call from Officer Brown just a few moments ago. Are you alright, Mikell?"

"Yes, I'm okay. A bit upset about the whole thing." "Yeah, I know man. Me too. I mean, we both have a lot to lose, and I don't want that to happen. How about we meet up later on today, and discuss this? Would that be, okay?" "Yes, that will be fine. Yes, we could meet there, okay." Mikell hung up his cell. Emmanuel and Mikell had decided to meet at Shine's Restaurant for the meeting.

"Is everything alright?" "Yes, we just have some loose ends to tie up. Thanks, Lee, for staying up with me. How did I get so lucky?" Mikell grabbed her waist and pulled her to him, hugging her tight.

It was already 7:00 in the morning. Ailese had dozed off beside Mikell on the couch, he didn't want to awaken her making his calls, so he went into the den. Mikell spoke with his assistant Leenah. She was wide awake and seemed alert, and she was ready to take notes on what needed to be done. Leenah didn't mind that it was a Saturday; she knew what she was signing up for when she took the job. You never know what your schedule will be.

Mikell left Ailese a note that said, "Hun, I will be back later. I am going to go to the police station with Lennah so we can give the information to the officer. We need to handle a few things. I will check in later. Love you, Mik."

The kids and Ailese were still sleeping when Mikell was finished showering and getting dressed. He left and locked the door behind him. He made sure that he had everything that he needed before driving off. His cell rang. It was Gabe he wanted to know if he would be at the meeting with Emmanuel at 2:00. Mikell told him that he would be there and that they would talk then.

Mikell wanted to make sure everything was done with Leenah before his meeting with Emmanuel; he liked to be punctual.

Lennah was punctual in meeting Mikell at the studio. She was given permission to enter the building so they could gather the books that she needed to take with her to show Officer Brown what was stolen from the studio. They spoke to Officer Brown and showed him what was taken: some laptops and music equipment. Officer Brown made a report on the missing items and had them look over the report to make sure everything was correct. He told them that he was looking into some leads that were called in and would let them know if anything checked out. Mikell was a bit relieved to know that the case was being worked on and someone cared about putting these punks away.

Mikell wanted this to be all over so he and his colleagues could get back to work. "Leenah, do you have plans now?" "No, I don't. What's up?" "Oh, I just thought that you could accompany me to this meeting with Emmanuel. I'm sure you'll need to jot down some info of the changes that will be happening, is that okay?" "Oh, that's fine, that will be a good idea, and besides, I didn't want to go home and do laundry anyway," she said with a grin and rolling her eyes.

When they arrived at the restaurant, Gabe, Jaden, and Nate were already there, waiting for everyone to arrive. "Hey guys, have you seen Emmanuel? He's usually on time, said Jaden. Maybe we should call him."

"No, he'll be here," said Mikell. "Let's go in and get a table. Maybe he made reservations." They all walked inside the restaurant, and Mikell asked the man at the front if he had reservations for Collins. The man checked and said he had reservations for Collins, and that he called to have him relay the message that he was on his way and when they arrived, he should seat them. The man seated the party and waved the waitress over. Emmanuel arrived and sat down as the waitress was taking their drink orders. "Sorry guys I lost track of time. I was attending my son's soccer game, and I had to take some kids home, including mine. Please forgive me." "We get it", they all said on cue. "Lunch is on me, so go crazy, guys. Don't be shy," Emmanuel grinned. Emmanuel was a well-groomed Caucasian man in his late thirties who wore casual slacks and button- down shirts. Emmanuel was tall and husky, with dark brown eyes. He was married and had one son, who was ten years old. His wife was a bit older than he was. Emmanuel and Mikell had been friends for over five years. They met at a jazz club while Mikell was searching for a new face to sign with his record label. They hit it off, and after two years they decided to go into business together.

They are pretty close, but they don't hang out a lot outside work because they both work together a lot.

"So I do believe that we should upgrade the security system, only the best. I think this was just a wake-up call. I also think that we should come up with a plan on where we should store the demos and the music equipment. Yes, a lap top could be replaced, but there's music that we don't want people to have rights to." "I agree, Mikell said. Everyone else agreed as well. "I could look up some people who could help us on this, said Leenah. I will get right on that", she said, writing on her notepad. Jaden began to talk about the security as their drinks arrived. "I think we all agree that we should look into having better security, but what about putting a 24-hour security officer in the building, not rent-a-cops, everyone laughed. No, guys, you know what I mean -not security guards that can't apprehend anyone who tries to break in. They have to be strong physically and mentally. We can't hire men who doesn't know anything about being a security guard; they need to be true to their job." Everyone agreed with Jaden. "Good thinking, Jaden," said Gabe. They continued to talk about the plans and agendas. Everyone agreed that there was a lot of work to be done and that it needed to be done fast. Leenah told the guys that she called all the people who were scheduled to be in the studio and canceled all the appointments and that there will be a meeting in a week or so to fill everyone in.

"Hey you, how's everything going?" "Good, Lee. How did you sleep? It sounds like you got plenty of rest. Am I right?" "Yes, babe I did. The kids let me sleep and they behaved well. Are you coming home soon?" "Yes, in a bit, I'm just wrapping up this meeting, and then I'll be home. Hey, ask the kids if they want to go out with us for dinner." "Okay, hold on. Kids come here." The kids all came into the living room, where Ailese was. She asked them if they wanted to go out to dinner with their mom and dad, and they all said yes, loud enough for Mikell to hear them. "Okay, Lee, tell them to be ready at 8:00." "Okay, I love you."

"Where are we going for dinner, Momma?" The girls asked. "Well, Dad says it's a surprise, but all I can tell you is to wear something nice, okay, and be ready at eight." "Okay, Mom, we'll be ready." The girls were more excited than Ailese. They loved it when their dad surprised them. Armont came into the living room and sat down beside his mother. He was a bit quiet. "Are you okay?" "Yes, I'm fine. I miss Dad, when is he coming home? I haven't seen him all day."

"He will be home soon. He had some important things to take care of." Armont had a look of disappointment on his face. Ailese told him that he would be able to spend some time with his dad when they all go out for dinner.

"Dad works too much, Mom, and it's Saturday Mom. He should be here."

"Well, hun, your dad is a very important person to his company, and when there is something that needs his attention, he can't say no. You know that, son."

Armont looked down at his shoes. "I remember when Dad took me shopping to buy these shoes for me, it was just he and I. We don't even have guy time anymore, mom." Ailese lifted her son's face and told him that his dad loved him more than anything. "Hun, I can promise you that Dad will make time for you as soon as he can, okay?" "Okay, Mom. Mom, thanks for making me feel better. I love you, Mom." "Well, I better start getting ready. I don't know what I'm wearing yet. Love you, hun." Armont headed to his room.

Ailese looked at the clock and thought that she should tidy up the house a bit since she slept in. Ailese loaded the dishwasher, vacuumed, and tidied up the bedroom. She smiled to herself when she came across Mikell's pajamas. She held them up to her chest, she missed him so much. She felt as though Mikell had been gone for a couple of days, then she heard his voice. "Hey, you." Mikell said excitedly. "I'm home. Where are the kids?" He kissed Ailese. It was a long, deep kiss that gave her chills. She looked at him as though she were examining him; she wanted to make sure he was okay. "The kids are in their rooms, so did everything go okay?" "Yes, hun, we can talk about it later. I just want to spend some time with my family." He kissed Ailese again and told her that he was going to check on the kids and that he would be right back.

Ailese could hear the kids down the hall. She could hear the excitement in their voices as they expressed their happiness that their dad was home. Mikell visited the kids for a bit and came back into the bedroom.

Mikell started to kiss his wife on her lips and made his way down to her breasts. He kissed her ear lobes, her neck, and her forehead. Ailese felt chills going through her body. She knew that her husband wanted her, and he wanted her badly. Mikell laid Ailese on the bed on her back, and he began to touch every inch of her body. Ailese wanted him too; she wanted to taste him and to feel every inch of him. "I love you so much," Mikell whispered in her ear. I don't want you to think about anything but us. Mikell took Ailese's hands and pinned them above her head, saying, Relax baby." Ailese didn't mind the roughness that Mikell was putting on her body. They both needed this to let loose and to focus on each other. Mikell made love to her like he did on their honeymoon and then some. Ailese let her husband take her; she let him lead, spoiling him. She loved letting Mikell have his way with her. Ailese wanted him even more now that Mikell was in between her legs kissing her thighs and vagina, feeling all her juices flowing, feeling her trembling, and hearing her moaning. Ailese and Mikell felt one another's thrust; he fulfilled her in every way, and she fulfilled him in every way. She felt warm, and when he was inside her, he didn't want to stop; he wanted to stay inside of her; he wanted this moment to never end. He told her how good she felt. It was hard for Ailese to be silent; she always had that problem. She didn't want the kids to hear them making love, and Ailese wasn't a quiet lover; she loved to show her emotions. Ailese grabbed the sheets and held on to them for dear life, like her life depended on it. She began to climax. She grabbed Mikell's body and buried her face into his shoulders. Mikell whispered to her, "Let's come together." Mikell began to move his body in a fast motion, and they climaxed at the same time. Mikell began to kiss Ailese on her neck and her breasts. Ailese kissed Mikell on his chest, and they held each other.

The restaurant was very packed with a lot of people. The place was very busy, with waiters and waitresses running around and bartenders hard at work as well.

Mikell had made reservations, so he wasn't worried about not getting a seat. The kids loved Ten Jayes restaurant. They served everything from seafood to Italian food, so everyone could order whatever they were in the mood to eat.

They sat in the middle of the restaurant, which had different types of art on the walls, beautiful lightning, and expensive chandeliers. The waiters dressed in different -colored polo shirts and black slacks, and the waitresses dressed in camel -colored slacks and different -colored ruffled shirts. There was soft music playing throughout the restaurant. There were tall black and white candles at every table.

"Excuse me, I will be right back I need to go to the little girl's room. Do you girls need to go?" "Yes, Mom, we're coming with you." Ashanee said as she got up from her chair.

Mikell looked as the girls disappeared out of his sight. "So, Armont, what's been going on with my main man, huh?" "Oh guess what Dad?" "Mmm … I guess that you have some good news for me, Mikell giggled. "I got an A+ on my English paper, you know the paper where I had to write about what would I do if I were President?" "Alright, they both gave each other high fives. I am so proud of you son. I knew that you were going to ace that paper." "Dad, I was talking to Mom earlier about you and me not having our guy time anymore; it bothers me, Dad, and I really miss you!" "I'm sorry, man; you're right we haven't been hanging out much lately. I've been really busy with work, and I work hard for you, all of you." Armont looked at his dad. They made eye contact, and Mikell was really touched to know that his son still needed him and enjoyed his company. Most teenagers become bored with their parents. How about we have a guy's day tomorrow?" "What about work? Armont said. "Work will be there, son, and you can pick what you want to do. We can get an early start." Armont eyes lit up like a Christmas tree.

"Wow, that dinner was so awesome Adrieana said. Everyone agreed with her. Can we have dessert, Mom and Dad?" "If you have enough room, you can. It's fine." When the dessert arrived, Ailese sipped her coffee slowly and carefully. As everyone was enjoying their dessert and talking among themselves, Ailese and Mikell stared at their children. They loved to see them getting along with one another. They loved spending time with the kids. They didn't want the evening to end.

"Dad, I'm ready to go whenever you are," Armont said to his dad, who was searching for his keys. "Okay, as soon as I find my keys, we can get going. Ailese, have you seen my keys, hun?" "I found them. You left them in the restroom. Are you okay?" Ailese handed Mikell his keys. "I'm fine. I do have a lot on my mind but spending some time with our son is more important. What's on my mind will have to wait. I will be okay. I promise I will stop thinking about work." Ailese smiled at Mikell and gave him a quick kiss on the lips, telling him that she was going to hold him to that. Ailese walked the guys to the door, and gave her son a huge hug, she noticed how happy her son was to be with his dad.

Ailese went into the bedroom to pick out an outfit for church. The girls were already getting ready for church. Ailese decided on a purple and black dress with gold trimming and matching shoes. Everyone was ready on time. Ailese called D'Andra to let her know that she was on her way to pick her up.

When they arrived, her mother Alonda greeted Ailese. They attended the same church and had been members for a few years now. Ailese always looked forward to Sundays because all the women would go out for brunch once a month and today was that day. "Hi Mom! You look gorgeous! Alonda kissed Ailese on the cheek. Ailese also greeted Don Zell, who she was surprised to see because he just had leg surgery and was walking with a cane. "How are you feeling, Don?" "Hey you, it's been awhile. I feel good, I have to go to the doctor next week. I'm hoping I can go back to work. I've never watched so much television in my life!" Ailese laughed. "You're a tough one, so I'm sure that you will be back to work soon."

Everyone enjoyed the service. All the women met at the usual spot called Ally's Café, which served the best American food in town. The café was known for its sandwiches, milkshakes, french fries, and out-of-this- world drinks. "Hi, how are you ladies today?" The waitress knew everyone. Since they ate at the café once a month, they all became friendly with her. Her name was Kaye, she had been working there for a while now, and she even knew what everyone liked to order.

Everyone said their hellos to Kaye as they were being seated. "So are we having the regular today?" Everyone agreed that they would have their regular meals. "I need to check on Don. I will be right back." Alonda got up from her chair and walked outside. "Are you doing okay Don?" "Yes, I'm good. Guess who's here?" "Who?" "Mikell and Armont called to see if they could visit me, since you were at your Sunday brunch, I told them that they could stop by." "Oh, tell them I said hello, okay. Don don't do too much, okay? I don't want you to overdo it. I know how you are. If you go anywhere, please be careful. See you soon. Love you." "I love you too, Alonda. Don't worry go have fun. I know I am." They both hung up.

When Alonda came back to the table, everyone's drinks had already been served, and everyone was talking among themselves. Alonda took a sip of her drink and began to talk to Ailese. "Everything's fine, guess what? Mikell and Armont are over at the house right now." "Oh, that's good. I know that Armont has been wanting to visit Don. He loves watching Don's old movies. I'm glad that Don won't be alone." "Me too, me too," Alonda said, smiling. Ailese's cell phone rang. She didn't recognize the number but answered it anyway. She stepped away to answer the call. "Hello, this is Mrs. LaShae." Hello, I am trying to reach Ailese LaShae?" "This is she. How can I help you?" Ailese was thinking about who this person was and hoped that it was important. She needed to get back to her brunch. "I apologize for calling you on a Sunday. This is Mr. Lee, Shane's father, and I am told that my son will be taking your daughter Adrieana to the school dance. I hope I haven't caught you at an inconvenient time." "No, how are you, Mr. Lee?" "I am good. I won't hold you long. I was wondering if we could meet you and Adrieana before the dance." "Oh, I do agree. Let me speak with my husband. Is this a good number to reach you?" "Yes, it is." "I will give you a call this evening. My husband and our son are on an adventure," Ailese chuckled. I am expecting everyone to be home this evening." "Okay, talk to you then." Ailese headed back to the table. She was lucky that the food hadn't arrived yet. She hoped that her phone wouldn't ring until after brunch. Ashanee and Adrieana were sitting next to D'Andra, who were talking among themselves, Ailese smiled.

Ailese waited until D'Andra looked up, and they both gave each other eye contact. They both headed to the restroom. "Are you okay, Ailese?" "Yes, I just got a call from Mr. Lee, he's Shane's dad. Shane asked Adrieana to the school dance. He wants us to meet his family. I just think that was sweet." "Wow, sorry to tell you this, but you do not have any babies anymore. Speaking of babies, Chris and I are ready to have one." "Oh my gosh, congrats! Ailese started to tear up. I am so happy for you guys. I will kill ya if I am not the godmother," Ailese said, frowning at D'Andra. "Now you know that you're already the godmother, you know that." They both laughed and returned to their seats at the table.

"Ailese, could you come over for a bit?" "Sure, why not. Where is Chris?" D'Andra looked at Ailese and paused. "He's on a business trip. He had an emergency and took the red eye. I miss him so much, and we need to finish packing."

"Well, you know I'm here, so let's do some packing girl!" The girls asked their aunt if they could watch movies in the entertainment room, and she told them that they could.

"Let me know if you guys need anything, okay. Your mom and I will be upstairs, okay?" The girls headed to the room to watch movies. "So, what's up sis? I know that look in your eye. I'm listening," Ailese said, raising her eyebrows.

D'Andra let out a long sigh. "I'm scared, Ailese, so scared, D'Andra started to cry. Ailese walked over to her and held her. "Speak to me. You know you can tell me anything, you know that D." I'm afraid to have children. I mean I want children, but I don't know, I just … don't know Ailese." "Well, first of all, you will make a great mom. You know why? Because you are my kids' second mom, I trust you with them. You have that motherly instinct already. I think you were born with it. Ailese smiled. You know whatever you need I'm there. Yes, having kids is a huge decision. Having kids is hard work, but I believe that you and Chris are going to make great parents!" Ailese picked up a tissue and handed it to her sister. D'Andra wiped her face and smiled at Ailese. "You really do mean that, do you? What will I ever do without you? Thank you. I'm so lucky to have you." "No, we're lucky to have each other. Please don't hesitate to call me day or night. Hey, get your purse. I know what we need to do. I'll get the girls." They ended up at a bookstore. D'Andra looked puzzled, she didn't know why they were at the bookstore. "Follow me, okay. Everyone stay together, okay?" Ailese let the girls look around while Ailese led D'Andra to the motherhood aisle of the bookstore. She showed D'Andra what books to get so that she could prepare for a family and that D'Andra and Chris could read them together. "These books helped me so much because my mother had brought me so many books on labor and raising a child the right way. I know she didn't want to explain some things to me she would have been embarrassed to discuss with me." D'Andra was fascinated with all the books about babies. The girls met them at the counter with some books that they wanted to buy themselves. "This is on me D, I don't want to hear a sound." Ailese paid for the books and headed back to D'Andra's house. Everyone helped pack a few boxes here and there and afterward they all watched a movie and headed home after it was over.

"Okay, girls, you guys need to get ready for school tomorrow. Adrieana, could you please come here?" Adrieana headed to where her mom was sitting in the spare bedroom. "Hey, Mom, what's up?" "I talked to Shane's dad, Mr. Lee. He wants us to meet before the dance." "When did he call?" "At brunch, he sounds like a nice man. I told him that I would have to speak to your father first. I just wanted to let you know that." "Okay, thanks, Mom. Could you let me know what day we'll be going to Shane's?" "Sure. Ailese gave Adrieana a kiss on her forehead, and Adrieana smiled at her mom as she walked back into her room. The phone rang, and Ailese answered it. "Hey girl, what's up?" "Hey, I miss you already. I just wanted to thank you for the books, there is so much information. Chris wanted me to thank you also. He and I have been reading since he got home." "Oh, when did he get home?" "A few hours ago, we've been packing, and we'll read the books in between breaks. Thanks for listening today. I meant what I said, Ailese, I don't know what I would do without you."

"I'm going to always be there until the day I die. We made a promise, remember? "I love you, D'Andra. You are truly my sister." "Don't make me start crying, Ailese, D'Andra said angrily and then laughed. Hey, I'm going to let you go and say goodnight, and we'll talk tomorrow." "You bet, love ya sis." "Ditto, bye." They both hung up at the same time.

Ailese always had a hard time getting along with females, period. They always loved stabbing her in the back, even though Ailese was never two-faced, and she never kissed anyone's ass to get on their good side because Ailese always treated people with respect. She always had a huge heart which would always get her in trouble. Ailese would give you her last dollar, shelter, and clothes if you needed them. For some reason, the males saw what Ailese represented and didn't take her for granted. The females on the other hand, were a different story. D'Andra was the only female that Ailese got along with. They both took each other under their wings. They've never fought; they don't agree on everything, but they've never disrespected each other.

They knew each other like the backs of their hands. They were both okay with that, and for the first time, Ailese was fine with that too. She considered D'Andra as her sister, the sister she always wished for. Ailese and D'Andra have been there for each other through the breakups, losing a loved one, and being the maid of honor when they both got married. Even though D'Andra's parents died in a car accident when D'Andra was very young, Ailese never left her side. Ailese's mom let D'Andra live with them for a few years until her aunt decided to come for her, after which her aunt just claimed that her parents' lawyer finally dug up a will that stated that D'Andra had to live with her aunt. As soon as D'Andra turned eighteen, she moved back to Shelby to be close to Ailese, and she never looked back.

Ailese was finished with the earrings. She was very pleased how they turned out; they were fabulous, she thought to herself. She put them in a gold shimmer box and put it away, thinking that she would make sure she brought the earrings with her when she had her appointment with Dr. Salvino next week. Ailese looked through her date book and skimmed over the appointments that she had for next week. She sighed and said to herself, "Another busy, busy week."

Ailese checked on the girls, they were both heading to the kitchen. "What's up, girls?" "We're just thirsty." Adrieana said as she kissed her mom on the cheek. What time are Dad and Armont coming home?" "Soon, come to think of it, I haven't heard anything from your dad since we were at brunch. I better call him." Ailese went to the phone that was in the kitchen and dialed Mikell's cell number. There was no answer, she left him a voice mail asking him to check in, then she called her mom's number. "Mom, are Mikell and Armont still there by any chance?" "I was just going to call you because Don isn't here either. He left me a message that he took off with Mikell and that he would be back before dinner. I called his cell and there was no answer." "Mmm ... okay, well, maybe they're in an area where the service is bad. I wonder where they could be." "I don't know Ailese if they don't return soon ... Ailese interrupted her mom and told her not to worry and that they were all responsible men. Ailese sat down on the couch and called Mikell's cell again. This time he answered. "Hey Lee, were stuck in traffic. I'm sorry that I didn't check in, time just got away from me." "Yes, I do understand that, but mom and I were starting to get worried, Don left her a message that he would be back before dinner and hadn't heard from him she called his cell but there was no answer, babe is everyone okay?" "Yes, yes, we're fine. We went to a ball game, lunch shopping and babe, hello, hello." The call had ended. Ailese called Mikell back but he didn't answer the phone, Ailese decided to just wait until he called her back, she called her mom to let her know that she talked to Mikell, her mom was relieved Ailese told her that they should be home and that they were stuck in traffic.

Mikell and Armont arrived at home an hour later. "Babe, where are you, we're home. Armont followed his dad to look for his mom, but she wasn't answering them. She may be in the shower. Go and get ready for school, son, okay. I will let mom know that you want to talk to her, okay?" "Okay, Dad." Armont headed to his room and closed the door behind him. Mikell heard the shower running as he entered the bedroom. He began to undress and decided to join his wife in the shower. He knocked on the door, and entered. "Baby, it's me. I'm home," he smiled as he opened the doors to the shower. Ailese turned around and welcomed him with open arms. "Mmm. I missed you so much. Where's my boy?" "Oh he wants to talk to you when were done, we had a blast!" "I'm glad that you all had fun, but next time, please try harder and check in at least twice, okay? Especially if you guys are taking my dad, you know how my mom gets. She tends to worry easily." "I know I'm sorry, baby." Mikell kissed her on the lips.

"Hey Armont, what's up, son? Dad said that you wanted to talk to me." "Hey, Mom. He hugged his mom tight. Thanks, Mom." Ailese had a puzzled look on her face. "For what, hun?" "For giving me the advice to talk to dad about spending guy time together, we had so much fun, and guess what Dad said? That Sunday's is guy days; our day after church." Armont had a big smile on his face. He showed his mom what his dad and grandpa bought him at the game and told her all the activities they did. She noticed how excited Armont would get just talking about his day with his dad.

"Well, hun, it sounds like you had a pretty eventful day, huh? You love your dad, huh?" "I do I love him so much, and I thought that he was too busy for me, and that kind of hurt my feeling but … well, everything's okay now. I just love spending time with dad, that's all." Ailese shook her head and gave her son a kiss before he went to bed. "Love you, big guy." "Love you too, Mom."

Ailese found Mikell lying on the bed in his boxers looking at some magazine. He looked up to see Ailese heading to the restroom, and he followed her into the restroom. "Armont was so overjoyed to have spent the entire day with you; he adores you. So, you're stuck with us for life; you know that"

Ailese said that as she was playfully choking Mikell. He jokingly gagged. "I know I don't mind. I love my family more than anything." "So, are you hungry? I could fix you something." "Oh no I'm stuffed from earlier I just want to relax, do you want to cuddle with me sexy?" "Sure, after we check in on the kids." They checked on the kids and went back to their room. Just as they began to lay down, there was a knock on the door. It was Adrieana.

"Mom Shane's dad wants to speak to you. We were on the phone already." "Give me a minute, okay? I need to speak to your father. Hun, what day are you free next week? It has to be before Adrieana's school dance." "Whatever day you need me, I'm there." "Okay, that was easy." Ailese picked up the phone. "Hello, Mr. Lee, I do have to apologize for not getting back to you sooner. I've been a bit side tracked today. How are you?" "I'm okay, and you?" "Good. I do look forward to meeting you and your family, Mr. Lee." "Well, are you guys free on Friday evening?" "Yes, we are free. Okay, we will see you then." Ailese told Adrieana that they would be going to Shane's on Friday evening and to make sure she came straight home that day and that she had to skip study hall. Ailese told Adrieana to let her brother and sister know that they didn't need to go to study hall on Friday.

"Oh, Mom and Dad, you guys are the best! Thank you, thank you so much!"

Adrieana kissed them both and skipped out of the room.

The next morning Ailese and Mikell got everyone off to school. Since Mikell drove the kids to school today, she had a little extra time to herself before she left for work. Ailese didn't have a set time to be at work, she liked to arrive no later than 9:00 a.m. Going in after nine was too late for her, she thought the earlier she started the better.

She decided to fix a lunch and take some coffee with her today, being that she may not have time to get a bite to eat. Ailese made some phone calls and headed out. As she was walking to her car, she heard a female voice call her name. She turned around and it was Evette, who lived a couple of houses down. She was a single parent who had one daughter named Heather, who was ten years old. She had never been married. Heather would visit the girls every now and then. Evette would sometimes come to Ailese's for drinks and conversation from time to time. They would even play games for entertainment. But lately they haven't been spending time together since Evette's mother has been sick. She had been staying at the hospital every day.

Evette parked her car next to Ailese's, got out, and walked over to Ailese. "Hello, my friend." They both greeted one another with a hug. "How's your mom doing?" "She is getting better, we're hoping that they will release her in a week or so." "That's good to hear, Evette, and hey did you and your mom get the flowers that we sent?" "Yes, thank you. I'm sorry. I should have called." "No worries you, have a lot on your plate right now. I just wanted to know if your mom got them." "Maybe we can get together soon?" "You know it, Ailese said as she hugged her friend. You need anything, please don't hesitate to call; you and your family are in our prayers." Ailese could tell that Evette was very stressed out. She felt for her.

When Ailese arrived at work, she was ready to tackle whatever came her way, whether it's documents to sign or meetings to attend. She was determined to complete everything today. Her day went by really fast, so she thought, until she received a call from a client who argued with Ell and Ailese that their appointment was for today and not tomorrow. They both tried to make the client understand that it may have been their secretary's error and misunderstandings happen. The client had threatened to pull their business from the company, and Ailese knew that Mr. Saxx would not like this at all, so she compromised with the client and invited them for a late lunch to go over the details. "I hate to ask you this, Ell, but you're going to have to push everyone else back an hour or so, and if they give you a hard time, transfer them to me." "I understand, boss. No problem, I will get right on it. Did you need me to attend the meeting?" Ailese looked at her watch and sighed. She was thinking to herself how much she needed Ell at the meeting but didn't want to keep her. "I do." Ailese had a sad look on her face. I hope I haven't ruined any of your plans." "No you need me, so I'm there, you know that, now let me start making some calls okay?" Ell walked away before Ailese could say anything else.

Ell buzzed Ailese's desk to let her know that she didn't have any problems at all pushing the client's appointments back and that she was getting the files together that they needed for the meeting. Ailese was a bit irritated; she really didn't like to inconvenience anyone, but she knew that she was doing the right thing, and most of her clients were troopers.

Ailese was relieved when the meeting ended. "These clients are something else, she thought. I have my work cut out for me." She thanked Ell for all her hard work and for being there when she needed her the most. Ailese decided that she was going to make sure she was early tomorrow so she could have a huge bouquet of flowers on her desk, to show her that she really appreciated her. Maybe I will take her to lunch tomorrow and give her the rest of the day off, Ailese reasoned. "Ailese, Mikell's on line 2 for you." "Thanks, Ell."

"Hello, hun, how's your day going?" "It would be perfect if you said yes to my question that I am about to ask you." Ailese raised her eyebrows and wondered what it could be. "Oh man, I don't like this. Go ahead and shoot, and I can't promise you that I will say yes, hun." "I know Lee, just hear me out, okay? I need someone; a female with a great voice to sing a couple of hooks on one of my artist's songs, baby please, I need you to do this for me." There was silence on the other end. Ailese closed her eyes and hit her desk gently with her hand. She wanted to say no, but the desperation in his voice made her know that she couldn't say no. "Okay, Mik, but before I set it in stone, I don't want this coming in between our family and my work. If you can promise me that it won't, then we have a deal. I do need more details though." "Thanks, babe. You won't be sorry, baby. Why don't you come by the office tomorrow?" "I don't know what my schedule looks like. I'm not near my book. Hey, let me patch you through Ell, okay? She can let you know the time and date." "Okay, baby, but I do want to talk to you after I talk to Ell, okay?"

"Guess what? I will see you tomorrow at 2:00 p.m. Mrs. LaShae." "Oh okay Mik I look forward to seeing you tomorrow at 2:00 p.m. Ailese said in a serious voice. Mikell assured Ailese that he would make sure that she had time for the kids, and her work, and that he would work around her schedule. He would do whatever it took.

Ailese called D'Andra to let her know the good news; she was very excited for her. "I wish I could work with my hubby; you're so lucky! Don't forget to invite me to come to the studio, girlfriend. I want to see you in action." "I won't. Ailese assured D'Andra. You know you'll be there. I won't forget you, sis. I'm excited and nervous at the same time, you know." "You're a fantastic singer, Mrs. Laydee. You have nothing to be concerned about"

Ailese noticed that Mikell was already home when she pulled into the driveway. She was shocked that he was home so early. Ailese was greeted by a familiar smell in the kitchen. It was Mikell's famous Parmesan Chicken. She knew that smell anywhere. Mikell was concentrating on dinner when she walked into the kitchen. He didn't even hear her come in. She came up from behind him and hugged him. He turned around and said dinner would be ready in twenty minutes and he went back to what he was doing. Ailese had gotten comfortable and checked on the kids before she went back into the kitchen.

She began to set the table for dinner and asked Mikell if he needed any help. He told her that he just needed her to make sure there were drinks in the fridge, which she did. She decided on water and maybe a little wine for Mikell and herself. She filled up the serving jug with ice-cold water and went to the wine cabinet and pulled out a bottle of wine. She then placed them on the table. She watched Mikell finish dinner. She thought that he was so thoughtful to get home early to cook her favorite; how sweet was that? She could smell all the spices, and her mouth was watering for his Parmesan Chicken, but she was waiting patiently. "Dinner was sooooo delicious, babe, thanks. You're so sweet, you know that?" "Yep, I do, and you're welcome, anytime. It was the least I could do being that you saved my butt today, Mikell said, touching her face. I wanted to properly thank you. I'm so excited you have no idea." He took her hand and led her into the living room sat her down on the loveseat, and sat next to her. I just wanted to talk to you about the artist that we're working with. He does a little bit of everything, and I can't wait for you to meet him tomorrow. He's excited too, because I talk about you a lot! Ailese kissed Mikell and laid her head on his shoulder. I don't want to overwhelm you. I know you have a lot on your plate, but I wanted to ask you. Remember that song you and I wrote a few months ago?" "Yes ... I do. I still have it, why?" "I loved that song. I still remember most of it." Ailese started singing. "What will I ever do without you baby? There is no one else that could do the things that you do." Mikell smiled and began to join her on the next chorus. "Oh, my word, we do remember it, huh?" "Well, I had an idea. You trust me, don't you?" "No, sorry, I don't." Mikell began to tickle Ailese. "What did you say, huh, huh?" "Stop, please Mik stop." Ailese was laughing uncontrollably. "I'll stop if you take back what you said." "Okay, I trust you. For real, I do." Mikell stopped tickling Ailese. "I think using our song, is a terrific idea, but I think I'm a bit rusty so, I better practice in my spare time. I don't want to disappoint anyone." "You won't, sweetie." Ailese and Mikell talked for a while about the meeting and headed to bed, it was late.

Ailese woke up, her body jolted, she was out of breath, she had another nightmare, and she began to sob. She had gone to the restroom because she didn't want to wake up Mikell. The dream seemed so real that she had thought about calling D'Andra but didn't want to wake her up either. She sat on the bathroom floor and sobbed more. She couldn't stop. She told herself that she'd better get it together, that she wasn't and shouldn't be afraid of this man, and she refused to let this bastard take control of her life. Why am I having these dreams about him. She started to think about what Dr. Salvino had said to her, that it could be stress or something else that triggers our dreams as well. She woke up Mikell and began to sob some more. Mikell held her. "Tell me what's wrong, Lee, please." It took everything she had to get the words out of her mouth. "I had another bad dream. I'm so scared Mikell. Please hold me tighter. Don't let me go." "Tell me what the dream was about, baby. I'm here for you. I won't let no one hurt you ever!" "I'm scared that if I talk about it and go back to sleep, I will have a bad dream again." Mikell wiped her tears from her face. "Look at me. Baby, it may help you, but I won't force you." "I just want you to hold me, Mik." He held her and told her that he understood, and when she's ready to talk about her dreams he'll be there to listen. Ailese finally fell back to sleep, but a few hours later, she had another bad dream. This time she was screaming, "Don't hurt me, don't hurt me!" She punched Mikell when he tried to wake her up. "Baby, it's me. He grabbed her hands and held them tight so she wouldn't punch him again. Lee baby wake up. Mikell gently shook her, and Ailese began to cry. She tried to come back to reality and realized that her dream wasn't real. She was shaking uncontrollably. Mikell slowly hugged her and whispered in her ear. "I'm right here." He repeated himself over and over again. He began rocking her as he held her in his arms. Mikell didn't like to see his wife like this, scared and afraid, not sleeping well because something or someone is controlling her dreams. What could it be? Mikell didn't let his wife go. He held her all night. He felt helpless. She's seeing Dr. Salvino, which was a start. She needed to talk to a professional like Dr. Salvino. He knew that she could help her, but she just started her sessions with her. Mikell would do anything in his power to protect his wife from harm or from anyone. Mikell was her protector. If he could have a wish right now, it would be to erase all of her bad memories.

Last night was a long, hard night for Mikell and Ailese; they haven't had a night like this in a long time. "Lee, we need to talk," Mikell said as he led her into the spare bedroom and shut the door. I'm not sure if you remember what happened last night, but we need to talk. I'm worried about you." He had a worried look on his face. "No, we don't need to talk.

What is there to talk about? Yes, I had another episode. I'm sorry. Maybe it would be better if you slept in the spare bedroom." Ailese knew she did not want this at all. "Ailese, what are you saying? You know that's not an option. Baby, please listen. I just love you so much. I hate seeing you like this," Mikell said in an angrily voice. "I'm sorry," Ailese said as she massaged her temples and put her head down. Mikell lifted her chin so she would look at him. "Hun, I just think that you should take some time off from work to spend more time with Dr. Salvino so she can figure out why these dreams are returning. We need to know." Ailese could see the hurt in his eyes and how much he wanted all his questions answered for his wife and for himself. "I do understand what you're asking, but I've only had one session and it takes time, one session isn't going to answer all of our questions." She looked at Mikell, hoping that he'd agree with her. Mikell was silent for a few seconds, then he responded. "I think that we should just focus on your sessions with Dr. Salvino and hold off on starting our project together. What do you think about that?" "Okay, that sounds good, says Ailese, crossing her arms. I do have an appointment this week, and I know that these things take time, so we have to be patient. I don't want you to delay your artist and what was already planned, I don't like to let people down, you know that. My sessions have to come first, and then my sessions with you." "Ailese, please, I am concerned about my wife, and my work should be the least of your problems, hun." "Yeah, you're right," Ailese said with a slight grin. She poked Mikell playfully. "I love you, Lee, so much. Please don't think that I'm trying to tell you what to do, but we're a team, and we need to always have each other's backs, okay?" "I love you too, Mikell, she hugged him and whispered to him, I'll always have your back." "I'm sorry that you had a rough night." Mikell kissed her and held her tight. "Thank you for being so caring. Baby, we will get through this. I just feel bad waking you up." Mikell interrupted her. "That's not how I see it. If I have to lose sleep to get us through this, then so be it."

Mikell couldn't stop thinking about the conversation that he and Ailese had earlier. He began thinking that if he knew where this bastard lived, he could get someone to take care of him, but Mikell knew that wouldn't solve the problem. He wasn't a violent person, not a mean bone in his body, but when it came to his family, he would do anything to protect them. This guy hurt his wife so badly that she has these bad dreams -dreams of him hurting her. Ailese told Mikell earlier on when they were dating, Ailese had to tell him because she would withdraw from Mikell a lot, and sometimes when Mikell would stay the night with Ailese, she would have those same dreams, so she had to tell him. Mikell had to hear about the mental abuse, physical abuse, and the emotional abuse that this bastard put his wife through. Because of this guy, Ailese had a hard time trusting men in general. Mikell was very patient with Ailese, he understood. Mikell was gentle with Ailese and still is to this day. After Mikell heard Ailese's story, he wanted to kill this man! He wanted to whip him off the face of the earth! You never disrespect a woman like that, never! No one was allowed to speak this bastard's name, ever. It would give Ailese the chills, and she just wanted to move on and forget about him.

"Hey baby, I just wanted to check on you. How's your day going?" "Hi, I'm just trying to stay awake. I may have to have Ell run and get me some more coffee. I've had two cups already today. I'm glad you called. I wanted to let you know that I love you and thank you for always being there for me. Please don't ever think that I feel like you're telling me what to do. I know that you care about me, and you only want what's best for me, Mikell." "That makes my day hearing that, babe, and once again, I want you to know that I only want what's best for you. I don't like to see you suffer, that's all." "I know I love you, Mikell. What will I ever do without you?" Ailese gave Mikell a kiss over the phone, and he gave one back. "Ell, could you run and get me some more coffee, please?" "Okay, oh, boss, thanks for my flowers and the nice gift. May I ask why?" "For being the best assistant in the entire world, silly," they both laughed.

Ailese heard a knock on her door. She stood up from her chair and opened the door, and to her surprise, it was Mikell standing there with bags in his hands. "Hi, have you eaten yet?" "This is a surprise. Hi, baby, and no, I haven't eaten yet." She was so happy to see him, and she was in a bit of shock. Mikell sat the bags down on her desk, which was clear of papers and very tidy and neat. He smiled when he saw the pictures of him and his family.

"I got us some Asian chicken rolls and salads with Asian sauce, and some iced teas. I'm having the same." He placed the food carefully in front of Ailese, and he handed her some napkins. "Mmmm, this smells so good. How did you know that I was craving this, huh? Are you living in my head?" She said with laughter. "No, he said laughing. I just thought that you would like your favorite for lunch, that's all." "This is so sweet of you. Thanks, baby." Mikell could see the joy in his wife's eyes.

They ate and talked. Ailese even told Ell to hold all her calls until Mikell left. "Hey, boss, sorry to interrupt. I just wanted to thank Mikell for lunch, it was so delicious." "You're welcome, Ell."

"So what time are they expecting you back?" "I didn't give them a time. They'll call my cell if they need anything. Gabe and the boys will be fine without me."

"Thanks, I'm so stuffed. That was so delicious Mikell. We need to do this more often, you think?" "I agree, my dear." Mikell said in a french accent.

Mikell had already left a smile on Ailese's face, and she couldn't stop thinking about her husband, how lucky she was to have him, and how good he is to her. She called Mikell to thank him again, and he told her he couldn't stop thinking about her.

Later on in the day, Mikell received a call from Officer Brown. He had some new information about the robbery that took place at his business, and he wanted to speak with him in person. "Hello, Mr. LaShae, I want to thank you for squeezing me into your busy schedule. I just wanted to follow up with you on this case." "No problem at all Officer Brown. I am glad that you're here; good news I hope?" "Actually, I do, Officer Brown said as Mikell offered him a seat. I do want to warn you, you may not like what I am about to tell you. Mr. Lashae, we viewed the video footage very carefully and thoroughly, and we also had pictures of all the employees that your assistant provided us, and we concluded that this was an inside job, Mr. LaShae." Mikell went numb and silent at the same time. He knew that the officer made a mistake. He knew all of his employees like the backs of his hands. No one would betray him.

"Are you sure, officer? I mean no disrespect, sir. I'm not doubting that your investigation was done correctly, but I just can't believe that someone who works here will be that immature to steal from the company. Please just tell me who it is, please." Mikell felt himself getting upset and angry and he told himself not to. He needed to stay calm. "I know how you feel, Mr. LaShae, but sometimes these situations happen more often than we think, and again, Mr. LaShae, I do apologize. Mikell interrupted him and told him that he didn't have to apologize, because it wasn't his fault.

"You do have options. First of all, we can confront them together, or I can escort them off the premises and book them. This all can be done if you want to press charges." Mikell was a laid-back person, and avoided confrontation when he could. He didn't want to have to fire an employee. He began to remember the days that he had to steal and rob places just to eat or when he needed shelter; that was wrong, but he had to do what he to do to survive in the streets, so he thought that maybe the person who stole the equipment was in trouble. What could be the reason? They could have come to him or Emmanuel. They would have helped him or her; they were a family.

Officer Brown stood up and walked over to Mikell and told him that he could give him a few minutes to think about whether he needed to be alone or talk to his partner about making the decision. Mikell found himself daydreaming. Officer Brown called his name to get his attention. This has really thrown Mikell for a loop. His day was going great until this happened. "Okay, yes, I do need a few minutes if you don't mind." Officer Brown told Mikell that he needed to make some rounds and would be back soon. He told him to take his time.

Mikell called Emmanuel and asked him to come into his office as soon as possible. Emmanuel could tell from Mikell's voice that it wasn't good.

Emmanuel was there in Mikell's office in a flash. He could see the look on Mikell's face as he entered the office. Mikell walked over to the window and rubbed his chin. "We have a decision to make. I just had a visit from Officer Brown. They found the persons who robbed the studio and do you know. Mikell paused to keep his composure. He turned to

Emmanuel, who was sitting in the chair that was by the desk. Do you know that it's one of our own?" Emmanuel's heart sank to his feet. "Are you serious, man? No, that just can't be right. I mean, were all family here." "I do have the names. I decided that we should hear what the officer has to say together, so we could decide, right then and there.

So, I want both of us in this together. We need to come to an agreement and be on the same page with this." "I totally agree, so when will the officer be coming back?" "I'm going to call him in a few minutes, he said he was going to make some rounds." An hour passed, and Officer Brown came back to Mikell's office ready to hear the decision. "These are the names that we have: Leon McCray and Andre' Strickland, Officer Brown showed Emmanuel the video and the pictures that Mikell had already seen, as well as the evidence that the police department had to prove their case. After looking at the video and the evidence carefully and thoroughly, they both agreed that the robbers were Leon and Andre. They were both in shock. The guys decided to fire them and speak to them. They couldn't afford to have thieves as employees because too much was at stake. "Thank you, officer. We will need for you to escort them from the premises because if I do it, it won't be pretty. These guys were very trustworthy, and I don't expect to get back what they took. I know that's long gone." "Officer if we press charges, how long would they be in jail?" "Well, it depends. Both men do not have criminal records, so they may not get much time. It will be up to the judge." "Wow I think these guys thought that they were really going to get away with it. They even showed up at the meeting excluding Andre, who works in another department here in the building but who does help us out in the studio from time to time." "Wow, this is serious." Emmanuel said with a look of disgust. "Yeah, you think you can trust someone, and you think you know them; think again. You really don't, Mikell said.

Mikell buzzed Leenah on the phone. Leenah, could you please come into my office right away." "Yes, I'll be right there." Leenah entered Mikell's office with an anxious look. She could feel something was going on. It had to have been something serious, since the officer was present. Mikell and Emmanuel spoke to Leenah and gave her instructions on what to do as far as the paperwork and procedures that they needed to go through before terminating the men. Leenah was surprised herself that Leon and Andre would get themselves into all this trouble. She was fond of Andre' and Leon. Why would they want to jeopardize their jobs? Mr. La Shae treated his employees very well. The men talked amongst themselves until Andre' and Leon arrived in the office. Leon and Andre' were both in their late twenties, they were very educated young men. Looking at both men, you would think they wouldn't hurt a fly. They spoke with gentle voices. As the men sat down, they looked confused and wondered why Emmanuel and Mikell, called them into the office. Officer Brown sat in a chair by the window and was quiet until it was his turn to speak.

"We called you guys into the office because we have a serious matter to discuss with you. I need you both to be honest with me. Do you understand me? Both men agreed. This is Officer Brown, Mikell said. He has been investigating the break- in that we had not too long ago. He has been a very big help in cracking the case, Mikell continued. Today he visited me with the evidence that he has, and I just want you to know that Emmanuel and I also went over the evidence that the officer and the police station came up with; they know what they're doing. Mikell noticed the men's expressions on their faces changed. I was very disappointed to see what I saw with my own eyes. I was and still am disgusted." Emmanuel took over. He could see that his good friend needed a break. "So, I am going to ask you, young men, why? There was silence in the room. Why, why, why? Who wants to go first?" Emmanuel said as he shrugged his shoulders.

Leon put his head down and looked at the floor. He had been caught and there was no room for lying. "My daughter is sick our medical bills are so expensive. Andre' poked Leon and gave him an angry look. "No, man, this was your idea, and I was stupid enough to believe that we were never going to get caught! You told me that the cameras were fake. Now I've ruined my life! I'm sorry."

Leon sobbed, knowing that he shouldn't have betrayed Mikell and Emmanuel. They gave him a chance when everyone else closed their doors in his face because he didn't have a degree in music, but a degree didn't matter to Mikell. He knew Leon was very smart and passionate about making music. He was very creative. "Now, we're not going to press charges because we feel that you have learned your lesson, Leon. Why didn't you come to us, man?" "Because I was embarrassed, I didn't feel like a man because I couldn't take care of my family. I mean, we were going to lose everything, and I didn't want us to live on the street. Please forgive me." "We do forgive you. I just don't think that Mr. Strickland doesn't feel bad about what he has done, do you?" Emmanuel walked in front of Andre; he stood there until Andre made eye contact with him. "I do feel bad about what I did. I'm truly sorry for getting Leon in trouble and betraying you guys as well. I'll do whatever it takes so that you won't press charges."

Officer Brown told the men that they were lucky that no one was going to press charges and that they should have gone to their boss, and this may have all been solved. "Leon, you knew that I would have done whatever I could to help you. I would have made sure that you didn't lose anything you know that!" Leon stood up and became face-to-face with Mikell. "I know I swallowed my pride, and look where it got me, -the one relationship and the one role model I had in my life. I let him down." I deserve whatever's coming to me."

Mikell was hurting inside. He wished he could turn back the clock for these young men, but he couldn't. "Don't beat yourself up, okay? I'm here for you, but unfortunately, we have to let you guys go. Mikell went back to his desk, picked up two gold envelopes, and walked back to the men. You will find everything on the checklist, please look it over before you leave. Officer Brown will be escorting you out of the building." Mikell went back to his desk, and told the men that if they promised not to come onto the property, they would not press charges but needed to sign the document. The men looked over the document and signed their names. Mikell called Leenah to his office so she could be a witness to sign more documents. Everything went fine. The men didn't disagree with anything and were very apologetic to Mikell and Emmanuel. The men didn't mind that the officer escorted them off the premises.

Mikell was ready to go home and see his family, even though he thought that he should have stayed at work longer, but he wasn't in the mood at all. Mikell just wanted this day to be over so he could start over tomorrow. It bothered him that Leon couldn't come to him with his problem; he could trust him, and whatever they discussed would always be between them and no one else.

Mikell felt he let Leon down. Was there something he did to make Leon feel he couldn't trust him? Mikell shrugged his shoulders. He took the long way home; he needed to get some things off his mind. Mikell thought that he would stop and get some coffee before he headed home. Maybe that would calm him down. The coffee did calm him a bit. Mikell told himself that he did his best and that it was good enough. He would call Leon soon to check on his family, if they needed anything. He would still help him out. He didn't want to stop being there for him. He just couldn't have Leon work there anymore.

Mikell was surprised to see that Ailese wasn't home, but he was early. He put his things down by the door and headed to the kitchen, thinking that he would finish his coffee and wait for Ailese and the kids to come home. There was a knock at the door. Mikell answered the door. It was Evette. She looked like she had been crying. "Hello, Evette, are you okay?" "I'm very sorry to bother you, but is Ailese here?" "No, she should be here soon. Come in, please, and have a seat. Evette sat down at the kitchen table, where Mikell had joined her. Can I get you something to drink?" "Water, please, if you don't mind." Evette didn't make eye contact; she felt that she was intruding and that she should wait until Ailese came home. Mikell sat a glass of cold water in front of Evette. "Please, tell me what's wrong? You look very upset." Evette took a long sip of her water and looked around the kitchen. "Are you sure that I'm not barging in on you, Mikell?" "No, please, go on." "I thought that my mom was getting better until today, when I got a call from the hospital that she had taken a turn for the worst. She has a fever that they are having a hard time keeping down, and she's back on a feeding tube. No matter what the doctors explain to me what happened to make my mom take a turn for the worse, I don't know if I'll ever understand it." Mikell reached for Evette's hands from across the table and held them in his; he felt her pain. "I'm so sorry, Evette, it looks like we both had one of those days.

Your mother will remain in our prayers. Do you go to church at all?" Evette paused and looked down. "Well, I used to, but taking care of my mom doesn't leave me much time for myself, you know?" Mikell told her that he did understand. "Hey, I have an idea maybe you can come with us to church this coming Sunday. I know Ailese would love that. I'm not trying to make you believe that everything will go back to normal with your mom, but just knowing the Lord gets you through a lot. I know trust me, Mikell said with a smile on his face. I mean, you don't have to go to church to speak to the Lord or have a relationship with him. He wants you to have a relationship with him, but God wants you to lean on him when in doubt or when in need." Evette was beginning to feel a lot better, talking to Mikell.

Ailese came home to find Evette at her kitchen table with her husband. She was very happy to see her friend. "Hey you, how are you?" "I came by to let you know that my mom isn't doing well at all, and your hubby here is a wonderful listener, "Evette said with a smiled at Mikell. "Yes, he is. I agree. Why don't you stay for dinner?" "I can't, I already feel like I'm imposing." Ailese interrupted her friend and demanded that she stay for dinner and that they had a lot of catching up to do. "So let me get out of these clothes and make a couple of phone calls, okay? I will be right back, hun. Could you please keep Evette company for me?" "Sure. Mikell kissed his wife before she headed to the bedroom.

After dinner, Ailese and Evette went into the family room to catch up. Ailese made herself comfortable and curled up onto the sofa. She invited Evette to do the same. Evette sat down next to Ailese, and they both found themselves curled up on the sofa. "I am so sorry to hear about your mom, hun. I'm praying that she gets better and comes home soon. It's all in God's hands now, even though the doctors say that she may not get better. It's not all up to them. It's up to God, you know?" "Thanks for being here for me, and yes, I do agree. I just don't know what I would do if I lost her, you know? I mean, I had to explain to Heather why her grandmother wasn't coming home. She calls her Mama, and calls me Mom, I think it's so cute. She's been calling her that since day one. She loves her my mom so much." "I can't imagine what you're going through. I remember when my best friend D'Andra, do you remember her?" "Yes, I do." "Well, when she lost both her parents in a car accident, I was there for her, and I felt her pain. Losing anyone close to you is very hard."

Evette told Ailese how much she appreciated her listening, and just being there for her through all the tough times meant a lot to her. She didn't have anyone to talk to because she was the only child. She only had Heather and her mom. Ailese assured her that she would be there for her and not to hesitate to call her or stop by if she needed anything. Ailese had always been a good listener; she was the best friend anyone could ever have, and you could always count on her. Before Evette headed to the hospital, she thanked Mikell for letting her wait until Ailese had gotten home and for his kindness.

After Evette left, Ailese went looking for Mikell and found him sitting in the kitchen drinking a glass of water. She didn't like the look he had on his face. She knew something was wrong because he was quiet at dinner. "Mik, tell me what's wrong, please?" Ailese sat at the kitchen table next to Mikell. She turned her chair around so that she was facing him. "I had the worst day today. You wouldn't believe it baby. I had a visit from Officer Brown, he cracked the case, and everything went to H-E-L-L. Sorry, you know I don't like using that word. I couldn't believe my ears or my eyes. From the look on Mikell's face, Ailese knew what he was about to tell her wasn't good-not at all.

So basically, I find out today that the people who broke into the building and stole the equipment, well, get ready for this one Lee. Mikell shrugged his shoulders. Well, it was Leon and Andre' who broke in and stole the equipment. Can you believe that?" Ailese's eyes widened with surprise. "Are you kidding? I don't believe you! Those guys? Aren't these the same young men that you believed in? You gave them the time of day, and they go and stab you in the back?" "Yes, that's exactly how I feel, babe; I mean, I was very surprised. I had all these emotions inside." Mikell told his wife what happened. She was sympathetic. She knew how much trust and time Mikell had put into Leon and Andre' and how fond Mikell was of them. She didn't like that her husband's kindness was taken for granted. The one thing that they both had in common was their huge hearts, and people would take advantage of their kindness. They give their hearts very easily and they put faith in people. It wasn't a bad thing to have a huge heart, but there had been lots of times where people that Ailese and Mikell helped and put their faith in ended up stabbing them in the back. They took their kindness for granted. They always managed to pick themselves up and move on, but they still tend to lend their hearts to people, no matter what happens. They just couldn't get off the welcome wagon.

"I am beat after the day I had. I'm surprised I'm still standing, but I won't let this keep me down." "I know you're my strong man," Ailese said as she playfully tried to flex a muscle. Mikell laughed at her and grabbed her. He thanked her for being the perfect wife. "I'm going to turn in, do you want to come with me, hun?" "Yes, Mik. Ailese stood up, and Mikell grabbed her from behind and gave her a huge bear hug. "Have I told you that I loved you today?" "Tell me right now, my love." I love you." "And I love you too, sexy."

As Ailese and Mikell were getting ready for bed, Mikell's cell phone rang, and he wondered who it could be. "Hello, hey, hold on for one second, okay?" He looked at Ailese and told her that it was Emmanuel and that he needed to take the call and would be right back. "Hey man, what's up?" "I just wanted to check on you. I know it was a crazy day today, and I also needed to let you know that my son isn't feeling too good, and my wife already left for her business trip. I gave him some medicine, but it seems that he's not getting any better. I'm actually calling you from the emergency room. He has a throat infection, so I have to find an all-night pharmacy to get his prescription filled, so he can feel better." "Hey, take care of my boy, okay? I need Junior to get well. That's my buddy. We have a guy's day coming up soon. Tell him to get better, okay?" "I will he love you to death, and I hope that tomorrow will be better for you, Mik. Just remember tomorrow is a new day, okay buddy?" "Yeah, Amen. Talk to you soon. I'll call you to check on my boy. Okay? I don't want you worrying, okay, I know how you get when you're not in the office." "Shut up, man, you're not right, it's all good."

"Junior's not feeling well, so Emmanuel wanted to let me know that he won't be in for a few days, and he wanted to check on me; you know that whole ordeal today, wow, what a day." "I understand, hun. I hope Junior gets better. He's the sweetest little boy." Ailese patted the bed, inviting Mikell to cuddle with her. He laid next to her. He thought that he should be tired, but he wasn't. They watched a little television and fell asleep. Ailese woke up in the middle of the night to check on the kids, who were sound asleep. When Ailese went back to bed, Mikell wasn't in bed, and she wondered where he was. She noticed that the bathroom light was on, so she figured he was using the restroom. She got back under the covers and waited for him to return to bed. "Hey, where did you go? Are you okay?" "Yes I went to check on the kids, Are you okay?" "Oh, yeah." They both went back to sleep. This night went smoothly. Ailese didn't have any bad dreams. She slept like a baby. Mikell slept like a baby as well.

Today was the day the family would meet Shane and his family. Ailese reminded everyone to come straight home. She figured Mr. Lee needed to meet the whole family, not just Mikell and herself. Ailese was a bit anxious to meet Shane and his family.

Adrieana wasn't nervous one bit. She was more excited than anything. This was her first school dance, and she was going with a boy. She knew how protective her mom was with all of her children, but she respected that; it didn't bother her. This day is very special. She knew deep down that her mom would like Shane and his family. As they pulled up in front of Mr. Lee's house, Ailese was in awe. She thought to herself, this house is gorgeous! She couldn't wait to see what awaited her inside. She began to picture it her mind.

Mikell knocked on the door, a butler answered the door and announced them, and the butler led them to a huge room with a lot of crystal. Everything in the room was white and burgundy -the prettiest burgundy Ailese had ever seen in her life. The butler seated them and told them that Mr. and Mrs. Lee would be joining them in a bit. Mikell and Ailese talked about how beautiful the house was and that Ailese needed to know what the name of the color was. She had to know. She told Mikell that there are many different shades of burgundy and that this one was beautiful. The Lee family had joined them in the same room. They introduced one another and had tea and cookies as Shane gave the girls and Armont, a grand tour of the house. Ailese actually knew Mrs.

Lee, she worked with her when she would visit the colleges to speak. Mrs. Lee also was a speaker. She had long black wavy hair that went almost to her buttocks line. She was very pretty. Her makeup looked like she had just walked out of a magazine; it was flawless. She looked like a model, she wasn't too tall or too short. Mrs. Lee had long legs, which complemented the skirt she was wearing. Mr. Lee wore very thin glasses, and he too had long black hair that was pulled back in a ponytail. Ailese thought that his voice didn't fit him in person, which happened to her a lot. She would place a voice with a face, and when she met them in person, she was always wrong. Mr. Lee was in a white tailored suit, which looked very expensive, Ailese thought; he liked to put his hands in his pockets a lot. Mrs. Lee wore the pants in that house. Even a dummy could figure that out. Ailese was always fond of Mrs. Lee. She knew her by the name Ryann, and she never paid much attention to her last name.

"So, you two know each other from speaking at the colleges. It's a small world, huh?" Mr. Lee said. "Yes, it is Ailese said. Your wife gave such great speeches, I learned a thing or two from her." "Well, no, I think it's the other way around, Ailese." They both smiled at each other. "Adrieana is so excited about the dance. What about Shane?" "Yes, he is, Mr. and Mrs. Lee agreed. That's all he's been talking about. He's tried on his suit so many times that I had to hide it from him," laughed Mrs. Lee. The kids came back to the room where all the adults were. Ashanee asked her mom if she could go outside for a while, and Ailese told her that she could, and to stay in the front yard. Shane and Adrieana stayed behind and ate cookies and drank milk. "I have to tell you, you have such a beautiful home, if you don't mind, please tell me about this burgundy, it is so beautiful, I was telling my husband that this is the most beautiful burgundy

I have ever seen." The Lees thanked Ailese and told her that the color was called Marquee Burgundy. Ailese was already planning on finding that color the first chance she got, and she was going to tell D about it. "I can also tell you the places that have the color if you do me a favor. "Okay, what is it?" Ailese thought. What could the favor be? "Please call me Ryann and call my husband Robert." "You got it." Ailese said, Mikell agreed as well.

The dinner went well, everyone got along, and it was agreed that Ailese would pick up Shane and take them to the dance. Ailese and Mikell were very proud of Adrieana for picking a nice boy and a nice family. They knew that she would be in good hands.

"Adrieana, where are you?" Mikell looked for her to ask her if she wanted to go to the supermarket with him and her sister.

"I'm in the family room, Dad." Mikell walked in the family room and asked her if she wanted to go to the supermarket. She agreed. "Dad, can we get some more stuff for lunch to take to school?" "Yeah, Dad we do need more stuff," said Ashanee. "Okay, let me tell your mom where we're going. Here are the keys. I will be right out, okay?" Mikell handed the keys to Ashanee, and the girls went to the car. "Hey you, the girls and I are going to the supermarket. Did you need me to get you anything?" "Can I see your list?" Mikell took out his notepad and gave it to Ailese. She looked it over and added a few things to the list. Mikell kissed her and went out the door. Ailese cuddled into a blanket and read a book. She was a bit thirsty, so she went into the kitchen and poured herself some water, and she thought that she'd go and see what's up with Armont. She walked down the hallway to Armont's room. She knocked softly on his door. She could hear him talking to someone. "Hey, Mom," he said as he opened the door. Come in, Mom. Sit down. Hold on, Mom." He told the person that he would call them back and hung up his cell. "I could have come back later. I hope I didn't interrupt anything." "No, Mom, you never could interrupt anything. You come first." "So, why were you so quiet at the Lee's? Are you okay?" "Yes, I'm okay. I was a bit bored, but I got through it." Ailese gave him a playful punch in the arm. "Are you going to your dad's this weekend?" "No, I just got off the phone with Dad, and he said that he needed to put in some overtime at work, so he won't even be home this weekend. Dad said it was best if I stayed here this weekend. I don't mind." "I agree with your dad, hun, so maybe we can find something to do this weekend, okay?" "Okay, Mom, but if you wanted to rest, that's fine. I was actually thinking about catching up with some friends if that was okay with you and dad." "Okay that's fine, but make sure that you speak to your dad and make sure it's okay with him." Armont had agreed with his mom. Armont had always been a momma's boy when was little. He was his mom's shadow, even though he has become a young man. He still respects his mom's feelings and will never put her last for anyone.

When Armont was young, he used to have a hard time sleeping in his own bed. He would always sleep with his mom, but Armont would sleep in his bed until the middle of the night. Ailese would wake up with Armont sleeping next to her. She would be too tired to put him back in his own bed, so she would let him stay. Armont is a very smart young man. He was never a problem child, and never hung around the wrong crowd, even when he would stay with his biological father. He didn't stay in a very good neighborhood. Ailese would worry herself to death when Armont went to his dad's, but as Armont got older, she felt she could trust him to make good decisions.

Ailese and Armont's father agreed that they would get along for the sake of their son, and even though Ailese regretted ever having a relationship with Irving, she did love him at one point in her life. Irving and Ailese met at a Stevie Wonder concert. Irving sat in her seat. Ailese asked him politely if he could move out of her seat. She even showed him her ticket that had the set number on it. Irving thought Ailese was so beautiful with a bit of an attitude, but that's what he loved about her. It didn't offend him at all because she only used it when it was necessary. Irving was determined to meet Ailese, no matter what he had to do. Ailese went to the restroom, and Irving followed her and pretended that he had to go the restroom also. He couldn't talk to her inside the concert, it was way too loud, so this would be a good time to try and talk to her. Ailese had dropped her makeup bag and didn't realize it. Irving picked up the bag and caught up to her. He asked Ailese if the bag was hers. She told him that it was, and the rest was history.

Irving and Ailese hit it off, they dated for a while, and moved into an apartment together. Everything was going well until Irving became a bit obsessive. Ailese would tell Irving that she didn't have to answer to anyone, that she was her own person, and that if he couldn't change it was over. When Ailese gave Irving the ultimatum, he did try to change, but he then started telling Ailese what not to wear because his friends would look at her in ways he didn't like. Ailese would tell Irving time and time again that she was with him, that she was faithful, and that he was very insecure. They broke up until Irving asked Ailese for a second chance and convinced her that he needed her in his life. He missed her. He was a better person. Irving was given a second chance by Ailese because things were going well and he was content. They broke up because Armont's father couldn't handle the pressure of being a new dad. Irving told Ailese that he wasn't happy that it was him, not her. Ailese took her son and left. She didn't hear from Irving until Armont was a year old. Ailese wanted Armont to know his father and have a relationship with his father. She didn't want Armont to hate her for keeping that from him. Irving and Ailese made a promise that they would get along for the sake of their son.

Ailese never dwelled on the past. She just wanted to leave all the bad things that happened to her in the past. Having these dreams from her past bothered her a lot, and she was very anxious about her session with Dr. Salvino tomorrow. Ailese had hoped that these sessions with Dr. Salvino could have a bit of a breakthrough on why Ailese was having these dreams again. It had to be more than stress. Ailese still feared this man who hurt her, but she wouldn't show it. The only person that knew that she feared this man was D'Andra, not her husband or anyone else. There was only one other man that Ailese feared, and that was GOD; her life was in his hands!

She hadn't seen this man who hurt her in years. She had no idea where he lived or worked; she didn't want to know. She knew that she was safe, her husband, family and friends would protect her, and even if he wasn't in jail but permanently removed from her life, he would be a fool to try and find her and hurt her again. Ailese just wanted tomorrow to get here fast so she could get more answers from the doctor about these dreams. She prayed that she wouldn't have an episode tonight.

"We're back, Lee. Where are ya?" Mikell began to search for his wife as the girls were putting away the groceries and talking among themselves. Lee, the girls, and I are back." There was still no answer. Armont came out of his room and told Mikell that mom went to pick up something she needed from the art store and that she said that she would be back in a bit. "Hey there's some junk food in there, you better get it before your sisters do," Mikell said as he hugged his son. Armont ran to the kitchen. Mikell took his cell phone out of his pocket to call his wife. "Hey, baby, are you on your way home? Because we're home, we miss you." "Yeah, I'm not too far from the house. Did Armont tell you that I went to the art store?" "Yes, he did, hun. I would have picked up the supplies for you. I wanted you to rest while we were gone." "I did, I just needed some air, that's all. I'll see ya in a bit, okay?" "Okay, love ya." "Love ya too, bye." "Mom will be home in a few minutes, so don't eat too much junk food. You know your mom will kill me if you eat too much." Mikell decided to fix himself some ice cream. He had let the kids fix themselves banana splits and sundaes, and as he was fixing his sundae Ailese had come into the kitchen and met him with a kiss. "Man, I missed you, babe," she said as she hugged him. The kids were all sitting at the table, making funny faces at them as they ate their ice cream. Ailese walked over to the table and kissed them one by one, then went back to where Mikell was putting the finishing touches on his sundae.

Ailese started to fix her a sundae as well and joined her family at the table.

Ashanee and Ailese were putting ice cream on each other's faces and giggling so hard that it looked like they were crying. Everyone else was laughing as well, and as time passed, everyone started putting ice cream on one another.

"Okay, since we all made a huge mess, we all need to clean it up, okay guys." Everyone cleaned the kitchen. After the kitchen was cleaned, everyone had agreed to watch a movie together. Mikell had popped popcorn for everyone. As they watched the movie, Ailese would sneak a look at her family, and she would think about how lucky she was to have her family in her life; she felt so blessed. After the movie, Ailese made sure everyone was ready for bed and had everything they needed before heading to her room, where Mikell was. She found him lying on his stomach on his side of the bed, reading a magazine. Adrieana screamed for her dad. He ran out of the room, and Ailese ran after him to see what was wrong. "What's wrong, kitten? Mikell ran to his daughter. Her finger was bleeding. What happened? Did you hurt yourself? Ailese ran into the bathroom to get the first aid kit. She came back with it and gave it to Mikell. "What happened to you, and why are you bleeding, kitten?"

"I was trying to sew these flowers, Adrieana pointed to the flowers on her bed. I was trying to put the needle through the thread, and the needle poked me really hard. It hurt dad." "I know you have to be more careful, okay?" Mikell nursed her finger and kissed it, and stayed with her, he helped her sew on the flowers onto her shirt, that made Adrieana happy.

"Is everything okay?" "Yes, she's fine. I helped her sew the flowers onto her shirt. She's asleep now. She's going to be fine. I think it just scared her, that's all."

"You know when she gets an idea, like her father and her mother, she has to get it done while it's fresh in her head. Can't knock her for that."

"Nope, we can't, huh?" Mikell and Ailese agreed and finished getting ready for bed. The next morning, Adrieana had the shirt on that her dad helped her with, and everyone complimented her on her outfit. Adrieana loved fashion. She was always complimented on her cool ideas, like adding rhinestones to a plain t-shirt, and putting silk flowers in her hair. Adrieana could turn anything into something.

"You and Dad worked hard on that shirt, huh? It looks great on you, my little fashionista," Ailese said as she pretended to walk a runway like a model. "Mom, you're so silly."

Mikell hadn't come to eat his breakfast. Ailese went to check on him. He was still getting dressed and was moving slowly. "Baby, you don't look so good. What's wrong?" Ailese began to feel his head for a fever, he wasn't hot at all, but he looked a bit flushed. "I don't know, I hope I'm not coming down with anything. I can't get sick, not today of all days, damn it!" "Sit down. I think you need to stay home. Mik, you don't look to good. I will call Emmanuel, okay?" "No, baby, I need to go run a business. A little bug isn't going to stop me." Ailese interrupted him and told him that he was being stubborn and that he didn't need to go to work and get everyone else sick. Ailese called Emmanuel and Leenah. She had their numbers for emergencies like this one. Emmanuel and Leenah understood. Leenah assured Ailese that she would take care of everything and would call later to check on Mikell. Ailese was confident that Leenah had everything under control, and she wasn't going to worry herself. She needed to focus on Mikell. Ailese called Ell to let her know that she had a family emergency and would be working from home and to call her if there were any problems. She knew that Ell was capable of handling things.

"Baby, go to work. I will be fine. I probably just need to take some Pepto-Bismol. I think I ate to much ice cream. I don't want you to miss any of your important client's. Please go ahead. I'll be fine." Mikell all of a sudden ran to the restroom and threw up. Ailese went into the restroom to wet a face cloth for Mikell. "Hun, do you really think that I'm going to let you stay here by yourself in your condition? You need me. Now let me help you, okay?" Mikell rose slowly from his knees, and Ailese took the warm washcloth and wiped Mikell's face with it. Mikell did need her, and he was happy that Ailese had known that before he did. He knew that his wife would do whatever she needed to do so her husband could get better. Ailese made Mikell comfortable with extra blankets, and she put a bucket next to his side of the bed and went to make some chicken soup to settle Mikell's stomach.

As Ailese was making the chicken soup, she went to her laptop case, pulled it out, and set it on the kitchen table. She did some work in between making the soup, and so far, everything was fine at work. Ailese served the soup to Mikell. She fed him some soup when he was feeling weak, and she gave Mikell plenty of fluids and checked on him from time to time. Mikell hardly ever got sick, not even a cold. He took care of himself. He would splurge every now and then, so this must be a virus.

When Ailese checked on Mikell, he was sound asleep, so she turned off the television and the lights and went back into the kitchen and fixed herself some hot tea. Ailese checked her emails and voice mails throughout the day, and so far, everything was going smoothly. She thought that she would call D'Andra to let her know that she was home today, but D'Andra was very busy and couldn't talk, so she told Ailese that she would call her back later. "Hello, hello you, wow, what's going on? Why are you home? Are you okay?" "Hey you, man. I'm fine. How are you?" Ailese said with a giggle. "I'm good." "Mikell came down with something this morning. He's been throwing up. He may have some kind of stomach virus or something, so, I am working from home today." "Oh no, tell Mikell that I hope he feels better. Well, that explains why Chris couldn't get a hold of Mikell this morning. I'll tell him that he isn't feeling good. I guess they were supposed to go to the gym before work or something." "Oh yeah, you're right, that is today. Yeah, just tell Chris that the guys will have to schedule it for another day."

"Ailese, did you need me to come over to help you out?" "Actually, do you think that you could pick up the kids from study hall today? I don't want to leave Mikell alone in his condition." "Oh yeah sure, no problem, so I will see you when I drop off the kids, and sorry, I couldn't talk earlier. It's been crazy here, I have to say that God has blessed my business. I mean, we are doing very well." "Yes, God is good, and I know why you're doing so well. I just received my magazine the other day, and you guys always have interesting people on the cover, and the gossip column is off the hook, girl!" "Well, thanks. I'm glad my girl is feeling the same because if there's anybody who will always tell me the truth, it's you Lee. As long as I own this business, you'll never have to pay for the magazine. You know that I gotcha, right?" "Yep, hey, I must go. I hear Mikell. He needs me." "Okay, hun, see ya soon, much love." "Much love, bye." "I need you to hurry, Ailese!" Ailese ran into the bedroom where Mikell was hovering over and was in a lot of pain. When Ailese asked him what was hurting him, he pointed to his belly. Mikell looked a bit flushed. Ailese thought that she should call the doctor, so she picked up the phone and called their family doctor. Ailese had explained to the doctor what symptoms Mikell was having. The doctor told Ailese that he felt that he needed to come and examine Mikell and make sure that she put him back into bed. "Hun, the doctor is on his way, okay?" Mikell was groaning and moaning and was in a lot of pain. Ailese went into the bathroom to wet the towel with warm water to try and ease Mikell's pain. She put the towel on Mikell's stomach. He was sweating a lot. He could barely speak, but when he did, he told Ailese to keep the warm towel on his stomach.

The doorbell rang. Ailese looked into the peephole. It was Dr. Chaddman. Ailese opened the door. "Hello, Dr.

Chaddman. Thanks for coming over on such short notice. Mikell is in here." She led Dr. Chaddman into their bedroom. Dr. Chaddman was a tall, attractive, doctor, his dimples even made him more attractive. When Ailese and her family would visit Dr, Chaddman, he always made them feel like family. He cared very much about all his patience. Dr. Chaddman was in regular street clothes, which meant he was off duty from the hospital. He was one of the most prominent doctors at Shelby Memorial Hospital. He had finished top of his class, Ailese always looked at his awards and certificates probably hundreds of times when she would go for a visit.

"Hello, Mikell, it's Dr. Chaddman. I hear that you're having stomach pains?" As the doctor examined Mikell, he shook his head yes. Ailese explained to the doctor that she gave Mikell some chicken soup and plenty of liquids. She also told him that she had given him some Pepto-Bismol for his stomach. After Dr. Chaddman examined Mikell, he led Ailese into the hallway and told her that he may have food poisoning or a stomach virus, but to be on the safe side, he would feel more comfortable if he was checked into the hospital. "I will call the ambulance to pick him up, and I will meet you at the hospital, okay?" "Okay, Doctor, thank you so much." "Don't worry, Ailese, we will take care of Mikell. He's going to be fine." Ailese was a bit worried but was confident that Dr. Chaddman was going to take care of Mikell.

"Baby, I need for you to try and sit up, okay? Dr. Chaddman wants to run more test, at the hospital, okay?" Mikell was a bit disoriented, and couldn't make out what his wife was saying. He trusted his wife to do whatever she needed to do. The ambulance had arrived fifteen minutes later and loaded Mikell into the ambulance. Ailese was sitting right next to Mikell. She let the emergency team work on Mikell. They were putting IVs in his arms. They were talking to the hospital on the dispatcher's radio. It seemed like it took forever to arrive at the hospital. Ailese was anxious and didn't want anything to happen to Mikell. What would she do without him? She shrugged her shoulders and told herself that she was getting ahead of herself, and she shouldn't think the worse. She took a deep breath. She needed to stay calm and strong. As they rolled Mikell to a room that was already prepared for him, they transferred him to another bed. Dr. Chaddman walked into the room, put his hand on Ailese's shoulders, smiled at her and walked over to Mikell and started speaking with the nurses. Ailese thought that she needed to make some calls. She excused herself and noted to herself the room number that Mikell was in. She called D'Andra and told her what was going on, and that she didn't want the kids to come to the hospital, so they both agreed that the kids would stay with her and Chris and to call her with any updates. Ailese called her in-laws to let them know that Mikell was in the hospital. They were actually in town doing some shopping and would be right there. Ailese walked back to Mikell's room. He was asleep, and she figured that the doctor had given him something to ease the pain. Ailese walked over to the recliner that was sitting by Mikell's bed and watched Mikell sleep. She too was feeling a bit tired. She didn't want to leave his side to get coffee, so she thought that she would wait until Verneil and Johnnie arrived, then she could go to the cafeteria for coffee. "Hi. Ailese looked up, and it was Evette. Ailese was so happy to see a familiar face. Evette walked over to her and gave her a hug. "I hope you don't mind me being here. I bumped into Dr. Chaddman, and he told me that I should look for you. He couldn't tell me why Mikell was here, so here I am." "No, I don't mind at all. Thank you that was so sweet and kind of you." "Well, it gave me an excuse to catch my breath. You know, being in that room with my mother ... well, it makes me a bit claustrophobic." "I understand Ailese said, as she stood up to give Evette a hug. How is your mom doing? Is she getting any better?" "Actually, she's getting more tests done as we speak. We hope that some good news is on the way." "I've never stopped praying for her." Evette smiled at Ailese. "Mikell is going to be okay, I know it, and Dr. Chaddman is a great doctor. Mikell is in great hands." Evette stayed with Ailese until Mikell's parents arrived. Evette and Mikell's parents really hit it off. They talked until Evette had to go back to her mom's room to check on her.

"So what's going on with our son?" Mikell's mom asked calmly. Ailese explained to them what was going on and assured them that Mikell was in good hands. Ailese went down to the cafeteria to get coffee for everyone. She had seen a familiar face but didn't know if she should speak or not, but he looked like he needed a friend. She took a chance and walked over to him. "Leon, are you okay? Leon looked up to see Ailese standing beside him. She saw that he had been crying, and that he was picking at a tray of food that was in front of him. May I sit down? Leon nodded yes and went back to picking at his food. What's wrong, Leon?" Leon was a bit floored that Ailese would even speak to him after the incident that happened. Leon took a deep breath. "My daughter is very sick, and it doesn't look good I'm not sure what my wife and I will do if she doesn't get better. She's so innocent, and little, you know," Leon said his voice trembling. "Oh no, I'm sorry to hear that. Please if there's anything that I could do, please let me know." Leon looked at Ailese and thought that there may be hope after all. "Thank you. Can I ask you a question? Why are you here?" Leon wiped his face with a handkerchief. "Well, Mikell is sick. They're running some tests on him right now. I mean, he woke up feeling sick, and then he started having stomach pains, so our doctor, Dr. Chaddman, checked Mikell into the hospital to be on the safe side." As Ailese began to drink her coffee, she felt herself getting overwhelmed again. "I'm so sorry to hear that. He's a strong man, so I know whatever it is he will fight it, so you don't have anything to worry about, Mrs. LaShae." "Please call me Ailese, okay?" Leon smiled and asked if he could see Mikell later if he was up to having any visitors. Ailese said that he could, and that she had to get back to Mikell.

When Ailese walked into Mikell's room, Dr. Chaddman was there and told Ailese that Mikell was going to be okay, but he had to have his appendix taken out. The surgery would be done in a few hours, and if the surgery went well, Mikell would be going home in a few days. This made everyone happy that it wasn't life-threatening. "We're going to stay here in town for awhile just until Mikell gets better." "Okay, that sounds great." Ailese told her in-laws that she needed to get some things done and would be back soon. Mikell's parents told Ailese to take her time and that they would call her if anything changed.

Ailese was a bit happy to leave that hospital. It seemed as if she had been in there for days. Ailese needed new scenery. When she got home D'Andra's car was in the driveway, and Ailese was so happy that she was there that she needed her best friend. She needed to let her know what was going on. "Hey guys, I'm home." D'Andra met Ailese at the door and gave her a huge hug. They both held each other tight, and they both needed this. "Oh, hun, are you okay? I know you've been through so much today." "I'm great now that you're here, and yes, it's been a crazy day, Ailese said as she rolled her eyes and shook her head. The best thing is that Mikell is going to be just fine. The doctor said that he needed surgery. He needs his appendix taken out." Are you serious? Wow, because Mikell never gets sick, thank God it's something simple, how will he going to react to, well, not working for a while?" "Well, he's been sleeping most of the time, so he doesn't know what's going on. I'm sure the doctor will let Mikell know what has to be done. Mikell will have to deal with not working for a while. He has no choice." Ailese shrugged her shoulders. She didn't want to start thinking about how Mikell wasn't going to like staying at home and depending on people to wait in him, etcetera. Ailese knew how he would react when he found out that he had to push back a lot of sessions and meetings. "Well, you're right, Lee. I know that he would eventually understand," D'Andra said in a sarcastic way.

"Hey, where are the kids?"

"Oh, they're with Chris back at the house. I came here to get them some change of clothes, and Adrieana needed a book for school. They're fine, Lee. I told them what was going on. All I told them was what you told me, that Mikell wasn't feeling well, and the doctor checked Mikell out and suggested that he needed to be checked in to the hospital to be on the safe side. They took it well, and Chris has been keeping them busy, hun. Stop worrying. I mean, yes, they're worried, but I told them that when I knew something, I would make sure they were the first to know. You know how mature your kids are." Ailese called the kids to give them an update on their dad, they were relieved and told Ailese to give their dad hugs and kisses and tell him that they loved him.

Ailese made sure that the guest room had plenty of blankets and towels and was thoroughly cleaned for her in-laws; she wanted to make sure that they were comfortable. The last time her in-laws had stayed with the family was two Christmases ago, and Ailese didn't want them to go home;

she had so much fun with them. Ailese headed back to the hospital. When she entered the room, her in-laws were sitting in the chairs and watching television. Mikell was actually awake, and Ailese smiled and was happy to see that handsome face. Mikell looked up to see his wife walking towards him. "Hey baby, Mikell said as if he hadn't seen his wife in weeks. I hear we've had quite a day today, huh?"

Mikell patted the bed to invite Ailese to lie down beside him, and she took off her shoes to lie down next to him. "Yes, we did and don't ever forget how much I love you, remember, I had to put up with all your crap today, young man," Ailese said, as she gently punched Mikell. Everyone laughed. "The doctor told me that I have to have surgery and that I needed to have my appendix taken out, Mikell said as he wiped his face. Wow, I'm just glad that it wasn't anything really serious." "So, you're okay with having to stay at home for a while, baby?"

"Yes, but I have to do what my doctor says. I don't want this to come back because I didn't properly let my appendix heal, right?" "Right, and we'll be there to help, okay?" Johnnie said to Mikell. "I will make sure that there will be no being bullheadedness coming from this one." Mikell's mother laughed. "Verneil, let's let them have some time alone before Mikell goes into surgery, okay?" He took her hand and led her outside. Ailese was initially quiet, but she told Mikell that she was scared; she knew that he would not judge her, and that confession will never leave that room. Mikell and Ailese just held each other and talked about the kids and what needed to be done before he came home.

"Okay, Mr. LaShae, we're ready for you," a nurse said, coming into the room. Another nurse followed her in, and they began getting Mikell ready for surgery. Ailese told Mikell that she would be waiting for him in the recovery room. She asked the nurses if they knew which recovery room Mikell would be in after surgery, and they gave her all the information that she needed. When they rolled Mikell out of the room, Ailese walked with them until they went through the double doors that lead to the surgery room. Ailese called D'Andra to let her know that Mikell was in surgery and to check on the kids. Chris had talked to Ailese and wanted to tell her that he was thinking about her and Mikell.

When Ailese decided to get something to eat in the cafeteria, she saw Leon again. He was leaving the cafeteria. She asked Leon if he'd had something to eat yet, and when he said that he hadn't, she asked him to join her for a bite to eat. "Leon, where is your wife? Is she here?" "Well, she had to go back to work earlier. We can't risk her losing her job because if she did, we'd lose everything; the house, I mean, we couldn't survive; we were barely getting by as it was." "I do understand completely. Ailese said as she took a bite of her salad. So, has your daughter made any progress since the last time we spoke earlier?" "No, Mrs. LaShae, and time is running out. They want to send her to specialists, but our insurance only covers so much. The doctors said that if we could get her to these specialists, there is a huge possibility that she would get better." Ailese's heart just sank in her stomach; her heart was hurting for this family, and she wanted to help. "Tell you what, give me the names of her doctors and I can guarantee you that I'll be able to speak with them, okay?" "That would be great, Leon said, smiling from ear to ear. Ailese thought that this was the first time she'd seen him smile, and his smile was beautiful. She wanted to see that smile a lot more. Leon wrote down all the information that Ailese needed, including his phone number. Please tell Mikell that I'm praying for him, and to get better, please let him know that." "I did let him know that he said that he wanted to see you; I can come and get you when he's out of surgery if that's okay?" "That would be great. See ya then."

After finishing her food, Ailese walked to her car to get her book that she had brought from home and headed back inside the hospital, where she saw her in-laws walking towards her. "Hey what you got there?" "Oh, a book that I am dying to finish one day," Ailese said, smiling. "We've been so caught up with Mikell, I didn't get to ask you if it was okay for us to stay here and help out. We don't want to get in the way," Johnnie said. "Oh, no, don't ever think that you're intruding, besides, I already have your room ready, so I hope you did not make any hotel reservations." "Oh well, we were going to, but we were so worried about Mikell that it slipped our minds, Mikell's mom said as she took Ailese's hand and held it up to her face. You're so good to us, thank you." "I love you, Mom and Dad." Ailese told her in-laws that they could go to the house if they wanted to if they were tired, they decided to stay at the hospital a while longer. "Have you guys eaten anything?" "Oh yes, we went to the deli down the street and had some sandwiches and tea. It was very delicious." "Oh good, because if you hadn't, I would have run out to get you guys something to eat. I actually ate at the cafeteria."

Mikell was asleep when they wheeled him into the recovery room. Dr. Chaddman had his clipboard in his hands and was writing information before handing it to the nurse. "The surgery went well, though you will need to look over and sign some paperwork. It's just procedure." "Okay, no problem. I thought that I had signed all the necessary paperwork, but I will be right back." Ailese went down the hall to the nurse's station, where she saw two nurses who were both on the phone. One of them told Ailese that she would be right with her in a moment. "Yes, I'm supposed to sign some more paperwork for Mikell La Shae?" "Oh yes, I do apologize. I just forgot to have you sign a few more documents. Please forgive me, madam. The nurse handed Ailese a clipboard with the documents attached. You could have a seat if you like." The nurse pointed to the chairs. Ailese decided to sit down while she filled out the paperwork. She read each and every line and made sure that she didn't miss anything. When she was done, she went back to the nurse's station and handed them the paperwork. "Thank you, Mrs. LaShae, have a great evening, and again, I'm sorry for the delay." "No problem, but I was wondering if you could help me with something. Ailese took out a piece of paper and read off the doctor's names that Leon had given her earlier. Do you know if I could speak to these doctors as soon as possible?" "Sure, you're in luck. Give me a few minutes, okay, and I will be right back." The nurse disappeared down the hallway. Ailese waited patiently. A few minutes passed, and the nurse had the three doctors that Ailese had requested. "Hello, I'm Dr. Lewis." The rest of the doctor's introduced themselves: Dr. Thomas and Dr. Corbell. They all brought Ailese up to date on Leon's daughter's condition and what needed to be done. Ailese processed all the information and wanted to get back to the doctors before she went home for the night, but she had to speak with Mikell and wasn't sure if he would be awake any time soon.

Ailese headed back to Mikell's room. Dr. Chaddman was still in the room. He was speaking to Mikell's parents. "Oh, I'm glad that you're here Ailese. I was just explaining to Mr. and Mrs. LaShae that Mikell should be fully recovered in a week or so. He needs to stay in bed, and he has to be careful when he does get up. The stomach is very sensitive. I do have his prescriptions ready because he will be in some pain, and please call me if you have any questions. I will be dropping by to check on Mikell in a few days, okay?" "Thanks, Dr. Chaddman, thank you so much for all your help." "Mikell will be out probably the rest of the evening, so if you guys want to go home and get some sleep, you can, okay?" Dr. Chaddman gave Ailese a hug and left the room. Ailese was trying to decide if she should make this decision without Mikell. Or should she wait, but Leon's daughter's time was running out. She thought that she should focus on Mikell for now. "Mom and Dad, I will be right back. One of Mikell's friends wanted to come and see him. I promised him that I would let him know when he was out of surgery, okay?" "Okay, we'll be right here," Johnnie said to Ailese.

Ailese reached Leon's daughter's room, where she found Leon sleeping in the rocking chair. She didn't want to wake him up, but she knew how much he wanted to see Mikell. There was a baby crib. Leon's daughter was sleeping, and she had numerous tubes coming from her body. This just broke Ailese's heart. Leon's daughter was so little and innocent. "Leon, Leon, wake up. It's Mrs. LaShae, sorry to wake you up." Leon woke up and looked at Ailese. He looked around the room. He had been asleep for a while. I'll give you a minute, okay?" "Thanks, I will be right out." Leon washed his face and checked on his daughter. The nurse had stayed with her until Leon came back.

When Leon and Ailese entered the room, Mikell was still asleep. She introduced Leon to Johnnie and Verneil, who all gave Leon some privacy. Leon sat down in the recliner and spoke with Mikell. He told him to get better and that his daughter wasn't doing too well. Even though Mikell was asleep, he just wanted to tell his good friend that he was in his prayers.

Ailese went back to the nurses' station to leave them an important message about Leon's daughter, and the nurse assured Ailese that she would make sure they got the message.

When Johnnie Verneil and Ailese made it home, they were all beat and headed to bed. Ailese made sure she kept her cell phone next to her. She didn't want to miss Mikell's or the doctor's call. The bed felt so empty, she was so used to Mikell always being there next to her. She tossed and turned most of the night. Ailese couldn't sleep, so she watched some television and decided to call the hospital and check on Mikell. The nurse patched her through, and she was surprised that Mikell answered the phone. He sounded like he had just woken up, but he knew his wife was on the other end. "Hi, baby, she said softly. Man, I miss you so much. How are you feeling? Are you doing okay?" "I've had better days, but I'll live. What are you doing up so late for? You should be resting, sweetie." "I can't sleep, Mik. I need you here with me in our bed. I am worried about you, and besides, I'm scared that I might have one of those bad dreams. You know your mom and dad are here. I had them stay in the spare room. I don't want to scare them away." "Hun, you won't scare them away, and if you have a bad dream, you call me okay, Lee."

"Could you talk to me until I fall asleep, please?" "Okay," Mikell said as he let out a long yawn. They talked for a while. Ailese hung up when she had finally gotten tired.

The next morning, Ailese had been woken by the smell of bacon and coffee. She figured it was still early, but when she looked at the clock, it was after 9:30 in the morning. "Oh no, I overslept. I wanted to get to the hospital early, and I needed to make some calls." She hurriedly got out of bed, put on her robe, and headed to the kitchen. "Good morning, Mom, and Dad, I usually don't sleep in this late. I had a rough night last night. I would have made you guys' breakfast." Ailese kept rambling on until Verneil sat her down and put a plate in front of her. "Eat, you're fine, okay? I thought maybe we could all go to the hospital in one car. Would that be okay, Ailese?" "Yes, that would be a great idea, Mom." Ailese finished her breakfast and headed to the room to get dressed. She had to take her laptop and reports with her and would have to make calls from the car on the way to the hospital. "Verneil, do you mind driving to the hospital?" "No, not at all." Ailese sat in the back and worked on her laptop and made calls. She had to go into the office today. It had to be done. There was no way around it. Ailese called Dr. Lewis to check if they had gotten her message, which they had. Dr. Lewis had agreed to give Ailese a few more days to get back to them, being that she had to attend to Mikell, and they understood. Ailese had her appointment with Dr. Salvino, and Adrieana's school dance was today. D'Andra had already agreed to pick up Shane and even take Ailese's place and chaperone. Ailese didn't want to miss Adrieana's dance, so she would make sure to call Adrieana before she left for the dance. Her days would be very busy, and she needed all the help she could get.

They had finally arrived at the hospital. Mikell was actually awake but looked like he was in pain. "Hey son," Verneil said as she kissed her son on his cheek, and Johnnie shook Mikell's hand. "How's my boy doing today?" "I'm in pain, but they are on the way with my pain medicine." "Hey, you. I know that this may not be the right time to ask you this, but I wanted to talk to you about Leon. I bumped into him, here at the hospital, his daughter isn't doing too well. They really need help. Mikell interrupted Ailese, lifted her chin, and told her that he was going to leave the decision to help Leon out up to her because he trusted her. "You know why I'm leaving it up to you, my dear?" "Not really, why?" "Well, knowing you, I'm sure you've already done your research and have all the information you require, am I correct?" Ailese smiled. The nurse came in and asked everyone to leave so she could change Mikell's dressing on his stitches and change his bed sheets. Ailese kissed Mikell on the forehead as everyone headed out into the hallway.

While they waited for Mikell to be done, Ailese decided to make some phone calls. She headed outside to her car, where she got her laptop and cell phone. She had a couple of messages from Ell and some clients with no major disasters, which didn't surprise her. Ell has never let her down. Ailese responded to some emails that needed her attention, and when she was done, she called D'Andra to check on the kids. "Hey you, how's it going? Are my kids driving you guys crazy yet?" Ailese said as she giggled. "Hey sis, how are you? And how's Mikell?" "Oh, he's fine. He should be home tomorrow or the next day. I thought I would take a break while the nurse is checking on Mikell. So, are you getting some practice?" "Yes, I am, and I hope my children are as well behaved as yours. I took them to school today and made sure that they had everything. I also wanted to make sure that the salon that Adrieana's going to is The Right Touch. Is that correct, Ailese?" "What will I ever do without you, huh? I love you so much, sis. Take care, okay. Are you sure there isn't anything else you need from me?" "Mmmm. No, I think that's it if I think. Oh, wait, please confirm with me the address where Shane lives. I have 2356 Markson Road. Is that what you have, sis?" "Yes. Hey, I will call you soon, okay, love you."

"Hey baby, I miss you so much. Hey, where are your parents?" "Oh, they went to look at the gift shop. They will be back. Come here you sexy woman, Mikell said, blowing Ailese a kiss. Ailese walked over to him and sat next to him on the hospital bed. You know what would happen if I wasn't feeling like crap and could move like I wanted to. You would be in so much trouble. Mmmm. I just want you in my arms and to make love to you. You know you're teasing me, don't you?" "No, I don't. What am I doing to tease you? I'm coming here to make sure my baby's doing okay and being taken care of, that's all. What am I doing, Mik?" "You are so damn sexy you don't have to do anything, you should know that by now." He touched her face, and as much as he could, he leaned toward her. Ailese met him the rest of the way, and they kissed; it was a passionate kiss, like they were on their honeymoon. Ailese looked at Mikell like she hadn't seen him for months. She studied his face, and he studied hers. "I can't wait until I have you home. I don't think you've stayed away from me this long, huh?" Mikell was thinking long and hard. "No, I don't think so, because I don't think I could do it. I miss you so much, just being away for two days," Mikell said. He kissed Ailese on her lips. They both talked among themselves and watched television.

"Baby, I do need to go to the office in a minute and I'll be right back," Ailese yawned. "Lee I will be fine. I know that you have to run your business too. I do understand that, and you need to get some sleep, okay? Please promise me that you will get some sleep, okay?" "I can't. I'm so used to you sleeping next to me that I can't sleep Mik. I'll be okay. Besides, I have so much to do. My appointment with Dr. Salvino is today, and I have to be there at 5:30. Okay, so I will see if your parents are still at the gift shop, and I will give them my keys, and I will take a cab to work, okay?" "Okay, give me some sugar, baby. Ailese gave Mikell a long, sensual kiss. Lee don't worry if you're not able to come back here. Just call me, okay?" "Okay, said Ailese. Mikell grabbed her hand. "Hey, isn't tonight the dance?" "Yes, all is taken care of. I will call you baby. Love you, bye."

Ailese called a cab and waited ten minutes for one. On the way to work, she leaned her head back on the seat and relaxed, closing her eyes for a bit. She knew the drive would be about 20 minutes or so. She paid the cab driver and entered the building. She kind of missed work. She hadn't been there for two days, and it felt like weeks. She was ready to get to work.

"Hey Ell," Ailese said, as she walked to her office, and Ell followed her in. "Ailese, hey. I wasn't expecting you. How is Mikell?" "He's doing fine. He should be able to come home tomorrow, maybe. So, let's get to work. I need a full report from you, please, and oh, by the way, you're doing an awesome, awesome job, which doesn't surprise me. Thank you for holding the fork down."

"No problem, boss, and thank you for noticing all my hard work," Ell said as she patted herself on the back when Ailese wasn't looking.

Okay, I took care of all your meetings. I updated your calendar, and no one gave me any trouble. Everyone was very understanding and cooperative. Mr. Saxx did call. He just wanted an update on something, so I emailed them to him, and he said to call him as soon as possible because he was worried about Mikell."

"Okay, so how are we doing on the Clarkson account?" Ell smiled. She was very excited to deliver the good news to Ailese in person. "Well, we're going to Ally's Café for lunch, isn't that great? I know we can reel 'em in. I know we can." "That is great." Ailese was very excited about the Clarkson account, they owned a salon, and this would be a challenge for Ailese and the company. She knew that if they signed on with her company, she would make them very happy after she saved their business.

Ailese finished up some loose ends and made some calls from the office after the meeting, and she began to think about Adrieana. She was getting ready for the school dance, and Aunt D'Andra would be fussing over Adrieana, just like Ailese would. I hope D takes a lot of pictures, Ailese thought. Ailese had some time to kill, so she decided to call Dr. Lewis so they could discuss Leon's daughter and what would be the next step. "Hello, Dr. Lewis. It's Ailese LaShae. How are you?" "Hello, Mrs. LaShae. I am fine. How are you?" "I'm good. I thought that I would give you a call and discuss Leon's daughter's case. I want to help in any way I can, Doctor."

"Okay, great, Mr. McCray's daughter will need to see a couple of specialists, most of them are in Rory, and she would have to stay there for a few weeks, maybe even months. If she sees these specialists, there is a huge chance that she could get much better. So, I know that Mr. McCray has insurance, but it only covers so much, and I know that he is worried about the expenses." "Yes, I understand, Dr. Lewis, so what I want to do is write a check for the expenses, hotel stays, meals, transportation etcetera." "Okay, Mrs. LaShae, let me get all that info for you, how about I call you back in a few hours, okay?" "That would be great. I am at work right now. I'll be here for a few more hours. I do have an important appointment at five, so if you could get back to me before five that would be great, if not, please leave me a message." "Okay, sounds great. You have a good heart Mrs. LaShae. We all want to thank you for all your help. Take care. Talk to you soon."

"Boss, are you hungry?"

"Actually Ell, I am. I don't even remember the last time I ate today, I believe breakfast." "Do you want me to go to the café up the street, the one that you like that has the gourmet sandwiches?"

"Oh, that would be fantastic. Could you please get my usual?" "No problem, boss." "Ell, could you come here before you go, please?" "Sure, I'll be right there."

Ell entered the office. "You wanted to see me, boss?" "Yes, Ailese picked up her purse and gave Ell a fifty dollar bill, Ell pushed her boss's hand away. "I gotcha, boss. Put your money away, it's fine, see ya in a bit, bye." Ell disappeared down the hall before Ailese could say anything.

Ailese didn't realize how hungry she was until now. She would usually take the rest of her lunch home, but not today, she finished all of it. Ailese loved the food at the small café up the street from the office, even if it was crowded, she would wait because it would be worth it. They had the best sandwiches and salads, they even had delicious desserts, sometimes, Ailese would distract herself so she wouldn't go crazy and buy all the sweets.

"Boss, a Dr. Lewis is on line two. He says it's urgent." "Hi, Dr. Lewis, it sounds like you have some information for me." "I do, so before I start, do you have something to write with?" "Yes, I'm ready, Dr. Lewis." When Ailese hung up with Dr. Lewis, she began to look at all the information and wondered if she should still discuss spending that large amount of money with Mikell even though he left everything up to her. She decided that she would just write the check to the hospital and discuss it with Mikell when he was feeling better and more alert.

"Hello, Mr. Saxx, how are you?"

"Hello, my dear, how are you holding up? I hear that your husband had to have surgery? What happened? Is he okay?"

"Yes, he had to have his appendix taken out. The surgery went well, and he should be coming home soon." "Good to hear, good to hear. Hey, please take all the time that you need, and why are you at work, my dear?" "Well, you know me, I have to check on things with my eyes and not just my ears," Ailese laughed. "Oh yes, I know, Mr. Saxx said, but seriously, please take all the time you need Ailese, because I know that your husband will need your assistance". "Take care, Mr. Saxx, and thank you for the flowers, they're lovely." "You're welcome. Talk to you soon."

When Ailese headed back to the hospital, it was already close to four. She thought that she would stop by for a few minutes to check on Mikell and then head to her appointment. Ailese visited with Mikell and found out that he wouldn't be released until tomorrow evening. The drive to Dr. Salvino's went smoothly. Ailese thought that she would hit traffic. She was so excited to give Karen the earrings that she made for her mom. "Hi, is Karen here today?" Ailese asked the woman who was behind the receptionist desk. "Give me one moment. I'll go get her for you," the woman said. "Hi Ailese, how are you? It's good to see you again. Do you have time to come into my office?" Ailese looked at the clock before she answered Karen. "Oh yes, I have time." She followed Karen to a room that was off to the side of the hallway. "Have a seat; I will make sure I won't keep you long." Karen opened a drawer, pulled out her purse, and took out her wallet. Ailese was already holding the box that had the earrings in it; she was going to surprise Karen with a bracelet and necklace to match. Ailese sat the box down on the desk and told Karen to open it. "I hope you like it." "I'm sure I will. Oh my gosh, I am so excited, Karen said as she opened the box. She gasped with excitement when she saw the beautiful jewelry. Ailese this is the most beautiful jewelry I have ever seen in my life! You did a terrific job!" "Oh, I'm glad that you love it. I hope your mom does as well." "Oh, I know she will, thanks a million!

So do you have the bill so I can pay you?" Ailese looked at Karen with confusion. She never remembered discussing a price to make the jewelry.

"Karen, please, there is no charge. Put your wallet away. I told you that I just make jewelry for fun it's not a business." "Well, I want to give you something. I know that this took you a long time, and time is very valuable, so please let me pay you, Ailese, Karen pleaded.

Ailese kept telling Karen that there wasn't a fee. She didn't want the money. It was a gift for her mom, and Ailese didn't mind doing the work.

Finally, Ailese and Karen came to an agreement that Karen would take her somewhere and for her to take plenty of pictures at her mom's birthday party.

"Ailese, Dr. Salvino is ready for you, the receptionist said, and she was led to Dr. Salvino's office. "Hello Ailese, how are you doing?" "I'm a bit overwhelmed, but I'm okay." "So, let's pick up where we left off at the last session. We were talking about the abuse that you've experienced. Now, tell me how old you were when you first experienced any type of abuse." Ailese took a deep breath and cleared her mind of everything. She wanted to focus on this and this only.

"Well, I was in high school, an old boyfriend had gotten angry with me, and he pushed me on to the sofa. I never told anyone this, not even my mom.

His name was Aaron, and I immediately broke it off because he hurt me, and I knew I deserved better." "Right, that's correct, so in high school, when did you have any other occurrences, Ailese?" Ailese didn't like talking about her past, but she had to be honest about it. "Well, I was in fists fights, because I was bullied a lot in school, mostly by females, but not until I met." Ailese paused. She stopped talking and closed her eyes. She didn't want to say his name, and it wasn't going to just roll off her tongue either. "Ailese, are you okay? It's okay, take your time, I'm here, okay?" Ailese began to tear up; it was so hard for her to say his name or even speak about what he did to her. "I can't say his name because I'm afraid if I do, he'll find me and really hurt me, bad this time, or even kill me." "Okay, how about you write the name down, but that's only if you want to. If you're not ready, we can wait until you are ready." "I haven't said his name in years. No one speaks of him or even mentions his name. It's a rule that no one who knows about what happened says his name. Ailese's tears began to fall down her face; she could no longer hold them back. Ailese took a tissue from the tissue box that was sitting on a table next to her. I'm not ready, Doctor. I can't even write his name down. The things that he did to me are unforgivable." "It's okay," Dr. Salvino said as she leaned over and touched Ailese's hands. She went back to making notes on her notepad.

When Ailese got home, her in-laws had already made dinner, Johnnie was folding the laundry, and Verneil was washing dishes. Ailese hated to get behind on chores, but so much was going on. As Ailese sat down to eat her dinner, the phone rang. Verneil answered the phone, and motioned for Ailese not to get up. "Hold on, please, one moment. This is D'Andra," she said as she handed the phone to Ailese. "Hey you, how's everything going?" "Hey sis, it's going great. We're on our way to pick up Shane. Adrieana wanted to come and see you if you were home. I see that you are." "That would be great. I would love to see her."

When D'Andra came over with Adrieana, Ailese had just finished her dinner, and she was so excited to see her daughter all dolled up. "Hi mom, so what do you think?" Adrieana modeled her outfit for her mom so her mom could see how she looked.

"You look so beautiful! Hey, stay right there. I'm going to get my camera. I'll be right back. Ailese came back with her camera. Smile for mom." Ailese took a dozen pictures until it was time for them to go. Ailese walked D'Andra and Adrieana outside to the car. "Have fun, honey. See you tomorrow." Ailese hugged D'Andra and Adrieana and went back into the house.

"She looks so pretty, Johnnie said, those kids are growing up so quickly." Ailese said, smiling and thinking to herself, "Wow, were they ever babies?" Ailese's cell phone rang, and it was Mikell. He sounded better since she last spoke with him. "Hi love, I just wanted to tell you that I love you, and Leon came by to visit me. We had a long talk about his daughter and how she wasn't doing so well. My heart goes out to him, you know?" "Yes, I know I'm working on some things that may help him and his family. I'll fill you in when I pick you up from the hospital, okay?" "Okay, well, I'm a bit tired, so I'm going to take a nap, and babe, could you please do me a favor?" "Yes, anything for you, my love." "Could you make some of your home cooking? This hospital food isn't getting it at all, Mikell laughed. "Aw, you poor thing. Of course, I will make sure that I make all your favorites before I pick you up tomorrow. I love you, bye."

"Ailese we're going to go and pick up some things from the house and check on the house as well. Do you need anything?" "Well, to be honest, I do. Mom, do you mind if I give you a list of things that we need?" Verneil reached into her purse and handed Ailese a notepad. "Take your time, Ailese. We're in no hurry. Besides, your dad loves to drive, and he wants to get some fresh air so he can stay occupied." Verneil grinned. When Ailese was done with her list, she handed it to Verneil. "I need to give you some cash. Just give me a second." Ailese stood up, and Verneil took her hand and told

Ailese not to worry. "Well, Mom, that's a lot of stuff. Let me," Verneil interrupted Ailese. "It's no problem. Now you just relax, okay? We will be back later on, okay?" "Thanks, Mom and Dad. Be careful, okay?" "We will. Verneil and Johnnie hugged Ailese goodbye.

After Johnnie and Verneil left, Ailese was a bit bored, so she wondered the house looking for something to do. There wasn't anything to do; all the chores were done, so Ailese decided to surf the net for a while. After a while, her eyes were getting heavy. Ailese made sure all the doors were locked before she went to the bedroom to nap. Being alone it bothered her sometimes, especially when she was taking a nap. What if she had one of her dreams? There would be no one there to comfort her, to tell her it was all a dream. Ailese tried to stay awake, but her fatigue had won, and before she knew it, she was sound asleep. Ailese began having one of her dreams. It seemed so real she couldn't wake up. She pleaded and pleaded with him. "Don't hurt me! Don't hurt me!" Ailese began to run as fast as she could, but he would always catch up to her. He pulled her down to the hardwood floor. Ailese had seen this look before. His eyes were black, and evil. He could smell her fear like a dog could. She could feel his sweaty, clammy hands around her neck. She yelled, "Please, I'm sorry!" At the top of her lungs, she's pleading for her life. He has no mercy for her. His face was absent; the only thing on his mind was to hurt her, make her more and more afraid of him. Ailese couldn't wake up. She began to moan and move her head right and left over and over again, because she was so scared. He was beginning to take the breath out of her body. Ailese tried to fight him off of her, but he was so strong, that she began to get some strength; it took everything in her to get this man off of her. When Ailese was able to free herself from him, she knew she had to move quickly. She needed to flee to the front door, where maybe someone could hear her screaming. If she could get someone's attention, they could call the police for help. Ailese didn't make it to the door. She felt his huge hands grab her neck from behind her. She began to scream. He covered her mouth and told her to shut up, and if she didn't, she would regret it. He whispered in her ear. "You love to make me mad, don't you? I'm going to show you what happens when you don't listen." He still had Ailese by her neck. Ailese was sobbing uncontrollably. She tried to free herself from him again, but couldn't. The more she tried, he would grip her neck tighter and tighter.

Ailese still couldn't wake up from her nightmare, and then the phone rang. Ailese screamed and started to sob. She couldn't stop shaking. She was so scared she didn't want to move. What if he was in the house?

Ailese couldn't answer the phone, because she was still too scared to move. The phone kept ringing, then she remembered that she turned off the voice mail service and forgotten to turn it back on. What if it was Mikell or her in-laws? She took a deep breath. It took everything in her to get herself together. She looked at the caller ID. The number was unfamiliar. It was Verneil. "Hun, it's Verneil. Are you okay? You sound funny, hun." "I'm okay. I was asleep, that's all. Is everything okay?" Ailese wiped the tears from her face. She was still shaking. She tried to hide all of this from her mom. "Okay, I'm sorry to wake you up, but I just wanted to be sure. I'm picking up the dry cleaning, and I needed to know the exact number of items I should be picking up." "Oh, it should be ten items in all, and please wake me up if you need to. It's no big deal," Ailese said, still trying to keep her composure. "Okay, hun, we'll see you soon." Ailese hung up the phone. She began to sob even more. She couldn't stop crying. She began to feel her neck. She got out of bed and headed for the shower. ""Why, why me, Lord? Please give me the strength not to let him run my life. Heavenly Father, I need you to be my counselor, and my *Strength*. Lord, as your child, keep me safe from danger seen and unseen." Ailese closed her eyes and prayed even harder. She didn't blame God for the dreams. Ailese felt that only God could protect her from these dreams. Ailese looked at herself in the mirror. She studied herself for a while. She began to cry again. She went into the fetal position. She began to pray some more. "I have got to get it together and keep it together. I know I am strong. I refuse to let this man take control of me. I won't let this happen!" Ailese took a shower and changed into some comfortable clothes. She began to think about her session with Dr. Salvino and how desperate she was to find out why she was having the dreams after so much time had passed. Is having the dreams a sign that he's trying to find her to hurt her? Is he here in Shelby? Ailese shrugged her shoulders and began to get chills down her spine. She began to think of good things. Ailese decided that she would check on Chris and the kids. Chris and the kids weren't home, so she tried Chris's cell phone. "Hello, Chris. It's Ailese, what's all that background noise?" "Hey Ailese, the kids and I are at the Game Room Arcade, you know, the one next to the mall? They're playing some video games, and they're having a blast. Sorry for all the noise." "Oh no problem, I can still hear you just fine, so it sounds like everything is going well on your end." Ailese missed the kids deeply, and she couldn't wait to pick them up tomorrow. "Oh yeah, yeah, I'm just keeping them occupied, and don't worry, I will have them home in time for bed. Hey, how is Mikell doing?" "He is doing better. I'll pick him up tomorrow evening, but I think I'll pick up the kids first and head to the hospital, is that okay?" "Yes, hun, that's fine. I'll let D know. Hey, what if I let the kids call you when we get home, unless you prefer that I go and round them up?" "Oh no, Chris, you can have them call me when you guys get home. Have fun. Love you guys." "Hey Ailese, are you alright? You sound like something's bugging you." "Oh no, I'm a bit worn out, but I will be okay once Mikell is home." Ailese wanted to tell Chris, but she didn't want to be a burden, so she held it all in, tears and everything.

"We're home Ailese, Verneil and Johnnie called to Ailese they were back from their outing. Ailese met them in the living room, where Johnnie and Verneil were putting away the items that they bought. "Let me help you guys! Ailese took several bags from Johnnie and headed to the kitchen. Everyone worked together to put all the items away. "So how was your outing?" "Oh, it was lovely," Johnnie said as he sat down in the recliner that faced the television. "I see that Shelby's been building a lot of new shops; a lot has changed since the last time we were here." "Yes, I know. I'm glad though. Now we don't have to drive so far to get what we need. Did you see the new mini mall?" "Yes, we did. We went to every store. Your mom did some damage, though," Johnnie said and laughed. "Oh, you be nice. I couldn't help myself, and everything I bought was on sale, so I didn't do too much damage." "I love you too, hun," Johnnie said to his wife, and they both laughed. "That reminds me, I bought you something. Verneil walked over to some bags that were sitting by the front door and handed Ailese three bags. Here you go, my love. I know I shouldn't have, but I love spoiling you." "Thanks, Mom." Ailese gave her a kiss on the cheek. There were a few things that cheered her up. Ailese loved gifts. Ailese opened all her bags, and Verneil wanted her to try on what she had bought her. Ailese loved everything that Verneil had bought her. "Thank you, mom, everything is so beautiful. I can't wait to wear them all." Anytime, I'm glad you love them." "You do know my taste."

Ailese made turkey meatloaf, green beans, mashed potatoes, and lemonade. After dinner, Ailese thought she'd work out to get her mind off of things. She went into the workout room and worked out for an hour, and she did feel a little better. There was a knock at the door. As Ailese got up to answer the door, she wondered who was at the other end. "Who is it?" "It's Evette." Ailese was happy that Evette had come for a visit. "Hello, come on in." Ailese hugged Evette. "Hello, I'm sorry that I didn't call you before I headed over, but I have something for you. Evette took out a book from a shopping bag and handed it to Ailese. Here ya go, sorry it took me so long to return the book. I was going through some stuff at home, and I came across the book." "Oh, thanks, did you like it?" "Yes, I actually just came back from the bookstore. I bought some of the author's books, and she is pretty good, thanks." "I'm glad you enjoyed it."

Have a seat. Do you have time to visit Evette?" "Actually, I do. But if you're in the middle of something, I don't want to keep you." "Oh no, you're not keeping me from anything. I just finished working out, which did me some good. We just have to be mindful not to wake up my in-laws, they're resting. I just finished working out." "Oh, good for you, wow, I don't even remember the last time I had time to work out. So are you excited that Mikell's coming home tomorrow?" "Yes, I am very excited. I miss him being here, you know?" "Yeah, you have a great guy." "Thanks Evette. How is mom doing?" "She is hanging in there. I know it's because of the Man above. He's watching over her. She pulled through the surgeries, and everything's going well." "Oh, I am so happy to hear that. That made my day. I always kept you and your family in my prayers."

"I know, I know, hun. So, where are the kids? Are they here?" "Oh no, they are with Chris and D'Andra, they will be home tomorrow."

"Oh, I bet they're having lots of fun. They are really good people." "I don't know what I would do without them." Evette and Ailese caught up on what was happening in their lives and sipped tea. They watched a movie and ate popcorn. They didn't want their visit to end, but they knew that it had to come to an end.

After Evette left, Chris called Ailese. She talked to the kids, and Adrieana's dance went great. She said that she would tell Ailese all about it once Mikell was home. Ailese looked at the time. It was after 9:30. She decided to drink a bit more tea and turn in. After she was done with her tea, she went and checked on her in-laws to see if they needed anything. They were fine. Ailese didn't have anyone to take care of, so she didn't know what to do with herself. She didn't want to watch television read, or even go to sleep. She decided to get her laptop and check her emails and look at some websites. She was doing everything she could to stay awake, but she began to yawn, and her eyes were beginning to feel very heavy. Ailese had always prayed before she went to bed, but this time she prayed even longer than usual because she didn't want to have another bad dream. She just wanted to have a normal night. She couldn't wait until Mikell was home. He was her protector, but for now, she had to rely on God and herself.

When Ailese met Mikell, she didn't want to give him the time of day because she had had it with men and relationships. Mikell was the only man that was patient with her, no matter what, even if she swore at him or told Mikell to give her space. Even though it would hurt him to leave her, not seeing her, also hurt him. Mikell was too good to be true,

Ailese would always say that to herself. What does he want from me? She would have all those crazy thoughts in her head; she just knew that a good man did not exist. Ailese felt as though all the men in her life had let her down, even her dad. If her father had just stayed home like her mother had asked him and not gone out with his drinking buddies, maybe her father would have been in her life longer. His life may have been spared. Ailese would always wonder how things would be with him in her life. Her previous relationships with men always consisted of giving, and if she didn't, they would leave. The men in her life didn't like how strong headed Ailese was, because she used her own brain. She was her own person, and never experienced a man telling her what to do and how to do it. She wouldn't even let a man tell her how to dress or what looked good on her. Some of the men did not like that about her. They were very intimidated by her. Ailese always stood up for herself, but that did not bother Mikell, he loved that about her. She fought her battles, no matter what she went through, and in the end, she stood on her own two feet. If Ailese was wrong, she would admit it. She was never an argumentative person. She had always felt that yelling and screaming were a waste of her time. She disliked lowering to their level. Mikell was the same way, he stood his ground, and if he was wrong, he would admit that he was wrong as well. They both treated people with respect. It didn't matter who or where you came from; respect meant a lot to both of them, which is one of the reasons they clicked.

Ailese didn't always treat Mikell like a king. She would compare him to previous relationships. Mikell wouldn't like this at all. He didn't like being compared at all. He was his own person. Mikell was a good man. He was truthful and kind, and her friends and family would tell her to give him a chance. They had a good feeling about Mikell, and they were right.

Ailese came to realize that as time passed, Mikell was a good man, and he was truthful and kind.

Ailese once asked Mikell. "Where have you been all my life?" Mikell would tell her, "I'm here now, and I'm not letting you go."

Ailese turned off the lights in her room. She left the bathroom night light on just in case she needed it. She was a bit chilly, so she got the extra blanket that she kept at the foot of the bed and went to sleep. Ailese could feel him breathing. She didn't want to open her eyes. She was very afraid. It took everything in her not to move, she knew that he was standing over her.

He didn't move for a few minutes. He continued to stand over her. Ailese began to pray to God silently in her head. "Please God protect me from danger seen and unseen." She said this over and over again, then suddenly she felt the covers come off her body. She stayed still. He grabbed her off the bed until her body landed on the cold floor. Her body was in the fetal position. He yelled at her to wake up. His voice sounded fury, she knew that he was going to hurt her. "Get up! He screamed. He was screaming at the top of his lungs. Get up now!" He began to drag her to the other side of the room, where she was yelling at him. "Okay let me get up, please!" He finally stopped dragging her when Ailese was on her feet. She couldn't even look at him, and she would always keep her head down.

"Look at me you bitch! Look at me! Ailese looked at him, he was naked.

Ailese was still praying silently in her head, when he walked up to her and grabbed her neck. As he was grabbing her neck, he began to swear at her. I want to know why you didn't do the laundry today. You better have an answer right now!" "I didn't have time. I was going to do the laundry in the morning because I had to work late." He yanked his hands away from her neck and tossed her onto the bed. His heavy body was on top of her. Ailese will never forget what he said to her. I'm going to have my way with you, even though you disgust me!" He stayed on top of her. He made Ailese touch him in ways that no one could ever imagine. He made her do things to him; this made Ailese sick to her stomach. She sobbed quietly the whole time. She'd rather touch him then have him beat her. Ailese woke up sobbing and shaking uncontrollably. She ran into the restroom and vomited. She washed her face with warm water. She couldn't take this; she had to talk to someone.

"Hello?" The voice sounded sleepily. "D'Andra, I need to speak with you please," Ailese sobbed. "Ailese, hun, what's wrong? Hold on one second, okay? Let me go into the other room. Ailese could barely get the words out. She was crying to the point to where she was out of breath. Hun, take a deep breath, Ailese, okay? Ailese took a deep breath and wiped the tears from her eyes. What's wrong? Talk to me, please." "I had a bad dream, it was about him," Ailese sobbed even more. "Oh my gosh, hun. I can come over right now. I know that you need me. I'm on my way." Before Ailese could say anything, D'Andra had hung up. D'Andra knew how bad the dreams would get. Other than Mikell, she had experienced it firsthand. She knew that Ailese needed her more than ever. She didn't care how far she had to travel or that it was in the middle of the night.

Ailese wiped her face with the warm face cloth. Her eyes were red and puffy. Ailese couldn't stop herself from shaking. She began to pray to God silently in her head. She picked up the blanket and wrapped her body in it. She closed her eyes and prayed some more. When she heard the front door close, she felt warm. She knew her best friend was there. D'Andra had let herself in and walked into Ailese's bedroom. She was in a trench coat and sweats. She walked over to where Ailese was. She didn't say a word. She just held Ailese and waited for her to talk. Ailese knew that when she was ready to talk, D'Andra was all ears. Ailese held on to D'Andra for dear life. She took a deep breath and began to tell D'Andra about the dreams that she had been having.

"Hun, I am so sorry that you're going through this. I wish there was something I could do." "You're doing it right now." Ailese whispered. "So how are your sessions going with the doctor?" "Good, I just started but… Ailese paused. I have to tell you something, and I'm telling you because I know that you won't think that I'm crazy." "Okay, shoot, I'm listening." "I truly feel that the dreams are a sign; they're telling me that this man- oh my god, after all these years, I still can't say his name. Ailese paused again. I truly feel that my dreams are telling me that he is trying to find me, and when he does, he will hurt me, D." Ailese looked at D'Andra with fear in her eyes. "No, Honey, he is long gone, we know that for a fact. He can't hurt you any longer. These dreams," Ailese cut her off. "No, I can feel it, D. He's going to hurt me, and it kills me not knowing when and where." "Stop it, Lee! I don't think you're crazy, but this man knows what would happen to him if he tried to come back into your life."

"Have you ever stopped to think that I don't have a restraining order and I never reported all those incidents to the police?" "I know Lee, but we all know what will happen to him if he even tries to hurt you."

A few days later, after the man who hurt Ailese left, a few mysterious men had tracked him down and beaten him senseless, and to this very day, no one knows who those men were, but one thing for sure: it was someone who cared about her very much that they would risk everything for her. One day she got a threatening phone call from him, and he told her that he didn't appreciate her sending people to fight her battles and that she had better watch her back, that scared her, but nothing became of it, he didn't carry out his threats to her. Eventually, time passed, and he wasn't heard from again. Who knows, those men might have beaten him again if they had known he was brave enough to return.

"Ailese, sweetheart, Mikell will not let anyone hurt you. Come here." She hugged Ailese and told her that she would stay with her until the morning. She called Chris to let him know that she was staying with Ailese. "Where are you going, D'?" "To the restroom, hun. I am not going to leave you." D'Andra touched her face and kissed her on the cheek.

When morning came, Ailese was up before D'Andra. She woke her up to ask if she was going to work, she told her that she would work from home, she wanted to stay and help her. She knew that Mikell would be home soon, but she couldn't leave her sister with that look in her eyes, she couldn't leave her.

"Are you sure you want to stay here?" "Yes, all I need is some coffee, and I have to get some stuff out of the car. I will be right back." "Okay, I will start the coffee. Do you want decaf or regular?" "Either or it doesn't matter." After Ailese was dressed, she noticed that her in-laws weren't up yet. She decided to make everyone breakfast, this would keep her busy, and she didn't want to think about what happened last night. Ailese made eggs, toast, and sausages, and just as she was done, everyone was dressed and ready for breakfast. "Good Morning, everyone, Ailese said. I fixed breakfast.

There's juice, milk, water, and well, you guys know where the fridge is. Please help yourselves."

"Hi D'Andra how are you? Give me a hug." D'Andra stood up and gave Verneil and Johnnie a hug. "When did you get here this morning?" "Yes, I did earlier this morning. I'm going to help Ailese cook for Mikell, and besides, I haven't seen my sister in like forever." D'Andra didn't want Mikell's parents to know the real reason why she was there; she knew that Ailese didn't want them to know.

"Oh well, that's nice of you. You guys, I can pitch in too." "Okay, thanks," D'Andra and Ailese said, and they looked at each other with a smile.

When breakfast was over, Johnnie was sitting on the couch reading the newspaper, and Verneil was watching television. "Hey, let's go for a walk," D'Andra suggested. "Okay, that sounds like a good idea. I could use some fresh air. Let me change, it's a bit chilly out. Did you want to change too, sis?" Ailese changed into jeans and a t-shirt, with a hooded jacket. D'Andra was in jeans and a hooded sweatshirt. "Wow, it is pretty cold out, huh?" "Yeah, D, it is, but I know we will warm up soon." They walked down a few streets. Ailese waved to the people that she knew. They didn't talk about last night, but if it came up, no one would be scolded for bringing it up in the conversation. "Stop for a minute," D'Andra said. What is it, D? Are you alright?" "Yes, I'm fine. Ailese faced D'Andra, I just want you to know, Lee, that I am here for you, and if you have to call me in the middle of the night, day, or whatever, you do that, okay? Don't hesitate, we're going to get through this, and I'll be damned if this bastard tries anything. He's going to have to get through me and a whole bunch of folks, you hear me?" "Yes, D'Andra, I do, "Ailese told her. D'Andra and Ailese hugged each other and headed back to the house.

"Let's start on the things that are going to take the longest to cook, so here's what I am making for my hubby: parmesan chicken, spaghetti with marinara sauce, sourdough bread. You know how Mikell likes it, he likes it to be toasty and crisp. Um, okay, what else. Oh, for dessert he wants a York Cheesecake." "Wow, I heard that. I know you love your man, huh?" Ailese and D'Andra laughed. "So, if you want to help, what do you want to start on?" "How about I make the cheesecake, set the table with the special China, and chill the drinks? Is that okay?" "That would be great. I love your cheesecake. Heck, I got the recipe from you." "Yes, you did, huh?" The phone was ringing. Ailese had answered it. It was Mikell. "Hi, baby, how are you?" "I'm good. I just can't wait to see you guys and get out of this hospital bed." "Hey Mikell I miss you." D'Andra said in a playful voice. "Tell my sis I said hi." "He said to be quiet he's talking to his wife Ailese began to laugh. "Whatever," D'Andra said. "Hun, you'll be home soon, and I will be there at 5:30 on the dot, okay?"

"Okay, Lee, I love you so much." "I love you more."

When it was getting closer to the time that Mikell would be home, D'Andra had left to pick up the kids, and she was going to meet everyone back at Ailese and Mikell's around 6:30. Mikell's parents had stayed behind just to make sure all the final touches were all taken care of, before Mikell came home. They wanted Mikell's arrival to go perfectly. Ailese ran into Dr. Lewis and Dr. Corbell, who thanked her for her generosity and informed her that Leon's daughter was about to leave for Rory to begin her treatments, which made Ailese feel much better. When she arrived at Mikell's room, he was already dressed and ready to go. He was sitting on the neatly made bed. "Hey sexy, I see you didn't waste any time, huh?" Ailese gave Mikell a long kiss. She kissed him on his mouth, then she began kissing him on his neck. "You are so sexy- bad, but still sexy." "I know, baby, so let me call the nurse so we can get you home." Ailese didn't want to tell Mikell about all the nights she had been afraid, all the nights that she wished he could hold her; she just wanted to focus on getting him home. The nurse came in with a wheelchair and told Ailese that they needed to wait until Dr. Chaddman arrived. He just wanted to make sure Ailese knew how to take care of the dressings, etcetera.

After Dr. Chaddman gave Ailese instructions, he gave her the prescriptions that needed to be filled, and they signed the release papers.

The nurse helped Mikell out of the wheelchair and into the car, and they all said their goodbyes.

"Are you comfortable?" Yes I'm fine, thanks." "We have to stop off at the pharmacy for your meds. I will go in and get them for you, okay?" "Okay, so how are mom and dad?" "They're keeping busy. They have been a huge help. They stayed behind so that your homecoming is perfect. They've been making sure you have everything that you need. Just the other day, I gave them a list of things that were needed, and do you know that they didn't even let me give them any money for all those items? It was a lot too." "Yeah, I believe you. They're so kindhearted and they would do anything for us." I know they would, and we would too." "I will be right back, okay?" Ailese went inside the pharmacy to get Mikell's prescriptions. She looked at her cell phone, and she was making good on time.

She filled the prescriptions and headed home. She helped Mikell out of the car. His parents had met them at the car to carry the bags in. Mikell was surprised when he saw everyone that meant so much to him sitting at the dinner table. Everything looked so nice, that he smiled when he smelled that familiar aroma. Ailese had invited Emmanuel,

Chris, D'Andra Gabe, Jaden and Evette, and the kids were there, of course. "Hey, Daddy, I missed you. I know that I have to be careful when I hug you. Mommie said that you got stitches."

"That's right, Ashanee, daddy missed you so, so much." Mikell gave her a hug and kissed her on the cheek. Mikell greeted everyone until he got tired and needed to sit down. Johnnie helped him get situated and made him comfortable at the dinner table. The kids made sure that they all sat close to their dad at the dinner table. "I just want to thank everybody for coming. I just wanted Mikell to be surrounded with love when he came home. Please enjoy yourselves." Ailese fixed Mikell's dinner and told him to let her know if he needed anything.

Everyone ate and talked amongst themselves. Some people went back for seconds, even thirds. Mikell had seconds, so Ailese knew that his appetite was back for sure. He told her how delicious the meal was and that he appreciated her and D'Andra's hard work. "I would like to raise a glass to all my friends and family, for always being there for me, and a special thanks to my sexy, lovely wife, come here hun. Ailese walked over to where Mikell was sitting at the dinner table. Thank you so much for being there for me. I can't say it enough how lucky I am to have you and the kids. I love all of you."

"Cheers to that," Ailese said with a smile. Everyone toasted one another's cup or glass. Evette had to excuse herself, she needed to get back to the hospital and check on Heather, who was at the sitters.

After everyone had gone, Chris and D'Andra stayed back to help clean up, and the kids were watching a movie with their grandparents in the game room.

Chris and Mikell chatted about the surgery and how Mikell was anxious to get back to work. "Hey, man, please call us if you need anything, like me to drive you to work or come over, whatever, okay?"

"Thanks, man, I appreciate that. I will take you guys up on that offer."

"We have to head out, guys. Chris and D'Andra went into the game room to say goodbye to the kids and Mikell's parents. D'Andra and Ailese went outside to talk for a bit before she left. Ailese told D'Andra what she had done for Leon's daughter and how the doctors told her that Leon's daughter was getting ready to start her treatment. D'Andra told her that she was the only person she knew who had such a huge heart.

It took a while for Ailese to get her heart back and her strength back. When this man hurt her, he took everything from her: her pride, her confidence, her strength, and most of all, her heart, it was shattered. Ailese was determined to get all this back no matter what! He was the reason why she couldn't sleep at night; he was the reason why she was terrified of closing her eyes at night. He was the reason why she couldn't trust anyone for many, many years. It took her a long time to put the pieces of her life back together. She had promised herself that she would never ever let anyone abuse her again! He took away her inner and outer beauty; she felt ugly, and no one would have known this because Ailese kept her secret. She didn't tell her close friends or family until one day she couldn't hold in that secret any longer. She broke down in tears and told her family about being abused. Yes, her family was shocked. They knew that Ailese would never let a man, or anyone abuse her, she was too damn good for that! This man made her feel powerless. He made her feel ugly, like she was trash, and as time went on, Ailese had begun to believe it.

Mikell knew how fragile Ailese was. When he would make love to her, he took his time, and if Ailese told him that she couldn't, he would just hold her. Every time Ailese thought about sex, she would get sick to her stomach because of all the things this man made her do to him sexually. He would make her have sex with him even when she was menstruating and would get mad at her because the sheets were bloody. One day, when Ailese came home from work, she decided to take a bath because he was not home; this would give her some peace and quiet. She didn't hear him come home, he stormed into the bathroom where she was taking a bath and made her get out of the tub. He threw her on the floor and forced himself on her. Ailese begged him not to hurt her, and after he was done her wrists were black and blue from him holding them down with all his might. Ailese wore bracelets that covered the marks so no one would see them. Having sex with this man was always painful for Ailese because he was so rough, never gentle, and he would tell her that she would never find any other man that was well endowed as he was. Ailese would be in so much pain that she would take a lot of pain killers to relieve the pain, luckily, she never overdosed on them.

There was a knock at the door. It was Leon. He wanted to thank Ailese and Mikell for helping him with his daughter. When Ailese opened the door, he had a huge bouquet of flowers, wine, and balloons in his hands. "Hello, I knew that I should have called first but." Ailese interrupted him. "Let me help you. Ailese took the balloons out of his hands. Come on in, and have a seat. Mikell is on the couch in the living room. Thanks for the lovely flowers and gifts; you shouldn't have Leon, but I am so glad to see you." Leon walked into the living room, where Mikell and the family were. "Hey buddy Mikell said with a smile on his face I would get up, but … well, you know, it's good to see you." Leon gave Mikell and everyone a hug and sat down. "How are you feeling, Mikell?" "Oh, I am doing okay. I am so full, my wife fixed all my favorites for dinner again, and I ate like a pig. That hospital food doesn't do me any good." Leon laughed and agreed with Mikell. Ailese had walked into the room and hugged Leon again. "So, tell me, how did you remember that I loved silk flowers and purple is my favorite color." "Well, I have a good memory, and I am glad you like them." "No, I love them; they are so gorgeous." Ailese sat next to Mikell as they chatted with Leon. "I just wanted to tell you both in person how much my wife and I appreciate what you are doing for our daughter, Kayla. Because of you, my daughter has a chance at life. Leon began to get emotional, tears rolled down his face. He was not ashamed of showing his emotions.

There are no words to explain how I feel right now. God is good, you're forgiving people, and I know that I messed up by betraying you. Mikell started to say something, but he decided to wait until Leon was done. I never meant to hurt you, Mikell, but I had to do what I had to do, and I know that what I did was wrong, Leon paused. I had to get the money for Kayla to stay in the hospital longer. Please forgive me and find it in your hearts to forgive me. When I thought that this was the end, you two showed up and helped me and my family. You gave us hope, and I can't repay you enough." Leon began to cry even harder. Ailese sat next to him and consoled him. "You're welcome. All we want is for Kayla to get better so she can go outside and play with her friends, kiss you and your wife goodnight have her experiences, have her first love, graduating." "Yes, Leon, that is all we want, man, and please don't beat yourself up for what happened; that was why I didn't press charges, and yes, I am not happy about us not working together, but please call me if you need to talk. I'm here for you, we're here for you."

After Leon had left, Mikell headed to bed he was exhausted. He took his medications and went to sleep. Ailese didn't want to go to sleep, but she was exhausted herself, and as always, she prayed before she went to bed. She knew that there would be a lot of work tomorrow. Mikell tried to wake his wife up, but he was unsuccessful. He shook her as hard as he could, and Ailese was moaning and sobbing, words were coming out of her mouth. "No, no, please, I'll be good!" She was pleading with this man, pleading for her life. "Ailese, Ailese, wake up! Baby you're dreaming, wake up! Ailese woke up, but the dream seemed so real that she had forgotten where she was; she looked at Mikell. Baby, it's me, Mikell, your husband. Mikell held her as she sobbed. It's okay. I've got you. It's alright. I'm so sorry he hurt you, baby. Please, baby, talk to me, please. I'm here." Ailese sobbed even harder and confessed to Mikell about the nights that she was alone when he was in the hospital. She told him how difficult it was for her to sleep and how she had the dreams. She told him what had happened. "I hope that Dr. Salvino can help you with your sessions. When do you go back?" "Tomorrow, I have an appointment tomorrow. This time I'm going right after lunch, and she said that the session would be longer; she needs more time with me. Mikell. I don't want to take medications just so I can sleep. You know how I feel about that." She put her body closer to Mikell's body. "I know, baby, I am behind you 100 percent in whatever you decide to do, and you know that I am here for you, okay?" "I know, Mik, I'm so scared," Ailese whispered. "I know I am too baby, and it worries me that you're having these dreams again. I'm not worried about losing sleep, you know that."

Ailese was surprised to see Mr. Saxx waiting in her office when she arrived. She was jittery and sleepy, but she knew she didn't show it. "Hello, Mr. Saxx, how are you?" "I'm fine, my dear. I know that you just got here, but I need you to meet me in the conference room as soon as possible, and don't worry, Ell already prepared the conference room." "Okay, thanks, Mr. Saxx. I am right behind you." When they arrived, a few of Ailese's colleagues were sitting in the chairs, and a man that Ailese had never seen was standing next to the big white board with coffee in one hand, talking to Seth, who was a colleague of Ailese's. The man was tall and very good looking. He was Caucasian with deep green eyes and slicked black hair, he reminded her of an ex-boyfriend of hers back in junior high school. "Hello, everyone. There's doughnuts, juice, and coffee on that table. Mr. Saxx said as he pointed to the table. Ailese and a few others grabbed coffee and doughnuts. Ailese needed coffee so she could stay awake. I am Mr. Saxx, if anyone has, forgotten. I called everyone here because I have added someone to our company that I am sure everyone would appreciate. I give you Mr. Andrew McGee II." Mr. McGee walked over to the podium, spoke into the microphone, and introduced himself. He told everyone that he would be working under Mr. Saxx; basically, he would be Mr. Saxx's eyes and ears, and that he would be in the office every day.

Mr. McGee said that he graduated from Maryland University, and he was the number one student in his graduating class. Ailese had thought that he was a bit snobby, but she knew firsthand, that she would have to work with him, so they both had to get along.

After Mr. McGee was done with his long speech, he came around the table to meet everyone and get everyone's name. When it was Ailese's turn, he paused and stared at her like she was a piece of meat. Ailese stood up and said, "Hello, Mr. McGee, my name is Mrs. Ailese LaShae." He finally stopped staring at her. "Hello, nice to meet you. Mr. Saxx told me that we would be working together a lot, and I hope that you don't mind." "Not at all. Congratulations and welcome to the company." Ailese left Mr. McGee standing there. She could feel him looking at her ass, but she didn't let it bother her.

Mr. Saxx called Ailese into his office. Mr. McGee was already in Mr. Saxx's office. Ailese sat in the chair that was next to him. "So, I just wanted to go over some things with you, Ailese, if you don't mind, and by the way, how is Mikell doing?" "He is doing well. Guess what? His parents are down, and I know that they would love to see you." "Oh, my yes, I will give them a ring today. I haven't seen Johnnie and Verneil in a long time." Johnnie knew Mr. Saxx from college, and they remained friends. "So how long will they be here in Shelby?" "For a while, they're helping me look after Mikell, so, yeah, just give them a call."

"Okay, I will, my dear. So, I just wanted to let you know that you will be working with Andrew, and please know that your title will remain the same. I do need you to help Andrew catch up on everything, you know, like the clients. Introduce him to everyone; make him feel at home. I know that you'll do a good job as always." "Okay, Mr. Saxx, no problem, I will take care of all that, no worries."

After the meeting was over with Mr. Saxx, Ailese had Ell email Andrew the files that Ailese was working on, client names and so on. Andrew knew the company, but he had to learn the ropes because every company was different. Andrew asked Ell if he could see Ailese, and Ell had let Ailese know that he was there to see her. "Hello, what can I do for you, Mr. McGee?" "It's Andrew, please. I just wanted to let you know that I admire your work. Mr. Saxx knew what he was doing when he made you president of the company. I mean, your credentials, wow! I even noticed that you had you had a stake the Inergy. Wow, if anyone could turn that company around, they are very smart and know what they're doing. I mean, I thought nothing could save that company, but you did, wow. I'm sorry to ramble, but I just wanted to let you know that your work is awesome, and I look forward to working with you." "Me, too. Have a good day, and if you need anything just let us know. I do have a lot of work to do, Andrew. I don't mean to be rude, but I do have to get back to work. Andrew just stared at Ailese. It made her feel uncomfortable, and she didn't like it. Andrew, are you alright?" "Oh, I'm sorry I'll be in my office," Andrew was embarrassed to say.

Mr. Saxx had come over to Ailese's office. He told her that he wanted her to join him and Andrew for lunch. Ailese tried to get out of it, but Mr. Saxx insisted. "I want to let you know, Ailese, that you are doing a beautiful job and that I have decided to give you a generous raise. I feel that you've deserved it." "Well, that is great Mr. Saxx. Thank you, and thank you very much." Ailese was shocked and surprised at the same time. She made a generous salary already, but she felt that she deserved the raise.

"I'd like to make a toast; to Ailese and Andrew, my partners in crime." They all picked up their glasses and toasted, when Andrew touched Ailese's glass, he absently began to stare at her again. "Andrew, are you okay?" "Oh yes, please forgive me, but I must say that you are so beautiful. I hope that I'm not making you feel uncomfortable." "No. Thank you, but I have to remind you, I am married," Ailese smiled. "Yes, she is so hands off, mister," Mr. Saxx said as he grinned.

"No, I never will … Andrew paused as the waiter began to place the platters of food on the table. "It's okay, I'm not trying to give you a hard time, but I just wanted to let you know that I am married and dedicated to my family, and I do appreciate the compliment." Andrew took a sip of his drink and changed the subject.

Ailese, Andrew, and Mr. Saxx talked about the company's goals and expectations as they enjoyed their lunch. After lunch they headed back to the office. When they arrived, Ell told Ailese to call Dr. Salvino as soon as possible. "Hi, Dr. Salvino, how are you?" "I am fine, Mrs. LaShae, how are you?"

"Good, I can't complain." "I couldn't reach you on your cell, so I called your office. I hope that you don't mind." "Not at all, I'm sorry. I must have left my cell here at the office." "I was wondering, could you come to my office in an hour. I had two cancellations, so I thought that I would give you a buzz to see if you could come earlier." "That would be great. Could you give me a minute and I can call you back? I need to look at my calendar to make sure I don't have any important meetings today." "Oh, okay, I will be waiting for your call."

Ailese called Mr. Saxx to let him know what was going on, and he told her that she never needed his permission to leave early, because she was her own boss, but he did appreciate her letting him know that she was leaving for a couple of hours.

Ailese called Mikell to check on him, he was eating lunch when she called, and she told him that she was on her way to see Dr. Salvino and that she would call him later. Mikell told her that he had some good news to tell her when she got home. Ailese was a bit anxious to get to Dr. Salvino. She wanted to tell her about the dreams that she was having. When she passed by Karen's office, Karen had caught up with her. "Hey Ailese, how are you?" "Hey Karen, it's good to see you!" "I have something for you. Karen gave Ailese an envelope. When Ailese opened the envelope, it had some pictures of her mom's birthday party wearing the jewelry set that Ailese made for her, inside there was a thank you card from Karen's mom, it was very beautiful. My mom wanted to know if you could make her more jewelry. Our family and friends really loved the jewelry, Ailese." She wanted Ailese to sell her jewelry in her store. "Wow I will definitely call her. That sounds like a great idea. I am so surprised at how much people really loved the jewelry." Karen walked with Ailese until she arrived at Dr. Salvino's office. They hugged each other, and Karen went back to her office.

All these wonderful blessings that God gave Ailese were great, and Ailese knew that God would get her through anything, even these dreams. He is her protector, and Ailese never felt like some people feel about God when bad things happen to them. Some people felt that God let them down by not listening to them. Ailese never felt this way because, even when this man hurt her, she never felt God let her down. Ailese knew God still protected her, she was still alive, still strong and without the help of God, she knew she would not be able to get through life period. She got through her trials and tribulations with God.

"Ailese, I want you to take a deep breath, okay?" "Okay, Ailese took a deep breath and let it out slowly, closed her eyes, and said a prayer to God. "Now I want you to tell me about the man who abused you. Tell me when the abuse began okay." "It started after we were together for two years, in the beginning, he was so nice and sweet that he would move the earth for me if he could. I feel like it started when I began working for this company, somehow, he found out that I was making more money than he was, and I think he felt less of a man. I took the job to better myself. I felt like I never needed anyone's permission to better myself. The first time that he hurt me, we had a gathering at his apartment, and we were all talking about our jobs. He claimed that I was being big headed and thought that I was "all that," which I wasn't.

After everyone had left, he started yelling at me and saying mean things to me. I started to leave, but I loved him, and I didn't want to leave mad at him, you know? Ailese went on. So, I calmed him down eventually, or at least I thought that I did. He pushed me on to the couch, and when I tried to get up, he pushed me down again. I forgave him when he apologized to me. I knew that I should have broken up with him at that point, but I was stupid." "Let's not put ourselves down, okay, Dr. Salvino absently said as she went on writing on her notepad.

Remember, when people know that they're wrong, they will say anything to make themselves look good, and in this case, he knew that he was wrong, so of course he apologized, even if he didn't mean it. Dr. Salvino was still writing as she asked Ailese a couple of more questions. Tell me about a time that you started to fear him even more, because I know we talked about how you hid a lot from your family, like the bruises." "Well, one time I knew that I was going to die, this was my time. He came home, and by this time I had moved in with him, and I would help with the cooking and so forth. Well, he got really upset with me because he was hungry, and dinner wasn't ready yet. He said that I should have had dinner ready because I knew that he didn't like to eat late. It wasn't late. It was early. I remember it like it was yesterday.

I just ignored him, I didn't want to fight with him. I was setting the table when he took the plate out of my hand and grabbed me by my hair and told me to get into the room. I told him I didn't want to, and he became enraged. I didn't want him to hurt me. He started to choke me. He told me that if I didn't get into the room, I would never see daylight again. He finally stopped choking me. I went into the room, and all of a sudden, he pushes me on to the bed with all he had. He pinned me and straddled me. He wouldn't let me up. I begged him to let me up, but he didn't. He removed his tie and wrapped it around my neck, warning me that if I screamed or became too loud, someone would hear me. He ripped open my blouse. He stood up and took off his belt and began beating my upper body with it. He put welts on my breasts. I cried and cried. It was very painful. He didn't even care that the pain was unbearable, no matter how much I pleaded for my life. Ailese tried to hold back her tears and reminded herself of that thick skin that she has, but the more she talked about what happened, that thick skin didn't matter at all.

He then picked me up off the bed, like I was a rag doll. I couldn't free myself from him. He threw me into the bath tub and turned on the water. I remember praying to God that he wouldn't fill up the tub and drown me. I prayed and prayed for him to spare my life. Ailese felt more tears come down her face. She made a fist and felt herself getting angrier. This bastard took so much from her! All Ailese wanted to do was love him! The bath tub filled up pretty good, and all this time he's trying to choke me. I fought back as much as I could, but he didn't succeed choking me, so, that made him even more angry. He began to beat me some more with the belt, hitting me and telling me to shut up and stop crying. I never thought I would love to hear a sound that was so beautiful to me; the phone rang, and that phone ringing saved my life!

Dr. Salvino rose from her chair and sat next to Ailese, still holding her notepad. "Tell me how old you were when this man hurt you." Ailese paused and closed her eyes. She began to sob even more. "I was in my early twenties at the time. I hadn't had any kids yet; thank God, because I would never want to put my child in a situation where they feared for their lives every day. I would never want them to experience abuse." "I agree, Dr. Salvino said. Ailese, I want you to take a deep breath for me, okay? I'm going to get you some water. I think that this session went very well. Ailese took a deep breath and drank the water that Dr. Salvino had given her. It made her feel a little better.

Ailese, I think that it's best that we have two-hour sessions, because that would give me more time with you. Do you think you could do that for me?" "Yes, I can do whatever it takes for me to understand why I am having the dreams and to get this man out of my life all over again. Yes, I can make sure that I clear my schedule."

When Ailese came home, Mikell was resting on the couch. Ailese made sure that dinner was made, and everyone had everything that they needed. She wanted to spend some alone time with her husband. "So, tell me, what is this great news you have for me, sexy." Ailese smiled at Mikell as she waited for him to tell her the news. "Well, remember the huge favor that you agreed to do for me? Ailese shook her head, yes. Well, starting in two weeks, we're going into the studio to start recording with my artist, and I saved the best for last. He is a Christian artist." Ailese's eyes went big; they were filled with excitement. "Oh my gosh, hun, that sounds great. I am so happy! I am happy for you and me, that we get to work together." "I knew that you would be, and yes, our deal is still on. Everyone knows that they have to work around your schedule, okay?" "Okay great! That sounds good, but I do have to tell you I may be a bit rusty, hun, so be patient with me. I better start practicing, huh?" "I don't think you need to. I hear you sing in church and around the house. Your voice is still beautiful, Lee."

"Well, thank you." "Hey, tell me about your day today, Lee." Ailese really didn't want to ruin the good news and tell Mikell about her therapy sessions.

"Well, we had a meeting today at work. Mr. Saxx introduced our new edition to the company. His name is Andrew McGee II, and he was hitting on me. I told him that I was married, I thanked him for the compliments, and told him in a nice way not to flirt with me again." "You are so bad; I actually don't blame the guy; you're gorgeous, you know. Why do you think I married you?" Ailese punched Mikell playfully in the arm. "You married me because you were madly in love with me, right?" "Right, Mikell grinned, and because you were and continue to be breathtaking." "I had to eat lunch with the guy. I mean, don't get me wrong, he is very smart and has credentials that are out of this world, but he just bugs me. Like today, he came into my office and told me that he admired my work and that he looked forward to working with someone like me." "Really, well, you have turned so much around since you've been there, baby, and Mr. Saxx knows that he did the right thing picking you to work under him. Hey, I say take the compliments." "Yeah, and guess what? Mr. Saxx announced at lunch that he was giving me a raise! Can you believe that? I didn't even see that coming!" "Congratulations baby! Hey, you deserve it!" "Mr. Saxx went out of his way to tell me that Andrew was not there to take my job. Oh, no, he wanted to make sure that I knew Andrew was only working with Mr. Saxx, that he was only his eyes and ears, which helps me a lot in the long run."

Ailese was a bit quiet. She was contemplating if she wanted to bring up what happened at therapy with Dr. Salvino. "Baby, are you okay?" Mikell asked her. "Yes, well, I really didn't want to ruin the mood telling you about my session with Dr. Salvino. Mikell interrupted her and told her that he wanted to hear what happened and not think that he never wants to hear how her sessions went. Well, it was so hard today, Mikell, Ailese paused, and she told herself that she didn't want to cry anymore. I had to talk about an incident where I knew that I was going to die. I spoke about it, and it made me angry and upset at the same time, but I knew that I had to talk about it. A part of me was feeling guilty and stupid, but I was young, and my mom always warned me about men like him. Mikell comforted Ailese as she continued her story. My mom told me that I should never ever let a man abuse me in any way. I didn't listen, you know." Mikell kissed Ailese on the forehead. He wanted her to stop putting herself down. "Look at me. Mikell lifted her face so she would look at him. Please listen to me, and listen to me good. I am here for you. I am not here to judge you, no one is here to judge you, not even Dr. Salvino. You know and I know that we go through things in our lives, and we all wish that we could have made better decisions, but that is what life is all about. We make the mistakes, and we learn from them, but what is important is that we don't repeat those mistakes. Mikell could see the hurt in her eyes that she blamed herself for what she went through, and he was going to do whatever he had to do to remove that guilt. Baby, this man took so much away from you, but I don't feel like you're looking at the bigger picture here. You didn't let him win, he did not win, you hear me? You know why? Because you are here. You are strong. You have a huge heart. You have a beautiful family that loves you." Ailese never really looked at it this way, but he was making a lot of sense, and Mikell was right. Mikell hugged his wife; he wished he could make all her pain go away.

Ailese told Mikell how the sessions were going to be two hours instead of one, and he told her not to worry about anything. He wanted her to focus on her sessions, and he would arrange for the kids to be picked up, etcetera. Ailese also told Mikell about Karen's mother wanting to put her jewelry in her store; he was very excited for her, but he just didn't want her to get too overwhelmed, so he told her to take her time about making that decision. He assured her that he would stand behind her 100 percent and that it was solely up to her.

Ailese visited with the kids for a few hours. They played video games and read to one another. Adrieana and Ailese talked about Adrieana having a sleep over in a week or so. Ailese told her that when her dad felt better, they would talk about it then. Ailese made sure the kids were ready for school tomorrow. When she was about to head to her room, Ashanee called her into her room. She wanted to give her mom another kiss good night. She asked her mom to lay down with her, and she asked if she could read with her some more. After Ailese was done reading with Ashanee, she knocked on her in-laws' door. "Come in. We're still awake. Come in." "Hey guys, I just wanted to let you guys know how much I appreciate all your help." "Oh, you know that we don't mind," her father-in-law said. "You needed us. There is nothing that can stop us from being here for our family." Ailese smiled at them and thanked God for blessing her with great in-laws. "Hey, how about we all go do something this weekend?" "That sounds great, do you think that Mikell would be up to it?" "Well, I'll talk to him, and I'll see what his schedule is like. We could go and see a show or something. I will let you guys know, okay?" "Okay, Johnnie said. Verneil explained to Ailese that she would love it if everyone could come, but she just didn't want to put any more strain on Mikell.

"Hey, baby, how do you feel about doing something this weekend? Do you think that you'll be up to it?" "Oh yeah, sounds like a plan to me as long as it's after ten. I have to do a few things. I have some conference calls scheduled." Ailese knocked on her in-law's door again. "Mikell is fine with going out this weekend. I'm thinking maybe a show? It's our treat." "Alright, it's a date," Verneil said. "Good night, love you guys." Ailese went back to her room and told Mikell about the plans for the weekend. "You promise to let me know if we need to go home, okay? I know that you've been tired lately." "Yes, mom," Mikell said it jokingly. "I just want us to have some family time together, especially before your mom and dad go home." "I know I'm excited about this weekend."

After Mikell and Ailese finished getting ready for bed, the phone rang. It was Alonda, Ailese's mom. "Hey, Mom, how are you? I miss you so much. How's Don?" "Oh, we're doing good. I was calling, because I wanted to know what everyone was doing after church." "So far we don't have any plans, why?" "Well, I was wondering if we all could meet at my house. Mom's birthday is coming up, so, I thought that we all should take a family portrait as a gift to her." "Wow, Mom, that is a great idea, so what can I do to help?" "Oh, just show up after church, okay? However, I was wondering what you thought about this: all the women wear silver and black, and all the men wear silver and red?" "Okay, Mom, that sounds good. Have you told everyone?" "Yes, I have, and so far, everyone loves it. I do too! I mean, everyone doesn't have to worry about getting a gift, and we all know it's hard to shop for Mom. Alonda wanted to talk to Mikell to see how he was doing.

"Hey, Mom, how are you doing?" "I'm hanging in there, just busy, busy." Alonda chuckled. Well, I wanted to check up on my sweetie, and you're feeling good?" "Yes, I am. Thanks, Mom."

"We'll be seeing you on Sunday, right?" "Of course, I hear that were doing a portrait for Mommie, she's going to be sooo happy." "Yes, she will be."

Well, I am going to let you guys go. Tell Ailese that I love her. See you guys on Sunday after church at my house. Love you guys."

"Baby, um, we're going to have to go shopping before Sunday because I haven't bought a suit in, I don't know how long," Mikell said as he examined his closet. Mikell really wasn't up to going shopping for a suit. "Hun, if you're not up to shopping, I could have my friend Terrence come over and show you some suits. I could give him a call."

"Oh, baby, that would be great, could you?" "Sure, anything for you." Ailese looked at the clock. She thought she'd take a chance and call Terrence, she may catch him. "Hey Terrence, it's Ailese. How are you? I hope that I didn't catch you at a bad time." "Ailese, wow, how are you and your family?" "We are fine, thanks for asking, and how are you and your family doing?" "God is continuing to bless us every day." "I was wondering, what your schedule look like this week?" "Well, you're in luck. We're closed tomorrow because we have a fashion show to attend, but I'm not flying out until the late evening. What can I do for you?" "My husband needs some suits, and I was wondering if you could bring some by here at the house." "Hold on one second, okay? Terrence retuned to the phone. Are you still in the same house?" "Yes, I am." "Okay, what about tomorrow at seven?" "That would be perfect, and Terrence, I will make sure I have my special coffee that you like ready for you, okay?" "Sounds good to me. Is there anything specific you wanted me to bring?" "Anything that you recommend because we always trust you, could you also bring some suits that are silver and red because we're taking a family portrait?" "Okay, got it, so I will see you then. Take care, Ailese." "All done, baby. He'll be here tomorrow at seven." "Come here, you. What will I do without you? I do need more suits. Is it okay if I splurge tomorrow?" "Oh yeah, I could go to the bank after work, no, before I go to work, and get some cash, okay?" "Thank you, baby, Mikell said, gently kissing Ailese on the lips and neck. I better stop. It sucks that we can't make love for a while because I want you so bad." "Use your imagination, baby, Ailese said as she motioned for Mikell to lie down on the bed. He was in his boxers, so she took them off. She could see the gauze that covered his stitches, so she had to be careful.

Relax, baby, and close your eyes, but you have to promise me that you'll let me know if you're in pain, okay?" Ailese took off her robe and her night gown that was under it. She told Mikell to get under the covers with her. She took his hand and put it on her breasts. Mikell began to massage her breasts. He didn't care if he felt pain. He wanted to touch every inch of her body. He kissed her breasts. He was rough but gentle. He opened her legs and touched her thighs, his hands massaging her inner thighs, touching her, he opened her legs even wider. Mikell moved down in between her legs, and he began to taste her. He wanted to taste her all over, every inch of her body. Ailese began to moan and kept her legs open wide for him. Her body was like ice cream to him, it always tasted so good.

Ailese began to breathe heavily. Her heart was racing, and she wanted him even more. He felt the same way. Mikell kissed Ailese on her lips. His kisses were deep. She didn't want him to stop, so he didn't, when she climaxed, Mikell kissed her even deeper. Ailese whispered to Mikell that he felt so good that he told her the same. "Lie down, baby." Mikell interrupted Ailese. "Shsh …come here. I just want to hold you." "Mikell … I want you." Ailese kissed him. She kissed every inch of his body, down to the gauze that covered his stitches. I love you, she said as she massaged and pampered him. She could feel his heart beat, hear him moan, and her tongue moved all over his body, giving him chills. Hold me, Mikell." They held each other until they both fell asleep.

"Come on, kids, time to go to school. Meet me in the car in five minutes, okay?" Ailese gave Mikell a generous kiss before he left. "Hey, I love you, baby, and I just wanted to say that I really enjoyed that a lot. Could we keep that up until I'm 100 percent better?" "You bet, baby. I guess you forgot what we used to do. Do you remember how long I made you wait to make love to me because of my trust issues that I had?" "Oh, yes, that's right, I forgot how much I enjoyed it … Mikell paused. You were worth the wait." Mikell and Ailese kissed. "I don't know why you put up with me." Because I loved you so much." Ailese smiled at Mikell and gave him another kiss. "All right baby, I will call you, okay? Oh, by the way, Mr. Saxx asked about you. He actually wants you to give him a call, okay?" "Oh, okay, I will call him today." "Yeah, you're like his son. He loves you to death. When you were in the hospital, he told me it didn't matter when I came back to work. He didn't care if it was a month. He wanted to make sure you were okay." "I love that man. He's been so good to us. He sent me so much stuff when I was in the hospital." "Yeah, I know I had to carry all that stuff to the car, remember?" Ailese said in a sarcastic voice. "I do. I love you for it." Mikell said as he kissed her.

"Love you guys. Have a great day, okay?" The kids said their goodbyes as they got out of the car. Ailese looked on as the kids headed to the school ground. She started the car and drove off. She began to reflect on all the difficulties she had caused her husband prior to their marriage and how much he must have loved her to be as patient as he was and still is with her. Ailese smiled to herself as she thought about all the dates they went on, the late- night drives, and the late- night talks she and Mikell had.

Mikell has been the only male in her life who has never let her down.

Mikell had always been this loving man who had never disappointed her, never cheated on her, and most of all, never hurt her. Ailese always felt safe with Mikell; he would do anything for her to protect her and the kids, no matter what.

As Ailese was driving, she saw a familiar face. It was Andrew. It looked like his car wouldn't start, and he looked very frustrated. Ailese pulled over to where he was and walked over to him. "Good Morning, Andrew, can I give you a lift?" "Well, Good Morning to you, Mrs. LaShae." "Please call me Ailese." "Okay, Ailese, it is. I can't believe this car. I just had it serviced, and it won't start. I'm a bit embarrassed." "Oh, don't be silly, I'm parked right here, Ailese said motioning to her car. I can give you a lift. I mean, that's if you're going to the office."

"Yes, I am, but I was going to stop at the coffee shop that's just up the road, and if that's okay with you, the coffee's on me." "Okay, it's a deal." "I really appreciate it. I will call the tow truck when we get to work." "Yes, okay, don't forget, you don't want your car out there on the street all day."

Ailese's phone started ringing, so she answered it. It was D'Andra. "Hey sis, Good Morning." "Good Morning, sis. Hey, I know you're driving to work, but I had a question for you." "Okay, I'm listening." "Mom called me about the family photo, which I am so excited about, and I was wondering if I could stop by and get your opinion on some outfits I picked out." "Okay, sure, you know that you didn't have to call me to ask me that. Are you stopping by tonight?" "Is that okay?" "Yes, Terrence may be there. He's coming over at seven." "Oh, really, is he bringing some suits by for Mikell?" "Yes, he is, so hey, listen, I will call you later to check in with you, okay?" "Okay, love ya, sis." "Love you too."

"Sorry, I didn't mean to be rude. I had to take that call." "Okay, no problem; family is important, Andrew said as he made eye contact with Ailese. Are you the only child?" "Oh no, I have one brother, D'Andra may as well be my blood sister." When they went into the coffee shop, Andrew opened the door for Ailese, who thanked him and went in. "Anything that you want, I'm buying. You do like coffee, right?" "Oh yes, it's just that they have so many flavors and the Danishes look delicious." "Yes, I know, and you should try them, be my guest." The lady took their orders, and after they got their coffee and Danishes, Andrew, and Ailese headed to the office. "Thank you so much, Ailese. Have a good day, okay?" "Okay, and you have a good day too." Ailese could feel him staring at her as she walked away.

"Good morning, Ell. How are you?"

"Good morning, boss. I'm doing great."

"Do you have plans for lunch today, Ell?"

"Um, no, boss, I don't."

"Well, now, that you do, I'm taking you shopping and out to lunch today."

"Okay, thanks, boss. Oh, I almost forgot, Mr. Markson is waiting for you in your office, and he's early."

"Okay, thanks, Ell."

"Hello, Mr. Markson, how are you today?"

"Hello, Ailese, I hope it's okay that I'm a bit early."

"Better early than late, right? Will Ann be joining us today?"

"Yes, she will. She should be here shortly."

"Okay, could Ell get you anything to drink, coffee, tea, or water?"

"Water would be great. Do you have any spring water?"

"Yes, we do. Let me have Ell get that for you." Elle brought in the spring water for Mr. Markson.

When Ann arrived, they all headed to the conference room. Andrew was there as well. He had asked Ailese if he could sit in on the meeting. "I have all the information that you need in these folders that I am giving you. Please look them over and let me know if you have any questions."

The room was silent for a while as everyone read the documents.

Ailese had a good feeling that the Marksons would love her plan.

"Mrs. LaShae, this is so awesome." Ann was very excited. "We're excited to do business with you." Mr. Markson agreed as well. Andrew walked over to Ailese and told her that she did a good job with the account and to keep up the good work, then he headed back to his office. After the meeting, Ailese headed back to her office to look at her schedule. She knew that she had some phone conferences today, but she wasn't sure of the times. "Congratulations, boss, I knew we could land that contract with the Marksons; I'm so happy for you." "Thanks, but I couldn't have done it without you." Ell smiled.

Ailese told Ell that she could go to any store she wanted and that she could pick whatever she wanted.

They shopped and shopped until they were hungry, and they ended up at Ten Jayes. They chatted and sipped drinks.

"So, boss, tell me the truth what do you think about Andrew McGee? Oops, the second?" "I mean, he's okay, I guess."

"Yeah, I see how he looks at you. Boss, he has a crush on you." Ailese started to laugh. "Well, I guess that's just too bad because I am a happily married woman. You know what happened this morning? I actually gave him a ride to work today. I saw him this morning after I dropped the kids off. I guess he had some car trouble." "Really? Ell's eyes were getting bigger by the minute. Ell gave Ailese a look. "No, Ell, please do not read more into this, and I hope he would do the same if I were stranded." "Boss, I am telling you he has a thing for you. I know men, and when they want something, they will get it no matter what." "Yes, I agree Ell, but can we change the subject, please?" "Okay, fine, boss. Hey, I got your back okay." "I don't need any help, Ell," Ailese smiled. "Boss, please just hear me out. I had this friend, and we were very close. She was in your position, and she said the same thing to me, that she was happily married, and this man couldn't have her no matter what he did, and before you knew it, bam! Her marriage was in shambles! Ailese looked at Ell and shook her head. "Ell, I know that you're trying to be a good friend, and I do appreciate that, but mark my words, Mr. Andrew can say and do what he wants, hey, it's a free country. I don't care not one bit if he has something for me; nothing is going to happen." Ell took a sip of her drink. "Okay, boss, I hear you." "I'm not trying to belittle you; it's just that I've been through a lot with men, and the majority of them have brought me down and made me feel this small. I've always given, and when Mikell came along, I promised myself that no one and nothing was going to stand in my way. What I'm trying to say is that I am happy, okay."

When Ell and Ailese made it back to the office, Andrew had called an emergency meeting. Ailese wondered why he would schedule an emergency meeting. "Please take a seat, everyone. My name is Andrew McGee. I've met some of you, and some of you I have not. The reason for this meeting is because I believe that getting to know people that you work with is very important, so next Friday we will be having a luncheon for everyone. We will provide the food etcetera, and all you have to do is show up. The luncheon will start at 1:00 p.m. Are there any questions?" Stephanie from Human Resources had raised her hand, and Andrew pointed to her. "What time does the luncheon end?" "Well, there isn't any time, and just so you know, please don't worry about not being paid for the luncheon. It's not going to hurt anyone."

All the employees talked among themselves until Andrew dismissed everyone.

"Ailese, could I talk to you for a minute, please?" "Yes, what can I do for you, Andrew?" "I just wanted to say thanks again for the ride this morning. You saved my life," Andrew said with a grin. "Oh, no problem, is there anything else?" "Oh, no, that was all." Ailese walked back to her office. She remembered that she was supposed to go by the bank this morning, but giving Mr. Andrew a ride sidetracked her. "Hey Ell, I will be right back, okay. I have an errand to run."

Ailese decided to check on Mikell and see if he needed anything. "Hey baby, I miss you!" "Hi sweetie, how's your day going?" "Busy, it's really busy, but busy is good, right? I wanted to know if you or your mom and dad needed anything?" "Well, I was craving something from Ten Jayes, but I could wait until later." "No, baby, I can pick it up for you. What about Mom and Dad? Would they like something from there?" "Hold on baby let me ask them. Mikell put the phone back on his ear. Yes, they would. I'll have them look at the menu and I will call you back. Is that okay?" "Yeah, hun, that's fine." Ailese went to the bank, and to her surprise,

Don was there as well. She walked up to him, and he too was surprised to see her. "Hey you, how are you?" "I'm good, and you?" "I am much better, hey what's missing?" "Oh, your cane, huh?" "You're right, and I'm back to work too. Today, they have me in your neck of the woods. It's funny. I was going to stop by your office just to say hello." "Well, I guess I saved you a trip. It's funny, I was going to come to the bank this morning, but then I got sidetracked."

"Mom says everyone's excited about Sunday, huh?" "Yes, we all are. Hey, I meant to ask Mom. Do you know if she got a hold of Allen?" "Oh yes, he will be there."

"Well, baby girl, I have to get back to work. See you on Sunday." Don said as he hugged Ailese. "Okay, I love you, Dad."

Ailese went to Ten Jayes and picked up food for Mikell and his parents. When she arrived at the house with the food, Johnnie helped her bring in the food and drinks. "Hey guys, here's the food you guys wanted, so dig in. Ailese helped Mikell to the kitchen and made sure that he was comfortable in his chair. Baby I can stay a while." Mikell kissed Ailese on the lips and thanked her. Johnnie and Verneil pulled out a tray from the closet and ate their food in the living room to give Ailese and Mikell some time alone. "Thanks, baby, mmmmm, this is so good. Do you want any?" "No, thank you. I actually had Ten Jayes for lunch today, and I am still stuffed." "Baby, Terrance called to confirm our appointment today, and Chris and the guys stopped by earlier." "Oh, okay. I know that you're going to love the suits that Terrance is bringing, and I went by the bank. Ailese took the money out of her purse and handed Mikell an envelope. "Thanks, baby, he said, looking in the envelope. Baby? Ailese kissed him and told him that he deserved to spend the money, and she didn't want him to make a fuss about it. Ailese put the money in a safe place. She went back to the kitchen and helped herself to a bottle of water.

"Okay, I will see you guys later on, okay." Ailese headed back to the office.

D'Andra showed up with her outfits, so Ailese could help her decide which one she should wear. Her and Ailese headed to her room so that D'Andra could try on the outfits while Chris and Mikell watched television. Terrence showed up at seven sharp. Terrance was always on time. That was one of the reasons why he was so popular. He never made his clients wait. Terrence dressed very neatly. He was six feet tall, and he always kept his hair cut low, almost bald, and lined up, with a goatee. He had light green eyes and a million-dollar smile. "Hi Terrance, come on in." Terrance and his assistant came with suits cradled over their arms.

Ailese assisted in placing the suits on the couches and unzipping the huge green covers that the suits were in. Mikell studied the suits very carefully, one by one. Ailese fixed everyone coffee and gave Terrance his special cup of coffee like she had promised him. "I love this coffee, Ailese, and I don't know why I always keep forgetting to pick some up." "Hey, I gotcha. Remind me to give you some before you go, okay?" "Are you serious? Okay, well I will give you a discount for that!" "You're on, hun."

Mikell had picked out ten suits, and Chris ended up picking out some suits as well, luckily, D'Andra got a hold of Terrance to ask him to bring some suits for Chris. "Wow Ailese I really appreciate you guys. I mean, I have been so busy ever since you helped me reinvent my business. I owe you so much Ailese." "It was my pleasure, and by you coming here to help my family out, you're doing me a huge favor because Mikell didn't want to go out shopping." "Oh, I understand anytime ... anytime."

"No! No! Leave me alone! Let me go, let me go!" These words came from Ailese, who was yet again having a bad dream. He was hurting her, he was pulling her by her hair and kicking her in her stomach. She tried to free herself from him, but his grasp would get even stronger. Mikell tried to wake her up, but Ailese wouldn't wake up. "Baby, wake up, it's me, Mik. Wake up baby, please!

Ailese still couldn't break loose from him, his grip was too strong. She could feel the blood dripping down her legs from the carpet burns that she had from him dragging her. Her whole body felt like it was on fire, she began to scream even more, and he finally stopped dragging her and told her to get up. Ailese struggled to get up. He had lost his patience and stood her up on his own and threw her into a wall. Ailese hit her head and fell down on the floor.

Mikell was still trying to wake her up. Ailese, wake up! He shook her body as hard as he could, and when she finally woke up, she screamed and screamed. Her body was shaking uncontrollably. She began to scream even louder. Mikell shook her body and tried whatever he could to get her out of that dream. Ailese, baby you're safe, you're safe. Mikell repeated. Ailese was gasping for air, she was dumbfounded. Mikell grabbed her and held her; he rocked her back and forth. I'm here, Lee, I'm here." When Ailese caught her breath and could talk, she began telling Mikell about her dream. "He was, Ailese said after a brief pause. He was hurting me, he was pulling me and dragging me. I tried to free myself from him, but he was too strong. Ailese began to sob. I was bleeding so badly from the burns that I had on my legs. I pleaded with him to let me go, but he didn't even care. He threw me into a wall because I couldn't get up because I was in so much pain."

SHELBY LIES

Mikell wiped the tears from her face and kissed her forehead. "I'm so sorry that he hurt you. I'm so sorry that you're going through this. I wish I could take this all away. You didn't deserve to be hurt like that; he is a coward! I do feel that he will be punished somehow. I don't mean to be mean, but I hope this bastard has already paid for what he did to you! Mikell began to imagine the things he would like to do to this bastard who had hurt his wife.

"Look at me baby, Mikell said, lifting Ailese's face. I love you. We're going to get through this together. Everything will be fine." "Mikell, I can't keep putting you through this! I just can't! "Baby, please! We're in this together, and I love you more than anything! Please, don't ever say that again. You're not putting me through anything; were a team!" There was a knock on the door. It was Mikell's mom. "Is everything okay? I heard screaming." "I'm sorry I woke you. I had a bad dream." Ailese felt embarrassed. She wanted to throw up. She wanted to hide under a rock.

"Oh, honey, are you going to be okay? I'm so sorry." Verneil grabbed Ailese and hugged her. "Yes, I think so." "I'll fix you a glass of warm milk that usually helps." "I don't want you to go through any trouble." Verneil interrupted Ailese and told her that it wasn't any trouble at all. "Baby, let mom fix you the warm milk, okay?" "Okay."

The warm milk seemed to help, and Ailese slept the rest of the night peacefully. Mikell would wake up just to watch her sleep soundly. He held her the rest of the night. On Saturday morning, everyone was excited about the family outing. Everyone woke up early and headed to breakfast. After everyone ate, they looked in the shops nearby. They watched a movie and went to the Marina, that was nearby. The girls loved watching the boats go by.

"Dad, Dad." Adrieana grabbed her dad's hand and led him to where the boats were. "Look at that boat, it's nice, huh?"

"Wow, that's a beauty." Ailese had noticed the boat's name, *The McGee Winds II*. She noticed that the owner of the boat was Andrew. She started to think, "Mmmm … Is he following me?" Ailese didn't mention to Mikell or anyone else that she knew the person that was on the boat. He couldn't be following me. I mean, why would he be following me?" She shrugged her shoulders and watched the rest of the boats. She hoped that Andrew wouldn't spot her. She didn't feel like talking to him. She just wanted to have fun with her family. Johnnie and Verneil were enjoying themselves as well. They had suggested that they stop at the café and get coffee, so they did. "Kids, look at the menu and see what you guys want, okay?" "I'm still stuffed from the food we had at the movies. Armont told his mom. Could I get a shake mom?" "A small one, yes, you may, Armont." "We, too, Mom, can we just have a small root beer float?" "Yes, Ashanee, you guys may have a small root beer float." "Mommie, Mikell began to speak like a young child. Could I have a banana split, please?" Everyone began to laugh at Mikell.

"You're not a kid, Daddy." The kids began to tease their dad.

"I am exhausted. Wow, I had a lot of fun. Johnnie began to yawn. I think I am done for the day." "Guys, I need you to make sure that all the items that we bought today are hanging up in your closets or put away, please. Mommie doesn't want anything going wrong tomorrow, so hop to it. I will be there in a bit, okay."

The kids went into their rooms. Ashanee told her mom that she needed help. Ailese told her that she would be right there.

Ailese gave Mikell his medication. Mikell laid down in the room and watched television. "Hey, Ashanee, what did you need help with, huh?" "I need help organizing my jewelry box. Could you show me how you organized yours, Mommie?" "Sure, okay, let's start by separating the jewelry by color. It will help you find things much easier." Ashanee appreciated her mom teaching her how to be more organized, and now she could find all her jewelry much easier now. The girls loved jewelry like their mom does, so there was a lot of jewelry to organize. Ashanee asked her mom if she could help her put away the rest of her things. They both reorganized the closet so that Ashanee could find things much easier. "Thanks, Mom, you're the best!" Adrieana called her mom, she too needed help. "Hey kitten, what do you need, honey?" "I need more hangers. Do we have any?" "Oh yes, I'll be right back, okay?" "Okay, Mommy." Ailese came back with some hangers and gave them to Adrieana. "That's all, Mom, I'm fine now." "Okay, hun, let me know if you need me, okay?" "Okay, Mom." When Ailese headed back to her room, Mikell was asleep. She smiled at him and gently put a blanket over him. Ailese decided to take a long, hot bath to relax, after all that walking made her muscles ache. Ailese ran her bath water and lit some candles. She decided to read her book; it was very peaceful and quiet. She stayed in the bathtub for over an hour. She would have stayed longer if she didn't have to check on the kids. When she finished lotioning her body and putting her hair up in a bun, she got dressed. She checked on Mikell. He was still asleep. She didn't want to wake him up. She could hear the kids and Mikell's parents in the game room. She walked into the game room and found them playing Pictionary. Ashanee and Armont were in their giggling modes, and Adrieana and Verneil were trying not to laugh so much, they were trying to draw something. Ailese smiled. She watched them for a while until she interrupted them. "Looks like you guys are having a lot of fun, huh?" "Mom, Grandma was trying to draw this, look, it was supposed to be a jungle." Ailese laughed and told Verneil that she did a better job than she would have.

"Hey guys, Daddy's sleeping okay, so if you need anything let me know. Come and get me, no yelling down the hall, okay?" "Yes, Mom, the kids went back to playing the game Ailese took out her laptop to work on the guest list that she was working on for D'Andra and Chris's housewarming party. She felt an arm around her neck. It was Mikell. "Baby, how long have I been sleeping?" "Hey, sleepy head, oh, about an hour or so, why?" "I didn't want to sleep that long. I wanted to keep you company." "Oh, it's okay, I took a long bath and read my book, it was so peaceful." "You smell so good, baby." "Why thank you, baby."

"Where are the kids?" "In the game room with your mom, I think your dad's resting." "I'm going to check on the kids and everyone else." Ailese went back to her laptop and went back to working on the list. Verneil sat the table and gathered everyone up for dinner. Ailese made turkey meatloaf, peas rolls, and scalloped potatoes.

"Mmmmm ... Mom, dinner smells so good," Armont told his mother. Mom, you made my favorite turkey meat loaf, huh?" "Yes, I did, big guy, so dig in." "Mom is the best cook in the whole world," Ashanee said. "Well, thank you, baby. Ashanee, please make sure you eat all your veggies." "Okay, Mom, I will, I promise."

Ailese fixed Mikell a plate and sat next to him. She wasn't that hungry for some reason, and she had a lot on her mind. "Babe, what's wrong?" "I'm not that hungry, Mikell; I'm fine." "You look a bit tired. Why don't you lay down and rest, hun. I don't think you've sat down since we've been home." "No, I'm not tired. I just don't have much of an appetite." Mikell whispered in Ailese's ear, "Baby, I know there's something bothering you. Please tell me. I know you like the back of my hand." She just didn't want to sound like a broken record, but the dreams were bothering her, and she still had a bad feeling that this man was trying to hurt her again. He was out there somewhere, he's coming back to find her, and this time he was going to kill her. "I don't want to talk about this at the dinner table." "Mom, could you please make sure that the kids eat their dinner? Ailese and I need to run to the drug store." "Oh yes, go ahead." "Thanks, Mom."

Ailese helped Mikell into the car. She sat down in the driver's seat, and Mikell took her hand and put it up against his face. There were tears in his eyes, and Ailese could see the hurt and pain in his eyes. "I never thought that we would keep anything from each other, please, we've been through too much to start now; don't shut me out." Ailese was silent, she didn't know what to say. She knew that he was right; they never kept anything from each other.

Ailese started the car and began to drive down the road. She was still silent.

"Mikell you're right, okay? I just have this gut feeling that…. Ailese stopped talking. She took a deep breath. I just feel that this man is out to hurt me, Mikell! I am so scared!" Ailese could feel the tears coming. She didn't want this man to break her down again! "Baby, you're safe." Ailese interrupted him. "No, I am not safe! Please understand what I am telling you. These dreams are telling me that he is trying to find me, to get some kind of revenge! Ailese looked at Mikell for a quick second, then she kept driving. Please don't think that this is crazy; don't think I'm crazy. Remember that those men beat him badly, and I do mean badly, and I know that he would never let anyone, you hear me, get away with that."

"Baby I do understand where you're coming from, but that was a long time ago, and I'm sorry, but he deserved what happened to him. You never ever, no matter what, put your hands on a female. I don't have any sympathy for abusers." Ailese pulled into the parking lot and turned off the car. She wanted Mikell to understand how she was feeling. She faced Mikell so he could see the fear in her eyes. "Mikell, I know that you will do whatever it takes to protect me; I know that, but this man will do anything to hurt me. I mean anything; he would kill if he had to, I know it! "Okay, baby, then tell me what you want me to do." "I want you to really understand that there is a possibility that he is looking for me. They say that your dreams have meanings, and the meaning of my dream is that he is coming for me. I know it!"

Mikell was in a bit of pain, but he reached over to hug his wife and he told her that he loved her and believed in her. Ailese let all of her emotions out. She cried while Mikell held her in his arms. "Please look at me, Ailese lifted up her head to look at her husband, whom she adored, and she didn't want anyone to hurt him or her family. I know that I say this a lot, but we are going to get through this, okay? Trust me, I will not let any punk come into our lives to run our lives. We've worked too hard to have someone like this take it away. I know that you're scared, but if it makes you feel any better, we could hire someone who could help us find out where he is so we can have peace of mind."

"Okay, I think that should be okay, as long as we don't have to use our names. I don't want him to know where I am. He is one of the reasons why I moved to Shelby." "I know, baby, I am sure that we could remain anonymous. Mikell brushed Ailese's hair from her face. Do you feel a little better, baby?" "Yes, a little. I love you so, so much, Mikell."" "I love you with all my soul. I'm here for you, and I'm not going anywhere."

When everyone arrived at the photo studio, D'Andra was helping Alonda, and they were making sure everyone was present and neat. When Allen arrived with his wife, Ailese ran over to him to hug him, -oh how she missed her brother. "Hey sis you're looking fine. Looks like a lot has changed. Are you losing weight too?" "Um, I don't think so. You're looking so handsome. How are you?" "I'm doing very well. I'm blessed." "Hi, Mya, how are you?" "Hey sis you look great, and I agree with my hubby, that you have lost some weight since the last time I saw you." "Well, thanks. Mya. I love that outfit, you're wearing it, sis."

Allen and Mya made their rounds to say hello to everyone. Alonda made an announcement that everyone was there, so the photographer was ready for them and to follow her. They entered a huge room with florescent lights. There were props here and there. Some of the photographer's work was on the other side of the room. The photographer told them to pose in different ways and suggested that all the women take a picture by themselves, and all the men and children take a picture by themselves. The photographer even took a couple's picture; he was a very good photographer. After they were done with taking pictures, everyone parted ways. Ailese asked her brother to come over for a visit, so they followed them to her house. "I'm glad your brother's coming over. I haven't seen him in a long time. He looks really happy." "Yeah, he's doing really good. I wish that he would move out here, but I know he won't. I'm always begging him to move here, but he always says no." "Well, his work is there, and he's been living there for a while."

"Come on in and make yourselves at home." "Wow, I always loved the way you brought things out, sis. I have always loved your house. It's so cozy." "Is anyone hungry or thirsty?" Everyone was more hungry than thirsty. Verneil made sandwiches and fruit salad. After everyone was done eating, everyone was in the mood to watch a movie, so Johnnie popped some popcorn for everyone. There was a knock on the door. Ailese went to answer it. It was Chris and D'Andra. "Hey, we didn't get invited to this party, D'Andra said as she walked over to Allen to give him a hug. Hey, bro, what's up? It is so good to see you! I miss my brother so much. He needs to move to Shelby. Ailese and D'Andra agreed and laughed. I came over to see you because I didn't get to talk to you much, so mom told me that you were here." "Yeah, I know I was going to call you and stop by to see your brand new house, sis." "Oh, yes, that's right, you haven't even seen our new house. You could just follow us there when we leave." "Congratulations to you, Chris. I am so happy for you guys." "Thanks, man, I appreciate that."

"Wow, your home is so gorgeous," Mya said as she walked up the four steps.

Chris and D'Andra showed Mya and Allen around the house. They shared with them what they were going to do with the extra rooms. "Were going to have a family soon, Chris exclaimed, the next time we see you, we may be pregnant." Mya and Allen congratulated them and wished them all the best.

"I wish that you didn't have to go. Hey, don't wait too long to see us, okay?" "I won't sis, it's just that I've been really busy with work, but we will get together soon." Allen kissed his sister on the cheek, shook Chris's hand.

"I miss him already. I remember when we were kids, and this boy would pick on me all the time. One day when we were walking home from school, this boy hit me on my bottom. I remember my brother knocking him to the ground and telling him if he ever touched me again, he would kick his butt. He was always so overly protective of me. He always treated me like I was his blood sister, and I will always love him for that." D'Andra hugged Chris as they headed inside.

"I can't wait until this house is filled with kids and pattering feet. I can't wait to be a dad, and I don't care if it's a girl or a boy as long as our baby is healthy."

"Aw, that's sweet, baby. I love you for saying that. I'm so lucky to have you."

"No, I'm lucky to have you. Hey, how about some champagne?" "That sounds good. I'll get it. Be right back." D'Andra came back with the champagne and two glasses. She poured the champagne in both glasses and joined Chris on the couch. "I want you to know that there's no rush to have kids. I just want it to be soon, you know?" "Yes, I know. I've been reading those books that Ailese bought for me, and I am learning so much about parenthood, like you'll never believe baby. The books are very helpful." "Hey, guess what I've been reading them when you haven't," D'Andra teased Chris. "Oh, have you, huh?" "Yep, and I agree the books are very helpful. I even read about what your body is going to go through while you're pregnant and afterward. D'Andra took a sip of her wine and frowned at Chris. "Oh no, so you've already prepared yourself for the heart burns and the strange cravings?" "You know what Ailese craved for when she was pregnant with Armont?" "What?" "Okay, this is the honest truth. She would crave for Beefaroni, and with the girls, she craved Chinese food all the time. I think we ate Chinese food so much I ended up hating it! Chris and D'Andra laughed. Sometimes she would also get weird cravings, like one time she ate chips and dipped them in chocolate pudding, ha!" "Wow, are you serious? Well, I don't mind making those late-night runs for you. I can't wait to see what your cravings are going to be," Chris said smiling at her from the rim of his glass. "I'll be right back, Chris." "Okay, where are you going?" "Well, come and see." D'Andra pulled Chris's hand and led him into the kitchen. She went to the refrigerator and grabbed some whip cream and strawberries. "What are you up to, hun?"

"You'll see. Follow me, big boy, we have some work to do."

"Mikell, we need to get ready for your doctor's appointment. You don't want to be late for your checkup. Looking at your stitches, I have a good feeling that you'll be released to go back to working out. I know how much you miss your regimen, huh, don't you?" "I do. I am surprised I haven't gained any weight. I haven't worked out in a long time." "You're healing very well."

"I hope so, baby, because I'm going a bit ballistic! No offense, I enjoyed spending a lot of time with all of you, but you know how I am."

When they arrived at the hospital, Dr. Chaddman saw them promptly. "Hello, Mr. and Mrs. LaShae, how are we today?" "We're good doctor, Mikell said with a smile.

Dr. Chaddman examined Mikell and gave him the okay to go back to his daily regimens and to take it easy and try not to have too much stress at work, and he advised him to take the medication that he had prescribed if needed.

Mikell was one happy camper. "You guys take care, and Mikell, please don't overdo it, okay?" "I hear ya, Doc. Hey, babe, do you need to get back to work soon?" "No, I'm taking a personal day off today, so I don't have to go back. Why?" "Well, I was hoping that we could grab a bite to eat and swing by the office." "Okay, that sounds good." When they arrived at the office, everyone was very happy to see Mikell, especially Emmanuel, who was very surprised to see Mikell.

"Hey, big guy, are you supposed to be here?" "Whatever, man, I'm here, and I am released, my man. I thought that I'd just swing by for a few minutes to see if our building was still standing, Mikell grinned. "Oh, okay, you got jokes, huh?" Emmanuel pretended to box with Mikell.

"Hey, pretty lady, how are you?" "I'm good, and you?" "I'm doing good. I can't complain. Have a seat, Ailese." She sat down in the chair and looked around the office. Mikell and Emmanuel began talking about what had been done and what needed to be done. Ailese's cell phone was ringing, and she motioned to the guys that she was going to take it outside. "Hello, this is Mrs. LaShae. How can I help you?" "Hi, Ailese, it's Andrew. I know that you're on personal leave today, but I was wondering if you could come by the office. The Sheldon contracts are ready to be signed. I spoke with Mrs. Sheldon, and she would like to get started as soon as possible." Ailese really wanted to give Andrew a piece of her mind because she was on personal leave today and this could have waited, but she smiled and told herself not to. "I could be there in an hour or so." "Okay, that sounds great." "Andrew, I'm signing the contracts, and that is it. I am not able to change my schedule today," Ailese said in a firm voice. "I do understand that. Have a good day, and I will see you in an hour or so."

"Baby, I do have to go into the office in a bit, okay? I just got a call from Andrew, and we need to sign some contracts. I need to leave in an hour." "Okay, baby, no problem. Mikell saw Ailese frown. Lee, what's wrong? Did he upset you?" "No, but he knew…. Ailese stopped talking. We'll talk about it later, okay." Mikell took Ailese into the hallway. "Tell me what's wrong." "It's my personal day today, and he couldn't wait to sign these contracts? I don't like it when I plan something and someone or something gets in the way!" Mikell kissed Ailese on the lips.

"It's okay. I don't want you getting all worked up over this guy, okay?" "Okay, I know you're right. I told him that I was only signing the contracts and that was it."

"Okay, as long as you made it clear to him."

Mikell and Emmanuel took Ailese to Studio E to meet the artist that she was going to be working with in a few days. "Ailese, this is Sedrick Johnson. Sedrick, this is my beautiful wife, Ailese." Ailese and Sedrick shook hands. "Nice to meet you, Mrs. LaShae. I've heard so much about you." "Please, it's Ailese. I am looking forward to working with you." Sedrick was a young man who looked like he was in his early twenties. He had short wavy hair, and was tall and slender, but you could tell he hit the gym from time to time. Sedrick was a very attractive man; he was very respectful. "Hey Lee, I wanted you to hear how good this man sounds. I mean, he has a beautiful voice." Mikell sat down in front of a laptop as he and the engineer started to do what they did best. They played a track for Ailese. Ailese loved the music. It made her more excited. She knew that they would have no problem working together because this was her kind of music.

"You are so blessed; that voice, my goodness!" "Thank you so much."

"So, how long have you been singing all your life?" "Basically, I love the Lord, and I just want people to know how much I love the Lord." "You're very special, Sedrick, I am so excited for you." "I owe it all to Mikell. If it wasn't for him believing in me, I wouldn't be where I am today." "Yeah, my hubby has a gift; he knows when someone is dedicated and ready, because this business isn't all roses and candy. It's dedication and hard work, and you have to have thick skin too. I hope I'm not scaring you away, am I?" "No, Ailese, I agree. That was the first thing I prepared myself for because I knew how hard it was going to be to have the doors slammed in my face. I just prayed, and I knew that when God knew it was time, he would open those doors for me." Ailese was amazed by Sedrick. He had a good spirit.

When Ailese headed to the office. Mikell waited in her office while Ell kept him company. "I'm here, Andrew. Where is Mrs. Sheldon?" "Hello Ailese, you seem distracted, are you okay?" "I'm fine. Ailese sat down in the chair. She absently took the file that was in front of Andrew and began looking it over. Where is Mrs. Sheldon?" "Oh, she is in the ladies room." Andrew got up to close the door. He sat back down in his chair. Ailese didn't pay any attention to what he was doing, but she could feel him looking at her. "Hello, Mrs. LaShae. Ailese looked up to see that it was Mrs. Sheldon with her hand out, waiting for Ailese to shake her hand. Ailese shook her hand. "Have a seat, Mrs. Sheldon. How are you?" "I'm doing great. It's nice to see you, Ailese."

Ailese made sure that Mrs. Sheldon was comfortable. Ailese gave her the contracts to look over. "I have a question about when this will take effect?"

"Good question. If you look on page three, you will see the date in the second paragraph, Mrs. Sheldon. Ailese pointed it out for her. "Oh, I see. I must have overlooked It. Okay that sounds great." "Ell, I need you for a minute. I'm in Andrew's office." "Okay, boss, I will be right there." "Ell, I need these FedEx to Mr. Saxx, please. I need it to be same day, okay?"

"I'm on it, boss."

"Thanks, Ell."

"Great job, Ailese." "Thank you. We look forward to working and getting things going for you, Mrs. Sheldon. You have a great day."

"You too, thank you so much. I can rest now that Ailese cleaned up the mess that my ex-husband left. Ailese, thank you so very much."

"Please call me whenever you need anything, okay."

Well, Andrew, if there isn't anything else I have to be going, my husband is waiting for me." "Have a seat, please, if you don't mind Ailese. This won't take long. Ailese became a bit irritated, but she sat down anyway. Please don't take this the wrong way, but I feel like you don't like me at all, and I want us to get along, Ailese. I've never had anyone not like me." Ailese was stunned, that he would say something stupid, and why should he care if she liked him or not, they only work together. "I'm not sure why you would think that, Andrew. I'm a very respectful person, and I also get along with everyone. I feel like we're getting along just fine. I'm here to work, not make friends. I take my job very seriously." "That I do know, but every time I ask something of you or stir up a conversation, I feel like you avoid me as much as you can."

"Well, I'm sorry that you feel that way, Andrew. I guess you need to get to know me better." "I guess so, huh? Well, I know you have to go. See you soon."

Ailese didn't dislike Andrew. He was just upset that she wasn't kissing his ass like everyone else was. Kissing ass was something Ailese would never do. She didn't need to. She felt like we have ten fingers and ten toes, what makes you so special. Ailese never cared about people's titles that came after their names; even though her title was way up there, she never treated anyone any differently. Ailese didn't let Andrew get to her.

"Hey baby, I am so excited to work with Sedrick. He has such a good spirit, you know." "Yes, he does." "How are you feeling?" "I'm great, sweetie. Did I tell you I loved you today?" "Um, no, now you did." "Mikell, please don't overdo it when you go back to work. You heard what Dr. Chaddman said." Even though Mikell would work from home and sometimes go into the office for a short time, due to the doctor's orders so that he could heal, Ailese knew that since Mikell was released from under his doctor's supervision, she knew that he would overdo it. "Don't worry I got enough lectures from you and Emmanuel. Yes, I know." Ailese gave Mikell a look- a look that said he would be in huge trouble if he overworked himself.

"Hey, Mom and Dad called. They said that they were heading back tonight because Dad has some stuff to do back home." "Okay, well, what time are they heading back?" "They said they'd be leaving around six." Oh, okay, that gives us plenty of time to spend with them. I'm going to miss them, are you?" "Oh yes, I am." "Oh, I need to make that deposit today, or did you make the deposit already?" "Yep, I took care of it already, baby. Call your mom and have her check her bank, please." "Hey, Mom, it's Mikell. Could you check your bank? Oh, okay. Love you too. We'll be home soon. She said that the money was there; she forgot to let us know." "Good."

"So, what's on the agenda today?" "Well, I did want to go and buy a new laptop, but it's not for me. I wanted to buy one for the office, but I never got around to it."

"Okay, so are we going to the electronics store? Okay well, you know we'll be in there all day," Ailese laughed. "I can't get you out of there." "We do need to pick the kids up from study hall at 5:30 okay. It's still early morning, but I just wanted you to know." When Ailese would go to the electronics store, they could stay in there until closing time, even if they weren't buying anything. They had so many gadgets to look at, and sometimes Ailese and Mikell would get themselves into a lot of trouble; they ended up buying too much stuff, from music to cool gadgets.

"Hey kids, how was your day?" "Hi, Dad, it was good." All the kids piled into the car. "Dad, what did the doctor say?" "Yeah, what did the doctor say?" The girls were getting excited. "I'm actually dying." There was silence in the car. Ailese looked at Mikell and frowned at him. "What! Armont became angry and terrified all at the same time. "I'm kidding, I'm back. I can go into work regularly, but I do need to avoid stress. I'll be going back to work full-time, guys." "Dad, don't say that you're dying. That's not funny." Ashanee hugged her dad's neck. "I'm sorry, hun. Daddy, was joking, and I don't think I'm checking out for a very long time."

The kids told Mikell that they were going to miss him and that they didn't want him to go back to work. They loved it when Mikell worked from home. He would sometimes let them make music with him.

"Did everyone finish all their home work in study hall?" All the kids told Ailese that they had all finished their work. Good, because Grandma and Grandpa have to get back home, so they're leaving today. I wanted to make sure that we all spent time with them." "Mom, Adrieana said, I'm going to miss them so much. I love them so much."

It was time for Verneil and Johnnie to leave the kids; this wasn't at all easy for them. They all said their goodbyes. They gave their grandparents hugs and kisses. Verneil and Johnnie were sad that they were leaving and promised that they would come and get the kids for a visit in a few weeks. Mikell and Ailese said their goodbyes as well. Mikell's parents teased him. They told him that if he went back to the hospital, they were going to give him a good spanking. "I love you Mom, and Dad." Mikell watched them drive off.

After everyone went to bed, Mikell and Ailese just held each other. Mikell missed holding Ailese. He loved to feel her skin. It was the softest thing in the world to him. He loved smelling her Victoria's Secret or whatever she was wearing. Ailese and Mikell were silent for a while, they were just enjoying one another. Ailese raised up to get a drink of water. "Babe, where are you going?" "To get a drink of water. Do you want anything from the kitchen?" "I'll come with you." Mikell grabbed her waist from behind. Mikell went into the refrigerator and gave Ailese a bottle of water. He got one for himself.

"Let's go back to bed, babe." Mikell kissed Ailese softly on her lips, and she kissed him back. Mikell grabbed her by the waist and pulled her to him. He kissed her again and made his way to her neck. He wanted her right now and he didn't care where they were. Mikell took the clip out of Ailese's hair that held up her bun.

"You're so beautiful. I've never seen anything so beautiful, Lee. I love you." Mikell whispered in her ear that he loved her again, and Ailese whispered back that she loved him. Mikell kissed her lips, but this time Ailese felt his tongue in her mouth. Ailese couldn't resist his body. She felt every muscle. She could feel his heart beating fast. She led him to the room. Mikell kissed her with even more passion. He picked her up and carried her to the bedroom. He laid her down on the bed, and he began kissing her all over her body. He gave her chills. She could feel the chills going up and down her spine. He twisted her body, so she was lying sideways. He slowly slid his hands inside her silk robe. He slowly slid her underwear off her body, as she laid still.

He laid beside her and opened her robe so that her breasts were exposed, he began touching her breasts, he was rough but Ailese didn't mind it at all, it felt good to her; it gave her chills. Ailese could feel Mikell's arousal; it excited her. Mikell laid her flat on her back and took off her robe. Now she was naked. He loved to look at her beautiful naked body. He studied her for a while, then kissed every inch of her body again, until they became one.

When Ailese opened her eyes. Mikell was gone. "Where could he be?" She thought to herself. When she became more alert, she could hear noises in the restroom. She was too lazy to get up to see who it was. She rubbed her eyes and sat up, looking around the room. She looked at the clock. It was still early. Ailese went into the restroom. Mikell was in a sweat suit. He looked up and smiled at her. "Hey, baby I didn't want to wake you up. I thought I would get an early start today and make you breakfast." He kissed her passionately on the lips, and when he lifted his lips from hers, he told her that he loved her. "I thought that you were going to work out or something; being that you're wearing that sweat suit, you're not right." "No, no, babe, it's just a casual day today." "Oh. Well, making breakfast would be nice. Let me get dressed, okay?" "Okay, baby, how about some fruit eggs and toast and some turkey bacon?" "That sounds good, baby, thank you." "Baby, don't worry about the kids. I will make sure that they are up. I figured I would let them sleep for a few minutes. It's still early, and I'll let you know when breakfast is ready."

"Baby, breakfast is ready. Mikell took Ailese's hand and led her to the kitchen. Breakfast, is served, my love." Mikell placed her plate on the table for her, and sat down. "Mmmm, it smells good and looks good too. Thanks, hun."

"I'll be right back. I need to check on the kids."

As Mikell went to check on the kids, Ailese enjoyed her breakfast and made sure she had everything she needed before she left. "Mikell, did you want me to drive you to work or you could drive me, and you could take the car for the rest of the day?" "Okay, I could drive you to work, and I could take the car. That sounds good, but we better take the SUV. I will take the kids to school and pick them up." "Let's go, guys."

As time passed and Andrew and Ailese worked together every day, they had got used to one another's personalities, likes and dislikes, etcetera. Andrew learned a lot from Ailese, and as time passed, he began to understand more and more about why Ailese was good at what she did. Andrew began to understand why Mr. Saxx spoke so highly of her. Every day, he was in awe of her. He became fascinated with her, and on occasions, he would ask her to lunch, but Ailese would turn him down, despite his assurances that it would be strictly business, nothing less, nothing more.

Ailese would overhear women in the office speaking so highly and kind of Andrew. Some of the women said that they would love to date him and become his lover, and that he must be a good lover in bed. Then they would giggle about it. Susan in Human Resources had gone out on a few dates with Mr. McGee, but nothing serious. Susan loved to be seen with Mr. McGee, she made it a point to let everyone know that they were dating. He would sometimes shower her with gifts or have roses sent to her, and Susan would brag about it to her coworkers. Ailese had never agreed that you should date your coworkers; that was a pet peeve of hers. Whenever men fell at her feet wherever she worked, she would always turn them down and explain that dating someone she worked with was tacky to her.

One day Ailese had gotten a call from Mr. Saxx. He had an emergency and couldn't be at a meeting that was scheduled in Wellford. They weren't able to get any red- eye flights out to Wellford, so Andrew suggested taking his personal jet, which made Ailese feel very uncomfortable. Even though she and Andrew understood each other, she didn't think it was a good idea to accompany him on his private jet. She didn't know him in "that way." She knew very little about him outside of the office. "Ailese, I need you there at that meeting, please. I know that you didn't plan on attending the meeting, but I have a family emergency, and I need only my best people there at this meeting." After Mr. Saxx pleaded with Ailese, she called Mikell to let him know what was going on; she couldn't let Mr. Saxx down, he depended on her, and he had been so good to her; he would have done the same for her. Mikell never doubted his wife's trust, never! He was fine with her staying in Wellford overnight, even if it was with another man; it didn't bother him, not one bit.

They both trusted one another, and they both had friends of the opposite sex, and being that their love was so strong, anyone or nothing could break that bond- not even Andrew.

"Ailese, the car will be picking us up in two hours. Could you be ready, and I could send the car to pick you up?" "Yes, I am going to my house now to pack. Thank you, see you then." Ailese called Ruben so he could bring her car to the front entrance of the building. When she arrived at the front of the building, she was happy to see Ruben, who was waiting for her. "Hi, stranger, how are you?" "Hi, I'm fine. I just can't wait until my wife has the baby. Mrs. LaShae, how are you doing?" "I'm good. Yes, I know your baby will be here soon, huh?" Yes indeed, yes indeed." "Children are the most beautiful thing. You know they are so innocent, then they're in college before you know it," Ailese chuckled.

"You got that right, Mrs. LaShae, it seemed like my nephew was just born yesterday, and he's already five years old," Ruben said with a smile to Ailese. "Well, Ruben, I will be gone for a few days, but I'll see you when I get back, all right." "Okay, drive safely and have a safe trip."

When Ailese made it home, she was a bit irritated. She never liked to rush. She liked to check things over to make sure that she had everything, but she would always get over it. Ailese packed her suitcase and left Mikell a note. The note had information on where she would be staying in case, he needed to get a hold of her.

Just when Ailese was done packing everything, Andrew called her on her cell phone to tell her that the limo was outside. Ailese brought her bags to the car, and the driver put her bags carefully into the trunk of the limousine. "Hello Ailese," Andrew said as she got into the car and sat down across from him. "Hello, Andrew. Wow, is this your limo or the company's?" "It's my own personal limousine. I hope that you're not afraid of flying, are you?" "No, not at all. I haven't flown in a while, but I'm sure not much has changed, right?" "Right, Andrew smiled at Ailese. We should be at the airport soon. I'm not sure if I told you, but we'll both be staying at the Cottage Inn Resort. I hear that they have an apple martini that's to die for." "Yes, I got your info that you sent to me, apple martini, huh? Really? I've stayed there once, but it was a long time ago though." "Oh, well, you must show me around then if you don't mind." "Sure, Ailese said cautiously, taking out a bottled water out of the beverage cabinet. Andrew was drinking water as well. "Do you drink champagne, Ailese?"

"Um, sometimes, do you?" "I'm a water freak most of the time, but once in a while I like to enjoy some brandy or a nice bottle of wine. I like the wines that are old, like from 1920s." "Yeah, I heard that those are the best years when it comes to wine," Ailese said as she sipped her water. Ailese noticed that the limousine had stopped. "We must be at the airport," she thought to herself. The driver announced that they had arrived at the airport and that he would grab their luggage. When Ailese got out of the car, she saw a beautiful airplane, dark blue with gold trimmings and the letters AMGII in large letters. The letters were written in a fancy blue font. She was impressed.

Andrew helped Ailese on to the airplane and told her that she could sit anywhere she wanted and help herself to whatever she wanted while he went to talk to the pilot. Ailese picked up a champagne glass. It too had AMGII; everything had AMGII, from the napkins to the towels. Everything was so fancy and nice that the plane even had a bar and a kitchen. Ailese browsed the plane for a while until Andrew told her that they were about to take off.

Without thinking, Ailese sat next to Andrew and buckled her seatbelt. When she noticed that she was sitting next to him, it was too late to change seats, and the pilot told them that they were taking off. Ailese hoped that they'd arrive in Wellford soon. She just couldn't understand why she couldn't trust Andrew; he'd done anything but be nice and respectful to her, and she didn't understand why she didn't like it when he would strike up a conversation with her. "What's wrong with me? I need to just sit back and relax and focus, focus," Ailese said to herself. She thought she'd make conversation to make the trip go by faster. "So, Andrew, do you have any children?" "Oh, I don't. I wish I did have kids. I don't have any kids because of my crazy schedule.

I've had long-term relationships, but no one could deal with my schedule and me being away all the time, so I guess I never found the right person you know?" "Yes, I understand." "Mr. Saxx told me that you have three beautiful children, is that right?" "Yes, I have two girls and one boy; they're great kids." Ailese smiled.

"I imagine so. I know that we haven't known each other long, but I know I could tell that you're a great mom." "Well, thank you." Ailese's stomach began to growl. She hoped that Andrew didn't hear it. "Are you hungry? I could make something … I mean if you want me to." "Um, sure, please, if you don't mind, I could come help you if you want." "That would be good, let's see what we got." "Is it okay to get out of our seats?" "Yes, we're fine. Come on, I'll lead the way."

"Let's see here, we have eggs, bread, cold cuts, cheese, TV dinners, we have it all, what would you like?" Andrew moved to the other side of the refrigerator so Ailese could pick what she wanted. She looked into the fridge and saw that there was some thinly sliced turkey. She decided to make a sandwich, she didn't want anything too heavy in her stomach. "What about turkey sandwiches?"

Andrew agreed, and they both made their own sandwiches. Andrew had cut up some fruit for him and Ailese, and they went back to their seats to eat.

"That was scrumptious, Ailese. I never thought that a variety of meats on a sandwich would taste so good. Wow, I am so stuffed." "I'm glad that you liked it. I have always loved sandwiches that had more than one kind of meat, and you know what else tastes good with salami?" "What?" "Okay, you promise not to laugh?" "Okay, I won't, tell me," Andrew said anxiously. "Okay, you get some nacho cheese chips, and you wrap a piece of salami around the chip and eat it. My cousins got me so hooked on it that my mom had to ban salami and chips from the house because I ate them so much." Ailese and Andrew were laughing hysterically. "Hey, you said that you wouldn't laugh." Ailese gave him a playful punch in his shoulder. "I'm sorry. Don't be mad at me, but that was funny. I'm really enjoying your company, Ailese." "Me too, Andrew."

When they landed, another limousine was waiting for them to take them to the hotel. "Ailese, are you okay?" Andrew noticed that she was a bit quiet. "Oh, I'm fine. I just miss my kids. I'll call them in the morning. I know that they're asleep right now," Ailese looked at her watch. "Yeah, I'm sure that it's hard to leave them sometimes, huh?" "Yeah, I mean, even though they are older, they're still my babies, you know." Andrew smiled at her. "So how long have you been married?" "A long time. I love him to death too. Ailese shook her head. He's one of a kind. I'm so lucky to have him." Andrew shook his head and looked out of the window. "I hope that I can get up for the meeting tomorrow. It's getting pretty late. I better hit the pillow as soon as we check in to the room." "Me too. I think with a lot of coffee, we will be okay."

When they got to the hotel to check in, Ailese was so exhausted that she didn't even pay attention to what the hotel clerk was saying to them as they were checking into the hotel. She hoped that it wasn't anything important.

Andrew's room was three doors down from hers. "Well, let me know if you need anything. Please don't hesitate to call my room. I do have a bit of a confession to make, Andrew said, putting his hands in his pockets. "What's that?" Ailese asked. I don't like hotels, so don't be alarmed if I'm not in my room. I don't sleep very well when I have to stay in hotels. I always end up roaming the halls or the bars; I like to take a drive, and sometimes, if I'm lucky, I get some sleep."

"Oh, I understand." Ailese bit her tongue. She didn't want to tell him that she too had trouble sleeping, but she decided not to share that with him.

Ailese's eyes felt so heavy that as soon as her head hit the pillow, she was asleep.

"No, please leave me alone!" He was so strong, strong enough to pick her up and throw her across the room. Her body had landed on the hard floor. She knew something was broken. She tried to get up, but she couldn't. All of a sudden, she felt this excruciating pain in her stomach. He had kicked her in her stomach and grabbed her like she was a rag doll. She could see the anger in his eyes. He then cursed at her and left her alone in the room. He came back a few minutes later, with a knife in his hand. Ailese wasn't sure if it was a knife in his hands, her eyes were so puffy from crying, and she was in so much pain from him kicking her in the stomach, that she couldn't sit up. He leaned over her and threatened her with the knife. He put it up to her face and told her that he was going to kill her. He told her that no one would miss her anyway. He had told her that she would never see her family again! At this point, Ailese knew that she had to get some energy to fight him off; it took everything in her to fight back. Ailese tried to wake up from her dream, but she couldn't; she began to moan and ball her fists. He held the knife up to her face, and pressing the blade on her cheek. She pushed him away. "Get off!" At this moment, Ailese woke up screaming. No one was there to comfort her; she had forgotten that she was in the hotel alone. There was a knock on the door. "Ailese, open up, it's Andrew, are you all right? When Ailese didn't answer, Andrew saw a maid. He told her that it was an emergency and asked her to open up Ailese's room. When she did, Andrew found her sobbing and hugging the covers tightly. Ailese, what's wrong? Are you okay?" Ailese just sobbed. She didn't speak, but Andrew knew something was wrong. He wanted to hold her in his arms, but he didn't want her to think he was making a move on her, so he laid her back down and went to the restroom to wet a face towel. He sat next to her on the bed and wiped her face. "Please help me." Ailese was out of breath and shaking. "What do you want me to do?" "Please help me. He's going to hurt me! Please don't let him hurt me!" Andrew was confused, he didn't know what to do he considered calling her husband; something, he didn't like seeing her in this state.

Andrew took it upon himself to stay with her; he couldn't leave her, not knowing if she was okay. Andrew could hear her sniffling, and he could feel her body shaking. He wondered, what or who had her so scared? When he got up to wet the face towel again, Ailese pulled on his pants tightly and looked at him. He then knew that she wanted him to stay in her room with her, so he did.

When the alarm clock went off, Ailese stirred around for her robe, and then she noticed that someone was in her bed with her.

"Oh my God, she whispered to herself, what happened last night? When she pulled the covers from Andrew's face, she was relieved that it was him and not some stranger, because the last thing she remembered was going to sleep. "Andrew, she whispered to him, wake up, she shook him, but he didn't move. He just let out a groan. Andrew, you have to wake up. She shook him again, and this time he opened his eyes and tried to focus. Andrew, what are you doing in my room?" Andrew had finally sat up and regained focused. He looked at Ailese and noticed that even in the morning she was still beautiful, but he shrugged at his thoughts. He cleared his throat, and said "I heard you scream, and I thought that someone was hurting you. I had the maid open your door, and you wouldn't tell me what was wrong. You were shaking and crying. Andrew pushed his hair back from his face. I hope that you didn't mind, and yes, I was a gentleman. You didn't want me to leave, Ailese, and please don't be mad at me for staying here. I never touched you, I swear!" In some crazy way, Ailese believed him. "I know it's fine, but I don't remember much of last night. I am sorry that I frightened you." "You didn't frighten me, I just thought that you shouldn't be alone. I mean, you were crying and shaking, and you kept saying, don't let him hurt you. Who were you speaking of?" Ailese had shrugged her shoulders. She was upset with herself because now he knew her secret, but she didn't want to talk about it. "Andrew, I want to thank you for staying here with me, she said touching his face. But I do need to get dressed." Andrew noticed that she avoided the question, and maybe she had her reasons. He didn't bring it up again. He got up, put on his shoes, and told her that he would see her at the meeting.

Ailese called Mikell, but she didn't tell him what had happened- not yet. She would tell him later. She needed to stay focused. She told him how much she missed everyone and that she would call later. When Ailese was dressed, she figured that she had better eat something. She didn't know how long the meeting would last but was sure it would last a few hours. As she pushed the number on the elevator, Andrew called to her. She turned her head around and turned back around, because she didn't want him to ask her any more questions about what happened last night, but by the time the elevator door opened, Andrew was standing next to her, and they both went into the elevator.

Ailese tried to focus on something else that was in the elevator so that she wouldn't have to look at him. "Would you mind having breakfast with me?" "Okay, that's fine," Ailese said, looking down at her shoes. "You look lovely, Ailese." "Thank you.". Ailese didn't say much at breakfast; she was too focused on what she should say if Andrew brought up last night. "Shouldn't you be eating? The meetings could go on forever, and you wouldn't want us to hear your stomach growling, huh?" Ailese smiled and chuckled. "Yes, you're right about that, I better eat." This made her feel a lot better; Andrew did care about her. She smiled and finished her food.

Ailese was so exhausted from all the meetings. Every bone in her body ached. She talked so much that her mouth even ached. When she got home, there was no one home, but there was a note on the fridge that read, "Hi, baby, I took the kids with me. I needed to pick up some things. Be home before bedtime. I love you. P.S. Please call your mom, xoxox. Ailese picked up the phone and called her mom, but she had gotten her voice mail. "Hello, Mom, it's me. I was returning your call. Call me back when you get this message. Love ya."

Ailese was very tired, and she wasn't hungry, so she thought that she would take a shower, throw on some pajamas, and hit the sheets. She didn't think about the dreams because she couldn't think or see straight. She took a shower and went to bed. "Ailese, we're home, baby," Mikell whispered in her ear, but she didn't move. Mikell went into his studio to get some work done and told the kids that they needed to let their mom sleep. The phone had rang, Mikell hopped up to answer it. "Hello, hey, Mommie, how are you?"

"I am fine. How's everyone doing?" "Were good Mom. What's up?" "Well, I was returning Ailese's call. Is she there?" "Yes, Mommie, but she's sleeping. I know she's exhausted from her business trip. She just got back. I could tell her to call you in the morning. Is that okay?" "Yeah, that's fine, okay, love you guys."

"Dad." "Yes, Adrieana." "Could I lay down with Mom, please?" "Well, I don't want you to wake her up. Maybe next time, okay?" "But I missed Mom, and I promise I won't wake her up, Daddy." "No, Adrieana, next time, kitten." "Okay, let me know if Mommy wakes up soon. I'm going to go in my room and make something for her. "Ashanee, do you want to come and help me?"

"Okay." Ashanee followed her sister. Mikell went to check on Armont, who had been very quiet for some reason. Mikell had knocked on his door, and Armont had opened the door and invited him in. "Hey Dad, what's up?" "Oh, I was just checking on ya. Hey, are you okay? You seemed a bit quiet. Is there anything I could do?"

"Oh, I'm fine, Dad, but I'm a bit worried about my French test this week."

"Okay, show me what you've got? Armont went to his desk and pulled out some papers. See, I'm going to tell you a secret, okay?" "Okay." Armont sat down at his desk, waiting anxiously to hear what his dad was going to say. "Now, a lot of people do not know this, but my dad is half French. I know he doesn't look it because he takes after his mother, so that makes me part French. One summer, my father challenged all of us kids to learn French, and if we did, he would give us a surprise, and my dad's surprises were always cool. So, I took it upon myself to learn French verbatim, and by the end of summer, I had it down pat. My father tested me, and he was so proud of me, and guess what my prize was?" "What, Dad? Tell me." "My dad gave me $300. All of my siblings hated me that summer, and right to this day I still know how to speak French." "Wow, Dad, I never knew that about you. That's awesome."

"So, let me help you. Tell me what you're getting stuck on, and we can take it from there." A few hours had passed. Mikell helped Armont with his French test and gave him some tools to use until he had the test down pat.

"Thanks, Dad, because of you, I love French, and I know I am going to ace the test." "Anytime my son. Hey, I am going to check on Mom if you didn't need me for anything else." "No, Dad, go ahead, and please let us know if she's awake."

Mikell went into the room. Ailese was still sleeping. He didn't want to bother her, so he went back to his studio room, he wasn't tired at all.

He told the kids that they would have to wait until the morning to see their mom.

"Ailese never sleeps this long, she must have had a long trip," Mikell thought to himself. He missed her so much, all he wanted to do was wrap his arms around her and hug her and tell her how much he missed her, but he would have to wait until tomorrow. Mikell's associates would tease him because he loved Ailese so much. They would tell him that no one could love someone to death; only Mikell could, no one else. Mikell would tell them that when they find that special person, they will understand and the love that he had for his wife was real and that it does exist.

He adored Ailese. He couldn't imagine his life without her. She had been so good to him. She understood when he had to leave on long trips, even if they were last minute. The long hours, it never bothered her. She was always there when he came home.

She knew that Mikell wasn't in it for the money; it was something that he loved to do. It was like finding an old run -down house and making it your own; Mikell was good at turning nothing into something.

The phone had rung again. It was D'Andra. She wanted to talk to Ailese, but Mikell told her that she was asleep and that he would have her call her back in the morning. She told Mikell that it was important that she speak to Ailese first thing in the morning. He told her that he wouldn't forget to tell her.

SHELBY LIES

When Mikell went to touch his wife, she wasn't there. He had heard her singing in the shower. "You're always on my mind, you're always in my heart, even if you're miles away." Mikell smiled to himself and listened to her sing. Her voice was so beautiful. He remembered that song, she wrote that song in ten minutes. He rubbed his eyes and sat up. He stalled a bit and went into the bathroom. He opened the shower door. Ailese was so busy singing that she didn't even hear him come in. She turned around and saw Mikell's sexy naked body standing there. "Hi, baby, I missed you so much!" Ailese grabbed him and gave him a bear hug. She then kissed him on the lips.

"My, this is a surprise, a nice one." "Mmmm, yes, it is." Mikell hugged her tight and he began to wash her back with her loofah. Baby, I guess you were so tired, huh? You slept until morning. The kids want to see you." "Yes, I was so exhausted. I haven't been that tired in ages. Oh, my gosh, Mik, those meetings were so long, and I talked so much that even my mouth was aching." Mikell chuckled. "I know what you mean, but hey, before I forget, D'Andra needed you to call her as soon as possible, and your mom called also." "Okay, thanks, baby. I will make sure that I call them back." Mikell began to wash her body some more. They kissed so passionately that Mikell kissed every inch of her body as he washed her naked body. Ailese kissed Mikell passionately as her tongue explored every inch of his body. "I love you so much," she whispered in his ear.

"Hey, D, what's going on, sis?" "Hey, how was your trip first of all?" "It was good. I am so exhausted though." "I feel ya, sis, hey, I was wondering what your schedule looks like for…. D'Andra paused. Hold on one sec, okay?" "Okay." D'Andra came back on the phone. "I know that you have a lot on your plate, but I need your help. I want to redecorate a couple of offices here, and I love your taste so I was wondering if you could help me out?" "Yeah, when are you thinking to do this?" "Well, I was wondering what your schedule looked like next weekend." Ailese took out her laptop to look at her schedule. "It looks good, hun."

"Okay, could you pencil me in so we could have that weekend to discuss the ideas for the offices?" "Yep, sure can. If you don't mind me asking, why don't you just hire an interior decorator, sis?" "Well, I don't want to. They are a pain in the rear, and they always end up making you buy more than what you initially asked for in the beginning, you know, and I want someone who knows what I like, and I will pay you for your time, okay?" "Okay, we will talk numbers and all that good stuff later, so yes, I would be honored to help you."

Ailese called her mom. They were playing phone tag, so she left her another message.

Mikell was so impressed with how well Sedrick and Ailese were getting along. They clicked together, and they were always on the same page when it came to changing or rearranging a song. They didn't have any disagreements.

"Okay, guys, let's take a break." Emmanuel told Ailese that she was doing a great job. He loved her voice, and he told her that it was beautiful. "Baby, I am going to pick up the kids from the mall, okay?" "Okay, did you want me to come with you?" "No, it's okay, I'm going to bring them back here." Mikell kissed her and left.

"Hey Sedrick, why don't we go over the last song again?" Ailese suggested.

"You got to know him, know him. He's your best friend. He's someone you can always count on. He will never let you down." Sedrick and Ailese felt their music in the same way. Their voices were like angels singing. "How was that, Emmanuel?" "That was great. You guys are great together.

SHELBY LIES

It looks like we'll be finishing this album sooner than we thought. I'm so glad that Mikell came up with the idea to work with you." "Thanks, Emmanuel, that means a lot to me." Ailese and Emmanuel gave each other a hug.

As time passed, Sedrick and Ailese were almost finished with the album, and everyone was pleased with all the dedication and hard work. They felt like the album was going to be a hit. Working on the album distracted Ailese. She didn't worry about her dreams, even though she did have them on occasion, and Mikell was always there to comfort her. She made sure that her schedule at the studio never conflicted with work or her sessions with Dr. Salvino. So far, everything was going great, and she was very excited about the album. Ailese only told a few people about the album that she was recording with Sedrick. Everyone was so excited for her. Sometimes D'Andra and her mom would come to the studio to hear her sing. They too were fond of Sedrick. Sometimes Sedrick, Emmanuel, Mikell, and Ailese would stay up for hours on the weekends. They would occasionally sleep there and order food. The kids would sometimes stay with D'Andra and Chris.

Ailese was never too tired to go to the studio, even if her schedule had been crazy; it gave her a rush. She would sing some of the songs while she was in the shower or on her way to work; she couldn't have thought of a better person to work with than Sedrick.

Today Ailese was able to meet with Dr. Salvino right after work. She didn't need to be in the studio, because Sedrick had a concert to perform, he was the opening act. Ailese had already sent him a large basket filled with colognes, fruits, and other goodies and wished him luck. Mikell and Emmanuel would call Ailese to let her know how the concert went when it was over.

"Now, I want you to tell me more about the dreams you've been having. I know that we discussed over the phone the other day that you were having more dreams, but these were different, I want you to tell me more about them."

Ailese took a deep breath and folded her hands. "Well, the first dream was when he put the knife to my face and told me that I was never going to see my family again. Here I am in so much pain because he kicked me in my stomach so hard that I could hardly breathe. I didn't want to die, and he knew that. When I would fight back, he still had power over me. It took everything in me to push him off of me. He had landed on the floor pretty hard. Only God decides when it's time for me to leave this world, not this man. Ailese had so much hatred in her eyes. No matter what I do, I cannot wake up from my dreams, doctor. Ailese began picking at her nails. But I'm here; he didn't win; I won! But sometimes I feel that he won, because I feel like he's taking over my life. I know that it sounds crazy." "No, Ailese, it doesn't. We sometimes feel like other people can take over our lives, and in your case, you feel like this man has taken over your life because you're here talking with me. You can't have a normal life, and that's understandable." "He even made me take drugs a lot. I took the drugs because they made the pain go away, you know? One day he wanted to have sex, and I didn't want to have sex. I had taken some drugs. I don't know what I had taken, but it made me feel like I was flying; my eyes were so heavy. I was laying down on the bed. I mean, this drug had taken over me. He told me to take off my clothes, but I wouldn't take off my clothes, so he started cursing at me and asking me what the hell was wrong with me. I didn't answer him, so he got even madder. I could feel him taking off my clothes. I couldn't move or fight him, so he had his way with me. When he was finished with me, he told me to clean the house because it was dirty. I was still laying on the bed. He told me again to get up and clean the house, and when I didn't, he told me that would be my last time ignoring him. He still didn't know that I had taken some drugs. He locked me in the room and told me that I couldn't come out until I agreed to clean the house, then he'd let me out. I don't remember what happened after that. I didn't tell my mom that I was doing drugs while I was with him. He did tell my mom one time, but she didn't believe anything that came out of his mouth." When Ailese was finished, she returned to the time when she used drugs, and it took her a long time to forgive herself for doing so. "You've had a hard life, Ailese, and talking about it helps, but I want you to think about what you've accomplished and to remember that this man had problems, and yes, he hurt you tremendously. You are a very strong woman; you're stronger than you think, so I want you to try and remind yourself of that." Ailese began to think about the conversation that she had with Mikell. She felt as though this man was going to hurt her. Dr. Salvino told her that she was very proud of her today, that they were making progress, and that she was determined to help her through this. Dr. Salvino made Ailese smile when she told her that she admired her strength.

After leaving the doctor's office, Ailese figured she would pick up something for dinner tonight. She wasn't in the mood for cooking, so she called the kids to ask them what they wanted for dinner. They all decided on picking up some food from the deli not too far from the house. Ailese picked up the food and went straight home. She had missed the kids. She didn't pick up any food for Mikell because she knew that he was going to be home late. She was happy that it was Friday. She didn't have much planned for the weekend.

Adrieana and Ashanee watched TV with Ailese in her room and popped popcorn while Armont was getting ready to go to his dad's. "Mom, Dad's here. I have to go." "Wait I want a hug. Ailese got up to give him a hug and kiss goodbye. The girls told their big brother bye, as well. "Call me okay, big guy." "I will, Mom, love you." Mom, let's watch *Grease*, please." "Okay, you know where it is. Go get it." Ashanee jumped off the bed, went into the living room to get the movie, and came back with it. "Ashanee, how many times have you seen this movie?" "Oh, be quiet, Adrieana. I love this movie." "Behave, guys, okay? I don't mind watching *Grease*. I'm the one who got your sister hooked on the movie anyway." Ailese began to tickle the girls. "Mom, stop tickling us. Mom look, the movies starting. Ashanee took her mom's hands away from her stomach so she wouldn't tickle them anymore. The girls all sang the songs to Grease and danced to the music. They all knew all the moves, so they mocked the characters too.

The girls had fallen asleep in her bed. Ailese didn't want to wake them up. She actually enjoyed their company. Mikell had called to let her know that the concert went great and that he would be home soon. Ailese decided that she wanted to wait up for Mikell, so she made some coffee and watched television until he got home. Later, she heard his car pull up into the garage. She met him at the door. When he saw her standing there waiting for him, he smiled at her and gave her a huge kiss on the lips. "Here, this is for you." He handed her an envelope and some purple silk flowers. "For me? She sat down and opened the envelope. It was from Sedrick, thanking her for the gift. The flowers were from him as well. Aw that was so sweet of him. You must have told him that I love silk flowers, huh?" "Yeah, I did" Mikell smiled at her. "Are you hungry or anything?" "Oh, no, I am so tired. I am bit thirsty though." Mikell went into the kitchen to get himself a drink of water. "The girls are asleep in our bed. I didn't have the heart to wake them up. We were watching movies all night, and I just loved watching them sleep. They are growing like weeds," Ailese chuckled. "Yes, they are. Tell me about it. They're going to be tall girls."

Everyone had slept in, and when Ailese woke up, it was already 10:00 in the morning. She just lay there thinking about her session with Dr. Salvino, and for the first time in a long time, she really began to feel that the sessions were working and that the only thing that she had to deal with were the dreams.

Maybe the dreams will eventually go away, she thought to herself. She needed to give it more time. She was happy and was determined to stick to the sessions with Dr. Salvino; patience was what she needed to work on, and that is what she will do. Mikell was still sleeping when Ailese got up to see if the kids were awake. She checked on Ashanee. She was still sleeping, but Adrieana was up reading her book as she lay lazily in her bed. "Are you hungry, sweetie?" "No, I'm not hungry yet. Mom, could we go to the art store today? I saved my money and I wanted to get some new stuff." "Well, why don't we go in a few hours, okay?" "Thanks, Mom, I'll be ready. I will make sure all my chores are done." "Okay, hun." Ailese went back into the bedroom, where she found Mikell still sound asleep. She took a shower and got dressed. She left him a note by the alarm clock. "Ready girls, let's go. Try not to wake Dad, okay?" They all tip-toed out of the house and piled in the car. On the way to the art store, D'Andra had called to see what Ailese was up to, so Ailese swung by her house to pick her up. D'Andra needed a break from unpacking. "Are you done unpacking yet?" "I'm on the last box, wew. Unpacking is so much fun," D'Andra said in a sarcastic voice. "Well, that's great! Now you can find everything that you need, right?"

"Yes, and you know how I get when I can't find anything. It drives me crazy."

"Girl's, don't go too far, okay? We're right behind you, okay?" "Mom, I want to go and look at the beads first. Follow me." Adrieana took her mom's hand and led her to the aisle where the beads were while everyone else followed.

Adrieana began picking the beads and materials that she needed, and Ashanee went to join her. "Hey, Ashanee, do you want to help me?" "Yes sure! They both began to pick up more beads. Ailese heard someone say hello. She looked up and it was Andrew. He was holding a young child's hand. It must have been his niece or a friend's child. "Oh well, hello, and who is this cutie pie?" "Oh, this is my god niece. Say hello, Dana. Dana waved to Ailese. "Hi, my name is Ailese, and these are my girls, Ashanee, and Adrieana. The girls said hello to Dana and invited her to pick beads with them. "Oh, I'm sorry, this is my sister D'Andra. D'Andra, this is Andrew McGee II." "Nice to meet you," they both said as they shook hands. "Looks like Dana has made some friends, huh?" "Yes, it looks like it. We come here every weekend. We go for ice cream afterward, and I dedicate my weekends to my god niece." "That is great, Andrew." Ailese had no idea Andrew was a softy when it came to children. He appeared to be a great father someday, as if he had fatherhood down pat. He was so good with Dana. Andrew looked over at the girls to see that they were having lots of fun; they were giggling and talking to one another. "Dana, we have to finish shopping, okay." We have to go say goodbye to the girls, okay. Andrew looked at Ailese and smiled. "Uncle, I don't want to go yet. I want to play with the girls please." This just broke his heart, and he didn't want to ruin her time with the girls, but they had to finish shopping. Dana asked her Uncle, if the girls could come to lunch with them. "Dana maybe another time." Ashanee interrupted Andrew and asked her mom if they could come to lunch with them because they wanted to play with Dana some more. Ailese didn't know what to say or do. She just met this young girl, and the girls were in love with her. They had a lot in common, but she didn't want to seem snotty if she said no. "Andrew, could you excuse us for a minute, please?" "Oh sure, take your time." Ailese rounded up everyone and went outside to discuss if they should go to lunch with Andrew and Dana. "What do you think, D'Andra?" "I think you should go. We all could go. I don't think there's any harm in going to lunch with them. We have our own cars, and the girls are getting along great." "Please, Mom," the girls pleaded with their mom, until she gave in. "Well, I do know Andrew. We do work together, and he hasn't done anything to make me think that he could." Ailese paused and told everyone to go back into the store. Ailese found Andrew and Dana where she had left them. "Okay, it's a date, for the girls, I mean." "Yes, thank you, Ms. Ailese," Dana said with excitement.

When the girls had finished picking out what they wanted at the art store, Andrew asked if they could follow him to one more stop. Ailese was fine with that. They pulled up to an office building, and Andrew told Ailese that he would be right out, that he only needed to pick something up. Ailese told him that Dana could sit in the car with them until he came back. Ailese had a small conversation with Dana. "So Dana, how old are you?" Dana smiled, "I am nine years old. My birthday is next month." "Oh wow, so you're almost ten. You're a small nine-year-old." "Yeah, my mom calls me her ladybug. She says that I'm small like her." Dana and the girls were playing in the backseat while Ailese and

D'Andra talked amongst themselves. Ailese saw Andrew exit the building, he walked over to her car to get Dana. "Okay, come on, Dana, let's get back in the car so we can eat some lunch." Ailese watched Dana walk with her uncle back to the car. The girls were excited when they pulled up to Fun World. It was a pizza/ fun center place. "Girls, I need you to be on your best behavior, okay? Adrieana, I need you to look after your sister." "Okay Mom." When they all sat down, Andrew told everyone that he would be back, because he was going to order the food. "Mom, after we eat, could we play?" "Yes, Ashanee, be patient, okay?"

"Okay, I will. Mom, look, at that, Ashanee said, pointing to a large ceramic horse on which a child was riding, Mom I want to ride that!" "Wow, that's cool, huh?"

"Ailese, this is cool, huh?" "Yeah, I know the girls are going to have a blast."

"Hey, D, could you watch the kids so I could call Mikell and check on him?"

"Yes, of course, take your time. Tell him hello for me."

"Hey sleepy head, did you get my note?" "Yes, I did. Why didn't you wake me up?" "Because you needed your rest, and besides, the girls wanted to go out, I just wanted to let you that we ran into Andrew, you know, from work?

Well, we're having lunch with his god niece, Dana. The girls struck up a friendship with Dana, his god niece and she invited us to lunch." "Okay, tell the girls hello and give them a big kiss for me. Have fun. Ailese?" "Yes, Mike." "Please don't think that I have a problem with you hanging out with Andrew. You know that's not me. I can tell that you hesitated to tell me, but I don't have a problem with you guys hanging out, jealousy isn't me. Have fun, and I love you, baby."

"Mikell, it's just that having lunch with him and his niece, made me feel a little awkward. I mean, I know that you wouldn't mind. I don't know. I'm rambling, anyway, we'll be home later, and oh, were at Fun World." "Wow, I know the girls are excited, huh?" "Yes, they are—oh, and D says hello. She's with us as well." "Tell sis I said hello." "Baby, did you want to meet us here?" "No, baby, have fun."

When Ailese came back to the table, Andrew and the kids were all getting along. "Sorry about that, I had to make a phone call. Where's my sister?" "Oh, she went to the ladies' room. Our food should be here soon. I apologize I should have asked you guys what kind of pizza you guys wanted instead of ordering a little bit of everything." "Oh, we're not picky at all. I'm sure it's fine whatever you ordered." Ailese didn't know why she was nervous. This wasn't a date.

The waitress brought out the food, and everyone ate until they were full. The adults ate more salad than pizza, while the kids devoured most of the pizza. A while later, the kids went on rides and played games. Ailese Andrew and D'Andra made sure the kids were in their sight. Andrew even helped the girls win some prizes. He helped them win stuffed animals and a bowling game that gave you lots of tickets to redeem. Ailese was having more fun than the kids were. She loved playing the games and beating Andrew and D'Andra.

They stayed at the Fun World for hours. Everyone was having such a blast that no one was keeping up with the time. "Ailese, could I talk to you outside for a minute?" "Sure, Ailese said, with a puzzled look on her face. "I just wanted to say thank you. Dana has made some great friends, and I mean, your girls are so beautiful like their … I'm sorry, I didn't mean to say … Andrew paused and looked away. Ailese interrupted him. "No, it's okay. Don't worry about it." Andrew wanted to tell her that she was the most beautiful woman he'd ever seen in his life, but he couldn't, he wouldn't, and he didn't want to jeopardize what they had at this moment. Thank you for inviting us. It was so much fun. Thank you again."

When Ailese turned away, Andrew stood in front of her. "Don't go. There's something I want to tell you."

"Okay, what is it, Andrew?" "I just want us to be friends, confidants, no more, no less; can we do that?" Ailese didn't know what to say. She took a step back from Andrew and didn't say a word. Ailese will always have that trust issue, no matter what that was instilled in her. She didn't want to get hurt anymore and she made it a point not to. "What does he want from me? Why does he want to be in my life?" These were the questions that Ailese asked herself. "Well, our kids, well, your niece loves the girls, so I suppose they'd want to play together occasionally, I suppose. Ailese paused and took a deep breath. I can't make you any promises. There are so many things that you don't know or understand about me, Andrew. We can see what happens, okay?" Ailese put her hands in her pockets and looked away. "Okay, that sounds good. Thank you again, Ailese." Andrew opened the door for Ailese, and they both went back in.

"Okay guys, let's make sure that no one forgets anything, so make sure that you have everything." Ailese took the girls to redeem their tickets while D'Andra and Andrew threw away all the trash that was on the table. When she came back to the table, she reminded everyone to make sure that they had everything, before they left. "Thanks, Andrew, the girls loved it, and I had a ball watching them play." "I think my inner child came out, D'Andra said to Andrew. "Oh, my pleasure." D'Andra took the girls to the restroom and left Ailese and Andrew alone. Andrew asked Ailese to sit down. Ailese sat across from him, and there was silence until Andrew stirred up a conversation. "So, Dana's already planning a playdate with your girls. Is that okay?" "Yes, that would be fine. My girls already mentioned having a playdate with Dana," Ailese said with a smile. "Dana doesn't have many friends that are around her age that live in her neighborhood, so playing with the girls was a treat for her." "She is so sweet." "Thank you. Sometimes I think having her is the closest I'll get to having my own." "Well, you never know."

D'Andra came back with the girls, and everyone started to leave the restaurant.

"Bye, Dana. See you soon." The girls said their goodbyes to Dana and Andrew.

"Bye, Andrew. It was nice meeting you, and thanks for inviting me. Take care." "Same to you, D'Andra. I hope to see you soon." "Bye Ailese I'll see you on Monday."

"Monday, yes, take care, and thanks again." When Ailese walked to her car, Andrew watched her until she was in it. "Uncle, do you like Ms. Ailese?" "Oh, no, I just think she's cool, that's all." "Me too, and she is so, so pretty." "That she is, that she is, okay, let's get you home."

"There are my girls. Come give Dad a hug. I missed you guys so much." The girls ran to their dad and gave him lots of hugs and kisses. Mikell gave Ailese a kiss and told her that he missed her too. "Daddy, we had so much fun, you should have been there. Mommy's friend Andrew helped us win all these prizes. Oh, Mom, could we go get them out of the car?" "Yes, here's the keys and come right back, okay, guys." "Lee, what's bothering you? I can tell there's something bothering you, hun. What is it? Are you still worried about the dreams?" "No, I'm fine. I am a bit tired though, that's all." "No, I think.... Mikell stopped talking when the girls came back inside. The girls showed off their stuffed animals and the prizes that Andrew had won for them.

Mikell wasn't going to forget what he and Ailese were talking about. He knew something was bothering her and wanted to know what it was.

"Hun, now that we're alone, I want to finish our conversation from earlier."

"I told you that I am fine," Ailese started to yawn. Mikell looked at Ailese, waiting for her to spill the truth, but she didn't. "Lee, is this about you and Andrew spending the day together with the kids? I told you that it didn't bother me, Hun." Ailese was silent for a few seconds. "You know about my trust issues, and I feel that I kind of let my guards down today. It's just that the girls wanted to spend time with Dana, and now they want to schedule playdates. I told him that it was fine. I don't know why it's bothering me; everyone got along just fine, but there's just something about him I can't pin it down, you know?" "What do you mean? Are you saying that you don't trust Andrew?" "I don't know what I'm saying. I'm just rambling. I guess what I'm trying to say is, I need to stop thinking that someone is always out to hurt me. That I need to give people a chance to be in my life." "Okay, I agree, and I feel that you have good judgment. I haven't met Andrew, but I trust that you will never endanger yourself or anyone else because you have a huge heart, and if the girls and his god niece wants to have playdates, that's fine with me, but if you're not, just tell me, Hun." Ailese touched Mikell on the cheeks and said," I'm okay with it. Sorry for getting all weird on you." "You're not weird. Mikell kissed her on the cheek.

Ailese had a lot on her plate today. She kept busy all day. She worked through lunch. She wanted to get everything done. She had spent most of her day making calls and viewing properties for her clients. Ell told her that she needed to take a break, but she didn't. She never liked having to come back the next day and finish yesterday's work because she would have more on her plate. She would have to finish yesterday's work on top of today's work, so she worked hard. Ailese hated feeling overwhelmed; that was a pet peeve of hers. She just didn't like the feeling. "Boss, I'm going to lunch, I know that it's late. Did you want anything?" "No, thanks, Ell. Have a good lunch." "Boss, um, you haven't eaten anything today. I think you should eat something." "I'm okay, really. I need to get these contracts over to my client." "Okay, call me if you change your mind."

Ailese was a bit relieved that Andrew had sent her an email that he would be working out of the office today. Just when she thought that she wouldn't see him today, Andrew called to ask her to meet him at a property. It was urgent. Ailese shrugged her shoulders, gathered her things, and called Ruben so he could bring her car to the front of the building. Ailese had remembered that she needed to run some errands as well. Ailese left a note on Ell's desk to tell her she would be out of the office for a while. When Ailese had arrived at the property, Andrew was waiting for her outside. Two men that looked like construction workers accompanied him. "Why are they here? They shouldn't be here until tomorrow," Ailese said to herself. "Hi, Ailese, thanks for meeting me here. These gentlemen told me that they were supposed to start the work for the Grant contract, but here it says that they were to start tomorrow. Is that correct?" "Yes, you're right, Andrew but what seems to be the problem? They can't start work until tomorrow." Ailese had explained to the men that the contract clearly states that they cannot start any earlier than tomorrow, but the men insisted on starting today because for some odd reason, their contract started today. Ailese got out her Black Berry to pull up the original contracts, and she showed them that someone must have typed the date incorrectly, but the date on the original contracts was legit. After the men got into their trucks, Ailese heard one of them call her a bitch. She was livid. "Excuse me, sir. What did you just say?" "I called you a bitch. You walk around here like you own everything, like you people can never make a mistake, ha!" Before Ailese could respond, Andrew opened the truck door and pulled the man out of the truck, told him to never come back there, and fired him and his crew on the spot! "Don't you ever show your face around here, do you understand me? You never again disrespect this woman!" Andrew pushed the man to the ground. "Andrew, that's enough. Ailese pulled Andrew away from the man and told him to walk with her to the car. Andrew, it's okay. I can take care of myself!" "Ailese, I'm sorry. Please forgive me. I don't like it when a man like him disrespects a woman." Andrew took a deep breath. "I don't waste my time or breath on people like that. I would have fired him myself if given the chance. Yes, you're right; he did disrespect me, but you know there's always someone who loves to test you, and you ... Ailese stopped talking. Andrew, let's pretend this didn't happen, okay?" "Ailese, please, listen to me. I am not in any way a violent person. Please don't think that of me. I just flipped, and I am sorry." Ailese had all of a sudden seen it in his eyes, those apologetic eyes. "I don't think that you're a violent person. You stood up for me. Thank you." Ailese could see it in his eyes: what Ailese thought of him meant a lot to him for some odd reason. He didn't want her to think anything bad of him. Andrew, I told you that we're good." Ailese put out her hand so he could shake her hand. Andrew gave her a look, and they both just laughed. I accept your apology, Andrew, as I previously stated, were cool." "Thanks, Ailese. I love your personality and your energy, and you always make me laugh." Ailese smiled at him. "Hey, I am going to go back to the office and take care of this mess since

I fired those guys, uh, I mean since you fired them, and mark my words, I will be making a complaint to his boss. We have to make this deadline. I will let you know who will be there tomorrow for the Grant contract." "Okay, call me if you need me. See ya."

Andrew was the type of man that women loved; they would always flaunt themselves just to get his attention, but Andrew didn't like when women would flaunt themselves in front of him. It was a complete turn-off, and he just never had the heart to tell them. Here is a woman that would be perfect for him, but she happens to be married; he respected that, but he thought about her every day. How could you fall in love with someone so fast? He loved the way that she smelled, the way that she looked and, how her outfits were always neat. He loved her curves too. Andrew was very wealthy. Sometimes he couldn't tell if people, especially women, liked him or if they liked him because he was wealthy. He was so used to every woman being so attracted to him, but no, not Ailese, not the woman he had fallen for, not the woman that would be perfect for him.

Everyone was talking about him on the news and in the newspaper! He was the talk of the town.

When the town of Shelby found out that he was coming to work for Mr. Saxx, there were reporters following him around, wanting to get that first interview. Maybe Ailese didn't read the financial magazines, he thought. If she knew who he was, maybe she could give him a break? He had to get used to being with a woman who didn't want or need his company. One time Andrew attended a party that was given by Seth Garner. He opened a publishing company that skyrocketed, and Seth was celebrating its ten-year anniversary and only invited the best and well- known people. A woman had spotted Andrew and struck up a casual conversation. After the party was over, she followed him to his car, undressed in front of him, and told him that he could have her anytime, anywhere. Ailese was a wealthy woman herself, but unlike Andrew, she wasn't always wealthy. She wasn't born with a silver spoon in her mouth. She had to work very hard. Andrew inherited his wealth, although he too had to work hard to keep his companies on track. Andrew's parents died, and he was the only child, so everything was left to him. You couldn't spend all of his inheritance in a lifetime. Andrew didn't let everyone know that he had planes and jets; if they knew, they had to have read it in a magazine. He was never the type of person to brag.

"Ailese, hey, I sent you an email regarding the Grant contract. Let me know if you have any questions." "Okay, got it, thanks. "I will come and sign the contracts if they're ready." "That would be great. See you in a sec." "Hey, Andrew. Ailese sat down in the chair that faced Andrew. She signed the contracts, and as she was about to go to her office, Andrew told her that he would have Ell FedEx the contracts to the clients. "Well, I'm going to grab a bite to eat. I haven't eaten all day. My stomachs on empty. Andrew, um, would you like to join me? I mean if you haven't eaten yet." "Actually, I haven't eaten yet, and yes, I would love to. Let me get my coat and make sure these contracts get to Ell." "Okay, great, just meet me in my office." A few minutes went by when Andrew came to Ailese's office. "I'm ready. Do you mind if we take my car? I hope you don't mind, that I've already called Ruben." "Sounds great." As Ailese and Andrew were waiting for the elevator, Susan stepped out of the elevator. She looked at Andrew and Ailese, she rolled her eyes, then kept walking. "Um, if you want too." Andrew interrupted her. "It's fine, we broke up a few weeks ago; it's no biggie."

"Do you mind if we went to a restaurant?" "Oh, not at all. I was hoping that you would say that." "I heard about a place called Brunelly's. I hear they have great food; do you want to experiment with me?" "Sure, why not?"

When they entered the restaurant, the first thing that they noticed was a wishing well. The water was the color of the sky, and there was a porcelain statue of a woman that cradled a baby in her arms; it was beautiful, Ailese thought to herself. "Hello, and welcome to Brunelly's table for two?" "Yes, please." Andrew answered the young waiter. "Follow me, please." Andrew and Ailese followed the waiter to the center of the restaurant. "Wow, this is very beautiful." Ailese looked around the restaurant, admiring every detail. "Could I start you two off with anything to drink?" "Yes, could I please have a raspberry iced tea, please?" "I will have the same." Ailese took off her jacket and placed it on the back of her chair. "I guess my people that told me about this restaurant were right; it's a gorgeous restaurant, and whoever was in charge of the decorating has a lot of talent." "I agree, so tell me what happened between you and Susan. I hope I didn't make things worse for you."

"Oh, well, first of all, please don't apologize, and it just didn't work out, that's all." Ailese smiled at Andrew. "I'm sorry to hear that. Do you mind me asking why?" "No, I don't mind at all. For starters, Susan started to spread our business around the office, Human Resources to be exact. I am a private person when it comes to who I am dating or who I spend my time with; that turns me off, you know?" "I do."

"So what looks good to you?" Andrew began to look at his menu. "Mmmm, they have a dish that I haven't had in years, wow." "And what's that?" "Shrimp in lemon- lime juice and cilantro, which my mom used to make all the time." "That's funny that you say that because my mom still makes it. That was the first time I even tasted shrimp, because when

I was a kid, I always thought of the ocean when I thought about seafood." Andrew laughed. "Really, well, I'm glad that you gave shrimp a try because I have a rule, if you don't like seafood, I don't like you," Andrew laughed. "Really, that's not nice." "No, I am kidding, no, you are missing out on a lot; seafood is good for you, and shrimp is my favorite."

"Well, I think that I'm going to order your favorite then. It does sound good." "Well, alright then, I like that." Ailese and Andrew drank their iced tea, ate warm bread with butter, and had nice conversations until their food was served. "You bless your food too?" "Yes, I do. Ailese looked up at Andrew. When we were in your jet, I was so hungry that I forgot to." "Amen let's pray together. Wow, I don't know very many people who say grace these days."

A woman who looked like she had just stepped out of a magazine came over to the table, and Ailese assumed that she knew Andrew. "Hello, hun, how are you?" Andrew got up from the table to greet the woman. He hugged her and kissed her on the cheek. "Hi, Denice, how are you?" "I am good, and who is this beautiful woman? You need to introduce us, Andrew." "Yes, Ailese, this is Denice. This is Dana's mom." Ailese got up from the table to shake Denice's hand. "Oh, so this is Ailese. My daughter has been talking about your girls all week. They seemed to have hit it off nicely." "Yes, they did. I enjoyed Dana. She is such a sweetheart and well behaved." "Well, thank you. I try you know. We must have the girls schedule a playdate soon. "Oh yes, very soon." It was so nice to meet you." "Andrew, I will talk to you later?" "Of course, Andrew kissed Denice on her cheek and told her that he would call her later.

"Well, that was a nice late lunch or dinner. Ailese looked at her watch. It was already after five. "Yes, it was, and I hope that I haven't kept you from anything. I saw you looking at your watch." "No, no, not at all. I had a nice time, Andrew, and thanks for introducing me to Denice." "Sure. "I can tell that you two are very close. Is she a model?" "Well, sort of. She does go on photo shoots from time to time. Spending time with Dana is the most important thing to her. We've known each other for years. It's funny, I didn't like her at first, but for some strange reason we became the best of friends. She tells everyone we're brother and sister. Her family practically adopted me."

"Really, that sounds like something out of a book. It's funny how you don't like someone and they're the ones that would always have your back, you know? I mean, D'Andra and my brother couldn't get a long, and now they are like two peas in a pod." When Ailese made eye contact with Andrew, he hesitated to say anything to her, so he turned away, and she turned her head to look out the window. Was Ailese growing fond of him?

Today Ailese and Mikell went to the studio, and when they got there, Sedrick was already in the booth practicing some tunes. When Ailese tapped on the window, Sedrick looked up and smiled when he saw Ailese's face. "Hey, you sound great!" Sedrick took his earphones off and exited the sound room. "Hey, Mrs. Lady, how are you?" "I am good. I can't complain at all. Hey, I brought the song that I told you about. I actually found it." Ailese reached into her bag and pulled out a notebook. She turned the page and gave it to Sedrick to look at. Count On Him was the name of the song that Ailese had written a long time ago, and she was very proud of it, still to this day. Sedrick studied the song and started humming to it as he sat down. "Oh wow, this is good, Ailese. Why didn't you become a superstar or a writer?" "Well, I did at one point in my life, but I guess that wasn't

God's plan, but his plan for me is for me to share my talents, and that makes me happy." Sedrick smiled at Ailese.

> *You Count on Him, give all your problems to him,*
> *Yes, you can count on him.*
> *For he will never, ever let you down.*

Sedrick sang the song with feeling; he sang the song with his soul, and that was how Ailese sang the song too, so she was happy with that. Sedrick was the person who made the song come alive, and she hoped that this would be one of the songs on Sedrick's album.

"Honey, I don't know if I've told you this, actually I'm sure I have, but you are so talented, and I appreciate you helping us on this project; it means so much to me, and it brings back memories. Ever since you've been working with Sedrick, I hear you singing around the house more like you used to, and that makes me happy, baby."

"Aw, you're sweet. I'm so glad that you didn't stop bugging me about working with you again, "Ailese said as she hugged Mikell. "Yeah, me too. You know when I get an idea or a vision, there's no stopping me. I know, I know I need to stop being conceited for you," Mikell chuckled.

"Hello, Mikell. How are you?" "Oh, I am good, and how is Don?" "He is doing great. Thanks for asking. Is my daughter there?" "Yes, she is. Let me get her for you, okay. Mom is on the phone. Are you out of the shower? When Mikell didn't hear Ailese answer him, he knocked on the door. Ailese? He opened the door and found her in the shower. Baby, your mom is on the phone for you, and don't scare me like that." "Like what?" "I called you, but you didn't answer. I thought something was wrong." "I'm sorry babe, I didn't hear you. Tell my mom I will be right there okay. Could you talk to her until I put on my robe really quick?" "Sure. Mikell stared at her body. Ailese pushed him out of the bathroom.

"Hey, Mom, what's up?"

"Hey you, we're just two people with crazy schedules. We've been playing phone tag for weeks." "I know Mom, I am so sorry about that, and yes, my schedule couldn't get any crazier," Ailese said picking up a face towel to wipe her face. "I understand, sweetie. Hey, I won't keep you long, but the pictures came back, and they look so good, and I wanted to get your opinion on something." Mikell whispered to Ailese that he told her mom that they were going to drive there today. "Oh, okay, we could meet at your house, besides, I would love to see Dad." "Okay, I am going to be here all day today, so just call me when you're on your way, okay?" "Okay Mom." "Oh, hun, your sister will be here too. I knew that she had some things to do, then she was going to come over afterward." "Sounds great. Love you Mom." Ailese hung up the phone and went back into the restroom to dry off. Mikell was in the shower humming a tune.

Ailese didn't know what to wear. She stood in front of her closet trying to decide what to wear, and she finally decided on a simple burgundy dress that she dressed in gold jewelry and a leather jacket with ankle boots. "Mmmm ... You always look so sexy." Mikell complimented her. "So what made you decide to drive to my mom's today, and what are you up to?" "Oh, nothing, I figured we needed to spend some time with Mom. We've been so busy, and the kids mentioned that they missed her." "Aw, you're so sweet. Yes, I miss my mom too." "Mom, Ashanee said to her mother. Look, I finally finished the bracelet that Adrieana started for me, Mom. I really like making bracelets. It's fun." "Let me see, hun. Ashanee passed the bracelet to her mom. Oh, wow, Ashanee, you're getting good at this. This bracelet is gorgeous. You did a good job."

Ailese handed the bracelet back to her. "Ashanee, you did do a good job," Adrieana told her sister, and Ashanee thanked her for the compliment. Adrieana was proud that she and her sister had something special in common now, which meant a lot to her because now she could make her jewelry with her sister and teach her everything that she needed to know. Even though they were a year apart, they both loved each other unconditionally; they took care of one another, which is what their mom taught them to do. Adrieana would read books to her little sister before bedtime and teach her what she knew. She was always so patient with her sister. One time Ashanee wanted Adrieana to teach her a dance routine from a music video that she liked. Adrieana and Ashanee practiced day and night until Ashanee got the routine down. They even put on a performance for their mom and dad.

"Mom, when would Armont be home?" "Oh, in a few days, kitten, he's staying at his dads for a few days, remember?" "But I miss him, Mom, and I hate it when he goes away for a while." "I tell you what we'll call him once we get to Grammies, okay?" "Okay, Mom." Ashanee smiled at her mom.

Ailese's cell phone was ringing. She pushed the button on her Bluetooth. "Hello, hey handsome, we were just talking about you. Your sister misses you and so do I."

Armont told his mom that he missed her too. "Mom, Dad has to go on a trip. He has to fly out to see Grandma, she isn't feeling well, and he has to leave tonight, so I was thinking I could have Dad drop me off in an hour. Would that be okay?" "Yes, but we're heading up to Grammie's right now. Do you think he could drop you off there?" "Let me ask Dad. Hold on, Mom. Armont came back to the phone. Mom, he said that it was a bit out of the way and that he couldn't miss his flight, and there's going to be a lot of traffic." Ailese almost said something that she would regret later, but she caught herself. "Okay, could you put your dad on the phone, please?" "Hello, hey Ailese, look, I would be more than happy to drop him off at your mom's, but I'm pressing for time here. I can't miss that flight. It doesn't look good. My mother is very sick, and I need to get there as soon as possible." "I'm sorry to hear about your mom." Mikell got Ailese's attention while she was on the phone. "Babe, we'll just pick him up, it's fine." "Okay, I will be there in about an hour, okay? Let me drop the girls off at my mom's because we just pulled up to the house." "Okay, thanks. I will tell Armont to get his things together. See you then."

Mikell took the girls inside while Ailese went to pick up Armont. As she was driving, her cell phone was ringing again. "Who could this be? She said to herself.

Hello, oh, hello, Evette, how are you?" Ailese stopped talking when she heard the hysterical voice on the other end. Evette was crying; she was very upset. "Ailese it's me, Evette. I didn't know who else to call. It's my mother, she passed away this morning." Evette began to sob even harder. Ailese was in shock. She couldn't believe that her mother had passed away. She had just known that she would make it. "Oh my, Evette I am so, so, sorry. What happened?" "She died during her surgery. Her body couldn't take it, I guess. Her heart wasn't strong enough. I don't know what I'm going to do without her, Ailese. "Evette, where are you now? You shouldn't be alone right now." "I'm at home. There's nothing I can do at the hospital, so I came home. Why? Why? Why?" Evette kept repeating over and over. "Hey, I am on my way, okay. You don't need to be alone."

Ailese picked up Armont first and headed to Evette's house. She knew what she must have been going through, and she wanted to be there for her dear friend. "Armont, I need to stop by Evette's for a bit, okay? Her mom just died, and I don't want her to be alone."

"That's really sad, her mother was a nice lady."

"Evette, I'm here now. Ailese grabbed Evette and hugged her tight. Evette, I'm here for you, okay?" Evette was silent. She hugged Ailese even tighter. When Evette saw Armont standing there, she gave him a half-way smile and said hello with her eyes. Have you eaten anything? You look pale, and you're shaking. Evette, sit down. I will fix you something." "No, I'm fine. I'm okay." Ailese walked into the kitchen and demanded that Evette eat something. "You need your strength, okay?" "Okay, Mom," Evette said in a mischievous voice. She then smiled. Ailese, what will I ever do without you? Only you could make someone smile, no matter what they're going through." Ailese made Evette some soup and a small salad. "Mom, your cell phone is ringing." Armont brought his mom her purse. "Thank you, hun. Hello, hey, Mik. Yes, Armont's with me. Could you please tell Mom that I am at Evette's. Mikell, her mom passed away this morning, and she doesn't need to be alone right now. I will be there later, okay?"

"Oh, no, please tell Evette that she's in my prayers and that I am so sorry for her loss. We'll see you when you get here. I was just a bit worried, that's all." "Babe, I'm so sorry for not calling you, I … Ailese paused. I needed to be here for her, okay. I love you too." As Evette and Ailese talked, Armont went into the other room to watch TV. "It's going to be okay. I know that you don't see it right now, but know that you have lots of people who love you and are here for you, Evette." "I know, I know, but she was all I had other than Heather, but I know that she is in a better place, and she doesn't have to suffer anymore." "Remember all the good memories. She will always be with you. Please do not hesitate to call me okay. I would stay longer, but I do have to get to my mom's. I will call you later. Evette, is there anyone that you could call to stay with you?" "Oh, I forgot to mention to you that my family will be here soon. You go to your family, I will be okay." They hugged each other, and Evette watched Ailese drive off.

"Mom, is Ms. Evette going to be okay?" "Well, it's going to take some time, but eventually she will be okay." When they arrived at her mom's, Ailese had to gain her composure because she was worried about her friend and she really didn't want to leave her, but she was going to make sure that she checked on her later.

"Ailese, how's Evette?" "Not so good, so I don't want to stay here long, because I told her that I would check on her later. I mean, her family will be here soon, but I just need to be there, you know, in her time of need. I don't know what I would do if I lost my mom. I know that I would be devastated. I can't and don't want to imagine it."

"Come here." Mikell grabbed his wife and held her in his arms, kissing her forehead. Ailese shrugged her shoulders and sat down on the couch. "Okay, Mom, I'm here now, is D'Andra here?"

"Hey, you, and yes, she's in the kitchen. Go and get your sister for me, please."

"Okay, Mom. Ailese walked into the kitchen and snuck up on her sister from behind, just like they used to do when they were young. Ailese tickled her side from behind and started to laugh. D'Andra was laughing uncontrollably. They gave each other a hug. Hey sis, mom told me to come and get you. I guess she's ready for us to help her."

Alonda had all the pictures spread out on the huge dining room table.

"Okay, guys, I need your opinion on which picture we should give Mommie for her birthday." She showed the girls the picture that she had in mind. It was a picture of everyone with a pearl white background. "Mom, I do like this one, Ailese told her mom. But I think Mommie would like this one. It looks like a glamour shot. You can see the glossy glare." Ailese pointed it out in the picture. "I agree, Mom, we should put this one in the frame." "Okay, D'Andra and Ailese, I think we got our picture. D'Andra, I do need you to pick the frame. You are so good at that, okay?" "Okay, Mom, no problem. I will work on that this week." They both smiled at each other.

Don came into the dining room. "Is anyone thirsty or anything?" "I could use some tea if you have it," Ailese said to Don. "And what about you, Missy? What do you want to drink?" "Tea, too, Dad, please." Don went into the kitchen, came back with the iced tea, and kissed both his daughters on the forehead. "Dad, what are the kids doing? They are very quiet." "Oh, everyone's in the garage playing some games, and the guys and I are teaching Armont how to play pool. He's a quick learner, you know." Don grinned and went back to the game. "Ailese, remember when we were playing phone tag?" "Yes. "Well, I was calling to tell you that the strangest thing has been going on for a while now, and I forgot to mention it to you. Someone has been calling the house late at night, and when we answer the phone, they just hang up. They always call from a blocked number. It's like clockwork, every night at the same time, and it's getting really annoying."

D'Andra took a sip of her tea. "Mom, that is strange. Did you want me to look into it for you and Dad? Because I can, or I could have the number changed."

"I actually called the phone company, and they said that since the number is a private number, they are not able to trace it, and your dad doesn't want to change the number. We've had the same number for years. I don't know who it could be? They don't say anything." Alonda had a puzzled look on her face.

"Mom, maybe you have to get the number changed. Ailese said to her mom. This way this person can stop calling you. You could get an unlisted number. People do it every day for reasons like this one. Daddy may just have to get used to a new number because it will drive you crazy, and besides, you two need your sleep." Alonda looked at Ailese and shook her head.

"Just think about it, okay. That's all I'm asking." "Yes, Mom, just think about it because now that I know that there's someone calling you every night and hanging up, that doesn't sit too well with me." "I agree, Mom." "Okay, I will think about it. Now let's talk about something else, okay?"

When Ailese arrived at home, she went straight to Evette's to check on her. Evette came to the door. She didn't look pale anymore. She had even changed her clothes and her hair. "Come in. I'm glad you stopped by. I just want to tell you thank you for worrying about my well-being." "Oh, anytime. Ailese noticed that there were suitcases near the door.

Oh, I see that you've packed for a trip or something," Ailese said indicating the suitcases. Evette walked into the kitchen, and Ailese followed her. "Yes, I'm going to live with my family. They want me to move back home. I only came out here to live here so I could take care of my mom. I mean, she had dreamed of leaving Hanley, because she had lived there all her life. So, we came to Shelby, and now that Mom is gone, Evette paused. I do need to go back home, you know, because that is where all my family lives. I mean, I don't have a huge family. I've always thought of mom, and Heather, as my family, you know?" Ailese hugged her and told her that she would be greatly missed. "I think that is a good idea. You do need to be with your family, and we will definitely stay in touch, my friend." Evette hugged her tight. "Yes, we have too, and we could visit each other." "You bet, so when are you leaving?" "In two days, I actually got lucky because I had mentioned to a friend that I was selling the house. She and her family were looking to buy a house, and they fell in love with this one, so they bought it. Can you believe that?" "That's great! "Well, we're going to fly Mom home to bury her … I miss her so much. She was my everything." "I know, we're never prepared to lose our loved ones, and it's hard to get over losing them, but they live on inside our hearts. Where's Heather?" "She's over at a friend's house. I am on my way to pick her up. I don't know how she is going to handle all of this." Evette said, shaking her head. "Honey, you're a terrific mom, and I know you will find a way for her to adjust. She will eventually adjust; we do it every day.

Please don't leave without letting the girls say their goodbyes, okay?"

"Oh, yes, I won't."

When Ailese came into the house, Mikell was on the phone talking with someone. Mikell was speaking to Leon. He had called to let them know that his daughter was feeling excellent, and he wanted to thank Ailese and Mikell. "Hey, you, that was Leon. He called to let us know that his daughter is doing great!" "That lifts my spirits, Amen. Thank You Lord!

That is great, Mikell! I am so happy!" "Me too. So, how is Evette?" "She's trying to hang in there. She's actually moving back to her hometown, and I am going to miss her." "Really, what about the house?" "Someone has already bought it- a close friend of hers." Ailese sat down in a chair and began to feel a bit sad. She and Evette were more than just neighbors. They were very good friends, and when her mom became ill, Evette and Ailese lost touch because she had to take care of her mother, which was around the clock. "I know you're going to miss her, but I'm sure you guys won't lose touch, right?" "Right, we already said that we were going to call and visit each other." "Good." Mikell leaned over his wife and kissed her."

Ailese tossed and turned, unable to stop thinking about her dear friend Evette and the phone calls that her mom was receiving. It made her worried and restless. "Mikell, I can't sleep, she whispered, but Mikell was sound asleep. She tried waking him up but didn't succeed. Ailese went into the kitchen to fix some warm milk. She had remembered that it helped her when her mother-in-law fixed it for her. When the milk was ready, she carefully poured it into a coffee cup and sat down. She was careful not to make any noise, so she didn't wake anyone. She walked softly to the second level of the house. She then pulled out her laptop and thought that she would surf the internet for a while until she got tired. She finished the invitation list for D'Andra and Chris's housewarming party, and ordered the invitations on line and looked at some gift ideas for the housewarming party. She was tempted to buy some items but decided not to. As she sipped her warm milk, she began to think about those awful calls- who could it be? Why would someone want to spend their time calling her mom and dad at strange hours? She wished that Alonda would have the number changed and the problem would disappear. Maybe she would call her mother in the morning to change her mind. When Ailese had finished her milk, she decided to go back to her room and try to get some sleep. Mikell was still sound asleep. Ailese closed her eyes and finally fell asleep.

Ailese began moaning in her sleep. She was having another dream, and it was one of those dreams that seemed so real! Ailese tried to wake up, but once again she couldn't. This time he was very, very, very angry! Ailese had gone on a trip with D'Andra, which he was against her going on in the first place. Knowing that there was going to be hell to pay when she got back, she prepared herself for whatever was to happen, or she thought. Ailese walked through the door and closed it behind her. She felt a blow to her face. He had slapped her so hard that she fell on the floor. He had caught her off guard. She struggled to get up, and when she did get up, he pushed her so hard on to the floor and pinned her down to the floor. His heavy muscular body prevented her from fighting back; he was just too strong, for her to lift him off of her, but she wasn't going to go out without a fight. He cursed her the whole time he had her pinned down, telling her she was a no-good slut, and he knew that she was sleeping with other men while she was on her trip. He spit in her face, cursing at her even more. Ailese then took her knee and kicked him in the groin. He let out a loud groan, he was in a lot of pain, but Ailese didn't care. Once she was free from him, she wanted to go to the front door, but it would take too long for her to open it. She would had to have a key to unlock it and lock it, and her keys were nowhere in sight, so she ran into the other room and tried to open a window, but it was stuck. She tried with all her might to get that window opened, but she just couldn't! He made his way into the room, and she picked up the first thing that she saw, a lamp. She held the lamp in her hand and made sure she had a good grip on the lamp. She wanted to be ready for him. He charged at her while attempting to take the lamp from her grasp. Ailese hit him over the head with the lamp, he was bleeding profusely, but that didn't stop him. He punched her in her stomach, and she went down. He grabbed both of her legs and began to drag her as she kicked and screamed. "No one is going to help you. Shut up! You made the mistake of putting your hands on me. Now I'm going to teach you a lesson."

He beat her badly. Ailese began to moan even louder in her sleep. She wanted to wake up but couldn't. "Please stop, stop!" Mikell shook her really hard to wake her up, and when she did, she became violent with Mikell. She called him by another name and told him to stay away from her. He finally reassured her it was a dream, and he held her until she went back to sleep.

When this man hurt Ailese, she was very young. She hadn't met Armont's father yet, and luckily she didn't have any kids with this monster, even though there were times that he forced himself on her. Ailese never became pregnant. She had always thought that the drugs and the stress were the reasons why she wasn't able to get pregnant. She still feels it was a blessing that she didn't have a child with this monster, and it would make her sick to her stomach just thinking about how her life would have been if they had a child together. When he beat her so badly, she had to lie to a lot of people that she loved and cared about, and she didn't like doing that at all. Ailese hid her bruises very well. Luckily, her bruises were mostly on her back or arms. He had a lot of people fooled. He would make people think that he was a gentleman, a caring person, that he loved her so much, but they didn't know the truth. He was a monster, an ugly person, disrespectful, and a violent person. Sometimes Ailese would come very close to wiping that smile off his face and showing people how he really was, but she didn't want another beating. She rather him lie to people than tell them the truth. She hated him for hurting her. Ailese never had any enemies, and she had people in her life treat her wrongly and she would never hate them, but she hated him for everything that he put her through, because of him. She had to reclaim her life and her priorities. She had to literally start over. If she didn't have God in her life, she would not have survived this monster's abuse. She never once blamed God for everything that happened in her life. She only felt that it was a lesson from God. God loved her too much, and she understood that he takes us through things in our lives.

"Baby, it's time to get up," Mikell told Ailese as he gave her a gentle shake. Ailese slowly opened her eyes and looked at Mikell. She was so tired, but she knew that she had to get up. "Mik, do you mind taking the kids to school? I'm going to sleep for a while, okay?" "Okay, no problem. Are you okay, Lee?" "Yes, I will be fine," Ailese paused. She knew that Mikell was going to bring up last night she could tell by the look on his face. "Baby, I feel for you, I really do, and it's driving me crazy that I can't make these dreams go away, but I want you to know that I am here for you and whenever you want to talk, I'm here. Please don't forget that." Ailese touched her husband's face and kissed him gently on his cheek. Her look told him that she would be okay. "I love you, Mikell, so much that I don't want you to feel helpless, okay? Please don't think that you haven't been there for me, because you are, and you always have been, and I love you so much."

"I love you too. Hey, how about I drive the kids to school and come back here? I just don't want to leave you alone." "Okay, sounds good, but I think you forgot that you had a lunch meeting with Kara Kabbs, remember? I remember because you mentioned it to me the other day because you wanted me at the meeting."

"I know, I am sure she'd understand if we postponed it. Baby you come first, and you need me. I am here. They'll understand. Besides, I want to stay here with you until you go to work. I don't care what time it is. Mikell kissed Ailese and stood up. I am going to run the kids to school and I will be right back." Ailese said goodbye to the kids and went back to bed.

When Mikell returned, Ailese was still up, she wanted to wait for him before she went back to sleep. "Hey, I stopped off to get your favorite." He handed her a coffee and a bag. She knew what it was before she opened it. It was a breakfast sandwich from her favorite coffee shop. They ate breakfast in bed, feeding each other. "Baby, I was speaking to D'Andra the other day, and she had mentioned something to me. She said that when I was in the hospital, you had called her in the middle of the night because you had a bad dream, and she came to stay with you." Ailese wanted to avoid this conversation, but she knew she couldn't. "Yes, she did. She came to stay with me because she was worried about me. That night was a … Ailese let out a long sigh. It was very hard for me, and I needed her that night. She could feel tears coming on. Damn it, she said to herself, no tears." I mean, I really needed you, but you were in the hospital, and D'Andra didn't want me to go through it alone, and yes, I didn't mention it to you because I didn't want to worry you, Mikell." "I understand that, but why didn't you tell me this?" "I know that I should have, but you were recovering from your surgery, and I didn't want to put any more stress on you," Mikell interrupted her. "I don't care about the stress, baby. You needed me, and you didn't call me. Mikell took her hand and put it on his face. He kissed her fingertips. Ailese, remember when we were talking about hiring an investigator so we could find out where this guy is?" "Yes, I do, why?"

"Well, I don't think that we should. I feel like we may be opening a can of worms. I don't know if I want to know if he is alive or dead. I feel that you're focusing on your sessions with your doctor, and we will get through this, like I said before, please believe me. We will get through this, we will." Ailese could see the determination in his eyes, and she did believe him. "I agree with everything you just said. I do."

"Ailese I am not going to let him, or anyone else hurt you, ever. I hate him for what he put you through, and if you asked me, let him stay wherever he is!"

Ailese got up with a spring in her step, telling herself that she wasn't going to let this bastard run her life, her day was going to go as planned, and that she wasn't going to let it happen again. He wasn't going to control her, he wasn't going to ruin her, he wasn't going to be an inconvenience, she kept telling herself. Even though she couldn't control her dreams but, she could control her life and what she wanted, and she didn't want. She didn't want him controlling her life and putting fear in her anymore.

"You look so beautiful. Is that one of the outfits you picked up when we went to the shops with Mom and Dad?" "Yes, it is you like?" Ailese pretended that she was a model, modeling an outfit. "You are so funny, Mikell grinned.

Let me call Karen, okay, then we can go." "Okay baby." Ailese went to the kitchen and decided to fix a lunch. If she wasn't needed at the lunch meeting, then she would have a backup. She contemplated if she should take some coffee with her. She decided to put some in her thermos. She placed her belongings on the table by the door and went in to the bedroom to double-check her hair and makeup. "So guess what?" "What?" Ailese was anxious to hear what Mikell had to say. "Um, well, some things came up on Kara's end, so the lunch meeting is cancelled. She was just about to call me, but I beat her to it." "Oh, well, these sorts of things happen." "Yes, they do, and she did confirm the date and time, and she wants you present at the meeting. I made sure that it didn't conflict with your sessions, and I emailed the date, and time, and the location to Ell." "Oh, thank you, sweetie. You're so good to me." "Well, I try, Lee." Ailese smiled.

When Ailese got to work, Ell was so buried into her work that she didn't even notice Ailese. "Hey Ell, any messages?" "Oh, hi, boss. Yes, I put them on your desk. Could you please sign off on the contracts that are on your desk, please?" Ell dragged her voice. "Okay, I will have them signed today. I promise, just give me a few minutes, and I will deliver them to you myself." "Oh, thanks, boss."

As soon as Ailese sat down, there was a knock at her door. It was Andrew. He was anxious to see her. "Hello, you look refreshed and ready to work today, huh?" Ailese didn't respond to the comment. She just looked up and smiled at Andrew and went back to what she was doing. Andrew was making small conversation, and her responses were short and quick. He wanted to just stare at her beautiful face, but he knew that it would be rude. Andrew sat down in the chair across from Ailese and crossed his legs. Ailese looked up from the folder and closed it. "So, what's up, Andrew? Anything new?" "I just wanted to know what your take was on the Nelson contract? Have you seen the numbers and the relocation information?" "Actually, we could go over that right now together if you want." "Okay, meet me in the conference room so we can discuss it in private." "Okay, I am right behind you." Ailese grabbed the file and walked out with Andrew. When they got to the conference room, Andrew turned on the lights and offered Ailese a seat. They both went over the contracts very carefully because Ailese was deliberative about a few things and Andrew was too.

Ailese let out a quiet yawn. Andrew looked at her and lifted his brow.

"I am so sorry. That was so rude. Please forgive me. My sleeping pattern is a bit off." Ailese wanted to kick herself for telling him that it was something that she could have kept to herself. "Oh, I hope we're not working you too hard. I mean, I know that it could be a bit overwhelming." Ailese shook her head, no. "I'm fine. My life, it's just …. Ailese paused. My life and my schedule are a bit crazy, so I do, from time to time, get a bit tired." "I can only imagine, -you're a wife, a mom, a provider. Maybe you should go to a spa or something. I hear that spas can relax you. I know Denise goes to the spa, and always feels like a new person."

"Well, thanks. I will have to look into that. So, let's make sure we're on the same page with this contract. We need to rethink the location and redo some numbers, right?" Andrew agreed. They worked hard and put their heads together, and before they knew it, they were done, and they were happy with the contracts. Ailese heard Ell's voice on the phone intercom, and she picked it up. Ell called her to let her know that D'Andra was there to see her. "Are we done here, Andrew?" "Yes, we are. I'll walk back with you."

"Hello Andrew, nice to see you again." "You too, D'Andra." Andrew walked back to his office. "Hey sis, what brings you here? Ailese noticed that D'Andra had a huge shopping bag in her hand. Come on, let's go into my office." They hugged each other and chatted a bit. "So, I have something to show you. D'Andra took the huge square package out of the huge shopping bag. Here is the picture frame, for Mommie's birthday present." D'Andra took off the brown paper that covered the frame. "Wow, sis, it's so beautiful.

This is Mommie. You know it has her name written all over it. You did a terrific job, like I knew you would."

D'Andra was pleased that her sister loved the picture frame; they admired it together. D'Andra, Mommie is going to love it. I can't wait for her to open this gift with the picture of all her family in this frame." "I know, I can't wait either." "Ell, could you come into my office for a minute, please? I want to show you something." "I will be right there." "Ell, isn't this the most beautiful picture frame you have ever seen?" Ell let out a gasp. "Oh, my yes, it is; it is the most beautiful picture frame, and the picture is even more gorgeous. Your family is so beautiful, boss." "This is for our Mommie, well, she's our grandmother, but we all call her Mommie. Her birthday is in a few weeks, and this is a gift for her." "Wow, D'Andra, you have great taste." "I know, doesn't she? I tell her that all the time, and she doesn't believe me."

After D'Andra left, Ailese called her mom to try and talk her into changing the phone number, but she had got her voice mail. Ailese had just remembered that her mom had taken Don to the airport. He was going on a business trip. She would try her later, so she went back to work. Ailese finished the contracts that Ell needed, so she thought that she would hand -deliver them to her, so she stepped out of the office, but Ell wasn't at her desk, so she sat them on the desk. All of a sudden, she hears a voice coming from Andrew's office; it was Andrew. He seemed a bit irritated and upset with whomever he was speaking to on the phone. She heard him threatening someone his words were, "Get it done, or else." Ailese had never seen him so agitated and demanding before. She shrugged her shoulders and went to the break room to get a bottled water. She saw Ell in the break room pouring coffee. She looked like she had been crying. Ailese walked over to her. "Ell? She looked up at Ailese halfway so she wouldn't see that she had been crying. "Ell, are you okay? Sit down." Ailese led her to a chair and sat her down. What's wrong? Talk to me, please."

"I can't, boss, I just can't." Ailese felt that they needed to talk somewhere private. There were a lot of people in the break room. Ailese grabbed Ell's hand and led her back to her office. Ell followed her.

Ailese gave Ell the box of tissues that were on her desk and waited patiently for Ell to speak. Ell let out a long sigh and looked at Ailese. Andrew's voice was on the intercom, "Ailese, are you there?" "Andrew, I have to call you back, okay." "Oh, okay, bye." "It's okay, boss, go and see what he wants." "No, now tell me what's wrong." Before Ell spoke, she took a sip of her coffee, which was still hot.

"I've been seeing this guy for a while now, and we're very serious, so I thought. Ell took another sip of her coffee. He even asked me to move in with him, and I told him that I wasn't ready yet. He respected that, so he gave me a key and said that I could come there whenever I wanted to. He said that he was committed to me. He told me that he loved me, and I really believed him. Ell sniffed. I planned to surprise him by cooking for him yesterday because he had been working long hours, you know, I wanted to surprise him. When I walked into the house, he was with another woman; they were having sex on the couch! Ell began to sob even more. Her hands were shaking. He had the audacity to apologize for being drunk; that sick bastard, I gave him everything! He was my first. I was a virgin, and I let someone like him take that away from me." Ell's voice was in distress; she felt like he betrayed her.

Ailese took Ell's hands and put them in hers. "Ell, I am so sorry that he took you for granted, that he wasn't appreciative of your kindness. You know, sometimes we do go through things that aren't your fault, and it's his loss. Please know that you will get through this. I want you to walk with your head held up high because you will find that very special human being who will love you, respect you, and value you as a person. I know that it doesn't appear to you that everything will be okay, but it will be okay."

"I didn't want to burden you with this, and I tried to stay strong, but when he called me a little while ago, I just lost it." Ell finished her coffee and threw the cup in the trash can. "Hey, why don't you take some time to get yourself together and forward all the calls to me. Take as long as you need, okay?

I know what you're going through, and you feel like everything is in disarray, but give it time, and I am here for you." Ailese hugged Ell and smiled at her. Ell smiled back. "Thanks, boss." Ell took her tissue and wiped her face as she left the room.

"Andrew, you needed me to call you back. What can I do for you?" "Hello, yes, I was just going to let you know that I took the liberty of finishing the Nelson contract. Would you like to see it? I mean, that's if you have time." "Yes, but could you come into my office? Ell had something to take care of, so I had her forward all my calls to my office, and I don't want to miss any important calls." "Oh, I will be right there. So, these are the changes that you and I made. I think I forgot to tell you this, but this is just a rough draft, so please feel free to make any changes, Ailese." As Ailese reviewed the contract, Andrew noticed that she was smiling a lot. It looks like someone is pleased with the changes, huh?" He looked around the office and studied the pictures and art that were on the walls while Ailese looked over the contract. "Andrew, wow, this scares me." Andrew was shocked to hear those words. He thought that she would be satisfied. "What do you mean, is there something wrong?" "No, what I meant was that this scares me because we work good together, and hey, I am excited, so let's do this. When we put our heads together, we can't be stopped. To be honest, this is fantastic. It was executed flawlessly, and we did an excellent job on the contract. I must say, I am very impressed ... with us," Ailese smiled. "Well, thank you, Ailese, that means a lot to me. So, we both agree that the Nelson contract is ready then?" "Ditto, that means yes.

Like I said before, I think we make a great team." Andrew walked over to Ailese and shook her hand, and they both agreed that they make a good team.

Ailese was pleased how her day at work went. She hoped that her session with Dr. Salvino would go well. She was early, so she stopped by to see Karen.

Karen was talking to another worker at the front desk when she saw Ailese walk in. She asked Ailese if she had time for a short visit. Ailese told her that she did have time for a short visit "Sit, sit. How are you?" Ailese sat down in the comfortable, soft chair. "I am good, and you?" "Working really hard and we are so busy; hectic is good, though I don't remember the last time I worked a habitual schedule." "Really, wow, when was the last time you took a vacation or a day off?" "Like, never, Karen said, laughing. I mean, I am dedicated to my work, you know, but you know how we sometimes want a break." "Trust me, I have been there. How is the family?" My mom has asked about you a few times, and you know she loves you to death. The family is doing great. My sister is due to have that baby any day now. We're just counting down the days. I can't wait for her to have that baby." Karen smiled. "I am so happy to hear that your family is doing great and that bundle of joy will be here soon. Well,

I have to get going. I will talk to you later and tell everyone hi." "I will take care." Karen walked Ailese to the door.

Hello, doctor, how are you?" "I am just fine." Ailese hung up her coat and sat down in her usual spot. "Hello, Ailese, how are you today?" "I am very well."

"Ailese, could you give me a minute? I need to call my husband. It will only take a few minutes, do you mind?" "Oh, not at all. I need to use the restroom, so I will give you some privacy." "Thanks Ailese."

Ailese went into the restroom to freshen up. She brushed her hair, touched up her makeup, and used the lavatory. She took her time so she could give her doctor some privacy, and when she went back to the office, Dr. Salvino wasn't on the phone. She was waiting patiently for Ailese. "I hope I didn't take too long." "Oh, you're fine, actually, that was perfect timing, Dr. Salvino said with a smile.

Ailese sat down. She said a prayer to herself and took a deep breath. She was prepared for whatever Dr. Salvino was going to ask her. She wanted these dreams to stop and to understand why she was going through this! Ailese was there ever a time that he didn't beat you? I want you to recall a time when he didn't touch you and made you feel happy, okay." Ailese shook her head and closed her eyes tightly, trying to remember a time when he didn't hurt her or make her happy. At first, she had a hard time remembering but then, she started to remember. "He had gotten a promotion at his job and was making good money, so he knew that he couldn't mess up. He had to attend a lot of meetings, and he traveled a lot, so we didn't see each other a lot. Not seeing him a lot made me very happy."

"Okay, good, and was that the only time?" "Yes. "I want you to work on something for me. Think of this as a massive stepping stone; I want you to try and write his name down. This way you are facing your trepidation, and I know that this will be a challenge for you, but I want you to try. Even if you write the first letter of his name, it's progress." "Okay, doctor, I think I can do that; I feel confident enough." Dr. Salvino told Ailese that they needed to rebuild her self-esteem and to keep surrounding herself with people who were positive, valued her, and loved her. Dr. Salvino said that Ailese's self-esteem was not low, but her relationship with this monster had taken some of her self-worth. All this was true even though Ailese told herself every day that she was strong and that no matter what, she was going to live. Her self-esteem had always been a 7, no higher than that. No one knew that. Only Dr. Salvino saw it. She saw that 7 and was determined to make it a 10.

When Ailese was driving home, she thought that she would pick up Mikell's favorite magazines. He had mentioned that he didn't have time to pick them up, so she stopped at the bookstore. She bumped into Andrew. He was picking up some books himself. "Are you following me or what?" "I swear I'm not, don't call the cops." They both laughed. "Are you going to read all those books?" "Oh no, some are for me, and some are for Dana, see? Andrew showed Ailese the books that he picked out for Dana. Yes, I know I spoil her to death. I can't help it." "I don't think buying a child a lot of books is considered spoiling them. I think you're giving them knowledge. They can never ever have enough books." "You're right. So, what are you buying, huh? I see someone loves old school cars." Andrew took a magazine out of her hand. "Well, yes, but it's not me; it's my husband." Andrew gave the magazine back to her. Ailese's cellphone was ringing. She excused herself and took the call. "Hey, baby, I am so sorry. I have been really busy today that I didn't get to call you." "Hey to you too, it's okay, same here. I am so sorry to do this to you at the last minute, and I know that you're still out. Chris wanted me to work out with him, and the kids can't stay with their aunt, so I was wondering if it would be okay if Armont could watch the girls until you got home?" "Oh, yes, that's fine. I should be home soon. Okay, I love you too. Have a great workout."

Ailese returned to the bookstore, but she didn't see Andrew anywhere, so she went over to the romance section to look at some books, then over to the young adult section, where she felt someone come up from behind her. She turned around and it was Andrew, being silly. "Oh, I thought you had left." "Oh no, I'm still here. I'm going to let you in on a little secret. I stay in here for hours," he whispered in her ear. Ailese lifted her brow. "Really, what's wrong with that? I do too. What was the longest you stayed in here?"

"Um, let's see, let me think, oh, four hours!" "Oh, my, you beat me. I'm not liking you too much." Ailese smiled at Andrew. "Hey, hit me if I am out of line, but would you like to join me for a cup of coffee?" "Hey, why not? That sounds good. Did you want to go to the one next door?" "We do think a lot alike. Are you done? Because if not, you could take your time. I don't mind."

"No, I am done. What about you?" "I am done, after you." Ailese started walking to the register, and Andrew was right behind her. They both stood in line, chatting with one another. When it was Ailese's turn, Andrew walked with her to the cash register, and as she put her books up on the counter, so did he. "What are doing? She asked softly. You're cutting in line, sir. Now you've got to get to the back of the line, mister." Andrew smiled. The lady asked him if she needed to ring up everything together or separately, he told her to ring it all up together. "Andrew, no, I can't let you do that. I just can't." Andrew overlooked her, and Ailese didn't want to make a scene, so she remained quiet until they left the store. When they were outside, Ailese confronted Andrew. She told him she didn't want him to pay for the books, but he still didn't reply and instead led her to the coffeehouse next door. Since Andrew avoided the topic, she dropped it and forgot about it the rest of the night.

An attractive woman came into the coffee shop. Ailese had noticed her eyeing Andrew the entire time that they were there, and she knew he would ignore the lady because she was trying too hard. She should have approached him in her own selfish way. Ailese enjoyed being the center of attention. She wasn't sure why she enjoyed people staring at them. He wasn't anything to her, maybe a friend? Andrew was enjoying their tête-à-tête, and Ailese felt the same way. "Andrew, I had so much fun. You are such a goof ball though. Oops, did that come out of my mouth?" "Um, sorry, I have bad news. Yes, that did come out of your mouth. Let me walk you to your car, okay?" Andrew took Ailese's hand, and absently they both began to walk arm in arm the whole way to the car. As Andrew was looking for his keys, Ailese took out her wallet and handed him some money, which he declined. Ailese tried to put it in his pants pocket, but he would always step backwards really quickly, and she couldn't catch him fast enough. "Okay, fine, but don't feel bad if I start to disown you, okay?" Ailese laughed, and so did Andrew. They both got into their cars and drove off. On the way home, Ailese realized that Andrew was and is a great person. He was full of life and surprises. She thought she'd give him a chance to be her friend, to get to know her. She didn't want to rush into anything. She'd take things slow. Mikell never minded Ailese having male friends, and the same went for Mikell. They both knew their male and female friends, and everyone got along fine. Ailese had always gotten along with males better than females. That never surprised Mikell because he knew 100 percent of the time females just got along with the opposite sex, and he never had a reason not to trust Ailese.

The next morning, Ailese was up before Mikell, so she fixed everyone breakfast. She wasn't too hungry, so she ate a light breakfast and made some coffee as well. She was happy to see the kids when they came in to the kitchen. They all chatted with one another. Adrieana reminded her mom that she needed help with her English assignment. Ailese told her that she would be picking them up from school today and that they would work on her assignment.

Mikell had dragged himself into the kitchen. He was complaining about him overdoing it at the gym. He sat down at the table while Ailese took his breakfast out of the microwave and served him coffee and juice with his breakfast. "Baby, did you get your magazines? I left them in the den." "No, I didn't, I haven't gone in there yet. Thank you so much, you didn't have to, but I know you love me so much. I'm going to go and get them right now." Mikell walked into the den. When Mikell came back, he had some aspirin in his hand and the magazines in another. "Baby, remind me the next time I go to the gym not to overdo it; every bone in my body hurts, ouch. It's killing me. I think I need to soak in the tub or something," Mikell said, rubbing his arms.

As time went by, Andrew and Ailese were becoming closer, and closer so she decided to have Andrew meet Mikell since he'd already met the kids, with the exception of Armont. Ailese talked to D'Andra a couple of times about how close Andrew, and she had become. D'Andra had suggested that Ailese have Andrew meet Mikell. "Hey Andrew, it's me. How are you?" "Heyyy, you. I am fine, and you?" "I will be good if you could do me a huge favor. Okay, just listen, okay, it's nothing bad," Ailese said with a laugh.

"You know how you get with those favors of yours." Andrew laughed back. "Okay, I was wondering how your schedule looks on Friday around seven?" "It looks good, and yes, I am looking at my schedule. I'm free, so what's the favor?" "I wanted to invite you to dinner at my place. Can you please come to dinner?" "Anything for you, of course. I will be there. What's the address, hun?" "It's 9269 Lenwood Valley Road, in Shelby, of course." "Okay, I will be there at seven. See you then."

Ailese was ready before Mikell. They were going to a lunch meeting. She made sure she looked extra fabulous for the lunch meeting. "Mikell, are you almost ready?" "Yes, in five minutes, baby." Mikell was in a fine suit, and Ailese wore a black dress with small silver diamonds going down each side. "We look fierce, don't you think?" "Yes we do, they both laughed. Karla was not yet at the restaurant when they arrived, but the maître d' showed them to their table and handed them their menus. The restaurant was very fancy; people paid a hundred dollars for a meal here or even for one dish. Ailese was happy with the restaurant that Karen had chosen; it was beautiful, it was just outside Shelby, and this was her first time there. Ailese thought that this would be a good time to remind Mikell that Andrew would be coming to dinner on Friday night, since they were alone. "Mik, don't forget to be home before seven on Friday. I invited Andrew for dinner." "Yes, hun, Mikell said, and went back to his menu. I won't forget Ailese. I am excited to meet him." "Are you? Ailese smiled. "Baby, why don't we order some wine or something while we're waiting." "Okay sure. Can you order it? I will be right back. I need to go to the ladies' room." "Okay." When Ailese returned, there was wine in her glass. She took a taste of it and complimented Mikell for picking a good one.

"Hello, I am so sorry I am late. Forgive me." Karla took off her coat, sat down, and made herself comfortable. Karla had black shiny hair, one side long and one side short, with the back tapered. She had dark brown eyes and wore expensive eyeglasses. She had a tiny figure. She was nothing that Ailese had pictured. "Hello, Mrs. Lashae I'm Karla Kabb; I am so excited to meet you and to meet the face behind that gorgeous voice." They both shook hands and smiled at each other. "You can call me Ailese. That's fine." "Okay, call me Karla, she laughed. A few minutes later, Emmanuel and Sedrick had arrived. Ailese loved those guys to death and was glad to see them. She gave them both a huge hug before they sat down.

They all greeted one another, ordered their meals, and chatted with one another. Karla began to start the meeting by introducing the topics that were to be discussed. She took out her briefcase and pulled out a folder that contained documents. She handed everyone their documents and explained to them that the company's own personal lawyer had already looked over the documents and they were legit. She asked that they look them over carefully before signing. Karla was going to be Sedrick's manager, and Mikell was going to be his manager/producer; he would be responsible for all of Sedrick's music, producing it, and making sure he meets deadlines, etcetera. Karla asked If anyone had any questions. No one had any questions. She handed Ailese a document and asked her to read it over before signing anything. The document explained the fee that she was to expect being on the tracks with Sedrick and so on. "Mikell, Ailese whispered in his ear. Look at these numbers," she said, pointing to the document. "I know, baby, and you're worth every penny. Go ahead and sign it. It's legit baby." "Yes, I know that, but this is a lot of money. I would have done it for free because it's what I love to do."

"Yes, I know, but you're worth it." Everyone signed their contracts, including Ailese.

When they arrived at home, Ailese checked on the kids, and Armont did a superior job of babysitting his sisters. "Here ya go, sixty bucks all for you," Mikell said as he handed Armont the money. "Thanks Dad and Mom." "You did an excellent job," Mikell said, hugging Armont. "Mom, the girls are in their rooms. I'll go and get them. Armont went to tell the girls that Mom and Dad were home and as soon as they knew, they came running to them and gave them huge hugs. "Hey guys, did you have fun with your big brother?" "Yes, the girls answered their mom. "Mom, Armont is the best babysitter ever," Ashanee said with enthusiasm.

"Being that you guys were good, you guys can have two scoops of ice cream if you'd like some." The kids thanked their dad and went into the kitchen to help themselves to some ice cream while Mikell and Ailese went into the bedroom to change into something more comfortable. Ailese answered her phone. It was her mother. "Hi, Mom, what's wrong?" "I think we should just change the number. This time I heard the voice, I didn't recognize it at all." Ailese interrupted the conversation. "Mom, what did this person say?" Mikell sat down next to Ailese. He wanted to know what was going on. Alonda was silent for a few seconds. "They said that we would be dead and that it was only a matter of time, and hung up. I don't know why people can't find something else to do with their time. I'm not scared. It's just that I am tired of getting these calls. I want the number to be unlisted."

"Okay, Mom, I will take care of it right now. It's still early, and I will call you back in a bit. I love you, Mom."

"What's going on with Mom?" Mikell had a perplexed look on his face. "Mom's been getting crank calls all hours of the night, and in the beginning, they wouldn't say anything but now they are threatening my mom and dad. They're not scared but tired of the calls, so I am going to call the phone company to change the number. I told my mom when we were there the other day to change it, but she didn't want to."

"What's going on here? Mikell shook his head. I just don't understand people, he said. Yes, I think you should just change the number."

Ailese called the phone company, fortunately, they were still open, so she was able to tell them what she needed, and it took no time at all.

"Mom, this is your new phone number. Are you ready?" "Wow, that was fast. Let me get a pen and paper. Okay, I am ready." Ailese gave the new number to her mother. "Mom, it should work in one hour, so please let me know if it isn't, okay." "Thanks, baby, I appreciate you. Love you." "I love you too, so don't forget to call everyone and give them the new number, and don't worry about Dad, he'll learn the new number in no time. If there's any problem, just call me." Ailese put the new number on her cell phone and on the house phone, and she gave it to the kids and Mikell as well.

An hour later, Don called to speak to Ailese. "Hi Dad, how are you?" Ailese dragged out "the how are you" part, because she knew what was coming next. "Hi, sweetie I just wanted to thank you for releasing the stress. We are grateful, and your mom seems better now. Ailese was shocked. She was expecting her dad to be a bit disappointed, but her dad was thanking her. Guess what? The phone number was easy to remember. It wasn't hard at all. Thanks, baby girl."

"You're welcome, Dad." Now that Ailese has a peace of mind because her mother and father do.

It was Friday, and Ailese was ecstatic about Andrew meeting Mikell and Armont. She even doubled- checked the menu and her grocery list to make sure she hadn't forgotten anything. She wanted everything to be perfect. She and Andrew made sure that the directions from Map Quest were correct and accurate. Andrew was excited. He thought about what Ailese would wear, what her house looked like, and what she would make for dinner. He couldn't stop thinking about the dinner. They had come so far that he felt so close to her more than ever before. He knew that it was a platonic relationship; he furtively wished that it was more, but he was fine with it. Andrew made sure that nothing went wrong tonight; he didn't want to disappoint Ailese and her family.

The doorbell rang at exactly 7:00 p.m. on the dot. Mikell answered the door while Ailese was putting the finishing touches on the dinner. Mikell opened the door, and Andrew stood there holding flowers and wine in one hand and a gift bag in the other. "Hello, you must be Andrew? I'm Mikell Ailese's husband. Come on in.

Andrew could smell the aroma when he walked into the house. Let me take these off your hands." Mikell sat the items on the table. "It's very nice to meet you. They both shook hands. Andrew was wearing a dark blue suit with a sky-blue shirt and a red tie. He looked very handsome. You have a gorgeous home; wow, it's a beauty." "Well, thanks, Andrew." "Hi Ailese, I'm on time." "Yes, you are. Ailese came out of the kitchen and into the living room and walked over to him and hugged him. He hugged her back. So, you've met my husband." Ailese put her head on Mikell's shoulders. "Yes, I have. Oh, I have something for everyone, is it okay if I get them off that table?" Andrew pointed. "Yes, go right ahead," Ailese said, with a smile. "Speaking of everyone, where are the kids? Are they here? I have something for them too." "Oh yes, they're here. I'll go and get them."

Ailese came back with the kids and introduced Armont to Andrew. Armont shook his hand, and greeted him. The girls were asking about Dana and why she wasn't here with him. Andrew gave Ailese silk flowers, and he gave the wine to Mikell. Andrew gave the girls the latest craft book that came with a necklace that they could make, and finally he gave Armont a new cover for his iPod, which Ailese had mentioned that he wanted. Everyone thanked Andrew for their gifts. "Well, I hope everyone's hungry because I made a feast for us to enjoy. Let's eat. Armont, could you please show Mr. Andrew where he can wash up for dinner and make sure your sisters does as well, and then lead everyone into the dining room when everyone is finished?"

Armont lead everyone into the dining room while Mikell helped his wife carry all the food to the table.

"Wow, Ailese, everything looks appetizing." Andrew looked at all the food and inhaled all the scents all at once with his eyes closed. He couldn't wait until he tasted them all. Mikell was in charge of saying the grace and blessing the food, and afterward everyone started to pass around the platters of food around the table. Ailese made sugar snap green beans, pot roast, romaine green leaf salad, and a fruit salad. She also made red potatoes, and for dessert, she made a plain cheesecake and a lemon cake. "So, Andrew, how do you like living in Shelby?" "I love it. It's clean. The people are nice and respectful. I can't complain. I hear that Shelby has come a long way." "Yes, it has, the population is growing every day, and Shelby is growing every day, you know." "Yes, I'm thinking about buying some property in a year or two. I don't know if I want to buy property and build a business or buy some condos and occupy them. Not sure yet." "That sounds like a good investment."

"I admire the work that you do, Mikell. I mean, you started something from the ground up and worked your way to the top; you must be a very smart man." Andrew took a sip of his wine. "Thanks, man." After everyone was finished with their dinner, Andrew and Mikell volunteered to clear the table, put up the food, and load the dishwasher.

Ailese took a load off, sat down in the living room with the kids, and watched television. "Mom, could I go into my room now?" "Yes, you can, Adrieana." All the kids had decided to go into their rooms. Ailese went to check on the guys; they were getting along very well, and she was pleased. "Ailese, would you like some more wine?" "Yes, actually, that would be nice." Mikell fixed her a glass of wine and brought it to her. Andrew sat down across from Ailese with a glass of wine in his hand and watched television with Ailese while Mikell was in the kitchen fixing himself a glass of wine. Andrew would sneak a peek at her when no one was looking, then stop completely. He didn't want to offend Mikell. "This show is so hilarious. Andrew laughed. Hey, Ailese, do you know who got me hooked on this show?" "Who?" "Denice, of all people."

"Really, yeah, it's one of my favorite shows. I don't get to watch it much."

"Andrew, do you like sports?" "Oh yes, I love hockey, basketball, and football."

Mikell was flabbergasted. He didn't know anyone who loved hockey and was a fan of basketball and football; this was his lucky day. "That's strange, we love the same sports. I don't know anyone who loves hockey. Have you been to any games?"

"No, because I don't know anyone who likes hockey, and I don't like going to a game by myself, but hey, we should hook up sometimes and go to a game."

"That sounds like a deal." Ailese smiled at the men who were admiring each other. Everything was going well so far. "Mikell you guys should definitely go to a hockey game. I'm sure you too would have a ball."

Mikell and Andrew shook their heads. Andrew and Mikell talked about hockey for hours. Ailese left the room a few times when the kids required her help with something. The guys sometimes didn't even notice that she left the room because they were so wrapped up in their conversation.

Andrew, Ailese, and Mikell stayed up until midnight talking. They didn't realize what time it was. Andrew called his driver to pick him up. He didn't drive himself, he had been drinking wine, and he didn't want to take a risk and drive. When his driver arrived at the house, Ailese and Mikell walked him to the door. Ailese gave Andrew a hug, Mikell shook his hand, and they had settled on going to a hockey game really soon.

"Andrew is a very nice person. I am glad that you guys became good, close friends. He's very respectful … I like him." "I'm glad that you do. You know you guys have so much in common; that's crazy, huh?"

"Yes, it is. Maybe we'll all become good friends."

Ailese hadn't heard from D'Andra since she returned from her business trip, so she decided to call her and check in. "Hello, hey, Chris. Long time no hear," chuckled Ailese. "Yeah, I know I've been gone on business. How are you?" "I am fine. You know you need to remind my hubby that he needs to take it easy when you guys go to the gym. I can't remember the last time he's ever taken medicine, but he had to this time; every bone in his body was hurting."

"Oh boy. Chris dragged his words. I better make sure he doesn't overdo it, or I'll be in trouble," Chris grinned.

"Yes, you will be in trouble. No, I am kidding. Hey, is my sis home?" "Oh yeah, let me get her, okay?" "Okay."

"Hello, sis, how are you? I've been meaning to call you, but I have been swamped! "Oh, it's okay, sis. I just thought I'd give you a call to see how things were going. How did your trip go?"

"It went well. I still feel a bit jet lagged, though. So how did the dinner go with Andrew?"

"It went excellent. Mikell and Andrew got along very well. They have so much in common that it was scary. I made a feast, and everyone was pleased with the dinner; Andrew was very impressed. He brought me some lovely silk flowers and even brought gifts for the kids and some expensive wine for Mikell."

"Wow, he did go all out, huh? Well, I am so happy that the dinner went well."

"Me too, sis, thanks for suggesting it."

"No problem. Hold on one sec, okay? Ailese could hear Chris and D'Andra in the background, but she could only make out a few words: something about Chris leaving town again. Sorry sis, hey, I have to call you later, okay, sorry, but I will call you back."

After a few minutes, had passed, D'Andra called Ailese back. She was a bit disconcerted. "I don't know why he has to go away so much. He never traveled this much. It's absurd! I mean, I know that he has a lot of responsibilities, but I am so ready to have kids, and we can't since we never see each other." D'Andra let out a long moan. "Oh, sis, I know how you feel. I do. You know how Chris is. He likes to get things done. I am sure things will settle down soon and you and Chris will have more time together."

"Yeah, you're right, I'm just venting, that's all. I mean, I get lonely being in this huge house alone." "You can come here, you know that, anytime, sis."

After Ailese hung up with her sister, her mom called. She was a bit frenzied and annoyed. "Mom, what's wrong? Is it Don?"

"No, honey, I am sorry to bother you, but we're still getting the crank calls. I don't get it. Our number is unlisted, right?"

"Yes, that's right, and no, it doesn't make any sense at all. What is going on here?" "I thought that if you had an unlisted number, no one would be able to retrieve the number. This person has a lot of time on their hands or something; we don't have any enemies, you know."

"Mom, I'm sure you don't have any enemies. I believe that. I just don't know what else to do. Let me look more into it. Mom, let me look into this more, okay?"

"Okay." "But, Mom, what do you guys want to do in the mean time?"

"We may just stay in a hotel or something because this is working my last nerves. I mean, this person is threatening our lives, and we can't sleep because they call at all hours of the night, and we need our sleep, especially Dad."

"Mom, I am on my way to pick you guys up."

"No, honey I won't hear of it. You know that Dad has a weird schedule, and we don't want to put the stress on you. We don't want to give this person an open invitation to stalk you guys too. It makes sense." "Okay, Mom, I'm going to put you guys up in a hotel. I will make your reservation, and I'll email you the confirmation, okay."

"Ailese, I can't let you do that. You've done so much already." Ailese interrupted her mom.

"Mom, please. I don't mind, and besides, I want you and Dad to be safe and sound, so I will send you an email so you can print out the information." Ailese hung up before her mom could argue with her.

Ailese told Mikell what was going on with her mom and dad, and he agreed that they should stay in a hotel just until things get figured out. He wanted them to be safe as well. He told Ailese that he would go to the hotel just to make sure they were settled in. Ailese made the reservations and emailed the information to her mom. Alonda called her to let her know that she got the email and thanked her. "Baby, why don't we all just take a drive over there. I need to make a run to the store anyhow. I'll get the kids."

"Okay, let me put on some shoes."

When they got to the hotel, Mikell and the kids stayed in the lobby while Ailese checked her parents into the hotel. "Mom and Dad, I gave the clerk strict directions. I told her not to forward any calls to your room, unless it's the cleaning lady or the desk clerk, okay? If we need to get a hold of you, we could always call you guys on your cell." "Okay, okay, baby, thank you." Alonda smiled at her daughter. She knew her daughter loved her and wanted her mom to be safe and feel comfortable. She knew that her daughter would take care of her. They all took the elevator to the third floor and checked into room 322. She waited until her mom and dad were settled in.

"Mom, Dad, please don't hesitate to call me or sis, okay?" "Okay." Ailese left and closed the door behind her.

"I don't know what I would do without her. I just hate that she's in the middle of this mess. I mean, we don't know who this person is or who keeps threatening us. Who do they think they are? It burns me."

"I know, honey, let's get some rest." Don hugged his wife and told her that it was going to be okay.

As Ailese was waiting for the elevator, she began to think terrible thoughts; the dreams came back, and maybe he was out to hurt the people that she loved. Ailese shrugged her shoulders, and shook her head, telling herself it was impossible. She put the terrible thoughts out of her head. When the elevator doors opened, Ell was standing there, all dressed up. "Hi, Ell."

Ell was astounded to see her. She had a look on her face like she didn't want to be seen by Ailese in a hotel anyway. Ailese could tell that Ell was a bit nervous, but she spoke anyway. "What brings you here, boss?" "Oh, I had to see someone, and you." "Oh, I'm here with a friend, for dinner. Ailese wondered why Ell was acting unusually. She said goodbye to Ell, who stayed behind in the elevator.

"Ailese, it's sis. What's this about Mom and Dad staying in a hotel? Why wasn't I notified of this? What's going on?" "Hey sis, I thought that Mom and Dad told you. Their lives were threatened, so I changed the phone number and it was unlisted, but they kept getting the calls all night, so it was my idea to put them up in a hotel so they could be safe."

"Who is this son of a bitch threatening our mom and dad? I would like to give them a piece of my mind. Who the hell are they?" D'Andra became livid. "I know, sis, I feel the same way. I want them safe. I'm sorry you were left in the dark. They probably didn't want to worry you. Did they call you or something?"

"Yes, they did. I told them that they should have told me what was going on. I don't care. This is important. Thanks, sis, for keeping them safe. I love you. I mean, who is this character, and how did they get an unlisted number?"

"I'm not sure sis, they're safe, maybe this will blow over." It's probably some kid that needs some attention. Who knows! "Well, I've got to get to work. We'll talk later." "Yes, okay. Love you."

When Ailese arrived at work, Ell was her usual self this time, and Ailese wasn't going to bring up why she had acted strangely toward her when they were at the hotel the other day. Ailese had a meeting with some clients today, so she made sure everything was ready, especially her. "Ell, is the conference room ready?"

"Yes, boss, it is, and yes, I remembered to get the herbal tea for Mrs. Johnson."

"Thanks, Ell, you're the best. Could you please let me know when they arrive, please?"

"No problem." Ailese didn't see Andrew in his office. When she checked her email messages, he told her he would be in the office later, because he had some things, he had to take care of. As always, Ailese kept busy until it was time for her meeting. Ell notified her when her clients had arrived. When Ailese was starting to head to the conference room. Ell stopped her and told her that she had an urgent call. Ailese took the call in a vacant office. It was Alonda, and she was very upset that Ailese couldn't understand what she was saying. Andrew got Ailese's attention, he saw that she was on an important call. He came into the office and wrote on a piece of paper that he and Ell would cover for her until she was done. Andrew touched Ailese's shoulder and gave her a fretful look. He then left the room. When Alonda had finally calmed down, she told Ailese the bad news. "This morning your dad had to come home to get something that he needed, and he found the house destroyed. Everything is in disarray. Everything that we cherished is destroyed; gone. Everything we worked hard for!"

"What! Ailese couldn't believe her ears; who could do such a thing? Mom, did you guys call the police yet?" Alonda began to sob even more. "No, not yet." "Mom, listen to me ask for Officer Brown. Tell him that I recommended him. He may remember Mikell and me from the break-in that Mikell had. I'm just glad that no one got hurt. Alonda was silent. Mom, did anyone get hurt? Mom, please tell me what happened and if anyone was hurt."

"They killed all of our beautiful birds and emptied the fish tank. Honey, I'm scared. Who wants to hurt us? Thank god we weren't home. It could have been worse." Alonda began to cry hysterically. Ailese felt antagonism come upon her. She needed to stay calm, cool, and collected so she could stay focused. "Mom, it's going to be alright. Did you need me to come over? Because I can."

"No, honey, your dad and George are here. George just got back from being was out of town, so he didn't see or hear anything. I'll call the man that you told me to call. Officer Brown, right?"

"Yes, mom, please call me and don't hesitate, okay?" "Please don't leave work. We will be okay. I will call you later."

"Mom! How could I focus on work knowing that someone is trying to hurt you and Dad? Tell me, huh?" Ailese was in ire. Someone hurting the people she loved sent her emotions flying off the handle. "Honey, I know that you're upset, but we are going to be fine, you hear me? Now, listen to me. After Ailese had sat down. She began to feel weak in the knees. We need to stay strong; we can't let this person get us down."

"Mom, please, they killed the birds and the fish. Yes, it could have been worse. This doesn't sit well with me at all, Mom, so please make sure you give all the details. Tell him what's missing, what's out of order. Tell the officer about the fish and the birds, and most importantly, tell the officer about the crank calls. Tell everything to Officer Brown. Mom, I can be there soon," Ailese said, Alonda interrupted Ailese. "Ailese, it's okay. We are okay. Now come over when you're done with work. Just come to the hotel. I will call you as soon as we get back to the hotel."

After Ailese hung up with her mother, she began to feel sick. She looked up, and Andrew was standing there in the doorway with arms folded. "Ailese, is everything okay? I came to check on you. Andrew walked over to Ailese, pulled up a chair, and sat down next to her. Ailese, you don't look so good. Are you sick or was it the call?" "I will be fine. We need to get back to our client's. I'm sorry that my phone call took so long." Ailese rose from her chair and began to walk out of the office until Andrew pulled her back in. He closed the door and asked her politely to have a seat. "Now, I know that you're a bit of a private person, and I respect that. Please know that what we discuss will never go past these walls. Anytime you need to talk, I'm here." Ailese looked at Andrew and saw how genuine he was. She wanted to tell him what was going on, but she couldn't. She didn't want him to think that she was weak. That she couldn't handle situations like these; she would never cry or show weakness in front of him. She didn't want to show it today, especially after that night when she had that awful dream. Andrew put his hand on her shoulder to let her know that he was there for her. "Whatever it is, I am sure it will work itself out." Andrew gave her shoulders a light rub.

After the meeting was over, Ailese called Mikell to let him know what was happening. He too was upset, and they both agreed that Alonda and Don should never go back to the house ever again. Mikell and Ailese met at the hotel to check on her parents. She felt a little bit better, she'll feel even better once she sees their faces. "Hey, Mom. Hey, Dad." Ailese hugged both of them. D'Andra and Chris were already there. Ailese and everyone acknowledged their presence. "I'm so sorry you guys are going through this ordeal. I love you guys so much. How did it go with Officer Brown?" "He asked all these questions, and we had a lot of answers. He was very helpful. They dusted for prints, and we're waiting to hear what the results are. You know all that, et cetera, et cetera. I hope they catch this sick asshole! "We feel the same way, Mom," D'Andra said as she hugged her mother.

When Ailese was leaving, she ran into Andrew, who was also leaving, and he asked her to walk with him to his car. Ailese was very quiet. She wasn't focused on what Andrew was saying. Sometimes he would have to repeat himself. When they got to Andrew's car, he gave her another chance to open up to him and to get whatever was bothering her off her chest, but Ailese didn't take the chance. Ailese was anxious to get to D'Andra's; she needed to be there.

Driving to D'Andra's seemed like it took forever to get there; there were more red lights than green ones. Finally, Ailese pulled up to the driveway, and she noticed that Mikell's car was there. When she rang the doorbell, Mikell answered the door and gave her a huge hug and kiss.

Alonda and Don were sitting on the couch, and D'Andra wasn't in sight. Ailese sat next to them, gave them a hug, and began to chat with them. A few minutes later, D'Andra came down the stairs, and Ailese could tell by the look on D'Andra's face, that something was wrong. Ailese walked over to her sister to comfort her.

"D, what's wrong?" D'Andra let out a long sigh. "It's Chris. I need him here, and he's out of town on business. I begged him to come home because we all need to be together as a family. I'm upset with him. He said that he couldn't come home early. I even told him that this is a family crisis, but he wouldn't budge."

Ailese took her sister's hand and put it up to her face. "Sis don't get all worked up. Maybe he couldn't come home. You know how demanding his job is. I'm sure that he wanted to be here. We all know that he wants to be here."

"Mikell has a demanding job, sis. We all have demanding jobs, and we're all here, sis, so tell me what's wrong with this picture? He's been acting weird these past few months, you know, and I can't figure him out." "Sis, he's probably a little stressed. Remember how it was when you started your own company? You were stressed out a lot, you had to put in long hours, and there were a lot of sacrifices made." "I don't want to talk about this anymore; I don't want Mom and Dad to see me upset. They have enough to worry about."

Ailese dropped the subject, as her sister had requested. She focused her entire attention on her mother and father. She wanted to know who was out to hurt her mother and father. Alonda had explained to everyone what happened when Officer Brown took the report. Officer Brown had called in a special team to take fingerprints, but they were unsuccessful. Officer Brown said that the burglar may have worn gloves and wasn't new to burglarizing people, and had committed these crimes before. Officer Brown suggested that Alonda and Don didn't come back to the house now that it is a crime scene.

Alonda and Don made sure they answered every question honest, and meticulous, so that the police had enough information so that they could catch the criminal. The officers also went around the neighborhood to ask questions, but no one heard or saw anything. Officer Brown will be keeping in contact with them with any new information.

"Mom, do you want anything to drink or eat?"

"No, Ailese, I am fine. I am going to go and make some calls, and then I'm going to lie down. I am a bit exhausted," Alonda said with a long yawn as she stood up to give everyone a hug before excusing herself.

"Mom, let me make sure you're comfortable, okay?"

"Oh, you're so sweet. That would be great."

"Let me help you to your room." Mikell took Alonda's hand and led her upstairs to her room. "Dad, I told Mom the same thing that I am going to tell you, so I want you to listen, D'Andra said in a stiff voice. I know you and Mom have your pride, and I am not mad at that at all, but if you need anything, please don't hesitate to ask. I want you guys to feel at home.

If you guys never want to go back to the house, that's fine with me. I love you guys. D'Andra began to sob. Don wiped her face and gave her a kiss on her cheek. I don't want anything to happen to you guys. I mean, when I lost. D'Andra paused. I don't know what I would do if. She paused again, and began to sob even more. "Sis, it's going to be okay; we're going to be okay."

Ailese kept in touch with Officer Brown and the Shelby Police Department regarding the investigation. She would call them at least once a week to check if they had new leads. She felt that the investigation was not going well. They had no leads so far. Ailese felt that the Police Department was doing their job, but since this criminal had covered his tracks, it wasn't going to be easy.

Alonda and Don were still staying with D'Andra, and Chris. Alonda and Don made it their home as best as they could and helped out a lot around the house and with the cooking as well. Ailese would come over to visit from time to time to check on them; she would call them as well. D'Andra loved that Alonda would have dinner ready when she got home, and when Alonda went back to work, D'Andra missed her mom's cooking.

Today, Ailese was going to see Dr. Salvino. She had missed some appointments due to her family crisis, but Dr. Salvino understood.

When Ailese and Andrew were eating lunch, she had gotten a call from Sedrick, who was so excited. "Ailese, guess what we're done with picking all the songs for the album, but I wanted your opinion on some things. I know that you're not my manager, but your input means a lot to me. Do you think that you could come by the studio later?" "Oh, sure, I am so excited for you. I could come by around eight. Is that okay?"

"That would be perfect. I will see you then. Oh, hey, Mikell wants to speak to you."

"Hey beautiful wife, hey, if I am not in the studio when you arrive, please wait for me, I have some things to take care of, see you later?"

"Okay, love you too." After Ailese hung up the phone, she could feel Andrew looking at her, so she made eye contact with him.

"What? Why are you looking at me like that?" "Nothing, so what's going on?"

When you were on the phone, you sounded ecstatic."

"Oh well, Ailese said after a brief pause. Well, that was Sedrick. He is a nice gentleman. I actually did some work with him."

"Work? What do you mean?" "Well, I have a secret to tell you. Promise you won't tell anyone, but I'm a singer and songwriter, and I don't like to brag or appear arrogant, so not many people know." Andrew smiled at Ailese, took her hand in his, and told her that she should be proud of herself. "You just told me, and I don't feel like you're being bigheaded.

That is great. I would love to hear you sing sometime. I am serious. I bet your voice sounds like an angel." Ailese took a bite of her salad and smiled.

"Hey, come to the studio with me. It would be great. You could hear Sedrick and me."

"Okay, are you sure I won't be in the way?"

"Yes, I'm sure, so let me give you the address. Ailese reached in her purse and pulled out a piece of paper. She wrote down the address and gave it to Andrew. "So meet me there at eight, okay? Call me if you need to."

"Okay, thanks. I will be there." Andrew put the address in his jacket pocket. They finished their meal and headed back to the office. When Ailese was leaving, she stopped by Andrew's office and reminded him of their plans. He offered to walk her to her car, which Ailese accepted. They talked about their plans and how excited Dana was to have a playdate with the girls this weekend. "I will see you in a few hours, okay."

"Okay, bye, Andrew."

"Hi, Dr. Salvino, I do want to thank you again for understanding when I had to miss our sessions." "Family is important. Is everything okay now?"

"Yes, so far. My mom and dad, are staying with my sister for a while."

"That seems like a good idea. I am just grateful that your mom and dad are okay.

Let's start the session, okay. I want to talk about your real father, because it seems like a lot of the men in your life have let you down, but first I want you to tell me why you had the self-esteem issues. Let's start with that."

"Okay, well, I was teased in school by some classmates. I mean, it bothered me, but it didn't bother me because I would just ignore them. They would say that I walked funny, with a hump. Some girls called me a snob because they said that I was conceited, and I wasn't. The guys would always look at my breasts. I've always been big- chested. When the guys would ask me on a date, I would always decline because I felt that they were only after one thing. Actually, as time passed, I did end up having a lot of male friends more than female friends. There were a few guys that I dated here and there."

"Okay, so talk about your dad. How was your relationship with him?" Ailese closed her eyes; this was a very hard subject for her to talk about. "Well, I was a daddy's girl. I still remember it like it was yesterday. Every Saturday he took me to breakfast. It would be him and me, no one else. He'd spoil me so much, Ailese laughed, imagining the scene in her head. And she could see her dad's face- how handsome he was. When I would get into trouble, my dad would protect me. Ailese opened her eyes and focused on Dr. Salvino writing on her notepad. He was always there for me when I needed him until his job required him to travel a lot. He would call me, but that wasn't the same. I needed to feel his arms wrapped around me. I knew that he had to work; I missed him so much. I miss my dad so much; I wish he were here. We begged him not to get in the car, but he wouldn't listen. He told us that it would be fine, but it wasn't. Now he's gone, all I have are memories. I want more. I want him."

The room was silent for a few minutes until Dr. Salvino began to speak.

"All these feelings are good to get out and never hold them in, but it's also important not to feel like it's your fault that your dad got in that car. That was his decision; you were helpless. I want to talk about the abuse some more. Did your dad or anyone in your family ever abuse you?"

"No, never. I was disciplined, spanked, but not abused."

"So, tell me. You stated that you kept your abuse a secret. How did you keep it a secret?"

"Well, I had gotten so used to the abuse and had gotten very good at hiding it. I had become a master at it, good at being insincere. I would wear enough makeup to hide the bags under my eyes. I would wear more clothing to hide the scars. I would be very careful never to undress in front of anyone because my family and I would go shopping, but I would never ever try on clothes. My mom would always ask me how we were doing, and I would always tell her that we were great and that I always had a smile on my face."

"Tell me what is the number one reason why you are not able to say this person's name."

"To be honest with you, it's like playing Bloody Mary. Do you know that game?"

"No, I don't why don't you tell me about it."

"Well, you turn off the lights and stand in front of the mirror, and you say Bloody Mary three times, and she is supposed to appear in the mirror. It's a very scary game. Dr. Salvino shook her head. Well, if I say his name, he will appear and hurt me again, and this time he may kill me. I know that it sounds crazy."

"No, it doesn't, but facing your fears is very important, so I want you to work on facing your fears. I want you to work on saying this person's name; I know that it's not easy. You can take baby steps, like I said before; even if you write the first letter of the name, Ailese, it's a huge step."

There was traffic on the way to the studio, but Ailese remained patient. She didn't mind the traffic. It gave her some time to think about what Dr. Salvino expected from her. *I don't know if I can do this- write his name. I can't even say his name, Ailese thought to herself. Focus, focus, try, try, try, Ailese. You have to. Your life depends on it.* She kept repeating these words to herself until her phone rang. "Hey Andrew, yes, I am on my way, but I am stuck in traffic." Andrew could hear in her voice that something was wrong. "Same here. I don't know what's the holdup. I can't see it from where I am. Ailese, are you okay? You sound a bit troubled, and don't tell me it's nothing. What's wrong?"

"I'm okay, really." Ailese tried very hard to shift her voice from distracted and troubled to happy, but she couldn't; she couldn't fool Andrew. Andrew and Ailese had spent so much time together, that he knew when something was bothering her.

Andrew told Ailese on many occasions that he wished she would open up more; she still hasn't, and they have been friends for a long time now.

Andrew wished she would put more trust in him; he would ask her. What did he have to do to gain your trust? Ailese would always avoid the conversation. Yes, Ailese trusted him, but in a different way. If she asked him a question, she knew that he would give her an honest, truthful answer, or if he was visiting her at home and she had to leave the room, she knew that he wouldn't steal anything. When it came to opening up to Andrew, Ailese shut down. She cared about Andrew a lot. She saw him as a confidant, someone that she could always count on.

"Andrew I am fine. I am just anxious to get to the studio, that's all, really!"

"Ailese, I want to know something; why do you always shut me down when I ask you what's wrong? Is there something that I did to make you feel this way? I care about you a lot. I consider you one of my closest friends, but I can't be there for you in your time of need because you always shut me out."

"I told you, Andrew, it's complicated, and I don't expect you to understand that. You are such a great friend, and I value our friendship. I value the time that we spend together. Like I said, it's complicated."

"You've never explained that night at the hotel. I didn't bring it up because I didn't want to upset you; I still don't know what happened that night and why it happened. You have no reasons to be afraid to tell me anything, and you know I will never ever judge you, right?"

"Yes, I do, Andrew."

Ailese massaged her temples and shook her head. "I don't mean to pry, but look, I am here okay, and I will see you at the studio." Before Andrew hung up Ailese asked him to stay on the line for a few minutes. "Andrew, thank you so much. You're there for me now, more than you'll ever know."

Ailese and Andrew had arrived at the studio at the same time and parked next to each other. "Hey you, we need to talk before we go inside, okay?" Andrew stood in front of Ailese, just waiting to hear what she had to say. I meant what I said earlier. I meant every word. Please don't think that it's you because it's not. Look I can tell you this; I have been through, so much in my life, and I am just a cautious person, that's all. Ailese grabbed Andrew's hand. Please understand.

I've had people judge me all my life, and they still judge me, Ailese said, pausing.

So, I choose not to discuss my personal life and what I may be going through. If it's something that I'm going through involves my family, then it stays within the family." Andrew smiled. "I understand, I do."

When they walked in to the studio, Ailese didn't see Mikell anywhere, but she did see Sedrick sitting at a table and listening to his iPod. Ailese motioned Andrew over so that she could introduce them. Ailese tapped Sedrick on the shoulder, and when he saw that it was her, he stood up and gave her a huge hug.

"Sedrick, this is my good friend Andrew McGee." They both shook hands.

"Nice to meet you, Sedrick. I've heard so much about you. You're going places, and thank you for letting me come here to listen to your music."

"You're welcome, but this is the star here," Sedrick said, pointing to Ailese.

"No, you're the star. I just helped, that's all."

"Have you heard this amazing woman's voice? It is incredible. As soon as Mikell and Emmanuel get here, we could get started. In the meantime, could I offer anyone something to drink?" Ailese and Andrew asked for a beverage, and Sedrick came back with their drinks.

Sedrick Ailese and Andrew were a having great conversation. Sedrick bragged about Ailese's beautiful voice the whole time, and Ailese blushed the whole time. "See, Ailese likes to keep secrets from me," Andrew said softly as he rested his head on Ailese's shoulder. "I do not; I don't really. I'm not a bragger, guys."

As time passed, Ailese wondered what was taking the guys so long, then she got a call from Mikell saying they were on their way and would be there in five minutes. Andrew was enjoying himself and was anxious to hear Ailese's voice.

He had already begun to imagine what her voice would sound like- a mixture of one of his favorite female artist, J. J. Canton, or Mareah Coles; they both had beautiful voices and were both very talented. Ailese's singing was one thing he did know about her.

As everyone listened to the music, everyone was very elated and delighted with the music and the voices. Ailese wasn't expecting her voice to sound as good as it did. Sometimes Sedrick and Ailese would sing along to the songs that they were listening to. Mikell told Ailese how proud he was of her and bragged about her. Ailese loved getting lost in her music. She felt that she was in another world. Music got her through a lot in her life. Ailese listened to music whenever and wherever she could.

"Oh, wow, look at the time. Andrew said, looking at his watch. I need to get going." Andrew stood up from his chair and shook the guy's hands, and hugged Ailese, and told Sedrick to keep up the good work. Andrew talked to Mikell for a few minutes. Ailese walked him to the elevator. "You are very talented. You should really think about singing full-time. I think you're in the wrong profession, honey." Ailese shrugged her shoulders and blushed.

"So, I will see you tomorrow at noon, right?"

"Yes, you will, and Dana will not let me forget about their playdate tomorrow, he said, rolling his eyes, and they both laughed. I am so proud of you, Ailese, I really am. You are the most talented person I've ever met. Why did you stop singing? I'm sure you would have gone very far." "Well, I just decided that I wanted more, and my life changed, and I had to change my lifestyle. Having kids can do that to you."

"Oh well, that's true, but seriously, honey, you have a wonderful gift."

They talked for a bit and discussed their plans. Ailese hugged Andrew; he was a bit surprised because he would always hug her first. "Okay, see ya tomorrow."

"Bye."

"Ailese, we make a great team together, do you think so?"

"Yes, I do, Sedrick, and I just wanted to thank you for involving me in making the final decision on picking the songs for your album. That means a lot to me."

"No, it means a lot to me. I am so glad that we were able to work together."

"You know what would be great, baby?" Mikell made eye contact with Ailese.

"What? "If you could go on tour with Sedrick, at least perform at a few of his shows, what do you think?" Mikell knew that he was pushing it a bit, but it couldn't hurt to ask. "Yeah, that would be great, but I don't want to take away his shine, you know? I'm beginning to miss performing and singing like I used to ever since we've been in the studio. I'm just not sure, honey. I mean, I have responsibilities, and you know what they are. I don't want to get ahead of myself. I don't want the kids depending on someone else to take care of them other than me. I want to be there for them."

"Yes, I know, baby, but we could make it where the tour is in the summertime and the kids could travel with us, and I am sure the kids would love that!"

"Yeah, actually, I didn't think about that. Well, I can't make any promises, but let's just see what happens."

The next day everyone slept in, including Mikell and Ailese. Everyone was a bit exhausted from school and work. When Ailese woke up, she looked at the alarm clock that was by her bed and it said 9:30 a.m. She had thought it was later than that. Mikell was still sleeping. She checked on the kids, and they were still sleeping. Ailese would have to wake them up soon so they wouldn't be late for their playdate with Dana. Ailese went back into the room and thought that she would take a hot bath. She wanted to use her new bath gel. As she closed her eyes to relax, she heard the door open, and when she opened her eyes and saw Mikell coming toward her, she reached out her arms to him. Mikell accepted the invitation. He undressed and joined her in the tub. Mikell washed her back, and she returned the favor. Mikell kissed every inch of her naked body and washed every inch of her body. They kissed each other and touched each other; he loved her soft skin, she loved everything about his body; it excited her and he excited her. Mikell kissed her as if he hadn't tasted her for months, and he didn't want to stop. What stopped him was hearing both their cell phones go off. Mikell shook his head. "They'll call back if it's important. He picked up the sponge and squeezed the water from the sponge over her thighs. The warm water on her thighs felt good, and it felt even better when Mikell squeezed the water all over her body. As Ailese began to wash him, she heard both cell phones ringing again. I'll be right back. Stay right there. Mikell went and got the phones and brought them back with him. He handed Ailese hers, and he looked at his. Baby, I'm sorry but I have to call this person back. It's regarding Sedrick." He dried off his body and put on a terry cloth robe and went into the room. Ailese had a few messages, so she retrieved them and listened to them. One of the messages was from Alonda, and the second one was from an unknown number, and there was no message left.

Ailese finished her bath and got ready. When she was done, Mikell had already made sure the kids were up and had breakfast on the table.

"Thanks, hun. Breakfast was delicious!" Everyone agreed with Ailese.

"Baby, I don't know what time I will be home, but I will definitely call you.

Girls have fun, okay? Be good for mommy." "We will." Adrieana and Ashanee gave their dad a huge hug and a kiss goodbye. "Are you ready, Armont?"

"Yes, Dad, I'm ready. I will see you guys later. Bye Mom." Mikell kissed his wife goodbye.

Before Andrew arrived with Dana, Ailese did some last- minute chores around the house, and ran an errand to the store, dropped off the things that Alonda needed, and headed back to the house. The girls were very anxious and kept looking at the time. Ailese and the girls previously prepared lunch and snacks for their playdate and stored them in the refrigerator for later, by the time they were finished, it was nearly noon. Andrew was on time as usual, but this time he looked different because he was wearing jeans and a polo shirt, and he looked very handsome. "Hey, girls." Andrew told them that he had a surprise for them, but it was also up to their mom to say yes.

"So, Andrew, what's this surprise?" Ailese hugged him. "Oh, well, Andrew paused. I hope that I haven't overstepped my boundaries, but if it's okay with you, I'd like to take the girls and you, of course, on an adventure. What do you say to that?" Andrew looked at Ailese guardedly. "That sounds like a great idea. We were planning on watching movies and playing games, but it's such a beautiful day out, why not?" The girls all jumped for joy and were screaming because they were happy that Ailese agreed with Andrew to take them all on an adventure. We could take the lunches and snacks that the girls and I made. Is that okay?" Andrew shook his head, yes. He was on cloud nine right now. He was shocked that she had agreed to go on this adventure.

Andrew was prepared. He even had an SUV so that everyone could all ride together. "So, Andy, where are we going?" Ailese laughed because she never called Andrew by his nickname. Andrew looked at her, raised an eyebrow and rolled his eyes. "Because you called me Andy, I am not telling you. Call me that again, and I will be letting you off in a desert somewhere," Andrew laughed. "Ha, ha, you're so funny. No, seriously, where are we going? I hope I'm dressed for the occasion." Ailese looked at her outfit. She was wearing caprice, a nice top, and tennis shoes; she was casual.

"Ailese, would you shut up and just enjoy the ride like the girls are?" Ailese playfully punched Andrew in the shoulder. "Ouch! That hurts, hey, leave the driver alone."

"Fine, keep on being mean to me!"

"Never, I love ya too much!"

Ailese smiled.

When they arrived at their destination, everyone was in awe when they found out where they were; they were at the Explore-Thorium Zoo, and the girls were so excited! Andrew and Ailese gathered the girls and told them to hold hands. Ailese held Ashanee's hand, who held Adrienne's hand. Adrieana saw some of her friends at the Explore-Thorium Zoo and she wanted to go with them. Since Dana was closer to Ashanee's age, Ailese thought it would be okay just this once. Ailese knew her friends and their parents very well, so she trusted them with her daughter. Ailese made her promise that when it was time to go, she would meet them at the exit, and Adrieana promised that she would.

They looked at all kinds of animals and got to feed some of them, like the giraffes. Ashanee would laugh when the giraffe would lick her face.

They even saw a dolphin show later in the day. The dolphins showed off their tricks. One audience member was picked to feed the dolphins and was taught how to make the dolphins dance back and forth by the instructors. Andrew and Ailese asked the girls if they were hungry, and they all replied, yes. "Let's go over here and eat our lunches." Andrew and Ailese picked a bench to sit on to enjoy their lunch. They enjoyed their food and great conversation. When everyone was done with lunch, they just talked amongst themselves. "Why don't we go and ride the merry- go-round, guys, before it gets too crowded?"

"Good idea," Ailese said to Andrew as she sipped her iced tea. "Did everyone get enough to eat?" Andrew asked everyone, and everyone was satisfied. Everyone followed Andrew to the merry-go-round. "Andrew, you really think that you're slick, huh?"

"What are you talking about?" Andrew tilted his head. "You distracted me so I wouldn't know that you were paying to get on the ride."

"No, it was my idea to come here, so it's my treat and I don't mind. I am very fond of the girls, and so is Dana." When Ailese was about to finish the conversation with Andrew, her cell phone rang. It was Mikell. She asked Andrew to watch the girls while she took her call.

"Hi, baby, are you guys having fun?"

"Yes, what about you guys?"

"Oh, lots. Guess where we are?"

"Um, at a concert?"

"Ha, you're funny, no, Andrew surprised the girls and me by taking us to the Explore-Thorium. Can you believe that? The girls are having so much fun." "Wow, that is so cool. Tell Andrew that he's definitely on my Christmas list, Mikell chuckled. Wow, I know how much they love the zoo. Tell Andrew thanks."

"Okay, I will. Hey, could I talk to Armont?"

"Hello, Hi Mom, guess what Dad and I are about to do?" "What? Do I even want to know?"

"We're going to race cars, and don't worry, Mom, it's not dangerous." Ailese's heart fell to her knees. "Be careful, honey, promise?"

"I will be extra careful; here's Dad." "Mikell, please be careful, okay?"

"You know I will, you know that. We'll be fine, trust me. Okay, I gotta go. Love ya."

"Love you too. Tell Armont I love him too."

Ailese walked over to Andrew and the girls. They were standing in line waiting to go on the merry-go-round, and Ailese stood behind Andrew. Ailese looked around and saw Adrieana with her friends and their parents. Ailese called her over.

"Hey, Mom, are you guys having fun?"

"Yes, and you, kitten?"

"Yes, this is so much fun, Mom. Can I spend some of the money that I brought with me?"

"Honey, it's up to you. It's your money."

"Okay, thanks, Mom." Adrieana began conversing with Andrew. She hugged her mom and went off with her friends.

On the way home, the girls were asleep. They had a long day. Ailese thought that she would be tired, but she was actually wide awake. "Mikell wanted me to tell you thanks for taking the girls to the zoo. He knows how much they love the zoo. I mean, they love the zoo."

"I am glad that they had fun. It was no problem."

"You're such a good friend, you know that?" Andrew looked at Ailese and focused back on the road.

Andrew began to yawn. "Hey, do you want me to drive? You look tired."

He pulled over to get gas and let Ailese drive the rest of the way. Ailese asked him if he wanted to stay at her house and drive back in the morning. Andrew agreed. She didn't want him falling asleep at the wheel. "We didn't bring any pajamas with us, Ailese." Ailese gave Dana a pair of Ashanee's pajamas and gave Andrew a pair of Mikell's pajamas. They both thanked Ailese.

Ailese showed Andrew where he would sleep and told him not to worry about Dana, who was sleeping with Ashanee in her bed."Hey, come here. Andrew patted the bed with his hand, inviting Ailese to sit on the bed with him. Ailese sat down on the bed. Hey, I just wanted to let you know something. I don't want you to think that I'm flaunting my money around when we go out. I just don't mind. I don't mind treating. It means a lot to me that we all get to spend time together. It means a lot to Dana too. Her mom's been going through a lot lately, and she needs positive people around her."

"Andrew, I don't think that about you. I just don't want you to feel compelled to treat us all the time, because I can pitch in too."

"I know that. Come here, Andrew kissed her on the cheek softly. We're buddies for life," he whispered in her ear. "Yes, we are, Ailese whispered back. You're so good to us, Andrew, you are, and I thank you for that. I mean, you've made me see a whole new side of myself. I'm more open than I've ever been. Sometimes it takes a special person to broaden your horizons," Ailese laughed. "Yes, indeed," Andrew said.

When Ailese called Mikell, Armont and Mikell were settling into the hotel.

Mikell told Ailese that they would be home on Sunday, in the late afternoon.

Ailese told Mikell that Andrew was spending the night and explained. Mikell didn't mind that Andrew and Dana stayed the night. Ailese checked on the girls. They were sound asleep. Ailese heard a noise in the kitchen. It was Andrew getting a drink of water. "Hi, sorry if I startled you. I have to take my medication." "Medication? "Are you okay?"

"Oh, yes, I am fine. When I was a kid, I had gotten really sick, and the doctors couldn't figure out what was wrong with me. They ran all these tests, and to make a very long story short, they sent me to a dozen of specialists, and they finally figured out what was wrong with me.

Andrew paused. They diagnosed me with a rare disease, and I don't talk about it much because I don't want pity, you know?" Ailese shook her head.

If I don't take my medication to keep my strength up, I will be in a lot of trouble."

"You don't have to tell me your diagnosis, but are you?" Ailese paused. Andrew already knew what she was going to say. "No, It's not fatal. I make sure I take care of myself, and no, you don't have anything to worry about. I will tell you this. When I did have an episode and I thought that I was dying, I skipped my medication, being all macho. I had the worse headache imaginable, and I learned my lesson."

"You'd never know that you had a disease. You're so carefree and you don't let it get you down."

Ailese prayed and went to bed. She was very tired, and when her head hit the pillow, she was out like a light. "Please! Please! Don't kill me!" Ailese began to scream even louder as he put the gun to her head. Ailese knew that he would pull the trigger, and it would be the end for her. Ailese pleaded with him, but he ignored her pleading. "Why don't you ever listen to me, huh? Answer me!

He begins to count: 1, 2, 3." "Okay, okay, I'm sorry I didn't listen to you. I'll do anything, anything. I promise I will listen to you, please! He still had the gun to her head, telling her that he was going to pull the trigger. Ailese closed her eyes. God, I need you. I need you right now. Protect me!" "Get up!" Ailese got up with the gun still pointing to her head. He told her to go into the bathroom and wash her face. She washed her face and waited for his instructions. He told her to go back in the bedroom, so she did. He told her to lie down; he took the gun from her head for a brief minute. She didn't dare move. He handcuffed her to the bed. She was handcuffed for hours. He didn't check on her. He didn't even let her use the restroom; she couldn't talk because he covered her mouth with a scarf.

"Please, let me go," she would murmur. Finally, he came into the room and put the gun to her head again. He took the handcuffs off and tortured her. This went on for two whole days. Ailese couldn't wake up, and when she did, she let out the faintest scream ever! She was out of breath she screamed so loud that she woke up Andrew, the kids slept right through it.

"Ailese, let me in. What's wrong?" Andrew opened the door and ran to Ailese. He grabbed her and held her in his arms, and he knew just what to do. "Let go of me, please!" Ailese began to sob and scream. She still thought that she was dreaming. She thought that Andrew was him. She thought that he was the man who hurt her. She began to punch Andrew in the back. He shook her lightly. "Ailese, wake up, it's me!" When Ailese came to, she was delusional and perplexed. "Andrew, please, please don't let him hurt me, please!" She was weeping so hard that she couldn't see Andrew's face. "Honey, who wants to hurt you? Tell me. Please." Andrew wiped her face with his outer hand and soothed her. It was quiet in the dark room. Andrew stayed calm.

He rocked her in his arms and began to wonder who wanted to hurt her. Who hurt her? He was angry inside but didn't want to show it.

Finally, Ailese opened up to Andrew. She told him everything from beginning to end. He held her and comforted her the whole time as she told her story.

Andrew was very angry and upset. He had so many emotions! Now that he knew all of this, he felt overly protective of her. He wasn't in the dark anymore, and he was going to do all he could to assure her that he wouldn't let this man hurt her, ever! He told Ailese that she shouldn't be ashamed of what happened to her. He told her that that we all go through a lot in our lives, and he assured her that the conversation stayed between the two of them. Andrew felt tears travel down his face; it was so hard for him to listen to everything that she went through. How could anyone treat someone like a dog, like they were worthless? He couldn't understand why anyone would want to hurt Ailese; he thought that she was the sweetest person he'd ever known.

Andrew would apologize to Ailese a dozen times for what she went through.

"Wow, you're a very, very strong person, and a lot of people that have been in your shoes don't make it, and you know that right?" Andrew softly touched her face and caught the tear that was about to come down her face. Ailese sniffed and shook her head in agreement. "Now, do you understand the way that I am?" He shook his head and hugged her, holding her tightly.

You put your walls up because no matter what, even though you had lots and lots of therapy like me, you will always have a hard time trusting anyone."

I feel like he controls my life sometimes because of my dreams. I have them on a daily basis. My dreams did go away, so I thought," Ailese sniffed again.

"I understand. I always understood why you had your walls up. Everyone has their reasons, but I just didn't know why. You know?" "Yes, Ailese shook her head and shrugged her shoulders. Andrew asked Ailese if he could go into the bathroom. She told him that he could, and he came back out with a warm face cloth and handed it to her. He took her into the kitchen and fixed her some warm milk. Andrew never left her side. After she was done with the warm milk, Andrew walked her back into her room. He put the covers over her body and told her that he would stay with her if she wanted him to. "Andrew, please stay with me. I don't want to be alone, not now."

"Okay, I'll sleep here on the floor." He began to get the blanket from the foot of the bed until Ailese asked him to sleep right next to her. "Are you sure? You know that I am a respectful man; there will be no funny business," Andrew made her smile.

Ailese had planned to go to church, but she had overslept. She heard the alarm and shut it off. When she woke up, she had a huge headache. She didn't remember everything that happened last night, but she did remember some of the conversation with Andrew. "Now he knows my secret, she thought to herself. Andrew knows." She looked at Andrew, who was still sleeping, and she didn't want to wake him up, so she slowly got out of bed and walked to the girl's room. She could hear voices, so she knew that they were up. "Hey guys, who's hungry?" Ashanee and Dana raised their hands, and Ailese told them to watch television until breakfast was ready. When Ailese went to Adrieana's room, she was still sleeping. Ailese smiled at her and closed the door. She would wake her up when breakfast was ready.

As Ailese was finishing up making breakfast, Adrieana came into the kitchen and hugged her mom. "Mom, I already washed my hands. Could I help you?"

"Sure, honey, could you put the biscuits in the oven for me? That would be a big help."

"Sure, Mom, do you want me to do one can or two cans of biscuits?"

"Um, one would be good, unless you think you guys are going to want seconds."

"I'll do two cans." "Okay, be careful, okay?" When breakfast was done, Ailese went to wake up Andrew, but he was already up. She heard water running in the restroom. She knocked on the door. "Andrew, breakfast is ready, okay?"

"Okay, thanks. I'll be right out."

After breakfast, Mikell and Armont had arrived home. Armont was happy to see his family. Ailese made Mikell and Armont a plate. They told Andrew and Ailese what they did over the weekend. Mikell wanted Andrew to stay longer, but he told them that he needed to take Dana back home, and he too needed some fresh clothes. "Why don't you come to my house later?" "Oh, okay, I mean, I don't want to intrude if you already had plans."

"No plans. Let me write down the address. Do you have some paper?"

Mikell handed Andrew some paper to write on and gave him the piece of paper back with his address.

"Honey, did we have plans today?"

"Um, no. I was just going to relax today."

"So it would be okay for me to hang out with Andrew then?"

"Yeah, honey, that's fine with me."

"Okay, great thanks." Mikell kissed her on the cheek.

"So, come by whenever. I'll be there."

"Mikell, I need to talk to you, please." "Okay, baby, he followed Ailese to the room.

"Um, I need to tell you what happened, last night," Ailese said, pausing. I had an episode, and it was really bad. Andrew got me through it." Mikell interrupted her. "I knew that I should have stayed here with you. What the heck was I thinking?" Mikell stomped his foot. "Baby, please don't beat yourself up. I have to deal with this, and besides, you guys planned that trip months ago. You know that. You can't always rescue me. I know that, and you know that, Ailese whispered. So please don't feel like Andrew took over your job, because he didn't. He happened to be here, and I had to tell him everything that happened." Ailese started to cry again, and Mikell held her tight.

"Don't cry, baby. I'm here now. What did Andrew say?"

"He was upset that I went through the abuse, and he was angry all at the same time. He stayed with me the rest of the night, and he didn't judge me- not one time. He understood why I put up my walls, you know? I'm kind of relieved that I told him; I mean, it wasn't fair to leave him in the dark. He's been a great friend. I know that I can count on him."

"I'm glad that he was here for you. Please forgive me."

"For what?"

"For not being there when you needed me."

"Mikell I've already explained that to you and told you that you can't blame yourself, so stop blaming yourself, and you can't be in two places at the same time," Ailese's tone in her voice changed. "I know that, but…Mikell paused. My heart hurts for you!"

Ailese turned to Mikell and hugged him. "Remember what we promised ourselves- we are going to get through this."

Mikell, aren't you supposed to be hanging out with Andrew today?"

"Yes, I don't think that I'm going to go. I've changed my mind, I'm going to stay here with you."

"Mikell, I'll be fine, and besides, I have a lot of work to do to keep me busy until you come home. I want you to go and have fun. Ailese smiled at Mikell, but she knew that he was worried about her. "Baby, Andrew and I can hang out another time, and besides, I just got home. I haven't spent any time with you."

"Mikell, I don't mind."

"Are you sure, Ailese? If you need anything, call me, please."

"Yes, I promise. Just don't come home too late, okay?"

"Okay, I won't. I'll be home at a decent time."

Ailese couldn't get it out of her head that Andrew knew what a lot of people didn't know about her, and she sighed. She didn't know why it was bothering her that he knew, because she actually felt better that she finally got it off her chest and told Andrew. He didn't judge her at all; he didn't judge her when he stayed with her the first time she had an episode. Ailese knew that he cared about her, and he was upset when she told him what this man had done to her. She felt closer to him now, than ever.

Ailese did the laundry, put it away, and cleaned up the house while Armont took the girls to the park that was nearby. When Ailese was done, she thought she would take a long, hot bath to relax. Just as she began to run her bath water, she heard the phone ringing. "Hello, sis, what's wrong?"

"I need you. could I come over? I need to talk to you."

"Sure, of course, are you okay to drive?"

"Yes, I'm okay to drive, and I will be there shortly."

When Ailese opened the door, she could tell that her sister had been crying a lot. Ailese hugged her sister, sat her down at the kitchen table, and fixed her something to drink. "I love Chris so much. I have given him everything. D'Andra began to weep even more. You know, I knew that he would be traveling a lot, but not like this. I mean, I knew what I was getting myself into before I married him. Ailese looked at her sister, wishing she could take her pain away. Ailese knew that whatever happened between Chris and her sister wasn't good. I thought that we were going to grow old together, and I thought that I was the only woman for him- no one else, you know?

We were going to start a family, and he looked me dead in the face and lied to me- and he's been lying to me for years! I wonder if he ever loved me." D'Andra wiped her face. "Sweetie, are you saying that Chris is cheating on you?

I can't believe this! What the heck is going on here? I mean, what the heck is he thinking? You've been nothing but good to him, sis. I'm here for you. If you don't want to go home, you know that you're welcome here. I will make room for you, whatever you want, sis." Ailese hugged D'Andra and told her that it was going to be okay; she was going to get through it. "Right now, my head is pounding, do you have some aspirin?" Ailese gave her some aspirin and told her to lie down and rest. Ailese put her in the spare room that Andrew slept in.

"Let me know if you need anything, okay? I'm going to start dinner. Now get some rest." Ailese decided to fix her sister's favorite dish to cheer her up. She couldn't believe that her brother-in-law was cheating. She wanted to call Chris and give him a piece of her mind, but she didn't want to get in the middle; there are always three sides to a story: the truth, his side, and her side. Ailese hoped that the two of them would work it out.

When D'Andra and Ailese used to live together, they both used to make up recipes on their own, and most of them came out pretty good. D'Andra loved Ailese's dish that she discovered: rice, ground turkey, Worcestershire sauce, onions, and green peppers. The dish also had special seasonings. Ailese taught D'Andra how to make it, and when she became a wiz at it, she made the dish every Sunday for dinner, and Ailese would beg her to stop making it so much.

SHELBY LIES

"Mmmm, Mom, that smells so good. Didn't I see Aunt's car here? Where is she?" Armont asked. "She's sleeping right now, so I need you guys to use your inside voices, please, and try not to wake her up."

"Mom, need any help with dinner?"

"No, but thanks. Actually, could you make sure that your sisters wash up for dinner?"

"Sure, no prob, Mom." Armont headed to the girl's room.

Ashanee and Adrieana, Mom wants me to make sure that you guys wash up for dinner. You could go first while I get Adrieana." Armont went to Adrieana's room to let her know she needed to wash up for dinner. "Thanks, big bro."

Ailese checked on D'Andra. She was still asleep. Ailese kindly shook her to wake her up. She opened her eyes and was disoriented. When her eyes were more focused, she sat up in bed and smiled at Ailese. "Hey, Lee," D'Andra let out a lengthy yawn and stretched her body. "Hey, I have a surprise for you in the kitchen, so do you want to wash up for dinner?"

"Sure, be right out, thanks." When Ailese returned to the kitchen, she heard the key enter the lock- that's Mikell she thought. When the door opened, Mikell was happy to see his wife. He gave her a long, passionate kiss and helped her set the dinner table. "So, how was your visit with Andrew? Did you have fun?"

"Yes, wow, his house is immaculate! I mean, he doesn't have to go out of his house because he has everything. I gotta tell you, I was so amazed. He still lives in the house that he grew up in, he didn't change anything in the house everything is original, like the furniture, except for a few things he upgraded, like his entertainment room."

"Wow, really?"

"We're going to a hockey game in a few weeks. You should see his hockey collection."

"It Sounds like you both had fun."

When D'Andra walked into the kitchen, she spoke to everyone and sat down sluggishly in the chair. "Hey, D, are you okay?" Mikell whispered in her ear.

"Nothing that I can't handle. We'll talk about it later."

At the dinner table, D'Andra was a bit quiet, but every now and then she would joke around with her nieces and nephew while she ate.

"Thanks, sis, dinner was so delicious. You know that is my favorite dish. You are so talented. Did you ever come up with a name for your dish?"

"Um, no, I haven't, but I'm glad that you enjoyed it." "Let me help you with the dishes. D'Andra began rinsing off the dishes and staking them in the dishwasher before Ailese could even answer her. Ailese knew that D'Andra needed and wanted to keep busy to keep her mind off of Chris, so Ailese didn't argue with her, which she normally would because she was a guest.

"Hey, sis, could I open a bottle of wine?"

"Sure, you know where it is."

"Thanks." Ailese sat down and turned on the television. She was watching the news and couldn't believe her ears. A man broke into a couple's house and killed all their animals. Ailese wondered if this was the same man that broke into her mom and dad's home. She picked up the phone and called Officer Brown to let him know that he may have a suspect: this man on the news could be who they were looking for. "Yes, Officer Brown, please?" The operator put her through to Officer Brown, and Ailese was lucky that he was there in the office because he told her that he was actually on his way out. "I'm watching the news, and the same thing that happened to my mom and dad, happened to another couple. I don't know if it helps or not." "I'm glad you called. I was going to call you once I had enough information, but I am on my way to make an arrest. There were several witnesses that spotted this guy the same night that the robbery took place, you know, the one on the news."

"Really, okay, could you please keep in touch with me about the arrest, please?"

"Certainly, yes. Talk to you soon."

"Mikell, come here, please." Mikell came into the living room, where Ailese was. "What's up, baby?"

"I just saw the news, and a couple had the same thing happen to them that happened to my mom and dad. I just spoke to Officer Brown, and he said he was on his way out to make an arrest. He said he would keep me updated. I hope this is the guy, so he can be off the streets."

"That's good. He needs to be locked up.

Officer Brown will get the job done; I know that he will."

Ailese told D'Andra the good news, she too hoped that the guy would be captured. "I don't understand people these days, coming into people's homes and robbing them and hurting them; what in the heck is this world coming to?"

We're not even safe anymore."

"I know, sis. I hear ya, I hear ya."

Ailese and D'Andra watched television together and chitchatted with one another. "So, how's it going with your new best friend, Andrew? I know you guys have been spending a lot of time together that it makes me jealous." D'Andra pouted. "We're doing great. Guess what he did yesterday? You would have never guess."

"What? Tell me sis, what!"

"Well, he surprised us and took all of us to the Explore-Thorium Zoo! You know how much the girls love that place. I mean, they had a blast! He is so sweet to the girls too. We had lunch, and we fed the animals all kinds of things."

"Wow, that does sound like lots of fun. D'Andra shrugged her shoulders and began to tease her sister. Aw, he likes you, he loves you." D'Andra began to bat her eyes. "No, we're just friends, you know that that's all, and stop teasing me." "I know, sis, I'm just joking, but I know that he has always had a crush on you." D'Andra whispered in her ear.

Ailese debated on whether she should tell D'Andra that Andrew knows about what happened to her. "D'Andra, I need to tell you something. Um, Andrew stayed here last night, and well, I had an episode, and that wasn't the first time that he was there. Remember when we went on that business trip a while back and we took his private jet?"

"Yes, I remember that. What about it?" "Well, we had to stay a few days, so we had to check into a hotel; his room was right across from mine. I had an episode, and he thought that someone was trying to hurt me. I mean, he was determined to get into my room, so he told the maid that it was an emergency and to let him in, which she did. He asked me what was wrong. I wouldn't stop screaming. I was surprised that no one called the police. Anyway, he finally calmed me down, he stayed with me the whole night. The next day, we both didn't bring up what had happened and why. I had another episode last night, and he was there for me again. What I am trying to say is that Andrew knows what happened to me."

"Okay, D'Andra paused, he does huh? Well, what was his reaction?"

"He had a lot of emotions. He didn't judge me. He said that he was happy that I let him in, that I finally put my wall down; that I opened up to him. He felt disturbed, livid, and sad all at the same time. I do feel much closer to him. At first it bothered me that he knew, then I thought, he needed to know. He's been there for me, you know?" "Yes, I do know. He's a great person inside and out, even though I think that he still has a huge crush on ya." D'Andra laughed. "Oh whatever, stop!" "You're growing up, sis!"

The next morning, Ailese was woken up by a knock at the door. It was Chris. he wanted to talk to D'Andra. Ailese let him in. She made sure that she didn't show any animosity toward him. "Hey, Chris, come on in. I'll go and get D."

"Hey, sis, how's everyone doing these days?"

"We're doing good." Ailese went to D'Andra's room. She was awake but still under the covers. "I know, I know, Chris is here. Tell him I died! I don't want to see him; he's a goddamn cheater!"

"Calm down, D, and watch your mouth. The kids are here," Ailese said, gnashing her teeth. D'Andra rolled her eyes at her sister. "Tell him that he can go back to that woman who thinks she's better than me, or maybe he thinks she's better than me. I am done, you hear me done!"

"D, please. You know that you have to talk to him sooner or later. Come on. Ailese grabbed D'Andra's hand and told her to put on her robe. Go and take your time. Just take Chris into your room because the kids and I need to get ready for work and school."

"Okay, fine, I will listen to what he has to say."

D'Andra walked into the living room, where Chris was standing in his usual ball cap, jeans, and T-shirt. "Hey, Chris said in a whisper. D'Andra didn't answer him. "What do you want, Chris? Why are you here? There's nothing left to discuss, and there's nothing I want to say to you, D'Andra said, folded her arms.

Come on, if you want to talk to me, we have to go into my room," she said. Chris followed her. D'Andra sat on the bed, and Chris sat next to her. I'm listening, and I ain't got all day, so spit it out, honey."

"Please stop being such a butthead, D. This isn't you. Please listen to what I have to say. D'Andra frowned at Chris and folded her arms again. Look, I don't know what else to tell you, but I am not cheating on you. I love you so much. You are my world, D. I don't know why you think I am cheating on you just because I am never home. I'm never home because I have high demands, and I'm doing it for you and for us, baby."

"I don't care what you say. I know that you're cheating on me, Chris, and how could you? We're working on having a family, D'Andra said, pausing. I feel like I can't trust you anymore and that you're lying. Until then, we have nothing, nothing!"

D'Andra stood up and walked over to the window. She didn't know what else she could say, she could think of some things to say, but she would regret it later. Chris came up from behind her. D'Andra pushed him away from her. He tried taking her hand. She pushed his hands away from hers.

"D'Andra, please. Don't do this to us, by believing something that isn't true. I love you and I'm not going to let anyone, or anything take that away from me or from us. Come home, come home now. Here, get dressed. Chris picked up her clothes and gave them to her. Please, I need you. I am not cheating on you, I'm not!" D'Andra began to cry. She hugged her husband and told him that she loved him. "I want to work our problems out. I don't know what happened, but I feel like … you don't love me anymore. I feel like I've lost you forever. We don't have that thing that no one else has. Only we know what it is; it's not there anymore, Chris, why?"

"Baby, I love you, and yes, we still have that thing that no one else has. Honey, it's there."

When Ailese and Mikell left for work, Chris was still there at the house; Ailese hoped that they would work things out. "So, I hope that everything is okay between those two." Mikell said as he got into his car. "I hope so too. I know I am staying out of it, and I pray for the best." Mikell smiled at Ailese. Ailese kissed him goodbye, and they drove off.

When Ailese got to Dr. Salvino's office, she bumped into Karen. They had a casual short conversation because Karen was heading home. She had come down with something and didn't feel good. Ailese told her to feel better and get plenty of rest. When Ailese checked in at the front desk, the receptionist was surprised to see her. "Hi, I'm here to see Dr. Salvino. My appointment is at 9:30." "Didn't you get my message?"

"No, what message?"

"I left a message with someone at your home number. I told them Dr. Salvino would not be in today because she had a family emergency and didn't know when she would be back. Mrs. LaShae, right?"

"Yes, I'm Mrs. LaShae. I didn't get the message."

"Can I verify your phone number, please?" "Yes, go ahead." "I have 333-0296." "That's me. Okay, I hope everything's okay. Will you call me when she gets back?"

"Oh, yes, I will. Sorry for the inconvenience, but I did leave a message with someone."

"Oh, I believe you. This sort of thing happens sometimes. Have a good day."

"You too."

Ailese called Mikell to ask him if he maybe took the message and forgot to tell her, and he told her that he didn't take that message. Ailese wondered who would forget to give her that important message. "Oh well, I guess I'll go back to work." When she arrived at work, Ell was already meeting her halfway, and Ailese knew something was up. "Boss, I need to leave early today if that's okay. I have to take a personal day. I could stay until two. Is that okay, boss?" Yes, that's fine, Elle. Are you alright?"

"Yes, well, no, it's a long story, but I do have to leave early."

"Okay Ell." Ailese sat down at her desk and let out a long sigh. She called her sister to check on her. "Hey, D, is Chris still with you?" "Yes, he is. He's right here. Hey, sis, um, please don't be mad at me. I just thought of it, but your doctor's office called yesterday while I was on the phone, and I." Ailese interrupted her. "I know, they cancelled my appointment. I just came back from there. D'Andra, please try and remember to write the message down, okay?"

"Okay, you're not mad? I mean, I know how much you," Ailese, interrupted her again. "Hey, I love you, and go and talk to Chris and call me later."

There was a knock on Ailese's door. It was Andrew. "Wow am I happy to see you. I need one of your hugs. Andrew smiled and walked over to her. Ailese stood up, and Andrew gave her a bear hug. Thanks, I needed that."

"Anytime, you're back so soon?"

"Yeah, my appointment was cancelled, and my sister forgot to tell me," Ailese shook her head. "Aw, you poor thing, are you going to be okay, huh? Ailese shook her head, yes. Hey, I wanted to talk to you about the Alston account."

"Okay, did you want to go to the conference room?"

"No, no, Andrew sat down across from Ailese. I have the file right here." He opened the file and handed it to Ailese. "What did you want to talk about?" "Well, look at the current location and look at the new location, which just can't be right. I thought that they had to foreclose on all that property on 198th Street. I know that they had some issues with the foreclosure." "Yes, you're right. This can't be right unless the research department didn't research it right. I'm calling them right now. Hello, Edward, it's Ailese LaShae. How are you?" "Good, good."" Hey, listen, I have the Alston account in front of me, and something seems a bit off. Now it says here that the new location was going to be 198th Street, am I correct?" "Yes, that's correct, and yes, that was foreclosed. Someone bought the property, and it isn't in foreclosure anymore. This just happened a few weeks ago, and I did confirm it, Mrs. LaShae. I know that it takes a while for this new information to show up in the system."

"Okay, I see. Okay, thanks Edward, for all your help."

"Well, I guess that answers all of our questions, so it's a go!"

"Yes, I guess it is, huh? This is going to be great. I mean the 198th. From what I understand, they are building a lot in that area, and the business should do excellently, don't you think?"

"Yes, I do. Hey, I have an idea. Let's drive over there just to be sure."

"Well, hey, why not? It couldn't hurt. Are you free right now?"

"As a bird."

When they arrived at 198th Street, it was better than they both had pictured it. It had colorful tall buildings and apartment complexes, and it was very fresh.

There was a coffeehouse that looked like a miniature house. The chimney was a huge coffee cup, something that you would see on television.

"Well, it looks like we hit the jackpot, Ailese. Let's head back to the office."

"Okay, but you drive this time, Ailese raised her brow. "You want me to drive your car, are you sure?"

"Yes, I trust you." Ailese tilted her head.

"Whoever had that beautiful plan to build the 198th is some genius. Our clients are going to be floored! I can't wait to see their faces, can't you?"

"Yeah, I agree. I don't see them not wanting to fly with us. It's a done deal."

When they arrived back at the office, Ailese noticed that Ell was not at her desk, and then she remembered that she was leaving early. With Ell leaving, it must be very important. She never asked to leave early. Ailese didn't expect her to come back, since she took a personal day.

"Ailese, is it just me or has Ell not been herself lately?"

"No, you're right. I don't know what's going on with her, but I hope that she'll be okay. All the times I've told her that she could leave early, she still wouldn't, and now she's asking me, could she leave early, or there is always something with her?"

When Ailese came home, the kids were eating dinner already, and Mikell was in the kitchen fixing himself a plate. "Hi, baby, sit down. I know it's a bit early for dinner, but I thought that I'll save you some time." "Thanks. Hey, is it tonight that you guys are going to the game?"

"Yes, baby, it's tonight. Mikell kissed Ailese on her cheek as he placed her tea on the table in front of her. Oh, Chris is tagging along too I guess he needs to get out of the house.

Actually, I spoke to him for a while today, and he said that both he and D'Andra are working things out."

"Yes, I suspected that they were since D'Andra moved back home. I mean, I want their marriage to work out. Ailese changed the subject she'd almost forgotten that the kids were sitting at the table. Hey guys, how was school?"

"It was okay, Mom, and how was work?"

"It was good, Adrieana. Thanks for asking."

"Mom, is it okay if I go to Dad's tomorrow? Grandmas in town, and she wanted to see me."

"Okay, that's fine. Hey tell her hello for me, okay." Armont smiled at his mom. "Okay, Mom, I will. Could I be excused? I have a math test to study for."

"Sure, clear your plate." Armont cleared his plate, cleaned up his area, and went to his room. "Mom, could you please help me with my English please? I'm stuck."

"Sure, kitten, as soon as I am done with my dinner, we can get started."

"Thanks, Mom, I'm done with my dinner. I'm going to go in my room and do my other homework until you come. Is that okay, Mom?" "Yes."

"What time are you guys leaving?" "Oh, 6:30 or so, Andrew said that he would call me when he's on his way. The doorbell rang, interrupting Mikell and Ailese's conversation. "Hey, buddy, look at you. I think you're ready, huh?"

"Yep, I am, Mikell said as he modeled the Glyndon outfit he was wearing. I love the Glyndons. They're my favorite hockey team, I hope your team loses and mine wins." Chris said chuckling at the thought of his team losing. "We'll see about that. The Caravels are going to kick your team's butt! When Chris realized that Ailese was sitting at the kitchen table, he started to blush. Hey Ailese, how are ya?" Chris walked over to her and gave her a hug. "I'm good. I see you're excited about the game, huh?" "Yes, I am, I know I'm a kid when it comes to hockey games." "I hope you guys have fun. Well, I am going to get out of these work clothes. Mikell dinner was good. Thanks so much for cooking." "You're welcome. I'll come and get you when Andrew's here."

Hey, are you thirsty or anything, man?" "Yes, sure. Do have any tea or bottled water?" "Actually, I have both. Which one?" "Water is cool. Thanks."

The doorbell rang, and it was Andrew. He was excited about the game as well.

"Hey guys, are you ready for the greatest hockey game ever?" Both Mikell and Chris answered yes. "I thought I heard you out here." Ailese gave Andrew a hug. "Hey you, why aren't you resting?" Ailese laughed. "Duty calls. You guys have fun, and Andrew, if you don't want to drive back, feel free to bunk here. You too, Chris." The guys both agreed.

"Wow, I thought that we would never get here with all that traffic!" "We're here now, Mikell. Let's go and find our seats. We can go to the concession stand later." The guys followed Andrew inside the stadium. Chris eyes were big. He'd never seen anything like it. He saw people in jerseys and hats, some even painted their faces, to let everyone know what team they were rooting for. The lights were as bright as streetlights in New York. The stadium was as big as he'd imagined it. The seats were better than everyone else's seats. They were in the box seats, and Mikell and Chris couldn't believe it! "I thought that we were sitting out there." Chris pointed outside the window. "Nope, we have the best seats in the house; enjoy it because it only gets better." A few minutes later, a man came in and gave all the guy's jerseys, hats, pucks, and autographed pictures signed by both teams. They had champagne, but Andrew didn't drink. He was the designated driver, so he drank apple cider instead. Food and drinks and whatever else they requested were brought to them; they were treated like royalty. When the game was over, a few of the hockey players chatted with the guys. Andrew knew most of them; Chris and Mikell were very impressed. The guys kept thanking Andrew over and over again; Andrew just kept saying it was his pleasure.

When they got home, they were all exhausted and were happy that they didn't have work in the morning. Andrew decided to sleep in the spare bedroom, and Chris slept in the other spare bedroom. Mikell woke up Ailese by kissing her. He wanted to let her know that he was home. Ailese went back to sleep. As soon as Mikell's head hit the pillow, he was out like a light.

When Mikell finally woke up, he realized that Ailese wasn't beside him. He looked at the clock, and it was nearly noon. Mikell jumped out of bed. He didn't want to sleep that late, and he thought that Ailese would have woken him up.

He could hear voices but was too sleepy to make them out. He shaved and showered and went looking for Ailese. When he entered the kitchen, no one was there, so he went into the living room, but she wasn't there; no one was there.

"Where could everyone be?" he thought to himself. "Ailese, kids," he called to them, but no one answered, so he looked for a note—there wasn't one.

He went to Chris's room. He was still asleep, and he didn't want to wake him up. He went into Andrew's room; he too was still asleep. He knew that he heard voices too. Did he? A few minutes later, Ailese and the girls were walking through the door, giggling. "Hey, sleepy head, you're up. Are the guys still sleeping?" "Yes, hey, why didn't you wake me up? I was concerned when you guys weren't here." "Oh, I'm sorry. I just figured that you were tired, Mikell, so I didn't wake you. I took Armont to his dad's and took the girls to the bookstore; we all just hung out." Ailese gave Mikell a bag. "Oh, thanks, Lee. You're so sweet. I have such a good wife. Ailese had bought the book that Mikell had told her about the other day. Come here." "What?" Mikell grabbed her close to him and gave her a kiss.

When Ailese started lunch, the guys were up. They had showered and shaved.

When they ate lunch, the guys told Ailese how much fun they all had at the game. Chris even showed her all the goodies that were given to them.

D'Andra rang the doorbell even though she opened the door with her keys.

"Hey guys! It looks like I'm in time for lunch." Ailese was happy to see her sister; she looked well rested; more her. "I'll fix your plate. Sit down, sis. I'm glad you're here." "Hi, I missed you last night, D'Andra kissed Chris on the mouth. "So did I, did you get my message?" "Yes, I did. Thanks for calling me to let me know where you'd be and that you were safe." "Anything for you."

Ailese placed the plate in front of D'Andra and sat back down.

After lunch, everyone decided to get out of the house and enjoy a movie.

Luckily Andrew and Chris brought back up clothes, so they didn't have to go home to change. Andrew had driven the SUV, so they took his vehicle, and everyone all piled in and headed to the theater.

Everyone had agreed on the same movie, so they could all stay together.

"I'll get the food. Ailese, could you please help me?" "Sure, I can, no problem." Andrew and Ailese went to the food court while everyone else went inside the theater to get seats. "I just have to have the junk food when seeing a movie.

I can't help myself." "So what? I'm with you, even though I know that I don't need it, and I usually pay for it later." "Aw, please, I disagree. Junk food agrees with you." Andrew smiled at Ailese. "What do you mean by that?"

"Just that well, please forgive me, but you have a banging body Ailese, I thought that you knew that by now. I mean, I know that I'm probably crossing my boundaries but you're so beautiful. Did I just say that out loud?" "Yes, you did. I should crack you right in your forehead, but I won't. I'll be a lady and say thanks." "No, thank you. I guess I forgot to mention that I love all body types, but my favorites are the curvy ones." "Really, Ailese looked surprised.

"Why are you surprised? Ailese just shook her head. She didn't know what to say, and besides, she was still blushing. Ailese, I apologize for crossing that boundary. Please forgive me." "No, it's fine." Ailese lightly bumped Andrew's shoulder. As they were ordering the food, a couple told them that they made an awesome couple. They didn't tell them that they were just friends. They just thanked them and giggled.

The movie hadn't started yet when they came back with the food. "Okay, guys, we've got food here. Pass it down, please." Andrew and Ailese began to pass the food and drinks to everyone. All of a sudden, the theater went pitch black, and Ailese couldn't see a thing, so she had to sit next to Andrew. When the previews started, Andrew whispered to Ailese, apologizing to her. "What are you apologizing about? She whispered back. "For, you know, I told you that you have a beautiful body. Forgive me if I upset you." "No, I'm not mad at you at all. Why do you think I'm mad at you?" "I just don't want to overstep my boundaries, sometimes I put my foot in my mouth." "We're good, Andrew."

After the movie ended, the girls begged their mom and dad to go to one of their favorite stores, and D'Andra offered to take them and meet up with the rest of them later. Andrew Ailese and Mikell found a coffee shop and decided to get coffee and chat. "Coffee and treats, are all on me guys," Mikell said, when they arrived at the coffee shop. "So, what did you want, Ailese?" "Oh, wow, let's see, get me a medium white chocolate mocha with no foam and soy milk, please."

"What about you, Andrew?" "Could I get a green tea with a few splashes of melon, please? Thanks, man." Mikell ordered the drinks while Andrew and Ailese went and found seats. "Wow, this tea is really good."

So, guys, what did you think of the movie? I thought it was well done."

"Well, I loved the movie," Ailese said, smiling. "Yeah, I agree, it was a good movie," Mikell said, as he sipped his drink.

"I am so exhausted, how about you guys?" Andrew looked back at everyone; they all agreed that they too were exhausted. After Andrew dropped everyone off at Ailese and Mikell's, he headed home. Chris and D'Andra stayed a bit but took off shortly after Andrew did.

A few hours later, Chris showed up at the door in a panic. "What's wrong Chris?" Ailese asked him in a disturbed voice. "Please tell me that my baby's here! Please!" "Chris, sit down. No, D isn't here. Now, what's going on?" Chris put his face in his hands. "She said that she was going to pick up some things and that she would be back. I offered to go with her, but she said that she wanted to go alone to clear her head. I respected that so I told her that it was fine; she's been gone for over an hour. I've called her cell phone, but it just goes straight to voice mail. I've called everyone looking for her, but no one's seen her."

"Oh my gosh, this doesn't sound like D. Okay, stay right here, let me get Mikell, okay."

"Mikell, please, I need you." Ailese grabbed him by the hand and led him to where Chris was. "What is it?" "D, she may be missing, and I know that you have to wait 24 hours to report her missing, but I think that we all should split up and go find my sister, Mikell." Ailese and Chris filled Mikell in on what had happened and why she might be missing. Ailese called her mom to let her know what had happened, but there was no answer, and Ailese didn't want to leave a message saying that D may be missing, so she thought that she would try again later.

When she got a hold of Alonda, she was so worried about D. Ailese told her that she needed someone to watch the kids so they could all look for D'Andra. Alonda left work and met Ailese at her house.

"We can't get a break. I don't know what's going on, but I know one thing: when I catch this son of a bitch, they better run! Excuse the language. I told your dad what happened, he's trying to get back here as soon as he can. He's all the way in Valora, which is five hours away from here." "I know Daddy will get here as soon as he can. We don't know if she's missing, but this isn't like her at all."

Ailese drove through alleys dead- end streets. She drove to different towns, some of which she hadn't visited in a long time. Ailese drove for hours, and still couldn't find her sister. She kept asking herself, "Why is this happening to my family? Please, God, wherever my sister is, keep her safe until we find her.

Protect all of us, Lord." Just as she was about to drive back home, she saw a crowd of people standing around. The police pulled up and started to move people back from the street. When Ailese parked her car, she prayed that whatever it was, she hoped that it wasn't her sister. She was wrong. The woman that was lying on the sidewalk had been beaten. Her face was so bloody she was unrecognizable, but not to Ailese. She knew her sister. She could pick her out in a crowd. As soon as Ailese saw her hair and the shoes that she was wearing, confirmed that it was D'Andra. D'Andra would be wearing these fluorescent pink shoes when she was going out for a quick run to the store. She loved these shoes. She owned them. "Oh my God, Ailese ran to her sister, but before she could get to her, the police officer grabbed Ailese by the hand and asked her if she knew this woman. Please officer, that woman is my sister. Her name is D'Andra Kooley. Please believe me, this is my sister. We've been looking for her for hours, Ailese said as she pleaded with the officer to let her tend to her sister. Ailese began pleading with the officer. When the officer let Ailese through, he followed her. Ailese wasn't prepared for what she saw. She screamed when she saw D'Andra's face up close and put her hands over her mouth. D'Andra's eyes were beaten shut; she was incoherent and couldn't speak. I'm here, baby, it's me," she whispered in a soft voice.

Ailese tried to hold it together. She tried not to cry, but she couldn't hold in her tears. This was her sister here. Seeing her sister like this, was something that no one should ever have to go through! No one should ever have to see their sister like this. It hurt her so much. She held her in her arms. "Ma'am, what is your name, please?" "Ailese, Ailese LaShae, please get her some help, please!" "The ambulance is on its way right now. They should be here any minute now. Miss, please, I'm going to need you to let go of your sister. This is a crime scene. Please just let my men do their jobs, okay."

Ailese couldn't let her sister go. D'Andra began to moan, and just as Ailese was about to let her go, the ambulance arrived. Ailese never felt so happy to hear that sound.

The officer brought back some blankets and put them over D'Andra, who couldn't move or speak. Her body began trembling. When the ambulance arrived, they put D'Andra on the stretcher, attended to her, and hurried her into the ambulance. When they finally got D'Andra into the emergency room, Ailese stepped out to call Chris and Mikell, and she knew that it was going to take everything that she had in her to tell Chris what had happened. "Chris, please, you guys need to get to the hospital, Ailese said, swallowing hard and closing her eyes. I found D, and it's not good. Please come to the Southbridge Worthington Memorial Hospital. It's in Myron." Just as she was beginning to tell Chris where the hospital was, he cut her off. "I know where it is. We're on our way."

Ailese wasn't allowed to go into the operating room. She knew nothing of her injuries. She just prayed and prayed that her sister would come out of it alive.

Ailese called her mom to keep her in the loop. She wanted to take a cab there, but Ailese didn't want the girls to be at the hospital. She had promised Alonda that she would keep her updated. Alonda was crying so much that the girls had begun to cry too. Ailese told the girls that their aunt had an accident and that she was looking after her. She told them not to be sad, and she assured them that everything was going to be okay. Ailese knew that it wasn't in her hands, it was in God's hands, but in her time of need, God had never let her down.

Ailese waited and waited, thinking that the guys would have been there by now. She picked up her cell and called Andrew, but he didn't answer, it went to his voice mail, and she left him a message. Even though her husband could always calm her down, Andrew had a special way of calming her down, like he had special powers. How she wished he were there, sitting right next to her, but he wasn't. He would have told her to be strong and stay strong; Ailese played that in her head a million times to reassure herself.

Ailese would walk around the hospital and read the flyers that were on the walls to pass the time. She would watch people and doctors go past her. Just as she was about to head to the cafeteria to get coffee, Chris and Mikell had finally arrived. She was so relieved that they had finally made it.

"Where is she?" Chris said, apprehensively. "She's in the emergency room, and I don't know anything -her injuries or if something's broken. We have to wait until the doctor comes out and tells us, only the doctor can answer all of our questions." Ailese hugged Chris and Mikell and told them that they all had to be strong for D'Andra. "Tell us how you found her, please." "Well, I was leaving Myron, and just as I was leaving, I saw a crowd of people, and something told me to go and see what was happening. Seeing D there was the furthest thing from my mind. I made my way through the crowd, and there she was. Ailese could feel the tears coming back, but she wasn't going to let them roll down her face. All I know is that it looked like she had been badly beaten. Her face was bloody. I don't ever want to see her like that again! I can't get it out of my head." Chris comforted her and hugged her tight."I thank you, Ailese, for finding her. Thank you, and I just thank God.

Who did this? Chris balled his fists and massaged his temples. I'm not going to do it; I'm not going to get upset." "Don't, man, we're here for you and we're all upset, and we want answers. We all have to be patient."

A few more hours had passed. When Ailese looked up to see the doctor walking toward her. She told Mikell and Chris that the doctor should have some news. "Hello, I am Dr. Vance. Thank you for waiting patiently. Please, have a seat.

Everyone introduced themselves to the doctor. Mrs. Kooley has lost a lot of blood. We gave her a blood transfusion, and she has suffered some head trauma. The operation was a very, very long process; we had to stop the bleeding. She is not able to see very well, her eyes are closed. But the swelling should go down in a few days or so. The doctor paused. Ailese noticed that he had an odd look on his face. She is going to need a lot of care and maybe a home care nurse; we will provide all the information that you need before releasing her." "Well, I will be the one taking care of her doctor." "Okay, very well then, but we can still be of service if you need us.

Mr. Kooley please, if there's anything that my staff or I can do, please let us know, okay? Chris shook his head. Now you can see your wife, now, but only for a while. She needs her rest right now. I'll lead the way." "Dr. Vance, is she really going to be okay?" "Yes, she will. That's my word. Now, she will need therapy to get her mobility skills up to par." "Okay, I see that's not a problem, not at all." "Okay, ready? I must tell you that she has a lot of bandages on her wounds, okay? Are you sure you're okay?" "Yes, doctor, I am sure."

When he walked in to D'Andra's room, he lost it, seeing her bandages. Her wounds. "Who would do this to you? But Chris knew he had to be strong no matter what. Chris had to hold back his tears as best he could. You're going to be okay, and we're going to do whatever we need to do to make sure of that okay. I can't leave you, baby. I just can't. It's all my fault." Mikell stepped in and told Chris that it wasn't his fault and not to blame himself, and to be strong, he had to be strong. "The doctor let us see D for just a bit, I hope that's okay." "Of course Chris said. Ailese kissed her sister on the forehead and prayed silently. "I'm here, baby, I'm here okay." Chris kissed his wife gently on her forehead and gently brushed her hair away from her face.

"I need to call Mom. I'll be back." Ailese said in a soft voice. Mikell went with Ailese because he needed some air. "I could call Mom for you, baby. You're to upset too even talk to anyone." "Thanks, baby, "Ailese said, leaning her head on her husband's shoulder as they sat down on the bench. Ailese could hear her mom's voice; by her tone, Ailese could tell she was crying but thankful at the same time. "I can drive you home so your mom can come see D. Is that okay?" "Yes, are you sure?" "Baby, yes, I'm sure. Come on, let's go and tell Chris."

When they arrived back in Shelby, Ailese was relieved because she needed to see some familiar places and faces. Alonda was ready to go to the hospital when they came home. Ailese hugged her mom and told her that it was going to be okay. Mikell and Alonda left to go to the hospital. Don was on his way to the hospital, he finally made it back to Shelby. The girls were asleep, so Ailese was alone. She just prayed and thanked God for not taking her sister away from her. Ailese thought that she was going to wake up from this bad dream and D'Andra would be okay, but this was real. This was not a dream!

Ailese started thinking about a lot of things that made her angry and sad all at the same time. Ailese began to cry. She knew that she needed to stay focused, but it was so hard. Someone tried to kill her sister. First it was her mom and dad, and now D'Andra.

She was lucky that no one was there to witness her losing it. Ailese had cried so hard. She covered her mouth and let out a scream. She let out all her frustrations. She stopped crying when her cell phone rang. She looked at the phone to see who was calling. It was Andrew. Ailese sniffled and answered the phone. "Hello." She was trying to make her voice sound calm. It took everything in her not to burst into tears again. "Hi, I got your message, and I am five minutes away. I am so sorry that I wasn't there for you when you needed me. I'm almost there." "Okay, I really need you right now. I'm here alone, and the kids are asleep." Ailese started crying again. "I know, it's hard, but I'm here, okay?"

When the doorbell rang, Ailese knew it was Andrew, but she still asked who it was, and she was right. It was Andrew. When she opened the door, Andrew grabbed her and held her, then closed the door behind him. Ailese felt warm and safe in his arms. "Let me fix you some of your favorite tea. Here, you're shaking." Andrew grabbed the blanket that was on the sofa and wrapped the blanket around Ailese. "Thanks, and tea would be great," Ailese sniffed again. When the tea was ready, Andrew carefully gave Ailese the cup and told her it was very hot and to be careful. Andrew sat down next to Ailese on the sofa, facing her. He could see that she had been crying a lot. "Ailese, what the hell's going on? Who would want to hurt D'Andra? If you don't mind me asking." "Well, they didn't say much, and they don't have much to go on. They asked me a bunch of questions. The officer said that someone called the police when they saw D'Andra lying in the street. He said that they would search the area and see what they could find. Hopefully, they would find some clues or something. I am so mad! I don't know how my sister got there, and who hurt her. I want all of my questions about my sister, answered. If I tell you something, please don't think that I'm crazy, okay?" "I will never think you're crazy. Tell me."

"Well, I think it may be the same person who tried to hurt my mom and dad. I can feel it, Andrew." "You may be right, and you may be onto something.

Did you tell the police?" "Yes, I did. I mentioned it to him. I don't have a name or anything for them to go on. It's hearsay to them." "I know that you're frustrated, but they will slip up, trust me. Criminals always do."

"I hope that they catch this monster too! He needs to be locked up so he can't hurt anyone anymore! The officer said without any evidence, it's going to be hard to catch this bastard, and that doesn't sit well with me at all."

Andrew and Ailese had talked and talked for hours and sipped tea. He didn't want her to be alone, so he stayed with her. She had fallen asleep in Andrew's lap while he watched television. He had the volume on low so he wouldn't wake her up. Andrew could hear Ailese moaning in her sleep. He stroked her hair gently to comfort her. Ailese began to moan loudly, then she began to clutch Andrew's thighs with her fingernails. "No, please leave me alone! I'll be good, please, please." "Wake up, Ailese, sweetheart, wake up." Andrew shook her body really hard, and she finally woke up. "Andrew, please don't leave me. He's going to hurt me, please!" Ailese started to cry. She put her head on Andrew's chest. Andrew comforted her and reassured her that no one was going to hurt her and that he was there for her. "I'm not going anywhere, I promise you."

Ailese cried and cried. "Andrew, I am so scared. I've never been so scared in my life!" "Shh … Shh. It's going to be okay, I promise." Before he could ask her what she meant by someone hurting her, Andrew heard the door unlock with the keys. "Hey, Ailese, I'm home." "Hey, Mikell, we're in the living room."

When Mikell entered the living room, he didn't expect to see Andrew and Ailese together like they were. Ailese was still lying on Andrew's lap.

"Hey, what's wrong, honey?" "I had a bad dream, Mikell. I'm so scared." Ailese burst into tears. Mikell comforted her. Andrew had told him what had happened. He didn't want him to think that anything sexual was going on between him and his wife. "Thanks, man, for being here for her. I do appreciate all your support. We're going through a lot right now." Honey, finish your tea okay. It will make you feel better." Ailese sat up and began to drink her tea.

"Hey Ailese, I'm going to take off, okay. Call me anytime that goes for the both of you. Please call me and don't hesitate if there's anything, anything, at all that I can do. Let me know." Ailese and Mikell both agreed that they would call Andrew if they needed anything. "Ailese, what was really going on before I walked in on you and Andrew?" "Mikell, please, you know that I would never go outside of our marriage, never! He came over because he got my message and he wanted to stay with me, and I fell asleep on his lap. He was concerned about me and you and our family, and he wanted to be here for us, that's all. Don't forget that we talked about Andrew for a while before I even let him into our lives- my life- and now you're accusing us of having sex." Ailese went to her room and slammed the door. Mikell followed behind her and opened the door. Ailese, please, it's just … I'm sorry. I guess this whole thing with D'Andra is stressing me out. Please forgive me. I know that you would never cheat on me. I'm sorry." Mikell took her in his arms and held her. Ailese and Mikell began to cry. Ailese told Mikell to hold her tight.

Ailese and Mikell didn't sleep much last night. They both tossed and turned all night. "Is Aunt D going to be okay, Mom?" "Yes, she is. If we all just pray, she will be okay." Ashanee hugged her mom. "Mom, I love you so much. You could sleep with me tonight if that would make you feel better." "Aw, you're so sweet, honey. Thank you," Ailese said, kissing Ashanee on her forehead.

Armont was still at his dad's house visiting his grandmother. She would tell Armont about his aunt when he came home. She didn't want to ruin his visit with his grandmother. Ailese, Mikell, and the kids headed to the hospital. Ailese was a bit uneasy about taking the girls to see their aunt, so she had a talk with them before they left the house. She had prepared them because they had never seen anyone in the hospital in D'Andra's condition.

Ailese didn't want the girls to be scared or anything.

When the girls were allowed to see their aunt, they were speechless. They didn't believe that the woman lying in the bed was their aunt. Mikell could tell that the girls were a bit uncomfortable, so he took them to get something to drink while Chris and Ailese stayed behind. D'Andra's face was still in bandages, and it was still hard for D'Andra to speak. Chris was feeding her ice cubes while Ailese was making sure that her sister was comfortable.

"Ailese, D'Andra mumbled, I still don't remember a lot about what happened that night." "I know, honey, it's okay. You will remember in time, I promise." There was a knock on the door. Ailese got up to see who it was. Hello, Officer Brown, it's good to see you. What are you doing here?"

"Hello, everyone. Well, since I took on the case with your mom and dad and you feel that the same person or persons may be responsible for hurting your sister, I feel that it's my duty as a police officer to seek justice. Ailese smiled and felt a sense of relief. Now someone actually believes her, even though she didn't have any evidence. Sit down, Mrs. LaShae, I just spoke with the lab, and it isn't good. They're still working on getting some kind of evidence from the crime scene. They are still speaking with people in that neighborhood. Hopefully someone saw something. I am hoping we will come up with something soon. Whoever did this is covering it up very well. The only thing that I could suggest right now until we catch this person or persons, is that if you go anywhere, take someone with you. Don't go off alone." Chris and Ailese agreed with Officer Brown. "So, if we don't catch this jerk, then they're going to get away with hurting my family? I don't think so! This is bull!" "I do understand how you feel, but we need evidence to convict anyone. I'm sorry, that's the law." "I understand, and please don't think that I blame you at all because I don't; you've been nothing but helpful. I just don't think it's fair! My sister is suffering right now; my parents can't sleep at night, and they will never feel safe again because of this jerk coming into our lives. Ailese stopped speaking. I'm sorry, please excuse me." Ailese went into the hallway and took deep breaths. A few minutes later, she heard a familiar voice. She thought that it sounded like Andrew's voice and she thought that she would investigate.

Ailese walked over to where the voices were. She saw Andrew and Dr. Lewis arguing and it looked serious. She couldn't make out what they were saying. Ailese didn't want the two of them to see her, so she rushed back to D'Andra's room. The whole day it bothered her; why was Andrew having a heated conversation with Dr. Lewis? It seemed odd. She didn't want to get into Andrew's personal business; she didn't want him to think that she was spying on him. Maybe they were friends or old colleagues? Andrew claimed that he didn't know a lot of people, and when he and Ailese met, he was just starting to get acquainted with people. Was Andrew lying? But why would he lie?

D'Andra was coming home today. She had been in the hospital for weeks. When Chris arrived at the hospital, he was anxious to take his wife home.

Her bandages were all gone, and she was looking like herself again, but he knew it was going to take a lot of time and work for D'Andra to feel 100 percent like herself again.

He wanted her to get back her smile. Her goofy laugh that he always loved to hear, but this will happen all in due time. He was going to do whatever he needed to do for her because he loved her so much. While D'Andra was in the hospital, he would cry himself to sleep every night after D'Andra would go to sleep because he had missed holding her, kissing her. He had missed their date nights. He looked forward to these special times with his wife.

Why? Who? So many questions went through his head. One night he had a dream that he had caught the person who had hurt D'Andra, and of course he handled that person himself in a way a man would. Chris didn't want to have that dream ever again. He wasn't a violent man, but he would do whatever he had to do to protect his loved ones, especially his wife.

Chris signed all the release forms so that he could take D'Andra home. Chris helped her get dressed and get situated in her wheelchair. The nurse wheeled D'Andra out into the hallway. D'Andra was quiet the whole time until she saw her sister waiting outside the hospital. It made her smile.

"Hey, hun, how are you feeling?" "Oh, I'm okay, I guess," she said slowly. She began to smile just a bit, and she slowly put out her arms to her sister, who hugged her very gently and kissed her on her cheek and whispered in her ear, I love you.

Ailese and the nurse helped D'Andra get situated in the front seat, while Chris put the bags in the trunk. She looked at Ailese again. She was so happy to see her. "We're going to be okay, were fighters!" D'Andra shook her head, yes. Ailese took her sister's hand, put it up to her face, and kissed it.

Ailese stayed at Chris and D'Andra's for a few hours. She wanted to make sure she had everything she and Chris needed. Ailese even made some meals and put them in the freezer so that Chris wouldn't have to cook. Alonda and Don were away with their church group. Ailese insisted that they go, being that they paid for the trip before all this happened and she felt that they needed some time away from all this madness! "Sis, thanks. You are so sweet, D'Andra hugged her. I love you. She began to cry. I'm so sorry, so sorry. I didn't mean to worry you guys." "Hey, hey, stop. Please don't start blaming yourself, okay." "But only if I stayed here, maybe." Ailese interrupted her. "Sis, look at me. No one's blaming anyone for what's happened to you. You are alive, and that's all that matters, okay? Now I want you to get some rest. I will be by here tomorrow morning, okay?" "Okay, I love you so much, big sis, I don't know what I would do without you." Ailese made sure D'Andra took her medication before she went home.

"Mom, are you alright? You look really tired." "I'm okay, Ashanee, but I am a bit tired. Mom had a very long day today, that's all." "I was going to ask you if you could help me with something." "Sure, kitten, what did you need help with?" "I want to make Aunt D a get-well card, but I need some help making the hearts. I was going to use stickers. Ashanee showed her mom the stickers that she wanted to use. What do you think?" "I know for sure that Aunt D would just love these colorful hearts, sweetie, so let's use these." Ailese and Ashanee worked on D'Andra's get well card, and Adrieana helped as well.

"Wow, Mom, you should be an artist. This card looks great. Thanks, Mom!"

"Thanks, honey, I used to be just like you and your sister, remember?

I used to collect a lot of stickers and make my own stuff. Remember all the stuff Grandma showed you?" "Oh yeah, I remember. You still got it Mom," Ashanee said, as she skipped to her room.

Mikell had called Ailese to check on her and the kids and to say that he would be home soon. When Mikell came home, Ailese had fallen asleep on the sofa with the television on. "Baby, Mikell gently shook her. Ailese opened her eyes. "Hi, I must have fallen asleep, Ailese yawned, turned off the television, and followed Mikell to their room. "What time is it?" "It's close to midnight. So, how is D'? She did come home today, right?" Ailese yawned again. "Yes, she's hanging in there. I stayed at the house for a few hours getting her situated and making things easier for them. I think that took a lot out of me. I just don't know how she's going to get through all of this; she is so fragile right now, but I know that if we work as a team like we always do, she'll be okay." "Yeah, because she's one strong woman, Mikell said. So, I know she's going to be fine, but not knowing who hurt her is what gets me."

Ailese and Mikell were woken up by the telephone. "Hello, Mikell answered the phone groggily. The voice on the other end was a female's voice that he didn't recognize. "I'm very sorry to have disturbed you. Is Ailese home?" "Hold on, I'll get her for you." Ailese, it's for you. Mikell handed her the phone. Ailese tried to focus, but she was so tired. "Hello, she whispered, this is Ailese." "Hi Ailese, I am so sorry to wake you, but this is Dr. Corbell. I know that you were very close to Dr. Lewis."

"Yes, I know, Dr. Lewis. What's going on?" "There's been an accident. Dr. Lewis is dead. Someone murdered him in his home. They think that it was a robbery or something. I thought you should know. I'm so sorry. We're all going to miss him. She paused again. He was a great person, and I don't understand who would want to hurt him." Ailese could tell that Dr. Corbell was trying to be strong by holding in her tears. Ailese couldn't believe her ears, she thought that she was dreaming. "Thank you for telling me I am so very sorry. Oh, my God, do you know anything else?" "All we know is that someone came into his home and murdered him and … Dr. Corbell paused again. Dr. Lewis is dead! He's gone! I just thought you should know." The phone went silent. She had just seen him a few weeks ago, and he was alive! "Mikell, Dr. Lewis is dead. Someone murdered him in his own home."

Mikell took the phone from her hands and hung it up on the receiver.

"What? Oh my Lord, he's dead? Ailese couldn't catch her breath.

Look at me honey, let's take a deep breath and let it all out, come on, do it with me." They both inhaled and exhaled at the same time.

"Mikell, I didn't want to say anything because I couldn't make out what they were saying. But I was visiting D, and I saw Dr. Lewis and Andrew. They were arguing; I mean, they were having a very heated argument about something. I mean, Andrew claimed that he didn't know many people here in Shelby, but when he and I started a friendship, he told me that he was just starting to get acquainted with people here, but I have a feeling that he already knew Dr. Lewis."

"What were they arguing about?" "I couldn't make out what they were saying. All I know is that it's weird how he's dead after that heated argument with Andrew that day." "Well, I agree, but we don't know what they were arguing about, and I don't recommend you bring this up to Andrew. I don't want him to hurt you in case he is involved in this." "Of course not." They both agreed to keep this to themselves, and besides, they both couldn't picture Andrew as a criminal.

"Hey Andrew, what are you doing for lunch today? I know you're just itching to take your favorite girl to lunch, right?" "Of course, whatever your little heart desires. It's good to have the old you back. I know that it's been hard for you, but don't be ashamed to laugh sometimes." "Yeah, I know. Hey, I have people like you in my life to get me through it all, and God. Thank you, Andrew, for emailing D those inspirational quotes that really lifted her spirits. I mean, she looked forward to those quotes every day."

"Well, like I said, anything I can do, I'm there."

"It's good to see Ell back to her unusual self, Andrew said with a snigger. I hope that it stays that way." "Yeah, me too. I mean, she is a great assistant, and I don't want to replace her either." "So, I will meet you here in your office at noon." "I was kidding. You don't have to take me to lunch." Ailese gave Andrew a light punch in his arm. "Oh, alright, yeah right, I don't believe you, Andrew said in a sluggish voice. See you at noon." Andrew left the room before Ailese could say anything. Ailese was so caught up in her thoughts until Ell told her that Mr. Saxx was on the phone. "Hey, there, Mr. Saxx, it's so nice to hear your voice." "Hey there, I know you're wondering why I'm calling, right?"

"No, you know that you could call me anytime." "Well, I know that my love. Listen, I talked to Ell and your calendars free. I hate to do this to you, but I need you and Andrew in Sutton. Now, this is an opportunity for our companies to get more exposure. It's a three-day event, and you know that I only send my top people, and that's you and Andrew." "Okay, I will be there, Mr. Saxx."

Ailese really didn't like going on those three-day conventions- type meetings. It bored her to death, but it was her job. Hopefully she won't have any nightmares this time, she thought to herself, and hopefully Andrew won't have to rescue her again. She looked at her watch, and it was almost time for her meeting with Mrs. and Mr. Gowan. They were in the upholstery business and needed their help.

Andrew had taken Mrs. and Mr. Gowan to the conference room, where Ell and Ailese were waiting for them. Ailese could already tell right off the bat that Mrs. Gowan wore the pants in their relationship and that she may be a bit of a problem, but there was nothing Ailese couldn't handle.

After everyone was introduced, Mrs. Gowan interrupted Ailese. "I need another drink. My stomach can't bear to take another sip of this horrible coffee." Mrs. Gowan turned up her nose. Ell took the drink from her and asked her what she would like instead. She asked for hot water and green tea. She told Ell not to make the tea, she would do it herself. Ell came back with the hot water and the green tea bag that Mrs. Gowan had requested.

"Is everything okay, Mrs. Gowan?" "Yes, sure, I'm listening." Mr. Gowan had an embarrassed look on his face and gave his wife a mean look.

After the meeting, Mrs. Gowan told Ailese that they would have to think about it before making a decision, and Ailese respected that, but Mr. Gowan tried his hardest to change his wife's mind because he was ready to make a decision, but she wouldn't listen to him. Ailese knew this would happen, so it didn't surprise her one bit. "Mr. Gowan, you have my card, and when you decide, give me a call. I do understand that you and your wife need to talk things over, and that's fine." Ailese really wanted to tell Mr. Gowan that he needed to have some guts and stop letting his wife run all over him, but she couldn't.

"Boss, was it just me or does Mr. Gowan have absolutely no say in anything? I bet she picks his clothes out for him and tells him how to eat and what to eat," Ell chuckled. "You're so bad you know that and no comment to that, statement."

After lunch, Ailese had decided to go by D'Andra's to check on her. She told Andrew that she would be back later on. "Hi, you're looking well," Ailese said, hugging her sister as she put her things down on the table near the door.

"Hi, I'm so glad that you're here. What's in the bag?" "Oh, here, this is for you."

"You got my favorite makeup, awww, sis. Thanks, you didn't have to do that."

"Well, I know that you can't live without your apple candy lip gloss, so I thought that would cheer you up," Ailese smiled. D'Andra was already putting on her favorite lip gloss. "Remember the first time you turned me on to this lip gloss? I said candy apple lip gloss? You said, come here and try it on. I bet you would love it, and I did. I don't know what I'd do if they ever stopped making my favorite lip gloss." "You're still rockin' that lip gloss!

Hey, where's Chris?" "Oh, he's taking a nap. I couldn't sleep last night, so he stayed up with me all night. I'm okay. Don't worry. I just had a bad night, that's all." "It looks like you're getting around better, sis." "Yes, I am, slowly but surely. I've been sleeping down here because Chris doesn't want me to use the stairs, but he wants me to take it slow." "And I agree."

"Sometimes, I still you know … D'Andra paused. Let's talk about something else. D'Andra quickly changed the subject. So, how are my girls doing? I miss them so much; I bet they're getting so big." D'Andra began to cry. "Honey, what's wrong? It just hit Ailese that before all this chaos, Chris and D'Andra were trying to have a child. Honey, what's wrong? Talk to me? Please?"

D'Andra sniffed. "I'm so emotional right now, that's all. I'm sorry. I haven't said anything yet, but I think that I was sexually assaulted. Every time I close my eyes, I see this person on top of me, choking me and covering my mouth." Ailese couldn't believe what she was hearing. "Honey, oh my God!" "It hurts that I can't remember what happened, only what I just told you, sis. I am not sure how I ended up where I was. Is it true that I was lying on the sidewalk?" Ailese couldn't lie to her sister, so she told her the truth. "Yes. Ailese took her sister's hand. Honey, we need to call the police right away. No, we need to call Detective Brown.

I am so, so sorry, sis. I really hope were wrong. I mean, Ailese paused. She found herself rambling. Ailese grabbed her cell phone, but D'Andra told her to wait to call Officer Brown because she just wanted to be sure; she wanted to be right, and she didn't want to embarrass herself or her family.

"Honey, it doesn't matter if you have a little info or a lot of info. We need to take care of this as soon as possible, sis, please." "Sis, I understand that. I do, but please, D'Andra whispered. I just don't want to right now, and please let's keep this to ourselves please, please. Don't even mention this to your husband either, please!" Ailese shook her head yes, she didn't want to drop the subject of her sister confiding in her about possibly being raped. She couldn't hold back on this one even though she knew her sister wasn't up for the argument that was for sure to happen if Ailese continued this conversation, but this is her sister, this is important! "D, please listen to me, okay? Ailese whispered to her sister. We need to catch this person who's hurting us. We need to stop this person before it gets worse. Now, please, let me call Officer Brown."

"Sis, I do understand, but there is no proof. It's gone. They didn't do a rape kit when I was admitted. I know this because my husband asked them if they did. There has to be a reason why they didn't think it was necessary for a rape kit. I am okay with not knowing, and I know that this may sound crazy to you. I just feel bad because I can't remember the things that could help catch this person or whoever. Does this scare me, yes? I have a doctor's appointment in a few days. My doctor wants to see if I am making progress. I will be seeing my physical therapist as well. I love you, sis. I thank you for being very concerned about my feelings." While Ailese was listening to her sister, she had a quick flashback when the monster raped her. Ailese grabbed her sister and held her so tight that she didn't want to ever let her go.

Ailese had to be okay with her sister's decision.

"Hello, hey, Mom. How are you? Are you guys back from your trip?" "Yes, we are, and your dad said hello. I just wanted to check in on you to see how you're doing. I know that a lot has been going on. Chris told me that Dr. Lewis was killed. Are you okay honey? I know that you two had gotten pretty close." "Yes, I know, I can't believe it. He was such a great man. I don't know why someone would want to hurt him. The funeral is next week, and I decided to pay my respects to Dr. Lewis. I feel for his family." "Yes, I do too, and you should go and pay your respects." "Leon will be going with me. He's the father of the baby that I helped pay for her medical needs, remember?" "Oh, yes, I do remember. Wasn't he her doctor?" "Yes, he was." "How's Leon's daughter doing?" "Great, she's doing awesome. He sends me pictures of her from time to time." "We all need to make sure to keep on praying and honoring God. This is a time that we as a family really need to depend on him." "I agree, Mom, I do. I love you Mom, and as I've told everyone, we'll get through this." "Please call me, if you need me okay?" "I will, Mom."

Ailese was a bit exhausted when she came home. It was a crazy day at the office. Nonstop meetings, nonstop viewing properties with Andrew, and lots and lots of paperwork. Being that she was keeping busy, she hadn't had time to think about this mysterious death of Dr. Lewis, but she still wanted to know what Andrew and Dr. Lewis were arguing about that day, and there was something that she didn't think of: why was Dr. Lewis at Southbridge Hospital? That was a bit out of his jurisdiction. But sometimes he is called to work at other hospitals, so it probably wasn't out of his jurisdiction. What business did Andrew have there? Ailese had so many gaps to fill, and she wasn't getting anywhere, and she didn't want to go to the source. Maybe she could talk to Dr. Corbell. Maybe she could ask her if Andrew was on any of the committees at the hospital.

First, it was the dreams that were haunting Ailese, and that still remains a mystery, even though Dr. Salvino did say that something triggered Ailese's dreams, and that was why the dreams were coming back, but Ailese hadn't seen this man in years and years, so it wasn't that, or was it? Ailese still couldn't get the nerve to write the first letter of this man's name that hurt her. Dr. Salvino wanted her to at least write the first letter of his name and work up to the last letter of the name. Every time Ailese would try, she would start shaking, then she would get all upset. She couldn't take it, and she didn't like how it made her feel.

Ailese knew that Dr. Salvino would expect her to write the first letter of the man's name who hurt her, when she came on Wednesday. She knew that she was going to disappoint her, and she didn't want Dr. Salvino to think that she wasn't taking her therapy seriously, because she was. Ailese was a bit bored, so she figured that she would work on writing the first letter of this man's name. Ailese pulled out a piece of paper and a pen and sat down at the kitchen table and took a deep breath. She told herself that this was a project and that it needed to be done as soon as possible, like she would say to herself at work. Ailese put the pen to the piece of paper and closed her eyes. When she opened them, the letter R was staring her right in the face.

Ailese couldn't believe it, but she'd finally done it! Ailese felt like this was a huge stepping stone for her! She couldn't wait to show Mikell. Ailese stared at the paper for a few minutes, and then put the piece of paper away.

After taking a long, hot bath, she figured she would call D'Andra to see how she was doing. She was out with Chris earlier when she spoke with her mom. "Hey Daddy, I miss you so much!" "Hey you, I miss you too, baby. How are you?" "Well, I'm hanging in there, and you?" "Same here too, sweetie. Your mother is making dinner right now, did you need her?" "Oh, sis, is she there?" "Hold on, I'll get her for you. I love you, and I will talk to you soon?" "Soon, I love you too, Daddy."

"Oh, I just took a long, hot bath and now I'm waiting for the troops to get home. Mikell took the kids right after school to see his mom and dad."

"Oh, well, that was nice, so you're there by yourself?" "Yes, D, I'm okay. I don't want you worrying, okay?" "Okay, but remember what the officer said- that we shouldn't be alone, Ailese. Please make sure that all your doors and windows are locked, sis." "They are. I just doubled-checked all the doors and windows."

"So, how was your walk?" "It was great. It's a great day to go for a walk. It's not too cold or too hot, just our kind of weather." "Yeah, I know a bunch of us walked to this restaurant for lunch, and we all walked back. It was a very nice day." Hey, guess what?" "Tell me." "I get my bandages taken off next week. Do you want to come with me? I mean, if you're." Ailese interrupted her. "Of course, I will. I'll pick you up, okay? Let's just have a girls day out if you're up to it." "That sounds great. It's going to be on Friday, so don't forget, okay?

10:30." "Okay, I'm putting it in my Blackberry right now."

"Hey, Mom's calling us for dinner. We'll chat later?" "Yes, okay, I love ya, sis." "I love ya too."

Ailese was done with dinner when Mikell and the kids came home. "Mom, you haven't made sloppy joes in a long time, and you make the best sloppy joes, Mom." "Thanks. Eat up. Did you all finish your homework?" "Yes, Mom."

"Good. There's some ice cream cake in the freezer, but you can only have a little." "I think I'm going to have some myself," Mikell said, as he shoved down the last of his sloppy joe. Ailese fixed everyone a bowl of the ice cream cake. She had some herself, and afterward she was very full. Mikell and Ailese spent some time with the kids before disappearing into their room.

"Lee, I was thinking that I would go with you and Leon to the funeral, okay?" "That would be great. Honey, that would mean a lot to me." Mikell kissed her gently on the lips. Ailese told Mikell about D'Andra's progress and having her bandages removed, and then she showed Mikell the paper with the letter that she wrote. "Baby, look, this letter *R* is a start for me.

Dr. Salvino wanted me to write the first letter of his name, and I've been struggling with this forever! I finally did it. I told myself that it was a project and that it needed to be done right away, and here it is. I know that my doctor is going to be so very proud of me." "Come here, I am so, so proud of you, baby. I knew you could do it, but only you knew when you were ready. This makes me feel so good, Lee. I feel like this is a stepping stone for you. I am so happy!" Ailese and Mikell hugged each other.

"Mikell, come here and listen. It's Sedrick! His songs on the radio!" Ailese pulled Mikell into the den, turned up the radio, and started singing.

"It is Sedrick. We've been shopping his CD around, and they said that they were going to air it this weekend. I better go and call him." Mikell called Sedrick, and he was so excited that his song was on the radio. "I can't believe it. Where's my lady?"

"Hey, Sedrick, you sound so good! I am so happy for you!" "Now, if only we could get you to appear in a couple of my shows, then we'll be set, my lady."

"Sedrick I want you to shine, okay?" "I know." "Well, Mr. Big Timmer, how does it feel to hear your voice on the radio and know that everyone is listening?" "I'm so blessed, so blessed! We'll talk soon. We need to do lunch or dinner soon, okay, my lady?" "Okay, it's a date."

"Sedrick really adores you, Ailese. He really looks up to you as a person and a singer. He once told me that he has never met anyone who feels their music like you." "Aw, I feel the same about him too. I am just happy that we can celebrate something good; it gets all the bad stuff that's been happening off my mind." Ailese felt herself getting sad again, but she shrugged it off.

"Ailese, don't feel bad if you smile or if you're happy. I know that we're going through a lot right now, and I have to say we're getting through it as well as I'd hoped. We're there for each other, and that's what counts, okay?" "I know Mik."

SHELBY LIES

"Hey, boss, Andrew wanted to see you in his office." "Okay, thanks, Ell.

Ailese knocked on the door before she entered. Hey you, Ell said that you wanted to see me." "Wow, don't you look beautiful as always. Ailese started to model her outfit in front of Andrew. This is not work-related. I just been so busy that I had forgot to mention this to you. I happen to be on a committee called Saving Our Children. I don't know if you've ever heard of the committee.

Well, we throw charity events to raise money for a lot of hospitals. We usually have a lot of space from what I hear, but it is being renovated. My question is, could you make a recommendation for a place that has a lot of space and is very exquisite?" "Oh, sure, I could email you some places if you'd like." "That would be great." "How long have you been doing the charities?" "Oh, a few months now. Denice talked me into it." Andrew rolled his eyes. Ailese thought that this would be a good time to ask him what the names of the hospitals were that he worked with. "Do you only work with hospitals in Shelby or do you go to other hospitals?" "Actually, all throughout the county and then some." "Oh, wow, that sounds interesting." Ailese kept her cool the whole time while she asked Andrew questions about the hospitals. So maybe he did have a reason to be at the hospital that day. Ailese was sure that all the pieces would fit together soon.

Ailese sat at her desk and surfed the net to look for some rooms to show Andrew. It didn't take her long at all to send all the info to Andrew.

A few minutes later, after she emailed Andrew the websites, he emailed her back to ask her if she would take a drive with him to look at a particular room. He wanted her opinion on it. She emailed him back and told him that she could go with him. Within an hour, Andrew was ready to drive to the places where he was thinking about having the hospital charity.

After the tour was over, Ailese told Andrew that he should book the room today because it would be perfect for the charity. Andrew agreed as well.

As Andrew was booking the room, Ailese had to answer a call, so she stepped outside to take the call. It was Dr. Salvino's office reminding her of her appointment today at 4:00 p.m. Right after Ailese hung up with the doctors' office, her phone rang again. She was surprised to hear Armont's father's voice on the other end, he rarely called her. Armont's dad wanted to know if it would be okay if he picked him up from school today. He had promised him he would take him to pick up some things that he needed. Ailese told him that it would be fine, but he had to drop Armont back at home. Mikell called her to tell her not to cook, and he also had a surprise for her. He asked her if she could be home before 7:00. She wondered what he had up his sleeves, but that didn't surprise her at all. He was always full of surprises.

"Sorry about that duty calls, so how'd it go? Were you able to book the room?" "Yes, I was, and thank you for all your help. You are the best." Andrew put one arm around her waist while they walked back to the car. "So, are you ready for the convention that's coming up soon?" "No. Ssh! Don't tell anyone. It's not my favorite thing to do, but oh well, we can't have it all, right?" "Right, well, you'll have me." Andrew looked at her and raised his brow. "Yes, I will, and we can keep each other company." "Yep. You know, some people at work has asked me about our relationship, you know. They asked me if we were a couple or if we were we engaged or stupid stuff like that. I think it's funny," Andrew chuckled.

"Really, they do, and what do you say? Yes, and yes to both questions, right?" Ailese gave Andrew a valiant look.

"No, I tell them, hey, we're really good friends, and I end the conversation," Andrew chuckled. "Well, it's not any of their business anyway. Maybe they could get some work done instead of worrying about us." "You're so bad, Ailese." "Well, it's true."

"Have a seat, Ailese. I do want to thank you for understanding when I had to go out of state. I'm so sorry that we had to miss our sessions." "I understand, doctor." Ailese made herself comfortable in the chair. "So, how did we do with writing the first letter of his name?" "Actually, I did good doctor. I am so happy."

Ailese gave her doctor the paper that had the letter *R* written on it. Dr. Salvino smiled. "Wow, this is great, Ailese. I am so proud of you! It just takes some time. I want you to still work on the next letter, okay?" "Okay, sounds good."

"Let's talk about the feelings that you were feeling when you wrote that R."

"Well, at first, I felt nervous, petrified, like I just wanted to give up, and then I felt victorious. It took me this long to even write this one letter. I mean, it should be easy, right? Not for me, it was so hard. I felt like if I said his name, or wrote his name, something bad would happen to me. I know that sounds crazy. I know I keep saying that, but that's how I've been feeling forever!

I told my husband what I did, you know, writing the first letter, and he was so proud of me because he too wants me to get better and beat this, you know? He stands behind me 100 percent. I don't know what I would do without his support and without my family's support."

"I'm so glad that you do have that support. Often people do not have that support like you do. Now that you have finished that first step. I see that we are making some progress, and Ailese agreed with Dr. Salvino.

So, Ailese, I want to talk about Mr. R: that is what we'll call him okay. Ailese shook her head. Let's take one day at a time. Say that tomorrow you happen to bump into Mr. R. What do you think your reaction would be? But before you answer that, I want you to take into consideration your strengths, your perception, and how focused you are now. What would be your reaction?" Ailese took a deep breath and started to create a picture in her head. "To be honest, I may be a bit afraid because I know what type of person he is, but at the same time, I would stand up to him. I wouldn't so much bring up everything he has done to me because I know he knew deep, deep down inside, it was wrong. I would try my hardest to make him apologize to me, and maybe that would give me closure in some way.

He made me do things that are unforgivable, that hunt you forever, and even though I'm sitting here with you, it will be in the back of my mind, or something will trigger the emotions. But it took me a very long, long time to forgive him, because my mom always told me to never hate anyone, no matter what.

He treated me like I was a slave, like trash, like a dog, and I thought that he loved me, but he didn't. Having to lie to the people that I loved hurt me the most! I hid from the truth, I didn't want to see the truth."

Ailese went to the funeral with Mikell and Leon. It was very hard for her, but she stuck it out. When Ailese Mikell and Leon entered the church, there were a lot of people. There were people praying, sobbing, and comforting one another.

They all took their seats and waited for the service to start. A beautiful woman who looked like she was in her mid-forties sang the most beautiful song. It brought tears to everyone's eyes. The Reverend who started the ceremony, read some scriptures from the Bible, and talked about the kind of person Dr. Lewis was. Some family members and loved ones spoke about all the goodness that was in his heart. Ailese didn't want to say goodbye. She didn't want to see his lifeless body lying in that casket. It reminded her of when her father was killed. Ailese briefly talked to his family about how she had met Dr. Lewis and worked with him. She paid her respects and told them how sorry she was and that he would be greatly missed. Ailese began to tear up when she was waiting in the car for Mikell and Leon. It really started to hit her. She was never going to see Dr. Lewis again.

"Baby, let me drive you to work. I still think that you should just stay at home. You've had quite a day, Ailese." "Yeah, I hear ya, baby, but there's nothing I could do. I can't bring him back. Baby, I will be okay besides, I don't like getting behind on my work, you know that." "Okay, baby, I'm ready whenever you are."

Mikell dropped off Ailese at work and would pick her up whenever she was ready to go home. "Why the long face, boss? Are you okay?" "Um, well, could you get me some tea, please? That would probably make me feel better. I've had some kind of day today." "Okay, boss, I will be right there with your tea."

Boss, boss, where did you go? I've been calling you; it looks like you have a lot on your mind, boss. Now, what's wrong." Ell put the tea in front of Ailese very carefully. "I just came back from a funeral. He was a good friend of mine, and I miss him. I guess it just hit me, I'm never going to see his face again or hear his laugh. Losing someone is hard, but I'm going to be alright."

"I remember when my brother's best friend passed away. It was so sad because he was like family to us. I'm sorry to hear about your loss, boss." "Thank you, Ell."

This was the one day that Ailese just wanted to forget about forever! She wanted to sweep it under the rug. When she got home, Mikell decided not to go back to work because he knew that she needed him. He ran her a warm bath, lit her favorite candles, and told her not to worry about anything.

"Wow, I feel so much better, baby. Where are the kids?" "Oh, they're in the game room. I was beating Armont at soccer. I told them that they could play some games for a while. Come with me, my dear. Mikell led her to the kitchen, where he had lit tall purple candles. It looked like they were at a restaurant.

Sit down. I will be your server for the evening, anything your heart desires."

Mikell put together a fresh plate of salad with Ailese's favorite toppings. Mikell sat down as well, and he too had a plate of salad. "Mmmm, this is so good, baby. You've outdone yourself. I can't wait until the main course arrives." "Oh, trust me, it's worth the wait." Mikell wanted to get that smile that he missed so much back on his wife's face; he wanted to distract her. After they finished their salads, Mikell was ready to serve the main course. "Are you ready? Here it is." Ailese's eyes got big when she saw what was on her plate. The main course was, blackened tilapia, corn on the cob, and brown rice with Pico de Gallo. "Baby, I'm speechless. You make me feel like a queen. Thank you. I love you so much." Ailese stood up to give him a kiss, and it was a passionate one too.

Mikell and Ailese talked and laughed. They hadn't done that in a while, like they had no care in the world. They watched television and laughed so hard they got a headache. They really missed doing this. After the kids said good night to their mom and dad, they still continued to laugh and laugh until they got tired. "Hold me, Mikell, please. Mikell held her in his arms, and began gently stroking her hair. I love you so much. Thank you for being my husband, my best friend, and for being here for me, no matter what. Ailese turned to him and whispered in his ear. Make love to me, please." Mikell took her in his arms and held her tight, and he would never let her go. They made love all night until the morning, tasting one another, and feeling every inch of each other's bodies, climaxing, and raging with fire. Feeling her femininity and feeling his masculinity, feeling every inch of him inside her, him feeling her tongue going places it's never gone before. Hearing their moans, feeling each other's hearts beating as one.

Mikell and Ailese had overslept. Mikell jumped out of bed and woke up Ailese.

"Oh my gosh, the kids are going to be late for school. Mikell grabbed his clothes and threw them on and ran out the room to check on the kids, who were all ready and dressed and were eating breakfast. "Hey guys, Mom and I overslept. I'm sorry. Are you guys ready? I'll have to write you guys a note for being tardy." "Um, Dad, we have twenty minutes to get to school. We should be fine." "Okay, give your dad a minute, okay? Mikell came back into the kitchen. Well, is everyone finished with their breakfast? The kids started heading to the car until Ailese came into the kitchen to kiss them goodbye. I'll be right back, okay, baby. love you." Mikell grabbed his keys and headed out the front door. When Mikell came back, Ailese was still lying in bed. Today she really didn't care what time she got into work today. She had already checked her schedule and didn't have any appointments until later on in the day. "Hey baby, come here. Mikell walked over to her. He kissed her like he was hungry for her again, and he was. He kissed her greedily. Ailese could feel his teeth while he was biting her bottom lip.

He laid her down, and they became one again.

"Hey, Ell said that you were feeling bad the other day. Are you okay?"

"I'll be fine, Andrew. I just had one of those days, but my hubby made it all go away, like it didn't exist." "So, tell me what happened?" Ailese really didn't want to get into her losing a good friend, so she kept it short and sweet.

"Well, I lost a dear friend of mine, and going to the funeral was harder than I thought it would be, that's all, but I got through it." Andrew hugged Ailese, held her tight, and kissed her on the forehead. "Hey, look at me. Call me next time. I want to be there for you, and I'm sorry that I wasn't." "Andrew, you have nothing to apologize for. You can't be there all the time. You have responsibilities, and I would never hold that against you." "Hey, I got a call from Mikell today. He said something about a dinner party." "Oh yes, he wanted to invite you to our dinner party. He's having some of his artists there, family, and close friends. Are you coming?" "I can't make it, that's the night of the charity event. Man, I didn't want to let him down." "No, he'll understand. Just call him back. I'm sure you guys can hang out another time. Don't make that face, Andrew. I told you not to feel bad, sweetie." "You guys are always good to me. Hey, maybe I could stop by later after the charity." "Yes, do that."

Ailese and Mikell went shopping for the party on Friday night. They ordered lots and lots of expensive foods and shopped for the finest wines and spirits.

They even hired servers and bartenders for the party. Mikell was so excited last year when he hosted the party that a couple of record labels signed some artist on the spot, and he's had success with all of them. He had hoped for the same turnout. He loved hosting parties. He would hire the same DJ every year, and every year it was a success. People would wear tuxedos and ballroom gowns, shining like stars. Mikell and Ailese's house would transform to look like a red-carpet party, that you would see famous people attend.

"I can't wait. I know you're excited, baby, and I am too. Now we need to figure out the desserts, do you think we should switch things up this time? Maybe have a huge cake with frosting that says your record label in gold letters? Her phone ringing interrupted Ailese. Hold on, baby. Mikell kept driving. Hello, okay, we'll be right there. It's going to be okay, and I'm coming right now." When Ailese hung up the phone, Mikell immediately saw the look on her face, and it wasn't good. "What is it?" "It's D'Andra. She needs us. We need to go there like, now. She sounded so upset." "Did she say anything, baby?" "No, all I could make out was that she needed us. She was crying a lot, and you know how she gets when she's crying. You can't understand anything she says."

"D'Andra what's wrong? You're shaking, here, sit down." Mikell walked to the kitchen to get her a glass of water. He handed D'Andra the glass of water and told her to drink it. When she was calm enough to speak, she took a deep breath. "I don't know where Chris is. He left me here alone by myself. When I woke up, he was gone, and I've been calling his cell a million times, and he doesn't answer, so I don't know if something happened to him." "Okay, and you're sure that he didn't leave a note?" Ailese looked around for a note, but she didn't find one. "I'm sure he'll be back. Maybe he lost track of time," Mikell said.

"Mom and Dad are out. He should be here with me!" "Okay, get dressed. You're coming with us." Ailese took D'Andra upstairs to help her get dressed. She was going to let Chris have it when she saw him.

"Okay, I left a note for Chris on the fridge. In the meantime, we'll keep trying him on his cell." Mikell looked at Ailese and shook his head. He was upset with Chris. What was he thinking, leaving his wife alone like this?

Mikell and Ailese had to finish their errands, or they would be behind, and they didn't want to do things at the last minute. "Have you eaten today, D? Mikell asked her. "No, I haven't. I am hungry, though." "Okay, is there anything in particular that you would like?" "I would like to go to Ten Jayes. I've been craving their tortilla soup and bread lately, is that okay, Mikell?" "Of course, anything my sister wants." They all smiled. Mikell parked at Ten Jayes and escorted the women inside the restaurant. The waitress gave them menus and took their drink orders. "Maybe you should come back to the house with us, okay." "Okay, Mikell I will, and I don't mean to rain on you guys' parade. I know you guys are busy today. I know you're excited, Mikell. It's going to be your big day, huh?" "You got it, beautiful." "Hey, it's Chris! Where have you've been?" D'Andra whispered. Mikell and Ailese waited for an explanation from him.

After D'Andra hung up, she said that he was running some errands and thought that he would be back in time. He said that his neighbor was supposed to come and watch D'Andra until he got back, but she had an emergency, which he found out later, and as far as him not answering his phone, he was getting a new one. She was still going to give him a piece of her mind, in person, not over the phone. Chris was acting very irresponsibly, and that didn't sit well with Ailese at all.

"You're looking really good, D'Andra. So, Lee tells me that you're getting your bandages, removed huh?" "Yeah, I hope that everything goes well because I would love to attend the party because I had so much fun last time." "I would love it if you were there." "Hey, if you don't mind me asking, how are your sessions coming along? Are they helping you?" "I love my sessions and my group sessions too, and yes, they're helping me a lot! Speaking of sessions, I hear that my sisters making a lot of progress with Dr. Salvino, right?" D'Andra took a sip of her iced water. "Yes, you're right. Just like we said we refused to be victims, we're going to fight." "This monster that hurt me, will not run my life forever!"

When they arrived back at D'Andra's, Chris was sitting at the living room table, looking over some paperwork. He looked up from his paperwork when he heard voices. "Chris, please call me if you need to go anywhere. You had my sister scared to death. I don't want her to be alone, and what in the heck were you thinking?" "I'm sorry, and it won't happen again, Ailese." "You damn skippy, it won't, because if it does your wife will be living with me!" D'Andra was relieved that her sister gave Chris a new ass. He'd known better not to leave her alone and not to depend on a neighbor to watch her either. He needed to depend on his family, and besides, she didn't have the strength at this point to rip Chris a new ass, anyway.

Ailese woke up early so she could stay ahead of herself, and she didn't want to be late picking up D'Andra and Chris. "Hey sis, I'm on my way. Are you guys ready?" "Hi, yes, we're ready. Come on over." "Mikell, I will see you later. They kissed each other. Kids, I love you guys. I'm leaving now to pick up your aunt." The kids told Ailese to tell their aunt hello and that they loved her.

When they arrived at the hospital, D'Andra checked in at the front desk, and the receptionist told her that the doctor would be right with her. D'Andra was seeing her primary doctor today and had hoped that the news she received would be good news. "D'Andra Kooley, the doctor can see you now." Chris and Ailese, and D'Andra followed the nurse to the waiting room. A few minutes later, the doctor came in, greeted everyone. Before he started, he washed his hands. "Hello, D'Andra, you're looking well today." "Thank you, Dr. Lowell."

Dr. Lowell examined D'Andra, he decided it was time to remove all of her bandages. Everyone was excited for D'Andra. After all the bandages were removed, Dr. Lowell gave D'Andra a mirror. "Oh my, I healed very well. I mean, you could barely see the scars. Thank you so much. You're the best doctor a girl could ever ask for!" "Baby, you look awesome. See, I told you that everything would work out," Chris said, as he kissed D'Andra on the cheek.

Dr. Lowell asked everyone to exit the room because he still had to examine D'Andra in private. Everyone exited the room and waited until she was done.

On the way home, D'Andra explained to Chris and Ailese what the doctor said about her progress, which was a surprise to both of them. "Well, get this, guys. The doctor said that it may be possible to have kids and that it's always good to get a second opinion. What do you think about that?" "That is perfect, baby. We can try having kids soon. This is the best news I've ever heard!" Chris was so excited that he didn't know what to do with himself. "Baby, remember the key word is possibility. I don't want us to get our hopes up high, so we'll see what happens, okay?" "Okay, my queen, I love you so much." "I love you so much." "I am so excited for you guys, and I do believe in miracles." When D'Andra's accident happened, the doctor wasn't sure if all of the internal and external wounds would heal, so he had suggested waiting to have a child until he was 100 percent sure. This news was exactly what everyone needed right now-something awesome like this.

"Hello, Ruben, it's nice to see that you're back. How's the baby doing?" "Hello, Mrs. LaShae, the baby is doing awesome. I didn't even want to leave her. The baby sleeps through the whole night. We wake up the baby to feed her and change her, and she goes right back to sleep. I'm the happiest man on earth!" "Well, that is so good to hear. Hey, stop by my office later, I have something for you, okay?" "Sure, I'll see you then, and have a good day, Mrs. LaShae." "You too, Rueben."

Andrew came up from behind Ailese and frightened her. "Andrew, I owe you one big time. You scared me to death!" "I'm sorry, I couldn't resist. You're so cute when you're mad." Andrew laughed. "Whatever. Ailese rolled her eyes at Andrew and then smiled at him. Why are you in such a good mood today? New girlfriend last night?" "No, you're the only woman in my life, sweetie," Andrew chuckled. It's a special day today. You want to know what it is?" Andrew started walking backward, and then he stopped in front of Ailese.

"Mmmm, do I really want to know? Well. I guess I'll take my chances, so tell me, give it to me." "It's my birthday, and unlike some people, I get excited because it means I'm doing something right. I'm still here!" Andrew started dancing like he was in a Fred Astaire movie. "Andrew, wait, Ailese looked at her blackberry, and it was his birthday. She felt so bad. Oh, my it is your birthday. I am so sorry, so much has been going on. Please, let me make it up to you. Let's do something tonight." Andrew interrupted her and took her hand. "Don't feel bad. I know you don't have to say anything. So, meet me here at five, okay? Don't be late. Promise me that you'll be right here at this spot at 5:00, Ailese." "Okay, I will. You know I will."

Ailese didn't ask Andrew why he needed her to meet him at 5:00. She knew he had something planned and she wanted to spend time with her best friend, especially on his birthday, and it was the least she could do. She felt so bad about forgetting it was his birthday. She's been going through so much these past months. Ailese and Andrew were together the whole day, and not once did she mention or ask him what he had planned at 5:00. She told her husband not to expect her home early, because she was going out for Andrew's birthday. He told her to have fun and to check in with him later.

Ailese and Andrew worked right through lunch. They survived off of coffee and some sandwiches that Andrew had brought from home. They were in and out of meetings, conferences, presentations, and meetings with important people all day long. No one even saw Ailese and Andrew all day, not even Ell.

"I am so tired, what a day. Are you tired?" "No, I'm good. I must warn you, you're going to need your strength later, okay." "Okay, whatever you say, my friend." "Well, I will see you at 5:00. I have some things that I need to do in my office, and I need to return some calls." Andrew closed the door behind him.

Ailese returned calls and made some calls. Her mom called as well. Ailese picked up the phone and dialed her number, but she had gotten her voice mail, so she figured she would call D'Andra's. "Hello, Mom, I thought that I would catch you there. I left you a message. What's up?" "Hi, baby, my phones charging, so I didn't get your message. How's your day, sweetie?" "Oh, it's really busy and crazy. Thanks for asking Mom. Mom, how's Daddy?" "Oh, he's working hard. I haven't seen him all week. They have him supervising a crew in another county, and you know how those are." Yeah, I do. How is Daddy really doing, though? How is he holding up?" "Well, you know how your dad is. He keeps himself busy. From time to time, he will bring up the situation and what's been going on, and he does get angry. The thought of someone hurting your sister will never sit well with him. If it were up to your dad, he would take care of the problem for good, and you know what I mean, and since we don't have anything to go on, we are keeping our family in prayer. Don says that we need to give it to God. He hates that he doesn't know why someone wants to harm us because we've always treated people with respect." "Yes, I feel the same way, and I know that it is all because of God that we're all getting through these trying times."

Andrew was knocking on Ailese's door at five sharp. He decided to walk out with her, it was better that way than meeting her at the spot. "Are we ready?" Ailese made sure she had everything and made sure she locked up everything. "What are you up to, birthday boy? We better not be doing anything illegal." Ailese looked at Andrew with a baffled face. "I promise you it's not illegal, Ailese, I promise. Man, I feel so bad that my own best friend in the whole world doesn't trust me," Andrew chuckled. "Aw, you're sweet, and yes, you are my best friend in the whole world, but you can be crazy sometimes." They both laughed.

Andrew and Ailese ended up at a casino on the other side of Romanville.

Ailese had only been there once. She wasn't big on gambling, and the time that she and D'Andra went to the casino, she was more excited about the band that was playing there. "Honey, I know that you don't like gambling, but I have a huge surprise for you and me. Come on." Andrew took her hand and led her inside the casino. It was very shrill inside the casino. You could hear people talking and music all at the same time. "How could you even think with all this noise?" Ailese thought to herself. When Andrew grabbed a table, he offered her a seat and told her that he would be right back. Ailese looked around. She did know that a band was about to play here, and that was all she knew. When she was waiting for Andrew, some guys were hitting on her and wanted to buy her a drink, but she declined. She was happy to see Andrew walking back to the table with two drinks in his hands. "Sorry I took so long. That line was crazy at the bar. "Wow, my favorite. I should be getting your favorite. It's your birthday, you know." "No worries." "So, tell me, why you aren't out celebrating with some beautiful woman or women? How are you doing in that department anyway? If you don't mind me asking." "Well, to answer your first question, I wanted to spend my birthday with you. Is that okay? Andrew took a sip of his drink. I date when I have the time, but nothing exclusive, and I'm okay with that."

"Okay, okay, calm down." "I'm cool, and seriously, though I don't know if I will ever find that special someone. I blew it when I had the best woman in the world, so I'm okay with just dating here and there."

The music was getting even louder, and the lights went dim. A few seconds later, the announcer entered the stage. "We have a treat for you tonight, folks. Without further ado, I welcome you, Ms. Melodee Zion!" Ailese couldn't believe it. This was one of her favorite singers, and she was there in person! Everyone clapped when Melodee Zion walked on stage. "Andrew, are you serious? You know how much I love Melodee!" Ailese wanted Andrew to pinch her because she had to be dreaming. The crowd sang along with Melodee. They danced and they cheered. Andrew and Ailese slow danced, and sipped on their drinks.

When Ailese was singing, Andrew told her that her voice was beautiful as well. "I knew how much you loved her being that you play the CD in the car a thousand times. I saw the ad that she would be here and, on my birthday, how great is that?" "Like a dream!" Andrew took pictures of Melodee Zion for hm and Ailese. They danced the night away. It was like magic having the two of them together. They never got tired of singing and dancing.

Ailese wanted to do something special for Andrew, so when he excused himself to go to the restroom, she thought this would be the perfect time to work on that surprise. She hurried to ask the announcer if she could speak with the band or Melodee. She had explained that it was her best friend's birthday and wanted to know if Melodee could sing happy birthday to him. Her request was granted. Andrew had come back to the table just in time, because Melodee was about to announce that it was his birthday. "I want to wish Andrew McGee II a very happy birthday, and this special request is from Ailese, your best friend. She wants you to have many more birthdays, and she wants you to know that she loves you. This is for you, Andrew." Melodee sang her own version of the Happy Birthday song, which was beautiful! Andrew was in awe; he was moved by her voice as well.

Andrew and Ailese couldn't believe it. Melodee had released a live album that was more like the concert that they had just attended, so they rushed in line to purchase it. Ailese told Andrew that it was her birthday gift to him, and he agreed. "Oh, my, I had so much fun, Andrew! Thanks so much! I will never forget this night as long as I live!" "I'm glad that you had so much fun! That woman has a voice on her, that's for sure." Ailese started singing one of Melodee's songs: "I can feel your heart beating next to mine, mmmm ... don't ever stop loving me." "You go, girl!" Andrew smiled. They played the CD the whole way home.

When Ailese came home, she told Mikell all about her evening and went to sleep.

It was Sunday morning, and Ailese was determined to make it to church today. Nothing was going to stop her. "Mikell, please make sure that the kids are ready while I find my keys." "Okay, babe, no problem." The phone rang while Ailese was looking for her keys. She debated answering it or not, but she decided to answer it. "Hello, oh, hey, Daddy. How are you?" "Hi, sweetie, Dad's doing okay. I want to know how you are doing, honey?" "I'm hanging in there, Dad." Ailese smiled, her dad's voice could always make her smile and it made her feel good that he was so concerned about her. "I know my girls are strong, just like their mom. Ailese smiled. "Of course, Daddy, I would love to spend some time with you. I miss you so much!" "Okay, so I know that you're getting ready to head out, so call me later on so we can set the date, okay, and I love you." "Okay, Dad, I love you too, and I will call you later."

When Ailese and her family arrived at church, she was surprised to see that the church had made some changes. They had rearranged the pulpit, and there were new chairs and carpet. Ailese greeted members of the church as she found her seat. The pastor talked about trials and tribulations and why we all go through our trials and tribulations. Ailese took everything that the pastor spoke about and soaked it all up. "We're going to be okay, she said to herself. We just have to remain strong, that's all." Hearing the sermon made Ailese hopeful.

After church, Ailese and Alonda chatted about the sermon and how they both related to the pastor words. Alonda told Ailese that the family was going to make it through and that D'Andra was going to be okay. She just knew it.

"With God, all the love and support, Ailese, that's all we need. I love you, and I will talk to you later." "Okay, Mom, I love you more." Ailese hugged her mother and walked her to her car. "What are you smiling about, Lee?" Mikell asked her. "Oh, I was just thinking about today's sermon, that's all. God is good, and I know that he will never let us down. When things seem hopeless, you need to know that you can count on God." "Amen, and you're right, we all need to keep our faith in him."

"Hello, D, how are you feeling?" "I'm feeling great, actually. I was calling to see if you wanted to come over and watch a movie with me?" "Are you sure you're up for company?" "Yes, I'm sure. Come on over, and besides, it's been so long since we had some girl time." "Okay, I am on my way. See you in a bit."

Ailese used her key to get into the house. When she opened the door, D'Andra was waiting for her. "Hi, you look so pretty, D'Andra. You're looking great, and you seem happy." "I am sis, I'm so happy, and I don't know if I told you, but I'm going back to work next week. What do you think about that? I mean, I'm going to work from home for a while and then ease my way back into the office." Ailese smiled at D'Andra. She didn't want to ruin the mood that her sister was in, and she didn't want to be negative. "I think if you're ready, then that is great! I just want you to be sure; you need to consider all that you've been through these past couple of months. I love you, and I'm not trying to be negative or anything. I care about you, sis."

D'Andra poured two glasses of chocolate milk and handed one to her sister, and smiled. "I know that you love and care about me, and you have always only wanted the best for me. I thought that Chris wanted the same for me, but I was wrong." "What do you mean by that?" "Well, the other day I was in the shower, and something was eating at me the whole day, like something wasn't right, you know, so something told me to get out of the shower, and I did, D'Andra took a sip of her drink and sat it down on the counter. I hear Chris making plans-plans that he should have been making with me, but he wasn't. He couldn't lie to me because I heard everything that was said. I thought that I was dreaming, you know? Here's a man that I have loved all my life. Since the day that I saw him, I knew that I was going to love him forever.

I never cheated on him, and yes, I was a bit hard-headed, but that is who I am.

We decided to separate for now until he knows what he wants or what it is he wants. I guess it's true, sometimes men do wonder and let their curiosity get the best of them, but no matter what, Chris wasn't honest with me. Ailese didn't say a word. She let D'Andra vent and say what she wanted to say.

I wanted so much for us, you know, and I asked him straight up: Was he cheating on me? He lied to me, and I took him back because I honor the vows that we took, you know, so I was willing to make it work, but I am not going to blame myself, but what I do know is this: I love him so much with all my heart. Our communication disappeared. We fell off the communication wagon. It happens sometimes. You know what gets me is- when I was … attacked and when I needed him the most, he still continued to lie to me. He knew that I wasn't going to be focusing on him lying and cheating on me in my condition. I know that he was lying and cheating on me. I just didn't want to deal with it. I couldn't deal with it. He did fool me a lot, though. I don't know if we can save our marriage or if maybe our marriage is over, but he needs to figure that out because I can't and I won't let him hurt me anymore!" Ailese grabbed D'Andra and hugged her telling her that it was going to be okay, and that she was sorry that she had to go through this. "I'm here. Please don't ever forget that. I love you. You're so strong and I admire that in you.

Ailese let her tears run down her face at this point she didn't care. She'd been holding in a lot of tears lately. She wished she could take all D'Andra's pain away. You are a great person inside and out. Don't you ever doubt that, and Chris will see that, I know that he will.

Don't let him push you into taking him back. You go at your own pace, and I am going to stand behind you in whatever your decision is." D'Andra wiped the tears that were rolling down her sister's face and grabbed her by the hand and led her upstairs, where they watched movies for hours and they talked, cried, and laughed. Ailese confessed to D'Andra that a part of her wanted to rip Chris's head off, but she knew that it wasn't right, but, it was right to vent about it.

As time passed, Mikell's party was approaching, and in between helping her family out in their time of need, Ailese couldn't grasp what day it was or if it was day or night. Things at the office were going good, and Ailese stayed busy. She had gained a lot of new clients, which was good. But today was a good day because she and D'Andra were spending the evening with their dad. They had him all to themselves. Don was taking his girls to dinner; they all deserved it too.

Ailese was so excited to see her dad. She talked about this day all week.

Andrew even told her not to worry, that he would take over for her if she weren't done with all her contracts, so she could be with her dad.

Ailese hadn't seen Ell since this morning and was wondering where she could be? Ailese did send Ell on some errands, but it shouldn't have taken her this long. Hopefully Ell will be back soon because there is a lot of work that needs to be done today, being that they have a lot of new clients.

Ailese worked hard, making sure everyone of her clients were happy. If it meant working through lunch and taking minimum breaks, then that's what she would do. She loved her work, she loved helping people, and that raise that Mr. Saxx gave her didn't hurt either. It was very generous of him. Ailese loved it when her hard work was acknowledged. That meant a lot to her to have a boss that always recognized her hard work.

Ailese took a short break to call Mikell. "Hello, handsome, how's it going? Are you busy?" "Never too busy for you. Hold on for one second. Emmanuel, can you please take over for me, for a bit? So, how's your day?" "It's going good. I'm keeping busy. So, I thought that I would take a breather and call my favorite guy." Ailese smiled. "Well, I thank you for thinking of me. So, tonight's the big night, huh? Listen, I want you to have fun, okay? You guys deserve it, and don't worry the kids and I will be just fine, okay?" "Okay, I love you. I will see you when I get home, right?" "Yes, baby, I will be there before you get off."

After Ailese hung up with Mikell, she heard Ell's voice, so she called her into her office. "What took you so long? I was about to send a search party for you. Are you okay?" "I'm sorry, boss, the lines were crazy. I spilled my drink on my clothes, so I had to go home and change. My phone went dead, so I couldn't call you, and I am so sorry. I didn't mean to worry you." "It's okay, I understand these things happen sometimes, but please make sure you charge your phone just in case I need you or in a case like this, okay?"

"Yes, boss." Ell assured Ailese that it wouldn't happen again. "Ell, what does that C stand for on your necklace? I'm just curious." "Ell grabbed the necklace and put it inside her sweater. "Oh, it's nothing really. It's the initial of my boyfriend's name. We're back together now." "Oh, congrats, well, that's good that you guys are working it out." "Thanks, boss. Well, I better get back to work."

SHELBY LIES

Ailese and Andrew had to have a meeting with a few contractors. The meeting was going to be a very long one. Ell made sure that the conference room was ready and waited for the contractors to arrive so she could take their drink requests or whatever they wanted. "Ell, I think that I'm going to need more markers. Could you please get them for me?" "Oh, sure, boss. I will be right back."

"So, I think after the meeting you should head out. That way you could get some rest before your big date." "Well, I guess. That does sound like a great idea, and I could use some rest." "I'm not asking you, I'm telling you, okay?" "Yes, sir." Ailese raised her brow at Andrew.

When Ailese drove up to the house, Mikell was walking out, he was surprised to see her. "Well, hey, love isn't this a surprise? I was heading back to work but I'd rather spend some time with you."

"Okay. I got off work early. I was going to take a nap and rest before Dad picked us up for dinner later. I would love it if you stayed." "Okay, then it's settled. Have you've eaten lunch yet?" "No, I was going to make a salad. I don't want to ruin my appetite." "Well, have a seat. Mikell took Ailese's shoes off of her feet. I'll make some lunch. Why don't you get comfortable, okay?"

Ailese went into the bedroom to get out of her work clothes and came back into the kitchen. She started laughing because Mikell was dancing and making funny noises. "What? Are you making fun of me?" "No, no, baby, don't let me stop you; do your thing." Mikell and Ailese both started to chuckle.

"Here you go, and what would my queen like to drink?" "Um, just ice cold water would be fine, thanks." "Here ya go, Mikell sat the ice- cold water down on the table and sat down at the table with Ailese. So, I wanted to tell you, Emmanuel, and I have a really good feeling that the party is going to be another success. I can't wait until the party." "Yes, I know how excited you are, and I agree with Emmanuel, the party will be another success."

After lunch, Mikell cleared the dishes and loaded the dishwasher while Ailese was getting ready for her bath. "Honey, your bath awaits you." Mikell led her to the bathroom and told her to relax. "Hey aren't you going to join me?" Ailese smiled. "Are you sure? Because you know how I get." Mikell took off Ailese's bathrobe and helped her into the bathtub. "Maybe I want you to be naughty. Come here." "Baby, I love you so much. It's been so long since we've made love. Ailese began to kiss Mikell; she was once again hungry for him. She wanted to taste him. I want you so bad." "I do too baby." Mikell kissed and caressed every inch of her wet body. He could feel her excitement, by the way her body moved. He made his way between her legs, and she instantly felt goose bumps run through her body. She moaned even louder. She couldn't wait to feel him inside of her. Mikell picked up her body out of the bathtub and slowly placed her naked body on the bed. He needed her and he wanted her, right now at this moment.

"Baby, wake up. It's time for you to get ready, and I have to get back to work. Come here." Mikell pulled her to him and kissed her. The kiss lasted a long time, making Ailese want him again. "Hey, take a shower with me, beautiful." "Um, I think I need to take one alone, or I or we, won't ever leave this room," Ailese said, when she stood up and gave Mikell another kiss. They ended up taking a shower together and, to some extent, behaving themselves.

"Dad, you look so handsome." D'Andra agreed with her sister. Don was wearing a dark and light blue suit with a burgundy tie. The waiter showed them to their seats and gave them menus. "Could I start anyone with some of our fine wines or whatever your heart desires?" "Yes, please, can I get a bottle of your finest red and white wine? It's a special occasion." "Very well, sir. I will be right back with the wine." As the waiter walked away, D'Andra and Ailese's eyes met each other. They smiled, they both felt so important.

"Red and white wine, Daddy? Wow, this is an important night." "Yes, it is. I'm spending the evening with my favorite girls. I want you to order whatever you want, okay?" A few minutes later, the waiter came back with the wine and poured everyone a glass. Don took a sip of the wine and was pleased with the taste. They all agreed that the wine tasted great.

"Wow, Dad, they have so much food on this menu that I don't know what I should order. What do you think, Lee?" "Well, to be honest, I don't know either. Everything sounds so good, and I've never been here, so I can't recommend anything, Ailese said, taking a sip of her wine. I think that I'm going to get grilled tilapia. It comes with brown rice and veggies. It sounds good." "Oh, yes, that does sound good sweetie," Don said, continuing to look at his menu.

They all finally knew what they wanted to order before the waiter arrived back at the table to take their orders.

"I was thinking about going to our favorite ice cream shop afterward." "That sounds good, Dad." They enjoyed their dinner and talked about what was going on in their lives. They even talked about Chris. When D'Andra told her dad what had happened, he wasn't happy about the whole situation. Don told D'Andra that he would stand by her side, and that it didn't matter what her decision was. He would still stand behind her no matter what. He wanted Chris to man up and admit that he was wrong for what he had done to his daughter and that she didn't deserve that at all. Don also said that he hoped that they could work it out. After leaving the restaurant, Don took D'Andra and Ailese to one of their favorite ice cream shops to get ice cream and they all ordered the same thing:rocky road with a drizzle of caramel sauce.

After they all finished their ice cream, Don drove Ailese home. Ailese didn't want the night to end. It had been so long since they had time together like this. "I wanted to say good night to the kid. Are they still awake?" "I'm pretty sure they are, come on in, Daddy."

When they entered the house, all the kids were in the living room watching a movie, and Mikell was in the kitchen popping popcorn. "Hi Grandpa, Ashanee, Armont, and Adrieana hugged their grandpa. They asked if he could watch the rest of the movie with them, and he couldn't say no. Everyone watched the rest of the movie and chatted for a while. Armont showed his grandpa his new fishing rod that his dad had brought him, and the girls showed him all their new bracelets and earrings that they had made. Don had promised the kids that he would pick them up soon and go shopping and hang out. The kids hugged Don and D'Andra goodbye and told them that they loved them.

After Don and D'Andra left, Ailese was a bit bushed. It took everything in her not to go to sleep while the kids kept her up talking to her about school, their friends, and other things. After a while, she could not fight it anymore; she needed to rest now. Ailese was so tired that Mikell had to get her out of her clothes and into her pajamas. "Thanks, baby, I'm just so tired. Are you coming to bed?" "Yes, sure, I'm not that tired but you go to sleep. I'm going to watch some television until I fall asleep." Ailese gave Mikell a kiss and went to sleep.

Mikell had let her sleep in, and besides, she needed her rest.

Mikell made sure that he didn't make a lot of noise. He told the kids to try and be as quiet as they could. Mikell started the laundry and cleaned the whole house. He didn't want Ailese to worry about anything when she got up.

When Ailese opened her eyes, she focused on the alarm clock to see what time it was. She couldn't believe it. It was almost noon! She had slept most of the day. She jumped into the shower, got dressed and headed to the kitchen because she needed coffee. She didn't see Mikell or the kids. She was a bit groggy. She saw that a pot of coffee had already been made, so she poured herself a cup of coffee and sat at the kitchen table and sipped her coffee slowly. A few minutes later, she heard Mikell's voice. "Baby?" "Mikell I'm in the kitchen and why did you let me sleep so late? The day is almost over."

"Hey baby, I thought that you needed your rest, and you haven't slept this good in a long time. It's okay, sometimes we need to sleep in." Mikell kissed her on the forehead as he walked over to pour himself a cup of coffee. "Mik, where are the kids?" "Oh, they're in their rooms. I told them to be as quiet as they could, and they have been. Hey, do you feel up to going with me? I have to take care of some things, and I'll drive." "Okay, sure, I have to go to the bank and stuff. I'll get the kids."

"Mom, I missed you. You were tired, huh, Mom?" "Yes, I was so tired, Ashanee, but I'm all rested now." Ashanee gave her mom a huge hug.

Mikell and Ailese ran errands the majority of the day. They also went to check on the catering and the decorations. They were both relieved that everything was still in place for the party. They went grocery shopping and bought supplies for Adrieana's upcoming school project.

"I need to pick up our dry cleaning and then I need to head to the mall. Is that okay, honey?" "Whatever you have to do, baby, I don't mind." "Mom, Armont got his mom's attention. "Yes, Armont." "Could I go look in some stores if I promise to meet you guys in a certain place when we go to the mall?" "Sure, Mikell and Ailese had agreed that Armont could look at some stores while they were at the mall. "Armont, could I go with you?" Adrieana asked her brother. "Sure, why not? I don't care." "Does everyone have their cell phones with them?" All the kids had their phones with them.

"Okay, guys, stay together, okay? We'll meet here at the entrance in a few hours, okay? Call me or your dad if you guys are here before us, okay?"

"So, where are we going?" Adrieana asked Armont. "I want to look at some tennis shoes." "Me too. Let's go to BG'S. I saw the perfect shoes there, and I know that you'll love them. Come on." Adrieana grabbed her brother's hand and led him toward the store.

"I think we did some damage today, huh?" Ailese looked at Mikell with a semi- smile on her face. "Don't worry about it, baby, enjoy it."

After shopping and running more errands, everyone was exhausted when they got home. Ailese told the kids that she would let them know when dinner was ready. "Let me help you. I'll put these on the grill, and you could cook the side dishes?" "Okay, sounds good. I guess you couldn't wait to try your new grill, huh?" "No, I mean you can use this thing when it's raining season." Mikell grilled some chicken breasts, and when they were done, he poured teriyaki sauce on them. "Mmmm. Baby, that smells so good, I can't wait to taste them." Just as they were getting ready to say grace, the phone rang. "Who could that be? Ailese answered the phone.

Hello, oh hey, hold on." She gave the phone to Mikell. "Hello, oh, hey, Karen. What's going on?" "Well, I do apologize again for bothering you at home, but we need to meet. Mr. Cummings has to fly out first thing in the morning. He had something unexpected come up, so he won't be able to see us tomorrow.

I need you to meet us at his hotel. I know that it's last minute."

"No worries, I'll be right there. Give me a minute to change. See you then." I'm sorry I have to go to a meeting. I'm sorry, kids." Ailese followed Mikell into the bedroom. "Baby, do you know what time you'll be home?"

"No, I don't, but I will call you, okay?" "Okay, is there anything you need?" "No baby. Well, actually, could you put my plate up for me? I do plan on eating my dinner when I come back."

Ailese knew how business worked when it came to Mikell's business, but she just hated it when he had to go to last- minute business meetings. That burned her, but she would never tell that to Mikell! She needed to keep busy, so she folded laundry. When she was putting away her laundry, she had come across Dr. Lewis's business card, which brought tears to her eyes. She sat on the bed and stared at the card for a long time. Ailese could still see his face, and she still remembered his smile. She began to grip the card in her hand tightly, and she began to sob even more. "I'm not going to let this get to me. I'll be fine." Ailese still wanted to know who hurt Dr. Lewis and why? Ailese shrugged her shoulders, wiped her face, and replaced the card in its place. Ailese regained her composure and went back to what she was doing.

Ailese had almost forgotten that she had bought Andrew a late birthday gift. She decided to wrap Andrew's gift. After she was done, she went to her car and placed it in the trunk so she wouldn't forget it. When Ailese was done with all her chores, Mikell was home. "I'll heat up your plate for you. How did your meeting go?" "It went great, thanks for asking." Mikell started on the feast that was placed in front of him. "That chicken was excellent, honey. You did a good job. Even the kids said so." Mikell smiled, polished off his drink, and put his dishes in the dishwasher.

"You're tired, Mikell, you can't stop yawning, babe. I think you should go and lie down after your meals have digested." "I can't because I have a late conference call in like an hour, Mikell said, looking at his watch yawning. If I drink some coffee, I should be okay." Ashanee sat in her father's lap while he sipped his coffee. "So, how's my kitten doing, huh? Are you doing okay?" "Yes, I'm good, Daddy. What about you?" "Oh, Daddy's a bit tired, but other than that, I'm super." Mikell kissed Ashanee on her check. "Daddy, could we read this book that I checked out from the library at school, please?" "Okay, let's go and get it."

Ashanee was pulling on Mikell's shirt the whole way to her room.

When they passed Adrieana's room, Mikell knocked on the door and entered her room. "Hey, you, do you want to join your sister and I? We're going to read a book. We could take turns reading it if you like." "Yeah, okay." Adrieana followed Ashanee and her dad down the hallway to Ashanee's room.

"Here's the book Daddy. Ashanee handed her dad the book. It had to have been over 100 pages. "What made you want to check out a book like this? This is way over your age group, honey." "Because it's about wizards and princesses, and it has princesses and wizards on the front, and I love wizards and princesses, Daddy." "Okaaayyy. Mikell read the title of the book: the book was called 100 WIZARDS AND 101 PRINCESSES BY C. G. KANE.

Okay, girls, we can only read until it's time for Dad's conference call, okay?"

Mikell began to read, and when he was done, Adrieana would take over. They both took turns reading until they read all twenty pages. Mikell told the girls to tell their mom and Armont good night after they finished reading the book.

Mikell went into Armont's room to see how he was doing. He was surfing the internet and listening to music. "Hey, buddy, I just wanted to check on you and see if you needed anything." "Hey Dad, I was just downloading some music on my iPod. Dad, you look really tired. How did your meeting go?" "Oh, it was a meeting, Mikell smirked. Is school going okay? How's your new math teacher? Is he cool?" "School is going well, and my math teacher is okay. He's a tough teacher, but I can handle it." "That's what I wanted to hear." Mikell's cell phone rang just as he was saying good night to Armont. When he was done with his conference call, he went straight to bed and held Ailese until he fell asleep.

"I wasn't talking to him, I swear. Please let me go!" He had a good grip on Ailese's hair in his hand as he pulled her by her hair into the spare bedroom. He slapped her across her face and called her a liar! "And you wonder why I don't take your ass anywhere because you flirt too damn much! I saw what you did, you little whore!" "I wasn't doing anything. I wouldn't do that. Please let me go!" Ailese let out a roaring scream. "Shut up! You shut your mouth right now! I'm going to show you how whores are treated. He threw Ailese onto the bed and told her that she had better not move or else, so she didn't.

Open your damn mouth, now!" Ailese had her eyes closed. She didn't want to look at him. He made her give him oral sex. She cried the entire time, and this made him angrier. He slapped her across the face because she wouldn't stop crying. He made her apologize to him for flirting. When Ailese wouldn't apologize to him, he slapped her again; he slapped her over and over until she finally apologized to him. Ailese began to moan in her sleep, then she began to sob. "Stop, I'm sorry," she said repeatedly. "Baby, you need to wake up. It's only a bad dream. It's me, I'm here."

When Ailese woke up, Mikell held her in his arms. Oddly he noticed that this was the first time that he didn't have to shake her so hard to wake her up. Was that a good thing? "I'm sorry I woke you up. Go back to sleep. I'll be okay. I'm going to get a drink of water." "I'll come with you, and please stop apologizing for waking me up. Don't apologize ever." "Okay, I just … "Ssh, Mikell kissed her on her forehead and led her to the kitchen.

There were so many people at the party. The guest list was a mile long. It had to have been well over one hundred people. Mikell greeted people and made sure they were comfortable, while Ailese and D'Andra made sure that everything else was going smoothly. So far, the party was going as Mikell and Ailese planned. Ailese was introduced to so many people that her head was spinning! She caught up with Sedrick, who looked absolutely stunning and handsome. "Mrs. Laydee, that dress is you! Don't tell Mikell, but you look so beautiful I may just have to steal you away from him." They both laughed. Obviously Ailese looked like a million bucks; her dress fit her curves well. She had gotten so many compliments throughout the whole night.

At the party, there were music producers, artists that just needed some direction, and some that wanted to be signed to a label and wanted it bad. There were aspiring singers there who had just signed to a label or renewed their contracts. Some people were there just to show off and say that they attended the party. Ailese was so proud of her husband; he had worked so hard and deserved all the recognition and then some. Music was what Mikell and Ailese had in common. It was so strong that they both loved the same music. Sometimes they would stay up late talking about music.

When Mikell would get a breather, he would spend time with Ailese and give her an update on what was happening at the party. Ailese wasn't expecting Andrew to show up because he had other plans and didn't make any promises that he would show up. Ailese went out onto the terrace to get some air. As she looked at the beautiful view and sipped her wine, she started thinking about how lucky she was and how God had blessed her and would continue to bless her.

She thought about all the things her family had been through. She was happy that her family stuck together, and most of all, she couldn't believe that her sister was here with her at the party. She thought about how her sister didn't let anything, or anyone, stand in her way of getting better, and that she healed faster because she never lost her faith. As she turned around, D'Andra was standing beside Andrew.

"Hey, beautiful, I'm here. Ailese, are you okay?" "Oh, yeah, I'm good." Ailese hugged Andrew tight. "Hey, let's party! This is a party right, come on." Ailese D'Andra and Andrew headed inside.

"Andrew, have you seen D?" "No, not since earlier, so I haven't, anything wrong?" "No, she said that she'd be right back, but it's been a while since I've seen her." "Have you checked the bathroom?" "No, I'll check there. Ailese walked to the bathroom and knocked on the door. D, are you in there? It's Lee." Ailese heard D's voice and entered the bathroom. D was throwing up. Ailese felt bad for her and thought that she just drank too much, but as she recalled, her sister only drank apple cider or maybe not. She couldn't remember. "Honey, are you going to be okay?" Ailese wet a face towel and handed it to D'Andra. After D'Andra was done throwing up, she wiped her face with the warm face towel. "I'm not drunk. I only had one glass of white wine. I've never felt this miserable in my life, oh my gosh!"

Ailese helped D'Andra up from the floor and studied her face.

"Why don't you go in one of the rooms and lay down, it'll do you some good."

"But what about the party? I'm supposed to be helping you. I feel so bad, but I think I need to lay down." Ailese made sure that D'Andra was comfortable and went back to the party.

Ailese danced with Sedrick, and surprisingly he kept up with her. They danced until they were worn out, then she danced with Emmanuel, Mikell, and Andrew. She even danced with some of the guests. When Ailese went to check on D'Andra, she was sound asleep. Ailese put an extra blanket on her and put some pajamas on the chair that was next to the bed. Nine times out of ten, D'Andra is going to wake up and get out of those clothes and change into her pajamas. D'Andra did not like sleeping in her clothes.

The party went on for a few more hours. Ailese and Andrew sipped wine and talked. Occasionally, they would check on the food, and the bar, and surprisingly, the servers and the bartenders were doing their jobs well. Everyone at the party was very well behaved. They all were having lots of fun.

When the party was over, it was close to three in the morning. This time it went longer than last time. Ailese

SHELBY LIES

Emmanuel and Mikell thanked everyone for coming, as they exited the party. Mikell made sure everyone had a designated driver, and if they didn't, he called a cab for them or grabbed a designated driver and gave them some cash to drive that person home.

Andrew had stayed to help cleanup. "Hey man, I think you should crash here until morning. It's really late." "Okay, man, cool, thanks." "Hey, let me show you which room you can sleep in. D is in one of these rooms sleeping. She's not feeling too hot, so Ailese told her to lay down. I checked on her earlier and she was asleep." "I hope she feels better." Here it is, your room. Let me get you some extra blankets, okay?" "Okay, thanks. This room is nice. I like the way you've decorated it." Ailese walked in, smiled, and handed Andrew some extra blankets. She had given him a hug and a kiss on the cheek. "See you in the morning. I better get to bed before I fall on my face. Love ya, night." "Ditto. See ya in the morning, my lady."

"Well, I think that the party was perfect! Ailese whispered to Mikell. "Yes, it was. Thank you so much for making it perfect."

Ailese was up before anyone else, so she decided to make breakfast and brew some coffee. She knew that everyone would be thankful for her making coffee. She made cheese omelets with red and yellow bell peppers, sausage patties, and fruit. The first person to wake up was D'Andra, who was wearing the pajamas that Ailese had set out for her. "I knew that you would wake up out of your sleep and put on those pajamas, she said. They both laughed. How are you feeling?" "My stomach's feeling a bit weird. Maybe after I eat something it should feel much better. Mmmm, breakfast smells so good, sis, thanks."

D'Andra fixed her plate and then sat at the kitchen table with Ailese.

Everyone thanked Ailese for breakfast and commented on how good it was.

D'Andra had disappeared again, and Ailese found her in the restroom again throwing up. "Do you have the stomach flu? Maybe I should call your doctor. He does house calls, right?" "Not necessary. Something just didn't agree with me. That's all. I'll be fine; really, please don't worry. I'm going to lay down. Love you, sis."

"D'Andra hasn't been feeling well ever since last night. I think I better call her doctor just in case." "I think you should, but I would make sure it is alright with her first, though." Mikell gave Ailese a kiss as she went to check on D'Andra. D'Andra looked very flushed and was losing her color.

"Ailese, I need to ask you a favor, and I need you to keep this between you and me." D'Andra gave her sister a look that she hadn't seen since the attack, so Ailese knew that she was serious about what she was about to say.

"I promise, it's between only you and me, sis. What's wrong?" D'Andra began to weep, and Ailese put her arms around her. "There's a possibility that I may be pregnant. I mean, I've read those mother-to-be books a dozen times, and I have all those symptoms. I'm sure of it; my life's been so crazy lately.

Chris and I are separated, and I can't trust him and I don't know if I can ever will, and now I'm pregnant! D'Andra sniffed and wiped her tears from her face. I'm so conflicted right now. I want this baby to have a father because I had a father growing up and I was so fortunate to have that experience and I believe that a child should have both parents I don't know if our marriage can be saved. I don't know."

"Look at me, and I want you to listen to me, really good, okay? D'Andra shook her head. If you think that you're pregnant, we could go and buy a pregnancy test so we can be sure that you are pregnant, and if you are, we'll go and see your doctor and go from there, okay?" "Okay." D'Andra looked at Ailese with a sense of liberation. "If you want me to call Chris and speak with him, I will. Whatever you need me to do, I am here. I love you, and you know that I will always, always be by your side, no matter what. Whatever we speak about stays in this room and goes nowhere else, I promise." "Ailese, I love you so much. I know that I can always count on you. What would I ever do without you? I never want to imagine not having you in my life, sis."

"I want you to get some rest. I will go to the store and pick up a few things." D'Andra interrupted Ailese and told her that she would like to come with her to the drug store.

"Guys, we'll be back in a while. Can I get anyone anything while we're out?"

The guys joked that they needed Ailese to bring back a bunch of unnecessary junk. "You guys are too much. Andrew, are you going to stick around a while? "Sure, I will." "Okay, see you guys later." When Ailese and D'Andra left, Mikell and Andrew decided to walk to the park that was up the road and shoot some hoops. When they got to the park, there weren't a lot of people there, so they had the basketball court to themselves. "Show me whatcha got, Mikell, cause I'm ready." Andrew began to bounce the basketball to demonstrate his skills to Mikell. "I'm ready, I guess you'll see what I got when I kick your butt." Andrew and Mikell started the first round. Mikell won the first round, and Andrew was impressed. "Okay, this time I'm gonna win this round, so you better start crying now, man," Mikell laughed. Mikell won the second round as well as the last one. "Man, I have to bow to you. Wow, that was a great game, and you kicked my butt." Mikell gave Andrew a victory look, like real basketball players give their opponents when they win a game.

"Let's head back to the house. I don't know about you, but I could use a drink, and I think the loser should prepare lunch too." "Okay, okay, fine. What can I get you, my king?" Andrew and Mikell laughed so hard.

When Ailese and D'Andra made it back to the house from running errands, the guys were into a game of backgammon and didn't notice that Ailese and D'Andra had disappeared to another part of the house. "I'm so nervous, I'm shaking. D'Andra took a deep breath, Ailese handed her the pregnancy test, and they both waited impatiently. Oh, I can't stand this. I need something to distract me; I can't take this!" "Calm down. I know how you feel, but we can't rush things like this, stay right here, I'll be right back." Ailese came back with some playing cards and handed them to her sister. Here, let's play I-declare-war, you know, like when we were little." D'Andra appreciated Ailese getting this pregnancy thing off her mind. When they were done playing the game, it was time to find out what the results were. Ailese followed D'Andra to the restroom.

"Ailese, you tell me what it says. I can't look. I'm so nervous. Look, I'm shaking."

"You're pregnant! I am so happy for you, and it's a blessing, honey!"

"It is, huh? I'm actually happy and relieved all at the same time."

Ailese hugged her sister and gave her a kiss on the cheek.

"Can you call Chris for me, please? I don't want to waste another second. I just want to get this over with." "Sure, I'll do it right now."

"Hey Chris. How are you?" "I'm hanging in there," Chris said, in a gloomy voice. Ailese could tell that he wasn't doing so well. "Hey, I wanted to check on you, and I have D'Andra here with me. I'm her support system right now, and her voice, okay? I have to tell you something, but I need you to come over. Are you busy right now?" "No, I can come over. I'm on my way, and please tell D'Andra that I love her."

"Hey Chris, long time no see, Mikell said, as he closed the door behind him. You remember Andrew, right?" Mikell said sarcastically. "Oh, hey, how's it going?" "Hey, what's up, man. I am good." Andrew said, as he went back to the board game that Mikell and he were playing.

"So, what's going on?" Before Chris could speak, D'Andra and Ailese entered the room and greeted Chris. When Chris saw his wife, he thought that she was even more beautiful the last time he'd seen her. "Hi, beautiful, how are you doing?" "I'm okay. They both smiled at each other, and they were both nervous because they didn't know how this meeting was going to go.

"Hey, can we talk?" "Sure, my love." Chris followed Ailese and his wife into the backyard. Ailese looked at her cell phone and noticed the time. She would have to leave soon to pick up the kids. "Chris, there's something that we want to tell you. I want to say this: I love my sister dearly, and I don't want to fight her battles. All I can do is be there for her and pray that she makes the right decisions and learns from her mistakes. What I'm trying to say is that I don't hate you, because you know that's not me, but I feel like you weren't there for my sister when she needed you the most, I felt that you didn't stand by her when she was going through pure hell. You took your vows in front of God, and I'm upset that you wouldn't honor them. You are my sister's heart and soul. She has given you everything. You need to do the same. You should and need to be honest with her. I know that as humans we are imperfect and we make mistakes, and no marriage is flawless. It's hard, hard, work. Why wouldn't you be honest with her? Be true. Be truthful. I know you're a great guy, and when you lose your way, find it back to your wife, Chris.

Seeing other people? That's not the answer. I'm going to leave you two alone now."

"I do understand. I was wrong, and I hope that you give me one more chance." Chris looked at D'Andra, walked over to her, and hugged her.

"Hey, I want you guys to talk. I have to go and pick up the kids from Mom's. Stay as long as you want. I will make sure you guys have privacy. D'Andra let me talk to you for a minute, okay?" Ailese told D'Andra to tell Chris the news and that everything was going to work out, and whatever she decided, she was by her side no matter what. "Ailese, I love you," Chris said. He smiled at Ailese. She could read a million words from that smile.

"Chris, sit down please. We need to talk." Chris sat down on one of the patio chairs. D'Andra sat next to him. She took his hand and put it up against her face, studying his face until she could finally get out what she wanted to say to Chris. "I'm pregnant. We're having a baby." D'Andra leaned her head to the side to see the reaction on his face, and to her surprise, it wasn't what she'd expected. He picked her up so high, that she got scared that he was going to drop her. "Baby, you've made me so happy! We're having a baby, and Chris kept repeating it over and over again that he was the happiest man on earth at this point in time. Look at me, sweetie. I know that we have a lot of work to do, and I know that I have a lot of work ahead of me, but I am willing to do whatever it takes for us to be a family. I didn't mean to hurt you. You didn't deserve any of this, and I know that it's going to take some time, but I am willing to wait." "I love you so much." Chris burst into tears. He didn't care about his pride. He cared about D'Andra and was focused on their future.

D'Andra didn't go back with Chris. She wasn't ready, and he did understand that and why she felt that she wasn't ready to go back with him. She told Chris that she didn't know when things would go back to normal, but he was willing to wait. Although it crushed him that he didn't take her back with him, he promised her that he would be there for her and the baby, no matter what.

The idea of him seeing another woman made her skin crawl, and she wasn't sure if Chris was still seeing this woman. She wasn't going to let him hurt her again, so she decided that they needed to take things slow, baby or no baby.

After dinner and spending time with Ailese and the family, Andrew had to head back home. Ailese hated that he had to head back home; she loved spending time with him just as much as everyone else did. Andrew always made everyone laugh and kept you laughing. His personality alone was appealing.

"Hey, you know another hockey game is coming up. What do you say, Mikell?"

"I'm there, man!" Mikell gave Andrew the thumbs up. "I'm goin' to head to bed." D'Andra told everyone good night and headed to her room.

After Andrew left, Mikell and Ailese discussed Chris and D'Andra, and Mikell wanted to know if they were going to be okay. "I think with a lot of work, determination, communication, and trust, I mean, I'm really praying that they will be okay." "I am so drained I am going to bed now. Are you coming, Mikell?"

"I'll be right there. I'm going to check on the kids and D'Andra. I need to make sure everything's locked up." "Okay,

I'll be in the room. Don't be too long, okay?" I won't, I'll be there in a few minutes."

When Mikell went back to the room, Ailese was watching television. Mikell joined her. "Do you want anything from the kitchen? I'm going to get something to drink." "No, I'm fine." As Mikell was heading to the kitchen, the phone rang, and Ailese answered it. She didn't know who could be calling this late. "Hello, this is she." "Hello, my friend, it's me, Evette. I'm so sorry to call you so late, I'm still trying to adjust to the time differences." "Evette, it is so good to hear your voice. How are you?" Ailese looked at Mikell and shrugged her shoulders. Mikell gave her a hand signal to take the call and said he'd watch television until he fell asleep. "I am doing well, and you?" "I am doing well, keeping very busy. How's life treating you? Are you adjusting, okay?" "I am adjusting fine, like I said earlier, I just need to get used to the time differences, other than that, everything's falling into place. I'm working for a great company, and the pay is good. Heather loves her new school; she's already had a few sleepovers. How's your family doing?" Ailese didn't want to get into the whole ordeal with what happened with her family; she didn't want to bring it up just yet. "We're doing okay. I'm going to be an aunt in nine months. Can you believe it? My sister's going to have a baby. I'm so happy, and I know I'm going to spoil that baby like crazy. The girls are growing up so fast you know, before I know it, they'll be in college. My son is just such a handsome young man. All my children make me proud every day. Mikell's still awesome, as ever. We've actually been working together. It has been a great experience. I actually did some collaborations with Sedrick Johnson. I don't know if you've heard of him." "Oh, my gosh, I love him. I'm just waiting to see him in concert. So, how was it working with him?" "Great! We have a special connection for life. We're pretty close. He loves music, the same way that I do. We're a lot alike when it comes to a lot of things, especially music. I just saw him the other day. We talk at least three times a week." "Wow, that's awesome. Maybe I can meet him one day. I mean, I wish I could personally meet him." "Well, I can probably make that happen, and I will let you know, okay?" Okay, sounds great. So, I have to go now. I don't want to, but I have work in the morning. I was thinking about you and wanted to say hello." "Okay, I am so glad that you called. Take care, and we'll talk soon."

"Wow, so how's Evette doing?" "She's doing great. I miss my friend. Maybe one day I'll plan to go and visit her." "You should. You guys are pretty close, and I like her, so I think that you should keep your friendship close to your hearts." "Yeah, I agree, you don't find very many people like Evette."

"I'm going to go to sleep now, but if you want me to stay up, I can." "No, I'm going to go to sleep too. By the way, Andrew told me that you kicked his butt on the court; good job, baby." Mikell smiled at Ailese. Mikell held Ailese until they both fell asleep.

D'Andra went home to grab a couple of things and to tell her mom and dad the good news! D'Andra took the girls with her to keep her company.

Mikell had left early for a meeting and said that he would be back in a few hours. Armont was still in bed when Ailese checked on him earlier.

As she was getting ready for her shower, she heard her cell phone ringing. It was Andrew. "Hey, what are you doing like right now?" "Well, nothing really. I was just about to take a shower and lounge around the house. Why? What's up?" "Well, I know that we saw each other yesterday, but I need your help.

I need your help. I hope I'm not asking you for too much, but if you could please help me pick out some decorations. I'm not feeling the decorations that the decorating committee sent me. They're just not right for the fundraiser." "Um, okay, I'll be ready by the time you get here. I may have to take Armont with us." "Okay, no problem. Ailese, you're a life saver, thanks." "Anytime you know you can count on me. Just have my coffee waiting for me. That's all I ask." "Okay, I will. Love ya. See ya in a little while." "I love ya too, bye."

Armont reminded his mom that his dad was coming to pick him up in an hour. "Are you going to eat anything, honey?" "No, I'm not that hungry. I'll grab a banana on my way out. Thanks anyway, Mom." "Please make sure you eat something okay." "Yes, Mom, I have to go. Dad's outside. I can hear his car." Armont kissed and hugged his mother. Ailese went back into her room to finish getting ready. She settled on a pair of jeans and a nice blouse with some comfortable shoes.

Just as she was done getting ready, the doorbell rang. She knew it was Andrew. Only he would ring the doorbell like a madman. Ailese grabbed her purse and keys and headed to the door. "Hey you," she said, as she hugged him. Ailese locked the door behind her. "So, where is everybody?" "Well, D'Andra and the kids are at her house. Mikell's at his meeting, and Armont's with his dad." "Hey, do you mind driving?" "Sure, I don't mind. When Ailese saw the car, she was in awe.

When did you get a new car? Wow, it's so clean, it's … nice!" "I got this car a few weeks ago, and guess what? You're the second person to drive it other than me. I'm glad that you like it." "Oh yes, the color suits you well, Andrew."

"Oh, I have a question for you. I was so excited when I opened my birthday gift that I don't remember if I thanked you or not, did I?" "Yes, of course you did. I'm so glad that you loved your gift. So, we're going to this place called the Super Party Palace. They have some neat things there, um, you know, the decorations at the party. We bought them from there." "Yes, I loved everything at the party." "Okay, good, so we'll go to the Super Party Palace." "Okay, great, sounds like a plan to me."

"Wow, this place has everything that you need for a party and the fundraiser. See, I knew that I could count on you." Ailese helped Andrew pick out decorations to silverware. Andrew was trying on silly party hats, making Ailese laugh until her stomach hurt. They didn't care if they were attracting attention. They were having fun with it.

Andrew and Ailese thought it was fun to be someone else for a day.

"I'm hungry. What about you, wifey?" "I can go for something juicy. Ailese chuckled. Hey, we're near Shane's. Have you ever eaten there?" "Um, it sounds familiar, but if my wifey wants to go, then that's where we're going. Come my love." Ailese took his hand, and he led her to the car.

When they were enjoying the food and conversation, Ailese got a call from Mikell, he told her that his meetings would be longer than he had anticipated, and as always, Ailese understood. Andrew and Mikell spoke over the phone for a brief moment. Ailese called D'Andra to let her know that she was still out and about with Andrew. D'Andra, Alonda, Don, and the girls were out as well. D'Andra told Ailese that she wanted the girls to hang out with her the rest of the day and to enjoy herself. "Well, it looks like it's just you and I hubby, Ailese smiled at Andrew he smiled back. "Well, it looks like it's just you and I hubby." Ailese smiled at Andrew, who smiled back. "You picked a great restaurant. I actually haven't been here before. I've passed by this restaurant, but

I've never tried it. The foods really good." Andrew took a bite of his fish. "Andrew, I just realized something. I don't think that I've ever seen you eat a burger, or any red meat for that matter. If I wasn't crazy, I'd say you're a health nut, huh?" "No, I'm not. Excuse me, you've seen me eat, and I can eat. I just don't eat a lot of red meat. It's not good for me in general and it interferes with my illness, that's all." "Oh, I'm sorry. I didn't mean anything by it. You never let your illness take control of your life." "No, I can't, and why should I let it take over my life?

I live for today. I can't be moping around and blaming myself, and if I do that, I only have myself to blame. I have to eat somewhat healthy, that's all."

"I understand, I'm sorry, I was only teasing you, and I just made a fool out of myself." Ailese put her head down, then she felt Andrew's hand on her face.

"Hey, don't ever apologize for asking me anything, and don't feel embarrassed, okay? Look at me, Ailese looked at Andrew. Ailese, you asked me that question because of how close we are, and you knew that I wouldn't keep anything from you. Hey, it's all good, wifey. Ailese smiled.

Sometimes I do wonder how long I have to live, but I just can't think about it. There's so much to do in life. I love my life." "I'm so glad that you're in my life, Andrew." "So where else are we going after this?" "I was thinking about going to this little art store. We could look at some paintings for your room that you were talking about redecorating. I had some things in mind, and I know that you'll love them. I have so much to show you." "I'm excited, and thanks again for all your help." "Oh, anytime. I'm having lots of fun, it's better than being at home alone."

Andrew loved the paintings that Ailese had picked out for him; he was very pleased. Andrew asked Ailese to come to his home so he could show her the room that he was redecorating, and she had agreed to come with him to his home.

"You know how much I love it here. It's so beautiful." Ailese stood on the terrace and looked at the wonderful view. Andrew stood right beside her.

"You know that you're welcome here anytime. You have the spare key. I'm surprised that you haven't used it yet." "I know I'm so busy, and by the time it crosses my mind, it's too late." When Andrew showed Ailese the room, she was astounded. She was immediately drawn to the room. She started touching the statues, touching every curve, and feeling the velvet chairs that were in the room. She even laid on the bed that felt like feathers. It was so soft. Andrew joined Ailese on the bed. She laid her head on his chest, and she could hear his heart beating. "I could lay here forever and ever, but I can't. Let's start hanging up the paintings." When Ailese and Andrew went to retrieve the paintings, Andrew's butler told him he had an important call and that it was urgent. Andrew had excused himself and told Ailese that he wouldn't be too long. The butler asked Ailese if she needed anything, and she told him she would like some bottled water if they had any. A few minutes later, the butler came back with a bottle of water, a glass of ice, gave them to Ailese, and left the room.

When Andrew came back, Ailese could tell that the call didn't go too well, but, she knew that he would tell her what happened, eventually. As they were hanging up the artwork, Andrew told Ailese that he needed a break.

"You've been quiet ever since your phone call. Are you okay?" "Yeah, I'm fine. Ailese knew he was lying. Okay, no, I'm not okay. It just burns me how people like to use me for my money, and when I don't give them what they want, I'm the bad guy." "Sit down, what happened?" "That was one of my cousins, well, he isn't my real cousin, his family and mine are very close, and he wanted me to give him money to start his own business. I told him that I wasn't going to because he still owes me money, and you know what he said? Oh, I was there for you all those times when I was sick. Could you believe that?" Ailese shook her head because she too could relate to that. "Look at me, Andrew, don't ever feel bad about saying no. I would have done the same thing. You can't always be nice, and you can't trust him. He hasn't earned your trust, by not paying you back, he needs to pay you back, before asking for anything else." "You're right, and I am going to drop it." Ailese gave Andrew a hug.

Andrew had dropped Ailese off at home and headed back home. Ailese noticed that Mikell and D'Andra's cars were parked in front of the garage. She thought she would be the first one home. "Hey guys I'm home, how was everyone's day?" "My day was crazy. I was in meetings all day." Mikell took Ailese's hand and led her to the couch where everyone was sitting. "Mom, Aunt took us to see Grammie and Papa. It was so fun." Adrieana said with excitement. "That's good. I bet it was fun, huh?" "Hey, I picked up some dinner. Are you hungry, sis?" "Um, a little bit. What did you pick up?" "Come here, and I'll show you." Ailese went into the kitchen and saw that D'Andra had picked up some Ten Jayes. "Here, let me help you." Ailese helped set the table and put the food into serving dishes.

"Hey everyone, go and wash your hands okay, and come and sit at the table."

Ailese and D'Andra followed them to wash their hands as well.

After dinner, D'Andra told everyone how excited Alonda and Don were when she told them the news and that Chris was picking her up for her first doctor's appointment. Mikell expressed his hope that she and Chris could work things out and that he wanted to see them happy. They talked about names, shopping for the baby, and who gets to spoil the baby.

It was getting close to the conferences, and Ailese was swamped with a lot of work.

She was confirming travel arrangements and schedules with Ell and Andrew that Mr. Saxx had set up for Andrew and Ailese. Ailese was dreading the conferences. They were so long, and she knew that she would miss Mikell and the kids. Andrew was looking forward to the conferences, which annoyed Ailese. He just didn't know what he was getting himself into. She knew that after the first day, he'd understand why she was dreading the conferences. Ailese had to go and see a property on her own, and Andrew had some clients that he had to take care of on his own as well. Ailese could have sworn that she saw Chris's car entering the parking lot where she worked, but she didn't have time to go back and check. He wouldn't be coming to see me? She thought to herself, shrugged her shoulders, and started thinking about her appointment with Dr. Salvino today. She was excited because she was able to write the second letter of his name, which was I.

Ailese has stayed motivated to get through this. She didn't want this man running her life anymore! Her dreams were getting better. She was having less of them, and she hoped that one day she could put this all behind her.

Dr. Salvino has helped her a lot. She couldn't ask for a better doctor.

When Ailese returned to the office, she saw Chris walking to the elevator. She called out to him, and he turned around, and smiled at her, before walking over to her to say hello. "Hey, Lee, I was actually coming to see you and go over some things with you. I wanted to let you know that I won the bid for the new shopping center over on Sky Drive." "Oh, wow, I'm sure that great news is on my desk as we speak. That is great! So, do you have time right now or do you have to get going?" "I do have to get going, but I am never too busy for you. I can squeeze you in with no problem." Chris followed her to her office.

"Hey, did I see your car earlier?" "Oh, yes, you did. You had already left, so I just waited for you, and I hope that was okay." "Of course it was." "I know I should have called but I was so excited to tell you the news." Chris would usually call her to let her know that he was coming over. Despite all his faults, he was a very respectable person when it came to work, and Ailese. This wasn't the first time that they had worked on a project together. She would sometimes recommend Chris for huge jobs, and they were always pleased.

"Hello, Ell, how are you?" "I am good, long time no see." What are you doing here? Oh, wait I know you've got that huge account with us on Sky Drive, huh?

Congrats to you, you deserve it." Ell walked over and gave Chris a huge hug. Ailese thought it was a hug that said "in love." She hoped she was wrong, so she zipped her mouth and didn't say anything. "Come on, Chris."

After her meeting with Chris, she headed to her appointment with her doctor. Ailese chatted with Karen for a bit until it was time for her session. Karen told Ailese that her boyfriend had proposed to her a few days ago, and she said yes. Karen was very excited. The entire office was excited for her. Karen told Ailese that she wanted her to make all the jewelry for her wedding, and Ailese was thrilled to do it for her. Karen told Ailese that she wanted her to meet her fiancé. Ailese told Karen that she would call her this week to set up something. Karen had taken Ailese's mind off the conferences, so she wasn't thinking about them anymore.

The session with Dr. Salvino went very well, and Ailese was so pleased with today's session. Dr. Salvino was pleased with Ailese's progress.

Every session, Ailese was getting stronger and stronger, and Dr. Salvino was even more pleased when Ailese showed her the same paper but with another letter. "This is great. Ailese. I knew that you could get to this point! Soon, I know, we will have all the letters on this piece of paper.

I do want to talk about your dreams. Are you having them more frequently or less frequently?" "Actually, the dreams are getting better. You know what, my husband noticed that as well. We were talking about it just the other day. I sometimes have control over my dreams. I can tell you this, though: I can wake up from them more easily now than before. Dr. Salvino I just feel like you've helped me make a lot of progress."

"So, how was your session today?" "Oh, it was fantastic. I told Dr. Salvino that she's helped me so much. I'm making progress. It feels good."

"Well, that's great, baby." "Hey, you remember my friend Karen?" "Yeah, doesn't she work like two doors down from your doctor?" "Right, well, she's getting married. I am so excited for her, and she wants me to make all her jewelry for her wedding! I told her that I would, and that I'd be honored.

We're supposed to set up a dinner, so we could meet her fiancé. I had such a good day today." "I love it when you have these days." Ailese smiled at Mikell.

"So, I wanted to make sure that you knew that next week were my conferences, or did you forget?" "No, baby, I didn't forget I don't think you'd let me forget, you've reminded me a dozen times already. Mikell said, smiling. You poor thing, I know how much you dread those conferences and those long presentations." "Oh, please don't bring it up, Ailese frowned.

Don't worry, we'll talk every day, and besides, I'll have Andrew there to keep me sane." Ailese laid down on the bed and pulled Mikell down with her.

I'm going to miss you guys so much. I hope it goes by fast, you know." "Yeah, I know, baby. Me too." Mikell kissed her on the lips, grabbed the remote control, and rolled over to his side of the bed. "Hey, get back here sexy, I wasn't done with you." Mikell scooted to Ailese. She grabbed him by the collar and kissed him passionately.

Today was an important day. It was D'Andra's first doctor's appointment, and everyone was very excited. Alonda called D'Andra just to make sure she was up on time and told D'Andra to call her once she got back from the appointment. Everyone, including Chris, was so excited about the impending arrival that they couldn't stop talking about it.

In celebration of D'Andra's pregnancy, her magazine company sent her tons and tons of flowers. D'Andra decided that she would work from home and the office. She didn't want to put any more stress on her body or on the baby. Ailese became increasingly happy as she saw more and more of Chris. Ailese just wanted her sister to be happy.

After leaving work, Ailese noticed that she had left her cell phone behind and needed to go back to the office to get it. She noticed that the light to her office was still on, despite the fact that she had sworn she had turned it off before leaving. She could hear voices coming from her office, as she got closer to it.

Who could be in her office? She wondered if the voices she was hearing were familiar. So she made sure that she was careful entering the office. She slowly opened the door,

Mr. Saxx and Andrew were talking. Andrew was sitting in her chair, and Mr. Saxx was sitting in the chair across from Andrew. "Well, hello, isn't this a surprise." Mr. Saxx stood up to give Ailese a hug. "I didn't know that you were going to be in town, Mr. Saxx."

"Oh well, me neither. Lin had some business to attend to, so I just tagged along, that's all. You're looking beautiful as always."

"Thank you. I just returned to get my phone. I'll leave you two to whatever you were doing before I interrupted." Ailese grabbed her phone and started walking toward the door until Mr. Saxx called her back. "Ailese, we were just talking about you and the 195th Broadway Project, and how you and Andrew have taken over all the empty spaces there. I just wanted to say congratulations! "Thanks, Mr. Saxx. That means a lot to me. It was a huge challenge. You know the Forsythes? They will be relocating to one of those locations, and all of the clients are very pleased with the Broadway Project."

"I told Mr. Saxx that you had a lot to do with this project and that no one could do what you did." Andrew looked at Ailese with a contented look on his face. "Well, thanks, but we did it together, Andrew. Well, guys, I do have to be going. Mr. Saxx, you know my mom and dad would love to see you." "We've already made dinner plans for tomorrow night." "Oh, great." "Oh, by the way, congrats on being an aunt soon. Your mom and dad are so excited for your sister, and so am I. I sent a gift basket already." "That was really sweet of you." "You know you guys are my family. I can't wait until I see your parents, we might get in until the next day, we have so much to catch up on," Mr. Saxx laughed, Ailese laughed with him. "I am so glad that you guys are able to catch up. Have fun, okay? Okay, I will talk to you guys later."

Ailese was craving something spicy and sweet, so she decided to treat herself to some Chinese food. She normally didn't like to travel far to get the food because it was out of her way and there was always traffic, but this time she didn't mind so much. She couldn't believe her eyes when she finally looked up from the menu. She couldn't be seeing this! She saw Andrew and Ell being lovey-dovey and having dinner, kissing, and being playful with another. This shocked her. She didn't know whether to go over there or pretend like this wasn't happening. She decided to order her food and get the hell out of there. She wasn't jealous, she just felt betrayed; first it was Dr. Lewis, and now Ell! Andrew still hasn't admitted to her that he knew Dr. Lewis. He has yet to bring it up. It was a high- profile case when Dr. Lewis was murdered. Could she trust him? Ailese would never get into Andrew's private life. She would tease him about it, and that was it, unless he brought it up. They all worked together, and she would never have guessed it. Ailese didn't mind that Ell and Andrew were dating, but it bothered her that Andrew didn't tell her. They never kept anything from each other and always told each other everything. Was Andrew hiding Ell from Ailese for any reason? Were they as close as she thought they were?

The number one thing that bothered Ailese was lying. Not being honest with her. She would rather you be honest with her than lie to her! She thought about the Andrew and Ell situation the whole way home. Coincidentally, Andrew called Ailese to thank her again for helping him decorate the room and to say that the room was done. He was happy with the artwork that brought out the room.

Andrew didn't mention Ell at all, and Ailese didn't push the issue. He even asked her what was wrong while they were talking, and she told him she was tired, even though he didn't believe her, but he let it go for the time being.

At work, Andrew knew something was wrong, even though Ailese did her best not to show how she was really feeling, even though she acted like she would every day. Andrew pressured her into having lunch with him. She didn't want to say no, then she would be a hypocrite. Andrew drove when they went to lunch. Ailese made conversation, but there was still some tension, and it was strong.

Andrew made sure that they sat off to the side of the restaurant so they could talk, and Ailese was ready, but she was going to remain calm the whole time.

"Ailese, please tell me what's wrong? Have I done anything to upset you?"

Ailese sighed and looked at her menu. She didn't want to get upset. She didn't really have a reason to be upset. "Okay, first of all, I feel like you've been keeping things from me. I mean, I don't expect you to tell me everything, but I thought that we could be open enough to always be honest, no matter what!

I don't care if what I'm about to say destroys our friendship. I just need to get this off my chest. Why didn't you tell me that you were dating Ell? I saw you two at the restaurant the other night, and you guys were kissing among other things." Ailese waited for a response from Andrew.

"Oh, Ell, well yes, we have gone on a few dates, but I didn't tell you because it's nothing serious, I apologize. Ell had a bit too much to drink that night, and I didn't want to reject her and hurt her feelings. I was a bit in need of her company, and yes, we've been intimate here and there.

Ailese, I didn't know that dating her would upset you like this. I mean, it's one of those things that just happened."

"It's not that I'm upset that you're dating my assistant. The point is that I felt like it was something that you should have told me, that's all. I don't want to talk about this anymore, okay?" "Okay, I respect that, but I just want to make something clear. When I don't tell you something, it's in your best interest. I'm sorry, Ailese, please forgive me." "You're forgiven." Andrew took her hand and squeezed it. "There is only one woman for me, and I told you what happened with that relationship- that I still love her." "Yes, I do remember that. I can't tell you who to date, but it's Ell, it was kind of important that I knew. I'm not trying to make your love life my business, and it's -none of my business, Andrew. I do feel that Ell shouldn't know that I know that you guys are dating. It may just freak her out." "I agree, but are you okay?" "Yes, I am straight, I'm cool."

Ailese did feel better that she got that off her chest. She was cool, calm, and collected now. "Look, I do apologize again, I'm sorry. You're not worried that Ell will come between our relationship, are you? Because if you are, put that thought out of your mind right now; it's not going to happen." Andrew felt like he cherished their friendship more than she did. He loved her so much that he would never let anyone come between them. Their friendship was far too strong to be broken.

"Hey sis, I'm on my way. Is there anything you need?" "No, come on over, and please don't forget to bring the movies, okay?" "I have them right here. See you in a bit." When Ailese arrived at D'Andra's, she had everything ready for movie night, including snacks, blankets, pillows, and drinks. "You're ready, huh? I would have helped you, sis. So, how are you feeling, honey?" "I'm great, and you?" "I can't complain. Where's Mom and Dad?" "Oh, they went out for dinner. I actually shooed them away. They're so overly protective now that I'm pregnant they won't let me breathe! I mean, I know that they mean well, but gosh! I need breathing room. I love them though." D'Andra let out a long sigh.

SHELBY LIES

"I know. I know what you mean. Trust me." "Ailese, you know when my accident happened?" "Yes, hun, of course." When Ailese looked at D'Andra, she had a solemn expression on her face. "I prayed to God. He and I had a long conversation. That's all I did was pray, and then I started thinking about you, that if I died, we wouldn't be able to have times like this anymore. Ailese started to cry. She took her sister's hand and held it. I know that we're not promised tomorrow, but I wasn't ready to give up. I know that it was in God's hands, and it's always in his hands, and he has the last word. God let me live, and now I'm having a baby. What I'm trying to say is that life's too short, and I've decided to maintain a stronger relationship with God, not just because he spared my life, but because I believe he deserves it, and I want to honor him." "Sis, that's a huge step, and I am so proud of you. I feel the same way he deserves our love, and we need to remember what he's all about." Ailese hugged her sister, and they cried together. "I'm thankful that Mom and Dad made us go to church, and listen to the word, teaching us all about God."

"Me too, sis. That's why I keep my bible close, and I make sure that I never stop hearing God's word." "I love you, sis. Hey, let's get this movie date started!"

Ailese and D'Andra watched movies and talked all night. Later on, Chris came over to check on D'Andra. She wanted him to bring her some French fries from Ten Jayes. "Hey girls, what's going on? Chris handed D'Andra her fries.

Oh, that's right, it's movie night. I forgot. I'm not staying. I don't want to rain on you guys' parade." "You're not, but I do want to spend some time with my sister." "I'll see you later." "I'll walk you to the door." D'Andra walked Chris out, and when she came back, she had a huge smile on her face.

"What are you smiling about?" "Nothing, what? He makes me happy, that's all. Stop looking at me like that." "I know you. What's going on?" "Oh, well, Chris asked if we could have dinner tomorrow night, and I said yes!" "That's good. I'm glad you guys are working on your marriage. I have to give it to you, sis, you're making him really work for it."

When Ailese came into work, she felt a bit apprehensive now that she knew about Ell and Andrew, but she did everything she could to ignore it. Why Ell of all people? Why couldn't it have been someone she didn't know. Ailese knew that she had better get used to it because there's nothing, she could do about it. What's done is done. Ailese wasn't going to treat Ell any differently than when she didn't know that she was dating Andrew. "Hey, boss. Good Morning. It's a pretty day today. Do you want me to get us some Frappuccino's later?" "Sure, that sounds like a good idea. Here, let me give you some cash, so I don't forget later." Ailese gave Ell some money from her wallet. "Thanks, boss, I will let you know when I leave." Before Ailese could make it to her office, Andrew cut her off to tell her that he needed her in his office. "Hey you," Andrew said as he shut the door behind him. "Hey yourself, so what's up?" "Well, I got some good news and some bad news. Which one do you want first?" "How about you just tell me the good and the bad news."

"Well, I just hung up with Mr. Saxx. Unfortunately, the place where the conference was going to be held had some bad weather and there's been some flooding, so the hotel is flooded as well, and therefore, the conference has been cancelled."

"Are you serious? Don't play, Andrew, are you for real?" "Yes, I am not kidding you, so there's the good news and the bad news. Everything's been postponed. I was thinking maybe you and I could go on a little mini vacation."

"Like where?" "Well, I was thinking we could go up to South City, do some shopping, get a little crazy. Just kidding. Then get this, we could go to Ashton Town City. I hear they have the best food and sightseeing. Let's go!"

"Okay, okay, wow, I guess you had this all planned out, huh? Let me talk to Mikell and see what he says. It does sound like fun. I'll let you know, okay? I don't know if we may make other plans since the conference has been cancelled."

"Okay, Mrs. Lady, let me know. Well, I'll let you get back to your office."

Ailese called Mikell to let him know that the conference was cancelled. He had to call her right back, because he was in a noisy elevator and couldn't hear her.

"Okay, sorry, baby, I'm back, so what happened?" "Well, the conference has been cancelled due to some bad weather, so I don't have to go." "Oh, okay, I know you're happy." Mikell said in a sarcastic tone. "Shut up. Ailese laughed. So, Andrew wanted to know, if I wanted to go on a mini vacation, what do you think about that?" "Well, it's up to you. Actually, that would give me some time with the kids because I already had a bunch of things planned for me and the kids. So, it's really up to you, baby." "You really wouldn't mind me going with Andrew?" "No, I trust you and I trust him, so have fun. It'll do you some good to get out of Shelby. How long are you guys going to be gone?" "A couple of days, that's all." "Okay, so give me all the details when you get home, okay? I do have to get going, they're waiting for me. Love ya." Ailese and Mikell blew each other kisses over the phone. "I love you too." Ailese was so excited about her and Andrew's mini vacation. Ailese couldn't wait to tell Andrew the good news, but something stopped her. She could see that Andrew was upset with the person he was speaking to on the phone. She could tell that he was chewing someone- a new ass- so she went back to her office. She decided to wait until later to speak to him.

Ailese received a surprising call from Officer Brown today. She hadn't heard from him in a very long time. "Hello, Mrs. LaShae. I mean, Ailese, did I catch you at a bad time?" "No, not at all. How are you, Officer Brown?" "I'm well. How's your family doing? I think about them a lot." "We're doing good, thanks for asking." "Ailese, I wanted to let you know that this case with your family has been a cold case. I'm sure you know what that means, right?" "Yes, I do. To be honest with you we even did some detective work of our own and we can't come up with anything. We've been very cautious and made some adjustments in our lives, and so far, everything's okay." "I do feel really bad about this. Sometimes these things happen. We do have a lot of cold cases, and if we have any new evidence, we do reopen the cases." "Okay, thanks for calling Officer Brown, and thanks for all your dedication and support. We could never thank you enough." After Ailese hung up with Officer Brown, she thanked God for keeping her and her family safe. God was and is the only reason why everyone was safe, and Ailese hoped that it stayed that way for a while.

"Knock, knock, hey, um, would you happen to be done with the Caldwell file? I was on my way to accounting, and I thought I would drop that off to them." Ailese was daydreaming a bit. "Oh, yes, the Caldwell, I'm done. Here ya go."

"Are you okay? I lost you there for a second." "I'm okay. I just got off the phone with Officer Brown. Andrew sat down in a chair. He said that our case is considered a cold case, and if any new evidence surfaces, then they would reopen the case. Until then, we may never know who tormented my family, and that just burns me." Andrew stood up and hugged her. "It's going to be okay. I hate seeing you so upset like this."

"I'll be okay. I mean, I have to accept it and move forward. That's why I'm going to go with you on our vacation." "Great, that sounds good! Listen, Andrew bent down on his knees and put his hand on her lap. I feel your pain, and I'm so, so sorry that you had to go through so much these past months, but you and your family are safe now, and I hope this person, this coward, has disappeared forever! I don't like that someone hurt you and your family. That doesn't sit well with me at all, but you're here and we're getting through it. I feel that you should live for today and that going on this vacation would do you some good." "What will I ever do without you, Andrew? You're so good to me, other than Mikell, and my family, you're so good to me." Ailese said, smiling. "I ... love that smile."

Since all the chaos was happening these past months, the tradition of going to Sunday brunch, once a month, hadn't happened in a long time, and today was a special day. Ailese and her family were all going to Sunday brunch, and D'Andra had a surprise for everyone. She didn't even tell Ailese what the surprise was. Ailese had invited Andrew to come to Sunday brunch. Today was all about family. Everyone ate, drank, and talked. "May I have your attention, please? Everyone's eyes are on D'Andra. I have a special announcement to share with you, or I should say, we have a special announcement to share with you. Well, as you all know, Chris and I are expecting ... but we're expecting twins! Everyone was shocked. Alonda got up and hugged Chris and D'Andra. D'Andra shouted, Amen!" Mikell made a toast and gave a speech that was very beautiful because it came from the heart.

Everyone was so excited. D'Andra was the first one in the family so far to have twins. "When the doctor told us that he was hearing two heartbeats, we were shocked as much as you were. We had the chance to know the sex of the babies, but we decided to be surprised and just make sure we prepared ourselves." "I am so happy for you guys. I'm going to have the best of both worlds, and I am going to be the best aunt in the world." "Yeah, we know, we know that you're going to spoil these babies." Chris winked at Ailese. "Not to the point that it makes your life harder, I'm just going to be there for them as you guys were for my kids." "Grandpa's waiting for those beautiful babies, and I'm with Ailese, we're all going to spoil those babies," Don laughed.

"Wow, twins, can you believe that baby?" "No, I can't. I'm still in shock.

Babies are a blessing. They just grow up so fast that it seems like just yesterday, I was teaching the girls how to ride a bike, and now it's almost time to teach them how to drive a car, whoa!" "Yes, I know. I feel the same way."

After Ailese's session was over, she went to see Karen, who had left her a message to come by and see her before she left. "Hey, Ailese, I'm telling you whatever it is that you're doing, it's working because you're losing more weight and you look great!" "Well, thanks. I really don't know what I'm doing but I can tell you this. I have been watching my portions a lot, and a lot of people have been telling me that I'm losing weight." "I just wanted to tell you that my fiancé is still away on business, so I didn't want you to think that I forgot about the engagement dinner that we talked about last time. It looks like he may have to stay there for a while." "Oh, I totally understand, and when you have the engagement dinner planned, I'm there, no worries. I'm looking forward to meeting him, though." "I will let you know as soon as he

SHELBY LIES

comes back." Karen and Ailese caught up on what was going on in their lives until it was time for Ailese to go home.

Before Ailese went home, she had a few things to pick up. She had to pick up the dry cleaning and pick up some things from the grocery store.

When she was in the grocery store, she ran into Emmanuel and his son, who were shopping as well. "Hi, Mrs. Ailese." Emmanuel's son was very polite.

"Hey, Junior, how are you? Wow, you're getting so tall, huh?" "Yeah, I'm good.

We had a game today, and we scored." Junior put his hands in the air and did a victory dance. "That's great! Hey, Emmanuel, how's it going?" "Good. Your husband and I have been working like dogs, but hey, I can't and shouldn't complain. I promised Junior that we could make ice cream sundaes and shakes." Emmanuel pointed to his shopping cart. "Mmm ... sounds like my kind of party. Well, have fun guys. Talk to you guys later." "Okay, bye, Mrs. Ailese."

Ailese was surprised to see D'Andra. She was supposed to be out with Chris tonight. "Hey sis, I made dinner. I hope you didn't mind. I know you're probably wondering why I'm here." "No, you're invited here any time, you know that."

"Well, Chris had to deal with something at work, and Mom and Dad took a drive down to see Allen, and I didn't want to be in that huge house alone."

"Honey, you don't have to explain to me why you're here. I'm glad that you're here." "Let me fix your plate while you get comfortable and give me those bags." "No, D, I'll get it. You relax." "I'm fine like they say, I'm pregnant, not handicapped. I'll be careful. Now go."

"Dinner was great D. Thanks a lot." "Yeah, Aunt D, dinner was sooooo good." Ashanee said, as she rubbed her belly and licked her lips. Everyone laughed. "Lee, you look tired. Why don't you take a load off and relax. I'll have the girls help me clean the kitchen, and besides, it's all my mess anyway." D'Andra said, in a comical voice. "I appreciate it, but I can't go to sleep just yet. I promised Armont that I would help him with something, but thanks." Ailese headed to Armont's room, who was hard at work, studying for his English test. "Hey, handsome guy, do you want me to come back later, when you're done studying?" "No, Mom, I'm done now. I actually needed your help with something." "Okay, shoot." "My English teacher wants us to interview someone that you feel is famous, and I chose you, Mom."

"Did you? That makes me feel proud. Thanks, Armont, that is so sweet of you. So what did you need me to do? Armont handed Ailese a piece paper that was clipped together with a huge paperclip. Oh, so these are the questions that I need to answer?" "Yes, I know that you're busy, but if you could finish those by the end of the week, that would be great, Mom." "No problem, I'm never too busy for you. Hey, I will make sure that I get this back to you as soon as possible." Armont and Ailese talked a bit. Armont mostly talked about school and what was going on in his life.

Armont should be more into girls, but he wasn't. He was more focused on graduating and going to a good college. Yes, girls adored him, and he adored girls too, but he never forgot what his parents taught him: that school comes first no matter what. Armont saw how focusing could bring you much joy in life, like his dad Mikell, for example. When Mikell focused on what he really wanted, he is blessed, and now he is the number one producer and has been for a long time. His mom inspired Armont too, and that's why he felt that she was famous! His Mom has worked with some pretty famous people in her lifetime, like Sedrick Johnson, Meena Stone, and Karoline Simms, just to name a few, and even though she turned down a lot of offers to live the life of a big star, Ailese was a star in his eyes. Armont still remembered times when she would take him to the studio with her. He loved it, and he drew a lot of attention, everyone thought he was the most handsome young man. The women would always kiss his cheeks for good luck, and Armont didn't mind either.

"Baby, what's wrong?" Mikell pulled Ailese to him. Ailese had tears in her eyes.

"Did you know that Armont picked me for his English project? He had to pick someone famous, and he picked me. I'm so touched, that's all." Ailese wiped her face and chuckled a bit. "I know he told me. He told me that he wanted to tell you himself. He loves you so much, Ailese, and it doesn't surprise me, one bit because I feel the same way. You are famous in a lot of ways. We've raised a fine, smart young man. He looks up to us, especially you." "I'm so touched, you know. I told him that I was honored that he chose me." "Come here." Mikell hugged Ailese and gave her a kiss.

"Hey, Mom, look what I got on my paper. Armont was so excited about the grade that he got on his paper. "An A+, honey, that's great! Armont, I am so proud of you. Ailese kissed Armont on his forehead. Hey, how about I give you a little something for this A+? What would you like?" "Mom, you don't have to, Armont said. Well, there is something that I've been wanting for a long time." "Tell me, what is it, Armont?" "I would like to get this cool keyboard. I will be right back, Mom. I'll go and get the magazines it's in." "Okay, I'll be right here." Armont came back with the magazine and showed Ailese the keyboard that he wanted. "Wow, that's a cool keyboard. What if we look at it tomorrow? Would that be okay with you?" "Sure, okay, thanks, Mom!" My teacher says that she admires you as well. She thinks you're awesome,

Mom." "Tell her I said thanks." Ailese blushed. "Mom, I finished all my homework. Could I please watch a movie?" "Sure, why not?" The girls joined their brother after they were done with their homework.

"Mom don't forget that Dana's coming over this weekend for a playdate. Could we all go to the mall?" Adrieana asked. "Sure, we can. I don't see why not. I have to pick up some things at the mall, anyway." When the kids went to bed, Ailese and Mikell cuddled under the sheets and watched a movie until they got tired. Ailese talked about the weekend and their plans. Mikell said that he was going to spend all day Saturday with Ailese and the kids because Sunday he had to work for a couple of hours. When Mikell turned the lights off, they both fell asleep. Ailese's moaning and talking in her sleep woke Mikell up.

Ailese kept mumbling something in her sleep. Mikell couldn't make it out, but he tried to wake her up, but she kept mumbling in her sleep. "Baby, wake up." Mikell gently shook her a few more times, but still no luck. "No, no, don't hurt me, I'll be good. I'll be good." Ailese kept repeating over and over, and finally she woke up. "Baby, are you okay? You were mumbling something in your sleep. I tried to wake you up." "I'm sorry, I'm okay. I need some water." Mikell stopped her and told her that he would get her a glass of water. After she drank her water, she felt much better. "Thank you, Mikell, I'm okay. Don't look at me like that. I'm okay. Go back to sleep." Mikell held Ailese in his arms. He needed to hold her. Holding her, always calmed he down. Mikell was used to holding her after she'd have a bad dream. Mikell took notice that she was more in control of her dreams now than before. "I love you." Mikell whispered in Ailese's ear. She whispered back. "I love you." They both went back to sleep.

Ell called in sick today, so Ailese was swamped. She was doing her job and Ell's at the same time. The phones were going crazy, and Ailese wasn't used to Ell's filing system, so it was hard for her to find anything. Eventually, she figured it out. "Hey, let me see if someone from Human Resources can help you, okay?" "Thanks, Andrew. If you could, that would be a great help." "I'll be right back. Don't move." Andrew didn't know why Ell called in sick. He hadn't seen or spoken to her outside the office in a few days. He didn't keep a leash on her, but with her calling in sick didn't sit well with Ailese, and he could see it in her eyes, and that didn't sit well with him either. Ell picked today of all days to call in sick, even though people do get sick sometimes.

"Ailese, this is Sheri. She'll be helping you out today." "Hello, Sheri I really do appreciate it." "Oh, no problem, just tell me what you need, and I'll get it done."

Ailese looked at Andrew, and he could tell that she was thankful and relieved that he brought Sheri to her. Sheri did a great job. It was like Ell never left. She was a very fast learner. Ailese appreciated all of Sheri's hard work, too.

"You are such a lifesaver. Andrew, thanks so much. You truly are a great best friend. You're always there for me no matter what. Thanks again."

"Now you need to go home and get some rest. You've had a long day. I'll see you tomorrow?" "Yep." Ailese looked at the time, then she thought that she would surprise the kids and pick them up. "Mikell, baby, I'm going to pick up the kids from study hall, okay?" "Okay, are you sure?" "Yeah, I just wanted to surprise them. I can't remember the last time I picked them up from study hall, and I didn't want you to go all the way there for nothing." "Okay. Hey, since you're picking them up, would you mind if I got a bite with the guys?" "No, go ahead, and I will see you later."

The kids were so excited to see their mom. They were expecting their dad to pick them up. Ailese decided to take the long way home so she could finish her conversations with the kids. When they arrived home, Ailese noticed that the answering machine was blinking, so she checked the messages. There was a message from someone named Lea Pines. She was from a magazine. Ailese figured that she would call her back to find out what she had to say. "Hello, Lea Pines. How may I help you?" "Hi, my name is Ailese LaShae, and I am returning your call." "Hello, well, thank you for returning my call. As you probably already know, I am the head publisher of Eshe Magazine, and I wanted to interview you. I know that you have worked with Sedrick Johnson, who's so big now; he has a great sound, and he's going to go a lot of places." "Yes, he is, and yes, I have worked with him. He's an awesome person. I think you should be interviewing him, not me." "Well, I see that you've worked with some great artists, and we would love to interview you. You're a very talented woman." "Well, let me get back to you in a few days. Is that okay?" "Yes, sure, you have my number. I hope to hear from you soon. Take care."

Ailese was still in a bit of shock. "They want to interview me?"

Ailese called Mikell, and he told her that she should think about giving an interview. Andrew agreed with Mikell, as did D'Andra.

Ailese wasn't really up to giving an interview, and yes, she had worked with famous people in her lifetime, and she enjoyed every minute of it; that made her very proud to have accomplished something big, because a lot of people told her that she couldn't do it, and she proved them wrong. Music is and will always be her life; she couldn't live without music. It's what helped her through a lot of rough times. She would just write her feelings on paper and never expect them to come to life in someone else's voice, other than her own.

As Ailese soaked in the bathtub, she started thinking about the conversation that she had with Lea Pines earlier that day. Is it a good idea for her to accept the offer or not? Ailese closed her eyes and relaxed to the soothing music that was playing in the background. Ailese started humming to the music. When there was a knock at the door, Ailese opened her eyes. "Who is it?" "It's Adrieana Mom, could I come in, please?"

"Sure, kitten, come on in." "Hey, Mom, Dad wanted me to check on you. You've been in here a long time. Do you need anything, Mom?" "No, sweetie, I'm just relaxing that's all. Thanks for checking on me." Adrieana smiled.

"Mom, I could wash your back for you." "Well, that would be great. Here's the sponge." Ailese handed Adrieana the sponge to wash her back.

Ailese closed her eyes and relaxed her body. "So, Mom, are you going to do the magazine interview? I think that's so cool, Mom." "Moms thinking about it. I don't know what I'm going to do yet. I mean, I'm very honored that they recognized my work, but I don't know if I want to do the interview."

Adrieana told her mom that she should do the interview, so that everybody could get to know her and what she's all about.

After spending hours at the mall, Ailese still had to go back to the office. She had a late meeting with one of her clients. She and Andrew would probably be working late. Armont and the girls were already in his room, fiddling with the new keyboard that his mom and dad bought him. "Baby, I'm going to lie down for a bit until I have to go back to work, okay?" "Okay, baby, I'll be in the den. I have some work to do as well. I'll hold down the fort while you rest."

Ailese slept until her alarm went off. She hopped in the shower, changed clothes, grabbed a bite to eat, and headed to work. She saw Andrew talking to Ruben when she pulled into the garage. She joined in on the conversation.

"So, how's that beautiful baby of yours?" "She's doing great. She's looking more like her daddy, and that scares me." Andrew and Ailese laughed at Ruben. "Why do you say that? She's beautiful, isn't she, and you're not bad-looking yourself." Ruben laughed. "She loves what you gave her because she goes to bed with it and wakes up with it." "Aw, my girls loved that toy when they were babies. I'm glad she loves it. Well, have a good evening, Ruben. Talk to you later. Andrew, are you coming?" Andrew followed Ailese into the elevator.

When the building was empty, the office looked so different. It was very quiet. Andrew waited in Ailese's office until their clients arrived. "So, I have our vacation all planned. All you have to do is pack, my love." "Wow, okay, I love your ideas. I think I've looked at those emails you sent me a thousand times." Andrew was smiling from ear to ear.

"You won't regret it. We're going to have lots and lots of fun." Ailese gave Andrew a worried look. It just hit her. She had been so into the vacation that she didn't stop to think about Ell. "What would she say?" "Ailese, why are you looking at me like that?" "Um, what about Ell?" "And?" "Andrew, I think that you should be planning this trip with her, not me." "Ailese, please, let's not go there. I can understand why you're so worried about how Ell would feel about us going on this vacation. Just so you know, I was never planning on asking her to go. So, please, we don't need to bring this up again, and besides, we're not that serious, I told you that. I just want to spend some time with my favorite girl, that's all,"

Andrew said, becoming a bit frustrated with Ailese. "Okay, okay, don't blow up at me for being concerned, Andrew, man!" "I'm sorry, sweetie. I didn't mean to get all mad at you. Sometimes, it feels like you don't listen to me, you don't want to listen to me, Ailese. I told you I didn't make any plans with Ell. I know that I kept the whole me and Ell thing, from you. I meant what I said. I don't want any more secrets between us. Ailese, what I'm trying to say is that our friendship means a lot to me, you mean a lot to me." Ailese was at a loss for words. She didn't know what to say to him. Ailese got up to hug Andrew.

"Our friendship means a lot to me as well. I mean, when you first came here, I couldn't stand your ass. I would never think, in a million years, that you out of all people, ended up being my best, best friend, and I don't ever want to lose that. You've been an inspiration in my life. I'm just respecting Ell, that's all." "I know, I know." Ailese interrupted Andrew. "Let's pretend that this discussion never happened, okay?" Andrew shook his head.

To make up for the disagreement earlier, Ailese took Andrew to dinner. That was the least that she could do. She kind of felt bad about how she doubted Andrew; he really meant everything he said about not keeping anything from her anymore. He was done with that. "So, the hotel that I booked for us is awesome Ailese, Andrew took a bite of his fish. "I bet, you should have been in the travel agency business because you know a lot about a lot of different places. I wish I had known you when I planned our honeymoon. I would have let you plan it." When Ailese looked at Andrew, he was bright red and didn't look too good. "Andrew, what's wrong?" Ailese didn't want to panic and make a scene, she went over to Andrew to make sure that he wasn't choking or anything. When Andrew pointed to his pocket, Ailese then knew that he was having an attack. She went into the pocket and pulled out the syringe, prepped his shoulder, and injected his medication. "Andrew, look at me, are you okay?" Andrew held his neck and shook his head. He was a bit out of breath. For as long as they'd been friends, Ailese had never seen Andrew have an attack. Luckily, he taught her what to do if he had one. Andrew got up to go to the restroom to get himself back together. There must have been something in his food to make him have an attack, Ailese thought to herself.

When Andrew came back, he wasn't as red as he had been earlier. He looked at Ailese, and sat down in his chair. "Andrew, are you okay? What happened?" Andrew cleared his throat before answering. "I don't know. I was eating my salad, when all of a sudden, I had an attack. There may have been something in the salad that set it off." Ailese handed Andrew some fresh water. Thanks, Ailese."

"Are you sure you're okay? I can have the waiter take the salad and bring you something else if you'd like?" "No, actually, I think it would be best if I just headed on home. I'll wait until you're done with your meal." Andrew finished off his water. "No, I'm done. Let me get the check, and we can leave. Ailese paid the check, and they both left. Ailese decided to drive Andrew home.

"Andrew, why don't I stay with you. I'm worried about you. I mean, I know you have your butler and maids there at the house, but I would feel better if someone was there with you." "No, just drive me home. I'm just going to hit the hay and rest. I'll be 100 percent in the morning. Ailese, I'm fine."

Ailese called Andrew first thing in the morning to check on him. When she spoke with Andrew, he was better. He sounded good; that was a relief for Ailese. "Stop fussin', woman. I am fine. I will see you later, okay?" "Okay, call me if you need anything." "Well, I'll be at the fundraiser all day, so I will call you tomorrow, okay, sweetie?" "Alright, have fun, my love."

When Ailese hung up with Andrew, she got an unexpected phone call from her brother Allen. She was very happy to hear from him. "So, sis is having twins, huh?" "Yes, can you believe that? Crazy huh?" "I can't wait. I'm so happy for sis. So, what have you been up to, other than working with Sedrick Johnson?" Ailese chuckled and procrastinated on answering her brother's question. "Well, I've been working hard, of course, um, and yes, I have been working in the studio. I may even go on tour in the summer, I don't know yet." "Oh, really, okay. Man, you always had that beautiful voice, sis. I brag about you to people all the time, but they don't believe me when I tell them that you're my sister." "Well, if you came around more often, maybe they would believe you. They probably don't believe that you even have a sister. How's my sister-in-law doing?" "Great, she says hello. She's cooking dinner right now. Say hello to everyone for me, and by the way, I will be in town shortly. I'll tell you all the details, soon, okay?" "Okay, I would love to see you. Hey, let's go shopping or let's do something, okay?" "We need to go see a chick flick or something, and catch up on some soap operas. They both laughed. Sounds like a plan. Love ya sis."

Ailese was a bit bored, so she decided to make some jewelry to pass the time, until it was time to cook. After she finished her jewelry, she decided to call her Mommie, to see how she was doing. "Hi, Mommie. How are you doing?"

"Ailese?" "Yes, Mommie, it's me. I know you're probably upset with me. I've been so busy. I'm sorry that I haven't called you in a while." "Oh, it's okay, baby.

Mommie's doing well. Did the girls get my package?" "Yes, did you get the card they sent you?" "No, not yet.

When did you send it, baby?" "Oh, the other day, I think it will show up soon. Mommie, do you need anything?" "No, baby, I'm alright. Your mom was here just the other day. She took me shopping, and I picked up all the things that I needed. How is everybody?" "We're sticking together and getting stronger each day, Mommie." "I'm glad to hear that because I know you guys went through some chaotic mess! I told your mother that I needed her to come get me so I could find that bastard that was torturing my family. Now, you know Mommie, don't play that! I don't care who you are, don't mess with my family. I may be old, but I'll puts ya out."

"Mommie, don't make me laugh. I know Mommie, but we're okay."

"It was good to hear from you, but Mommie has to get ready for her bath, so I'll talk to you later." "Okay, I love you." "I love you too, my dear."

Ailese loved her grandmother so much, and she was just like Alonda; messing with her family was not an option. Ailese's grandmother and Alonda stuck together when someone tried to hurt any of their loved ones. If you messed with one of them, you messed with all of them. It was in their blood when it came to their young; they were all animals protecting their young.

While living with her grandmother at a very young age, Ailese told her grandmother that a few bullies who were girls hassled her on her way home from school. Because of Ailese's hair and because the boys liked her, they were jealous. Ailese fought back best as she could. She had to fight four girls! When Ailese's grandmother saw her hair that had always stayed neat and the tears in Ailese's eyes, her grandmother took Ailese and washed her up and told her that it was going to be okay. The next day the bullies were messing with Ailese again, but this time they didn't touch a hand on her, because

Ailese's grandmother was there, and Ailese was surprised as well. Her grandmother threatened to cut off the hands of the bullies if they touched her granddaughter again. The girls all ran home and never touched Ailese again!

When Ailese went to bed, Mikell was still at work. Her cell had rang, just as her head hit her pillow. "Hey, Andrew, how'd it go?" "It went great. I hope that I didn't wake you." "Oh, no, I was just thinking about you. I'm just lying in bed right now." "So, how was your day?" "Um, I didn't do much today. I did make some jewelry, though. I'm just waiting for Mikell to get home." "Did you want me to keep you company until he comes home?" Andrew let out a yawn.

"No, you sound tired. I'll be okay. I'll watch TV or something." "No, I'll stay up with you. I want to know what you made." "Oh, I made some bracelets and necklaces. They're really pretty too. Andrew, I think I'm going to do the interview for the magazine. What do you think?" "I think that's a great decision, and I am so proud of you, and you deserve the credit." "Aw, you're too sweet, thanks. If Mikell can't be there with me, can you be there?" "Of course, I will. I'll be honored." "Andrew, are you still there? Hello, hello?" "I'm here. I dropped the phone, sorry. Like I was saying, I'm there if you need my support." Ailese and Andrew talked for a few hours until they both were tired.

"Good Morning. I didn't want to wake you when I came home. You were sound asleep. I didn't plan on being so late. I'm sorry, baby. Hey, what if you and I catch a movie or something today." "Well, the girls are having their playdate at Dana's today. Let me talk to Dana's mom and we'll go from there, okay?" "Okay, let me know." Mikell gave Ailese a kiss.

"Girls, are you almost done with breakfast? It's almost time to go, and you guys need to make sure you have everything that you need, okay?" "Okay, Mom."

"Hey, Denise, it's Ailese." "Hey girl, what's up? Please don't tell me that you're canceling?" "Oh, no, I needed to know what time you wanted me to pick up the girls?" "Well, I'm thinking in the evening. I know that's a bit late, but I could bring them home, so if you have any errands to run or whatever, go for it!"

"Are you sure? Thanks." "Yes, I am sure. You know the girls are in good hands."

Ailese went to tell Mikell that they could spend the day together, but Mikell was on an important phone call. Ailese had to take the girls to Dana's. She got Mikell's attention. Mikell put his call on hold. "It's a go. We can spend the day together. I have to take the girls to Dana's." "Okay, give me a sec and I will be right there, okay?" "Okay."

After they dropped the girls off at Dana's, Mikell and Ailese got started on their date. "I thought that we'd go to Greensville. Is that okay?" "Wow, I haven't been there in a while. Mikell, I have decided to do the interview for the magazine." "That's good. I am so proud of you. When will you know the date of your interview?" "Well, I have to call Lea Pines back, and I'm sure that she'll have a date set up, and I'll let you know." "Okay, sounds good. I'm happy for you, baby. Come here." Mikell hugged her tight and kissed her on the lips.

Ailese and Mikell spent hours talking after the movie at her favorite restaurant. They then rented bikes and went on a bike ride together, where they met a nice married couple that joined them on their bike ride.

They visited all the new stores that were in Greensville and saw a comedy show that happened to be in town. Ailese and Mikell laughed so hard. The comedians were so funny. Ailese and Mikell picked up some must-haves from the gift shops and headed home.

"I had such a great time, Mikell. Thanks, I really needed that." Mikell kissed Ailese passionately and held her in his arms. "I missed spending time with you. I needed to spend this day with you. I really did." Ailese kissed Mikell and rested her head on his chest. I love you so much. I love you, Ailese."

"I love you so much, Mikell. What would I ever do without you? I'm so blessed and glad that I have you." Mikell and Ailese kissed each other like they hadn't seen each other in years. Mikell carried Ailese to the bedroom, where they made passionate love.

When Ailese woke up, she didn't see Mikell. She called out to him. "I'm in the shower, baby." Ailese felt so sluggish that it took her a few minutes to get out of bed and focus. "Hey, you could have waited for me." Mikell's eyes studied Ailese's beautiful body as she stepped into the shower with him.

Mikell turned to Ailese. He wanted to look at her naked body. He loved her body. Mikell always told Ailese that he loved her body and that she was the most beautiful thing he had ever seen in his life, and that's why he was determined to make her his. But he loved her free spirit first. That was what attracted him to her. He loved that she was goofy and a bit off. Her laugh was amazing! Everything about her that made her who she was. "You're making me blush, Mikell, stop." Ailese turned the other way so Mikell could only focus on her butt. "What? I love looking at you. Come here. Mikell pulled her close to him. You're the most beautiful woman I've ever seen in my life. I love you." "I love you too." Ailese smiled at Mikell and gave him another kiss. He made love to her a few more times.

The girls told their mom and dad about their day with Dana. They had lots of fun. They all decided to make chocolate chip cookies and cupcakes, which they enjoyed after dinner. Mikell helped Ailese with dinner. Mikell made the Caesar salad and cut up all the vegetables. Ailese made her famous lemon pepper chicken and red -skinned potatoes.

When everyone was eating dinner and having good conversation, someone was banging very hard on the door. Ailese and Mikell looked at each other; it creeped them out. Ailese instructed the girls to eat their dinner in their bedrooms and not come out until their dad came to get them.

After Mikell knew that the girls were safe and sound, he went to retrieve his gun. The banging got louder and louder, and the person began turning the handle on the door. As Mikell motioned for Ailese to join the girls in the bedroom, she did so. Ailese didn't want to leave her husband, but she knew that their safety was important. Mikell aimed his gun straight at the door. He was ready for anything. He wasn't going to let anyone hurt his family. The girls and Ailese stayed together. Ailese told the girls that they had to be very quiet. Ailese held on to the girls. Adrieana is on her left, and Ashanee is on her right. Ailese always kept her cell phone on her. She dialed 911 and told them that there was a disturbance. The police were on their way.

Mikell didn't want to look through the peephole, so he looked out a window. He had to be very careful that this man didn't see him looking out the window. Mikell was not going to open the door to this stranger, as he continued to bang on the door, swearing and cursing. The police arrived and responded to the disturbance. The police talked to the man that was banging on the door, and the neighbor came out and told the police that he saw the man get out of the car and walk up to the front door, and he thought that Mikell and Ailese knew him, so he didn't call the police. The police officers spoke with Mikell and filed a police report just in case

SHELBY LIES

this man came back. After the police were done questioning the man, they told Mikell that there were drugs involved and he could press charges for trespassing on his property if he wanted to. Mikell told the police that he didn't have any reason to press charges and stressed that he didn't know why this man was trying to get into his home.

Mikell went to get Ailese and the girls to let them know that it was all over. "Come here girls. Mikell hugged his girls and told them it was okay. The man who was banging on the door was sick. Sometimes people don't know what they're doing. It's okay. Dad will always protect his family, no matter what."

"Dad, why did he want to hurt us?" I don't know, honey, but I talked to the police, and he shouldn't be bothering us anymore. They took him away. I'm proud of my girls. You guys were very brave." In an effort to distract the girls from the incident, Mikell took them into the kitchen to eat cookies and cupcakes they made. Mikell reassured the girls that everything was okay. As the time passed, the girls forgot all about it.

"I can't believe it. This man was trying to get in our home. What's wrong with people these days?" "I know Lee, but we're okay, and that's the most important thing." "It burns me, though, how bold people are these days. Ailese took off her jewelry and threw it in the box. She was angry. Angry that people were targeting her family, and for what? I don't feel safe anymore, Mikell. This man could have come into our home and done who knows what! I'm very upset. I didn't want to show it in front of the girls. This doesn't sit well with me at all.

This man was brave enough to turn the handle on the door, and luckily all the doors and windows are locked. I know one thing, if you had to use that gun on him, I wouldn't have blamed you one bit. He was trespassing on our property! So, if people want to come in here and try to hurt us, then they have another thing coming because I know how to use a gun too, and when I use my gun to protect us, I'm not going to have one ounce of sympathy for them either! I mean it!"

"Baby, calm down. I agree with you, baby, I do. Mikell kissed Ailese on her cheek. Hey, it's okay. I'm glad that you got out your frustration, but I don't want you to worry, okay?"

Ailese told D'Andra what had happened to them the other day. "I'm glad that you guys are alright, and I don't blame you for taking measures, if you have to. The weird part about it, is that this asshole didn't even know you guys; some drughead. Like I said, you guys are okay, and that's all that matters.

I feel your frustration though, sis, I do, and I know that you or Mikell will do everything in your power to keep the kids safe." "Yep, we are and we will."

It took a few days for Ailese to feel totally comfortable in her own home after that incident happened. She kept telling herself that it was over and asked God to watch over them. Still, she wondered, "Why? Why? Why?"

During early morning prayer, she asked a church member to pray for her and her family. That helped her feel a lot better. She visited D'Andra, Alonda, and Don. She needed to be around her family. They all pitched in and fixed a big lunch and had lunch out on the patio since it was a nice day. They played games and took pictures of each other, especially D'Andra, since everything about her was changing and she had the most beautiful glow. During their conversation, they discussed how they should plan for Allen's visit. The grown-ups drank wine with strawberries and D'Andra, and the kids had sparkling cider.

Ailese loved being around her family. She loved them so much and would do anything for them. They keep her going every day. They were excited that Ailese had decided to do the interview for the magazine. Alonda told everyone stories about Ailese when she would sing in plays and at church. Everyone loved those stories, except Ailese, who always felt like her mom was bragging too much, but she was just proud of her daughter.

Chris arrived as they were leaving. They chatted with him in front of the house for a bit. Chris was so excited about the babies. He had changed alot, and everyone noticed it. Chris told everyone that he would not be traveling much and that he had hired some new people so he wouldn't have to have so much responsibility. He was not going to let anything, or anyone get in the way of him raising his babies. Everyone was so proud of him. He'd even moved back in with D'Andra. Alonda and Don decided to stay there for a while to help out with the babies.

D'Andra had talked them out of moving, when they heard the magic words: rent free, no mortgage. D'Andra and Chris convinced them that they would miss them, and they could use their help. They were having twins and first time-parents. They all agreed that they would need them there.

"Hey guys, time to get ready for tomorrow, alright?" The girls went to get ready for school tomorrow. "Mom. Adrieana tapped her on the shoulder. I can't find my pink and blue shirt that you just bought me. I wanted to wear it tomorrow." "Um, let's go into your room to look for it. Come on." Ailese looked in all the dresser drawers, she wasn't able find the shirt, then she looked in the closet. It had fallen into the empty hamper, so she handed it to Adrieana. "Thanks, Mom." "You're welcome." "Mom, are you okay?" Adrieana looked at her mom with an inquisitive look. "Oh, I'm fine.

Why do you ask?" "Because ever since that man tried to break in, you haven't been yourself, and I'm worried about you. I saw that you didn't even eat all your food at Aunties, and you've been walking us to our class when you drop us off at school." "You caught me. I'm going to be just fine. I'm just a bit angry, a little shaken up, and more cautious, but I'll get over it in time." "Mom, I love you. It's going to be fine. We're okay. Daddy will take care of us." "I know, baby." Ailese gave her daughter a huge hug, and she got one in return. She really needed that.

Ailese was surprised to see Chris in her office. He wanted to go over the project with Ailese. "I hope that I'm not holding you up, Lee." "No, not at all. Let me get Andrew, and we could start. I will be right back." "Hello, Chris. How are you today?" Andrew took a seat. "I am great. How about you?" "Missing those hockey tickets." Chris chuckled. "Oh, I know I've been so busy that I haven't been to a game since we all went. We have to get back in there, huh?" Chris shook his head. I'm glad that you're in on this project. That way, Ailese and I can rest easily because we know that you and your guys will make us proud."

"Thanks, I appreciate that." Ailese, Andrew, and Chris went over the project until they all came to an agreement and the figures all matched, etcetera.

"I have to get going guys. I will talk to you guys later." "Let me walk you out, Chris." Andrew followed behind Chris.

"This project is a lot of work, but I know that it will be worth it in the end." Ailese let out a sigh and massaged her temples. "Take a break and go get some coffee or water." "Thanks, Andrew. Do you want to come with me?"

Andrew and Ailese walked to the deli that was down the street. They both needed some fresh air. "Are you okay.

Ailese? You seemed distracted the whole day." Ailese looked at Andrew and contemplated telling him what was bugging her. "Well, get this, we had a disturbance the other day. Can you believe that?" "What! What happened, Ailese, and why didn't you call me, and you're just now telling me about this?" Andrew stopped Ailese and told her to sit down. "This man was kicking in our door. I mean, I thought that he was going to kick the door down, but he didn't. He started swearing and cursing. He was on drugs. It was crazy, you know." Ailese could feel her eyes tearing up. She had held so much in that before she knew it, she was crying. "Come here, sweetie." Andrew held her in his arms. "I just knew that this man was going to hurt my family and me, but Mikell was there. Thank God." Ailese sobbed more.

"Please tell me that you called the police?" "Yes, I did. They said that this man was on heavy drugs, and they took him away, but I still don't feel safe, Andrew." "Look at me. You can't hold all this stuff inside Ailese. You just can't.

I know that you're strong. We all know this, and it's okay to be scared. Don't ever feel ashamed of being scared. Let it out. I'm right here. I'm right here."

Ailese didn't feel any shame that she was crying. The incident made her think about what happened to her sister, her mom, and her dad, and it upset her a lot. Her girls were in that house! She didn't care about the materials that were in that house. She cared about the girls and Mikell. Andrew was right, she can't always hold in to her feelings. She needed to let them all out.

"Ailese, I'm glad that no one was hurt. Andrew took more tissue from his pocket and gave it to Ailese. Ailese let out a moan. "I needed that from you, Andrew. Opening up to you is different from opening up to Mikell. What I mean by that is, you're the man in my life who hands me tissue, you focus on the moment, you remind me of my strength. Mikell, is the man who reminds that I can conquer my fears, and if I am going through something, we're going to go through it together. Both of you never judge me. Ailese paused. I'm not making any sense, huh?" "Yes, you are my love. I understand what you're saying, and sometimes that happens, so there's no need to feel bad about it. Come on, let's get something in that stomach of yours."

Andrew took Ailese's hand to help her up, and they headed to the deli.

"Hey, Andrew, I just wanted to say thanks again for earlier, Ailese said after a brief pause. You really made me see how much I keep inside Andrew. You're such a good friend, and I know I say that a lot, but you are." "I was only doing my duty as a friend, that's all. Now promise me that you'll try not to keep all those emotions inside." "Okay, I'll try." "Also, if some asshole wants to try and scare you guys like that again, let me know, okay? I have something for them. Andrew said, as he balled his fists. You know that I'm there." "Andrew, what am I going to do with you, huh?" "Mmmm ... I don't know Ailese, you tell me, "Andrew laughed.

"So what are you up to?" "Oh, just feeding my face right now." "So, how are you and Ell doing?" "We're good, why?" Ailese laughed. "I was just wondering, gosh. Why do you always get so defensive when I bring up your girlfriends?" "I don't get defensive, me? No, me? I don't think so. I just don't like to discuss my love life with people. It's private, and I need some kind of privacy." "Okay, gotcha, I understand. I went to the mall the other day and did some serious damage for the trip we're taking." "You are so bad. I know you did because I know, Ailese, has to look her best at all times." Andrew said, in a girly voice, teasing Ailese. "Shut up; stop teasing me." "So, did you find out when the interview will be?" "Oh, I haven't called her back yet. I've been preoccupied, but I am going to call her though." "I hope that you do, Ailese. This would be a great opportunity for you, I think." "Hey, did that friend of yours ever stop harassing you about money?" "No, he still calls every now and then, my answer will remain the same. No, no, and no." "Wow, he's still calling you? He needs to get the picture and find another way. I help my family sometimes only because they work hard and I know how expensive things can be, but when someone owes you money and is still asking for more, I would feel the same way that you do." "I am a very free-hearted person to an extent, but I have to draw the line somewhere, you know?" "Yes, I know. My heart used to get me in a lot of trouble, as I've told you this. I had to learn the hard way."

"Yeah. I know, but some people love to take advantage of people like us."

"Hey, I have to go, Ailese. I will talk to you later. I have to take this call, sweetie." "Okay, bye." After hanging up with Andrew, Ailese looked at the time. It was almost time for her to pick up the kids from study hall. She picked up her purse and headed out.

"Mom, could you make some chicken tacos tonight? We had some for lunch today, and they were good." "Okay, Ashanee, why not? Do you want to help mom make the tacos?" "Yeah, I will, mom." Ashanee began to make up a song about tacos: My Mommies making tacos, My Mommies making tacos." "Ashanee, you're so goofy, like your mom." Ashanee started dancing in the backseat. Armont and Adrieana joined in on the song and started dancing, they all were laughing hard. "Mom, I have a note for you to read when we get home." "Okay, I will look at it when we get home.

Armont, do you really want to go on this field trip?" "I do Mom. I mean, I know that it cost a lot, but I do want to go." "I know you do, but it's a whole two weeks, and how can I rest if I don't know if those teachers will make sure they keep an eye on you? I want to know that you'll be safe, that's all." "Mom, I will be fine. We have to stay with a guardian the whole time no matter what. Please Mom, can I go? You know me. You know that you can trust me." "You're right, and I do trust you. Your dad and I will talk more about this tonight, okay?"

"Okay, Mom. I'm going to my room now. Hey, Ashanee and Adrieana, do you guys want to come?" They both followed Armont to his room. A few minutes later, Ailese heard music coming from Armont's room.

Since the kids were keeping busy, Ailese decided to keep busy as well, and with Mikell working late a lot these days, she needed to keep herself occupied.

She caught up on laundry, even though she would normally catch up on laundry on the weekend, but this was one less thing that she had to do.

Just as she started the last load, her cell phone rang. "Hello, hey Mik, I miss you." "Hi, baby, I miss you so much. I just wanted to check in and see how everyone was doing?" "We're good, and you? I hope you're eating, and keeping fluids in you. Are you?" "I'm good, and yes to all those questions. I'm going to be home earlier this time. I'm shooting for, um, before the kids' bedtime, okay?" "Okay, I hope so, because I miss you." Out of nowhere, Ailese started crying. She didn't know why. "Baby, what's wrong?" "I just had a rough day today, and I thought that I got it all out, but I guess not. I'll be okay, just a bit emotional, I guess. I need you to come home, Mikell." "Baby, I'm coming right now. I love you." Ailese didn't know what was wrong with her, she was so emotional and fragile. Maybe she was working too hard? Maybe she just needed her husband.

"Hey baby, what's wrong? You scared me. Sit down, baby." "I didn't mean to scare you. I think I'm just a bit overwhelmed, that's all. I have a lot going on, that's all. I'm not going to lie; I am still trying to get over this whole ordeal with that man trying to break in. I don't know why, but it's still so fresh in my mind. I guess I feel like he took away my freedom to feel safe." "Come here. I'm so sorry. I know that you don't need any more stress." "No gun, no top- of – the- line alarm system, nothing, can ever make me feel safe anymore. I know that you will always protect us; I know that. I'm sorry. I know that I'm not making any sense."

"No, don't say that. You are making sense. You've been through so much these past couple of months, and that can change any person's mind about not feeling safe. Come here, Ailese." Mikell held her in his arms as tight as he could hold her.

It was getting close to vacation time, and Ailese was getting more and more excited about the trip. She was finally feeling like herself again.

She scheduled an appointment with Dr. Salvino for today and then she planned to go and spend time with D'Andra. Things at the office were a bit less stressful since the biggest project of all time was in progress; she could breathe now. Andrew and Ailese were discussing their plans nonstop. Andrew would email Ailese new things about the vacation every day.

Andrew even emailed her the schedule, from site- seeing to shopping.

For example, they would have to be showered and dressed by 8:00 a.m. every day. Luckily, Ailese respected Andrew and cared about him, so she didn't bother to complain.

Ailese needed some new files, so she buzzed Ell, but she didn't answer. Ailese went into Ell's drawer to get the supply key to get what she needed.

When she opened the drawer, she saw a picture of Chris and Ell. She couldn't believe her eyes. The picture looked like it was taken at a club or something.

She put the picture back where it was and took the key, got what she needed, and went back to her office. "What should I do? I can't spring this on my sister, not now. Chris and Ell? And now Ell and Andrew? What in the hell is going on? Should I confront her? I think I do need to confront her, but I don't want to cause a scene either." Ailese was furious with Chris and Ell. Ell knew that Chris was married to her sister. They had been introduced on more than one occasion. "This bitch, coming into.... No, Ailese, stop it. You don't know the whole story. Calm down, Ailese. Keep it together. Ailese could not believe that Ell would stoop that low. Mmmm ... Ell did have a necklace on with a C on it, and she did say that it was her boyfriend's initials. Okay, Ailese, back to work. You'll deal with this later. You need to stop talking to yourself."

"Andrew, do you have the Roland file?" Oh, hold on one sec, okay?"

Ailese went to Andrew's office to get the file. "Hey, I would have brought it to you." "It's okay." Ailese went back to her office, and when she was done, she went back to Andrew's office to give the file back to him. He was on a call and seemed upset. "Are you okay?" "Yeah, never been better." "Okay, here ya go."

"FYI, I would never want to make you mad. Your bite would rip my head off."

"I'm sorry, Andrew said, winking at her. Was the file, okay?" "Perfect. I actually forgot to add something, that's all.

I'll try not to bother you." Ailese said, as she chuckled and left the office. She could hear Andrew mumbling something.

There was Ell sitting at her desk, and Ailese was on the verge of telling her what she thought about her and Chris, but she didn't, couldn't, not yet.

When she arrived at Dr. Salvino's office, she visited Karen for a bit until it was time for her to go to her appointment. "Hey, I am so glad that you stopped by. Guess what?" "What?" "My fiancé is finally back, and I have a date for the engagement party. I have your invitation right here." Ailese opened the envelope that smelled like perfume and read it. "I'll be there with bells on."

The party would be before Ailese went on vacation.

Karen was getting pretty busy, so they had to cut their visit short.

Ailese made a call to Lea Pines to schedule the interview. The interview was scheduled for next week, and Ailese was a bit excited and looking forward to it. She was going to be very busy next week, between getting ready for her trip, the engagement party, and the interview.

The sessions with Dr. Salvino were going really well, so far. When she entered Dr. Salvino's office, she was surprised to see her on crutches. "Oh, you poor thing, what happened?" "Oh, I slipped and fell on my son's toy, grrr. Dr. Salvino growled. I'm adjusting, though the only thing that I don't like is having to depend on my husband to drive me everywhere. He drives too slow for me."

"I know what you mean." They both laughed. Ailese waited patiently while Dr. Salvino got situated. She had a hard time trying to rest her feet on a velvet-rose stool, so Ailese assisted her in resting her foot comfortably on the stool. "Thanks. I'm sorry. I'm the doctor here. I'm supposed to be helping you."

"Oh, it's no trouble. Hey, let me get you a pillow, okay?" "Thanks, Ailese, that's very kind of you." Ailese sat one of the pillows under her foot and the other behind her back." That's so much better. Now we can get started on our session.

So how have your dreams been? Are you more in control of them now?"

"It's funny that you would ask that because I am more in control of my dreams now, and I have less of them. I have something for you. Ailese pulled out a piece of paper and unfolded it, showing it to her doctor. The paper had a name on it. Dr. Salvino took the paper out of Ailese's hand and examined it; she smiled. "Ailese, this is great progress!" Dr. Salvino was pleased that Ailese was able to write the name of the man who hurt her. She wrote all the letters; his name was Rico: R-I-C-O. "Dr. Salvino I am determined to not feel like Rico's running my life any more. I refuse to feel this way. I'm done with running. I faced this problem head on. At first, I wanted to run away and never look back, but I couldn't ignore it. I don't think I've ever stopped blaming myself for what I've been though, and stopped being afraid of whatever I'm going to go through. Dr. Salvino shook her head and continued listening to Ailese. Rico is not going to ruin my life. I won't let him!" The session went well today, and her progress will continue to improve. That was the only way to go: improve, improve.

On the way to her sisters, Ailese was still unsure what to do regarding Chris cheating with Ell. She needed a decision soon. Telling her sister was her duty as a big sister, and if she didn't tell her and D'Andra found out from a stranger, then Ailese would feel bad. D'Andra was very fragile right now. She's pregnant, and her hormones are all over the place. She was damned if she did told her sister and damned if she didn't.

When Ailese pulled up to D'Andra's house, she saw Chris and D'Andra outside talking. "Hey Ailese," Chris kissed her cheek and hugged her. "Hey, where are you going with all that stuff?" "Oh, I'm taking all this to the dump or else." Chris looked at D'Andra. "Come on in, Lee. I'm so glad to see you. I'm working from the house today, and I've been really busy today, and I made sure that I got all my stuff done before you came over."

"How are things at the office anyway?" "Busy, busy. Do you know I'm still getting things from people at the office? Come here, and let me show you what Chris and I did." "Wow, a garden? This is so beautiful, sis." "Thanks, Chris, and I decided to do something with all the flowers that people were giving us, and here they are." Ailese smelled the roses and flowers and imagined that she was in a tropical place. "How long did it take you guys to do this?" "Oh, a whole weekend! Chris is so determined to make me completely happy, especially after he told me that he had an affair with Ell, your secretary." After picking a flower, D'Andra put it in her hair and continued walking. "D'Andra, we need to talk. Come here and sit down." "Sis, I'm okay. I just want to be happy. I just want to be a good mother and a good wife."

Ailese tried to tell D'Andra about Ell and Chris, but D'Andra just kept cutting her off. I know that you won't judge me for taking Chris back after what he did to me, but I believe in second chances, and I've worked too damn hard to let this relationship just die and go down the tubes. These babies deserve to have two parents because it took both of us to make these babies." "I agree, and no, I will never judge you for any decisions that you make, and I still love Chris no matter what. Well, Ailese said to herself. At least D'Andra heard it from the horse's mouth and not me or even Ell."

Ailese was having a bad dream, but this time it wasn't only about Rico, the man who hurt her. It was about everyone trying to hurt her. What did this dream mean? Andrew was in her dream as well, and he, too, was trying to kill her! Ailese ran and ran, trying to get to safety, but every time she thought she was safe, someone would chase her with a knife or a gun, trying to kill her. When she finally woke up, she was shaking like a leaf on a tree.

It seemed so real to her. It took her a while to fall back to sleep. She didn't want to wake up Mikell, because he had a long day at work today. He was so exhausted, that he didn't even eat dinner, he went straight to bed.

"Andrew, are you on your way?" "There's a bit of traffic, my love, but I will be there as soon as I can. We're still making good time though." "Okay, see you then."

Ailese paced back and forth, putting a hole in the floor. She checked her makeup and outfit a dozen times and looked in the mirror a million times.

The outfit suited her in every way. She wore a rayon burgundy- wrapped dress with a huge gold medallion necklace and gold studs; she looked elegant.

"Hey, you look beautiful, my love. Are you ready to go?" "Are you sure I look okay?" Ailese made a sour face and smoothed her dress with her hands. "Yes, I am sure you look perfectly beautiful. Now let's go and ace this interview.

Your hair looks great, Ailese. You look great!" "Thanks Andrew, Ailese looked in the mirror again. "I don't know why there was all this traffic. I thought that there may have been an accident, but there wasn't, who knows, huh?" "Yeah, I know. I guess everyone's out because it's a nice day." "Did you eat anything, Ailese? "Yes, I had something. I'm okay. Are you straight?" Andrew gave Ailese a quick look. "I'm straight, my love."

When they arrived at *Eshe Magazine*, Lea Pines greeted them. They followed her into the elevator. She pressed the number four.

"Follow me, please. Please let Kiley, my assistant, know if you need anything. Coffee, water, a sandwich, anything. I will be right back. Oh, have a seat. I'm sorry. I guess I'm excited that you're doing the interview." The room was huge, you could have lived in it if you wanted to. There were pictures of famous jazz singers on the walls, the furniture was red velvet with burgundy accents, the floors were bright white marble. Lea came back with a man that stood at least six feet five inches tall with fair skin. He wore expensive prescription glasses and an expensive tailored suit with nice cuffs. "This is Mr. Williams, our senior editor in chief for Eshe Magazine." "Please, call me Edward. Hello, how are you Mrs. LaShae? Thank you for being here." "Hello, this is Andrew McGee II. He's a good friend of mine, and by the way, you can call me Ailese." Edward smiled at Ailese. "So, let's get this show on the road. I bought everyone waters. Here you go." Edward passed around the waters to everyone.

"So, Ailese, how did you get your start singing with famous people?"

"Well, one day a friend of mine asked me if I wanted to sit in on a recording session, and I agreed to. One day, they needed a backup singer, because one of the singers had quit, so I was asked to take her place, though it was only temporarily. I first worked with Faye Chandler. She's a great person inside and out. I loved, loved working with her. She asked me to do some background vocals for her, and it took off from there." "How was it working with the famous Mr. Charles Day? He is one of my favorites too. I don't care what anyone else says." "One word to describe him is amazing. I was a bit nervous, I mean, I was very young and a bit inexperienced, is how I felt, but Charles told me that I needed to embrace my gift, and he thought that I was a great singer, which shocked me." "Wow, and you do have a great voice. Why didn't you ever get signed to a recording contract?" "Well, to be real with you, I did have offers and I did turn them down. I mean, don't get me wrong, earlier on I did want to be signed, but as I got older and wiser, it just wasn't for me. I was happy if I was singing, period. Music is and always will be my life. I have loved music ever since I was old enough to speak." Ailese felt Andrew looking at her, so she looked back at him, and they both smiled. They asked Ailese more questions about her life and other artists she had worked with in the past. They also talked about Sedrick's album and how they chose the songs. They even brought up Mikell. After the interview, they took some professional pictures of Ailese. After the photo shoot, Lea gave Ailese and Andrew a tour of the place. Lea told Ailese that the interview would be in next month's issue and she would have it FedExed to her.

"Well, that went better than expected, huh?" Yes, you were excellent Ailese. I told you that you had nothing to worry about." Andrew glanced over at Ailese. Andrew wanted to celebrate, but Ailese took a rain check. She wanted to spend the rest of the day with Mikell, since the kids were with her mom.

"Hey, Ailese, could I use the restroom before I hit the road?" "You know where it is." Ailese pointed down the hall. When Ailese checked the answering machine, she was disgusted when she heard the police officer letting them know that the man who tried to break into their home had made bail and the charges had been overturned. Ailese immediately called Mikell to let him know.

"Mikell, they released this bastard! They released this son of a bitch!"

Ailese was furious, and so was Mikell. "What's all the fuss about Ailese? What's wrong?" Ailese played the message for Andrew. What the hell is going on here? This system is fuc—" Before Andrew could finish cursing, Ailese stopped him. "Andrew. Don't curse. Please don't get me started!" "I can't let you stay here by yourself. I'm going to stay here with you until Mikell comes home, okay?"

"No, I'll be fine, and if I have to use a gun then so be it. I won't hesitate to kill somebody if I have to." "No, I'm staying here like I said, and I don't want to hear it, Ailese. I'm staying, and that's that!" Ailese started to have an anxiety attack; she couldn't breathe. Ailese, here, sit down and try to take small breaths. Look at me. Andrew began to take small, deep breaths, so that Ailese would do the same. Okay, good. There you go. Shh, shh, shh. It's okay."

Andrew got up after Ailese calmed down and gave her a glass of water.

"Andrew, please, just hold me, please," Ailese said, grabbing Andrew's shirt and pulling him to her. Andrew held her in his arms. He hated seeing her like this. He felt so helpless. What could he do to make it all better?

"Hey, hey, Andrew whispered. It's going to be okay. I'm right here," he whispered again, and before he knew it, Ailese had fallen asleep in his arms.

Andrew gently laid her down on the sofa. He was very careful because he didn't want to wake her up. As Ailese slept, Mikell came home, and she was still fast asleep.

"Hey, Andrew, what's going on?" "Oh, Ailese had an anxiety attack. She's okay, though. I calmed her down. She's not taking this whole thing about the damn crazy ass being released doesn't sit well with her, so I stayed with her, I hope you didn't mind." "Oh, no, not at all. I appreciate it. Can I offer you a drink or something?" "Sure, what do you have?"

"We have soda, juice water, mineral water, and wine. Oh, and we have a few wine coolers." "Mineral water with lemon. Is that okay?" "No prob, man, here you go, Mikell told Andrew as he handed him his drink. Mikell looked over at the sofa to make sure Ailese was okay.

So, the interview went good, huh?" "Yeah, it did, it did, and she was great."

Mikell shook his head. Mikell opened his soda, poured it into a glass of ice, and took a sip of it. "I'm sure that she will tell me all about the interview when she feels better." Andrew finished off his mineral water and took his keys out of his pocket. "Well, I better get going. Hey, call me if you guys need anything, anything at all." "Thanks, Andrew. Take care. Mikell locked the door after Andrew left. Mikell watched Ailese sleep and made sure she was warm enough.

Hey, baby, I'm home. How are you feeling?" Ailese looked around, but she didn't see Andrew anywhere. "I'm feeling a little better. How long have I been asleep?" "Um, for a while baby. Oh, Andrew said that he would call us later."

Ailese shook her head and yawned. "Are you hungry, Mikell? I can fix you something to eat." Just as she started to get up from the sofa, Mikell stopped her from getting up. "Baby, don't worry about that. Please talk to me. I know that you're upset, and I want to be here for you, so please talk to me." Ailese got back under the warm blanket and laid her head on Mikell's chest. "I just don't understand why this crazy man is out on the streets. He's going to torture someone else the same way that he tortured us. I know that you may think that I am taking this too seriously, but. Ailese paused. But this man's intentions were to hurt us, and he may come back and finish what he started all because of some goddamn overturn? Ailese let out a sigh, closed her eyes, and prayed to herself, asking God to forgive her for using his name in vain. Mikell didn't dare interrupt her. He just listened to her and shook his head every now and then. I am a good person, I respect people because I want to be respected; I don't hate anyone, and if I have any enemies, they never said it to my face. I feel like I've been violated and disrespected, and I don't know which ones are worse! I already let Rico run my life, and we all know where that's gotten me. I'm not going to let this son of a ... Ailese stopped herself from cursing like a sailor. No, I am not going there! Ailese had become angrier and angrier. Mikell had never seen her like this. Yes, he's seen her get upset, but not like this. After Ailese let out her frustrations and Mikell knew it was safe to speak, he let out a long sigh.

"Ailese, I know how you feel. I can't stress that enough to you, but I'm from the streets, and no matter what, if the dude was big, bigger, or smaller than me, I never let them disrespect me or anyone I cared about, and if I had to fight, I fought with all I had. Mikell balled his fists. We're going to fight with all we have to make sure that we're all safe, and we're going to start by making sure that you're not alone in this house. I know that you'll take out this man if you have to, but I don't want to take any chances because you and the kids are my world, and I don't want anyone hurting you if I can help it. First thing tomorrow morning, I'm going to get a new alarm system installed. Maybe it's time to update our alarm system. Baby, it's all taken care of. I don't want you to worry. This is my job, okay?" Ailese shook her head. "Mikell, I just feel like this. First, it was the dreams, Mom, and Dad, and then D'Andra, now this; all of this is bad, really bad! I feel like all these things are signs; that someone is targeting our family, for a reason, I just don't know the reason. I am scared out of my mind. It's one thing after another, and I feel like I'm losing it, Mikell." "No, you're not losing it, baby, you're not.

Come here." Mikell hugged her and reassured her that they were going to be fine.

Normally, Ailese wouldn't dare take any medicine. Sometimes, it made her think about the bad times when she depended on medication to keep her going, but today she had the worst headache. It felt like someone was hitting her over the head with something. "Hey, boss, how's your headache? Is it going away?" Ailese massaged her temples and looked up at Ell. "No, it's not. I don't know what's wrong with me. I haven't gotten these headaches in years. Could you please bring me some tea, please, Elle." "Okay, I'll be right back, boss."

"Oh my gosh, I wish this headache would go away now." When Ell came back with the tea, she also came back with some aspirin. "Here you go, boss, and here's some aspirin. It's been a few hours since you've taken them. Maybe if you take the second dose, you'll feel better. I'll come back and check on you later." Ailese took the aspirin and began to feel a little better. As she sipped on the tea, her headache seemed to slowly disappear.

Andrew was out of the office the whole day. Ailese missed him being around and harassing her all the time. The two of them would be going out to lunch right about now. Ailese skipped lunch, even though Ell invited her. Ailese had to decline the offer, she told Ell that she needed to catch up on some work. Ailese locked the door, laid down on the sofa that was in her office, and closed her eyes.

She had to be out for an hour or so because when she woke up, Ell was back from lunch. She knocked on the door and brought her something to eat, just in case she got hungry.

SHELBY LIES

Ailese wanted the day to end already. She had been feeling like crap all day long, even though her headache was better. She just wanted to go home.

Ailese ate the chicken salad sandwich, the apple and the drink that Ell had given her, and afterwards she felt a lot better. "Hey, boss, Andrew's on line 1."

"Thanks."

"Hello. Hey, Andy." They both laughed. "Excuse me, no, no, take that back. You know that I hate it when anyone calls me that." "I'm mad at you, so that's what you get?" "What did I do to you? I'm not even there, my love." "You left me all alone. That's what you did, you asshole." Andrew cleared his throat before he spoke. "Um, I must have the wrong number, sorry." Ailese stopped him from hanging up by giggling. "You know I love ya!" So, how's it going out there?" "It's going well. How's it going for you?" "I just got over a huge headache, but I think I'll be alright." "Are you sure? Need anything?" "Nope I'm straight," Ailese said, as she made a funny noise with her mouth. "You crack me up when you make that noise with your mouth." Andrew chuckled. Hey, I called to ask you if you needed me tonight?" "Um, no. Mikell's going to be home before me. So, I should be good." "Ailese, are you absolutely sure, my love?" "Yes, I am 100 percent sure." "Hey, call me if anything changes, okay?" "Done." "Hey, did you eat anything today? Maybe that's why you were having that headache." "Yes, Daddy, I did eat, Ailese groaned. I'm going to go now because I don't know you anymore. I love ya."

Ailese was able to see Andrew for a minute as he was picking up Ell. They talked for a few minutes, and Ailese headed home. Mikell and the kids were cooking dinner when she got home. She gave everyone kisses and hugs and headed to her room to get comfortable. She sat on the bed and looked around the room. She could tell that Mikell had already tidied up the room already. Everything was nice and neat. That was one less thing to worry about. Her cell phone was ringing, so she answered it. It was her mom reminding her that her brother Allen would be there tomorrow and they all needed to meet up at D'Andra's at 7:00 p.m. Ailese had been so occupied with other things that she actually did forget and was happy that Alonda reminded her.

As they were lying in bed, Ailese had reminded Mikell about meeting up at D'Andra's tomorrow at 7:00 p.m. "I can't wait to see my brother, I really do miss him. I'm so happy that we get to spend at least one of his birthdays together as a family." Mikell agreed with Ailese. Mikell and Allen have always got along. Allen stayed with Mikell and Ailese when they were living in Paisley. Mikell helped Allen get back on his feet and let him stay there rent- free. Mikell would give Allen money when he needed it, and he never asked for it back because he had faith in him and Mikell was right, because Allen put his all into what he has now. He is a very successful businessman.

Everything went smoothly at the gathering for her brother. Everyone showed up on time. They sang old songs and ate good food. Everyone was so amazed at how big D'Andra was getting. She was having twins! D'Andra told everyone about her weird cravings, such as salami, nacho cheese chips, and tacos with ranch dressing. They all sang Happy Birthday to Allen. His cake was shaped like a racing car because he loved cars. After eating lots of cake and ice cream and everyone's food having been digested, they played charades in teams. They watched old home movies. Everyone teased Ailese about her afro she had as a little girl. They laughed at how they dressed back in the day. Alonda brought out old pictures of Ailese, Allen, and D'Andra. Most of the pictures of Ailese were always singing, dancing, or performing. She has always been talented. Allen's wife, Mya, told everyone that this was the best birthday party ever! She wanted to do his birthday party with his family every year.

"Wow, that was so much fun! Ailese said, as she was getting into the car. My brother had a blast, and everything went perfect, just perfect." Mikell started up the car and made sure everyone was buckled up. "Yes, that was a lot of fun. I had a blast! "Yeah, I know me too. It's already one in the morning. I think we'll all be sleeping in." Ailese looked in the backseat to see that all the kids were already asleep. She took Mikell's hand and put it in her lap and kissed him on the cheek. "What was that for, huh, sexy?" "Oh, nothing, I just love you to death, that's all." Ailese looked at Mikell. "I love you so much, sexy." Ailese started to blush. I'm glad that your brother is down spending time with his family. I know that makes you happy." "It does, and I am happy."

Ailese knew that she was going to get a late start on things today, but her brother wasn't due for another couple of hours. Ailese and the kids had to go with Mikell because he still didn't feel comfortable leaving anyone alone in the house, even though the new alarm had already been installed. He wanted to play it safe.

"Ailese, are you ready, hun?" "Yeah, I'm putting on my shoes. I'll be right there."

Mikell came into the bedroom to get something that he needed. "Baby, if you need more time, just let me know." "No, I'm fine." "No, I know you, and you're irritated with me. So, what's wrong, baby?" Ailese hated to be rushed by anyone; it was a huge turnoff for her. "No, baby, I'm just tired, that's all. I'm ready … mmmm … I think I should change my shoes. Are we going to be walking a lot, Mikell?" "No, not really. The shoes you're wearing should be fine."

"Alright, let's go. I'll round up the soldiers and meet you in the car?" "Sounds like a plan." Ailese set the alarm and headed out.

"Hello, hey bro, what's up old man?" "Hey sis, I just wanted to ask you if it would be okay if we met up at J's Bistro instead of your house."

"Why?" "Well, James wanted … he wants all the family there. You know it's his restaurant, and we haven't seen each other in a while. I just wanted to be fair to everyone who wants to spend time with me while I'm down here, sis. That's all."

"Sure, I understand, and since I love James, I guess we can meet there, and if he's paying for the food, then hey, why not? Allen, give me the address."

"Thanks for understanding, sis. Okay, are you ready?" "Yep shoot."

"It's 1456 Island Place Road in Pineville. I know it's pretty far, but." Ailese interrupted Allen. "Pineville? You're lucky, it's your weekend, so I don't mind." Allen and Ailese chuckled. "I can send a limo service if you guys don't want to drive." "Really? Why not, send the limo service and we can swing by and pick up D, Mom, and Dad." "So, the limo service will be there at 6:30. Does that sound good?" Thanks, bro, love ya." Ailese filled Mikell in on what she and her brother had discussed. Mikell was happy that they didn't have to drive all the way to Pineville. Ailese called D'Andra to let her know what time to be ready and shared all the details with her.

"Dad, could we stop and get something to eat? I'm hungry." "Ashanee, in a bit, honey." "Okay, Daddy." "It'll be soon, kitten. Why don't you color in your activity book, okay?" "Okay, Mom." Mikell had to stop and pick up some things from the office. Armont went inside with his dad. Ailese noticed Sedrick coming out of the building and honked the horn to get his attention. "Hey, Mrs. Lady. Where have you been? I haven't seen you in a while." Ailese got out of the car to give him a hug. "Hi, my love. How are you doing?" "Oh, man, busy, busy, busy, but that's good though. Hey girls, how are you? The girls said hello to Sedrick.

A few minutes went by, and a limousine pulled up in front of the building to pick up Sedrick. He told the driver he would be a few more minutes. Have you given it any more thought about going on the tour with me?" "I don't know, I mean, I'm still thinking about it. I'll let you know. I promise I will give you guys an answer."

"Well, I think that you should get back out there. Ailese, you're just so talented, and I feel that everyone needs to know. I mean, they play our song all over the radio, baby!" Ailese was blushing as Sedrick started to tease her in a childish, playful way. "Well, we'll see, baby boy. I love you, and you better get going. I don't want to hold you up." "Ailese, I love ya, and please, please think about going on tour with me long and hard. "I will, I will. Bye." Ailese watched the limo drive away.

"Mom, what's taking Dad and Armont so long to come back? I'm really hungry." Ashanee whined. "Honey, I don't know, but you need to be patient, baby." "Ashanee, do you want to play a game?" "Sis, what game are we going to play?" Ailese smiled at Adrieana, she appreciated her keeping her little sister occupied. Mikell and Armont had finally come back to the car, and Mikell apologized for taking so long. When they got to the supermarket to do some shopping, Ailese was already exhausted and was hoping that she could rest some before leaving to meet her brother later. She looked at her watch, and it was only eleven in the morning, so she should have time to rest up before dinner.

"Baby, why don't I go and get some of this stuff on the list while you get the deli order?" "Thanks, babe, that will be a big help. I'll come and find you when I'm done. You can leave the kids with me so you can concentrate." Mikell kissed her as she grabbed the shopping cart. She was in the cereal aisle, getting cereal, oatmeal, and breakfast shakes that the kids liked. As she was putting some things in her cart, a woman approached her. "Hi, you probably don't remember me but I'm Mrs. Lewis, Dr. Lewis's wife." "Hi, you probably don't remember me, but I'm Mrs. Lewis. Dr. Lewis's wife." "Yes, I thought that you looked familiar. How are you, Mrs. Lewis?" I'm hanging in there. It's been a bit rough since Thomas is gone. I miss him so much. The reason why I remember you is because I will never forget the beautiful flowers that you sent, talking with you at the funeral, and the goodness in you." "Thank you, Mrs. Lewis. Dr. Lewis was a good person. We had gotten close before he died, and I will never forget him, never. He will be greatly missed, Mrs. Lewis. How are the children doing?" "Oh, they have their days, but we're sticking together and trying to be strong. I don't know if you know this, but they're naming the new facility that's being built after my husband." Mrs. Lewis' eyes began to tear up.

"Oh, that's great, Mrs. Lewis. Ailese took her hand and massaged her back. She wanted to give her a hug but wasn't sure how she'd react. Ailese took a chance and gave her a hug. Ailese could tell that was what she needed- a hug and someone to talk to. Please, take my number, and if you need anything at all, please feel free to call me. We can go have coffee or lunch sometimes."

"Thank you so much. You know you've made my day. I don't have very many friends. Several of my friends are the wives of doctors at the hospital, but they are so self-absorbed that I can't really talk to them. Thank you so much."

Ailese felt good that she was there for Mrs. Lewis and had hoped that she would call her sometime.

Ailese needed to rest for a while until it was time to get ready to spend the evening with her brother. She tossed and turned for a bit but had finally fallen asleep. She started to have some weird dreams about Dr. Lewis. She tried to get to him before he was killed, but someone who was very strong would block her from getting to Dr. Lewis. Dr. Lewis would frantically call out her name over and over again. When Ailese finally woke up, she shrugged her shoulders and called for Mikell, and when he came into the bedroom, she told him about her weird dreams and how they frightened her. He told her that she might have had those dreams about Dr. Lewis because she had spoken to his wife earlier. Before she went to sleep, she had him on her mind, which made sense to Ailese, because Dr. Lewis was on her mind. She desperately wanted to know who killed him, but there was still, no answers. It was a robbery, and the person who robbed their home, killed him. Ailese jumped in the shower to clear her mind, but she was still thinking about her dreams.

When the limousine arrived, everyone was ready to go, even Ailese. "You look so pretty, Mom." Armont said to his mother. "Thank you. Everyone looks very nice.

I don't want anyone ruining their appetite for dinner, so don't drink too much of that cider, okay?" "Baby, are you okay?" "Yeah, I'm okay." Ailese whispered to Mikell.

"You don't seem that excited about dinner anymore. Is it the dreams? Are they still bugging you?" "A little bit, but I'll be fine, Mikell, really I am."

When they arrived at the bistro, D'Andra could hear her brother's voice before they made it to the table. "Look at our brother. I think he's started the party without us, huh?" When everyone else arrived at the bistro, James let his staff take over and joined everyone at the table. "Hey, anything you guys want, it's on the house." "Alright, like he said, on the house, so don't be shy, guys, Allen said as he sipped his drink. Hey, we have a lot to celebrate tonight.

I'm going to be an uncle not once, but twice. Hey Chris, I commend you man, I really do. Let's toast to that." Chris and Allen raised their glasses and made a toast. Allen kept feeling D'Andra's belly and saying that he wanted her to name the baby after Chris if a boy, and Stephanie if a girl, but D'Andra said she didn't want a junior, and Chris agreed.

They ate lots of good food, drank a lot of good drinks, and toasted to everything. Everyone enjoyed themselves. "Allen, we need to do this more often and not just on your birthday. I miss you and I wish you would call and visit more." Allen hugged Ailese and told her that he would be visiting more often, and had promised to work on calling more.

Ailese's phone kept ringing throughout the night, but she didn't answer it because she was with her family, and whatever it was, had to wait. When she went to the restroom, she checked her messages, and all of the messages were from Andrew, who was in the hospital. He had been in an accident and needed her. Ailese felt really bad about not being there when he needed her because he had always been there for her. She didn't want to leave the party, but she was sure that everyone would understand.

When she got back to her seat, she whispered to Mikell that she needed to talk to him right away, so they went outside to talk. "What's wrong?" "It's Andrew he called, and he's been in an accident, and I need to get to him, do you mind if I leave the party to go and check on him?" Mikell understood that he really did and was okay with that, but tonight was different; tonight, was all about family, not Andrew. He really didn't want his wife to leave, but this was her best friend, and he understood Andrew and his wife's relationship. "Ailese, I understand how close you two are, and I do respect that, but this is a special night. I mean, your brother is in town. Can't this wait until morning?" "No! Ailese shouted. Andrew needs me. Could you please tell everyone that an emergency has come up, and I had to leave, please?" "No, I won't do it. I can't believe this; are you choosing Andrew over us, your family? I knew that this would happen eventually. Are you in love with him or something? Answer me! Mikell looked at Ailese, waiting for an answer. He stood close to her. "Please, Mikell, are you serious? This is crazy. Ailese put her hands on her hips and shook her head. No, and FYI, I only love you, and you know that," Ailese whispered. She didn't want to cause a scene. "You ... Mikell paused, you tell them yourself, and, FYI, Andrew is a grown man. He can take care of himself. Although you were open about how close you guys got, I never said anything. I'm putting my foot down now. I don't want you to go, Ailese, stay here with us." Mikell looked at Ailese and went back into the bistro. She followed behind him. "Hey everybody. Ailese picked up her fork and tapped her glass to get everyone's attention. I hate to do this to you, Allen, guys, but I have an emergency and I have to leave. I'm sorry." Ailese could feel Mikell looking at her. "Hey sis, do what you have to do. I understand." Allen hugged her and told her that he would call her, and that he would be in town for a few more days, anyway. Everyone in her family understood that she needed to attend to whatever the emergency was, but they probably wouldn't have understood if they knew what the emergency was, or maybe they would. She had the limousine service take her straight to the hospital, where Andrew was. What had seemed like hours getting to Andrew had only taken fifteen minutes. On the way there, she couldn't stop thinking about what her husband said, but right now, at this point, she couldn't fix it. She knew that there would be a discussion about it when she got home.

She told the driver that he could go back to the bistro and that she would take a cab home. Ailese looked at her watch and hoped that visiting hours weren't over yet.

"Andrew McGee II, please tell me where his room is." The nurse told Ailese the room number, and as she ran down to the hallway, she could hear something about visiting hours being almost over, but she didn't pay attention to what the nurse had said. The elevator took forever to open, and as soon as it opened, Ailese stepped in and hit number two. As soon as she was on Andrew's floor, she started walking vigorously until she got to Andrew's room. A doctor was coming out as she was coming into the room. "Excuse me doctor, I'm Andrew's close, close, friend. Can you please tell me if he's going to be okay?" "Are you Mrs. LaShae?"

"Yes, yes, I am." Ailese felt a bit relieved that Andrew knew that she would come eventually. That was why the doctor knew who she was. Andrew gave the hospital permission to speak to her about his condition. "He's a bit banged up, but he will recover in a couple of weeks, and he's going to need some help getting around. He's pretty damn lucky. He may have to have a bit of physical therapy, as well. He has been asking for you." "Thank you, Doctor."

Ailese smiled when she saw Andrew sound asleep in the hospital bed. His face had a few cuts, and bruises, and his arm was in a sling.

"Hey, Ailese whispered. Andrew, it's me. I'm here. I'm right here."

Ailese had fallen asleep in the recliner, that was in Andrew's room.

When Andrew opened his eyes to see Ailese sleeping in the recliner, he too was relieved that she was there and waited patiently for her to wake up.

When Ailese did wake up and was focused, she went to Andrew's bed to hug him. "Hi, how are you feeling? What happened?" "I'm fine. A car rear-ended me. Can you believe that?" Andrew groaned as he tried to sit up. "Honey, try not to move, okay?" Andrew looked at Ailese and squinted his eyes because he was in a lot of pain. Ailese fixed his pillows to make him more comfortable.

What are we going to do with you, huh?" Ailese said, smiling. Andrew just winked at Ailese. A nurse had come into the room to check on Andrew. She checked his blood pressure, gave him his medication, and left the room.

Andrew's pain is at level three now. Earlier it was at level ten. Despite having broken his arm, he was in a lot of pain in his back and neck from the car that hit him. Andrew didn't care about the car. He only cared that he was still breathing and alive. The car was only materialistic. The accident did shake him up a bit. There he was sitting at a red light and this car plunged into him out of nowhere, and this bastard that hit him was drunk and talking on his cell phone, not paying any attention. The man who hit him was so out of it, he didn't even know what was going on until the police took him to jail.

"Did they tell you how long they were going to keep you?" "Um, a few days or so. I hate hospitals, I don't like to tell people that, but I don't. Andrew shook his head and frowned. I want to go home now and get in my own bed and eat my own food." "I know, I know, but you have to stick this one out, buddy, and listen to the doctor." "Why aren't you answering your cell? That's the millionth time, what's going on?" Ailese walked over to the window and said nothing for a few seconds. Ailese didn't want to tell Andrew that she and Mikell had a disagreement about her leaving her family and the party just to see him.

Mikell had called and texted her several times, but she didn't want to talk to Mikell right now. She wanted to talk to him face-to-face. Andrew asked Ailese the same question over and over again, and she stalled again. Ailese let out a deep breath and walked back to Andrew's bed, regretting what was about to come out of her mouth. "Mikell and I had a stupid argument. I'm fine. I am more concerned about you. So, could we please talk about something else?

Andrew gave Ailese the look that he gives her when he knows that she's lying. My brother is in town, and when I finally got your message, we were still at dinner. We were having dinner and a birthday party at his friend's restaurant all the way in Pineville. You needed me, so I told my family that I had an emergency and had to leave early. They all understood except Mikell. He didn't want me to leave. Don't worry about it, okay?" "No, I am going to worry about it, Ailese. Andrew said, in a low calm voice. I don't want to be the reason why you guys had a disagreement." "I'm going to stop you right there; Mikell knows how close you and I are, and yes, you're a grown man like he said, and you can take care of yourself. Ailese rolled her eyes. But you needed me, and I didn't want to let you down. Besides, Mikell's looking at it as though I neglected my family, and that's not it at all.

I didn't choose you over him or my family. My family means everything to me. That's the truth. You needed me, and when a friend is in need, you need to be there for them." Ailese sat down in the recliner and crossed her legs, waiting for Andrew to agree with her.

"Ailese, my love, I appreciate you being here for me, I really do. I don't want to be the reason you and Mikell are having disagreements. I think that you should go home and talk this over with Mikell, Ailese." "Is that medication making you all crazy and stupid?" Andrew was shocked by what Ailese had just said to him. "No, my love." Normally, anyone wouldn't react this way, when they're calling you crazy, but Andrew loved Ailese no matter what came out of her mouth. I just think." Ailese cut Andrew off. "Don't worry about it, and this is the main reason why I didn't want to tell you. I knew that this conversation that we're having, was going to happen.

My marriage is not in trouble, and that's for real. I am still my own person, Andrew."

She walked down a few streets after leaving the hospital to see the new building named after Dr. Lewis that was being built.

The special project was well thought out, which delighted Ailese. "Nice, nice. Dr. Lewis deserves this, Ailese said to herself. I miss him, and he was a good man." She watched the men hammering, pounding, cutting, and shouting orders as they worked. As she walked back to flag a taxi down, she started thinking about Mikell and how she was going to stand her ground and tell him that he took the disagreement all out of proportion and that she only meant well. One thing that Ailese had learned over the years is that you never should let a man run you in your relationship. You should always be your own person and use your own mind. Ailese felt like Mikell had mixed feelings about her and Andrew's friendship, and that didn't sit well with Ailese at all. She needed to clear things up with Mikell, right away. She did know this: she didn't want to lose Andrew as a friend, and yes, Mikell means the world to her, but so does Andrew. For some strange reason, Ailese felt a bit guilty having these strong feelings for him.

When she was home, Mikell was in the bedroom on a call, and the kids were nowhere to be found. "Hey, I'm home. Where are the kids?" "Oh, I let them go to the movies with your mom, dad, Allen, and D. They should be back soon. Your mom said that she would call if they stayed out later." Ailese could tell that Mikell had just shaved and could smell his aftershave. "Oh, I see. We need to talk, Mikell," Ailese said as she took off her shoes and placed them neatly in the closet. "Yes, we do Ailese. We do." Ailese figured she would go first so she wouldn't leave anything out that she was feeling. "I know that you felt like I put Andrew first, but that wasn't and isn't the case, Mikell. I would never put him first, and you of all people should know that. Ailese stayed focused on Mikell's face. I cherish our friendship, and once again, like I mentioned the other night, I discussed having him as a friend before I sealed the deal, and I didn't know that you would have a problem with me running to his aid when he needed me. I mean, damn, he was in a car accident. Hell, I would have needed someone too. My point is I felt like you were taking this way out of proportion, Mikell. I feel like you don't trust me and regret agreeing to let me have this friendship. Ailese paused. Are you feeling that way?" Mikell got up from where he was sitting and walked over to the other side of the room.

"Lee, I don't have a reason why I shouldn't trust you. The bottom line is that I felt that you should have waited until the dinner party was over. It wouldn't have hurt you to realize that, Lee. I mean, I can't believe you, I really can't!

All I'm saying is that your brother was in town, and you know that he doesn't get down here as often as we'd all like him to, so I thought that you would want to spend time with him instead of running off to Andrew. I am sure that Andrew would have understood if you couldn't be there at the snap of his fingers.

Ailese folded her arms and kept telling herself not to get upset, and to stay calm. I don't have a problem with Andrew, and I don't have a problem with any males that are in your life, Ailese, because I am not self-conscious, not one bit.

I don't want you to think that Andrew is an issue, because he's not and never will be. Mikell walked over to Ailese and took her hand. Ailese stood up and faced Mikell, who took her hand in his and kissed it, then smiled at her.

I love you, and I just want to make you see and understand my side; he said softly. Come here." He pulled her hips to him. He wanted to kiss her, but Ailese pulled back. "Stop, don't touch me, just don't, kissing me and trying to get me in the mood ain't gonna work, Mikell!" Ailese shouted. Mikell was surprised to see his wife acting like a child. I am not going to let this go, not yet. You're sitting here saying that my family isn't important to me! You better think again because that isn't true! Yes, my brother was here, and I have been spending time with him ever since he got here, letting him do what he wants, and letting him plan things. Pineville was far, and I was very tired, but who still showed up his sister. So, act like you know, Mikell. Ailese started to bring out the "ghetto girl."

Twitching her head and neck. Wow, you're a trip. Mikell." Ailese shook her head.

You know me better than anyone Mikell, anyone! Humph. I would never imagine us having a conversation like this one! I care about Andrew a lot, yes, this is true, and I'll say it again. I love my family, and I would die for my family, you know this, Mikell. I'm sorry that you don't understand why I had to go to Andrew. I'm sorry." Mikell took her hand as she started to walk away, but this time she didn't let go.

"Baby, you've misunderstood. I know you, and I know what family means to you, Lee. I think we both weren't thinking straight. I'm sorry, baby." "I'm sorry too, Mikell."

Since Andrew was out of the hospital and resting at home, Ailese had to pick up the slack at the office for a few more days. Andrew was determined to still take Ailese on the trip he had planned for weeks, despite the vacation plans being put on hold. Ailese told him that if he wasn't 100 percent better, they had to put the trip off a while longer. He told her he was strong and would bounce back quickly; he did bounce back, but had a minor setback when he had three attacks from his sickness, which was fortunately treated by someone. Ailese visited him a couple of times. One of those outbreaks happened when she was visiting him. Andrew and Ailese would watch old movies together in bed and Ailese would cook for them sometimes. Ailese didn't mind taking up all the slack at work when Andrew stayed out longer than expected. He had some setbacks trying to recover from the accident, and he had a few more outbreaks, which worried Ailese. She prayed that Andrew would pull through.

Ailese was still trying to come to a decision about whether or not she and the family were going on the summer tour with Sedrick Johnson. Ailese would have to miss a lot of work, and she didn't feel that comfortable having everyone pick up her slack and their work as well. There would be a lot of conference calls, and all of this would have to fit into her schedule. What to do? What to do? Ailese would take a few breaks here and there to make sure all her work was done, and all her clients were satisfied, but going on this tour was a tremendous responsibility that she wasn't sure she was ready to take. She loved being in the scene and singing again, but just as she told the magazine, she was happy singing here and there even if it was in the background or even writing.

SHELBY LIES

She was fine with not having all these crazy demands and contracts. From the sales of Eshe Magazine and Lea, a lot of people loved the article on Sedrick and Ailese. They even blogged about it. Some people said that Ailese and Sedrick were like fire: hot, hot, hot. One of the blogs said they would pay top dollar to see Ailese and Sedrick in concert. Maybe she should go? Maybe this was her chance to get back out there, but she loved her life as it was now too.

Tonight, Karen's friends were going to meet her fiancé. They were all going for drinks and dinner. Ailese wore a black-and-white rayon pants suit with a white lace tank top underneath and two-inch heels. Her hair was up in a long, curly ponytail, decorated with rhinestone barrettes. When Ailese was done with her makeup, she looked at the time, and it was still early, and she didn't want to be the first one there. She decided to listen to some music instead of watching television. She put Mariah Carey into the CD player and sang along with it, looking in the mirror as she pretended to be on stage. She pictured herself in a sparkling long burgundy dress that had one split on the side. Her hair up in a bun, with a few curls in it. Everyone looking at her, yelling her name, cheering her on. She's singing a beautiful slow song, that she wrote from her heart and she's singing it with all her heart and soul. She could see her audience watching her as she sang each lyric like an angel. Ailese listened to a few more songs and headed to the engagement party.

An hour later, Ailese arrived at the engagement party. As she walked in, she spotted Karen wearing a tiara that read, "I'm Getting Married" in sparkling pink letters. She was entertaining the other guests. "Hey, Ailese, I'm so glad that you made it. My fiancé will be here in a minute, in the meantime, order whatever you want, okay?" Ailese shook her head. She greeted everyone that was sitting at the table. Karen introduced Ailese to the other guests. Karen told everyone that she would be right back. The music was a bit loud, but Ailese was used to it. The woman that was sitting next to her made casual conversation, sipped her drink, and kept her eyes peeled toward the front entrance of the club. After a few minutes, Karen showed up with someone who looked very familiar to Ailese.

It was someone that she really didn't seem to ever get along with for some reason. His name was Eric Wallace. They used to work together a long time ago. He and Ailese would butt heads a lot. Some co-workers told Ailese that Eric had a huge crush on her and just didn't know how to tell her, but Ailese would never believe all the rumors about Eric. Eric stood about five feet seven. His skin was caramel, and his eyes were hazel brown. He was a good-looking fellow, and he knew it. He was a bit conceited at times. Eric and Ailese's eyes met at the same time, and Ailese felt a bit awkward. "Why me, Lord? Why do I always find myself in odd situations, huh?" When Karen made her way over to Ailese to meet her fiancé, she had already decided to play dumb and act as if she didn't know him. Yes, that's exactly what she did too. "Hello, nice to meet you, Eric. I've heard that my friend here is in love with you, huh?" Ailese smiled. "Yes, she is, and I'm going to make her the happiest woman on earth," Eric said, smiling back at Ailese. Eric looked the same; nothing had changed about him other than not having a beard anymore. Now he had a nicely trimmed goatee, and his hair was cut military style. When Ailese excused herself to go to the restroom, she bumped into Eric on the way back to the party. "Hello, old friend. I must say, you're looking good. How have you been?" Ailese really didn't want to start a conversation with him, but she didn't want to be snobby either. "I am great, and you?" "I am great as well. You still look the same, in a good way that is, you really do." "Thanks. You're not bad yourself. So, how do you like the military?" "I love it. I've been in for eight years now and counting. If I had never was stationed here, I would not have met my Karen. I love her so much, you know. Ailese nodded her head. Eric stood closer to Ailese, making her uncomfortable; she stood there and didn't move or make a sound. You know what? I've always wondered what happened to you. Remember all those rumors? Well, they were all true, but I did regret not telling you my feelings back then, and we all have something that we regret." Before Ailese could say anything, Eric had already walked away. Ailese shook off what had just happened and headed back to the party.

Today, Andrew was scheduled to come back to work, and Ailese was looking forward to his return. Ailese was very happy when she saw Andrew leaning on her office door with her favorite coffee waiting for her. Ailese wanted to give him the biggest hug, but he had the hot coffee in his hand.

"Look at you, looking all handsome," Ailese said, as Andrew handed her the coffee. "Thanks, my love. I try. I guess somebody didn't miss me, or she would have given me a hug by now, huh?" Ailese didn't wait another minute. She gave him the biggest hug ever! "I needed that, my love. Thanks! Ailese laughed. "So, I was wondering if we could have some lunch later and go over some things. Would that be okay, or do you have plans?"

"Nope, I don't, but I do think that we should go over some important things right now." "Okay, sure." Andrew took a sip of his coffee and sat in the chair that was in front of Ailese. "I wanted to let you know that we had to change some things with the Brewer and Phillips contract. It was just too much when it came down to the renovations. I mean, the cost alone for the renovations was out of this world." Ailese pointed out to Andrew. "Oh, I see we could get them a brand spanking new building for this amount, and I see that you've already been working on that. That's great, my love, Andrew said as he looked up from the file. I totally agree, and I don't know why the guy lied to us. I mean, we would have found out eventually." "Yes, and I made sure he knew that we would never do business with him even if he was the last person on earth." "That-a girl! Yeah, you get 'em Ailese." "It's good to have you back, Andrew."

"Boss, I have a FedEx package for you. Did you want me to bring it into your office?" "Sure, Ell, that would be great." "Here you go, boss. It looks important. Is everything good with you?" "Yes, Ell, there's nothing to worry about. I'm sure there are some documents to look over." Ailese looked at the sender's address. It didn't have a name on it. She wondered who it was from. She opened the FedEx package, and inside there were airplane tickets, two envelopes, and some brochures. "Mmmm, I wonder what this is." She opened one of the envelopes first. It was a letter from Andrew. It read: Hey, my love. Here's what you're going to need for our vacation that I've planned for us. You will find another envelope that will have instructions for you to follow. Now, these instructions have to be followed just as they are in the letter, okay? I know, I know, I shouldn't tell you what to do, and I know that you hate it! Oh, well, tough! One more thing before I go. You have to bring the airplane ticket. This is very important! Love ya, Drew. (smile).

"Oh, wow," Ailese said as she looked at the brochures. These places were so beautiful. She had forgotten how beautiful they were. As she opened the other envelope, she read it and began laughing to herself. The instructions were a bit funny. One of the instructions told her what she had to do once they arrived at their destination: If people ask you if we're married, tell them yes and stick to that story. Another one said she had to have fun the whole time, and the first person that talked about work had to buy all the meals. Ailese loved this a lot. It was different. It was how Andrew was: goofy, laid-back, and creative. That's what she loved about him.

Ailese got a call from D'Andra who was working at the office today, since D'Andra had gone back to work they hadn't been spending as much time together. D'Andra was also busy with other things as well, like working on her marriage, which was up to par, and D'Andra and Chris even got themselves into marriage counseling. With so much progress made, they both owed it to their counseling. Ailese understood that things would change, because a lot has changed in everyone's lives, not just her sister's. Ailese was happy that D'Andra and Chris were doing great, and she really didn't want to see two good people who were made for each other put so much into their relationship, and then it goes downhill. Chris just made bad decisions and thought that since he and D'Andra had been together for so long, it was time to leave the relationship because he started to get curious about other women. That doesn't make him a bad person. It makes him human, but what he did when he finally woke up and realized what he had done was wrong is what matters. He admitted it and took the punches, meaning he did whatever it took to prove to D'Andra, his wife, that he had learned his lesson and that's what he did. "Hi, sis, how's your day going?" "Good, busy as always, but I'm not complaining. How's yours?" "Oh, great. The twins have been kicking me all day, and other than going to the bathroom every like, five minutes. I'm good." D'Andra laughed. "Aw, well, that's normal. How are you feeling, good?" "Yeah. I am feeling good. I have another appointment next week. When I went to my appointment a week ago or so, the doctor said that the babies and I were doing fine. I'm so excited, Ailese! I am!" "I am too. I can't wait until those little blessings are born. Ailese and D'Andra laughed. How's Chris?" "Excellent. I just feel for him right now, he's such a good sport. I have to have this special pillow for me, and it takes up a lot of room, but Chris doesn't mind. I know that he's not sleeping all that well because he is so used to holding me at night, and I just don't want to be bothered because I'm always hot, you know. I mean, I have to have air on me at all times. My hormones are all jacked up, Lee." "I was the same way, remember? So, don't worry about it, and I'm sure Chris will put up with whatever he has to put up with, no matter what."

"Yeah, and I do remember your hormones being all over the place, sis. Oh, well, it's called being pregnant." "Yes, sweetie, you're right. I know what you're going through, sis, and those beautiful babies are going to have so much love around them and a great mother and father." "Don't get me started, D'Andra said, as she started to tear up.

Despite being gone for hours, Andrew and Ailese accomplished a lot. They talked about a lot of things and caught up on a lot of things that were going on in their lives. They talked about Ell and how she and Andrew were getting serious, but he needed her to be there for him emotionally as well, not only physically, and mentally. Andrew told Ailese that Ell wasn't really there for him during his accident because she couldn't stand seeing him in so much pain. Ailese didn't like the sound of that at all. She told Andrew to give Ell some time, and if she didn't deliver, then he should think long and hard about their relationship, because you need someone to be there for you emotionally too. Andrew agreed with her. Ailese wasn't trying to butt in their relationship, but she wanted Andrew to be happy. They talked about the FedEx package that Andrew sent, and they laughed until their bellies hurt.

Ailese had gotten a surprise from Mikell. He had sent her some purple flowers, and the note read: I love you so much. I just wanted to let you know. Love, Mik. Ailese placed the beautiful vase on the table in her office. She picked up the phone and called Mikell to thank him for the flowers. "You're welcome. I meant what I said, baby. I do love you so much." "I love you too, Mikell. Hey, what if we plan something before I go on vacation, just the two of us, okay?"

"I would love that baby. I will see you later?" "Yep. Mikell?" "Yes, Lee." "I love you." Those flowers brightened up Ailese's day even more. She was so lucky to have Mikell. He was very hard to come by.

When Ailese drove home from her session with Dr. Salvino, she had decided to surprise Mikell. Since he had gotten her those beautiful flowers, she wanted to give him a surprise as well. She had to, and she wasn't expecting the flowers at all. Ailese stopped at the luggage store and picked up a new laptop case for Mikell, since he had misplaced his and couldn't find it anywhere, and Ailese knew that he hadn't been a happy camper about losing it. After she paid for the item, she then stopped at Ten Jayes and placed a to-go order, making sure that she ordered Mikell's favorites. Ailese and Mikell had their dinner in the dining room so they could have some alone time, while the kids ate at the kitchen table. "Thanks, baby, this is so good. I am so hungry." After Mikell finished his dinner, Ailese brought his gift into the dining room. When Mikell opened it, his eyes were like those of a kid in a candy store. "Wow, baby, baby. Thanks, this is so nice. Thanks, baby, and I promise not to lose it." Mikell kissed her gently on the lips. After Ailese and Mikell spent time with the kids, Mikell got a call from the studio from Emmanuel. There was an urgent meeting that Mikell had to attend. "I'm sorry, baby, I don't know when this meeting will be over, but I'll call you. Hopefully I won't have to take a rain check on that hot tub." "It's fine if you have to take a rain check, baby. I understand. I love you." Ailese gave Mikell a kiss and walked him out to his car. Ailese found herself bored and needed something to do. She watched some television but had gotten bored with that, so she decided to listen to some music and eventually fell asleep. Ailese fell into a deep sleep, and she couldn't wake up from her dream. Rico was angry with her as always, and this time his anger was on high. Ailese was trying to explain to him what had happened earlier that day. Ailese had forgotten to call him to wake him up for work. She didn't do this on purpose because she had a lot of distractions and just couldn't call him. "Now I'm late for work, you selfish bitch. Why can't you do one thing right, huh? Rico was furious! Now I'm late. All I'm trying to do is provide for us, so you don't have to go without. You stupid bitch." Even though Ailese could take care of herself on her salary alone, Rico never bought her much except for when it was her birthday, other than that, he was one stingy son of a bitch! "I am sorry Rico. I had so much to do today, and it had to get done. Why don't you just use the alarm clock?" Just as Ailese said this, she found herself on the floor. Rico had hit her and pushed her down onto the floor so fast, that she didn't even know what had hit her. Ailese got up slowly from the floor and pushed Rico back. That was a huge mistake. Rico took off his belt and whipped her like she was his stepchild. Please stop! "Shut up! Before someone hears you. Get out of my face, you disgust me." Rico pushed Ailese's head like she was a dog and left for work. When he came home, he woke her up by beating her some more. Rico didn't care how much Ailese would supplicate, cry, and beg for him to stop hurting her. Just as long as he got his point across and made sure she stayed afraid of him, was all he cared about. Ailese took the beatings and kept them a secret for a very long time. She kept them deep inside, but she still kept the promise that she made to herself: never again would a man disrespect her like Rico did. Ever again, never! She remained strong and has stuck with that promise.

When Ailese had woken up, she was shaking a bit but calmed herself down and went back to sleep. In the past, she couldn't go back to sleep because she thought that Rico would still come back and hurt her, but not anymore. The therapy has helped her a lot. She can somewhat control her emotions when it comes to the horrible nightmares. "Baby, I'm home." Mikell whispered to Ailese. "Hi, are you hungry or anything?" "No, go back to sleep, okay?" Ailese turned to Mikell and looked at him. "Baby, I missed you while you were gone." Mikell smiled and hugged her, and they held each other as they slept.

Ailese fixed breakfast, took the kids to school, and let Mikell sleep, even though it was his day to take the kids to school. Ailese went back to the house to check on Mikell. He was still sleeping. Ailese brought him breakfast in bed, because she didn't want him to miss it. "Hey you, I brought you food." "Hey, did I ever tell you that you are the best wife in the entire world?" "Aww, baby, I don't think so, not lately," Ailese smiled. "I love you, he said in a sleepy voice, as sat up to eat his breakfast. Lee, you didn't have to do all of this. I would have fixed something, but I do appreciate it." "I wanted to, because I love you." "You want a bite of my toast? Here, Mikell fed it to her and kissed the jelly that was on the crease of her mouth. What time are you going in today?" "Um, that depends on what time my hubby's going in," Ailese said, in a very sexy voice. "Whenever I feel like it, let's just spend the day together for a few hours. How does that sound?" "Sounds good, Ailese said, taking another bite of the toast that Mikell had fed her. An hour later, they found themselves at the coffee shop. They talked and joked around for a while, taking their own sweet time drinking their coffee.

"Hey, that was D. She wants us to come by for dinner tonight. Is that okay?"

"Yeah, of course, what time?" "Oh, six thirty. Can you get out of work?" "Sure, I can. Why don't I just take you to work and pick you up from work, and we can go straight to D's. Is that okay?" "Okay, yeah, that's fine. I'll tell her that it's a go." After they left the café, they decided to take a short walk in the park and feed the birds. It was such a beautiful day that they were both tempted not to go to work, but they had so much to do.

"Maybe we could play hooky one day soon, huh?" "Yes, and we will. I promise you that, baby."

"Hey, Ailese, are you ready? We need to get this show on the road." "I'm right behind ya, Andrew." Mr. Saxx had wanted Andrew and Ailese to meet with some investors just to see what and why they were interested in Lindell & Co.

"Hello, Mr. Kane, and hello Mr. Middleton. How are you fine gentlemen doing today? I must say, those suits complement you very well." Mr. Kane and Mr. Middleton both thanked Ailese at the same time. Mr. Kane flirted with Ailese the whole time, telling her how he liked how she carried herself differently from most women. He was a short, stalky older guy that walked with a cane but was a very attractive, dark- skinned man. Mr. Middleton was a very overweight man, was perspiring heavily, and spoke with a very soft voice. The meeting lasted about two hours, longer than they had anticipated. The two men were very interested in Lindell & Co. and wanted to do big things with and for the company, but as Ailese and Andrew had explained to the men, the final decision was Mr. Saxx's. "We'll get back to you soon. Thank you for coming." Andrew escorted them out and sustained the conversation as they entered the elevator.

Andrew didn't come back to Ailese's office like he said he would, they needed to finish their work. Ailese went to his office, and once again, he looked like he was upset about something. Ailese waited until she knew that he was done with his call. A few minutes later, Andrew was knocking on her door. "Hey, sorry, I had to make a few calls." Should Ailese ask him what that call was all about? "Hey, are you okay?" "Yes, why do you ask? Nothing, okay, let's. Andrew interrupted Ailese. Ailese, you asked me that question for a reason. Now spit it out, my love." "I saw you talking on the phone, and you looked upset. What's wrong? Is that friend still bugging you for money?" "No, not at all. I was talking to one of my employees. I mean, he keeps forgetting what his job is and showing up late, and then he gets mad at me when his paycheck is short, accusing me of trying to withhold his money. I hate getting upset, but sometimes I have to." "I just worry about ya. I don't want you to end up with high blood pressure." Andrew shook his head. "I may regret this one day for saying this, but sometimes I wish I was poor and maybe I wouldn't have so much drama to deal with." "Hey, hey, don't talk like that, Andrew, because there was a time in my life when I was poor, and I am not lying. I didn't like it, not one bit. Maybe you need to revamp your staff and be a bit more … harsh with your employees maybe?" "Yeah, I agree. I do need to be harsher. I just don't have the heart to fire people these days because I know there's less and less work out there every day." "Yes, that's true, but you want them to respect you as well." "Yes, you're right."

Ailese had gotten a text from Sedrick asking her if she had made a decision about the summer tour. She replied to him that she was still contemplating it and that he should give her some more time. Sedrick wanted her on this tour so badly that he could taste it. Ailese didn't want to think about the summer tour. She was more focused on other things, like being a new aunt soon. She was tired of everyone pushing her to go on that tour. Andrew had even suggested that she go on the tour as well. He said it would be a great experience for her, and she should get back into the music scene. She could show all these amateurs what singing really is, because she can blow. Ailese could sing a mixture of jazz, contemporary, and r&b, because that is what she listened to growing up.

One of her girlfriends from high school even got her into a little bit of country music as well. She even went to a concert or two.

"That dinner was delicious sis. I will talk to you in the morning, okay?" "It's a deal. Love you guys. Bye." "Hey babe, I need you to relax, and I'll clean up the kitchen." D'Andra let out a long sigh, sat down, put her feet up on the couch, retrieved the remote, and watched television. As the announcer on the news announced that there was a hospital that was named after Dr. Thomas Lewis, everyone was invited to the opening of the new hospital. It was in honor of Dr. Lewis for being a great doctor. The hospital was named after him: The Thomas Lewis Rehabilitation Center.

"Hey, babe, look here and come here." Chris sat next to D'Andra with a towel in his hand. "What is it, baby?" "Remember the doctor that was killed? Dr. Lewis?" "Oh, yeah, that was tragic. What about him?" "Well, they're having a hospital named after him, which is good. I know how hard Ailese took it when she found out that he was killed." They continued looking at the news, and then the reporter did an interview with the wife of Dr. Lewis. She looked really sad. "I just want to find my husband's killer. That's all, so justice can be served. I miss him every day. He was my best friend. The reporter asked her if there were any new leads. She shook her head no and looked into the camera and said: Please, if you have any information about the murder of Dr. Thomas Lewis, please call the sheriff's department. We've raised the reward to one million dollars for any new information about my husband's killer. No one, and I do mean no one, should have to go through this. I am honored and pleased that this hospital is named after a great man and a great doctor." "That's just so sad. You know, Ailese said that she ran into her in the grocery store, and they exchanged numbers, so they do know each other. I wonder how she's getting through all this. I hope she has a good support team. I think I'm going to interview her and do an article about unsolved mysteries or something. I don't understand how someone could just decide to take someone's life! D'Andra said, shaking her head, and Chris agreed with her as he went back into the kitchen.

"Baby, are you thirsty or anything? Did you need anything before I leave this kitchen?" "Um, no, I'm good, Chris." "Are you sure? Because you know how you are, as soon as I sit down, you change your mind." Chris yelled to D'Andra. "Yes, baby, come and sit down." D'Andra yelled back.

Chris had a diet soda in one hand and a bottle of water in the other, and he sat them both on the table. D'Andra looked at him and smiled. Chris smiled back at her. A few hours later, Alonda and Don had arrived from their church meetings. "Hi, Mom and Dad." Alonda went straight to D'Andra's belly to say hello to the babies. She wanted her grandchildren to get used to her voice. "Hi, babies it's Grammie. I'm home. I can't wait until you come into the world." "I put your guy's dinners in the oven if you're hungry."

"Thanks, D. Because your daddy is very hungry. Don went into the kitchen and Alonda followed him. You did good, D. Alonda yelled to D'Andra. This cashew chicken is really good." "Thanks, Mom."

Chris helped D'Andra up to bed and made sure she was comfortable and had everything she needed. Every night before Chris went to bed, he read to the babies, and sometimes, if he were lucky, he would feel the babies' kick.

They must've changed the nursery a dozen times, more D'Andra than Chris.

They were ready for anything that came their way. They had clothes, diapers, car seats, baby carriages, and changing tables. They also spent a pretty penny because their babies deserved the best. D'Andra was getting bigger month by month, and she just loved to feel her babies kick, it was the highlight of her day. She was ready to be the best mom that she could ever be. The babies were mostly active in the morning, right when D'Andra would finish her breakfast, and sometimes at night before she went to sleep. She would always tell her babies that she loved them and that they were going to have a lot of love around them.

"Hey, Allen, are you still meeting me for lunch today? I do apologize for not checking in with you. I've had so much going on lately." "Oh, no prob, sis, and yes, I'm still meeting you for lunch. Hey, I wanted to go shopping and get the babies, my nieces, and my nephew something. Could you help me with that?" "Sure, of course." "Perfect, so I will see you in a bit. I have to take this call. See you in a bit, sis. Love you." "Love you too."

Ailese was excited to spend most of her day with Allen. It was going to be just the two of them, no one else. Ailese had arrived at the restaurant that Allen had picked. The restaurant was elegant and rich, not the kind that you could walk in wearing jeans and a nice top. Oh no, not this restaurant. You had to be in your Sunday Best outfit. Ailese was happy that her brother told her ahead of time what kind of attire she should wear. When she walked in, she could feel all eyes were on her, but it didn't bother Ailese. "Reservations for Armstrong, please." There was a gay maître d' that wore more eyeliner than she did.

"Yes, Mr. Armstrong is waiting for you, he said in a very feminine voice. Follow me this way, please." Ailese followed the maître d' and tried not to laugh at his walk. He was "doing too much." He was switching his butt so hard.

"Hey, you look beautiful as always." Allen kissed his sister on the cheek and pulled out her chair for her. "Thank you. Thank you very much. This is an exquisite place. Wow, it's so nice. You know how to pick 'em. So, what are you going to order?" Ailese asked as she picked up the menu. She noticed that the writing was very fancy and there was a lot to choose from. "I don't know. I hear that the tilapia is excellent. I may have that, who knows?" Having ordered an expensive bottle of wine, Ailese and Allen sipped their wine until they were ready to order their meal. She had been to fancy restaurants before, but none like this. This was something you would only see on television. The prices were out of this world, but she knew that it didn't bother her brother.

Ailese and her brother had done well in their lives but had never forgotten where they came from. That was one of the things Alonda preached to them every day.

After lunch, Allen and Ailese took in a show. Allen had been wanting to see a movie. The ticket master was flirting with Ailese, and Allen didn't like that, one bit, so he told the guy that his sister was married, and he needed to leave her alone. Ailese told Allen that he didn't have anything to worry about because Mikell was the only man for her. "I am so excited and happy that we are spending the day together, Ailese. It brings back the old days, you know, when we were kids. I used to always hang out with you and your friends. I was a peanut- headed boy, huh?" "Yes, you were. Even though you got on my last nerves, I still loved your stinky butt." The movie was a comedy, and a very funny one. Ailese and Allen laughed so hard that their sides hurt so much.

"Hey, I wanted to take you shopping and buy some things for the kids. Would that be okay?" "Sure, on one condition. You come over afterward and give the gifts to the kids. The kids would love to spend some time with their uncle, and now you know I will never turn down a shopping spree, Ailese said in a sassy voice. I do need to change. Do you mind if we stop somewhere so I can change?" "Sure, you're like me. I like to be comfortable when I shop too. My wife teases me about that too. I keep an extra change of clothes in my car." Ailese giggled. "Me too, me too." After they changed into comfortable clothes, they headed out to Ella Drive, where all the best clothes were. There was a store on every block. Everyone was important, parking their Mercedes or Corvettes. "Whatever you want, sis, just give it to the lady, sis. I'm going to look at the men's section. I'll be around in that area." Ailese tried on blouses, pants, and jackets. When she was done, she tried on shoes as well. There was so much to choose from. Ailese shopped at the best stores but had only visited a few of the stores on Ella Drive. Allen and Ailese did some damage in all the stores that they went to, and Allen never told Ailese that her purchase was too much. He would just hand the cashier his American Express Card.

Ailese was so exhausted after her brother had spent some time with the kids and Mikell. She decided to soak in the tub since Mikell had some work to do and the kids were already in bed. Just as she was about to enjoy her bath, the doorbell rang. Ailese wondered who could be at her door unannounced and at this hour. Ailese looked through the pephole and saw that it was a delivery man with a package in his hand. "Baby, I got it. You go and enjoy your bath, sexy." Mikell kissed Ailese. Ailese went back to what she was doing.

Mikell disarmed the alarm so he could open the door. "Hi, I have a package here for a Mrs. La Shae. Could you please sign here?" The deliveryman pointed to the X on his clipboard. He signed for the package and thanked him. He closed the door behind him and turned the alarm back on. The package was very heavy. "Ailese, I sat your package on the bed. I'm going back to the den." Ailese was still humming, and in the middle of her humming, she told Mikell, it was okay. She was enjoying the smell of the strawberry candles that she had lit before she ran her bath water. "Man, can a sista get any peace? She grabbed her cell from the small vanity table that stood next to the bathtub. Hello, Ailese said in an agitated voice, rolling her eyes, thinking that this better be important.

"Did I wake you, Ailese?" Ailese didn't recognize the voice. Hey, it's your secret admirer. What are you wearing? I want to taste you so badly." The voice on the other end moaned. Ailese couldn't believe what she was hearing. "Don't ever call this number again, you sick bastard!" Ailese hung up the phone and shook her head. She looked at the caller ID on her phone, but the number was restricted, so she wasn't able to find out who was playing on her phone.

A few minutes later, her phone rang again. It was the same person. He continued to talk dirty to her, telling her what he wanted to do to her sexually, and once again Ailese hung up in his face. "This is one sick bastard. He needs to go and find a prostitute to get his fix and leave me the hell alone!"

Her cell phone continued to ring, and when restricted came on her caller ID, she didn't answer it. Ailese thought that she would be able to enjoy her hot bath and her book, but no, this son of a bitch wouldn't stop calling her, and this made her very angry! Ailese tried to ignore it, but she had to shut her phone off and pray that Mikell would just call the house if he needed her and that there were no emergencies while her phone was turned off.

Ailese used her new lotion and body mist that her brother had brought her when they went shopping. It was one of her favorites. It was called Silver Nights. It smelled so good and drove Mikell crazy when she would wear the scent.

"Mmm … this smells so good." Ailese said, as she sprayed the body mist all over her body. She put on a pink tank top with silver letters that read "I'm in Love" and a pair of capris and went into the kitchen. The phone rang, and Ailese was happy to hear Andrew's voice on the other end. She asked him to come over to keep her company, and besides, she was still jumpy from those weird, obscene phone calls. When Andrew arrived, he had a paper bag in his hand and placed it on the table. "Hey, what's all this?" "Oh, I picked up some salads for us and some drinks, and guess what else I picked up? Andrew had a DVD in his hands. I picked up a few movies. I hope that's okay." Oh, yeah, let's get this party started." Andrew couldn't help but notice that Ailese was distracted by something. "Hey, are you okay? What's wrong?" "I … I was in the bathtub earlier, and some perverted asshole kept calling my cell over and over again, talking dirty, and saying that he was my secret admirer and what he wanted to do to me." Ailese was a bit embarrassed and didn't make much eye contact with Andrew.

"What? Well, if he calls again, give me the phone, and trust me, he'll stop calling you. Come here, you're shaking. It's okay, my love." "But I'm embarrassed because I shouldn't even let that bother me. I'm better and stronger than that." "You can't be strong all the time. Any woman would feel the same way if that happened to them, especially if it wasn't their husband or boyfriend talking to them in a sexual way." Andrew comforted Ailese. He made her feel better. Ailese had forgotten all about it after Andrew assured her that she didn't need to be embarrassed. They watched movies, ate the salads that Andrew brought for them, and ate lots and lots of junk food. Ailese had not heard from Mikell, so she paused the movie while Andrew excused himself. She called her husband. "Hey, it's me. Please call me once you get this message. Love you guys."

"Did you get a hold of your hubby?" "No, I'm sure that he'll be home soon."

A few minutes later, Mikell called Ailese back. "Hey, I got your message. Ailese could hear the kids in the background. "Sorry, I was loading the bags in the car when you called. What's up, baby." "Oh, I was just checking on you guys. What are you doing anyway?" "Oh, I'm getting stuff for our trip. Are you okay baby?" "Yeah, I'm fine. Tell the kids I said hello and I love 'em." "Okay, I will."

Ailese could hear Mikell disciplining the kids, telling them to stay with him. "Okay, oh, Andrew's here keeping me company, so I'll be fine." "Okay, hey, really quick, how did the day go with your brother? Did you guys go out?" "Yeah, it was great. We had a great time." "Kids, sit down. Baby, I will be home later okay. I love you, and tell Andrew hello."

Ailese made popcorn for her and Andrew and watched more movies.

"Do you mind if I used your study for a bit? I need to make a couple of calls."

"Sure, go right ahead. You know where it is." Andrew went into the study and made his calls. He was gone for a while. Ailese went to check on him, as she had gotten closer to the door, she could hear his voice, which meant that he was still on the phone, so she gave him his privacy. She went into her room to freshen up a bit and fixed her hair. She looked in the mirror, examining herself. She didn't notice how long her hair was getting. She needed a trim, she thought to herself. As she looked into the mirror, she could see that she was a clone of her mother, Alonda. She made funny faces, then wondered why people told her that her eyes were so beautiful. Andrew's voice startled her, when he called her name. "I'm right here, I'm in my room. I'm coming out right now." Ailese found Andrew smiling at her, looking suspicious. What? Why are you looking retarded?" Ailese laughed. Andrew picked her up and twirled her around while Ailese was screaming at the top of her lungs, begging him to put her down. "I'm so happy because I'm in love. Elle told me that she loves me, and that makes me one happy fellow!" "Congratulations, see I told you. You just needed to give her enough time and she came around." "I have you to thank, my love. I have some more great news. Remember the property that I bided on? Ailese shook her head yes. Well, everything went through, and I'm one step away from building the after- school program that we talked about."

"I am so happy for you. This is great news!" Andrew and Ailese talked about Andrew's plans for the after -school program. This was a huge step for him. He's always wanted to help the schools and kids in his community, and now this was his chance. Ailese even gave him some ideas, and Andrew thought that the ideas were genius. Andrew had always admired how smart Ailese was; he could talk to her forever and would never get tired of hearing her.

"When Ell comes back from her trip, we have a lot to talk about, you know. I really hope that our relationship can survive for it to go to the next level; I care about her a lot." "I know you do. I don't know if I've ever told you this but I admire how conservative you are at work. I wouldn't have ever known you two were dating because you guys keep your relationship outside of work, and I really respect that." "Yeah, because you mean a lot to us and we respect you as a friend and a boss.

We don't want to put our relationship in the middle, you know?"

"Well, look who finally decided to come home. I thought that you guys deserted me forever," Ailese said, pretending to cry. The kids had bags and bags in their hands, and so did Mikell when he finally entered the house.

Ailese greeted him with a quick kiss as she headed to the car to retrieve the bags. When Ailese went back inside, Andrew was coming out of the house to help carry the bags. I don't think that the kids will be up for shopping with their uncle tomorrow, she thought to herself. Mikell out did himself she thought to herself. What is all this stuff? Ailese had retrieved the last of the bags and sat them down as she plopped down on the sofa, feeling like she'd just run a marathon. "Mikell, sweetheart, may I ask what's all this?"

Ailese looked at Mikell and Andrew as they were taking some items out of the shopping bags. "Oh, well, a little bit of everything. Come here, baby, I'll show you. Ailese gathered all her strength and got up from the sofa, and went into the kitchen. Well, Mikell said, taking a deep breath. He looked like he was going to pass out anytime now. I'm taking the kids camping, and then we're going to Disney Land. I promised Armont that we would do some guy things too." Mikell showed Ailese some of the stuff that he had brought. Tents, outside grill, sleeping bags- all the necessities that you needed to go camping. Ailese never liked going camping, it just wasn't her, the closest she's ever been to camping was sleeping inside an RV in a sleeping bag on a camping ground and you couldn't pay her enough money to sleep outside. She was just so used to having electricity and having all her necessities that she had always been used to them.

"Wowww, camping, huh? Oh, they are going to love it." Ailese said, hugging her husband's neck tightly. "Yeah, they are, Andrew said. "Hey, so what's the date of your guys' trip?" Mikell asked. "Oh, it's the nineteenth to the twenty-sixth, possibly longer, but we don't know yet," Ailese said. "Excellent, we're leaving on the eighteenth at 6:00 am. I've already rented an RV, and I'm thinking about buying one one of these days. Do you know that they have top- of- the- line washers and dryers? They look like an apartment. They have everything that you need." "Yeah, they are nice, Andrew said. A lot of people are buying RV's. I hear that they can't keep them in stock. It's a great investment." The kids came back into the living room after they were done getting ready for bed. "Hey guys your uncle wants to pick you guys up and spend the day with you. Would you guys be up to that?" "We love Uncle Allen. He makes me laugh all the time. He's a silly uncle," Ashanee said. "Guys, I suggest that you guys go to bed soon so you guys can be well rested for tomorrow, alright?" The kids agreed. "Hey, Andrew, do you want to see my new music equipment that I got?" "Sure, Armont, lead the way." Andrew followed Armont to his room. "Hey Mom and Dad, come here. I have something to show you." Armont was so excited to show his mom and dad this surprise. He started playing the drums and started to play along with the song that was playing on his CD player. The girls joined them in the room and started dancing. Armont sounded really good. Ailese and Mikell started dancing to the beat. When Armont was done, he took a bow as if he'd just finished a concert and they were his fans. "Thanks, Andrew. Armont shook his hand. Mom, Dad, Andrew taught me how to listen, I mean, really listen to the music, and now I can do it! "That's great, son. I'm so proud of you."

"You sounded really good. Keep up the good work." "Look at you, a part time music teacher huh? How much do you charge, Andrew?" Mikell said, laughing. "It's free for you guys." Andrew said as he chuckled. Armont played a few more songs until it was time to go to bed. "Hey, you're getting really good, kid. Andrew told Armont. We need to jam more, huh? We can drive your mom and dad crazy and start our own band, my man," Andrew said in a boastful voice. Ailese put up her fists playfully, threatening Andrew.

"Hey, guys, your Uncle Allen will be here in a few minutes, so make sure you have everything. The kids waited patiently for their uncle to arrive. Ailese looked them over to make sure nothing was out of place and fixed Ashanee's hair. "I know my best guys will be on their best behavior, right?"

"I'll make sure of that, Mom." Armont said, assuring his mom that the job would be done. *Beep, beep.* Allen honked his horn, and the kids popped up, grabbed all their stuff, and headed to the door, waiting for Ailese to disarm the alarm. Armont was holding Ashanee's hand as they walked outside to the car. "Heyyyyyy, my beautiful babies, Allen said as they climbed in the car. Hey, sis, you're looking beautiful as always. I don't know what time I'll have them home, but it shouldn't be too late. I'll call you, okay?" "Okay, have fun guys. I love you."

Ailese walked back into the house to find Mikell preparing a platter of cheeses, fruits, and spreads. Fresh out of the shower, his body was still glistening with pats of water on it. Ailese came up from behind him and hugged him. Mikell fed her a strawberry. "Mmm ... that's good," she said with her mouth full.

"This is for us. You have two minutes to get in that bedroom sexy, Mikell said, as he kissed her on the neck. I have plans for us." Ailese skipped to the bedroom like she was a child. There was candles lit in the bedroom, and soft music was playing. Ailese loved this, and she was about to enjoy every bit of it.

She prayed that there would be no interruptions until after their secret rendezvous. She did a quick check in the mirror to make sure that she looked her best and that nothing was out of place. She laid on the bed, making sure she didn't move, so she wouldn't mess up her sexy stance. A few moments later, Mikell was carrying a tray. He told her not to move from that position. He put the tray down, grabbed his cell phone, and took a picture of her. "You're so damn sexy, baby. I mean s-e-x-x-x-x-x-y." Mikell said, as he climbed on to the bed and fed her more food. Mikell and Ailese fed each other fruit, cheese, and crackers and sipped fine wine. Mikell had removed her clothes from her body and laid her on her stomach as he gave her a full body massage. He gave the important places more attention. Ailese loved when Mikell was sliding his fingers inside of her, it drove her up the wall. He made her climax a few times. Mikell then turned her over on her back, bathing her body in the massage oil that tasted like chocolate. Mikell began sucking on her nipples, and as he added more oil to her breasts, he would suck her nipples even harder. She let out a loud whine, arching her back. When it was her turn, she returned the favor, but gave even more than he gave her. She massaged his body all over, kissing and licking his body with her tongue. She loved how his body felt when she straddled him, kissing him and tasting him. She wanted to feel his nature inside of her, and she wanted it now: she never wanted to let him go. She never wanted their rendezvous to be over. When Mikell opened her legs, Ailese began to shudder. She could feel his nature rising by the second. She wanted him badly that she thought that she was going to go insane! When he was inside her, Ailese trembled and let out long moans. Mikell started off slow, and then he would be rougher and rougher, putting Ailese's body in all kinds of positions. When he would go faster and faster and get rough and more rougher Ailese climaxed even more. He turned her onto her side and told her how good she felt, telling her how much he loved her and asking her if it felt good. Mikell was the type of lover that could last a long time. He would make love to Ailese for hours, not climaxing until he wanted to. Ailese would always know when Mikell was about to climax. She knew his body language. His body language would change, and so would their position. Mikell was ready to climax. Ailese squeezed her vagina tight on Mikell's penis, and then there it was: Mikell climaxed, letting out loud noises.

They made love and laid in bed all day with no interruptions, not leaving the room. They sipped wine and ate the tray of goodies, and this made them both happy. They both needed this. It had been way overdue.

"Hey Sis, I just wanted to check in with you. Everything is great. Mom and Dad wanted to see the kids. They're in the kitchen baking cookies. I'll make sure that they don't overdo it with the sweets." "Okay, sounds good. Were they okay?"

"Perfect angels, you know that. If they were some bad kids, which they aren't I wouldn't be taking them anywhere." Allen said, as he laughed. "Thanks, Allen. I really or, we really, appreciate you taking the kids. I am glad that they are behaving like I knew they would." "So, we will see you soon. Love ya." "I love you too, Allen. Tell the kids we love them, and we shall see them soon. Give hugs to Mom and Dad for us." "Will do, Sis."

"Hey, do you want to go into the sauna, Lee?" "Yeah, Ailese said, with a surprised look on her face. That is a good idea. I'll get ready." "I'm right behind ya. It's a beautiful night, baby." "Yeah, it is, Ailese said as she carefully stepped into the sauna with a glass of wine in her hand. "Let's make a toast, Mikell said as he held up his glass to Ailese's. Let's toast to staying together, never stop loving each other, and keeping our marriage strong." Mikell kissed Ailese as if it had been so long since he last tasted her. "Mmm ... what was that for, sexy?" I love you so much; I love you more and more each day. Ailese saw the serious look on Mikell's face. Ailese didn't say anything until Mikell was finished. We've been through a lot, and our trials and tribulations only make us stronger. Tears began to fall from Mikell's face. Ailese touched his face with the back of her hand. You're the most beautiful, smart, sexy, savvy, intelligent, loving wife, mother, sister, and soon to be aunt I have ever known in my life. Will you marry me?" Mikell retrieved a black box with a purple ribbon from under a towel that was sitting next to him. "Mikell! Ailese's eyes filled up with tears. Mikell opened the box, and Ailese couldn't believe her eyes! The ring was multicolored, silver and gold, with a huge purple diamond in the middle. It was really big, bigger- than her wedding ring! Ailese knew that it had to be specially made. "Yes, I will marry you, baby! Yes, I will! Mikell put the ring on her finger, and they kissed.

Ailese thought that she was dreaming. We're getting married again. I am so excited." Ailese said, wiping the tears from her cheeks. She was excited- all of the happy emotions that one person could feel-she was feeling all the emotions all rolled up in one. "Yes, baby, we are and soon. I just felt like it was time to renew our vows and I needed to upgrade ya." Ailese smiled as Mikell started singing the song lyrics to Beyonce's "Upgrade You." "Baby, how did you find time to do all of this?" "Um, my secret Mikell said, as he kissed Ailese on her cheek. "I love you so much. I love your surprises. You're the best, Mikell, and I would marry you a hundred million times if you asked me too. You're my best friend and my soulmate for life. The only man that I want to spend the rest of my life with is you. I want to love you until the day that I die. I love you so much, Mikell! I love you; I love you; I love you!"

Ailese told everyone the news that Mikell and she were renewing their vows.

Ailese couldn't stop looking at the ring on her finger. It sparkled like magic. She couldn't stop smiling. Ailese envisioned what their wedding would be like: what she would wear and how she would wear her hair. How many people would be there? "Baby, I'm hoping that we could get married soon. It would be great if we could get married this summer. I mean, I know planning a wedding takes time, but I don't think I want to wait, Ailese." Mikell kissed her on the lips gently.

"Well, it could be done. We have some time, baby." Ailese kissed Mikell back.

When Ailese and Mikell were married, it was a simple but beautiful wedding, and all the people that they loved and cared about were at their wedding. Ailese was the most beautiful bride you've ever seen in your life! Mikell was the most handsome groom you've ever seen in your life.

"Baby, I still remember our wedding. I was so nervous; I couldn't even think straight." Ailese closed her eyes and pictured that day in her head. "I was nervous too, but it was all worth it. "Mikell smiled.

"So, you guys are renewing your vows, huh? Sounds so romantic, Ailese.

I hope I'm invited?" "Yes, you dummy, why wouldn't you be, huh?" Andrew let out a silly laugh. "I'm so happy for you, my love," Andrew said, hugging Ailese.

"Thanks, honey, I am so excited, you know?" "Yes, I do. You guys are great together. So, summer time, huh?" "Yeah, that's what we're pushing for. I mean, it may just be a simple wedding. We're not sure yet." Andrew shook his head.

"Well, hey, I'm there. Just let me know if you need me." Ailese brushed her hand over his face. "Andrew, Ailese took his hand and looked into his eyes. I just wanted to tell you thank you so much for always being here for me."

Ailese and Andrew spent the majority of the day viewing properties, going over documents, and signing off on them, making sure the documents were hand delivered to accounting and FedEx on time. They didn't want to leave any loose ends while on vacation. Today Andrew took Ell to lunch. Ailese reassured him that she would be fine. He felt kind of bad because they've always gone to lunch together, but every so often he would take Ell to lunch.

Ailese told Andrew that she wanted to go by some dress shops anyway, even though it was a white lie. Ailese took a walk and window shopped on her way back to the office to eat her lunch. Suddenly, she heard a familiar voice calling her name, and when she turned to see who it was, it was D'Andra.

"Hey, sis." They both hugged each other. They were happy to see one another.

"Hi Lee. Are you on your way back to the office?" "Yeah, hey, have you eaten yet?" "No, I haven't, why?" "Well, I'm sure this is enough food for the both of us. Ailese said, holding up the bag. Join me for lunch, or are you busy?" "Never too busy for my sister, and sure, I would love to join you for lunch. I feel like it's been forever since we've seen each other." Ailese and D'Andra walked back to the office. "Wow. look at my sister. You're glowing. You're even more beautiful."

"No, um, I think you need some new glasses, because I think otherwise, honey." D'Andra said, as she felt her belly. "No, I don't need new glasses. I'm serious. Ailese said, tapping her sister on her hand. You're beautiful!" "Thanks Sis. I can't wait to sleep like a normal person. You know? Wew! Okay, okay, I know you guys are hungry. Mommas sorry. She didn't mean to make you guys wait." Ailese smiled as she watched her sister have a conversation with her belly.

Ailese was able to feel the babies kick. This was the high point of her day.

"Hey, where's my boy Andrew? D'Andra asked, looking around the office. I thought you guys always ate lunch together. Is everything okay?" D'Andra looked puzzled at Ailese. "Oh, yeah, were good. He had some other things to do." Ailese didn't want to bring up Ell. She didn't want to upset D'Andra.

"Oh, okay. Tell him I said hello when you see him okay." Ailese shook her head and took a sip of her drink. Even though D'Andra is a tough woman and could handle Andrew dating Ell, Ailese didn't feel that it was appropriate to talk about Ell since she did mess around with Chris. Ailese didn't want to bring up the past either.

"Well, Sis, walk me outside?" Ailese followed her sister to the elevator.

"Hey, where's your car?" "Oh, it's a block away. I'll be fine and don't start babying me, please. I'll be fine." "Okay, alright, and yes, I am always going to fuss over you, so hush!" D'Andra shook her head. "Thanks for lunch, Sis. I will talk to you later." "Yeah, okay." Ailese watched her sister walk out to the lobby until she disappeared. Ailese went back to her office, finished the rest of her lunch, and went to the break room to have a cup of coffee. When she was in the break room drinking her coffee, a woman came up to her and introduced herself. "Hi, I'm Michelle Hines and I work in Human Resources. I'm new," she said nervously. "Oh, well hello." Ailese said, as she extended her hand out to shake Michelle's hand. Ailese started to introduce herself, but Michelle interrupted her. "I know you're Ailese LaShae, and I was wondering if I could get your autograph, please."

Michelle handed Ailese a copy of Eshe Magazine. Ailese didn't think people would want her autograph. "Sure, Ailese signed the magazine and handed it back to Michelle. "Thank you, Mrs. LaShae. I really hope to see you on tour soon," Michelle said, as she walked over to her friends to show them her autographed trinket. Ailese smiled, and unusually, she felt a bit embarrassed as people began to stare at her. A few more people asked her for her autograph. People were complimenting her and encouraging her to go on the tour with Sedrick. Is this a sign telling me that I should go on the tour?

Ailese finished her coffee and went back to her office. When she grabbed her cell phone to call Sedrick, she was interrupted by a knock on the door.

"Come in, Ailese said, as she stuck her phone back into her purse.

"Hello, how can I help you?" There was a tall dark-chocolate man standing in her office dressed to impress. He was beautiful, and Ailese couldn't stop staring at him. When she stopped drooling and staring at him, her focus was back on him and how she could help him. "Hello, my name is Dante' Fields, and I have an appointment with Mr. McGee. I'm sorry to disturb you, but there wasn't anyone at the desk." "Oh no worries. I'm Ailese LaShae, and please come in and have a seat. Mr. McGee should be here any minute." Ailese could feel Mr. Fields was looking at her when her back was to him when she picked up the phone to call Andrew. When Mr. Fields was caught looking at Ailese, he smiled at her.

"Mr. McGee will be here in a few minutes. He's here as we speak. He was getting on the elevator, Ailese said, as she sat down in her chair. "Mrs. Ailese LaShae, right?" Mr. Fields said, as he was pointing to Ailese. "Yes, it is. That's me," Ailese said, wondering why he had asked for her name again. "I knew that name sounded so familiar. You're that singer that was featured on Sedrick Johnson's joint, am I right?" "That would be me," Ailese smiled. "Yeah, I am a huge fan, especially after that interview. Wow, you're hot!" Before Ailese could respond, Andrew walked into the office. "Hot, yes we are," Andrew smiled. "No, I was speaking to Mrs. LaShae over here. I was telling her that she's hot, that I'm a huge fan of hers, and how beautiful she is, inside and out." "Thank you, Mr. Fields," Ailese said, as she stood up from her chair. "Yes, I do agree, Mr. Fields. Sorry, I am late. I don't want to make you wait any longer, so let me lead you to my office." "Okay, question, would Mrs. LaShae be joining us?" Andrew gave Ailese a quick look that said she needed to say yes to the invitation. Ailese played it off like it was already planned that she would be joining them. "Of course."

After the meeting, Mr. Fields signed the contract without thinking twice.

"Mrs. LaShae, could I speak with you for a minute?" "Sure, how can I help you, Mr. Fields?" "I was wondering, could you walk with me to my car? I have the Eshe magazine in my car, and I know that this is probably out of context, but I was wondering could I please have your autograph?" Ailese was caught off guard. "Um, sure," she said. Ailese knew he wouldn't try to hurt her, and besides, she would be safe because there were security guards everywhere. "I've gotta tell you I love your work, and I just have to know something: why are you working here? Of course you're a whiz at what you do, but don't you want to get back out there?" "Yes, sometimes, but I am happy where I am right now, but who knows?" Ailese handed Mr. Fields the magazine that she had autographed. "Well, I really think you are a very talented person and smart too, but I hope that we see more of you. Goodbye, Mrs. LaShae. Hope to see you soon."

"Hello, Sedrick, it's Mrs. Laydee, we need to talk so please return my call."

Sedrick called Ailese back a few minutes later. "Hello, Sedrick, it's Mrs. Laydee. We need to talk, so please return my call." "I am keeping very busy. Mrs. Laydee. How are you? It's so good to hear your voice." "You too, you too." "I hope you're calling me with some good news. Are you?" "Yes, I am a matter of fact. Well, it's good that we both get along because you're going to be stuck with me the whole summer tour ha!" "God is good. I've been praying and praying that you would agree to go on the tour. I am sooooo happy. Have you told Mikell yet?" "No, I haven't. I just made this decision today. I'll call and tell him as soon as I hang up with you." "So, there's a meeting in a few weeks. I'm sure it's about the tour, and I'm sure that I'll see you there, and we could catch up." "Hey, do you think that we could practice?" "Oh, we have too. That's no problem. I gotcha back." "So, I will call you soon, okay?" Okay, love ya. "Love ya, Sed."

"Baby, that's great. I talked to Sedrick earlier, and he seemed really excited about something, but he wouldn't tell me. Now his secrets out. Baby, this is so good and you won't regret it, and I know that you're going to be great." "I'm just nervous about performing in front of a lot of people, you know." "Lee, you'll be great, and besides, you'll have a lot of practice before the tour starts."

Hey, I will need you to be at the meeting in a few weeks; we'll be going over the promos and discussing this and that." "Oh, sure, no problem. Well, I guess our wedding will be on hold for now?"

"Hey, we are still going to get married, my love. That's a promise, Lee." "Wow, were going to have a great summer, together huh?" "I agree, Mikell said. I am so nervous and excited about the wedding!"

"Hey, Mikell I have to go. We'll talk when I get home, okay?" "Okay, baby."

Ailese was so excited that it was hard for her to stay focused on the conference call with Mr. Saxx. "Congratulations, kids! You're doing a fabulous job, and just to let you two know, I have been getting nothing but praise from our patrons, so keep up the good work." Andrew and Ailese thanked Mr. Saxx.

"He's pleased, and I want it to stay that way," Andrew said, as he laid his pen down on the table. "Like I always say, we make a great team," Ailese said, raising her hands in the air. How did lunch go?" "Great. Sorry I was late. We lost track of time." "Understandable. No problem," Ailese said. "I think Mr. Fields has a huge crush on you, though." Andrew said it in a whispered voice.

"Speaking of that, he asked me for my autograph, and you know what else happened to me today? Some people from the office asked me for my autograph today. See what happens when you leave me all by myself?

Ailese tilted her head and rubbed her temples. I was in shock. I read some of the blogs, and most of them were good, but I never knew how many people really read the magazine." "See, told ya that it would be a great idea. Aren't you happy that you did the interview?" Ailese looked at Andrew and rolled her eyes mischievously. Ailese was very nervous; she knew that this tour could make her or break her. What would the fans be like? Are they really ready for her? Ailese kept telling herself that she was in the best hands anyone could ever be in: her husband's hands, and Mikell would never let her down. He would protect her like a lion protecting its cubs. He would not let anyone disrespect his wife. He would have her back all the way.

Ailese knew that the ball was in Mikell and Emmanuel's court. They called all the shots. Ailese took a deep breath and told herself that this meeting was going to go well and would be in her favor. She was a little at ease when she saw Sedrick enter the room. He took a seat right next to her. Sedrick greeted everyone and went back to talking to Ailese. "Mrs. Laydee, it's all good. We're in God's hands. You're fine. We're all fine, okay. Now, don't be nervous," he whispered. Ailese smiled. "Sorry about that baby, I had to take that call. The meeting should be starting any minute now." Mikell put his arm around Ailese's chair to comfort her. "Mikell, tell your wife here that it's going to be fine. I gave her a pep talk, but maybe you can talk to her?" "Okay, thanks, Sed. She'll be okay." Mikell shook his head. When the meeting started, Ailese was relieved. Now she could breathe. They talked about what states, cities, and dates they would be touring.

They talked about how long the tour would be and who the sponsors would be. In addition to asking Ailese and Sedrick questions, they also asked if they would be able to handle the tour and if they needed to make any other arrangements. In the meeting were other artists trying to break through, they would open up for Sedrick and Ailese. Ailese remembered being in their shoes. There was an artist named Kyra. She reminded Ailese of herself a lot. She was a go-getter and felt her music. She took her music very seriously.

After the meeting, Mikell, Sedrick, Kyra, and Emmanuel all went out for drinks. Ailese and Kyra bonded instantly. They talked about their music and the tour. Kyra was a young artist who had been on her own since she was just fifteen years old. Her parents abandoned her at a young age, and she was left to fend for herself. Kyra told Ailese that her music kept her going, and a lot of her songs are about real experiences. Ailese loved Kyra's spirit and her energy, just like she loved Sedrick's spirit and energy when she first met Sedrick. After drinks, Mikell and Ailese headed home. It had been a long day, and all they wanted to do was go to sleep.

"Hello, hello, who is this? There was a male voice on the other end. It was the same person who called a few weeks ago, the same obscene phone call. Stop calling me and lose my number before I call the police! Ailese hung up the phone, put it back in her purse, and became angry. "Baby, what was that all about, huh?" Mikell kept his eyes on the road and waited for an answer from her. "It's nothing," Ailese yelled, wishing she hadn't yelled. "It's something, Mikell gave Ailese a quick look. Tell me." "Well, I keep getting these weird, obscene phone calls. It's nothing, and I don't want to change my number because some sick son of a bitch has nothing better to do!" "What? How long has this been going on, hon?" Mikell said in a calm voice. "A few weeks. I didn't mention it because the calls stopped for a while and now, they're starting back up again. Mikell, please don't worry about it." "No, I am, and I will worry about it. It doesn't sit well with me when a perverted person is calling my wife and saying who knows what!" "Well, you can't do anything about it because the number is blocked," Ailese said, folding her arms and looking out the window to find something to distract her. "Damn it, you may have to change your number, babe." "No, I'm not. I don't want to talk about this anymore," Ailese said. Mikell knew that Ailese meant what she said, so he dropped the subject, but when her phone rang again, he couldn't drop it. "Hello, Ailese hung up the phone and put it in the console of the car and didn't say a word, only to herself: "I am not going to stoop to this perverted bastard's level, and if I ever find out who you are, you better run for cover!" "Ailese baby, are you okay?" "Mikell, please stop asking me that. I am fine. We had a great day, and I don't want this asshole to ruin it." Ailese gave Mikell a look that said if he didn't drop it, he was going to find himself sleeping on the couch tonight. Ailese didn't answer her phone when the unknown number showed up on her caller ID. She could feel Mikell's eyes on her every time her cell would ring. She turned on the radio and sang along with the song that was playing on the radio to distract Mikell and herself; she just didn't want to think about it.

When it was time to get ready for bed, Mikell came into the restroom, where Ailese was putting on her night cream. "Baby, Mikell took her hand and stood in front of her. Please stop and listen to me. Ailese didn't want to listen to what Mikell had to say because she knew that it would be about the calls.

Ailese, look at me, please." "What, Mikell?" Ailese continued putting her cream on her face. "I just wanted to tell you that I am very proud of you. Ailese looked surprised.

She didn't expect this. You've been taking the punches that come at you and standing tall. I know that you can take care of yourself. I guess I'm still overly protective of you, only because I love you so much. Sometimes I forget that you took care of yourself before I came along. I owe you an apology, and I am sorry. Those calls … they just got me all upset. I do have a problem with this perverted punk talking slack to you, though. Just as long as he doesn't try to act on it, trust me, he's gonna regret it. I can guarantee you that! I love you, Lee." Mikell put his arms around Ailese's waist, buried his face in her chest, and whispered that he loved her.

Today was the first day of practice for the summer tour. Although Ailese knew the training would be very intense and she would have to work hard and sweat, she knew it would be worth the effort, despite her dislike of sweating. "Ailese, I need you and Sedrick, please." Ailese wore a tank top with a pair of rayon pants that flowed and didn't hold a lot of heat. "Yes, Bry, what's up?" Bry was a man that had a lot of soul and character. He was the stage manager/director of the tour. He was the person that told you where to stand and what to do while you were on stage. "I want to show you and Sedrick something. Follow me. Sedrick and Ailese followed Bry to the end of the stage. Now, I need you guys to make sure that you're connecting with the audience, so walk over here. As Bry talked, Sedrick and Ailese followed him as he walked the stage. See what I mean? You guys are doing great though. Okay, let's take it from the top." In the first part of the performance, Sedrick starts singing his verse, and Ailese comes out and sings her verse. They made sure that there was eye contact and chemistry seen throughout the whole performance. When they were singing the last verse, Ailese noticed Mikell was sitting in the second row, smiling at her and Sedrick. Mikell clapped when they were done.

"Good job, guys! You're gonna knock 'em dead, and Sedrick, that voice, is off the hook, and my beautiful wife sings like an angel."

"Yes, she does," Sedrick said, hugging Ailese.

After a couple of practices, Ailese felt comfortable. She was more confident and was going to deliver what the fans wanted and expected. Before she went to bed, she would take a long bath after getting home. Her whole body ached. Ailese would see the kids off to school, and Mikell would pick them up from study hall, and the kids would stay with Alonda or D'Andra. Sometimes after work, she would head to the studio to do some tracks that Mikell and Emmanuel suggested that she do, or practice on stage with Sedrick and the band. She was so tired, sometimes she couldn't even think or see straight. There would be times she wouldn't even get to spend time with Andrew. They would talk on the phone from time to time, and on a few occasions, he would come to the studio or to the concert hall and watch her practice, and then they would go for coffee. They would talk about their vacation that was coming up soon and how excited they both were. Ailese had already informed the managers and bosses that she had already planned a vacation, and they understood. Andrew would always remind her how much he didn't want to cancel the trip.

Ailese was losing weight too, just from all the practicing. That made her happy, now maybe she could feel a little comfy in some of her clothes, even though everyone told her that her curves were all in the right places.

"So, how's the concert going, hun?" "Oh, D'Andra, its going better than I thought. I am so excited. I just have so much on my plate, but I'm dealing with it though." "That's my girrrl. I knew you could and would do it. Don't worry, if you need the kids to stay with me sometimes, sis, it's not a problem, okay?" "Yeah, especially when it gets down to the last wire and we need to practice until sundown to sunup. I really appreciate all your help, sis. You don't know how much you've helped Mikell and me these past few weeks." "So, how's Andrew? Have you seen him lately?" "Oh, yeah, I saw him just the other day. He came to one of my practices, and we had coffee and chitchat. He told me that he misses spending time with me, and I told him that we'll get to spend time on our vacation, which is soon. We changed it twice already because of work being so demanding, but I am not mad at that, you know. I told him that I wasn't going to change it again. I think he thought that I was," Ailese laughed. "Well, you can't help what comes up, though, and Andrew, of all people, should understand that." "That's what I told him." "That man loves him some Ailese," D'Andra said, as she laughed. "Now wait a minute. Don't go there, sis. No, no, don't start that again!" "He loves you. Why can't you see that? But I think you guys are so cute though, that it makes me sick." "He loves me as a friend. We have been friends like forever, and the feelings mutual. I'm so glad he's in my life." "I know, I know. I was just giving you a hard time, that's all." Ailese laughed. "Whatever sis, I am going to end this conversation. I love you."

 Ailese was happy to have a day off today, normally she would be out of bed by now, but she didn't want to do anything but rest and lounge around the house. The girls stayed the night at D'Andra's, and Armont went on a fishing trip with his dad. Mikell was still sleeping, Ailese didn't get out of bed until late morning. "Mmm." She moaned as she stretched her whole body and yawned. Mikell moved a little but didn't wake up. Ailese was lazy and still tired, and found herself dozing off again. When midday arrived, Ailese and Mikell got out of bed. "Are you hungry?" "Yes, I'm starved.

Let's get dressed and go out for lunch, or do you want to stay in, hun?" "No, we could get dressed and go out to eat. That's fine." Ailese said, as she headed to the bathroom to take a shower. An hour later, they found themselves at a nice restaurant called the Juniper Diner. It was famous for its grilled chicken salad, and they served the best raspberry iced tea.

After lunch, they headed back home. The kids were still with D'Andra. She had called earlier to ask if she could get the kids hair done, and Ailese and Mikell said that it was okay. "I miss the kids. This house is way too quiet," Ailese said. "Yeah, I know, I miss them too, but they'll be back soon. In the meantime, let's enjoy this time together." Mikell smiled at Ailese. "Well, I guess I can figure out what we should have for dinner, huh?" "Okay, I can cook if you want me to, if you're tired." "Naw, I can cook. I slept enough today." Ailese went into the kitchen and opened the refrigerator to take out some steaks. She decided to make veggies, and red potatoes with salsa to go with the steaks. While Ailese prepared dinner, Mikell kept her company in the kitchen. "Hey, what if I put your favorite movie in and we could relax?"

"Okay, that sounds good, thank you."

After the movie was over, the girls arrived home. "Oh, wow you guys look so pretty. Thanks, D'Andra we really appreciate it." "Hey guys." D'Andra gave Mikell and Ailese a hug. "I hope it wasn't a lot of trouble?" "Oh, no silly, D'Andra said with a smirk. It was no problem at all, Mikell. They are never any trouble, these are my babies and I love spending time with them." "Well, I know they love you to death," Ailese said, agreeing with her sister. The girls modeled their hair for Mikell and Ailese, then headed to their rooms to unpack their things. After dinner, they all watched their mom's favorite movie. The girls were happy to be with their mom and dad.

"I could never remember Rico saying sorry to me or that he loved me, Ailese told Dr. Salvino. It took me a long time to tell myself that it wasn't my fault and that he was a sick man who needed help to get better. I mean, I remember one time I broke a vase by accident. His mother made it for us. He grabbed me by my hair and made me pick up all the broken pieces with my bare hands, and he saw the glass cutting my hands. He didn't care, and after I was done, he told me to get the alcohol for him, but it wasn't for him. It was for me. Ailese began to tear up. He put the alcohol on the cuts that were on my hands and said to me. This is for you being so damn clumsy and breaking the one thing that meant so much to me. I'm screaming and crying while he's saying this to me. Ailese took a tissue from the tissue box and wiped her tears from her face. It was just natural to me the way that he treated me. I deserved it. He brainwashed that into my head. Ailese sniffed and looked at her hands. She could still vaguely see the scars on her hand from the glass. She shrugged her shoulders, closed her eyes, and pictured something else.

I didn't mean anything to him. I don't even know why he had me there. I guess to control me." Ailese shook her head. "Surprisingly, there are quite a lot of relationships like this one. Some men and women love to be in control. They live for it, Dr. Salvino said, as she continued writing in her notepad. Some don't realize that it's a sickness; they think that it's okay to control a person.

They don't want this person to think for himself or herself. They continue to make the person feel like they need them to survive, and that is what happened in your case,

Ailese, and we've all been there. Please don't blame yourself. We're all human."

"Hello, may I please speak with Mrs. Lewis?" "This is she. How can I help you?"

"Hi, Mrs. Lewis. It's Ailese LaShae. How are you?" "Hello, how are you?" Mrs. Lewis was happy to hear Ailese's voice. "Good, good. I was wondering if you wanted to go for coffee?" "Sure, that sounds good. What time?" "Well, I was actually wondering if you were free for lunch today. Only if your schedule permits it."

"Actually, that would be great Ailese. I'm sorry, can I call you Ailese?" "Of course you can." "Ailese?" "Yes?" "Call me Cara." "Okay, Cara, so I will see you at noon?" Ailese gave Cara the address of the restaurant and told her that she would meet her there. Ailese really cared about Dr. Lewis and felt that she owed it to his wife to have and keep a relationship with her, and besides, she wanted to see how she was holding up. Ailese had a huge heart, and even though it had gotten her in trouble in the past, she still continued to take chances with people from time to time. She just couldn't help it. Although it had been over six months since Dr. Lewis was killed, Ailese could not imagine what Cara had been going through.

When Cara walked in, she immediately spotted Ailese sitting at the table. When Ailese looked up, she motioned for Cara to come and sit with her. "Hello, thanks for thinking of me, Ailese. I really appreciate it." "No, thank you for coming," Ailese said, as she sipped her lemon water. The waiter appeared and asked Cara if she wanted to order a beverage. "I'll have some mineral water, with a splash of cranberry juice, please. The waiter smiled and told her that he would be right back with her drink. I love your outfit, Ailese. It's very nice." "Well thanks," Ailese said, looking down at her attire. "There you go, miss. Are you, ladies, ready to order?" The waiter asked. "We need a couple of minutes." Ailese said as she picked up the menu from the table. When the waiter came back, they ordered their meals. Cara caught Ailese up on what's been going on in her life lately and how she's been getting through the death of her husband. "Cara, if you don't mind me asking, have they found any new leads at all?" Ailese said, frowning. "No, not really, Cara said shaking her head. There was a witness they clearly stated that my husband had been arguing with someone by the name of Richard something, but she wasn't for sure. When Ailese heard that Dr. Lewis had been arguing with someone, she began to think about Andrew, but she had never confronted him about it. There was a guy hanging around Thomas's office who was upset because he said that my husband didn't treat his sister in time, and his sister ended up passing away from a stab wound. They talked to the guy, and he had an alibi, so he was ruled out.

Cara sighed. I just wish that they find the person who killed my best friend, and then we all can rest. We can't rest because we know that person is still out there and may get away with it." "Yes, I feel the same way, Cara. Ailese said, shaking her head. I don't understand why someone wakes up and decides to take another life." "Me neither, I ... Cara paused as she took a sip of her drink, looking very sad. I don't understand it, and we had so many plans, you know? I must tell you this, though. I went through some bank records of Thomas's, and there was a lot of money in an account that I knew nothing about, Thomas and I were very open with each other, and for some reason he didn't tell me about this particular account, and I was so surprised because our finances is fine. The bank said that someone would deposit this money directly into Thomas's account. It came from someone named John Avery. I have never heard my husband mention this person's name. I didn't get much information from the bank." "Really, do you think it's a fake name this guy is using?" "Yes, I do. It just didn't all add up."

"Why don't you come back to the office with me? I actually have something for you. You can follow me there, is that okay?" "Sure, that's fine, and I would love to see where you work." "Have a seat, Cara. Cara took a seat. As she looked around the office, she thought it was decorated really nicely, and it fit Ailese's personality too. Here you go." Ailese handed her a purple envelope. Cara had a curious look on her face and wondered what could be in the purple envelope. As Cara carefully opened it, she smiled at Ailese and went to hug her. "How did you know it was my birthday?" Cara gave Ailese a surprising look, as if she knew she had been up to something. "Well, I talked to some of the ladies and I asked them what restaurants you liked, and they mentioned that it was your birthday today, and yes. I was sneaky. Ailese smiled with a laugh.

I just thought this would put a smile on your face, and please promise me that you will enjoy yourself." "Ailese, I can't accept this gift," Cara said, handing the gift cards back to her. "No, this is for you, Cara; please, I want you to take it, please." Cara paused and didn't say anything for a few seconds. "Okay, I guess so, but you really didn't have to do all this, Ailese." Ailese hugged Cara and made her promise to call her when she had gotten back from the spa.

Ailese walked Cara to the elevator, and as she was walking, she passed Andrew. Andrew spoke to Ailese and smiled at Cara. Cara studied Andrew like she knew him from somewhere but wasn't sure where. "Cara, are you okay?" "Oh, yes, Cara said as she got out of the trance that she was in. I think

SHELBY LIES

I know that man, the one that spoke to you. He really looks familiar. Um tell me, what's his name?"

"Oh, his name is Andrew McGee II. You may know him because he's a very well-known businessman, maybe?" "Oh, yeah, maybe that's why he looks so familiar."

"Do what I told you, you bastard, or else you will regret it! It better be done you have an hour!" "Am I interrupting something?" Ailese said, giving Andrew a strange look. Ailese frowned. Andrew motioned for her to come into the office. Ailese hesitated, then decided to sit down in the chair. "Hey love, what's up?" Ailese lifted her eyebrows, surprised at how Andrew went from mad to sweet in a matter of seconds. "Don't, hey, love me. What was up with that?" Andrew looked at Ailese as the room went silent for a moment. Andrew, hello?" Are you there?" "I'm here, my love. It was nothing. It was business, that's all," Andrew said, shrugging his shoulders.

"Andrew, I'm not trying to get into your business or trying to be your mother, but that didn't sound like a business call to me at all, Ailese said, making eye contact with Andrew. Her eyes said it all. It was obvious that she was not happy with him right now, especially because he was acting so unprofessionally at his place of business.

That sounded like you were threatening someone, and that wasn't the first time I've heard you speak to someone like that. Andrew was surprised to hear her say that. How was he going to explain himself to Ailese? This time she had confronted him about it. I didn't ask any questions, but something's going on, Andrew, and I want to know what the hell it is, huh?" "I told you it was a business call." Ailese interrupted Andrew. "What or who makes you this angry? Hell, you scare the hell out of me. I wouldn't want to ever piss you off, Andrew!"

"Ailese, please. I don't want to speak about this. Andrew felt himself getting upset, and he didn't want to get upset with his best friend. Not now and not ever. Andrew walked over to Ailese and sat down in the chair that was beside her. "I would never, ever hurt you, and you know that, right?" Ailese didn't speak, and for a second, she began to think about Rico and how awful he had been to her over the years, and it sent chills down her spine. Her best friend's attitude made Rico pop in her head. That was not good at all. Ailese, Ailese?" Andrew repeated her name because she failed to answer the question. "Andrew, yes, I know that you wouldn't hurt me. I know that, Ailese said, shaking her head. It's just that I don't like to see you get upset like that, and it kind of scares me." "I'm sorry, my love. I do apologize, my love. Andrew rubbed her back with his right open palm. I will try and keep my anger controlled, okay?" Ailese shook her head. "Please tell me that was a personal call." Andrew shook his head yes and promised her that from now on he would stop making his personal calls in his office and would make them somewhere more private.

Today was a special day! Ailese had gotten a call from Chris to let her know that D'Andra was in labor! Everyone was so excited that the twins were coming soon! Ailese couldn't be there for the birth of the twins because the girls both had colds and needed to be nursed back to health, so she stayed behind. "Hey, sis, your nieces are beautiful. I named them Christinia for Chris, of course, and D'Aunna for me. What do you think, sis?" "That's beautiful. Ailese said, with joy in her heart. As soon as the girls are better, I will come and see my girls, okay? I am so happy and one proud auntie. Did you get my packages, sis?" "Yes, all one million of them. They are all so beautiful. The babies are not even a day old yet, and Auntie is already spoiling them." "Of course, you know that is a mandatory thing for aunties to spoil them. Ailese laughed. Okay, sis, I love you." "I love you too." "Take care, okay."

"Mom, I need something to drink, please." Adrieana said, as she coughed.

"Okay, baby, I will be right there with your drink." Ailese took the drink to her daughter and made sure she drank it all. The flu was going around at school, and the girls were unfortunate to catch the virus, and they felt miserable. "Ashanee, it's time for your meds, okay?" "Mom, that medicine tastes really funny, and I don't like it." Ashanee said in a whining voice. "Baby, I know, but you have to take it. This time I'll let you drink a little bit of juice, so the taste won't be so bad, okay? There you go, see that wasn't so horrible. Now drink a little of this juice and rest. Both of you and I'll come and check on you guys in a bit. Here are your blankets, freshly washed. Mom needs to get some stuff done."

The girls thanked their mom for taking good care of them.

They talked about seeing the babies, and even though they both weren't feeling well, they were still excited to see the babies.

Ailese called the flower shop so she could send her sister more flowers.

She ordered a congratulations bouquet in pink and fuchsia pink with lots and lots of balloons and had them delivered to the hospital. Ailese couldn't wait until she could visit the twins. She imagined how they looked. One may look like Chris but have D'Andra's eyes, and the other may look like D'Andra with Chris's eyes. Ailese knew the babies were beautiful and healthy, and that was all that mattered. D'Andra and Chris lives were changing now, they were parents, and they had to make their relationship work more than ever. Ailese was so happy that she didn't know what to do with herself, so she called Andrew to tell him that the babies were born. "Wow, tell D'Andra I am so happy for her and Chris. I hope they wouldn't mind if I sent them something." "Oh, no, not at all, and besides, I'm way ahead of you. I know that they would appreciate it.

Here is the info you will need. Ailese gave Andrew the hospital room number and the hospital her sister was in.

"Thanks, my love. So, what are you up to? How are the girls? Are they feeling any better?" "Oh, just being nurse mom and doing laundry, and yes, they are feeling a little better." "Did you need anything, my love?" Ailese did need a few things, but she didn't want to be a pest. "Yes, I do, but I don't want you to get sick." Andrew cut her off and asked her what she needed. She gave him her list of things that she needed and told her that he would be there soon.

"Andrew, you're too sweet. Thank you. The girls will appreciate it. I will make sure they take you to a movie or something when they feel better. Andrew just smiled and gave her one of his looks that said it's not a big deal. Hey, do you mind keeping me company? I am a bit lonely. The girls are sleeping right now, that's all they do," she laughed. "Sure, I was hoping you would ask me to stay, Andrew smiled. I'm feeling a bit lonely too". Andrew and Ailese played cards and sipped on iced coffee. Andrew even finished the laundry and made her take a nap while he fixed lunch. Ailese was really tired. She slept for a few hours. She woke up in time for a late lunch. The girls were even starting to feel a lot better after Andrew made a secret soup and secret medicine for them. Everyone was very impressed. When it was time for Andrew to go home, Ailese asked him to stay the night. It was way too late for him to drive, so far. He agreed and stayed in one of the guest rooms.

"Oh my gosh, Chris, they're so beautiful," Ailese whispered as she held D'Aunna and gently kissed her on the forehead. "Thanks, I love being a dad. I even love getting up to feed them. I let D'Andra rest most of the time." "Mom, can I hold her, please?" "Okay, sit down and I'll show you how to hold them. They're very tiny, so you have to be very careful," Ailese said to Ashanee as she gently and carefully laid the baby in her arms. "I can't believe I was this little."

"Yes, I know, huh?" Chris smiled at Ashanee and Ailese.

"Hi guys, D'Andra was awake from her nap. She looked tired but beautiful. "Hi auntie, the babies are so cute," the girls said as they stared at the babies. "How are you feeling, sis?" Ailese asked as she handed Christinia to her mother. "I'm good. You know, I'm tired, but I'm okay, even better now that my sister is here, she said, giving her sister a kiss on the cheek.

Chris has been such a trooper, I don't know what I would do without 'em."

The babies needed changing. Chris scooped up the babies, one in his right arm and one in his left arm, and disappeared upstairs to change the babies.

"Well, I must say, you look good for just having twins, sis, Ailese said.

D'Andra disagreed as she held her belly and rolled her eyes.

Hey, why don't I give you guys a break and cook for you guys, or we could pick up something, whatever you guys want? Mom and Dad are out of town, so I can stay and help out whenever you need me too, okay?" "Thanks, sis, that would be great. I am so craving something grilled, and don't ask me why.

By the way, I have some errands to run, and I was hoping we could just hang out. What does your schedule look like this Friday?" "Um, I don't know, but I am sure that we could hang out. I can always make time for you, you know that."

Ailese came back from the grocery store with chicken, veggies, and pasta. She made grilled chicken with grilled veggies and pasta. Grilled chicken was her sister's favorite, especially when Ailese would make her special sauce. It was always a hit with everyone. "Sis, that was an awesome, awesome dinner. Thank you, and thanks for making extra." "No need to thank me, sis. I was glad to do it." When her sister started to clear the plates, Ailese told her to rest and not worry about anything. Ailese did whatever was requested of her before heading back home. She told Chris and her sister that she would be back tomorrow.

"Baby, I'm home." Mikell was back from his trip, and he had missed his family.

"Hey hon. Ailese hugged and kissed him. Dinners ready. Why don't you wash up, and I will have your plate ready for you, okay? We could talk about your trip?" "Okay, I'll be right back. Mikell went to wash up and change.

Thanks, Ailese, I didn't care for the food on the plane, and I am so hungry."

"The meeting went good, Daddy?"

"Yes, sweetie, it went good. Thanks for asking Adrieana. I'm glad you guys are feeling better too." Mikell talked about his trip with Ailese and the girls. He talked about the twins as well. After dinner, Mikell spent time with his girls. They played games and watched television until it was time for the girls to go to bed. Mikell called Armont to see how he was doing and he promised him that he would call him once he arrived back in town. Armont was excited to have his dad home. He told his dad he would be back home tomorrow after school. Mikell and Armont made plans to spend some time together.

"Baby, man, I missed you so much. You just don't know, and I don't think you should be getting undressed in front of me unless you want some trouble."

Ailese smiled at Mikell and continued to undress in front of him. She motioned for him to follow her into the bathroom, where a hot bath awaited both of them. "Trouble huh? Ailese said. She unbuckled the belt from Mikell's pants, kissing and teasing him. Before Mikell knew it, Ailese had undressed every article of clothing from his body. Shh." Ailese kissed Mikell on his neck, then on his chest, and worked her way down to his stomach. They both got into the tub, which was still warm. Ailese washed Mikell's body and massaged his neck, where there was a lot of tension. "Wow, baby, you're so tense right there, poor baby." Mikell moaned at the good feeling that tingled through his body.

"Come here. Ailese laid on top of Mikell. I just want to look at you, that's all. I love you so much."

"Hello, boss. How are you?" "Hi, Ell I am great, and you?" "I can't complain, boss. I got you some coffee. I put it on your desk, and it's really hot, so be careful." "Well, thanks, Ell. I appreciate it. Oh, by the way lovin 'your outfit," Ailese said, as she gave Ell a thumbs up. "Thanks, boss. Don't forget our lunch date; please don't cancel on me, boss." "No, I didn't forget and remember you e-mailed me like a hundred times." Ailese laughed as she went to her office, not giving Ell time to respond. Just as Ailese was getting settled in, Ell had already told her that she had a call on line six. It was Cara Lewis. "Hi, Cara. How are you? It's so nice to hear from you." "Hello, Ailese. Ailese could hear the joy in Cara's voice and hoped that the spa had done her some good. I won't hold you long, I just wanted to let you know that I had a blast at the spa, and I ended up taking one of my good friends with me, and she thanks you too. I would have called you earlier, but I had to take care of some business." "Great! I am so glad that you and your friend enjoyed yourselves." "I love your spirit, Ailese, and I hope that we stay good friends. You're hard to come by, Ailese." "Thanks, me too. Same to you."

"Boss, it's two. You have a meeting in conference room 3. I've already set up everything just as you requested." "Thanks, I do need you there though."

"Okay, I am right behind you." Andrew was already sitting comfortably in a chair in the conference room when Ailese and Ell arrived. Ailese noticed Ell and Andrew giving one another goo-goo eyes; she just smiled to herself.

The clients were fifteen minutes late. Ailese didn't like it when clients were irresponsible and didn't have the heart to call someone to let them know that they would be late. This made Ailese irritated. Ell could tell by the look on Ailese's face that she wasn't too happy with the client's tardiness, and the reason they gave everyone why they were late made Ailese more upset. They were late because they couldn't decide which car they wanted to drive and had gotten into an argument. "Too much info," Ailese thought to herself. Andrew introduced everyone to the clients. Ailese motioned to Andrew that he could do the presentation this time. These clients were tough people to please, and Ailese wasn't in the mood for it right now. Her patience was being tested and since she wanted to remain calm, she figured Andrew could take her place.

"These clients are a trip, Ailese," as Andrew threw the paper towel into the trash can. "I know, Ailese said absently. That's why I wanted you to do the presentation, and I don't mean to be a bitch or anything, but I didn't and don't have the patience for people like that. I don't like it when people think that they're better than you and their noses are all turned up," Ailese said, rolling her eyes and feeling disgusted. "Yeah, I know. Thanks a lot for picking me to deal with it," Andrew said sarcastically. "You're so welcome." Ailese smiled at Andrew, even though she knew he wasn't too happy with her.

"I owe you one, Andrew said jokingly as he opened the door to his office.

So, are you still excited about our trip, Ailese?" Andrew was hoping that she was still excited about their trip. "Of course, why wouldn't I be? I really can't wait until we leave, and I am praying- that nothing or anyone comes in between us going." Just the thought of that happening crawled under her skin. She was looking forward to spending some time away from Sabella Hills and Shelby.

"Hello, bro, how are you doing?" "I'm good, and you?" "I'm good."

"So, I hear that you accepted the tour, huh? I know that you're gonna knock them out, sis," Allen said proudly. "Well, thank you, and I hope you'll be at some of my shows or one of mine? I hope you bring my sister-in-law too." "Of course, I will, and yes, I plan on seeing my sis; we shall be there." "I'll make sure you guys get good seats." "Oh, thanks sis, that would be great! I am so excited! You know that I'm here for another week, and I wanted to see my sister again before I leave." "Oh, okay. I do apologize Allen. I didn't anticipate all these things happening. I mean, I am blessed to have the blessings that God has given to me, but I just wanted to tell you that I am truly sorry for my schedule being all crazy." Ailese really felt bad about not seeing her brother enough while he was in town. "I do understand. Trust me, I do, and please know that I am not mad at you at all. Things come up, and besides, you warned me about this anyway."

Ailese noted the date and time that she and her brother planned to see each other on her Blackberry. It made her happy that her brother wanted to spend more time with her. Today, Allen was going to spend some time with his new nieces and spoil them. As Ailese entered the limousine that was waiting for her, her cell phone rang. She looked at the caller ID. She did not recognize this number, but something told her that she needed to answer it. It was Alonda. "Hey Mom! She was excited to hear Alonda's voice. She hadn't talked to her mom in a while, since she and Don had been doing a lot of traveling lately. Are you back in town?" "Um, no hon, we're still out doing our own thing. I just wanted to say hello." "Mom, whose phone is this?" "Oh, mine, I had to get a new one because I had lost it. So, lock this number in, okay?" "Okay, where's Dad?" "Oh, he's sleeping. He said he had a headache, so I told him to take it easy.

I can't wait to see the babies. D has been sending pictures to my cell phone. They are so cute." "Yeah, I know they are cute, huh?"

"How's Mikell and the kids?" "Oh, they're good, and the girls are feeling better." Ailese had seen a boutique that caught her eye as the limo driver went past it. "I just wanted to call and congratulate you on the summer tour you'll be doing. I don't know if you know this, but it's all over the news, you know, and that's good, dear." "Wow, really, it's really no big deal, Mom. It's Sedrick that people really want to see, not me." "Nonsense, Ailese, they're coming to see you too, and your father and I are so proud of you, I know you must be very excited. I know how much you love to sing, baby." "Thanks, Mom. That means a lot to me. I am actually on my way to rehearsal as we speak." "Oh, that sounds good.

Well, we will be back shortly, and give my love to Mikell and my babies."

"Okay, Mom, I love you. Be safe, and tell Dad I love him too."

Ailese was very pleased with herself at rehearsal, and so was Bry. He told Ailese that she was doing an awesome job and wished that he could work with more talented people like her. Sedrick asked Ailese if she wanted to go for coffee, but she told him that she would take a rain check and that she had other plans. On the way to the limousine, Ailese noticed that a few people were eyeing her. As she walked to her limousine, one of the women stopped her. "Hi, could I please have your autograph, Mrs. LaShae?" Ailese looked surprised. She was surprised that the woman wanted her autograph. She smiled at Ailese and motioned for her other friends to join her. Ailese could hear her whispering. She's really nice. Come on, you guys." "Sure, not a problem." Ailese signed the *Eshe Magazine* and other items that the other women asked her to sign. "I can't wait to see you and Sedrick in concert! Are you and Sedrick an item, Mrs. La Shae?" Ailese gave the women a look as if they did not see the huge rock on her finger, which clearly stated that she was married.

"No, we are not an item. We just sing together, Ailese said, stopping herself from saying anything else. I have to get going. Take care, and thanks for all your support." As Ailese got into the limo, she looked out of the window and noticed people were waving at her!

Was this really happening? All this success is really happening! Ailese pinched herself. Her career was at an all-time high, and today she was getting married for the second time to the man that she loved so very much! As she laid her purple gown on the bed. She smiled. She felt warm inside. Her gown was made of silk, with spaghetti straps and a see-through silk wrap to go with it. The gown was detailed with lilac, white, pink, and purple small flowers that lay perfectly in front of it. Ailese took a sip of her orange juice. Mikell had sent her room service just so he could make sure that Ailese ate breakfast. Ailese was going to marry Mikell in two hours, two hours, she thought to herself. Ailese started to daydream until there was a knock on her door that startled her. She placed her juice on the table and walked to the door to open it.

"I have a package for you, Mrs. Lashae. Sign here, please." Ailese tipped the messenger and closed the door. She opened the package. It was something from a jewelry store-an expensive one. The card read: This is something new and blue for my baby. See you in a while, Mrs. LaShae. Love, Dad.

Ailese smiled. She didn't expect this from Don. She opened the box, and she was dumbfounded. It was a beautiful diamond necklace. She hurried to the mirror to see how it looked on her. "It's gorgeous!" She said out loud to herself.

But the necklace wasn't blue, so she went back to the box and found a blue garter belt that had one diamond in the center. She laughed to herself because she told her dad that she didn't have time to find this particular garter belt, and he did. She knew Alonda helped him find it, or maybe not. Don was a very smart man.

"Hey, sweetie, do you need any help with anything?" "Um, yes, I do. Can you please help me get my dress on without messing up my hair, which took forever?" Ailese said in an aggravated voice, thinking about how she had to wake up so early to make sure her hair was done for the wedding. "Okay, sure." "Hey, Ailese looked around the room. Where are my babies?" "Oh, Mom has them, of course," D'Andra said, rolling her eyes. I tell you, Mom's gonna spoil my girls.

She better not." D'Andra said, with a frown. Ailese laughed and agreed with her sister. "Okay, my hair is still perfect, Ailese said after the dress was on her, looking in the mirror. D'Andra, are you sure you had those babies because you look awesome! "Shut up, of course I have the video and stretch marks to prove it, honey." "You look so pretty, D'." "No, me, huh? No, she said, shaking her head.

Sis, you are the most beautiful bride in the whole world." Ailese hugged her sister. D'Andra helped Ailese put her flowers in her hair and helped with her jewelry.

When Ailese saw everyone that she loved and cared about, she tried to hold back her tears, but she couldn't. She was already in tears when she stood in front of Mikell. Ailese noticed that they were both in tears. As they stood in front of family and friends, they both were so emotional that they felt as though they were getting married for the first time. "I love you, Ailese Synaia LaShae, you're my heart, my soul, and my best friend. I believe that we're soul mates. I want to love you until the day I leave this earth, my love. And with these words I say to you, it still doesn't say it all: how much I love you. If I had all the words in the world, it still couldn't compare. I love you so much, Ailese."

Ailese could feel tears streaming down her face. "My love, my soul mate, my lover, my friend, my sun, my earth. I love you more than words can say, and I feel the same way you do. If I had all the words in the world, it still couldn't express how much I love you. Mikell Sean LaShae, these are only words from my heart and soul." Ailese looked over at Ashanee and Adrieana and smiled at them. When the pastor gave the okay to kiss the bride, Mikell gave Ailese a kiss that she would never ever forget. The crowd was in awe; they all clapped. Ailese hugged the girls and Armont. They all held hands and walked with Mikell and Ailese down the aisle, with D'Andra and Chris following them. Everyone cheered them on and blew bubbles as they exited the church. Ailese noticed Andrew looking handsome as ever and Ell standing next to him. Ailese stopped and gave them both a kiss on the cheek.

The reception was held at their favorite restaurant, Ten Jayes. Mikell surprised Ailese. She thought that the reception was going to be at their house. Mikell had the owner shut down the whole restaurant for the whole day so that they could have the reception there. "Baby, you're good. You kept this a secret from me, huh?" "I love you so much, baby." Mikell said, as he kissed her on the lips. Everyone was having a great time. When it was time to throw her bouquet, Ell surprisingly caught it, and Ailese gave Andrew the look. He smiled at her and raised his hands. Ailese teased him by saying that she would be their wedding planner and that she wouldn't charge them anything. Andrew just accepted the invitation and said that he does want to get married one day.

When Ailese woke up in Mikell's arms, she knew that yesterday wasn't a dream. Mikell had another surprise, but this time it was for the kids and Ailese. He booked a huge suite in Greensville, where all the theme parks, shops, famous restaurants, and best of all, the huge aquariums that the girls had been wanting to explore. "Guys were leaving in five minutes. I'll meet you guys in the car." Mikell said, as he was closing the door behind him. Five minutes later, the girls, Armont and Ailese, were in the car, ready to go. They ate a huge breakfast and headed to the theme parks. "Daddy, are you going to ride some rides with us?" Adrieana said. "Of course, I will. We're gonna have lots and lots of fun, guys!" "Dad, I hear that they have this funnel cake that's supposed to be out of this world." Armont said excitedly. "We have to try it, huh?" Ailese said to Armont, smiling at him. Ailese and the kids really needed this time away from home. Ailese loved to see her kids happy, and Mikell loved to see that sparkle in her eyes that he loved so much.

"Mikell, I'm not going to let this ruin our trip. Now, please drop it." Ailese whispered to Mikell. The calls had started once again, so Ailese turned her cell phone off and prayed that there wouldn't be any emergencies from anyone and that they couldn't get a hold of her. "Baby, change your number, please. I am sure everyone would understand, including your clients, so as soon as we get back home, we will change your number." "No. Ailese whispered, making sure the kids stayed occupied so they wouldn't hear what she and Mikell were talking about. I'm not going to do it. We've talked about this, hon, remember? Ailese said with a halfway smile. This son of a bitch can call all he wants to, she said, angrily. This discussion ends right now," she said in a serious midtone voice. Ailese, you're not listening to me." As he handed the woman money at the aquarium and she handed him tickets, Mikell smiled at her, hoping she hadn't heard the conversation. "Okay, gang, let's go and see my fish. Armont, keep an eye on your sisters, okay?" "Okay, I will, Dad." "Ailese, think about this before you make your final decision. Yes, I know that this may not scare you, but this guy does have a problem, and why is he targeting you? Why are you this jerk's problem? Why is this person calling you?" "I don't know Mikell, Ailese said as she focused on the kids walking in front of her. There is no way I'm letting some asshole who's horny and wants to fill me up ruin my life for the rest of my life." "Lee, I would think that these calls would have stopped by now and babe, I hate to mention this. Mikell took a deep breath. I hope that, and I pray that what happened a while back isn't stirring up again." Ailese shook her head. Deep, deep down inside, she hoped that her husband was wrong.

"Did you have fun, Ailese?" "I did Mom. We all had a terrific time. So are you and Dad here for a while?" "Yes, we are. Your father and I are back for good until we find another place we want to visit. I was actually thinking about going to Africa and Paris in a year or so." "That sounds good." "Will I see you in church next week, hon?" "Mom, no, did you forget already? I'll be on vacation."

"Oh, wow, where does the time go? That's right! We need to spend more time together, sweetie. Maybe when you get back, we could work on that, okay?" "Okay, Momma, that sounds good. Oh, by the way, I talked to Mommie today. She's doing well and she loves the DVR that D'Andra bought her." "Yeah, I talked with her a few days ago, and she was telling me the same thing. Mommie loved the wedding. She couldn't stop talking about it. She kept telling everyone how beautiful you looked and that she was your grandmother." "I know she had lots of fun, and she needed that you, know? So, how long did Mommie stay?" "Um, I took her home the next day. Can you believe it? I think she only stayed to spoil the babies. Speaking of babies, they're up from their nap and I need to go and check on them. I'll talk to you later, baby."

Ailese had decided to go into work later today since Mikell was working from home for a few hours. "Come on, baby, let's go." Mikell grabbed his keys off the table. "Huh? Where are we going?" "You'll see. Come on." Ailese followed Mikell as he held her hand, led her to the car, and opened the car door for her. "Great, Ailese said to herself as they pulled up to the cell phone store. Knowing that she couldn't get out of this one.

She slowly got out of the car and walked inside the store. As they were walking, Mikell pulled her to the side and told her that this would be for the best and to look at it as a fresh start. Ailese gave him a sad look. "Yes, hi. I would like to change my number. Would that be possible?" Ailese said to the woman who was ready to assist her. "Sure, could I have your account number, please?"

Ailese gave the woman her account number. Are you happy with our service, ma'am?" "Oh, yes, I am very pleased. It's just that, Ailese hesitated. Well, I've been getting weird phone calls, and I need to change my phone number, that's all." "Okay, I understand. Give me a moment, okay? Ailese smiled at the woman as she looked over at Mikell, who was checking out other gadgets that were in the store. Okay, I have a new number for you, and luckily, it's spanking brand new. Mrs. Lashae, would you like to upgrade your account with us today?"

"You know what, why not? I have been having this phone for a long time now, and there was a phone that caught my eye."

"See, now that wasn't so bad, huh?" "No, we all got new phones out of it. I love this phone. It's easier than my Blackberry. I cannot wait to play around with it. Now, I have to email everyone to give them my new number. Ailese let out a long sigh. I guess it won't be so bad. I could have Ell help me send out letters and new business cards." "Do you want me to drive you to work, or do you want to take your car?" "Um, I have to take my car. I have a therapy session today." "Okay, so let's go back and pick up the car."

"Hey, Ell, I need to see you in my office right away, please." "Okay, boss," Ell said, grabbing her notepad off her desk. "Okay, I need you to send out letters to all our clients because my contact number has changed, and make sure you get new business cards made please. Today would be great if it's possible, and notify Human Resources of the changes." "Okay, Ell said as she finished writing Ailese's requests on her notepad. Boss, is everything okay?" Ailese just shook her head at Ell. She didn't want to get into why she had to change her number. "It's something that has to be done since some asshole decided to crank call me and hasn't stopped, Ailese said, shaking her head. Ell's face said it all. Why and who would do such a thing? "Boss, I am on it right now, and I am so sorry."

"Knock, knock," Andrew said as he entered Ailese's office. He wore a double- breasted suit that Ailese thought he looked very handsome in. Tell me something. Why when I called your cell earlier, it said it was disconnected?"
"Oh, I had to change the number." Ailese looked down at her desk, not wanting to discuss why she had to change her number. "Oh, Andrew said, wanting to probe her for more information. May I ask why?" "Those calls." Ailese whispered to him. "What, are you kidding me?" "No, and I don't want to discuss it, and Mikell was on my ass and getting angry because I wouldn't change the damn number." "Okay, Andrew said defensibly, don't bite my head off, woman." Ailese gave Andrew the evil eye and scooted him out of her office. Wait, aren't you gonna give me your new number, my love?" Ailese wrote down her number, gave it to Andrew, and playfully pushed him out of her office.

"Boss, everything you requested is done, and all the letters and business cards have already been taken care of." Thanks so much, Ell." Ailese said, as she looked up from her papers. "Boss, are you okay?" "Yes, I'm fine. Why do you ask?" You seem irritated. Is everything okay, boss? I remember there was a time we shared a lot with one another. You can tell me, boss." "No, really, I'm fine, Ailese said. Sometimes I feel like my past is repeating itself, and it's something I don't want to repeat. Ell sat down in the chair. This past year, I just felt this way, and it scares me. It really does," Ailese said in a concerned voice. "Like what, boss? You mean, oh my, she gasped!" "Well, to make a long story short, it all started with my dreams. I started dreaming about the times when I was in a really abusive relationship many, many years ago. Ell was surprised to hear this from Ailese. He would beat me so badly, and I stayed for years. I mean, there were times he would rape me until I bled. I used to take medication just to get to sleep because I was so traumatized. Ailese held back her tears. I would see him everywhere. I would see him walking down the street or in the grocery store because he told me that he would find me and kill me. Ell gasped. Lately, a lot of weird stuff has been going on. First, I started to have the dreams again, which scared me so bad, Ailese said as she closed her eyes for a second, trying not to break down. Then, out of the blue, my mom and dad's house gets broken into, and someone kills all of their pets, and luckily my parents weren't there. Then, my sister was attacked and beaten by someone. Luckily, she was found. She doesn't even remember how she got there, and we still don't know. A man tried to break into my house while we were there!

This man was determined to get into our home, but the police said that he was on drugs and was disoriented, but it seemed as though he was there to hurt us and he knew we were there, like he was sent there to hurt us. Ailese took a deep breath. For a while now, I've been getting a lot of weird phone calls," Ailese said, as she shook her head and massaged her temples.

"Boss, I am so, so sorry that you've been through so much. Come here. Ell walked over to hug Ailese. Unknowingly, Ailese needed this hug. And so, you think that this man that hurt you may be responsible?" Ailese shook her head and prayed that Ell didn't think she was crazy. Okay, so I have a question. With all these weird events happening, what do the police say? They're there to protect us, boss," Elle said as she took Ailese's hand and put it in hers. "They couldn't even put the pieces of the puzzle together, and this person never left a trail or evidence- nothing."

"What about asking the police to look into this person who hurt you-his background?" "Yes, I did, and they couldn't find anything on this person. It was like he fell from the face of the earth." Ell shook her head and gave Ailese a puzzled look. Ell wished there was something she could do. "You have been working with the police ever since. Ell paused. Ever since the incident with your mom and dad, and I am infuriated that this person is getting away with hurting innocent people! I wish there was something I could do, boss." "You've been great, Ell. I appreciate you. I do.

So, that's my life. That's what's been going on lately, and I am sorry that I kept that a secret from you all this time. You're right, we could talk to each other.

I guess I was somewhat embarrassed because I never want to tell anyone that someone's taking control of my life and not me, you know?"

"No, don't think like that because you didn't let them stop you from being a fighter, and don't forget you're still standing, boss." Ailese smiled.

I mean, I only knew about your parents and the police still had no leads. I am so sorry that you are going through so much, but you're strong, and please don't forget we all love you and are here for you, okay?"

Telling Ell what had happened to her actually lifted a few monkeys from Ailese's back and now she was on her way to lift more monkeys for Dr. Salvino.

"Hi, Dr. Salvino, how are you today?" "I am good and you, Ailese? I love your outfit. Those earrings are cute," Dr. Salvino said, as she sat down in her chair.

"Well, thanks." Ailese made sure she turned off her cell phone and put it back in her purse before the session started. "Could you excuse me for just one moment?" "Sure, go ahead. It's no problem." Ailese sat in the chair and admired all the degrees on the wall in the office and thought how lucky she was to have a great therapist like Dr. Salvino. "I apologize for that, Ailese. I had to make sure my assistant took care of something."

"He would tell me how much he hated me a lot of the time, and I'm ashamed to say that I loved him even after everything he would put me through. Ailese glanced at her doctor. My self-esteem was at the lowest, it had ever been especially when the scars started to leave marks on my body. It was a constant reminder and I should have known better. He would never change. I wonder how I would come up with all those crazy excuses for why I was wearing a turtleneck in June, or why I would never wear short-sleeved shirts or low- cut shirts for that matter. It got harder and harder to keep lying to everyone. I never met a compulsive liar. I was my own compulsive liar, and I was. I would see right through them, trying to cover up lie after lie Ailese said. And sex, Ailese paused and shook her head. After Rico I refrained from sex. It scared the hell out of me. I would always think that every man would be just like Rico, so I buried myself into work, and the weird thing is that I didn't even miss sex at all.

When I met Mikell, I still remember how I slapped him across the face when he tried to kiss me. Ailese let out a small laugh. I mean the things that I put that man through. He shouldn't have gone through it, all because of one man that destroyed me."

"Hey, Sed, what's up?" "Oh, nothing, I was thinking about ya and thought I would give you a call. I'm going to miss you when you go on vacation, but make sure you don't have too much fun without me, and please, oh please, take care of that beautiful voice, Mrs. Lady." "I know, I will, and I'm going to miss you too, but just keep thinking about all the times we're going to have together, and I may just work your nerves with all my divaness," Ailese said as she laughed. "You're so funny, Mrs. Lady. I love you, and I just wanted to tell you that I am so glad that we met and we're working together. You're so awesome!" "Aww, I love you too, Sed, and I love working with you, and I hope we'll work together in the future. I love your spirit, and never change that for anyone." "And by the way, you could never get on my nerves." "I'll be bringing you back lots and lots of gifts!" "Can't wait!"

"Where are my babies?" "Oh, daddy's giving them a bath. Have a seat, sis."

"Don't you look all pretty?" Ailese said to D'Andra. "Oh, this old thing, I just never wear it, D'Andra said, looking down at her outfit. Hey, come here. I need to show you something. Ailese followed D'Andra upstairs.

Look, Chris and I finally finished the final touches for both of our offices. What do you think?" "Wow, you guys did a great job. It's really nice. Ailese looked around the room and admired all the things in it. She noticed an old picture of her and D'Andra when they were kids. Oh, my, this is such an old picture. I remember this picture. It was the day after we adopted you." "Yep, you remember, huh?" "Oh, wow, Ailese stared at the picture and began to go back to that very day. This has your name all over it. It is a good-looking office. Show me Chris's office.

Wow, this is great! It looks awesome, sis. I noticed the office was baby- proof and you guys have a "baby- proof office". "Yes, you noticed, huh? We can bring the babies in here, and we don't have to leave the room too much because we have everything that they need." "I like that idea. I do."

Hey, my sweethearts. Ailese took Christinia out of Chris's arms and into hers.

Hi, Chris," Ailese said, as she gave him a peck on the cheek. "How's everything going, Ailese?" "Oh, good, good. I can't wait until the concert starts. I'm ... actually excited." "Yeah, we are all excited and happy for you. We really are Ailese. So, what did you think about the offices?" "I think you guys did a great job, Chris." "Thanks," Chris said, as he put the babies down in their beds for their nap. Ailese looked on as Chris put the babies to bed. Chris loved being a father. Ailese could see it in his eyes, and that made her happy. She smiled at Chris and her nieces. "Hey sis, are you thirsty or anything?" "Yes, I'll get it. I know my way around." Ailese went into the kitchen and fixed herself a glass of iced water. When the babies woke up from their nap, Ailese fed them and changed their diapers. She enjoyed her twin nieces. The babies were good babies. They slept through the night, which was good. They never cried, not even when they were given a bath. They were laid- back babies.

"So, when are you guys going to let me keep the twins? I know it's been a while since you guys had a date, huh?" "Well, yes, it's been a long time, D'Andra said as she tried to remember when the last time, she and Chris went out on a date was. But you have a lot on your plate, Ailese. You have your concert and your own family. There's plenty of time for us to go out."

"Yeah, but I love my babies too, and my schedule has nothing to do with me babysitting for you two. Actually, I wouldn't even call it babysitting because we're family and I would love to have them over." "Okay, well, I am sure that will happen soon."

"Hi, Dana. How are you? I've missed you," Ailese said as she playfully pinched Dana's nose. "Hi, Mrs. Ailese I missed you too. I thought that I would never see you guys again," Dana said in a dramatic voice. "Aw, I'm sorry, sweetie, we just had a lot going on. You're always welcome to our home, okay?" Dana smiled, sat back, and buckled her seat belt. It had been a while since the girls had a playdate with Dana, so they were all excited to see each other. As soon as Dana arrived at the house, the girls headed straight for the playroom.

"Mikell, hey, I'm back. The girls are in the playroom, so they should be fine."

"Okay." Mikell kissed Ailese on the lips and went back to his laptop.

"Girls, what would you guys like for lunch?" "Were not hungry yet mom, Ashanee said. The girls decided to have turkey sandwiches and chips. "Okay, that sounds good. You guys be good while I go and prepare lunch, okay? Ailese's phone rang as she was preparing the girl's lunch. Hello, hello. There was no one there, so she hung up. Her phone rang again, and she hesitated before answering it again. Mikell, please come here." "Hey, what's up, baby?" "I think that those stupid calls are starting again." "What happened, babe?" "I just got an unknown call just now, and they didn't say anything, Ailese said in an angry, frustrated voice. The only people that have my cell number are clients and family, that's all." "Yes, I know, hon, and your number is unlisted. I really hope it's no one that you or I know. This is getting ridiculous," Mikell said. "Mom, were ready to eat now," Adrieana called out to her mom. "Okay, hon. Make sure you guys wash up for lunch."

Mikell, let's talk about this later, okay? I don't want the girls to worry."

Mikell shook his head as he helped Ailese put the drinks on the table.

After Ailese came back from dropping off Dana, Mikell wanted to finish their conversation. "Lee, I know that this seems like a little problem, but not to me. I still can't get it out of my head. The things that have been going on for a long time now, and I don't like them. When D'Andra was hurt, I wanted to find the person who did that to her, but maybe it was best I didn't find out who it was because they would have had to answer to me, and I know that it's wrong to take another person's life, but not when it deals with the people that I love.

I mean, this person is sick. It may be the same person who broke into Alonda and Don's house. I don't know, but I'm getting the feeling that there is a connection, and whoever this is, they're trying to break you and break us.

How much do you know about Andrew?" Ailese gave Mikell a harsh look. She didn't like what he had just said, and he had no reason to suspect Andrew. "Why would you ask me that?" "I'm sorry you're right, Mikell sighed. That was very stupid of me. You guys have been friends forever now. I am so sorry I asked you that question. I'm just ruling out people that are in your life and my life as well. But Andrew is the one person who is a newbie in your life, but what I don't understand is why, and what he would get out of hurting you." "You took the words right out of my mouth." I mean, they made sure that D'Andra didn't remember that night at all. They made sure that whatever they did, they didn't leave any evidence behind, Mikell said as he got up and paced the room.

Suddenly, there was a knock on their bedroom door. Come in," Mikell said.

Armont peered his head in. "Hi, Dad, hi, Mom, I just wanted to tell you guys that I was home from the mall." "Okay, did you have fun, and was the movie good?" "Oh, yeah, Dad. I got you and Mom something," Armont said, as he closed the door behind him. "Oh, you can leave the door open."

Armont handed his dad a small shopping bag. When Mikell opened it, he pulled out some pictures. Armont had taken some nice pictures at the mall and purchased a nice frame. Ailese and Mikell commented, "Nice pictures."

"Thanks, Armont smiled. I know that I've been promising you guys pictures for a while now." "You did this all for us?" "Yes, I did. I love you guys."

Armont and his parents talked about the pictures for a while and how thoughtful Armont was to think of them. Ailese hung the picture frame on the wall in the living room and admired it. It took her mind off the conversation that she and Mikell were having earlier.

When Ailese was getting ready for bed, her cell phone rang. She was too scared to look at the caller ID. She wasn't in the mood for these games. Low and behold, it was an unknown number. Ailese rolled her eyes and ignored it. "Hey, baby. Mikell startled Ailese when he came out of the restroom.

I'm sorry, did I scare you?" "It's fine. I thought that you were in the living room, that's all." Ailese was hoping that Mikell wouldn't notice that she was really shaking underneath and that her body had goose bumps, but she could not fool him one bit. "Baby, something's wrong?"

"Mikell?" "Yes, baby." "I got … Ailese paused. I got another phone call." She had a worried look on her face. Mikell sat down on the bed and motioned for her to come to him. Mikell comforted her, and he hugged her tight. "Lee, it's going to be okay. Look at me. I know that you may not want to talk about this, but I was thinking earlier. What about the man who hurt you? Could it be possible that he is the problem behind all of this? The reason why I am asking is because, even though you and I know what happened that night, remember, he may still be alive. There was never any evidence that he wasn't alive, and yes, the police said it looked like he fell off the face of the earth, but we need to accept that there is a possibility that the more and more I think about it, the more I think that this man may be out to hurt you." Ailese feared this man and hoped that what Mikell was saying wasn't true. Could Rico be the one causing her family to go through all this drama? Is he responsible for all those weird calls?

"This is crazy, Ailese. D'Andra said. I can't believe this after all these years. Do you really think that Rico would come after us, let alone you?" "I don't know, Ailese said in a sad voice. It's just speculations, that's all, but It does make sense. Remember all those times when I tried to tell Mikell the same thing, but he did not believe me, and he said it was me just being paranoid?" "Yes, I remember you telling me the same thing, and I believed you, but we couldn't come up with any evidence. The police said that there was no record of Rico, like he fell off the face of the earth, you know?" Yes, which is very weird. Sis, I didn't want to get you upset. I just needed someone to talk to." "I'm here, and please don't think that I'm upset. I'm just worried. I know what that man put you through, and no one should ever have to go through something like that, Ailese. Right till this day, I still feel so bad that I didn't see the signs. I should have seen them. D'Andra started to cry. That man took everything away from you, and you didn't have anyone to turn to because you were afraid and scared because of all the threats! It makes me sad that those days and nights when he hurt you, I could have been there. I wanted to be there, sis. I love you, and I would give anything if I could take that time in your life back. I would take it all away like it never happened!" D'Andra sobbed even more, just thinking about what her sister went through. She knew that Ailese was strong too.

"It's not your fault, hon. It's not. Please don't ever think that it is.

Ailese felt tears rolling down her face. I love you, sis. I just wanted to tell you what was on my mind. God will punish whoever is doing this."

"Kids, we need to load up the RV and get going." Mikell shouted to the kids, who were making sure that they had everything before they went on their trip with their dad. "Let me help you guys, okay?" "Okay, could you please grab those two backpacks please?" "Sure, Ailese said, as she picked up the backpacks, and followed Mikell outside to the RV. Wow, you guys are going to have a blast." Ailese said, looking inside the RV, imagining how much fun the kids were going to have. "Yes, I know. I'll miss you, a lot." Mikell kissed Ailese. "I'm going to miss you too, baby. I'm gonna miss you like crazy." Ailese said, as she hit Mikell on the butt. "Hey, you're so bad. Come here, Mikell pulled her close to him, and they began to kiss passionately. I think we need to break this RV in, don't you think so?" "Mikell, you're bad," Ailese said, hitting him gently on his shoulder. "What? Mikell laughed. Hey, I must say I think it would be nice if we made love in here, he said, nodding his head. I have it for two weeks, remember?" "Okay, we'll see what happens, lover boy."

"Kids, I want you guys to be extra good, okay?" The kids all agreed that they would. Ailese hugged all the kids and gave them lots of hugs. She walked them out to the RV and waved goodbye until they were no longer visible.

She missed them already. As she closed the door behind her, she looked at the empty house. What should she do with herself? She looked at the time, and her brother wouldn't be there for another hour. She looked through the mail, tidied up the house a bit, and made herself some iced tea.

She picked up her cell phone and dialed Andrew's number. She was happy that he picked up. "Hi, Ailese, did Mikell and the kids get off, okay?" "Yes, I miss them already." "Aw, poor baby, just enjoy your time alone." Alone, that word scared her a bit. "Yeah, I know, but I'm so used to them being here, you know?"

"I know. Hey, could you hold on for one sec?" "Sure." Ailese played with her necklace while she waited for Andrew to come back on the phone.

"Sorry, my love, I'm back. So, we're leaving in three days, my love, yes!"

"Wow, yes, and I hope those three days go by quickly. I made my checklist so I won't forget anything." "Okay, good, even though I know you're gonna shop until you drop, so make sure that you bring extra luggage. Ha, ha, ha," Andrew said, laughing. "Shut up, butt head, you're so mean. Why are you so mean to me, huh? I thought that you loved me, Ailese said, like she was a little girl pouting. Andrew, could you come over later after I come back from going out with my brother?" "Sure, just call me. Actually, I have a better idea. Why don't you stay here with me just so you won't come home to an empty house? What do you say to that?" Ailese was happy to say yes. She didn't want to invite herself and even if she did, Andrew wouldn't have seen it that way. "Okay, I'll call you after I get back, okay?" "Hey, what if I just pick you up?" "Andrew, that's such a long drive." He interrupted her. "No, I need it anyway, and you could take one of my cars if you need to." "Okay, thanks. I love you to death," Ailese said, hoping she didn't go too overboard. "I love you too, my love. Okay, I will talk to you soon." "Yes, talk to you soon." Mikell had suggested to Ailese that she should stay with someone until she went on her vacation so she wouldn't feel alone or scared, but she could be so stubborn at times.

After Ailese packed her overnight bag, her brother arrived to take her out.

"Hey, Allen, come on in." "Oh, I hope you don't mind that I brought Mya." "Oh, I would love to see my sister-in-law. Where is she?" "She's in the car." "Oh, okay, I'm ready." Allen, are you okay?" "Yeah, I'm good," he said, opening the door for Ailese. "Hi, Mya. How are you?" "I'm good. How are you, Ailese?" "Good. I'm good." Ailese said. She could feel there was a reason why Mya asked her that question. When they arrived, Ailese was surprised to see that they were at Allen's townhouse. She had thought that they were going to go for coffee. "Sis, I know that we were supposed to go for coffee, but we need to talk. Sit down. Ailese started to wonder what was wrong and what was so important. Sis, I need you to listen to me, and I need you to listen carefully. Ailese shook her head. Allen took a deep breath before he started speaking. I want to apologize first off, because I shouldn't have kept this from you, and I love you. Please don't ever forget that. Ailese shook her head. She had so many things swimming in her head.

When Mya came back into the room with coffee, she sat the tray on the table and began to pour coffee into the cups. She motioned to Ailese if she wanted cream and sugar, and Ailese shook her head yes. Mya handed Ailese her coffee, handed Allen a bottle of water, and sat next to Allen. "I know that our family has been through a lot, and we have remained strong and got through it. After the incidents, I started to have these weird feelings, like someone was out to get us. There's something that you don't know about that night, Ailese. The night that we made Rico go away." Ailese's eyes widened. "Allen, what are you trying to tell me?" Ailese took a sip of her coffee and sat her cup on the table. "Ailese. listen to me. Like I said, these bad feelings came over me and I started having these strange dreams, but I shrugged it off and told myself that it was only a dream, and went about my day. I was there that night, and I needed to be there that night." "Allen, you weren't there that night, and I know this for a fact. You were out of town on business. I remember it like it was yesterday. I remember crying for you, and momma reminded me that you weren't there."

"Mom called me and told me what had happened. She told me every detail, about how he hurt you, and I was not about to let this son of a bitch live, not while I'm alive, Allen said as he balled his fists. Nobody hurts the people that I love! Nobody! Mya massaged her husband's back as he spoke.

So, when Momma told me that she needed me, I came back, and I never made that meeting. I was willing to go down for my family, and I didn't care. I had to do what needed to be done that night. I mean, this man made your life a living hell, Ailese. He took everything from you, and I will never forget what you had to get through to be a person again or how we all had to pull together to be there for you, whether it was taking turns sleeping next to you because that was the only way you would sleep. I still remember how you would scream in your sleep because you would have all those bad dreams. I remember you being so scared out of your mind. You didn't deserve to be treated like a dog, sis.

Ailese could see the hurt in her brother's eyes. She was a bit shocked that he felt so strongly about the situation and how it hurt him this much. It was more than she had thought!

We all wanted to make sure that Rico would never mess with you again, and that was what we set out to do that night. Allen paused and looked at his sister and Mya. We waited for Rico to get off of work that night. I was ready for him. I wanted him so bad that I could taste it. Before he got the keys in to the car, he didn't even know what had hit him, but I did, Allen said, with a smirk. It felt good to see him fall on his face. I wanted him to feel pain like he made you feel pain." "Allen, are you saying what I think you're saying?" "Yes, I took part in beating the shit out of him. He deserved it. I'm saying that I had a lot to do with that asshole, and not once did I have sympathy for that fucking bastard!"

"Allen, watch your language!" Ailese couldn't believe what was coming out of her brother's mouth. He had always been so conservative, and she rarely heard him curse. "After we beat him senseless and threatened to kill him, we told him that if he ever stepped foot in this town again, we would kill him and wouldn't think twice about it! We took him to a secluded place and watched him all night until the morning. Hell, we beat him some more, especially when he would get smart and run off at the mouth! We all made sure that he got on that plane the very next day. The plane was a friend's personal plane. We used his plane so that no one would ask any questions later. Forgive me, sis, but it just still burns me for what he did to you.

One day, I got a message, from my secretary saying that a messenger had sent it to my office. I opened the envelope and it was a note that read: I got you son of a bitch. You're going to pay for what you've done, so watch your back.

I just ignored it. I didn't even tell my wife, Allen said. That stupid note didn't scare me at all, Allen said, shaking his head. I'm no punk.

I kept getting these notes about once a week, and then when all these weird things kept happening, I kind of put two and two together and thought maybe these notes were connected to Mom, Dad, D, and you. So, I had a friend of mine who works at the police station and is a police officer do a favor for me. I had him look into Rico's background, and he didn't come up with anything. His name wasn't even in the system, which was weird, like he fell off the face of the earth. Ailese." "Well, I got the same answer as you did when Officer Brown checked out Rico, so, what are you saying, Allen?" "I'm saying that Rico may be the one that's tormenting us." "Allen, that's crazy. You just said so yourself that he was nowhere to be found." "Yes, I know, but who else would want to hurt our family? Ailese, the letters, it all makes sense." "Allen, no, this isn't possible. Ailese said, as she stood up to pace the floor. Why did you keep all this from me, huh? Why?" Ailese began to feel like she had been betrayed by her brother, the one person that she thought she could always count on.

Ailese felt as though all of the men in her life had let her down, except her husband. Her father died and left her scarred for life, missing him and missing not seeing his face every day. Rico, let's not mention this bastard! She was feeling feelings that were unexplainable! Why is her brother keeping all these secrets from her? He knew that she was a strong woman and that she could handle taking bad news. She would have dealt with these secrets. Why would Allen keep this secret from her?

"Ailese, please, I'm sorry. Please forgive me. I wanted to tell you, I did, sis, Allen said as he walked over to Ailese to calm her down and hug her. Allen wanted Ailese to believe him. He wanted her to believe that he never meant to hurt her. Look at me, please, Ailese, there's more. Ailese's eyes filled with fear, as Allen gently stroked her face with the back of his hand. Allen saw the fear in his sister's eyes. The fear that he never wanted to see again, the fear that Rico put in her eyes. I got a call the other day. Allen hesitated. My friend at the police station called me, and he told me that he had kept the information about Rico from before, and he decided to do some searching again. Allen took Ailese's hand and put it in his. Ailese Rico is here, in Shelby." Ailese instantly felt sick to her stomach. "Allen, please I have to go. I need to get out of here!" Allen pulled Ailese to his chest and held her as she trembled.

Mya walked over to comfort Ailese and sat down next to her on the sofa.

"Ailese, please listen to your brother, okay? Please." Ailese shook her head. Mya handed Ailese a fresh cup of coffee. "Ailese, I don't know if your lives are in danger ... I went to the address that my police friend gave me, and the place was empty. I talked to some of the tenants that lived in the townhouses that Rico lived in, and they said that he was only there for a few months, and the manager told me that one day he just up and left and that he always paid his rent on time and never gave her any problems."

Ailese looked at Mya. She still had that fear in her eyes. Mya comforted Ailese.

Allen and Mya did what they could to reassure Ailese that it was going to be okay. Could Rico be right under their noses? Could she have passed him on a busy street? Most of all, did he know where she lived? All these questions raced through her head. Allen told Ailese that Rico may have gone back to wherever he came from and decided not to follow through on his plan to hurt her, and that maybe he got scared. Ailese didn't know what to believe anymore.

"Andrew, please come and get me, please." Ailese began to sob. "My love, please tell me what's wrong? Are you getting those calls again?"

Ailese couldn't answer Andrew's question. She was still shaken up by her brother's horrifying news. She tried calling Mikell, but his cell went straight to voice mail, so she left a message. My love, Ailese, are you still there?"

"Yes," Ailese said, trying to hold back her tears. "I'm on my way. I will be right there, and you can tell me everything, okay?" "Okay, bye." Ailese must have double-checked all the doors and windows a hundred times until Andrew came.

"Andrew." Ailese couldn't hold back her tears anymore. She fell into Andrew's arms and sobbed. He held her tight and didn't say a word.

Ailese woke up in the guest room at Andrew's house. As she sat up and looked around the beautiful room, she knew why Andrew had put her in this very room. It was her favorite room, and it made her smile. Ailese heard a knock on her door. "Come in," she said, yawning. "Are you decent, Ailese?"

"Yes, of course." "Hi, Andrew said, smiling at Ailese. He was already showered and dressed, wearing jeans and a blue and white striped polo shirt.

Hi, how are you feeling? Andrew said as he sat on the bed next to Ailese.

Ailese didn't know what to say, and she hoped that Andrew wouldn't think that she was crazy when she told him what her brother told her about Rico.

I think we need to talk, my love. You were so upset last night that it took me a long time to calm you down. I guess your brother upset you." Andrew said as he gave Ailese a quick look. "Andrew, I don't know what to do about this. I just don't," Ailese said as she gave him a puzzled look.

"I'll tell you what you're not going to do. You're not going to let this punk scare you, okay? You've worked to damn hard to get to where you are, and you know that—hell, I know that. This fucking bastard better hope that he is not in my town starting shit," Andrew said, heatedly. "Andrew, watch it," Ailese said as she covered his mouth up with her hand. "I'm sorry, my love, but I am pissed off right now! Ailese, please keep in mind that your brother was only trying to protect you, and I do understand that he had to do what he had to do, so please don't be mad at him." "I know, but he lied to me for all these years, Andrew, Ailese said as she grabbed the other pillow and laid it on her lap.

Andrew, my brother, is responsible for what went down that night, and he didn't tell me about all the letters that he was getting from Rico and that he had been looking for him all this time. Now I know why my brother came down here so quickly." Ailese began to replay all the events that had happened in her head.

"I know that you hate to be lied to, but your brother only meant well, my love."

A knock at the door interrupted their conversation. "Come in," Ailese said.

It was Andrew's butler letting them know that breakfast was ready.

At breakfast, Ailese didn't speak much. She had a lot on her mind. She wondered why Mikell hadn't called her back yet. He did say that he may not get a lot of cell phone service at the camping site that they were at. Ailese needed Mikell more than ever, but Andrew was someone that she could count on. She knew that no matter what, he was going to be there for her and do whatever he had to do for her.

After breakfast, Ailese and Andrew took a walk on the property and talked. They stopped at the pool house, where there was privacy.

"Talk to me, Ailese, please." Ailese sat down in the chair that was across from Andrew. Ailese's eyes began to fill up with tears, -enormous tears. The thought of Rico coming back to hurt her scared her. "I don't want to die. I'm so scared, but I know that I have to be strong. I know I have to stay strong. Just when I thought that he was completely out of my life, he's back again!

Wow, I guess he wins, huh?" "No, no, stop it. Don't say that, my love.

I am here, Andrew said. I am here for you, my love, and I am not going to let you deal with this alone, okay?" Ailese couldn't stop thinking about all the times that Rico hurt her. The times when Rico beat her so badly that she still had scars to remind her. "You see this? Ailese pulled down her shirt to where her cleavage was showing. There was a mark on her chest.

Ailese pointed to the mark on her chest. "Yes, I see it." Andrew said, feeling a bit shy that, he'd never seen Ailese naked or walked in on her by accident for that matter. He had never seen anything he wasn't supposed to see. Even though Ailese had seen him in the nude when she had to bathe him when he had his accident, it didn't bother her. They promised each other that they would never tell anyone. They kept it a secret. "This scar is from Rico getting the hot iron and burning me with it, and do you know why he did this to me? Andrew walked over to her and held her. Because I was late coming home, but I wasn't. It was a Tuesday, and he had forgotten that I had to stay late at work every Tuesday, and Rico had forgotten. I have to see this scar every day," Ailese said, as

Andrew brought her closer to him. He whispered to her. "It's going to be alright," he said repeatedly.

"Hello. Mikell, I can barely hear you. Hello." "Ailese, can you hear me?"

They lost each other. The signal at the campsite was bad.

Mikell knew that he had to find a way to call Ailese because she needed him.

"Armont I need you to stay with your sisters, okay? I have to try and get a good signal or find a payphone. I need to speak with your mom." "Okay, Dad, is everything okay?" Armont asked in a concerned voice. "Yes, everything's fine." Mikell said as he put on his parka and gloves. "We will be fine, Dad. Go and do what you have to do." Mikell knew that Armont was responsible and that the girls would be safe until he got back.

An hour later, after Mikell tried several different areas to get a good signal, he found a little convenience store that had a payphone. He was very relieved that he could finally speak to his wife. "Hello, Sir. There was a man behind the counter reading a newspaper. Hello, how are you today?" "Mighty fine, the man said. What could I do for you today?" "Please tell me that payphone works, Mikell said as he pointed to the phone, and if you say yes, you've made my day." "It works, sir. Go right ahead and use it." "Thanks, Mikell said as he smiled at the man. He reached into this pocket, pulled out a bunch of quarters, and sat them down. He dialed Ailese's cell phone number and was happy to hear her voice. "Baby, it's me, are you okay? I'm worried about you.

All I could get out of your message was that Allen said that Rico may be in Shelby and that you might be in danger?" "Yes, that's right, Ailese said, hoping that Mikell wouldn't hear the nervousness in her voice. I will be okay, Mikell. I will. I'm at Andrew's, so I am safe," Ailese sighed. "Ailese, what's going on?

No, you're not safe if this mad bastard is out to hurt you, not even at Andrew's, where this son of a bitch may be following you. I want you to stay there until I get there. I'm on my way home." "No, Mikell I told you I was fine, and besides, we leave tomorrow for our trip, and for the last time, I am not going to let this person who calls himself a man ruin my damn vacation. Mikell, I won't!" "Ailese, please, I don't want anything to happen to you." When Andrew had walked into the room, he could see that she was upset, so he gestured to speak to Mikell. Ailese handed Andrew the phone and folded her arms.

"Hello, Mikell, it's Andrew, how are you?" "Not to good, man. But how are you?" "I'm fine, thanks.

Look, I don't mean to pry, but Ailese is really upset about this whole situation. She called me, and I picked her up. I asked her to stay with me here so we could leave together tomorrow. I can take care of her, and besides, she is safe here." "I know that I just want her to understand that I don't want this man to try and hurt her, you know. I'm just concerned. I don't think she is safe anywhere. Hell, no one's safe!" "No, I do understand that man. I wouldn't want anything to happen to her. Mikell, I really think that she needs to get away for a while." Andrew looked at Ailese, shaking her head and agreeing with him. Mikell knew how much this trip meant to his wife.

"Okay, I guess it's okay since you two are together and I wouldn't want to ruin your trip. I know how much you guys are looking forward to the trip. Anyway, can you please do me a favor?" "Sure, man, anything, you name it."

"Please watch over her if your life depended on it, and please don't let her go off anywhere alone. You're a great friend Andrew, I do feel like I can trust you." "Yes, you can, and don't worry, we'll call you just to check in."

When Ailese got back on the phone, she was still in a bit of a bad mood.

"Yeah, I'm here." "Baby, I love you, okay, and I will see you when you get home, okay?" "Okay, I love you too. "I'll be fine." "Baby, please hear me out for a second, okay? This Rico situation, cannot be ignored, and I believe that you leaving town is best for right now, best for both of us, stay safe. I love you. Now, I will be calling you from wherever and from whatever phone works, okay?"

When Mikell hung up the phone, a part of him still felt that he should have rained on Ailese's parade and told her that she couldn't go on the trip with Andrew, but a part of him put himself in her shoes. Mikell knew that Ailese would have gone on that vacation no matter what, and he knew how strong Ailese was. Mikell headed back to the campsite and prayed the whole way there that God would watch over Ailese, his family, and his loved ones. He couldn't ignore it, he had to call Officer Brown soon!

"Hey, do you want to watch a movie, my love?" "Sure, sounds good, just as long as it isn't a gory movie." "Deal," Andrew said, as he took Ailese's hand and led her to the entertainment room. When they walked in, Ailese smiled at Andrew. He had her favorite snacks already prepared for her. "Andrew, you're so sweet, you know that?" "Yeah, I miss that smile that I'm used to seeing," he said as he motioned for her to sit down. A few moments later, Andrew's cell phone rang. He looked at the caller ID and turned it off. "Aren't you gonna answer that, Andrew?" "No, this is our time, and besides, it was a business call, and I am officially on vacation, remember?" Ailese shook her head as she popped an M&M in her mouth. "So, what are we watching, Drew?"

"It's a surprise, you'll see." Andrew hit a button, the lights went dim, and the movie started. When the movie started, Ailese looked at Andrew with excitement, he hadn't forgotten what her favorite movie in the whole world was.

"Dirty Dancing, Oh my gosh, Drew, I haven't watched this in a long time." "Aw, there's that smile that I love."

"Thanks Andrew." Ailese hugged him tight and laid her head gently on his chest. Andrew hugged her tight. He loved the smell of her hair. It always smelled like berries. Her hair reminded him of a good -smelling Concord grape wine. When Ailese pulled away from him, Andrew tilted her chin up and told her that she was going to be okay and that she should call her brother and work things out, and if she didn't want to sleep alone, he would sleep in her room with her. Andrew knew that under all that toughness, Ailese still had that dependent side of her tucked away, but he could still see it, and he was fine with that. He never once thought it was weakness. He knew what she had been through, a lot in her life, and that he wasn't fond of anyone hurting her and getting away with it. Ailese saw Andrew as a lifesaver because he was always there for her, no matter what. Ailese felt so safe with him, kind of like her protector, even though her husband was her protector too, and she had always felt safe with him. She had two men that she felt the same about.

Ailese had to wake up very early. She had to go by the studio before leaving for her trip. "Sedrick, let's do the last part over one more time." "Okay, sure."

They rehearsed the last song, went over a few more details for the concert, and did a few dress rehearsals. Bry was so pleased with Sedrick and Ailese. They work great together and fit like a hand in a glove.

"Hey, Ailese, could I speak to you for a minute, please?" "Sure Bry," Ailese said as she followed Bry to his office, as Sedrick started practicing his solo.

"Ailese, I just wanted to tell you that you are doing a great job, and like I always say, you always make my job easier. You never come in here like a diva with an attitude, and I love your spirit and you make me smile."

"Thanks, Bry, that means a lot to me," Ailese said with a smile. "I don't know if you know this, but they want us to extend the concert because of all the great feedback, and it's up to me to tell them yes or no, and the only way I will tell them yes is if you could keep going on the tour with us. I know that you only signed for the summer and you have your family, and I know you've stressed that to us how important your family is to you and your job as well." In the same breath, Ailese was honored and taken back. "Well, why not? I mean, wait, I better talk it over with my husband and Mr. Saxx, my boss. I mean, I am sure that my job will still be there after the tour is over. How long do I have to give you an answer?" "Oh, a week, just let me know, okay? You are a great singer, Ailese, and don't be shocked if music managers want to sign you. You have what it takes to be a huge, huge star," Bry said as he winked at Ailese. "Thanks, Bry." Ailese hugged him, and he hugged her back.

As the concert replayed in her head, so did Bry's wish for her on the extended tour. She called Mikell to say hello to the kids before she got on the plane. "Where are you guys?" "We're almost to Disney Land. Hey, how did rehearsal go, baby?" "Great, and guess what? Bry wants me on the extended tour with Sedrick and the gang. Can you believe that?" "Yes, I can, baby. I have a confession to make. I already knew, but I wanted you to tell me, and whatever your decision is, there's no pressure, okay?" "Okay, I think I want to do it, Mikell.

What do you think?" "Go for it, baby, do it! I am so proud of you and so happy for you, baby. We're blessed." "We are. I love you, Mikell, thank you for always believing in me." "Baby, that's my job. The kids want to talk to their mom, and if they don't, they're going to kill their dad." "Hi, Mom it's Adrieana. I miss you so much but we're having so much fun with dad." "Oh, baby, I miss you guys like crazy. I can't wait until we're together again. I need your kisses and hugs." "Soon, Mom, I'll make sure I send plenty of pics to your cell phone, okay?" "Hi, Armont, hey guy, how are ya?" "Missing you, but I'm having a blast with dad. I love you, mom. See ya soon." "Hiiiiii, Mom, it's your kitten, meow, meow," Ashanee said excitedly. "Hi, kitten, what's up, huh?"

"Oh, well, right now I'm drawing you a picture, and Mom, I have been drawing you lots of pictures, okay?" "Sounds great, kitten. I love you."

As they got on the plane, Ailese felt a bit sad. She really missed her family a lot. She reached in her purse and pulled out their family portrait that they had taken recently. It always made her smile, and if she was ever having a bad day, her day turned into a good one just by looking at the picture. "You miss them, huh?" "Yeah, I do. They grow up so fast, you know?" "Yeah, I know, every time I see Dana, I'm like, man, did you grow a few more inches? Are you okay, my love?" "Yeah, I'm okay."

"You thirsty or anything?" "Actually, I am. Ailese got up to get a bottle of water, but Andrew stopped her and told her that he would get it for her.

So, where are we going first?" "Not telling you, as bad as I want to."

"Drew, please come on," Ailese said, pouting. "No, you called me Drew. That's another strike, Andrew grinned.

Ailese sit back and relax, okay? You deserve to enjoy yourself, and are you sure you're okay with taking this vacation considering all that's going on? I didn't pressure you, right?"

"Andrew I am okay, and I don't want to sound like a broken record. I am not going to worry about Rico or anything that has to do with him, and no one pressures me into doing anything I don't want to do, mister.

Oh, my heavens, this is so gorgeous. Where are we?" "We're in Springsville. Beautiful, huh?" "Yes, it's gorgeous, Andrew." Ailese took pictures of all the beautiful flowers and scenery. A few minutes later, a limousine picked up Ailese and Andrew." "Are you tired, Ailese?" "No, why?" "Driver, we want to go site- seeing, please." "Andrew, where's your other driver?" Ailese whispered. "Oh, I'm using their limousine service because they know everything about the town. Why?"

"Oh, I was wondering. That's all. Smart, very smart. Ailese looked out the window and snapped more pictures. Beautiful! I can't stop saying it!"

"I knew that you would love it here, my love, but you haven't seen nothin' yet."

"Wow, are you serious? I don't know why I never took a trip here."

A few hours later, they found themselves in a beautiful café. The café was three stories high and smelled like coffee and paradise. All of the women that worked at the café wore all white with colorful flowers in their hair; they looked like they just stepped out of a magazine. While you waited for your order to arrive, there was great entertainment. There was a band playing great music.

It was out of this world, there was nothing like this, back home. This was paradise.

"Come on, Andrew, let's tour the entire place, Ailese said, as she pulled Andrew's arm and followed her. I bet this place could hold like five hundred people or more, huh? It's huge. Look, Andrew, there's even an area for the kids to hang out. Oh, I need to bring the kids here. They would love it," Ailese said, as she glanced around again. "Yes, I know my love. See, I knew it! I knew that you would love this trip." Andrew was happy that the trip was going as planned. Although he felt bad about the events that had occurred before they left, he didn't want to interfere with her happiness right now. Ailese was safe with him. He was like an animal on the prowl, following Ailese like a puppy. He never let her out of his sight.

"Ailese, please let me." Andrew wanted to buy Ailese's items that she wanted to purchase at the café' and bring them back with her. She didn't want to make a fuss, so she accepted the offer. "Thanks Andrew," she said as he handed her the bag that had all of the items in it. "Andrew absently replied, Anytime, anytime." "Where are we going now?" "Can't tell you, remember?"

"Did you like that play?" "It was a great play. Who was that woman that you were so fond of?" "Oh, we go back, way back. Sorry, I tried to find you to introduce you two, but I couldn't find you. Where did you go?" "Oh, I was admiring the place, so I took a short tour, and then I went to the ladies room."

"My love, remember we need to stick together, okay?" Ailese shook her head, and said, "I'm sorry the excitement made my brain freeze." They both laughed.

"Oh, did you take pictures?" "Of course I had too." "Melinda and I went to summer camp together when we were kids, and because she was a chubby girl, she was teased a lot, and I well protected her, and we've been friends ever since."

"Chubby? She has the body of a goddess, Ailese said with a grin. She's gorgeous and a wonderful actress." "Yes, she is," Andrew said as he took Ailese's hand to cross the street. As the driver opened the door for Ailese and Andrew, a female voice called out to Andrew. It was Melinda.

"Hey, I was hoping that I would catch you," she said as she caught her breath. "Hey, I want to introduce you to my wonderful best friend in the whole world, Ailese LaShae. Ailese, this is Melinda Brewton." "Hello, nice to meet you," Melinda said as they shook hands. "You are a great actress. I really enjoyed the show. Ailese pulled out her program. Do you mind signing my program, please?" "I would be honored. Do you have a pen?" "Yes, I do. Here you go." Ailese handed Melinda a pen. "Anything in particular you want me to write?"

"Oh, it's up to you. Surprise me," Ailese said with a smile. "Here you go." Melinda handed the program back to Ailese. When she read what Melinda wrote, Ailese smiled. It read, To: Ailese, my dearest friend, thanks for coming out to support me. Let's do lunch sometime. Xoxoxo. Ailese looked at Melinda. She was a bit puzzled. She had just met her. "A friend of Andrew's is a friend of mine." Melinda said to Ailese. "Hey, were going to dinner. why don't you join us?"

"Are you sure, Andrew? I mean, I don't want to mess up any of your plans."

"Please join us, Ailese said eagerly. I would love to hear about your career and how you got started." "Okay, then, since you two are twisting my arm." They all laughed as they got into the limo.

"So, you were supposed to be a vet, and you ended up an actress. Wow, that's so bizarre." "Well, if I hadn't listened to my friend who told me that I should try out for this play in our home town, I know for a fact that I wouldn't be where

I am today, Melinda said, picking up the wineglass. I mean I really love it. I mean, how many nineteen-year-olds see Paris? I got to travel at a young age. Sometimes God has other plans for us and I don't get in his way, because whatever God has planned for me I know it's good."

"Amen to that, Andrew said. Let's make a toast. To happiness and friendship." "I like that," Melinda said. They talked, ate, and reminisced over dinner. Ailese really liked Melinda. "Hey, let's all share the dessert," Andrew suggested. "Okay, I'm in. What about you Melinda?" "Sure, why not? Just as long as it has chocolate chips in it, then I'm really in." "Okay, Andrew motioned for the waiter to approach the table. Yes, we would like the dessert menu, please."

"Sure, I will be right back with the dessert menu." A few moments later, the waiter came back with menus and gave everyone a dessert menu."

"Mmm ... everything on here sounds good," Andrew said.

They all decided on two warm chocolate chip cookies covered with vanilla ice cream. When the waiter came back with their dessert, they all savored the smell of the chocolate chips when the waiter placed their dessert on the table.

"Melinda, thanks so much for joining us, "Andrew said hugging her.

"Nice meeting you Melinda." Melinda hugged Ailese as well. "I can't wait to come and visit you guys, and don't forget to put me on the VIP list for the concert, okay?" "We won't, I promise. We'll see you then." "Melinda, let me make sure you get in okay." Andrew began walking behind Melinda as she led the way to her penthouse. When Ailese's cell phone began to ring, she picked it up and looked at the caller ID. It was Allen. She didn't really want to talk to her brother, but she answered the phone anyway. "Hello, hi." Ailese said in a dry voice. She wanted to forget all this mess and pretend like it never happened.

"Ailese I just called to check in on you. How are you doing?" "I'm fine." Ailese said, rolling her eyes. "Sis, please don't shut me out and don't be mad at me, okay? I did what I had to do, and I am truly, truly sorry for what I did." "I know Allen, I love you too, Ailese said somberly. I'm actually on vacation with Andrew. Hey, you did get a hold of sis, right?" "Yes, of course. I did talk to sis. Everything is fine. Sis is fine. I am staying here until everyone is back home. I just wanted to hear your voice and tell you that I love you." "I will call you soon, love you."

"Dad, you can't catch me if you tried." Adrieana couldn't stop giggling as she played the game with her dad. "Give your old man a break, Mikell said as he tried to catch his breath. Mikell looked at his watch, and it was almost time for dinner. Okay, guys, let's wash up for dinner. I'm thinking that we'll go down to the diner. How's that?" Armont picked up his baseball glove and said, "Yeah, that sounds good dad." They all walked inside the cabin to wash up for dinner.

"Come on, Ashanee. We need to really get that paint washed off your hands. Okay. Come on. Mikell took his daughter's hand and led her to the restroom.

Okay, guys, is everyone ready to go? The kids all agreed that they were ready to go. Wait, wait. Ashanee, where's your jacket? It's a bit chilly, and I don't think that you want to get sick while you're on vacation, do you?" "It's in the RV, Daddy. It is, I am sure." "Okay, are you sure? Okay, let's put on your jacket." "See, Dad, I told you it was here." "Okay, good girl, now put on your jacket, kitten."

After they all ate dinner, they decided to watch a few movies until everyone was tired. "Dad, I'm going to go in my room to work on my music, okay?"

"Okay, but no drums after hours, okay? Remember what we talked about."

"Yes, Dad, I know." Mikell watched Armont walk upstairs and disappear into his room. A few hours later, he had to carry Ashanee to bed, she had fallen asleep in his arms on the sofa, and Adrieana had fallen asleep under Mikell on the sofa as well. He gently shook Adrieana and whispered to her that it was time for bed. He tucked the girls in and kissed them good night.

The cabin was very quiet now. He looked at the time and it was late. As a result of missing Ailese so much and used to having her beside him, he wasn't sleeping much. He picked up his cell phone and called his wife, hoping that he didn't wake her. "Hello, Mikell I was just thinking about you, sweetie." "Are you having fun?" "Yes, I am having so much fun. Ailese whispered. Andrew was asleep in the next room. Due to his promise to Mikell that he would take care of her, he chose to sleep in her room, so they shared a suite.

You should see this place, baby. We need to all come here for a vacation really soon." "Yeah, I got those pictures you sent me, and I agree, they're beautiful. The place is beautiful." "Hey, are the kids asleep?" "Yeah, I just went and checked on Armont, and he was asleep too. He fell asleep with his face on his keyboard," Mikell laughed. "He did? Give them huge hugs for me and make sure they call me no matter what time it is, okay?" "Okay, I will. Hey, I love you." "I love you too." "Baby, one more thing before you go." "Sure, baby." "Please be careful, okay, and I hope you and Allen worked things out?" "Yes, and yes," Ailese said, yawning. "Okay, good. I just love you so much." "I know and I love you so very much.

Allen and I talked, and we're okay. It still kind of bugs me that he kept that from me." Ailese said as she went back to the day that her brother confessed to her.

"Baby, I do understand and I know how you feel, and you're entitled to feel that way, but he means well, sweetie." "I know my mom made him promise not to tell me about that secret, but those letters still give me chills and knowing Rico may be living in the same town as we do." "I know, baby. Trust me, I don't like it either. Hey, get some sleep. I don't want to ruin your vacation, Lee. We'll talk about this soon."

"No, please. I promise that I'll listen. Rico, please! You're hurting me. Stop it! Ailese begged Rico to stop hurting her. He had her in a headlock, and she couldn't breathe. He was upset because he had told her not to burn the food that he was cooking while he went to run an errand. She could feel her circulation being cut off, his hands were so huge, he was holding her neck as well, and she was struggling to breathe. Rico, she said in a whisper, she pried his fingers away from her neck. He had finally taken her out of the headlock he had her in.

"Clean up this fucking mess right now, you stupid fucking bitch! I ask you to do one thing. He pushed her into the kitchen. You can't even do that!" He pushed her head halfway into the hot pot that was on the stove and pulled her hair so hard that Ailese thought that he had pulled her hair out of her head.

After Ailese cleaned up the mess that was in the kitchen, Rico had ordered her to make dinner, and if dinner wasn't on the stove by the time he was finished watching his show on television, he told her that he would beat her again. Ailese tossed and turned. She couldn't control her dream, and she couldn't wake up. She moaned in her sleep. "Stop, stop!" She would chant it in her sleep. Andrew got up to check on her, and just as he was going to wake her up, Ailese let out a scream. "Help me, please!" Andrew rushed to her and tried

SHELBY LIES

to snap her back to reality, and when he did, she started to cry.

"I'm here. I'm right here. Shh, shh, it's okay. It was only a dream, that's all."

"I'm so sorry, Andrew, I'm so sorry," she cried even harder.

I'm so scared, Andrew. Please don't let him hurt me, please!"

"Never, my love, he's never going to hurt you."

Andrew ended up falling asleep next to her. Ailese had finally fallen back to sleep, right in his arms. He hated this, he hated this Rico bastard. How he wished he could get a hold of him and really make him disappear!

"Andrew I need to talk to you, please." "Okay, what's up?" "I do apologize for last night. Andrew interrupted Ailese, but she put her hand up to let him know that she wanted to and needed to speak to him. No, please listen to me, okay? I rarely let people know my real fears because it's a sign of weakness, and that I'm not, not anymore, and I know that I can't be brave all the time, and right now I'm not, she said, sipping her coffee. I can't lie to you. If you weren't here with me, I don't know if I could make it. Andrew took her hand. Sometimes I can control my dreams, and sometimes I can't. It's something that gets the better of me, sometimes I don't have them for a while, a day or two. I don't know if you want to deal with all this?" "Ailese, please, you should never question that, never and never apologize for it, my love, never. We've talked about this over and over again, and it's still the same. You're thinking that this will end our relationship, and it still remains the same my love. I won't let this end our relationship. I see that look in your eyes." Andrew lifted her chin. "What look?" "The look that you get when you feel like someone's judging you and you know that I'm not. You fear that a lot, don't you?" Ailese shook her head, stood up, walked to the kitchen area to get a drink of water.

Her hands were shaking. Andrew took the glass from her and poured her a drink of water from the refrigerator. "Here, drink this, Ailese. You're shaking. Come here." Ailese pulled away from Andrew, and she didn't know why she did that. She desperately wanted him to hold her, but she was still feeling embarrassed and shameful. She took a drink of her water, and sat the glass down on the counter, and began to cry again. "I'm sorry, Andrew. I didn't mean to … she paused. Andrew held her, and they didn't speak for a while. He let her get all of her frustrations out and let her get all of her crying out.

"Andrew sighed. "My love, this man has hurt you so much, so much that you feel like he's right there," he said to her, pointing at her head. I wish I could turn back time so that man could never have hurt you. Please, my love, I know that I must sound like a broken record, but please know that I am here for you, always, he whispered. If I had a magic wand, I would take all your pain away, Ailese. I would. That's how much I love you." Andrew looked at Ailese and studied her face. He will always feel like she was the most beautiful woman he had ever set his eyes on. Andrew walked over to her, and kissed her forehead, and led her back to her bed. "Andrew, stay with me, please?"

It was as if Ailese was begging Andrew to stay with her.

"Of course, my love. Come here." Andrew stroked Ailese's hair, and they both fell asleep.

"How are you feeling this morning?" Ailese smiled, shook her head, closed her eyes, and shrugged her shoulders. "I'll be okay. Thanks for staying with me." "Anytime, you know that." "I didn't want to ruin our vacation, so could I ask a favor of you?" "Anything, well, except wearing ladies' underwear and having sex with another man." While Andrew was trying to finish his sentence, Ailese threw a pillow at Andrew. They both started to laugh. "No, I'm serious, you butthead!

Could we not talk about last night, okay? Please, I just can't right now; I just want to focus on our vacation, okay? Speaking of vacation, let's get out of here!"

"Are you sure you're up to it, my love? I will understand if you're not. Andrew knew that he had to agree with that. He knew if he didn't, Ailese wouldn't enjoy the rest of her vacation. Okay, deal, so let's get dressed. I'm taking you to breakfast." "Okay, sounds great." "Ailese, please don't take forever cuz I am starvin' like a Marvin." Andrew said in a country voice, rubbing his belly. "Shut up, fool," Ailese said playfully as she ran to the bathroom to hop in the shower.

An hour later, they were at a restaurant called the Spoon Factory, where they served humongous flapjacks and the best fresh- squeezed orange juice in the world.

"Mumm, this is delicious, Andrew. I feel like I've just died and gone to heaven."

Andrew raised his eyebrows and agreed with her. "I thought that we would do a little shopping. Our driver will take us to some places that are known for shopping, and he says that it would take us most of the day to look at all the shops." Andrew grinned when he saw the look on Ailese's face, like she was a kid in a candy store. "You want me to get into a lot of trouble, huh? Andrew took a bite of his eggs and shook his head. Yes, you do. I know you do," Ailese said as she tapped his hand. "No, my love, I would never do that."

"I am so exhausted. Do we have time to rest before we start another adventure?" "Mmmm, yes we do," Andrew said as he looked at his watch.

"Well, I don't know about you, but I am going to take a long bubble bath. Just knock if I'm not out within an hour or so just to make sure I haven't gone to sleep." "Okay, have fun. I'm gonna watch some tele." Andrew watched Ailese disappear into the restroom and walked back into his room to give her some privacy. As he turned on the television, his cell phone started to ring. He looked at the caller ID. It was Melinda, and he wondered why she was calling.

"Yeah, later, okay, I can't talk right now," he said, whispering. He hung up his cell phone and went back to watching TV.

When an hour had gone by, he remembered what Ailese had said, to check on her after an hour had gone by, just to make sure that she didn't fall asleep. Andrew knocked on the door. "Hey, my love, are you okay in there?"

"Hey, yes, I'll be out soon. What time is it?" "Don't worry about it, you still have some time. I'm going to be in my room if you need me, okay?" "Okay, thanks."

Ailese knocked on Andrew's door, and when he opened it, he was in awe.

Ailese was a knockout, she had on one of the dresses that the sales rep suggested that she buy at one of the stores that they had gone to.

Her hair was in curls that flowed down her shoulders as she wore a purple spaghetti strap dress, gold jewelry, and gold heels with straps. "Wow, you look awesome, my love. That dress is really beautiful on you. It really makes a statement." "Well, thank you. I just wanted to tell you that I was ready." "Okay, give me ten minutes. and I will be ready." "Okay," Ailese said as she walked slowly away from the door.

She double checked herself before they left for dinner, and Andrew complimented her the whole way there. Tonight was a special night for them. They were going to the Cameri Room. It was a ballroom that served dinner and had great entertainment, and you had to be dressed to impress or you would not be getting into the Cameri Room. Andrew wore a purple bowtie with his tuxedo, unaware that it would match Ailese's gown. In the ballroom, he led her by the hand and all eyes were on them, and neither of them mind the attention at all.

They danced all night. They had a lot of energy. They only sat down when a woman who went by the name Mrs. Rose sang a few songs with the band.

Dinner was out of this world, and Ailese decided to have some wine. Having surprised Andrew, he joined her and had some wine as well.

A lot of men wanted to dance with Ailese. Andrew was a gentleman and didn't mind giving Ailese up for a few minutes, but he remained close by.

Some ladies were eyeing Andrew all night. Some were bold, asking him to dance, and some just gave him looks from across the room. They danced so much that their feet hurt, but that still didn't stop them. Ailese felt like she was in another world. She had been a lot of places, but this place that Andrew had taken her was not the same at all, and she was thankful that he had wanted to share his world with her.

"Oh my gosh, Andrew, I had so much fun. I had a lot of fun. Thank you so much for a wonderful night. I felt like Cinderella." "You're more beautiful than that Cinderella," Andrew grinned. "You're so sweet, too sweet." Ailese had fallen fast asleep in the limousine. When they had arrived at the hotel, he carried her up to her room, took off her shoes, and laid her on the bed. Ailese had woken up, got out of her clothes, and threw on her pajamas. She was a bit thirsty, so she went into the kitchen. On her way to the kitchen, she could hear Andrew's voice, but she didn't disturb him. She knew that he was probably talking to someone important at this hour. She finished her water and went back to bed. As she lay awake for a while, she began to replay how she felt at the ballroom. It was all still in her head. Just thinking about it made her smile. Then Ailese began to think about Mikell and the kids, and how much she missed them. She had wondered what they were doing right this minute- probably sleeping. It was already morning. She thought about Mikell's reaction when he would see the Cameri Room, and how she knew how much Mikell would love it there.

Ailese and Andrew had slept in until noon. They were both tired from the night before. When Ailese finally woke up and focused, she took a shower and got dressed. She didn't see Andrew come out of his room, so she didn't disturb him. Ailese decided to go for a walk, but first, she knew that she had better leave Andrew a note so he wouldn't worry. After she left the note on the fridge, she grabbed the hotel key and left. She walked down a couple of streets and saw an art store. She knew that she had to go in to find out what was inside. She had promised the girls that she would bring them back some gifts.

"Hello, ma'am, how can I help you?" "Oh, I'm just looking for right now, but thank you," Ailese smiled back at the woman. After she purchased her items, her cellphone rang. "Hello, sleepy head, you're finally awake, huh?"

"Hey, where are you? Mikell's going to kill me if he knew that I let you out of my sight," Andrew said sleepily. "I'm okay. I'm not too far from the hotel. I'm okay, really. I'm on my way back to the hotel. I did some damage. Hey, why don't you join me? I would love to go for a walk. It's so beautiful today." "Okay, stay there." "I'm at the Donna's Arts Store, just right up the way." "Okay, I'm leaving right now, my love. See you in a bit." Ailese hung up her phone and went back to looking around the store.

A few minutes later, she heard Andrew's voice. "Hi, okay, I'm here now," Andrew said as he hugged Ailese. "Andy, I told you that I was fine, really."

The clerk smiled at Ailese and Andrew, thinking that they were in a lover's quarrel. "I know, I know, but I made a promise to Mikell, and I am going to keep that promise, and besides, our driver is waiting for us outside, ready to take us where we need to go. Are you ready?" "Yes, let's go."

Ailese had done and seen so much on this vacation, -things that she had never done or seen, -she sometimes felt as if she were dreaming, and if she was dreaming, she didn't want anyone to wake her up. They ate at different places, and all the places were elegant, neat, expensive, beautiful, different, and brand new to Ailese. Andrew showed her everything. He didn't leave anything out. They would talk for hours about their day and what they had planned for the next day.

"Hey, Mikell, how are the kids?" "Oh, they're good, and what about you?"

"Oh, I am good hun. I am having sooo much fun," Ailese said excitedly. "I'm glad that you're having lots of fun, and you deserve it, baby."

"Have you talked to your sister lately?" "No, why?" "She says that she misses you; haven't you called her, hun?" "I'll call her today; I've been on vacation, Ailese said. I miss her too. I just thought that she would be busy with the twins and everything, and she told me that she was also going on location for a photo shoot, so I didn't want to bother her." "I know, baby, just give D a call, okay?" "Okay, love you."

"Well, hi, there, stranger, I almost forgot that I had a sister." "I'm sorry, hun, how's everything going?" "Oh, good, it's good. I've been keeping busy with work and all." "What's wrong, hun? I can tell there's something wrong, are you upset with me?" "No, sis, I just miss you, that's all." "D, it's me you're talking to, remember?

So, tell me what's wrong, hun?" "Nothing, really sis. I want you to enjoy your vacation." Ailese wasn't going to let D'Andra off the hook. She knew that there was something wrong, and she wanted to know. "D, are you there?" "Yes, sis, I'm here, D'Andra said hesitantly. "Please tell me, sis, what's wrong? Is it the twins, Chris?" D'Andra took a deep breath. "Um, I don't know how to tell you this, sis, but I've always been open and honest with you." "Hun, please hold on for one sec, okay?" "Okay. Ailese went to tell Andrew that she would have to pass on having cocktails with him. He told her that if she changed her mind, he would be in the lounge.

Ailese, this is really hard for me." "Take your time, sis. I'm here." "Okay, I don't know why all of a sudden I've been having these memories of my attack." Ailese immediately felt chills down her back; going back to that night was still painful. "Okay, I'm listening. Go ahead." "I'm remembering some things from that night, and they are a bit scary. I remember getting a phone call from someone; they told me that I needed to get down to my office and that someone had broken in and the silent alarm had gone off. Now, I've never heard this person's voice before, but I did what I was told, and I should not have gone alone. Looking back now, I know why I didn't ask this person any questions. It was because Chris and I had gotten into this huge fight and I was all pissed off, so I wasn't thinking straight. All I wanted to do was get away from him. So, I went to the office and now that I remember, there was an officer there, sis. This officer was built like someone I knew, someone that I have come into contact with, you know?" "Okay, like who?" "I can't be sure, but the more I think about that night and the more memories I have, I do think that the man was Officer Brown, and the reason why I know this is because I remember that voice.

You know when there's a distinct voice, like Dad's laugh, no one could match his laugh. It's the same thing about his voice, and all the dealings that we had with him. I couldn't forget that voice … or face."

All this shocked Ailese. She was so angry. "You mean Officer Brown had something to do with your disappearance that night?" "Maybe, sis, I've been trying to put things together, so I don't know if he was. He could be. I know that seeing Officer Brown was the last thing I remembered, and the next thing I knew, I was in the hospital. There's something else that I remember. I remembered a smell that was really strong, like chlorine or something, so I was thinking that someone must have knocked me out with some kind of chemical or something. The chemical was so strong that it made my memory all fuzzy. I can be wrong. I really don't know what made my memory all fuzzy, and maybe I am just rambling about nothing. I knew that I was in a lot of pain, and you know what? My doctor said something to me. He said that whoever hurt me was really strong and knew what he was doing so he wouldn't get caught. Remember that, sis?" "That's what Officer Brown said, too, and why does he always show up when we call the police? I thought he was always there because he was determined to catch this person who was trying to corrupt our family. D, if he had anything to do with all these mysteries that are going on. Oh my gosh. He's going to pay some way! I don't care if he's a damn cop or not! This pisses me off!"

"Ailese, what if? D'Andra paused. She was shaking, terrified at all these thoughts that were going through her mind. What if Officer Brown knows Rico, and they're working together? What if he and Rico are the two people that have been trying to hurt us and drive us crazy?" "I hope not, D. I really hope not." "Do you think it is possible? Everything that we've just talked about may be true?"

"Anything's possible these days."

After listening to her sister's confessions, Ailese needed to be around Andrew right now, and she hoped that he was still in the lounge having cocktails.

Trying to maintain her cool, she looked in the mirror and grabbed her purse and headed down to the lounge. When she spotted Andrew, he was on his cell phone. She walked over and sat next to him. He acknowledged her and put up one finger, letting her know that he would be a few more minutes on his call. Ailese ordered a Long Island Iced Tea and sipped it slowly. She couldn't get all these thoughts out of her head. They were still fresh.

"Sorry, my love, that was Ell. Andrew smiled. She wanted me to tell you hello."

"Oh, okay, hello back. Ailese said smiling. Andrew, I will be right back. I need to go to the ladies' room." "Okay, and when you get back, maybe you won't mind sharing with me what's on your mind, huh?" Ailese looked at Andrew. Her look was dismissal and regretful all at the same time. The regretful look was because she sometimes regretted letting Andrew know her- her as in Ailese LaShae, who she was inside and out, so she couldn't put anything past him.

"It's weird, huh?" "Yeah, it is. I want your permission to kick his ass, please."

"No, the law- or God, for that matter, has to handle Mr. Brown." Ailese said, rolling her eyes. It burned her, that, deep down inside, they may not have a case and the judicial system was a bunch of bull. "You mean to tell me that this fucker may have hurt D'Andra?" Andrew wanted to take back the curse word he'd just used, but it was too late. "Andrew, Ailese whispered, take it easy, okay?" "I can't okay. I'm sorry, he said, taking a sip of his drink, and shaking his head. I will understand if you want to cut the vacation short, my love." "No, no, everything will be taken care of when I get back, and besides, I made a promise to D'Andra that I wouldn't let all this ruin my vacation." Andrew took Ailese's hand. "My love, I would surely understand if you wanted to leave. Please, don't worry about the vacation. This will always be here, and I know that you want to be there for your family." "No, I'm okay." "Are you sure?" "Yes," Ailese said, as she was looking down. She was still kind of sad that anyone would want to hurt her and her family. They were good people, and had always treated people with respect. Andrew and Ailese stayed in the lounge for a few hours talking, and they decided to have dinner there as well. Ailese didn't feel like getting all dolled up tonight to go to a fancy place, and Andrew as always, understood.

"Ailese, what's wrong?" "I don't know. I think I drank too much. Could you help me up, please?" When Ailese stood up, she felt very dizzy. Her body felt heavy, and her head was pounding. Ailese massaged her temples and felt very sick, and every time she tried to stand up, her head hurt even worse. She thought that she had over done it with the alcohol and needed to go lie down, and she would be fine in the morning. "Come on, I got you. Just be careful."

When Ailese woke up, her hands were handcuffed to a bed. She couldn't speak or scream because there was tape on her mouth, and she couldn't see because her eyes were also covered with something. She was naked. Her feeling senses were present, and she could feel the breeze on her body, but she wasn't sure what had happened, had anyone stripped her clothes off? Ailese didn't know where she was. Was she in her hotel room? But what she did know was that she had to stay cool, calm, and collected, no matter what.

She knew this was not right. Not right at all. She was in trouble!

The more she tried to move, the more it hurt. The handcuffs were on her wrists tightly. Where was she? Who put her there? Why would someone do this to her? All these questions went through her head. She was scared. Not knowing scared her, and not knowing who placed her there and why scared her even more! A few moments later, she heard a door close, and felt a presence in the room where she was. A person was breathing and pacing on the floor. Ailese didn't want to make this person any more upset with her than they already were; they had to be furious and upset with her to put her here.

All of a sudden, someone clapped their hands in her ear and yelled at her to wake up! All she could do was moan. She could barely move.

The person began to laugh. She wished she could make out who this was, but her head was still pounding. "Wake up, sweetheart." The person gently shook the bed. Ailese didn't move. She couldn't speak either. Ailese heard the door close. "Quiet, you're just in time. I haven't even gotten to the good part, honey. Have a seat," the man said to the person that entered the room. "I never thought that this day would come; me seeing you helpless," the man grinned and laughed. The man got up from the bed and walked over to the person that was in the room. Ailese could hear them whispering. She could not make out what they were whispering about. How she wished she could. She began to wonder, where was Andrew?

Did these people hurt him too? She needed him more than she had ever needed him.

She could hear more noises in the room. She felt like she was going in and out of consciousness, her head was pounding like someone put a hammer to her head. She was in so much pain, but there was nothing she could do about it.

Her body began to shake. She was cold and scared, and all she could do was pray, pray, and pray. "Mmm… the man moaned in her ear. I've got plans for you and me, baby. Too bad I can't tell you." He touched her breasts, and she instantly knew what she had thought earlier was true. Her body was bare.

She felt his nails digging into her skin as he touched her whole body, and all she could do was moan despite her desire to scream! She could not scream if she wanted to. Her mouth wouldn't open! When he got down to her vagina, it was more painful. She could feel his fingers entering inside of her. He was rougher this time. She couldn't move her legs. She couldn't move anything. Why is he doing this to her? So many questions played over and over in her head.

It made her sick to her stomach to feel this person touching her. She was used to Mikell touching her body like this and only him! When she felt him come back up to her, she prayed that it was over, but she was wrong. He took off the tape that was on her mouth before she could scream. His hands were over her mouth.

"I forgot how good you felt, he moaned. Now, you better not scream when I take my hand off your mouth. If you do, I'll have to hurt you, okay?" Ailese wanted to scream so badly, but she knew if she did, he would hurt her, and there was no telling what he would do to her. This man had no sympathy, no heart. When he removed his hands from her mouth, she let out a long, deep breath. She began to cough. She was gasping for air. Ailese lay in this bed for hours as he continued to torture her and have his way with her. She hated him for this, even though she didn't know who this person was. As he got closer to her, she noticed a familiar smell; it was like an aftershave or cologne that she was used to smelling. He suddenly slapped her face so hard that her whole face throbbed, she sobbed in pain. "Let me get some of that," a voice said. "No, man, stick to the plan, okay?" "Well, I'm not just gonna sit here and watch you, and I can't partake," the voice said angrily. "Leave then, you fuckin' punk!" "Fine, I'll stay.

Let me touch those huge-ass titties, man, something." "No, no one touches her. Do you understand me? No one! She's mine! I want your ass to shut the fuck up! Ailese was still crying as one of them began to touch her breasts. He kissed her on the lips and tried to put his tongue down her throat. She began to squirm and sob. He put the tape back on her mouth.

Sit down right now before I blow your head off!" He began yelling at the other person, giving him orders and threats if he didn't cooperate and listen to him.

Listening to the men talk, Ailese could bet her life on it that one of the voices sounded like Officer Brown. She knew that voice anywhere. Was Officer Brown working with this man? Did he want to hurt her too?

Finally, the men left the room but came back shortly after. She heard them talking about feeding her and making sure she didn't try anything, like trying to get away. "Here, you need to eat something. He took the tape off of her mouth, but before he did, he reminded Ailese of the rules. She was not to scream or he would hurt her. He took off one of the cuffs from her right hand so she could eat and drink something, but he didn't take off what was covering her eyes. Here drink this." Whenever Ailese would chew or drink something, it was painful, she could taste her own blood that was coming from her mouth. She needed to go to the restroom badly. She was lucky when he took off her cuffs and walked her to the restroom. With him right next to her, she did not try anything like getting away. The man stayed in the bathroom while she did her business, so she couldn't try anything.

After she was done, he wiped her from front to back, helped her off the toilet, led her back to the bed, put the handcuffs back on her hands and feet, he put the tape back on her mouth.

Ailese still wondered if she would ever see her family again. And where was Andrew? Who were these people? Would she ever see her beautiful children's faces? She wanted to get out of there, wherever she was. She was helpless, and no one can help her now. Ailese all of a sudden felt this excruciating pain in her arm, and she let out a moan. It was him! He had given her a shot in her arm, and it stung like hell! Ailese started to feel weak, like she felt before. Her head was pounding, her eyes felt heavier than before, and she couldn't keep them open. When she woke up, she was horrified to see Andrew standing right over her, but something wasn't right. He wasn't right. His eyes had coldness to them, something she had never seen and never wanted to see again. She looked at him, and she knew that he could see the fear in her eyes, what was going through her mind, and how pissed off she was at him for not being there for her, for not keeping his promise to her and to Mikell for letting these men take her! Andrew didn't react to the fear in her eyes. His eyes looked colder and colder, like he didn't care about anything, -was this the same Andrew that loved her, cared for her, was her best friend? Someone that she could always count on, -was this the same person that made a fuss over her and would never let anyone hurt her?

Even though she wasn't all there, she knew that this was not the same Andrew that she had grown to love and respect, the same Andrew that held her when she had those bad dreams and who would assure her that everything was going to be alright and that he would never leave her side.

"Hey, my love, how are you feeling? You may feel like shit, huh? Well, don't worry, it may wear off and it may not." Andrew grinned as he walked over to the window.

Ailese still couldn't speak. He hadn't removed the tape from her mouth, it was still there. The door swung open. It was hard for Ailese to tell who it was. A male was all that was known. When he spoke, it was Officer Brown! She knew it. D'Andra was right! Why would he pretend that he was working on the case when all along, he was the case and the problem? Ailese closed her eyes. She prayed and prayed that she would be protected and that someone would find her soon. "So, my love, Andrew said, as he walked over to her and sat down at the foot of the bed. You still love your Andy? Yeah, see, I had to find a way to make you pay for everything you put me through, he said in an annoyed voice. See, I had to plan it perfectly, so the story begins, and you'd better listen because I'm only gonna tell you this story once! Ailese didn't know what to think. Andrew betrayed her. She was in total dismay, betrayed, hurt. Why did he hate her so much? He tricked her, lied to her, and he did everything a friend should never do!

Why was Andrew so upset with her, and why would he want to hurt her?

She's only been good to him; all this just didn't make sense to her.

"See, my love, my plan had to work because I had a lot to lose if it didn't work, so I carefully planned my revenge. Andrew smiled like he had hit the jackpot.

It took careful, careful planning and lots of money. You're probably wondering how all this got started, huh? Well, one night I was leaving work to come home to you, but I never made it home that night. You wanna know why, huh! Andrew yelled. Andrew shook the bed until Ailese shook her head yes.

I'll tell you why," he said this as he took a seat next to her on the bed, and this time, he was really close to her. "Tell her ass why, boss," said Officer Brown as he cheered Andrew on. "Even though I should have killed the punks that did what they did to me that night, but I wanted you to suffer instead. They beat me. It was me against ten men. They outnumbered me. I fought those punks like a soldier, but they still got the best of me, and I will never forget what your brother said to me that night. He told me that he would kill me if I ever came back there, and no one would find my body because he would feed it to the sharks. I was out of ammo, and this soldier was down. They beat me some more when they put me in that car and took me somewhere. I was barely breathing. He told me that I better not ever show my face or else. I was beaten so badly. When some good Samaritan took me to a hospital and they found my wallet ... See, that's something that your brother who was supposed to be all smart and all, didn't take from me! Thank God! So they called my father, oh, this gets good. My father's old Mr. Saxx, surprising, huh? We did a good job keeping that a secret from everyone. My father he will do anything for me, anything. I was told that a woman found me, I was almost lifeless at some bus station, and took me to a private hospital that was nearby. Thank God for her, or I would have been dead!

The private hospital went with what I had on me, which was my wallet and a business card from a realtor that was very good friends with my dad, and they called my dad being that I was so smart to always carry info in my wallet. The hospital had told my dad that I had been in an accident and asked if he could come to where I was. When he came, he of course identified me as his son. Good old Dad! I was so badly beaten, and I do mean badly. It was bad, really bad, that when he got to the hospital, he couldn't recognize me, his son. The only reason he knew it was me was by my birthmark. Yeah, my birthmark. It's "original", he said, pointing to his left arm. Andrew had a birthmark that looked like spots that would be on a cheetah.

My dad was furious, and without my knowing it, he told the hospital to give me a new face, which they did. Yeah, they were good, huh? You'll be surprised at what money can buy. Andrew said. I changed my identity, even down to my name.

Ding, ding, does this ring a bell yet, huh?" Was Ailese dreaming? Was she going to wake up, and this would all be a nightmare, and everything would go back to normal? No, this was not a nightmare. This was her reality check.

Mr. Saxx was Andrew's dad; she couldn't believe her ears! She would have never put two and two together, but they didn't have the same last name, and from her recollection, they didn't look anything alike either. She trusted these men. She gave her all to these men, and why the hell would her boss, whom she had trusted for many, many years, betray her too?

"I was adopted by Mr. Saxx and his wife when I was five years old. My real parents hated me, and my momma, - well, not my real momma, the momma that has loved me since I was five- she wanted to give me a good life. See, no one knows this, but my father is married. He just won't let my mom get a divorce from him, and my mom has accepted it. Just as long as she can spend his money and live in the mansion, she's fine. So, my father gets to do whatever he wants to do, and my mom doesn't ask any questions. When my dad raved on about his new business associate, and yes, he spoke very highly of you. He told me that you were going to work for him, and he happened to tell me all of the details. How you lived in Shelby and you were married, smart, gorgeous, and how he wanted to have you in his bed, - yeah, he went on and on about you, until one day he told me your first name, and I was floored. I thought I was dreaming. I had looked for you for years, but I could never find you, even though you were using your married name. When my dad let me see a picture that you guys had taken at a Christmas party, I hit the jackpot, my love. I grabbed the chance of a lifetime to make you pay for all my pain, losing everything that I worked hard for, and yeah, my dad has money, lots and lots of it, but I was my own person and wanted to stand on my own two feet, so I worked hard so I would never have to depend on my father's money, so I made sure I depended on me, on me only," Andrew said as he gave Ailese a quick look. He then hovered over her, and now he is straddling her. He slapped her face again, Ailese moaned. She was silently screaming inside, but no one could hear her. Officer Brown looked on as if he were watching a movie; this excited him. He would give her looks like he wanted her all to himself, and Ailese hated that, but not more than she hated being betrayed by Andrew. She had overlooked Officer Brown, even though he had betrayed her as well. He made her think that he was going to find the person or persons that were responsible for all the weird things that had happened to her family, but no, he was working for Andrew, going against everything a police officer stood for. Ailese put her trust in Andrew, and that was very hard to do. She had given him a chance, and now he has her tied to a bed and helpless.

"Hey, go and do that thing I told you to do, man." Andrew said as he demanded of Officer Brown. "Okay, man, I'll be back later." After he left, Andrew started where he left off, telling his story. Ailese remained calm. "So, like I was saying before, my dad had a lot to do with me finding you. If he'd never shown me that picture of you, we wouldn't be here. I had to change my name to Andrew, move away, and get a whole new identity because of you and your family. I had to reclaim my life and get my revenge on you. I'm going to make your life a living hell! A living hell that you will wish you were in hell and not here!

Just when Ailese thought that he would never remove the tape from her mouth, he actually did, and once again he reminded her of his rules or else! Bit by bit, it came to her- this was Rico! The man who had abused her for all those years! "Yeah, it's me, and you've won a prize. Do you want your prize, my love?" Ailese couldn't speak. Now that she could, she was so speechless! She needed to think of a way to get out of there before things got any worse! This was Rico, but now he went by Andrew. Rico was the key word: crazy. He was crazy, deranged, and heartless. She knew that he was angry with her, and she knew that it would be a matter of time before he tortured her or, even worse, killed her!

"Andrew, she whispered. I understand that you want your revenge, but please, please think about my kids, please. Andrew didn't respond to her. I don't know what I did to you; I don't know, and whatever you think I did, I am very sorry. Please let me go, please." "You hurt me! Dr. Lewis wouldn't cooperate, he said in a firm tone. He decided that he didn't want to help me anymore and he was really close to ruining everything, so I had to teach him a lesson, so I had someone kill him. I bet his wife is dying to know who killed him, Andrew said absently. No one will ever find out who did it, Andrew whispered. I won't hesitate on killing you if I have to." Andrew had something to do with Dr. Lewis's murder; he didn't care about his family, or how devastated they were not knowing the answers to their questions. He was so heartless! It was very hard for Ailese to hear that Andrew had something to do with her friend's death, and a part of her wanted to stab him right where it hurt-his heart, even though he wouldn't feel it being that he was so heartless.

"All those phone calls to your cell, clever, clever, you are so good, Andrew, ha! All of those events were caused by Andrew, but he failed to tell Ailese who was responsible. He was responsible for Alonda's break-in, and D'Andra's disappearance, and now, she is starting to remember what had happened that night. He was also responsible for all those crank calls, that Ailese had been getting for months. He had something to do with everything that went on. All the strange events that went on. He managed to keep his composure, and he never slipped up, not once, so Ailese, let alone anyone else, didn't suspect him of being involved in any of this.

"So, my love, once again, it took careful planning." Ailese interrupted him.

Why, Andrew?" She snapped at him, and then he put the tape back on.

"Looks like someone's trying to get feisty, he said. Taking this vacation was the perfect timing, for me to follow through with my plans. I don't feel bad betraying you or your family. I had to do what I had to do, and I needed someone to help me with that, so I met Ell. Ailese's eye brows furrowed when she had heard this- could this get any worse? Yeah, Ell, I know, huh? She played her part well, Andrew laughed. We met by accident. She was horny and so was I, so we hooked up. It was supposed to be a one-time thing until she told me where and who she worked for. I mean it had to be fate. My dad showing me the picture and me meeting Ell. It made my job a lot easier. Ell needed to get out of debt or she would be out on the street, so, I made her a proposition, and she accepted it.

Ell, oh my Ell, she is hot, though. I have to give it to her. She didn't leave out one detail about you. She told me how to get into your life, and she was right. If I went by her rules, I would have you eating out of my hand. I knew what would scare you. I even knew what buttons not to push." Ailese couldn't believe it; Ell also had a part in this that bitch! Ailese took up for her when no one would, and this is the thanks that she gets?

After Andrew confessed to everything, he had felt a sense of relief, and he didn't care what Ailese had thought of him anymore now that he had nothing to hide. He pulled back the sheets and straddled her again, and this time Ailese saw a familiar look that she hadn't seen in many, many years. It made her body jolt and sent chills up and down her whole body. She shook her head, as in telling him not to do this, a plea, but he ignored her pleading.

"Yeah, I think it's time for me to reclaim something that's mine." All of a sudden, Andrew was naked as he straddled her. Ailese was so scared. She knew that whatever she did was not going to stop him from raping her. He told her to shut up as she started to moan, and the tears flowed down her face. He placed his elbow on her neck so she wouldn't squirm so much. She could barely breathe with his elbow on her neck. She began to sob even more when he entered inside of her. He was so rough with her, that she couldn't take the pain. He raped her for hours and hours for his enjoyment. Afterward, he took her into the bathroom and let her wash up and change into some of her clothes. She could barely get

SHELBY LIES

dressed because she was shaking so much, and she felt lightheaded. Her whole body ached all over.

"Ailese, I've been calling you for days. Please call me back. It's your sister. I'm worried. Where are you? I can't get a hold of Ailese, and that's just not like her. She wouldn't let days and days go by without calling. I know her like the back of my hand. D'Andra hadn't heard from her sister in a couple of days, and she was due back from her vacation today. This really worried her.

Chris, have you spoken to Mikell since he's been back from vacation?"

"No, hun, I haven't. What's wrong?" "I haven't heard anything from Ailese in a couple of days, and I'm worried," D'Andra said in a frantic voice.

"That's not like her, and isn't she due back today?" "Yes, I'm worried, and I don't know what to do." "Okay, I'll call Mikell and talk with him and see what I can find out, okay?" D'Andra shook her head and hugged her husband. I'm sure she just lost track of time. Chris dialed Mikell's cell number. Hey, Mik. It's Chris. How are you and the gang?" "Hey buddy, we're okay. I just actually walked in the door. What's going on?" "Hey, my wife's a little worried because she hasn't heard from Lee. Have you heard from her?" "Oh yeah, Mikell sighed. I am so sorry. I forgot to tell you guys that she called me and she lost her phone somewhere. Please forgive me. I've been so busy and all. Tell D not to worry, and right now she's not able to get a hold of her because they're on a boat ride. They are going straight to the airport after the boat ride. They are supposed to fly back in Andrew's private plane and I'm sure she will call you when she gets home." "Okay, man, I appreciate it, and I'll let my wife know. Hey, are we still on for the gym next week?" "You know it."

"Hun, are you okay now?" "Yeah, thanks babe. I feel better now. I'll just wait until she comes home tonight. D'Andra leaned over to give Chris a kiss.

I worry and you know why, this whole Officer Brown situation has gotten me all weirded out." "I know, baby, you don't have to explain," Chris said as he massaged her shoulders. "After I told her, D'Andra paused. I just don't want anything to happen to her. I don't want anything bad to happen to her." "Yeah, I know D, and hey, besides, she's in good hands. She's with Andrew and he will take care of her, that's no doubt." "Yeah, Andrew's a great guy, D'Andra said, shaking her head. When my sister comes home, we have a lot to sort out with this Officer Brown situation. I promised her that I would wait for her to deal with all this." As Chris pointed out, "I am this close to kicking his ass, so I can't wait until then."

"Chris, we've talked about this. I'm not sure what happened; my memory is coming back in bits and pieces, so we have to be careful about how we handle this, hun." Chris rolled his eyes and shook his head in agreement.

"Kids, it's time to go. We need to be on time meeting mom at the airport. Come on, let's go! Mikell was a bit irritated that the kids weren't ready when he had told them hours ago what time, they still insisted on making him run late. Seat belt guys, here we go." "Dad, can we buy mom some flowers at the gift shop?" Adrieana asked. "That sounds like a good idea, hun." Mikell smiled back at his daughter. Adrieana waited patiently as she held the bouquet of flowers in her hands. They all waited patiently for Ailese. Looking around at people greeting each other as they got off their planes became increasingly anxious, but Ailese was nowhere in sight.

There was no Andrew either, not even his private jet. This worried Mikell, and he didn't want the kids to panic. He told Armont to stay with his sisters as he went to find out what had happened to Ailese. "Hi, are those all the planes that were flying this evening, Miss?" "Why yes, but if you would give me a minute, let me double check, okay?" "Okay, great, thanks." Mikell waited patiently as the woman retrieved the information that he needed. The woman came back and told him that there was one plane that was delayed, and the name was Andrew McGee II. "Yes, yes, my wife was supposed to be on that plane this evening. Do you know what happened?" "I don't, sir; it just says here that the plane was supposed to land today, but it was delayed and it doesn't say anything else. I do apologize." "No, thanks for all your help." Mikell walked slowly as if he were waiting for the lady to call him back and tell him that she had made a mistake, but that didn't happen.

"Dad, where's Mom?" Armont asked as Mikell came back to where he had left him with the girls. Mikell didn't know how to break it to them that their mom wasn't anywhere to be found. Mikell threw up his hands at Armont and gave him a puzzled look. This wasn't like his wife, standing her family up like this, and he didn't know what the hell was going on. "Kids, mom's plane was delayed, so we will have to wait a little while longer," he told his kids, especially Adrieana, who was so excited to give her mother that bouquet of flowers. Mikell prayed that it would be soon.

He immediately got on the phone and called Andrew to find out what had happened and why the plane was not on time, but his cell phone went straight to voice mail, so Mikell left him a message, demanding that he call him back as soon as possible.

"Hey, D, are you busy?" "No, not at all. Hey, bro, what's up?"

"I just came from the airport, and there was no Ailese or Andrew to be found, and I don't know what happened to them either, so I left Andrew a message, and I'm waiting for him to get back to me." "Okay, well, maybe they got their days mixed up or they decided to stay longer and forgot to call, maybe? But Ailese is really good about keeping you informed of changes, that I know." "Yeah, I feel the same way. I just hope that is the case. I hope that she will call in any minute now. The kids are just sick about it."

"Why did you have me lie to my family like that? I hate you!" Andrew slapped Ailese across the face as hard as he could. Ailese couldn't fight back. She was still handcuffed to the bed. She spat in Andrew's face. This shocked him. He put up his hand as if he were going to slap her again, but he didn't. "Shut up! Don't you ever disrespect me like that again or else!" Andrew began unbuckling his belt, yanking it off and threatening her, saying that he would he would not hesitate to beat her with it. She remembered how much it hurt her when Rico would beat her with a belt. Ailese hated Andrew so much. She had never thought that she could ever hate anyone as much as she hated him. He had taken so much from her, and now here he is again as Andrew, but she still sees him as Rico. It didn't matter what he had done differently to himself, inside and out. He took so much from her, and now it's happening all over again. "Why did you have me lie to Mikell, huh? Tell me, you son of a bitch! Ailese became aggressive toward Andrew, but it didn't phase him at all. Andrew didn't answer her; instead, he gave her a grim look that said she had better calm down. "Let me go! "Let me go! Let me go!" Ailese said it over and over again, at the top of her lungs, and when she didn't stop, she found Andrew putting the tape back on her mouth so she would be quiet.

"Shut up, you hear me! No one's coming for you. No one's going to find you, so get over it!" After cutting off all her clothes, Andrew repeatedly raped her over and over again. Andrew made sure she couldn't fight back. No matter how much she would cry, moan, and sob and try to break free from the handcuffs that were on her wrists and ankles, he would love it when she would try and squirm so he would stop hurting her. He was so rough with her, like she was a rag doll, and her body became lifeless when she couldn't fight anymore. This time, he left her there. He would lie down beside her and hold her in his arms like they had just made love and they were lovers. All he cared about now was keeping her alive and torturing her, and making her pay for what she had done to him so long ago. He wanted her to feel his pain, and he was going to make sure she did, and he was going to make sure that his plan went accordingly. He didn't care about her family and loved ones. He didn't care about Mikell calling him every second and asking where his wife was. He was only focused on his revenge!

Ailese cried and cried. Andrew ignored her for a while. Then, all of a sudden, surprisingly, he had became somewhat sympathetic toward her. He wiped her tears from her face, and went to the restroom, and got a wet towel for her because he had knew how much she loved to feel a warm towel on her face when she was upset. "Now, I'm going to take the handcuffs off. Andrew paused and pulled something from the drawer, which was a handgun.

I don't want to have to hurt you with this, he said as he put the handgun to Ailese's breasts. I don't okay. I know that you're very smart, and I know that you won't try anything funny. Here." He gave her a warm washcloth. Ailese put it on her face and shut her eyes. When she opened them, she sat up on the bed and examined the room. She had never seen this room before, and it didn't look like a hotel either. Where was she? After all the time that had passed, she still didn't know where she was. She wondered if they were in another state or even another city. She began to examine her wrists; they were sore and red, and there was a huge imprint on her wrist. The cuffs were too tight.

As she motioned to Andrew that she needed to use the bathroom, she prayed he would let her go.

When she was in the bathtub, she could hear Andrew, who was sitting in a chair while she bathed. She hated that he watched her naked body. It made her sick every time he looked at her! He was talking to someone on his cell phone. She was so tired that she couldn't keep her eyes open enough to listen to his conversation. He let her bathe for two hours. During that time, she had some peace and quiet. She needed peace and quiet so she could think of ways to get out of there, but how? He was under her every second. She would be back in those chains, and no matter how much she tried to break away from the chains, she just couldn't, even with all her strength and determination!

Andrew made her lie to Mikell about losing her cell phone, and more than likely Andrew tossed it somewhere, -somewhere she couldn't find it.

She was sure that Mikell was worried by now, since she hadn't returned home on the day of her arrival. Maybe Mikell is trying to find her right now; she hoped and prayed he would, but those words that Andrew said to her couldn't stop playing in her head; he told her that no one would ever find her. Was that true?

"Hey, now this is what you're going to do, and you better do it, hear me?"

Ailese opened her eyes to see Andrew holding a cell phone in his hand, with a very serious look on his face. You're

SHELBY LIES

going to call Mikell and tell him that we decided to stay a while longer and that we're sorry that we made him worry and that we lost track of time. Put on your smiling face and get the job done. You better make sure he believes you and don't try anything funny." Andrew handed Ailese the cell phone and watched her like a hawk. Ailese gained her composure and prepared herself to be believable to Mikell and her family.

The phone began to ring. "Hello, Andrew?"

"Hey, baby, it's me. I'm using Andrew's phone. How are you?" Ailese gave a fake smile, but a believable smile. "Oh man, it's so good to hear your voice. What's going on, Lee? We went to the airport and you weren't there. We've all been worried about you, and not having your cell phone, so I called Andrew and left him a message. I've been waiting for him to get back with me," Mikell said in a calm voice.

"I know I am so, so, sorry, hun. I didn't mean to worry you. I didn't," Ailese said sadly. "I know, I know I love you, and we all miss you, Lee." "Not as much as I miss you and I love you so much," Ailese said as she swallowed, hoping that she wouldn't break down in the middle of the conversation. This ate her alive- having to lie to her husband and her family. "Hey, are you still there?"

"Yes, Mik, I'm still here. So, hey Mik, we're going to extend our vacation a little longer if that's okay?" Ailese prayed that it would be, and if not, then she would have to deal with Andrew's abuse. "Hey, I guess you guys are having way too much fun, huh?" "Yeah, we are. Do you mind baby?" "No, just do me a favor; please let us know what's going on, okay?" "I will. Hey, are the kids still up?"

"No, hun, sorry, they're already in bed. Just call them tomorrow, okay?"

"Okay, I will." Ailese prayed that Andrew would at least let her call her kids.

"Good job, baby. I knew you wouldn't let me down, Andrew said as he took the cell phone out of her hand. So, since you were so good, I guess I could reward you with something, huh?" Andrew was interrupted by a knock on the door. He went to answer it, it was Officer Brown. He had some bags in his hands and was complaining about something. Andrew came back into the room and took Ailese by the hand. She was still pretty weak, so she had to lean on him as he lead her to the kitchen. He sat her down in a chair across from Officer Brown, who looked at her like she was a piece of meat. Andrew sat her plate in front of her as he sat in the chair that was next to her. "You need to eat, Ailese," Andrew said, pointing to her plate. Ailese looked at her plate and then at Officer Brown and frowned. Officer Brown didn't look up from his plate to see her giving him dirty looks. Ailese didn't want to eat. For all she knew, the two men probably had put something in her drink, but she knew she had to take that chance, and she needed her strength.

Ailese felt like hell, and she was sure that she looked like hell. She hadn't groomed herself in a couple of days, and even though she took a bath, she still didn't feel like herself. Even though she was wearing her own clothes. Andrew didn't give her all of her stuff, like her face creams and all the necessities she needed to groom herself, and it wasn't something that she wanted to get used to either. "You need to eat, my love," Andrew said, as if they were still close- best friends, Ailese looked up at him and rolled her eyes.

He's full of shit, she said to herself. I want to kill him, and I hate him!

She was burning inside with anger. She wanted to hurt Andrew and Officer Brown. The one man, who took so much from her was controlling her yet again, and this did not sit well with her not one bit! No matter what she was going to do, whatever she had to do to get out of there and back to her family, that meant she had to stay alive!

"Okay, I'm off, Andrew said. This made Ailese look up from her plate. Where was he going? When she's done, you know what to do, right?" "Yeah, man, I'm the cop here, remember? Officer Brown said in a sarcastic voice. Make sure you're back here before my shift starts." "I got it. No worries. See you in a few." Andrew closed the door behind him. A few seconds later, Andrew came back. He looked at Ailese and grabbed her face, and kissed her hard on the lips. She pulled back from him and made a growling noise. "See you later, my love."

When Ailese was done eating, Officer Brown took her back into the room and he told her that he had the same rules that Andrew had. He pushed her on to the bed and took out his gun so she wouldn't get up and run. He handcuffed her to the bed, including her ankles as well. He put the tape back on her mouth and whispered in her ear, "Don't be scared. I won't hurt you."

Officer Brown was supposed to serve and protect. People are supposed to feel safe with him. People counted on him, and here he was playing the role of a -criminal, criminals that he was responsible for putting away. Ailese put her trust in him. She really thought that he was a genuine person and a good officer, but she was wrong. He's just like all the men in her life who let her down.

"I'm not sorry that Andrew put you here. Personally, I think you deserve to be right where you are. Man, the stories he told me, and what you did to him,- I think he's being a bit too nice if you ask me. Personally, if it were me, the minute that I found you, you would have been dead! Ailese didn't say anything. She couldn't. All she did was close her eyes. She wanted to give him an earful and tell him what she thought of him. He was nothing but a money- hungry punk! There was one thing that Officer Brown, had never seen, and that was her "I don't play" side. That was one side that no one liked to see, and if he had seen that side of her, he had better watch out! Man, Andrew's made me one rich son of a bitch; I was at the right place at the right time. I can say good-bye to this job, but I choose not to, because too many people rely on me." Really? People count on you, I really feel sorry for them, you sick son of a bitch!" Ailese said to herself. Ailese was tired of hearing his voice, so she closed her eyes and pretended to be at home with Mikell and the kids. She was making them breakfast and getting ready to go to work. Oh, how she missed them so much.

"I'm back now. You can go off to that so- called job of yours. I'll take it from here. I'll see you later." Officer Brown walked with Andrew to the front door as they talked amongst themselves. When Andrew came back into the room, he sat next to Ailese and took off her handcuffs and the tape that was on her mouth. She wondered why he had done this. Was he going to hurt her again?

Ailese still kept her cool, but deep down inside she was scared to death, and Andrew knew that she was. He knew that no matter how many therapy sessions she had had, Andrew could still scare the living crap out of her, no matter how strong she was, no matter how much she knew that she could stand up to him. He knew her way too well, and he knew he had her right where he wanted her, which was in the palm of his hands. Andrew's demeanor changed. He wasn't the same Andrew that always bended over backward for her, the person that held her hand when she needed that certain push, the person that she loved so much; she loved everything about him, and now he's this monster that she could never love. "It's time to call Mikell and your family, and I don't want any bullshit coming out of that mouth of yours, understand?"

"Yes, Ailese said in a hoarse voice. Before I do that, could I please have some water and I need to take my pills. I'm feeling light- headed, please?"

"You'll get all that later, after you've met my demands, and then I'll meet yours, got that?" Ailese didn't say anything at first. A few seconds went by. She took a deep breath before speaking. "No, I don't got that, okay? Now, I don't give a damn about your entire damn demands. You got it?" Ailese said this, forgetting about the gun that Andrew threatened her with, but she was tired of him treating her like a dog! In a flash, Andrew pinned her down, took the gun out of his jacket, and put it to her head. Ailese began to breathe heavily, this frightened her. She shook her head, her eyes pleading for her life, like it were her last days on earth. "You got it now, right?" "Yes, I do," she whispered. She was relieved once Andrew unpinned her. "Here, do what I told you to do! He yelled at her.

Now, that's my baby. Looks like everything is going my way, and it feels so good. Andrew grinned. Here, Andrew handed Ailese her grooming bag. She snatched it from his hand and took out her vitamins and pills. After washing them down with water, she felt a little better.

That night, Andrew slept right under Ailese. When she moved, he moved, and he kept the gun on the other side of him. Ailese thought about heading to the front door, but she couldn't. She was still chained to the bed. She could barely move. She shook Andrew, to wake him up, because she needed to go to the restroom. "What?" he whispered back to her. "I need to go to the restroom, now," she demanded.

"Okay, he said, and he set her free to go to the bathroom, and she wasn't surprised that he was one step behind her.

Why are you making faces?" "It hurts when I use the bathroom, and I don't know why. I'm really sore. Andrew, I may have a bladder infection or something. Could you please get me something for this?" "I know why you're sore. You know why? Ailese didn't say anything. She just wished he would give her privacy. Yeah, that's why you'll get used to me. I'll make sure of it."

Ailese hated him touching her. She hated it so much! The things that he would say to her as he whispered in her ear just sickened her. She wanted it all to stop, now!

A few days had already gone by, and Ailese missed her family more and more each day. She would picture their faces when Andrew would try and hurt her, or try to touch her. Picturing her family's faces got her through these days and nights. Each time she would call Mikell, each time, her heart would break. Lying to him, broke her down so low; she hated it so much. Here was Mikell thinking that she was on this adventure with her best friend. He had no clue because she was herself when she called him. She was with someone that they both trusted and for whom she grew to love, wanting to love him, her best friend for all the days of her life. It was what she needed. He came into her life at the right time, despite her reluctance to let him in, but she did, not knowing that this will happen- her ending up here. Hopefully Mikell will tell her to come home the next time she talks to him, but Mikell respected the person that she was. When Ailese wanted to do something, she was going to do it, like extend her vacation, or change her hair every week; it was her decision, no one else's. All she could think about was going home, how the kids needed her, how the twins must be growing so fast, or how she really didn't get to tell her brother that she loved him one last time after their disagreement. She wondered if Alonda and Don went off to Canada somewhere on one of their long sightseeing trips, and if they did, she would want to hear about their trip. Should she risk it all to try and get away, or should she play it out? These were the questions that went through her mind every second of the day. Yes, she was scared to die, but she would die fighting; that thought scared her. She knew that she was never promised tomorrow, but she didn't want to leave the earth in Andrew's hands.

Ailese could feel the wind on her face, but she couldn't see anything. She knew that she was in a car but didn't know where it was going. She could hear Andrew's voice, and she knew he was there because she could smell his aftershave. He sat her up and pulled her to him as he began to massage her hair, which was down and went past her shoulders. Andrew had finally let her groom herself after explaining to him that she could get lice if she didn't wash her hair, even though it was a little white lie. He let her wash, condition, blow dry, and even let her flat iron it as well.

"I love your hair like this, my love," he said as he stroked and took a sniff of her hair. He took the tape off her mouth slowly but gently, then he took the blindfold off. She didn't want to make any eye contact with him. It just disgusted her; his keeping her away from her family disgusted her. All the things he had done to her disgusted her! Andrew held her face, so that she had to look at him. He kissed her gently on her lips. Ailese didn't kiss him back, instead, she bit him on the lips. He slapped her and pushed her so hard that her body went all the way to where the door was. Ailese grinned. She didn't show him any fear this time. She just laughed at him. "Go ahead, hit me again. Give it your best shot, you punk!" "I don't think you're serious. I'm going to pretend that I didn't hear that." Andrew took a tissue, from the tissue box and wiped his mouth with it. He was bleeding from when Ailese bit him.

"You think you're the shit, huh? You're not. You wish you were! Ha! ha ha ha! Well, I have a news flash for you, boy. You're not the shit. Never have been and never will be," she laughed again. Andrew was getting angry, but he still remained calm. He didn't have to listen to this bull. Ailese began to show how she really felt about him, once again, forgetting that he had a gun and wouldn't think twice about hurting her, but she took that chance anyway, without thinking about the gun!

When the car had stopped, Andrew grabbed her and put the blindfold back on her eyes and the tape back on her mouth. He told her she'd better not try anything funny or else, and she knew that he was serious! He led her up some stairs carefully and slowly. Where were they going? Ailese was so tired of being in the dark, not knowing what the hell was going on, and being ordered around all the time.

Ailese didn't know that Andrew bought a lot of properties, some of which were still vacant, and trespassing was not permitted, so no one would know that Ailese was even there. "Andrew, where are we?" She snapped at him. Andrew looked up quickly from the glass that he was drinking out of and frowned at her. "We're somewhere safe, and that's all you need to know, my love. Here, watch some television while I get us something to eat." Ailese rolled her eyes at him. She didn't get the answer to her question, and she didn't like that at all. "I asked you a question, and I want an answer, Andrew, and I want it now," she said, folding her arms. "You do, huh?" Andrew said in a sarcastic voice as he opened the door and closed it behind him. A few minutes later, Officer Brown opened the door and closed it behind him.

"So, you're still keeping your head above water, huh? Ailese didn't respond to him, she sat back down on the sofa, stared at the walls, and didn't speak to him at all. Oh, so you want to play that game? Okay, I see. Officer Brown said, walking over to her as he stood in front of her. Ailese looked up at him and shook her head. You don't want me to tell Andrew that you weren't being nice to me, do you? He said this pointing at her. This didn't scare Ailese, not until Officer Brown grabbed her hair and dragged her into another room. She was kicking and screaming and trying to hold on to something, but she couldn't. His strength was greater than hers, even with all her might and muscle, he still was stronger than her. Just as he let go of her hair, he grabbed her from behind and put his arm around her neck. Don't move, you hear me? You stupid bitch! Ailese was able to hit him in the stomach with her elbow, but just as fast as she did that, he just as fast punched her in the face and then he threw her on the bed and said, I'm going to teach you a lesson. This is what happens, when you screw with the wrong person. You ain't nothing but a rich piece of ass to me, he said to her, as he took out his gun and put it to her head. You think you are all that, huh? Yeah, I know your type. You look down on people like me who have to work their asses off because we ain't born with a god damn silver spoon in our mouths. Well, I know what to do with bitches like you!" The nerve of him to say something like that to her, and it wasn't true. If only he knew. If anyone knew her, they would have known that she worked very hard, to get to where she was.

With her pinned against the bed, he was so heavy on her that she couldn't move, but she was damned if she let him. Ailese had something in mind for him when he kissed her on the lips, raping her was not an option. She bit him on his lip so hard that he screamed at the top of his lungs, and just when he was about to let her have it, the door flew open, and there stood Andrew, mad as hell. "Get the hell off of her!" Andrew pulled Officer Brown off of Ailese and pushed him into the wall. They began to argue.

Ailese could barely catch her breath. She got up and ran out the door as fast as she could, not knowing that Andrew was half a step behind her.

"Help, help! Ailese screamed and shouted her lungs out as Andrew unexpectedly grabbed her by the hair as she reached the door. "Come back here!" Ailese fought him, kicking him, and scratching him, but he still overpowered her.

She woke up when Andrew told her to get in the shower, unaware that he would join her. She couldn't make eye contact with him and did not want to. Her breasts would not show because she folded her arms to cover them up or faced the other way. Andrew would turn her body around to face him when she did, and he would look at her and touch her, and he would still come after her despite her crying or attempting to push him away. "Please don't do this," Andrew, she whispered, looking away from him and trying to focus on something else other than his naked body. She didn't want him to see her get weak again, but she was hurting so much inside, it was so hard to keep all her emotions together. The one person that she loved so much other than her family was hurting her. He was determined to bring her down at her lowest, and he was doing a damn good job of it. "Please, Andrew, don't do this. I am begging you. It's me. I'm still the same person that you met a long time ago, the same person that would do anything for you. It's me, Andrew, it's me, Ailese. She pleaded with him. She tried to make him remember who she was, not who she used to be. She was a different person, but Andrew wasn't. He tricked her into believing that he was a changed person.

Stop it! Let me go! Stop it! Andrew, please don't hurt me, please! Ailese cried. Help me, somebody!" She cried out, hoping that someone, or anyone would hear her. There was nothing that she could do. He had her shackled to the bed. She closed her eyes and screamed and screamed, even though, it made him more and more angry. She screamed until he put tape back on her mouth. Ailese opened her eyes and what she saw terrified her. Andrew had a knife in one hand, and a belt in the other. She was so scared, and no one could help her, and she's done all the pleading in the world. She didn't have any left!

"Shut up, be quiet. I don't want to have to use this, he said. His eyes were cold, absent, and devious, something no one would ever want to come across.

Keep quiet, and I won't hurt you," he said, slapping her across her face. He then began to whip her with the belt so hard, and as she screamed through the tape that was on her mouth, and anyone with a brain would know that this was killing her, killing her inside and out, but he didn't care. All he wanted was his revenge, and it felt good to him. Nothing else mattered. He intended to make her life a living hell, and he was succeeding.

"Yes, may I please have room number, um, 218, sir?" "Yes, just one moment, please." The man transferred the call to Ailese and Andrew's room, but there was no answer. This puzzled Mikell. He just had a bad feeling about something, but he couldn't pin it. "Maybe they're out, huh?" "Yeah, I'm sure that mom will call you back as soon as she gets the message," Armont said in a convincing voice. A few minutes later, Ailese called Mikell. It was very hard for her to keep lying to him like this. Andrew paid all the desk clerks and the staff a large sum of money to work for him. The man at the front desk called him to let him know that Mikell called for him.

Every time Andrew or Ailese would receive a call, Andrew knew about it. "Hey, hon, I was just trying to call you guy's room. Did you get my message?" "Yes, we just walked in. I miss you guys." "If you miss us so much, why don't you just cut your trip short and come home?" "I know, but I don't like to waste money, Mikell," she said, convincing him that was the real reason why she couldn't cut her trip short. "Okay, I understand. Baby, are you okay?" "Yes, I'm just a bit tired, that's all. How are my babies?" This made Ailese tear up, but she held her tears back. "They are getting so big. You should see them. I've been feeding them nothing but junk food." Mikell laughed. "Yeah, right. Can I please talk to them?"

"Hi, Mom, I miss you so much. When are you coming home?" "Soon, baby, soon. She couldn't promise Armont that she would be home. All she could say was soon, hoping that Andrew would come to his senses and let her go.

I love you so much. Hey, how's the music coming along?" "Really good, mom. I can't wait to put on another show for you." "That would be great.

Andrew motioned for her to cut the conversations short. Ailese ignored him, she needed this. Hi, kitten how are you, huh?" "Missing you, Mommy, come home. We miss you. It seems like you've been gone forever," Ashanee said in a sad voice. "Mom, it's Adrieana. I just wanted to tell you that I love you, and when you come home we all have a surprise for you, so please come home soon." Hearing all the pleas from the kids hurt Ailese; it hurt her heart so bad, even more than her whole body, which was filled with bruises cuts, and scars. Nothing could compare to the hurt that she felt right at this moment.

Ailese cried herself to sleep. She cried so hard that her eyes were so puffy from crying so much. Her body ached, and she was in so much pain that she couldn't endure it anymore, so she didn't have a choice but to ask Andrew to give her something for the pain when he woke up beside her the next morning. She soaked her body in a warm bath and took the painkillers, they helped some but not much. As the days went by, the harder Andrew made it harder for her to get through the days and the nights, and oh, how she prayed that he would let her go back home to her family and apologize for doing what he had done. There were times that he would overpower her and force himself on her, raping her over and over again. One day he raped her, and she was bleeding a lot. He still wouldn't stop hurting her. He made her change the sheets, and with her being very weak, it made her move slowly, and that upset him, so he took the belt and hit her on the back with it. She screamed, and he told her to move faster. Ailese began to not look like herself. She wasn't herself. He had made her his slave, and that was part of his plan- to bring her down so low, to take everything away from her- Mikell, the kids, and D'Andra, her whole family. She had to come to terms that she may never see them again. It was too much to bear that she even thought about killing herself at one point, but what good would that do? It wouldn't solve anything, and it would be like giving up. Ailese had to be strong. She knew that she was a very strong person, but when it came down to Andrew, it was a different story.

"I'm so upset with Ailese mom. She goes on this trip and drops me like a hot pancake, and I don't like it. I think she lost her marbles or something, and just because I have two babies to take care of doesn't mean that I don't have time for her, you know?" "Don't feel bad, baby. I haven't heard from her either. I know that she's having fun, but she can at least check in with us and see how her nieces are doing." I know, it's just not like her. I hope that she's not having an affair with this Andrew character. I mean, I like Andrew and he's a great guy, but they've always been a little too close." "No, not at all, mom, and yes, they are really close, but that's it. I know that Ailese wouldn't cheat on Mikell. She loves him with all her heart and soul. They just renewed their vows." "Yes, I know it was just a hypothetical question or theory, I shall say. Maybe she just needs some time to herself." "I don't know mom, but I hope that she has a really good excuse for blowing us off."

"Hey, Chris, could I come over? I need to talk to you guys." "Sure, man, we're here. I'll see you when you get here. The babies are actually with Alonda, so this is a great time for us to catch up." "Okay, hey, is your wife there?" "Yeah, she's here." "Okay, I need to talk to both of you." When Mikell arrived at D and Chris's, they immediately knew that something was wrong. "Sit down, Mikell," Chris said as she handed him a soda. "Thanks man. I don't know how to tell you guys this, and you may think that I am crazy, but this is really bugging me."

"Okay, we're listening. What's going on, Mikell? Is it the girls or Armont?"

"Oh, no, Chris Mikell said, shaking his head. It's Ailese. Now, I'm not for sure, and I don't have any proof, but I think there's something going on with Ailese, and I think she's in trouble. I've been feeling like this, but I just can't pinpoint it, you know? I've been feeling really weird, especially about the whole Officer Brown thing, so I'm here to ask for your help. I need all the help that I can get. I need someone to go with me where Ailese is; I need to know if she's okay. I have to know for myself." "I agree, D'Andra said, shaking her head, and agreeing with Mikell. It's not like her not to call me or mom and dad or Allen, and losing her cell phone is a bunch of crap. She can't live without that damn phone. I know this, and I know my sister." "I'm in, Chris said, but I think Allen, you, and I should go down there just in case anything jumps off, and I don't want D'Andra to get hurt." "But I need to come. I'll stay in the hotel room. I promise that I won't get in your way. Come on, guys." "Baby, I can't let you do that. I need you to be safe, here, the girl's need you baby." "Fine, D'Andra said, and she had a disappointing look on her face. Please be careful and keep me posted, guys." "We will," they all agreed. "I just have this feeling, and I can't explain it. I have this lump in my heart, and I can't seem to get rid of it, you know? I feel that we need to check on Ailese. Something's just not right. I know that she's her own person, but I know that she wouldn't want to stay away from us this long; she would go crazy. I remember when we went to San Francisco, and she was ready to go home before we even arrived there because she was missing the kids. I hope she's okay. I really do." "Me too, and I agree with you. I guess I never took a step back and really noticed that my sister hasn't been herself, and I just thought that she was being a bit selfish for once in her life, and I didn't pay any attention to her not wanting to come home because I haven't spoken to her much since she left to go on this trip with Andrew. I feel pretty bad not catching any of this," D'Andra said, looking down and feeling sorry for herself. "Hey, hey, Chris hugged his wife. Don't feel bad."

"I will be there at the airport in twenty minutes. I will see you then. Let's meet up at the main entrance so we can all stay together." "Alright, sounds good. Chris and I are on our way right now." Twenty minutes later, Chris, Allen, and Mikell found themselves at the airport, and ready to fly to Springville. They talked on the airplane and agreed that they would stop, and take showers, rest a bit when they arrived. They decided to start their investigation as soon as possible. The sooner the better. They checked into the hotel. The hotel that Ailese and Andrew were staying in was booked up any way, but they really didn't want to draw too much attention. Besides, the guys wanted to surprise old Andrew. They wanted to catch him off guard.

"Okay, let's rent a car and head over to the hotel that Ailese is staying at, guys."

"Sounds good," Allen said, as he gave the clerk his credit card to pay for the rental car. They arrived at the hotel where Ailese and Andrew were staying a half hour later. "Wow, nice. I bet this is a twenty-star hotel, huh, guys? I've been in really nice, expensive hotels, but none like this one." Chris was in awe over how beautiful the hotel was. Allen and Mikell teased Chris; he looked like he was a kid in a candy store. "Hello, I am looking for my wife. Mikell handed a picture of Ailese to the desk clerk, hoping that she would be able to help him out. I hope that you can help me. Have you seen her?" The desk clerk studied the picture. "Yes, I've seen her. Are you a cop or something? What's going on?" "Oh, no, I guess you didn't hear me. I am her husband, and this is my wife." Mikell said, pointing to the picture of his wife. "Oh right, I'm sorry. Please forgive me. I did hear you say that, sir. How can I help?"

"Well, can you tell me if she's registered here?" "What's her name?"

"Ailese LaShae, but it may be under Andrew McGee." "Let's see here. Give me one second, sir. Mikell just smiled at the desk clerk and waited patiently.

The desk clerk knew that she couldn't have Mikell suspecting anything, so she played it cool. Yes, they are staying here, but that's all the info that I can give you." "Okay good. Now what I need is for someone to open the room for me, so I can make sure my wife is alright please." "I am sorry, sir, but we can't do that. It's against the company's policy sorry. You can leave a message if you like, and I can make sure that your wife gets it," she said, handing Mikell a piece of paper and a pen, and he handed the pen and paper back to her. "Your policy, Mikell said, clenching his teeth. Right now, your policy means nothing to me. l, Mikell paused. Now look, I think that my wife is in danger, and I have to see if she's okay. That's all I am asking. Mikell was trying really hard not to get upset and he knew that he needed to stay calm.

Mikell took a deep breath and closed his eyes for a second to gather his thoughts. Mikell shook his head. Look, I'm going to say it again. My wife may be in danger, Miss, and I need you to give me the key or I will bring in the authorities if I have to, Mikell said in a calm voice. Give me the key or I will bring in the authorities if I have too, Mikell said in a calm voice. Mikell looked at Allen and Chris in disbelief. He couldn't believe that this person didn't give a damn!

I need your manager please, right now, Miss." "My manager is on her lunch break right now, sir," the clerk enunciated, giving Mikell a nasty look. She kept saying it is not the hotel's policy, leave a message, did she not understand the seriousness of the situation, or was she just dumb? She would turn up her nose at them when they became more and more demanding. "Miss, tell me when will your manager will be back from her break?" "In an hour, sir." "That's not going to work for me, Miss. I need someone right now," Mikell said, pointing his finger at the desk. "I'm sorry, sir, but like I said earlier, if you wouldn't mind putting your info on this paper, the clerk pointed to the notepad that was in front of her. I will make sure that my manger gets back to you as soon as possible." "Listen to me. I don't think you're really listening to me. My wife may be hurt, or even worse, and I need to know if she's okay." The clerk just shook her head and said nothing because she knew that whatever she said, Mikell wasn't going to give up. "Give me a sec, okay, sir?" "Sure.

Why not?" Mikell said in a cynical voice. "This is crazy man. Chris stated to Mikell and Allen. I think we're gonna need that favor, Mik." The men remained patient as the clerk kept them waiting for over fifteen minutes. This time there was another clerk, not the young lady from before. A thin, tall older man came to assist them. "Excuse me, where is the person that we were speaking to earlier?" "She had to handle something else, so I see that you needed to get into your wife's room, huh? The man kept tapping his pen on the desk as he spoke to Mikell. Well, we can't help you with that, sir. Is there anything else that I can help you with?" "You know what? I don't need this. Come on guys." Mikell had had enough of the running around that they were giving him at the hotel, so he knew that he needed that favor right away and fast!

"The nerve of those people, to have the audacity, um, they're supposed to be a what, five- or ten-star hotel. Let's rate it a zero!" "I know Chris. Please remind me not to ever stay there, Allen said. My sister may be in danger, and these assholes are becoming even bigger assholes. I'm so irritated right now."

An hour later, they arrived back at their hotel to talk about Plan B.

"I'm on the phone. What's up Chris?" "Oh, it can wait," Chris said, closing the door behind him. "Are you sure?" Chris shook his head.

A few minutes went by, and Mikell had some great news to share with the guys. "Hey guys, the favor is a go."

"These cuffs are making my wrists bleed, Andrew. Please loosen them. I'm asking you nicely." "No, do you really think I'm that stupid, huh? Andrew yelled. I'm going to make sure that you can't try anything else like you did earlier. Hell no! I don't care if you bleed. Hell, bleed to death, then I wouldn't have to kill you myself." Andrew looked Ailese in her eyes and walked away from her. This is the man who would let a spider go free if it was in his house; when Dana would get an owie, he could make it all better. He was so sensitive.

Now he's this raging bull that's out of the cage, and no one was going to stop him, and he was not going to go back to that cage either.

"You do your job, you hear me? You better do what I pay you guys to do. I don't care. Do you really think I care about that? Handle it!" Andrew pressed the button on his cell like madman. The workers at the hotel were trying to back out of the plan, being that Mikell was persistent on finding his wife, but the workers were running out of things to say and running out of lies to make up to tell Mikell. Mikell would show up there every day, and every day he would ask for the same thing to open Ailese's room, but they still would not meet his demands. Mikell didn't bring the police in, not just yet, but he had a great plan, and soon that plan will be put into motion.

"Why must you do this? Please, I miss my family, and I know that they're worried sick by now. Just let me go please. I know that you don't want to go to prison for the rest of your life, so do the right thing." Just as Ailese said this, Andrew took a blow to her face. She never saw it coming. He beat her for hours. He beat her with his fists, leaving her to feel the pain. Every time he would beat her, it would be either with his fists or an open hand. He even kicked her a few times, leaving her to experience every bit of pain and then some- every taste of her blood, every blow that he took to her. Ailese was reliving her nightmare- the nightmare, the nightmare that she never ever wanted to relive again! He loved that she was hopeless and helpless. He really enjoyed seeing her in pain, beckoning to his every command, and he felt like no one could take this power away from him.

"Oh my God, man, what did you do to her? She doesn't look good man. Is she still alive?" Officer Brown asked. Andrew didn't respond. Ailese just moaned and sobbed. She would rather have labor pains any day than the pain she was in right now. She could feel blood coming from every part of her body, even her nose. The blood would go down to her mouth, and she wouldn't have any choice but to lick it from her lips. Is he going to make her lay there like this? Was he going to clean her up? Ailese had to prepare herself when she was able to look into the mirror. She had already known that her face and her body were in really bad shape. Andrew would always take his fists to her face because he knew that her face meant a lot to her, and he hated it when other men would look at her. Her beauty and self-esteem were being taken, and when he was done, she wouldn't have a pot to piss in! "Man, you better get her to a hospital or something, because, man, she's losing a lot of blood here."

"Man, just shut up and go and get me a first aid kit and whatever else you think we need, "Andrew said as he handed Officer Brown some money.

"I'll be back as fast as I can," closing the door behind him.

Andrew didn't want her dead-not just yet. He still wasn't done with her or his plans! Anyone would think that all the things that he had done to her would be enough and then some, but not for him, he was just getting started!

As he went back into the room where Ailese was, he could hear her moaning even before he opened the door. "I want you to shut up! Shut up, goddamn it!

I need to think!" Andrew massaged his temples; he had a bigger problem on his hands now. His father, Mr. Saxx, was upset that his son wasn't returning his calls, so he flew down to where Andrew was, and the crew at the hotel had told Andrew that his father was looking for him, and luckily he wasn't staying in the same hotel that he had stayed in. What could he say to his father? He was due to arrive back in Shelby some time ago. He couldn't lie to him, he would see right through Andrew. What, what should I do? Andrew told himself. He took a deep breath and cleared his head. He looked at the time on his watch and thought that Officer Brown had been gone for a while now and wondered what was taking him so long. He knew that his father would be determined to find him, and he had no idea that Andrew had bought a lot of private properties in the area, which meant that no one was allowed on the property unless you were the owner. Andrew knew what he was doing; he had worked too damn hard to mess this up now.

"Double check to make sure we have everything, please." "Okay, I got the checklist ready." "Yes, we have everything that's on the checklist, Chris said.

I just hope that we can count that favor in as well." "Sure, man, I'm positive that we can. No worries, alright? Now, let's go to the airport, and we'd better leave now if we want to get there on time." Allen, Chris, and Mikell loaded the car and headed to the airport. They were all anxious to get things started and get Ailese home safely. When they arrived at the airport, Mikell was relieved when his friend walked through the terminal. "Hello, man, I can't thank you enough. Let me introduce you to my brother-in-laws. This is Allen and Chris. I'd like you to meet Chief Jacob Kenion. He's a good friend of mine, and he's here to help us out." Allen and Chris shook Jacob's hand. Jacob introduced the men that he had brought along with him. Jacob didn't look like a chief, let alone in law enforcement. He had a face of an angel. Hs skin was the color of chestnuts, and his eyes were a forest green. Jacob stood tall and proud, and when he would speak, you just knew that a good family raised him; he was very respectful.

Jacob lived in Mikell's neighborhood, and they became good friends. They were inseparable until Jacob decided to join the Air Force. They wrote letters back and forth. Mikell even attended Jacob's graduation when he graduated from the academy. Jacob served four years in the Air Force before becoming a police chief. They had a very good relationship, but Jacob didn't have much time to hang out with Mikell because of his job and he lived in another state, their schedules never agreed, but they talked on the phone periodically, it was a brotherly relationship between them.

"I need to talk to you guys, Jacob said as he sat down on the sofa. On my way here, I found out some things that I think everyone needs to know. Jacob pulled out his brief case, sat it down on the table that was in front of him, and pulled out some files. I found out that Andrew McGee II, has a lot of properties out here. The problem is they're all private properties and there's no trespassing, so I'm going to be the one who will need to check all of these properties out, being that I have the authority to do so. Is that clear?

Everyone agreed with Jacob. Now my guys are on their way to the hotel that you believe your wife is in, and don't worry, I only work with the best, and I know that they will get the job done." "Thank you. I don't know how to repay you, Jacob. Thank you so much." "No problem, I can't wait until this scum is in prison and then I can rest. I'm glad you called, Jacob said, as he put his hands on Mikell's shoulders. I won't let you down." "I know you won't, I know."

Ailese was still in a lot of pain. Andrew was so busy trying to figure out how to avoid his father that he wasn't paying her any attention. He didn't care if she was still in pain. Even though Officer Brown had cleaned her wounds, bandaged her up, and gave her some aspirin for the pain, it still didn't help. Ailese had a strong feeling that something was broken. Every time she would breathe, her rib cage pulsated with so much pain. She needed to get to a hospital, but Andrew wouldn't hear of it, so she had to deal with the pain. She had no choice. Andrew's cell phone rang, "Hello, what do you mean? I'm not hearing you repeat that again." "There were law enforcements officials here, and we didn't have any choice but to do what was asked of us, Mr. McGee. Look, I am sorry, but we have to obey the law. I don't know why I ever let you talk me into letting my staff work for you. As of today, our services have expired, Mr. McGee."

"Oh, really, after I paid you damn good money, you're telling me that you're quitting. I will make sure that no one steps foot in that goddamn hotel. Do you hear me? You're done! Hello, hello! Andrew threw his phone on the bed. He was very angry. He looked at Ailese, who was terrified. She just knew that he was going to hurt her again, and she prayed that he wouldn't.

Get up and get yourself together," he said, taking the handcuffs off of her. Ailese needed help getting to the bathroom, but it hurt her to even talk, so she gestured to him that she needed help, but he just ignored her. Instead, he called Officer Brown into the room. Ailese didn't know that he was still there.

"Yeah, man, what's up? I was taking a nap," Officer Brown yawned. "There's no time for napping. I need for you to stay focused. That was the plan, remember?"

Officer Brown's eyes remained on her for a few seconds, remembering that she was a huge part of their plan. He saw how much pain she was in, how much pain Andrew put her in, and how much pain he put her in. I need you to help her get cleaned up. We need to leave here fast. Just as Officer Brown opened his mouth, Andrew cut him off. No questions, just do as I say and hurry up!

Ailese was so weak that Officer Brown had to literally carry her into the restroom so she could get cleaned up. Andrew had given her all the necessities that she needed. "Could you please ... Ailese paused. It hurt so much to even talk. Could you please clean my wounds? That's all I ask, please," she said whispering. He shook his head and began to clean her wounds.

"Please, you don't want to do this. Don't! Officer Brown began to touch Ailese's breasts. Part of her wanted to scream, but she didn't have the strength to do it, and she didn't want Andrew to get upset and hurt her again. "You need to do something for me now, baby," he whispered to her. Tears fell down her face as he touched every inch of her body. He whispered sweet nothings in her ear, telling her what he would do to her if she did scream and what he was going to do to her. Ailese was saved by the bell. Just when he tried to force himself on her, there was a knock at the door. It was a female voice.

"Hey, Andrew said to hurry up in there, she said as she continued to knock on the door. What the hell are you doing, Damon?" "Nothing. We'll be out in a second. I'm just helping her get dressed like the boss told me too, stay outta my business! This gave Ailese plenty of time to slip away from him. "You can consider yourself lucky this time, but I won't promise that you'll have any luck the next time," he said as he sloppily gave her a kiss on the mouth and shut the door behind him. Ailese knew that she had to move as fast as she could. She didn't want Officer Brown to come back for more. She got dressed best as she could and came out, and it was to her surprise to see Melinda standing there with her arms folded. What was she doing here? "You cleaned up nicely, for a battered -looking bitch, she smiled at Ailese. So, you're the bitch that's got my fucking man all roused up, huh? That's what I wanted to say to you the first day I met you! Mmmm ... You ain't all that, honey," she said, snapping her fingers in Ailese's face. Ailese was so surprised that she didn't even respond like she should have. If Ailese were "herself" Melinda would have heard an ear full, and her mouth would have been shut, and would have stayed shut when Ailese was done with her. What the hell is going on? Ailese wondered.

"Melinda, calm down, Officer Brown said. You know how Andrew is when it comes to her." "Don't remind me, Melinda said, clenching her teeth. Shut up. I don't want to hear what you gotta say." "Stop all the damn arguing, you two. Did you guys do what I asked?" They both shook their heads. "Yeah, baby, I did everything you asked me, and guess what?" "What? Andrew said as he kissed Melinda. "My sister is going to be here in a few hours." "Good, I knew that you wouldn't let me down." Ailese was trying to process everything. For starters, Andrew was not who he claimed to be all this time; he was Rico, the man who controlled her and made sure he had her under his thumb. Then there was Officer Brown, or Damon Brown. Was that his real name? He was this sweet person who was into his work, determined to get these thugs off the streets, and yet he was one of them! Now there's Melinda, she didn't know what to think of this, and Andrew would play this innocent game. The last relationship he was in, he had told her that he had loved this person so much and that it was hard for him to even want to get serious with anyone, and here he is practically married to Ell and Melinda. Where does she fit in, in all of this? Was Andrew playing Ell, was he in love with this Melinda person?

Melinda walked over to Ailese and made a smart comment to her. "So, this is, or shall I say was, my competition, huh, Andrew?" Ailese didn't respond to the comment. She was still trying to grasp everything. Why would she say that Ailese was her competition? As Ailese began to come a bit more focused, she realized something that she hadn't realized before: Melinda dressed like Ailese and somewhat carried herself like her as well, and most of all, besides the nasty things that came out of her mouth, Melinda also had her demeanor as well. When Ailese first met Melinda, she was so into getting her autograph that she really didn't study who she really was, but now she could see that they had some things in common. "You don't have anything to worry about baby. It's all good, and we're all good, Andrew said as he gave Ailese a quick look. Come on, Andrew said, helping Ailese out of the bed to stand to her feet. We've got to get outta here before shit hits the fan."

Ailese found herself blindfolded again. As she sat in the limo, all she could hear were voices. She could hear sirens and people outside. Ailese despised that damn blindfold. She couldn't see anything. She would just pray and thank God for her sight because she didn't know what she would do if she ever went blind. She didn't know who else was in the limo, but she knew for sure that Andrew and Officer Brown were in the limo, and she had wondered if Melinda was there. All these questions rushed through her head, and she hated not knowing. She hated being in the dark. Ailese missed her family, she needed them so much, but would she ever see them again?

Why was this happening to her? How could her past creep back into her life when it's been so long? How could this happen to her? She did everything right, or so she thought she did. She was going on a tour, a tour that would change her life! Ailese had so many people depending on her, and now she would have to live with the guilt of letting everyone down all on her own. She gave Andrew her heart and her soul. He told her that he would never ever hurt her no matter what, even though she gave him a tough time in the very beginning of their relationship, but she decided to give him a chance, and now he's holding her captive, taking her place to place, beating her, taking away everything that she had, and why? Because of what her family and friends of her brother's had put him through. Andrew was angry and bitter, and he decided to break her down, making her feel so low- lower than she had ever felt in her life- just like he made her feel when he hurt her.

Andrew played the game perfectly! His money talked, and he made sure that he walked the walk. He made sure that he'd picked the perfect people that would join him on his quest and that they would never back down no matter what. How did Andrew get to Ailese? How did he win her heart? He was very careful, very careful. He had some assistance. If Mr. Saxx, who is his father, had never shown him that picture of Ailese, he would have never figured out where she was. Andrew dreamed of this day for so long. Andrew would ask his father questions about Ailese in a casual conversation, and when his father asked why Andrew asked those questions, Andrew would reply that he just wanted to know things about Ailese since he was going to work with her. Mr. Saxx didn't raise a monster. He had no idea of Andrew's plans. Andrew had never shared a lot with his father. He loved him, and even though he always wanted to do things on his own, his father would always try and talk him into working with him. When he'd seen that picture of Ailese, Andrew pretended that he was ready to work with his father just to get close to her. Over time, Andrew had become very obsessed with hurting Ailese and wanting to be with her again, just the two of them, and he had gotten his wish when he had befriended her.

Now Ailese could hear Melinda's voice, and it sounded like she was very close to her. Ailese heard her talking to Andrew, and she could have sworn that they had mentioned Ell's name. She hoped that Andrew wasn't going to hurt her too, being that she and Ell were pretty close. A few minutes later, the car had made a stop. "I'll stay here with her while you go and get your sister, Andrew said this as Melinda kissed Andrew and got out of the car. Hey, make sure you park somewhere else so we don't get a ticket," Andrew told the driver.

Ailese didn't move or make a sound until Andrew rolled up the privacy window in the limo for privacy. Ailese was scared. Was he going to hurt her again? He picked her up and sat her next to him, and then he began kissing her on her neck, whispering to her not to move, so she didn't. Ailese hoped that it would be over soon, but she was wrong. Andrew told her to lay down, and in a matter of seconds she found him on top of her, and she began to weep, shaking her head and pleading with him not to hurt her. Andrew was so strong, he put her hands above her head and began lifting her shirt up and putting his hands all over her body. She wanted to scream, but she knew the routine: his routine: make him mad. He will slap her or punch her, and he had done so much damage to her that she knew that she couldn't take it, she just couldn't!

This was the first time that Ailese wanted someone to come back from somewhere, like Melinda, why she wasn't back yet? Maybe if she came back, Andrew would leave her alone, but there was no Melinda, it seemed like she had been gone for hours. Luckily, he didn't rape Ailese. He only touched her body, gone down her pants and had made his way into her underwear, touching her vagina and her breasts. He had let her up when he was done. "Don't be afraid, my love. I still love you, I've always loved you."

How dare he say that to me! She reflected to herself. How dare him! He doesn't love me. He doesn't give a damn about me! A part of Ailese wanted to scream at the top of her lungs for all the things that Andrew had done to her, keeping her against her will, but she remained calm. Anyone that had been in her position would have screamed, kicked Andrew in between his legs and run off and kept running, or even worse, found a weapon and cut Andrew with it!

So why hasn't Ailese tried doing all these things? For one, Andrew had always kept a gun or a weapon on him no matter what, and for two, he would overpower her, and she didn't have the strength to overpower him. Andrew was a very strong man. She had been lucky when she was able to overpower him, and that was only because he was caught off guard or he had a bit too much to drink.

"Looks like we're here, guys, yes, this is it. We're here," Chief Jacob said as he motioned for his guys to get into position. They had parked a couple of streets away just in case Andrew was on the property that they were at and to avoid any distractions. The men took their positions while Jacob and another man had their guns drawn as they walked slowly to the front door. The house looked vacant, but they wanted to make sure. Jacob knocked on the door. "Open up this is the police, he knocked a few more times, but there was no answer. He then motioned for the woman who had the keys to the property to open the door while all the other officers made sure she was safe. "I want you to open the door just a bit, he whispered to her. I'm right here. The woman shook her head. She was scared, but she opened the door just a tad bit, like Jacob told her too. One of the officers escorted her back to her car and made sure she was safe.

This is Chief Jacob. We have the property surrounded. As he's speaking, the other men surround all the rooms in the house. I have a warrant to search the premises. If there's anyone here, come out with your hands up now!"

Officer Jacob drew his gun at every angle that he covered, and there was no one inside or outside of the house. Officer Jacob and his men were a bit disappointed. He told some of his men to stay there just in case someone came back to that house and to notify him if someone did.

Although Andrew had been at that very same house early on, he made sure nothing was left behind. He made sure he covered his tracks 100 percent of the time, wiping everything down making sure he didn't leave any articles of clothing, hair, anything else behind. He even had maids come in to clean after he left and paid them a good sum of money to do it. "Hey, Mikell, it's Jacob. No luck at the first property, but we are not giving up, okay?"

"Thanks. I was sure that you would bust him there." "Yeah, me too, man. Don't worry, we'll find Ailese. I have some of my guys there at the property just in case anyone comes back there." "Jacob?" "Yeah, man?" "Thank you. I know that I keep telling you that." Jacob interrupted him. "We're brothers, and you'll do the same for me. I know that. Talk to you later."

"Okay, were here now, Melinda said as she opened the car door, and climbed inside. Come on girl, the driver will put your stuff in the trunk. We have to get moving we took up too much time as it is." Ailese could feel her staring at her, but Ailese didn't acknowledge Melinda. She wasn't worth her time. Andrew had finally taken off her blindfold. When she sat up as best as she could, considering her hands were in handcuffs, she found something to focus on, which was a woman and her child getting into a cab. This made her miss her family tremendously. She started to cry, but something stopped her. She heard a very familiar voice. It couldn't be she said to herself. It just couldn't be!

"Hey, boss, miss me? It was Ell. What in the hell is going on here? Ailese gave Ell the dirtiest look she'd probably ever given in her lifetime. She balled up her fists and was ready to punch her lights out, but damn, if she wasn't wearing those damn cuffs! I missed you so much, boss. Damn, you look horrible. Ell laughed. Perhaps you need a drink, boss. Here, let me hook you up." She laughed again. Ailese had a smirk on her face, rolled her eyes, and didn't respond to Ell's juvenile behavior. "Leave her alone," Andrew said in a calm voice. Ailese made eye contact with him, but she quickly turned her attention to something else. Ailese looked out the window the whole ride.

She was all alone, and everyone in this limo had betrayed her! What could she do? She had no one by her side. She was beside herself. She couldn't take another shocker. She just couldn't!

"Please, my wrists are bloody. Could you please give me a damn break from these cuffs?" Ailese said in a still voice, looking at Andrew, hoping that he would pay attention to her wrists. Andrew grabbed some rope and tied her hands behind her back. He didn't even let her wash off the blood. "Sit down and stay there until I come back," he said as he left the room. Ell and Melinda entered the room with a look that said they didn't want Ailese there. When Ailese looked up, they were standing there staring at her and whispering in each other's ear. "I oughta blow your damn head off," Melinda said as she pointed the gun at Ailese's head. Ailese just closed her eyes. Naw, she ain't worth it. I'm not cleaning up all that mess off the carpet and the walls, Melinda said, laughing. Man, we have so many plans for you. I have a surprise for you. You get to take a bath and make your self look presentable. Melinda spoke politely, using the same tone she used when Ailese first met her. Get up, bitch, and you better do what I tell you to do, you hear me? Now get into that tub and wash yourself good. We'll be back in an hour." She pushed Ailese into the bathroom, threw her clothes and her overnight bag on the floor and told her to hurry up. An hour went by, and there was a knock at the door. Ailese had just finished getting dressed, and Andrew entered the bathroom, but this time he wasn't alone. Ell was with him. Ailese just stood there and didn't make a sound; she barely took a breath.

"Wow, now that's the lady that I know, Ell said with a pleasing look on her face. It's your lucky day, huh? Do you feel lucky, boss?" Andrew motioned for Ell to leave him and Ailese alone, so she did. "Come on," Andrew said as he opened the door, and Ailese followed behind him. When they entered the living room, Ailese could feel everyone staring at her. She even heard Melinda cursing at her. Andrew put on some soft music and handed Ailese a glass of wine. The look he gave her said it all. It said that she had better drink it or else.

A few hours later Officer Brown joined the party as well. They pilled into the limo and went to a restaurant. Maybe this would be her chance to get away, but everyone watched Ailese like a hawk. She had four hawks watching her, and she was outnumbered. They were the only ones in the restaurant. Andrew demanded that Ailese sit right next to him. She was sitting so close to him, that she could barely move. At one point, he even fed her food. He would kiss Ailese just to make Melinda and Ell jealous, and Melinda would swear at Andrew. He would just laugh. When Ailese had to go to the restroom, someone went with her, so she could not escape if she tried. "Here, I want you to eat. You need to eat," Andrew said in a firm voice. Ailese shook her head, and when Andrew slapped her hard on her thigh. She would eat. She would eat when he would threaten her.

"So, I know you're probably wondering what the hell I'm doing here, huh?"

"You don't owe her no damn explanation, sis. She ain't no body." Ell put up her hand, and Melinda stopped talking. "Well, as you probably already know, this is my oldest sister," Ell said, pointing to Melinda. She's beautiful, huh? Well, you know what? I'mma get right to the point. You see, Andrew and my sister have been together for a long time, off and on. They almost got married at one point, but somebody got cold feet, Ell said, making eye contact with Andrew and shaking her head. You know why he got cold feet- he was still hung up on you, the bitch that treated him like dirt, like shit!" Ailese was puzzled by this. She was the one that was beaten every day, and where was Ell getting all this misinformation from? What was Andrew telling these people? Despite the fact that Andrew was not the victim here, she did not appreciate people down talking her character in any way, which upset her deeply. "Excuse me, Ailese said, clearing her throat. I don't know what Andrew told you, but I never hurt him, never. It was the other way around, you stupid bitch! Andrew squeezed Ailese's thigh really hard this time until it hurt. He didn't want her to make him look bad, which was one of his rules: never make him look bad. Andrew took a sip of his drink, and sat it back down on the table in front of him. He grabbed Ailese by the arm so hard that she thought that he broke it. He had her in a corner, still holding on to her arm, and the more that he got angry at her, the tighter his grip was. "Ouch, you are hurting me," she said, clinching her teeth and trying to loosen his grip on her arm. "Shut up, shut up. You hear me, he said in an angry voice.

You know what happens when you piss me off. Do you want me hurt you, huh?"

"Go ahead do it, Andrew. I don't care anymore! Ailese yelled. I don't give a rat's ass what you do to me! I don't care what your so-called posse out there does to me either; I don't care because you've already taken everything from me. You got what you wanted, Andrew! Even though I hate you so much, I thought I could never hate anyone!

"Calm down, D. We're going to find her. I need you to stay strong."

D'Andra was sobbing. She missed her sister so much and feared she would never come home. Ailese wouldn't see the twins grow up. "I know. I know that I need to be strong. Please just find her, please," D'Andra sobbed even more. "I'll be home soon, Chris said. Hearing his wife crying and upset, his heart was torn into pieces. Kiss our babies for me. Baby?" "Yes, D'Andra sniffed. Yes, what is it, Chris?"

"I love you so much." "D'Andra's a mess, man," Chris stated to Allen and Mikell.

I can't do anything but bring her sister home and safely. That's the only thing that will make her happy right now." Mikell consoled his brother-in-law and told him that they couldn't give up on Ailese. They just couldn't.

A few hours later, Chief Jacob called Mikell to give him an update, and the update was going to take Mikell to a different level. "Mikell, we need to talk. We all need to talk. I'm five minutes away from your hotel. I'm going to warn you, prepare you for some mind blowing news bro." "I'll see you when you get here, Jacob. Jacob's on his way. He said that he needed to talk to us, and it's not good, so just prepare yourself. We're all here for one another, and whatever it is, we'll

SHELBY LIES

survive it. Whatever it is, we can handle it. We can handle anything, right guys?" Allen and Chris shook their heads. Jacob's serious look was the first thing that everyone noticed as soon as he arrived at the hotel. "Hey guys, Jacob sighed. I think you guys better sit down. Jacob sat next to Mikell. Now, we've been questioning the hotel staff, but get this; they were paid money to help Andrew cover up whatever he's doing, as we speak. The manager broke down right in front of me and spilled all the beans. We got lucky." "What? What does Andrew have to do with this?" "Actually, Mikell, he has a new identity, and I am told that his real name used to be Rico." "Rico? Mikell said, interrupting Jacob. Oh my God, Rico? Rico? What? Is it?" Mikell paused and focused on Jacob's face. Mikell had never seen that look on his face before, but he knew that this was serious and to be taken seriously! If the manager from the hotel hadn't told Jacob everything that Andrew was planning on doing, they would have been totally clueless and may have hit some rough patches, being that Andrew has pretty much covered all the bases.

"She's in deep trouble, and we've got to find her. You told me a bit about what happened to her, and how he hurt her. Look, this guys paying off a lot of people here, so we need to be extra careful. We can't trust anyone but ourselves. From what the hotel clerk told me, Mikell, Andrew has it out for Ailese. I mean, he went as far as changing his name, his whole demeanor, and where he lived. He even covered up who his father is. I mean, this guy went to the extreme, Mikell, and I don't know what we're dealing with. We may be dealing with a crazy person."

"Wait, who's his father?" "Ailese's boss, Mr. Saxx." "What, are you kidding me?"

"What the hell's going on here? Allen said. My sister is in danger, and I do know what this Andrew or, Rico, or whoever he is capable of doing, or whatever his name is." Allen stood up, grabbed his keys, and headed for the door. "What are you doing, man? Jacob asked, but Allen just looked at him. Hey, please sit down, Jacob said, as he walked over to Allen, leading him back to his seat. We have to stick together, no matter what. I know that this is a lot to take in." "Look, I don't think you understand, Allen said, after a brief pause. But maybe Mikell didn't tell you everything about this man, this, this monster, Allen said as he massaged his temples. This monster hurt my sister, and I was there. I was there when she couldn't function. I was there when Ailese went through withdrawals because he had her on so many drugs, and I refuse to let this son of a bitch put her through … I cannot let that happen. I can't! I am willing to risk my life to get her safe man. I hope that we're not too late." "I really do understand where you're coming from, I do. What good are you to her if you're behind bars? I know what you're thinking- you want to find him and bash his head open- but we can't. We've got to stay and be on the same page, here. Hey, I am on your side. This guy needs to be behind bars, and that's what's going to happen as soon as we find him. I need everyone to stay on the same page and hopeful, please. We all can't afford to mess up here." "I agree Mikell said. Yes, I do want to kill this guy, but that's not the answer. I know that we all need to stay strong-minded."

"Look, there's more, that you need to know. I got a tip from someone that he has an officer working for him. The person wouldn't give me a name though, but that does explain some of his power that he has. From what I gather, this guy has a nudge for Ailese. Jacob looked at Allen. He was expecting him to tell him that he was right, but Allen just shook his head. He wants revenge Mikell, and it's not good. Mikell, not good at all, Jacob said as he closed the file that was in front of him. Look, from what I got out of the interviews with the employees from the hotel, that this guy has been planning to get even with Ailese for years, and that he's obsessed with this!" "Bastard, son of a bitch! Mikell screamed out in a rage. He was upset. This scum has been in my house, around my kids, and he has been plotting against us the entire time. Well you know what? He better hope that you get to him first before I do," because if I do, Mikell paused. Mikell knew that violence wasn't the answer and that Ailese wouldn't want him to act on his feelings either. He wanted his wife home and safe, far away from Andrew! Mikell was enraged that Andrew befriended them. He had befriended Ailese, and he had fooled everyone, including him. Mikell wasn't going to let Andrew get away with this. Either way, he was going to have to answer to Mikell, and it wasn't going to be pretty. Everyone was in shock, trying to take in all this information about Andrew. Andrew was the one person they would never have guessed to be Rico. It was out of this world! It was unheard of; strangely, it was a lot to deal with and take in!

Jacob's cell rang. "Hello, this is Chief Kenison. Give me a second. I need to take this call. I will be right back. Thank you for waiting." "Hello, this is Naomi French, returning your call from F&N Properties. I hope I'm not disturbing you." "Oh, no, miss, I'm all ears." "Well, I do have that information for you. Do you have a pen handy?" "I sure do, shoot." "Okay, these are the properties that were sold to Mr. McGee." The woman gave Jacob all the addresses that he needed to make his move. This was great news.

"Jacob, please call me the minute you know something." "You know that I will, man." Allen and Chris walked Jacob downstairs to give Mikell some time to calm down. "Jacob, I just wanted to apologize for my behavior. Look, I'm sorry and I can't promise you that it won't happen again. This is my sister, my heart."

"I know, Allen, you don't have to apologize. It's cool. I understand. Please don't think that I don't, I do," Jacob said as he placed a hand on Allen's shoulder.

Jacob and his men had to drive to another city that was a few hours away.

When the men showed up at one of the properties that Andrew owned, it was time to move in, and the time was now. They couldn't waste any time. They needed to find Ailese in a hurry before it was too late!

"Officer Sharp, I want you and Officer Mann covering the back door." Jacob gave his orders to the rest of his men; all the troops had the whole premises covered. There was a parked car in the driveway, and Jacob was hopeful that this time they were going to catch Andrew. Jacob gave a quick knock on the door. "Open up, this is Chief Jacob, representing Greensville Police, Department. Please, open up." Jacob and his men waited a few minutes, but no one came to the door, so Jacob kicked the door in and drew his gun while his other men combed the other areas of the house. Was the car there just to throw them off? There was no one there, and it appeared as if nothing had been touched, and no one had been there for weeks or even months. This didn't set to well with Jacob. He was an officer, a smart one, and how in the hell was Andrew was more smarter than him? Jacob was determined to find his best friend's wife, and no matter how smart Andrew was, that wasn't going to stop Jacob from keeping a promise.

"Hey, Mikell, it looks like this bastard wants to play cat-and-mouse or hide-and-seek, and I guess we're it." "So, I take it that he wasn't there?" "No, Mik, he wasn't, and there was no sign of Ailese either and the house looked like no one had lived there for quite some time. Sorry, buddy, but we have more to scope, so let's not give up. We still have some hope. Please don't give up on me." "Never, man, never."

What Jacob, Mikell, Chris, and Allen didn't know was that Andrew was a few hundred steps ahead of them. Andrew was no longer in Greensville, so it would take Jacob a while to catch up with him. Andrew only knew that his father was looking for him, not the cops, but he was still ahead of everyone.

With Jacob's determination, all of Andrew's plans will soon come to an end.

Andrew made sure that Ell and Ailese kept their distances. He didn't want her talking to Ailese because Ailese had known too much, and he didn't want her putting the puzzle pieces together too fast on why Ell was there. Ailese knew that Melinda and Ell were related, and she had a hunch that Ell was the person who fit perfectly in the puzzle. Melinda had a chip on her shoulder. This was a daily thing for her. She complained so much. Her biggest complaint of all was Ailese, Ailese. Could you believe that? Melinda would accuse Andrew of making up excuses just so he could spend time with Ailese. One day she threatened Ailese with a knife, but Officer Brown stopped her from making a huge mistake and ended up taking her home. When Andrew heard about what had happened, he made Melinda apologize to Ailese and told Ailese that it would never happen again. She wasn't scared of Melinda, even when she was tied up at times, she stared her straight in the eye and didn't back down. Ailese was so confused about how he held her captive, against her will, but at the same time he would be very protective of her, and sometimes she would see that old Andrew, and sometimes he was the devil!

Andrew would tell Ailese that she'd better get used to everything because this was her life now and that he had plans for her. One time, Ailese brought up Melinda. "Melinda's your girlfriend, or did you forget that? I don't know about them, but I have respect for myself, and I'm not going to disrespect myself and be with someone like you, who loves to take advantage of women. I don't share, sorry to burst your bubble," Ailese said, rolling her eyes. "You think I give a damn about what you want and this respect shit? I don't. You're mine, and that will never change my love, and besides, Melinda's just for show, that's all. Andrew began to say more, but he stopped himself. I love you. You're the only person that I have loved all my life. My love. Even though it took me a long time to find you, I have you now, and this time I'm not letting you go. Ailese thought to herself: This son of a bitch is going crazy, or am I going crazy? He really thinks that we have a future together, I don't think so. Andrew's plans were changing. Was he going to let Ailese live? Or was he just pulling her chain to buy more time? Andrew wasn't planning on keeping Melinda around for long. She was in the way, and if anyone was getting in the way of his plans, that wasn't good at all. He knew what he had to do. Andrew had to let her loose, and soon Andrew was serious when he told Ailese that he loved her and she was his now. He was living in a fairy tale world. Did he really think that she would be his? That she had forgotten all about her husband, and her life? He was a fool if he did!

"I don't want you here! Get out! Ailese screamed. Andrew was forcing himself on her. Ailese was once again helpless. No one was there to help her. It was just Andrew and her, and it wasn't by accident either. He knew exactly what he was doing when he sent Ell, Officer Brown, and Melinda out on errands. He wanted his privacy. He wanted Ailese.

She pleaded and pleaded with him. "Andrew, please don't do this, she begged. Her face was wet, her tears streamed down her cheeks; she barely had the ability to focus her eyes. Please, listen to me! Please!"

"Stop screaming, baby, my love, shhh ... I'm not going to hurt you," Andrew said, as he tightened the cuffs on her wrists even tighter. Ailese gave everything she had, but she couldn't win. He was always more powerful than she was, and she despised him for it. She hated when he touched her, and kissed her. She wanted him to just leave her alone. She couldn't take anymore!

Being that he was as powerful as she was, he took advantage of that so much that he loved it; it made him feel like he could do anything, it made him feel good. Andrew was more obsessed with Ailese, yes he does love her, but in a psychotic, crazy kind of way, but this was normal to him.

"You feel so good," Andrew whispered in her ear, and Ailese lay there, hoping and praying that it would be over soon. Soon didn't get there soon enough. It was hours until she was allowed to take a shower, and once again, Andrew watched her take a shower, and even after doing his dirt to her, you'd think that he would be done, but no, he'd make her do things to him while in the shower. She was trying to get away from her past, leaving all her skeletons in a locked closet that no one could open, but she couldn't, as her past was staring her right in the face. Ailese needed Dr. Salvino more than ever. She wondered if she was trying to get a hold of her, it's been a while since her last appointment. Dr. Salvino would make sense of all this madness, and she would be able to explain to her why Andrew was doing all these horrible things to her.

After Andrew dried off and put on some clothes, he went into the kitchen to fix something to eat but was never too far away, making sure Ailese wasn't trying to escape or anything. It wasn't that Ailese didn't want to escape. She knew that Andrew would kill her, beat her, or, worse, both. Andrew was quick,-too fast for Ailese. He had thugs posted all over the place. You wouldn't think that they worked for him because they dressed in regular clothing. If Ailese were to get away, they wouldn't hesitate to shoot her. One day, one of Andrew's guys put a gun to a guy who was just delivering something, and Andrew forgot to tell the men that he had someone delivering something to him. Andrew had to intervene.

"What's wrong? Why are you walking like that?" When Andrew had gone to get her, he told Ailese to follow him into the kitchen. She was in so much pain that she was walking slowly. Ailese just stared at Andrew. She was stunned that he would ask her such a question, especially since he was supposed to be so intelligent. It would never occur to you that he could be so cruel to people, hurt people like Ailese, from looking at him. Andrew hurt her, but he would still tell her that he loved her, even when he would force himself on her or force her to do things that she didn't want to do, and he did whatever he wanted to do to her. Ailese was living in the past, and it looked like she was never going to live for the future. "Sit down. The foods going to be ready soon.

Ailese please pull yourself together." Andrew walked over to Ailese, sat across from her, and looked at her. Ailese was crying, and no matter what she did, she couldn't stop crying. "Why? Why? Ailese said as her voice trembled with fear. I just want my life back. Please I won't tell anyone. Andrew, it's me, remember?" Andrew was silent, he didn't say a word. He sighed and shook his head. He wanted to say some thing but he didn't. All he said was that he loved her and that she should be happy that he decided to spare her life. He went back to preparing the food. He had no emotions- no emotions about how upset she was.

Just as Andrew placed the plates of food on the table and sat down, his cell phone rang. "Hello, what's good? What? You need to handle that, handle that fast, and call me back." When Andrew hung up the phone, he started to swear. He punched his open hand with his fist. He just kept on swearing.

Ailese didn't say anything, but she did hear him say something about his dad.

One of Andrew's sources just told him that his dad, Mr. Saxx, was still trying to find him, and was still asking around about his son, so he told his source to handle it, but Andrew wasn't too worried about it because Mr. Saxx didn't know anything about his whereabouts and he would never know.

No one, not even old Daddy, was going to mess up Andrew's plans.

"You need to eat, and you know you need your strength, please." Andrew was getting upset with Ailese because she wouldn't eat, and when she didn't listen to Andrew, he wasn't a happy camper. She would just sob frenziedly, complaining that she was in a lot of pain and that she wasn't hungry and needed to lay down, so Andrew took her to the bedroom, hand cuffed her arms and legs to the bed like always, and laid next to her. She wanted to be alone, alone with her thoughts. Ailese would open her eyes every time Andrew moved because she was still scared. She wanted to be alone. She wanted to think about her family in peace; and maybe, just maybe, come up with an escape plan. Why was she kidding herself? Ailese had a gut feeling that her husband should be looking for her. She knew that everyone, especially Mikell, was so worried about her, and when they said those beautiful vows, he meant it. He meant every word. She knew that, and knowing that it helped her stay somewhat calm reassured her that there was hope, but she had to be patient. She missed everything about her life,- her children, her friends, the babies. Will she ever see anyone she loved again? She wasn't going to accept that this may be her life. She didn't want it, at all! She was only used to one man and one man only for years, and that was Mikell.

Oh, how she missed him. She missed smelling his cologne, hearing his voice, and being with him. Ailese closed her eyes and thought about all the times that she and Mikell shared. It brought a smile to her face, and it brought her some peace, and this made her fall into a deep dream.

It had been a while since Andrew trusted Ell and Melinda to stay with Ailese alone, and that was a big mistake, Ell spilled her guts to Ailese. Ell told Ailese everything. Melinda would remind Ell how upset Andrew would be, but Ell didn't care. "Yeah, he thinks that he's the master mind. No, I am. I am the one who taught him everything about you so he could be in good graces with you. I told him your dislikes and likes, Ell said as she took a sip of her wine. My sister thinks that she and Andrew are going to ride off into the sunset, and I keep telling her dumbass that he loves you and only you." Ell laughed.

"Shut up you stupid bitch! Melinda yelled. He loves me, not this bitch here, Melinda said, pointing to Ailese. It's just a matter of time before this bitch's smile disappears, and that's if I don't get to her first." Melinda stood up, put her hand on her hips, walked closer to Ailese, and spat in her face. Ell gasped. Ailese couldn't do much because she, as always, was handcuffed, and as always they were on so tight. She could move her legs a bit, so she kicked Melinda in her leg, this surprised Melinda, that was the last time Ailese saw Melinda and Ell. She was happy that she didn't see them again. Andrew was so upset with Melinda. Ailese had seen him angry before, but not like this. He was so angry at her that he could have beaten her to death and thrown her in a ditch somewhere.

Andrew looked like he was going to kill over. What was wrong with him? He didn't look very good. He lay beside Ailese for hours, moaning and groaning. He didn't even try anything with her for a few days, thank God; she didn't even want to think about the lines he had crossed with her.

Andrew shot up so fast and ran to the restroom. Ailese could hear him throwing up. He was in there for awhile. All he kept saying was, "No, not now, no not now!"

Andrew was sick. It was bad. His sickness was catching up with him; it made him so weak, and he hated that. He was powerless now. This was a setback for him. Ailese had to see him suffer, and she didn't have one sympathetic bone in her body for him! She used to be sympathetic, not anymore. She had lost everything she had for him. It was long gone! He was suffering and as far as she was concerned he deserved it.

Even though he was suffering, he somehow still made it a point to make sure all the rules stayed the same, sick or not.

It didn't look like Andrew was going to ever get better. Instead, he was getting worse. "I need you to come here fast. It's happening, and I need your help." An hour later, a man showed up. He took Andrew into another room to examine him. He had Officer Brown look after Ailese. Luckily, he behaved himself.

"You need to take better care of yourself you know, you know that don't you? Andrew shook his head. Now you need to rest. Those meds will help you, and if you do what I told you to do and eat what I told you to eat, that should help. Call me if you need me. Now the key is to rest, okay?"

"Thanks, you're a lifesaver."

Ailese lay there thinking about all the betrayal. She started thinking about Ell, and how she pretended to be the best assistant, but all the time she was getting personal information for Andrew. She told Andrew personal things that she shared with Ell, things that only she would know- her secrets.

Ailese despised Ell for that; she chose money over their relationship, she chose greed over their relationship, as well. Ailese had to get over it, and besides, Ell was the least of her problems; it only bothered her because she had put so much trust and faith in Ell when some people didn't. Ailese played their conversations back in her head. She could remember the times that she could have fired her for some things that Ell had done, especially the affair that she had with Chris, but she believed in her and gave her a chance-more than once. All the times when they would go to lunch and talk about private things, Ell would tell Andrew everything. Just thinking about it hurt Ailese. So many people had betrayed her, and the minute that she told herself stop living in the past and move on and try, just try, to put some trust into people; they're backstabbing her. She was lucky that she was still alive. She could feel the knife in her back. The minute that she trusted these people, they didn't waste any time deceiving her.

Ailese's head was pounding so badly that she had tears in her eyes. The migraine was getting worse and the aspirin wasn't helping. "Here, take these; they're stronger and they should make you feel better, and besides, we need to get moving. I've already packed your things, Andrew said as he handed Ailese a glass of water and the pills. Hello, what's good? The look on Andrew's face was one look that Ailese had never wanted to see ever again.

Okay, bye." Andrew took her by the hand and literally dragged her out of the room. One of Andrew's goons was waiting at the door and escorted Ailese to the limousine and told her not to make a move or a sound, so she didn't. What the hell's going on? She asked herself. A few minutes later, the driver and Andrew were in the limo, and before she knew it, they were off. Someone had given a tip to Andrew that the police were at one of his properties, so he left.

"Don't go too fast, man. I don't want to attract any attention, understand?

I need you to stay cautious and take the back roads, okay?" The driver agreed and did what Andrew told him to do. Ailese had fallen asleep, and when she woke up, they were at their destination. Unlike last time, Andrew removed the blindfold from Ailese's face and took off her handcuffs as well. Was he now prepared to let her live, or had he changed his mind? Did they come here so he could kill her and put her body in a ditch somewhere?

"Why are you shaking? I'm not going to hurt you. Now follow me." He took her by the hand and led her up to some stairs. Ailese looked around, she could feel it in her gut that they were not in Greensville, South City, or Ashton City. She had a feeling that they were somewhere far, far away. Nothing looked familiar to her.

They were down to the last place. Jacob was sure that he would have good news to tell Mikell because he was getting so impatient that Jacob suggested that he get out of that hotel before he went crazy, so Allen and Chris talked him into going for a drive and picking up something to eat. Even though it was hard to get Mikell out and about again, he had finally agreed. Jacob had promised him that he would call him if anything new surfaced.

Everyone wanted Ailese home and home safe. Everyone was praying that she would be home soon. Alonda and D'Andra were staying strong and positive and keeping their prayers powerful as well.

Sometimes Chris would have to calm his wife down because she would cry, and cry she would call him when she would have a bad dream about Ailese. The dream would be about Ailese not ever coming home, but Chris would eventually calm her down and reassure her that it was only a dream.

Ailese was missing, which really upset her family. They just couldn't believe that this was really happening, and they just wanted it to be all over. She needed to be where she'd belong, which was with their family. The kids missed her so much, but Alonda and D'Andra would reassure them that it was going to be okay and their mom would be home soon.

"I can't believe how many different properties this guy has," Jacob said to himself. When they arrived at the last one, they were in luck! They had to get through Andrew's goons that were posted everywhere. Jacob hoped that he brought enough men and ammo, and that they would be prepared for anything, and besides he had only brought the best men. "Open up. This is Officer Kenison. I have a warrant to search the premises." An older woman opened the door, startled and confused.

"May I help you, officer?" "Yes, I have a warrant to search the premises, and I have reason to believe that the fugitive that we were looking for is keeping a woman here against her will." "Well, that's nonsense. I just bought this house a week ago, officer and my husband is the only other person that lives here. You can check the house, please come in." The older woman invited the men in.

They checked every inch of the house, and there was no sign of Ailese or Andrew. The old lady was telling the truth.

Jacob was sure that they would find Ailese there and bring her home to her family. What happened? How was he going to tell his best friend that he didn't find her and that he was coming back empty- handed? How was he going to explain that? He had gone to every house on that list, and she was nowhere to be found. He didn't want to give up. Did he miss something? Jacob's stomach was in knots. It made him sick to his stomach, letting Mikell down. He prayed that he would find her soon. He needed to go back over all of his information. He must have missed something. How could he and his men go to all these places and didn't find Ailese?

"Chief Kenison, I have the man's father on the phone. I think that you should talk to him." Jacob took the phone and prayed that Mr. Saxx wasn't wasting his time. "This is Chief Kenison. How can I be of help?" "Yes, this is Mr. Saxx. I am Andrew McGee II father, and I understand that you are looking for him.

I hope that you don't mind that I went to your superiors. I just wanted to let you know that I don't want to offend you in any way, and I know your background, which by the way is very impressive, Chief." "Thank you, I appreciate that, Mr. Saxx." "When I heard that you were looking for my son and the charges that are allegedly against him, and being that he had never come home from his trip I knew something wasn't right. So I started to look for him. He wouldn't take any of my calls, and that really bothered me. What really got me was that this wasn't like him. What I am trying to tell you is that I want to help you find my son. I'm worried about him, and he needs to come home."

It came to Jacob that Mr. Saxx didn't know the whole story because he didn't mention Ailese, who was like a daughter to him, and they were pretty close.

"Mr. Saxx, I must tell you that we believe that your son is holding Ailese LaShae against her will and she is in danger, so if you could help us in any way to get her back home safely to her family, I would, well, we would appreciate it." Mr. Saxx was silent for a few seconds. "Oh my god, what the hell's going on here? I need to know, and I need to know now! No one told me that Ailese was in danger and that my son was the cause of her being in danger. Your men didn't tell me that." "I figured that they didn't, being that you didn't mention it, Mr. Saxx, and please know that we're doing everything in our power to find her." "Oh, my, Mr. Saxx said as his voice trembled. I can't believe this is happening. I mean, what ... Why would he want to hurt her?" "Mr. Saxx, where are you now? Maybe we could meet up and I could fill you in, and I will make sure that all your questions are answered." "Thank you, that sounds like a plan. I can meet you at your head quarters or where ever. I am in Greensville. Are you anywhere near there?" "Actually, let's meet in Ashton. Would that work for you? How does that sound?" "Okay, I know that there's a café on the corner of Brools Avenue. Do you know that place?" "Quite well. See you then."

"Mikell, I need you guys to meet me in Ashton. If you leave now, that would be helpful. I will fill you in when you get there. Oh, there's a café on the corner of Brools Avenue. You have the GPS still, right?" "Yeah, I do, Jacob. Is everything alright? You sound frustrated?" Jacob took a deep breath before he answered Mikell. "Yeah, look, Mr. Saxx will be joining us. He's going to help us find Ailese. We've been all over the place. We've been to all of his properties, and we haven't found her yet, so we need all the help that we can get. Do you agree?" "I agree. Jacob?" "Yes?" "Please don't think that you've failed because you haven't. You've done so much, and no matter what happens, I want to thank you for everything. Please know that, bro." "I do, Mikell. I do."

Everyone arrived at the café. Mr. Saxx was right on time, and as soon as he saw Mikell, he hugged him so tight and gave him his commiseration. He felt so bad that all this was happening. He knew that Andrew and Ailese had planned this trip for months, and he knew how close they had become, but putting her in danger? Why? He thought to himself, that Ailese had never done anything but good in her life, as long as he had known her. She was the sweetest person he had ever met. He had always wished that he had a daughter like Ailese, but he was only blessed with one child, and that was Andrew. Mr. Saxx knew nothing of his past. Andrew shut his father out of his life. He didn't know about what he had done to Ailese. He had no idea but there was still guilt.

Andrew kept a lot from his dad. He only told him some things, not everything. He never really opened up like that to his dad.

"Thank you all for meeting me here. Mr. Saxx is joining us because he has offered to help us find Ailese." "I am hopeful that we will find Ailese. I really am, he said in a confident voice. I have information that the police don't have, and I want her home just as much as you do, Mikell. You know that I am willing to do whatever I can, and I mean that. Mr. Saxx made eye contact with Mikell and winked at him. Now there is a place that I think that my son may have gone." "Where's that?" Allen asked raising his eyebrows. "It's just outside of Arcosta. We used to go there around this time. We have a cabin up there, and that is Andrew's favorite place to visit. I wouldn't doubt it if he's there."

"Arcosta? I don't think I've ever heard of it where is I don't think I've ever heard of it. Where is that?" "It's a little town just outside of Reddington." "Oh, I have heard of Reddington, but I haven't visited there in a long time," Mikell said. "So, Jacob, how long do you think it would take to get this ball rolling so we can scope out the place?" Chris waited for an answer. He was ready to go, and he was ready to get the ball rolling as soon as possible. "Well, I have to make some calls and get all set up." Jacob looked at his watch and thought to himself that he wouldn't have enough time to head down to Arcosta today, and he hoped that everyone would understand. "Hey, guys, we need to be patient and remember that these things take time, Mikell said. Jacob I do understand." Jacob didn't have to say anything or explain himself. Mikell already knew, and besides, Jacob's expression told him that it wouldn't be tonight anyway. He knew that Jacob needed to rest so that he could strategize, and that was fine with him.

"Here is where I'll be staying. Call me when it's time to head to the cabin, and please, if you guys need anything, anything at all, please call me don't hesitate. I feel responsible for all this. I can't tell you enough how sorry I am. Mikell, please listen to me. I am here for you. I hope that you don't have any bad blood against me." "Thank you, Mr. Saxx. Mikell stood up to hug him and thank him. I don't blame you," he said as he hugged him. I don't have any bad blood either. You should know that you had absolutely nothing to do with Ailese's kidnapping.

You love her like a daughter, and it's not your fault that Andrew decided to this. Mikell actually said "kidnapped," which gave him chills. I just want her home ... I want her home."

"Were going to find her," Mr. Saxx whispered in Mikell's ear as they hugged each other. "Jacob, I just want to thank you for all you've done. You're a good man," Mr. Saxx said as he touched Jacob's shoulder as he walked out of the café.

SHELBY LIES

Andrew carried Ailese to the bedroom. She wasn't feeling well and had been throwing up a lot. "Here, take this. It's for your stomach, and it will help with the nausea." "I think I need to go to the hospital," Ailese said, her voice shaky and soft at the same time. "You'll be fine now. Please take the medicine and the ginger ale that I gave you and rest. I think you just have a little case of the stomach flu. You'll be okay." When Andrew left the room, he had three missed calls on his cell phone. "Damn it, what is it now? Hello, why are you calling and what's going on? I have nothing to say to you. It's my life!" Andrew became very upset. "Don't hang up. You need to listen to me. What happened to you?

We need to talk, and now, where are you?" "Why do you need to know?"

"I'm worried about you, and you need to listen to what I have to say."

"I don't want to hear what you have to say. Dad." Andrew hung up.

Andrew began to swear and curse. He didn't trust anyone, not even his father, the man who loved him. Deep down inside, Andrew loved his father, he just couldn't face him. His father always ruled him, and that was the main reason why Andrew left to start his own life. He didn't want his father's wealth; he wanted his own, so his father couldn't have a say in what he did with his life- with his own wealth. He knew that if he kept avoiding him, his father was a smart man, and he will track him down. If he did all this, keeping Ailese against her will, it will be all over. That was the main reason why he didn't want his dad to get into his business; he hoped that Mr. Saxx didn't find him at all!

Andrew paced back and forth a million times until he made a hole in the carpet, so to speak. "I can't believe him. Why must he upset me? Get a grip, Andrew," he mumbled.

He hated when he would let his father get to him. Andrew played the conversation back in his head over and over again, until finally he shrugged his shoulders and focused on something else. He went to the room where Ailese was asleep and when he felt her forehead, he startled her, and she woke up. "Sorry, I didn't mean to wake you up. How are you feeling? Are you strong enough to eat?" Ailese shook her head. Okay, I will be right back. I made some chicken soup while you were sleeping. Come with me, please," he said as he looked at her. Even though she didn't want to eat, maybe the soup would make her fever go down and settle her stomach. Ailese and Andrew ate their soup. They both were silent until Ailese all of a sudden started to cry. Ailese cried and cried. Andrew didn't know why she was crying. He'd never seen her like this. "Please, just tell me what's wrong?" Ailese shook her head and she began pleading with him. "I just want my family. I just want to go home. I won't say anything. I'll make up something. Please, please. I'm begging you she sobbed. Andrew was silent. All you could hear was Ailese crying. I miss Mikell. I miss my babies. I know they must be so scared, not knowing where I am." Ailese sobbed even harder this time, but Andrew still said nothing, like his heart was cold and made of stone.

Ailese couldn't sleep. She tossed and turned all night. She would cry and cry. She missed her family. She hadn't seen them in weeks. She needed Mikell. She wished that she was lying in his arms, and she wished that she could kiss the kids good night. She wondered how they were holding up. She knew that Armont was strong and a huge help to the girls, and Mikell and her family were there for them, encouraging them, that she was going to come home soon. Andrew entered the room as Ailese got up to wash her face. Andrew looked at her as he followed her to the restroom. Ailese didn't say anything to Andrew. She pretended that he wasn't even there. When she looked at him, he had his gun in his other hand. She just ignored the gun and him, and went back to what she was she was doing. Ailese dried her face with a towel and looked at herself in the mirror. She didn't like what she saw in the mirror. She looked tired and worn out. She didn't look like Ailese. She looked like she hadn't slept in weeks; she disliked what she saw in the mirror, but she just didn't care anymore. She hadn't groomed herself in a long time, and for once in her life, it didn't bother her. All she cared about was her family. Her scars were slowly disappearing. She had lost so much weight, that her face was so thin.

Andrew leaned up against the basin and studied her. He loved her so much in his own sick way. He would at one time move heaven and earth for her, and never in a million years did Ailese ever imagine that he would be standing in front of her with a gun in his hand- maybe flowers or her favorite candy- but not a gun. "What?" "You're so beautiful. You're the most beautiful woman I've ever seen in my life." The thought occurred to Ailese that he must be crazy, what is he on about? Am I supposed to thank him? Please! Ailese looked at Andrew like she wanted to choke him. Excuse me, I need to get by. Andrew wouldn't let her get by. He grabbed her and pulled her to him. Ailese's body went limp, and instead of making eye contact, she looked the opposite way and studied the designs that were on the shower door. "Look at me, I said. Look at me!

Andrew grabbed her face and forced her to look at him.

We're stuck with each other, so I suggest that you get over it and accept the fact that this- you and me, -is it. This is your life and you must accept it.

Ailese shook her head and told herself that she wasn't going to ever accept it.

Get dressed. Here," Andrew handed Ailese a bag. It was obvious that he went out shopping while she was sleeping, she took the bag from him and went to the bedroom to get dressed. Being that Andrew had made it clear that she had better get used to "them," and what he said sickened her, she simply refused! Her life was not Andrew's. It was Mikell's. She had to believe that. She wasn't going to believe Andrew's sick beliefs. He was in control, and Ailese hated herself. She blamed herself for everything. She was the reason why she was in this horrible situation. An hour later, they were at a restaurant. Ailese hadn't seen a restaurant in weeks. She hadn't seen daylight in weeks!

Their orders were taken, and their menus were retrieved by the waiter. "Please eat and enjoy this," he said, giving her one of his looks that she disliked. Ailese had excused herself to go to the restroom, and Andrew became a bit annoyed. He told her that she had better come back or else and trust that he would find her if she tried to run, so of course she came back. "Excuse me, sir. I just wanted to tell you that your wife is very beautiful, and you guys make an awesome couple," a man told Andrew.

"Thank you, thank you very much, and yes, she is very beautiful." Ailese was in awe. She just kept what she wanted to say to herself.

"Let's go guys! We're meeting Mr. Saxx for breakfast so we could go over our plans." The guys grabbed their things and followed Jacob out the door.

The guys knew that they had a long drive to Arcosta, where Mr. Saxx said that Andrew would be. They wanted to take an airplane or Mr. Saxx's private plane, but they didn't want to attract a lot of attention, being that Andrew had so many people looking out for him, and they didn't want to risk Andrew leaving again, they were hoping that he was in Arcosta.

"I really appreciate you helping us, Mr. Saxx," Allen said. "No, it's my pleasure. I'm on your side. My son is wrong for what he's done." "I need to call my wife. I will be right back." Chris left the table to call his wife. He had promised D'Andra that he would call her as soon as they arrived at the restaurant.

"It was hard, but I pulled some strings and managed to pull up some extra backup- some men in Arcosta,- that's going to help us out, and don't worry, they're not going to move in until we're there, so we're covered in that area." Mikell and Allen shook their heads and looked at each other. Jacob shared his plans with everyone and why it was important that Allen, Chris, and Mikell stay in the hotel because things may get violent and he didn't want them to get hurt. Mr. Saxx shared with Jacob the house plans as far as where the bedrooms were down to the exits; which would help out a lot.

"What did I miss?" Chris said as he joined everyone else. "Oh, I was just explaining to everyone how important it is that you guys stay at the hotel; I don't want anyone hurt." Oh, oh, yeah. I agree, and besides, I kinda promised D'Andra that I would come home in one piece, so I am not disagreeing with you on that at all," Chris said. The men finished their breakfast, and chatted for a while, and headed to Arcosta with Mr. Saxx, who led them there.

"I miss my wife so much. I know that this sounds crazy, but I feel like a piece of me is missing, you know?" "We know," Chris said, in a caring voice.

We all miss her deeply." Chris looked at Mikell. He was worried about him. He could tell from the look on Mikell's face that he was losing hope, and he didn't want him to lose hope. "What if I never had agreed to her being friends with Andrew, what if I never approved of this guy this bastard! Mikell screamed at the top of his lungs. It was well overdue. He had been keeping his cool. He had been cool, calm, and collected for way too long. "Hey, hey, please don't blame yourself, because we all had no way of knowing that he was Rico. We had no way of knowing, you hear me?" He told Mikell that no one blamed him for anything, not even him, and that he had a good feeling that with Mr. Saxx's help, they were going to bring her home. "Chris, I need her and the kids need her. She just has to be alright. She has to be alive!" "I commend you, man, for staying so strong throughout this whole ordeal," Allen said. "It's hard not knowing, you know, if I'll ever have my wife back, and the kids not having their mom back. Mikell began to cry even more. He wasn't ashamed of crying, he wasn't ashamed of not having it together, and he wasn't ashamed of letting his emotions out in front of everyone. I don't know if she's hurt or worse. Mikell said as he sniffed. I don't know if she's even alive." Mikell began to cry even harder. "My sister is a very strong woman, and resourceful. She would do whatever she could to stay alive. I know that, and you have to know that, Mikell. We all love her so much and we're all determined to find her and find her alive."

"Wake up, Ailese, Ailese." Andrew shook her, but she didn't respond. He shook her again, and she finally woke up, opened her eyes, and looked at Andrew as if she wanted to punch him for waking her up. It was the best sleep she'd had in a very long time. "What?" "I need you to get dressed, and I don't want to hear nothing coming outta your mouth. Hurry up," Andrew said in a firm voice. Ailese let out a long yawn and looked around the room. She didn't feel like doing anything, especially when it was dictated to her. Finally, she hopped in the shower, got dressed and met Andrew in the living room, where she found him pacing the floor. "What took you so long?" Ailese noticed that he had that damn gun in his hands. She didn't have the strength to think about what was going to happen now or where he was going to take her. Surprisingly, he didn't hurt her, but he did take her somewhere. "Where are we going?" Ailese said as she yawned. "Oh, you'll see," Andrew said, smiling. An hour later, they arrived at their destination. When Ailese got out of the car, the first thing she noticed was how beautiful it was. It was so green, and the air was cool and crisp. She took in the air and reminisced about the times when she and her husband would go for their walks when the weather was perfect. "Come on, this way." Ailese followed Andrew very closely, and besides, she wasn't up to arguing with him, so she did what he said. "Oh my," she whispered as they entered a hair salon. I haven't been in one of these in so long," she whispered. She wanted to smile, but she didn't. She just wondered why they were there. He didn't give a damn about how she looked; he was up to something. She was shocked that he would do this for her. She needed this, and she needed this badly. She thought that she would just enjoy the day and pretend that she brought herself there and not Andrew. She wouldn't try anything funny, and she would pretend so she could get through this ordeal.

    A young lady greeted them at the door, and said, "Hello, how are you?" "Fine," Andrew and Ailese both responded. "Yes, I'm Mr. Mc Gee. I called earlier. My wife here needs her hair, nails done, or whatever she wants." "Oh, yes, yes, we're ready for her. I must warn you that it will take a few hours. There is a deli up the street. We know how much husbands hate waiting." "Oh no, I'm fine, but I may take you up on that deli suggestion later. Is the food good?" "Yes, sir, it is." Andrew sat down and all of a sudden he decided to get a haircut, himself. He made sure that he kept an eye on Ailese.

"Your husband is such a sweetie, surprising you and all," the woman said to Ailese. Ailese just smiled. If only that woman knew the truth, that she was being held against her will. She wanted to tell the woman the truth and nothing but the truth, but she couldn't and she didn't. Ailese put on her "happy face" "because every second and she hated it, especially when the woman would say, "Oh, your husband loves you so much, I can tell." That burned her. She imagined her slapping that woman and Andrew at the same time. Oh, what she wouldn't give for a few punches to Andrew's teeth and a kick between his legs. It would serve him well.

"Wow, baby, you look gorgeous," Andrew said to Ailese as he gave the ladies who dolled up Ailese a huge tip and then some. She picked out twenty colors of finger nail polish and told Andrew she wanted them all; this was the best way to get him back.

"Baby, I just love these colors," Ailese said. She spoke as if she was so in love with Andrew. Andrew smiled and paid for the items. Ailese could tell Andrew was a little annoyed, but she didn't care. She could play games just as well.

The women were still admiring Andrew and telling Ailese how lucky she was to have a husband who spoiled her. "Let's go eat. I am starved." Andrew demanded. They headed to the deli up the street to eat and headed home.

Ailese was surprised to see a car parked in the driveway. She wondered who it was. "Hey." She heard the voice, but she hadn't made her way to the kitchen yet, and when she did, she saw Officer Brown standing there like he owned the damn place. "I was wondering when you were gonna haul your ass over here," Andrew said to Officer Brown. "Sorry, you know how my work is. It's difficult. I am drained. I had to work a double shift." "Like I said, dumb ass, I don't know why you won't quit that dumb ass job. You're a millionaire now, man. You could do whatever you want, come on." "Shut up, I know. I know I don't need to keep repeating myself to you, do I?"

Andrew and Officer Brown laughed. Ailese just stood there admiring her beautiful makeover, so she figured that she would go upstairs and admire herself more in the mirror. "Damn, you looking mighty fine there. Mmm." Officer Brown let out a moaning noise. Ailese just ignored him. "Where are you going?" "Upstairs, calm down," she told Andrew, rolling her eyes. "Whew, she's a piece of work man," Officer Brown said as he shook his head. Ailese gave him a harsh look before going upstairs.

"You want a beer?" "Naw, I think I'm going to have a glass of wine. What about you? Do you want some wine instead, and why don't you have that wifey of yours join us?" "Yeah, wine sounds good, Andrew said. I'm going to check on her, I will be right back." "Cool, I'll pour the wine." Andrew found Ailese looking into the mirror. She had changed clothes and was modeling in the mirror not noticing that Andrew had entered the room. "Hey, Andrew startled Ailese. She stopped modeling in the mirror, and sat down on the bed. She felt a bit embarrassed. Hey, come down and join me for some wine, please.

I mean, the least you could do is join me for a drink. I took you to get all dolled up." Andrew made sure he made his point. What's with all the niceness? In some cases, Andrew was nice, and in others, he was cold-hearted, but Ailese accepted the invitation and prayed he wouldn't turn evil. "Okay, fine, wine sounds good, just as long as Mr. Brown isn't joining us?" "Um, well, he is so come on, and he was the one that suggested it, Ailese." "Really huh?" Ailese was going to speak her mind about Officer Brown, but she decided to let it go and followed Andrew downstairs. Since Andrew had put a little trust in her, he didn't have her in cuffs today. He gave her a little freedom from time to time, and when he did, she took advantage of it. It's not that she wanted to spend time with him, she just didn't want to be in cuffs and in pain, and when he gave her freedom from those awful cuffs that hurt her wrists and gave her bruises, she was grateful.

"Oh, by the way, you look hot," Officer Brown said to Ailese as she picked up her wine glass and sat down on the sofa. "Thank you," Ailese said in a sarcastic voice. They chatted and watched television, but Ailese didn't speak much. She didn't feel comfortable around Officer Brown. She had wished that she wasn't there, and besides, she had to watch her back when he was around. She didn't trust him, especially after the last time when he tried to force himself on her, and working with the man who was holding her against her will was a good enough reason why she felt this way about him.

"I think I had too much wine. I think I'm going to bed," Ailese said. "Hey, it's early, Officer Brown said. Stay a while longer. Let's play cards or something." "No thanks, like I said, I'm a bit tired. You guys have fun." "Hey, did you hear me? I asked you to stay, and when I ask a person to stay, I expect them to."

"Well, hun, I'm sorry, but I am not those people, Ailese said as she made eye contact with him and started heading for the stairs, but Officer Brown blocked her from going upstairs. Excuse me, I need to get by," Ailese said, but he wouldn't move. "I know what you need. You need a stronger drink. Let me get you one." "No, thank you, I'm good. Now move." He still didn't move, and Andrew hadn't said a word the whole time. Ailese came back down stairs to find Andrew knocked out sleep. Now she was very nervous, now it was just Officer Brown and her. She tried to wake up Andrew but he wouldn't wake up, he would just moan and go back to sleep. What was she going to do now?

She knew one thing: She was not going to let him take control or do anything to her that she didn't approve of, or she would have to kick him "where the sun don't shine," meaning she would have to kick him in the balls as hard as she could if he tried anything, and she wouldn't hesitate either.

"I'm not going to bite you. Sit down, it's all good," Officer Brown said as he pointed to the sofa, motioning for Ailese to have a seat. Ailese decided to try and wake up Andrew instead, but no luck. He wouldn't wake up.

Ailese cleared her throat and told Officer Brown that she would have to take a rain check on that drink and she was very tired. Officer Brown just looked at Ailese, and the way that he looked at her gave her the creeps. Ailese went upstairs so fast that she probably skipped most of them.

Ailese got ready for bed. She couldn't get that look that Officer Brown had given her. She just knew that he was up to something and she should keep something next to her pillow just in case he came into her room, but she couldn't find anything, and she didn't want to go back downstairs because if she did, she would have to deal with him, and she wasn't in the mood.

Ailese decided to lock the door, but to her surprise, there weren't any locks on the door for some reason. What was she going to do? She already had enough to deal with when it came to Andrew, and now she had to worry about Officer Brown too. She decided, if he came into the room, she would let him have it! She cleared her head, prayed, and went to sleep.

Ailese had heard someone walking into her bedroom. She swore that it was Andrew checking in on her or wanting to sleep with her, so she didn't get up or open her eyes. Then, she felt a hand on her mouth. It happened so quickly, that she didn't have the time to react. She couldn't speak, and when she opened her eyes, it was Officer Brown, and he was naked. This wasn't good, and for the first time in a long time, she wished Andrew was there right beside her, but he wasn't. She had to do something, and she needed to do it fast! "Don't you think about it! Ailese remained calm. She had to figure out how she was going to get away from this perverted asshole! I dare you to try anything, and trust me, you'll regret it." Ailese noticed that he had a knife in his other hand. He put the knife to her throat. Ailese gave him a good kick between the legs, which freed her. She ran out of the room so fast!

She bumped into Andrew in the hall as she was running. He asked her why was she running, she pointed to the room. Andrew went to the room and picked Officer Brown up with all the strength he had, threw him up against the wall, and began punching him over and over again. At this time, Ailese ran into the bathroom that was down the hall, luckily there was a lock on the door. She locked the door behind her so fast that her head was spinning. She could hear them fighting and yelling through the door. She felt something going down her skin. She looked and saw that she was bleeding. She didn't know that she was hurt. Everything was happening so fast! Her wound wasn't too bad. She looked around for a first aid kit. She found one under the sink in the bathroom. She opened it up and started to clean her wound. She closed her eyes when she put the peroxide on to her cut, thinking that it was going to sting, but it surprised her that it didn't sting at all. She cleaned it really well. She kept her eyes closed, even after she was done cleaning her wound. She stayed in the corner curled up in a fetal position. She was very scared. She could still hear them fighting. The whole time, she was shaking so badly that she remained in a fetal position. She waited until it was safe enough to come out, or when she didn't hear them fighting anymore, but what if she was wrong and Officer Brown had gotten the best of Andrew and he was standing right outside the door waiting for her? So she waited and waited until finally Andrew knocked on the door. "My love, open the door. It's me, Andrew. I won't hurt you, and I made him leave for good! Ailese opened the door. As a result of hearing Andrew's voice, she was crying, or perhaps she was frightened. Ailese I promise you, he's not going to hurt you. I made him leave for good. But she didn't believe him. Ailese finally stopped crying. I'm sorry that he did this to you. I made him leave. He won't be coming back, okay? Ailese was shaking. Andrew took the robe off the hook in the bathroom, put it around her body, and carried her into another room.

I just want to check your wound, please." Ailese shook her head.

He checked her wound, and Ailese saw a sense of relief on his face. He was relieved that her cut wasn't too bad and that she attended to it nicely.

"We are here, finally, Allen said, yawning. Boy, that was a long drive." Okay guys, I need, well, I think we all need to check into a hotel and get some sleep. Do you guys agree?" "Yeah, Allen, we do. That's a good idea, Jacob said. We'll leave at 6:00 a.m. guys, no later. We'll pick up some breakfast on the way. The sooner we leave, the better." "I agree," Mikell said. The guys checked into their room, as so did Mr. Saxx. He had a separate room as well. After he was done showering, he went over to Mikell's room to talk to him. "I know it's late, but do you have a sec?" "Sure, come on in," Mikell said as he closed the door behind him and locked it. Mr. Saxx sat down on the couch. At first, he was silent, then he started to talk to Mikell. "You know, when we adopted Andrew, we were so excited we couldn't wait until we could bring him home, and his mother, my wife, was more excited than a kid in a toy store. We had all these plans you know.

When he turned sixteen, he ran away from home, and we tried everything to make him come home, but he just wouldn't listen to us. I think my wife died of a broken heart, so to speak. Oh, how she loves him. I mean, we thought that we did our best raising him, and we raised him with goals, morals, you know, Mr. Saxx said, as he wept a bit. Then I find out that he's living in Shelby, and the reason why was because he had gotten into some trouble and lots of fights, and one accident, almost cost him his life. I think that's the only reason why he let me back into his life. I just want you to know that I am determined to get all the answers and fill in all the holes. I love my son, but I do love Ailese like she's my own, but Andrew's wrong, dead wrong. I just can't believe that he would stoop to something like this." "Hey, please don't blame yourself for this. You had nothing to do with his decisions." Mr. Saxx shook his head, stood up, and shook Mikell's hand. He assured Mikell that everything was going to go back to normal really soon.

Mikell kept thinking about Ailese. She was all he would think about, as were their children. Thanks to D'Andra keeping their minds off of their mom for the time being, he wouldn't know what he would have done without D'Andra, Alonda, his mom, and dad. All the family just came closer together because they wanted to protect the kids, even though they were old enough to understand. Mikell wasn't ready to tell them there was a possibility that they would never see their mom again. He told them that he had to be away for a while longer, to look for their mother, and the kids understood. Mikell promised the kids he would check in periodically.

Mikell prayed and prayed that he would come home with his wife and the mother of his kids, and he hoped he didn't have to tell anyone bad news.

Mikell cried sometimes just looking at her picture because he missed her so much. He had lost his best friend, and his heart was empty. She was his backbone and his best friend in the whole world. Looking at her picture, he cried even more. He needed her so much, he needed her alive and well. If Mikell didn't have Ailese, he felt that he didn't have anything. He loved her that deeply. He wiped his tears and went to sleep.

After breakfast, the guys headed on their way. This time, Mikell did most of the driving as he followed Mr. Saxx. When Mr. Saxx called Mikell's cell to let him know that they were an hour away, he started to get very anxious and prayed the whole time, asking God to watch over his wife and saying that he needed her to be okay. The guys stopped for a few minutes to stretch their legs and went on their way. Time was ticking. "I have some bad news, Mikell. I'm sorry, but I am short one guy. He had a family emergency to deal with, so I am going to need a volunteer to go in with me." "Well, I am in," Mikell said. He wasn't scared of Andrew or anyone for that matter. He was willing to risk his life for the woman that he loved. "Are you sure?" Mikell shook his head, yes.

"Mikell I need you to suit up. Come with me." Mikell followed Jacob.

Jacob handed him all the gear that he needed, down to a bulletproof vest.

"I want you to stay behind me at all times, bro. I don't know what we're dealing with here, as in how many guys we have to fight to get in there. So I want you to make sure you're good. Remember when you helped me with some of my training?" "Yes, yes, I do remember it like it was yesterday. Why?" "Well, you need to be in the "take no bull from anyone mode. You need to be in cop mode, SWAT mode on blast, bro. Can you do that?" "Yes, I can. I am not afraid at all. I have to do what I have to do." They went over everything more than once, and when everyone agreed that they were ready, they were off!

"Mikell, bro, please be careful. I wish we all could gear up for this son of a bitch. Bring that son of a bitch to me. I know he doesn't want a piece of me." "Allen, I hear you, man. I do. I won't let you guys down." Mr. Saxx would be the first to show up at the cabin, and besides, he had a key. Mikell, Jacob, and the other men were waiting in a secluded place not too far from the cabin. They could all hear what was going on. Mr. Saxx was wired. No one, not even Andrew, would know that he was wired. It was time to take this monster down. Andrew couldn't lie to anyone if he tried because they were going to have all the evidence that they needed to put him where he belonged.

Ailese stared at the calendar. She knew that today was a special day, she just couldn't put her finger on it, and besides, she hadn't looked at a calendar in forever. Finally, she remembered, and her eyes filled up with tears. It was Karen's wedding day. She had saved the date and prepared for this day way before she took her vacation. Karen and Ailese had become very close before she left, and Karen raved how important it was to her to have Ailese at her wedding. She was going to miss her close friend's wedding day. She had let her down. That was something that Ailese hardly ever did. If Ailese was invited to an affair, she would be there with bells on, so to speak.

She began playing in her head what she would say to Karen- that's if she were to ever get out of this place, get away from Andrew. Would Karen really believe that she was kidnapped by her best friend and held captive?

A knock on the door interrupted her thoughts. "It's me, Andrew, Mr. Saxx said as he turned the key in the door. I need to talk to you, my son. Are you here?" Ailese didn't know what to do. It sounded like her boss, but as she started to walk to the door, Andrew grabbed her so fast and motioned for her to go upstairs and not say a word. She knew something was wrong. Judging by the look on Andrew's face, he just stood there and said nothing. "I told you I'm fine. Now why are you here? What is it, father?" "I need to speak to you, and I know that you're lying to me. Now, I want the truth. Why did you just leave like that, Andrew? I have been worried sick about you." Andrew was silent for a few seconds, his dad waited patiently for him to give him an answer.

"Look, I am my own person, and don't treat me like a child either. I said I am fine, old man. Now go and never come back!" he yelled, but his father wasn't backing down. "Why are you pushing me away? Are you forgetting about what we talked about?" His son said nothing. He wanted to be left alone.

"Get out!" he screamed. "No, my son, listen to me! You went on vacation, and you never showed up to work, never called. He began to cough. I need some water. Could your father please have some water? Andrew went into the fridge to get a bottle of water and gave it to his dad. Sit down and let's talk. Please sit down. I missed you. Andrew decided to sit down. Maybe after answering all of his questions, he will leave soon.

Son, are you okay? I am worried you wouldn't just leave your father in the dark like you did, so what's going on, huh?

I had to move a lot of meetings around to be here, so time is money, is time, so spill it!

Andrew was not going to tell his father the real truth- that he kidnapped Ailese and was holding her captive in this very house! He had to come up with a lie that his father couldn't see right through; that was going to be hard.

"I want to know why you never came back, my son. I am waiting for my answer, and it had better be good."

Ailese was careful that she didn't move at all. She barely took a breath, so she laid there on the bed until it was safe for her to come down the stairs.

She eventually fell asleep. She dreamt about Mikell and the kids. She even smiled in her sleep. The dreams felt so real. She dreamed about their wedding when they renewed their vowels no too long ago. She dreamt about their last family vacation, about having Sunday, their special day, about church, her mom, dad, the babies, and her sister. She was at peace for now.

"Dad, I told you I just needed some time alone. I didn't need to tell you or anyone else for that matter. I was doing what I had to do. Is it a crime to want some time alone?" At this point, Jacob and Mikell and Jacob's men were still waiting for a clue that he had Ailese in this cabin, but there was no indication that she was there with him. They didn't want to mess up anything that would put her in more danger or set Andrew off. They came too far for that to happen.

"I never said that you had to answer to me, my son. I am simply saying that you need to keep me informed. You are a very important piece of this company. You have demands that you need to meet. It doesn't look good when you have to lie to your clients and your staff when they ask you where one of your employee is, -son, -an important one at that." Andrew just shook his head.

SHELBY LIES

"I am sorry your precious reputation was ruined by me, he said in a sarcastic voice. I am sorry. What else do you want me to say, huh?" "I want you to mean it when you apologize to me! Andrew shook his head again at his father.

Andrew, you need to come back home and get it together. Get you together. There's work to be done." A knock at the door stopped his father from finishing his scolding of Andrew. Andrew quickly went to the door. He knew that it wasn't his men that watched the property. He had sent them all away. Who could it be? He looked out of the window and saw Officer Brown standing there. Andrew quickly went outside to see what the hell he wanted. He made it clear to him to never set foot on his property ever, so what was he doing there?

"Dad, give me a minute. I will be right back." "Fine, son." "What the hell are you doing here? What do you want, man? My father is here. It's not a good time at all. What is it? Did you not hear me when I told you to never come back here? I don't trust you! Now, what do you want!" I want the rest of my money that's owed to me. Oh, don't think I forgot man. Remember you told me I would get an extra ten thousand dollars if I did that one favor for you, which I did, so where is it?"

"Does it look like I have that kind of money on me? No, see you later, man, and if that's what it takes for you to stop coming around here, it will be in your account in the morning. Now leave, go!" Officer Brown walked away, giving him a look that said he had better give him his money or else.

"Who was that at the door, son?" "No one, father." "Don't you no one me. Who was that?" "A friend. He is gone now." Mr. Saxx knew that the guys were still waiting to move in, but there was still no sign of Ailese, so he knew that he had to go to Plan B. It needed to be put into motion now.

When she woke up, Ailese decided to take a shower, but she remembered that her boss was there, and she didn't have confirmation that she was able to come out of the room, so she didn't move. She tiptoed to the bathroom. She needed to use the restroom. She washed up, and tied her hair up, and went to the vanity mirror. She stared at herself in the mirror. She was beginning to get her color back, and she was really beginning to look like herself again. She dropped her makeup bag and it startled Andrew, she knew he would be angry because he told her to be quiet, but was there going to be hell to pay for making a noise?

"What was that?" "Nothing probably ... something falling, it's nothing, father."

Mr. Saxx started to head to the stairs until Andrew talked him out of it and told him that he would see what it was and will be right back. He found Ailese sitting on the bed. She looked up at him. He was angry with her. He whispered for her to be quiet. While Andrew was upstairs, Mr. Saxx was listening to Jacob in his wire. He was telling him that they needed to move in soon, and Jacob needed him to get Andrew to tell him where Ailese was, and that he needed him to bring up Ailese in a casual conversation just to see what Andrew would say to his father.

"I told you dad, something fell in the shower. It always happens. I think this cabin is haunted." Andrew laughed, and his father just shook his head. Mr. Saxx knew what he had to do, and he had to do it now. There were people counting on him. "Son, your mom and I miss you a lot. Your mom sends her love and was hoping that you would come home and spend some time with us. How does that sound?" Andrew never admitted to anyone that he had a soft spot, a special place in his heart for his mother. He would move the earth for her. "Dad, tell Mom I love her and that I promise I will come home soon to visit her, okay?"

"So, tell me son, did you have fun on your trip?" "Yes, Andrew said. He cleared his throat. It was, you know, exciting." "Didn't my Ailese go with you? I'm still waiting for those pictures she promised me. I guess she's still on her own vacation. She called me and asked if it would be okay if she took another few weeks off. I granted her that request. She deserves it." As Andrew played along with this, he thought to himself, how could she have called her boss, her only privilege was to call her family. "Yes, I know she sent me an e-mail, and some pictures look like she was having lots of fun with her family."

Mr. Saxx was shocked at how Andrew just lied to him and was good at it.

"No, I think that she went with her sister, right?" Andrew didn't know what to say. He just shook his head and changed the conversation. "Why were you bringing up Ailese?" "You know how close we are, and I just miss her around the office, that's all." "Oh, I see." Andrew felt his heart drop in the pit of his stomach when Ailese's name came up. Little did he know that his father was the one who was more than two steps ahead of him.

Ailese was thinking to herself that she should have run downstairs and told her boss that his son was holding her against her will. Would he have believed her? Would he have saved her? She contemplated back and forth. She didn't know what she wanted to do. She knew that Andrew wouldn't hesitate to "deal" with her no matter what. He didn't care if his father was there; she had better not cross that line, but should she? She decided not to. Was she crazy? Crazy not to take advantage of her boss being right down the stairs? This was her chance, and she knew that she will regret it later. She had better not cross that line, and besides, she was lucky that she was still alive! Andrew had spared her life. Should she be grateful or was it a curse? Did he have more plans up his sleeve? She hoped that he didn't. She hoped that he was done hurting her physically, emotionally, and mentally. Ailese just prayed that God would keep her safe; he's kept her safe for this long.

As Andrew and his father talked and talked some more, Andrew still did not admit that Ailese was there in the cabin; time was running out. "I need to use the restroom. I will be right back." When his father began to head upstairs, Andrew asked him to use the restroom downstairs. His father questioned him. He asked him why he didn't want him to use the restroom upstairs. "You're not acting like yourself. When I come back from the bathroom, you better be ready to tell me what the hell's going on! Do you hear me, son?" Andrew didn't answer his father; he just gave him a stone-cold look.

"So what's going on? I didn't think that this bastard would take this long to confess that he has your wife. This is crazy. I think we may have to go with Plan C. I can't remember the last time I had to go with a Plan C. This guy's in denial, big time. I'm sorry, bro. I don't mean to be mean, but he has some serious issues."

"No, let's just give Mr. Saxx the benefit of the doubt, okay, bro?"

"If you say so."

"I think he's almost gott 'em. I can feel it." "Mikell, just be prepared mentally, physically, and emotionally. Can you do that?"

"Of course I can. I am ready and focused, bro. I am. I can't wait to see the look on this loser's face when he sees me, and sees us. I want to kill 'em is what I want to do! But I want this sick bastard to pay for what he did to my family and my wife. He messed with the wrong person, the wrong family," Mikell said as he checked his gear. Jacob and Mikell sipped coffee as they waited patiently for that one signal that they needed to take on Andrew and end this nightmare.

Ailese still didn't move from her bed. Now she could really hear their conversation because Andrew was infuriated with his father. He wanted an answer; he wasn't getting anywhere with Andrew. He just kept on telling his father to leave and to butt out of his life, but he wasn't backing down. He promised before going in there that he would do everything he could do to get his son to confess—and he was giving his all and then some, but he still wasn't getting anywhere. He knew that Ailese was somewhere in that cabin. He just knew it, but where was she? Did he get rid of her? Did he have her hidden somewhere else? These were the things that he needed to know. He felt responsible. He felt that he owed this to Ailese and her family.
"Oh, so you want to play that game, huh? Andrew, it's your father, or did you forget that? I am not leaving here until you tell me what the hell's going on here. Sit down! You have been acting weird since the minute I got here. I feel like you are hiding something, something that you choose not to tell me!"
Andrew pushed past his father and ran upstairs. His father followed him and he tried to keep up with him. When Andrew made it to the room where Ailese was, he hurried up, closed the door, and motioned for her not to say a word. Andrew hurriedly put a chair under the knob of the door; his father began banging on the door. "Andrew, for the love of God, open this door now!"
Ailese and Andrew were already gone. They went down the ladder that was behind the house. Andrew was always

prepared. "Where are you taking me? You're hurting my arm." He didn't say a word. He went to the garage in the back of the house and put her in the car. He had gone too far, and now it was her turn to go too far with him. You better stop this freaking car right now or else, you son of a bitch," she said in a very firm voice that took everything she had in her to say that to him, being that she had been so calm. Not anymore—she had enough! Enough of the demands. Enough of him hurting her in every way possible! But now she was fighting for her life once again.

It was confirmed to the guys that Andrew had escaped and that they needed to keep an eye out for him. They were on the move- something Andrew didn't even know! Jacob's men were told not to approach Andrew if he had Ailese because if they did, he knew for a fact and he bet his life on it that would set Andrew off and he would kill her where she stood, so they stood down and told Jacob that Andrew was in a car and they needed to be right behind him. His men were not far as well; they were determined to get this guy just like everyone else was. Andrew didn't even notice that they were following him. He was driving so erratically and wasn't paying any attention. He was only concerned with getting far, far away from his father, from the cabin. His father was asking way too many questions!

Andrew had become a whole different person; he wouldn't stop, and he was driving more and more witlessly. Luckily, there wasn't a car in sight, at least not now. "I said pull over, you bastard! Pull over," she demanded. Andrew had a smirk on his face, like he was enjoying being the asshole that he was.

"You want me to pull over, huh? Hell no, you spoiled-ass bitch! You're never gonna learn, huh? No one tells me what to do! You want to get out? Then I suggest you jump out, ha!" He laughed and laughed like some madman! I'm in control, damn it. What's it gonna take for you to understand that? I own your ass. Do you hear me?" Andrew gave Ailese a quick look and focused back on the road. She tried to take over the wheel, but every time she would try to steer the wheel the other way, Andrew would push her hands off the steering wheel. "You stupid-ass bastard, let me out! You no-good son of a bitch, let me out now! I've had enough. You hear me. You do not own me!"

Andrew was slowing the vehicle down. She had thought that he was going to pull over, but she was wrong! He made sure that the childproof locks were enforced so that Ailese couldn't get out of the car.

"Guys, he's not pulling over. We cannot afford to lose him. I don't care if we drive all night. We need to do this. Is everyone with me?" All the men agreed and agreed to stick with the plan unless Jacob changed them. This punk is driving crazier and crazier. He's going faster and faster. He doesn't care if he hits someone or, worse, kills someone. We're staying on his tail. He thinks that he's got this in the bag, but if only he knew. Stay on him, guys. Hopefully, we won't be doing this all day and night. Let's hope that he stops somewhere, maybe."

"He's a deranged son of a ..." Mikell paused. He felt like they were in a -movie, the scene where they're chasing the bad guys and the cars are going super fast!

This was a real-life movie. They were chasing Andrew and trying to get Ailese back where she belonged.

"You're crazy! Get the hell away from me!" Ailese began to scream as she pulled on the door handle, but she couldn't get out. Andrew had gotten out of his seat belt. He had grabbed her arm tightly. "I love you. I love you, goddamn it. What do I have to do to make you see that, huh?"

"Let go of me, and you don't love me. You want to own me. You've never loved me. You are a sick, sick bastard! Let me go!" Andrew grabbed Ailese, pulled her close to him, and pressed his lips against hers. She pushed him away, but Andrew, as always, kept coming back over and over again.

"Get off of me, she mumbled as his lips pressed against hers. Get off, you sick, son of a bitch!" Ailese pushed Andrew so hard that he hit his head up against the window, he let out a smirk. Big mistake.

Andrew became so furious that his eyes became huge, and horns were growing on his head. He grabbed her by her hair and pulled her to where he was while she was kicking, screaming, and yelling for help. During all this, Andrew was still driving like a madman! Ailese didn't want to die, not like this, not in the hands of Andrew. She knew that she had to find a way to make Andrew stop driving and pull over! She was so scared that if he didn't stop this car, her life will end, and she pleaded and pleaded with him, but he didn't care.

Andrew wouldn't let her go. He wouldn't stop the car. He wouldn't stop driving like a lunatic. He had almost hit a car. Luckily, the car swerved the other way. He kept telling her that he loved her and that they were made for each other, and carried on about spending his life with her. She couldn't believe her ears; he was really telling her this? At this time, really? Ailese was trying to convince him to stop the car, but he just wouldn't.

"Tell me that you love me! Tell me that you've always loved me!"

No, never, please stop this car! You're going to kill someone or, worse, us! Please, I am begging you, stop it!" Andrew just looked at her and laughed.

"Aahhhh!" Andrew let out a yell. Ailese had punched him in the eye as hard as she could. He was going to stop this damn car if it killed her, and that made the car slow down. She was surprised that she punched him in the eye so hard. He had become incoherent; this was her chance to grab the wheel and pull over, so she did as Andrew moaned, holding his eye. "You are going to pay for this!" he yelled. Ailese didn't say a word; she just kept her hand on the steering wheel. She made no eye contact. Andrew was like Dr. Jekyll and Mr. Hyde; there was no telling what he would try and do to her now, but Ailese wasn't going to give up. She was going to fight until the end. She wanted to go home to her family, and that's what she was going to do.

When Andrew became more focused, he made sure that Ailese couldn't get away from him. He pushed her so hard that her hands were no longer on the steering wheel. Her head hit the window so hard, that her head began to pound, she was sure her head was bleeding. He was going to make sure she didn't cross that line again! He was not having that at all! He wasn't going to let her ruin his plans for her, and boy did he have plans for her, and being that he decided to let her live, he felt that she should be thanking him for letting her live and not taking her life. "I let yo ass live, and this is the thanks that I get from you," he said in a sarcastic voice, wiping his eyes with the back of his hands and making sure his eyes were still in their sockets. He took out his gun and ordered her to get in the backseat, or he will pull that trigger, and she could forget about him sparing her life. He told her that he had changed his mind, which frightened her.

"Are you ready to do this, guys? I need one of you to ram into this fool's car on three. We need to end this now! I have a gut feeling that something's going down in there, I need you guys to be ready. Jacob said. One, two, three, go!"

The SUV swerved into Andrew's car. "What the—who the hell is this? What goons are brave enough to ram into me? I'll give them something. Oh, you wanna play, huh? Let's play. Little did he know he was playing with the "big guys."

As he met Ailese's face with the gun, he told her to fasten her seatbelt.

One more time, you've got one more time, he said, pressing the gun to her face and giving her the evil eyes. I dare you to try anything! The SUV rammed into Andrew again. Andrew was infuriated with this person ramming into his car, not knowing who this person was. Ailese even wondered who was hitting Andrew's car. She decided to stay in her seatbelt and prayed that whoever it was, they would save her from this delusional psycho!

You're not going anywhere if I have anything to do with it." Andrew swerved into the SUV even harder. He rolled down his window to see who it was, but the windows were tinted. All of a sudden, another SUV ran into Andrew. He almost lost control of the car. Ailese was holding on for dear life. Her body shifted in every way. Her head hit the window a few times. Andrew was determined to get these punks off his tail. "Do you know who these punks are? He asked Ailese. She shook her head, no. You're lying. Who are they? He put the gun to her face. She didn't back down. She stood her ground; fear was not an option for her.

I'll give you something to remember me by," Andrew said as he swerved once more into the SUV, hitting it really hard, with all his might, and the SUV skidded off the road. "Stand down. Stand down. Are you guys okay? The men told Jacob that they were okay. Mikell, are you ready? It's our turn to give this punk a taste of his own medicine." "Yeah, I have been ready. Buckle up tight, bro!" When Jacob caught up to Andrew, he was ready. He was more than ready. Andrew didn't know who he was dealing with. He was going to regret he ever coming in contact with Jacob. "Ughhh! Take that,

SHELBY LIES

Jacob said, and as he rammed into Andrew, he was fortunate that there were no other cars on the road when Andrew's car hydroplaned, he had lost control. Ailese screamed. She knew that they were in trouble when he couldn't stop the car. She knew her life was over. She saw her life flash before her eyes! When the car had finally stopped, Andrew tried to gain composure, and when he did, he stopped the car and pulled over. His head was pounding so much that he didn't realize that Jacob and Mikell were walking toward his car. They had their gear and were ready for whatever came their way.

"Open up. This is Chief Kenison. You are under arrest for kidnapping. Let me see your hands, and get out of the car slowly! Do you understand these demands? At first, Andrew didn't move. He was thinking about making a run for it, but the car wouldn't start. I am going to count to three. If you do not comply, you leave me no choice, to use this gun! One, two," before Jacob got to three, Andrew showed him his hands. He thought that he was going to get away with all the chaos he caused, but he was wrong. "Who the hell are you? Some rent-a-cop?" "Do you have any weapons on you?" Before Andrew could answer that question, Ailese began screaming. "Help me, please! I'm stuck! Please help me!" Mikell heard her voice and ran over to her, but the door was locked. He motioned for her to unlock the door, but she couldn't. Andrew still had the safety locks on, and he never took them off. Jacob had already had Andrew in handcuffs, and he wasn't going anywhere. "Come on, baby. I got you, baby, I got you." Mikell told Ailese not to move, that he would be right back. He had some unfinished business to take care of. "Please don't leave me!" She clinched on to him so tightly that he could see the terror in her eyes that she was so scared. "Baby, I will be right back. It's okay. He is not going to hurt you anymore. I just need you to stay right here for just a sec. Okay, baby, can you do that for me?"

When Andrew saw Mikell, he was in disbelieve. He had no idea that he was the second master mind; Jacob was the first.

Mikell walked slowly and walked around Andrew, and all of a sudden he punched him in the face as hard as he could. He deserved it. Andrew let out a noise and then laughed. He thought it was funny. "Is that all you got?"

Mikell punched him again, this time in his stomach. He didn't stop. It felt good, and since he couldn't kill him, Mikell gave him his best shots.

"I hope you burn in hell, you sick son of a bitch, he said as he punched Andrew one last time. You should have known not to mess with my family!"

Andrew began to shake uncontrollably. What was wrong with him? His nose started to bleed, and all of a sudden he passed out and fell to the ground! Was he faking? Should they just leave him there? "He has a weak pulse. I need to call it in, Jacob said. It doesn't look good." "Is he dead?" Ailese asked. He didn't deserve to live in her opinion he put her through so much heartache. "I hope not baby. I hope he is still alive. He needs to be put away for life."

"Hey, bro the ambulance are on the way, and I am sure the police is on their way too. Don't forget, we need to have our stories straight. Remember what we talked about, right?" "Yes, I do. I won't let you down, man. I won't. I owe you my life." Mikell sobbed as he hugged his angel. That's how he saw Jacob. They were really bonded for life.

"Are you okay?" Ailese shook her head no to Jacob. Her body was shaking like a leaf on a tree. She was so terrified, but both Jacob and Mikell reassured her that she was out of danger and it was over. "I need you to go to the hospital, baby. You need to get checked out. I will be right there with you, okay?" She shook her head. "I can't stand here with him here. Please, I want to get away from here, please. He's going to wake up and hurt me again! Please, she began to cry. She couldn't stop crying or shaking. Please Mikell." She begged him to take her away from Andrew. She was afraid he was going to wake up and rape her again, or put his gun to her face and maybe this time pull the trigger. "Okay, baby, come with me. We're going to wait in the truck, okay?" Ailese followed her husband. He put her in the truck and rested her head on his lap. He didn't say much. He just stroked her hair and face. He did not want to think about what Andrew had done to his wife, and what he had put her through. There was no doubt that Andrew had made his wife's life hell on earth! It killed him when he thought about it, and he knew when she was better and willing and able to talk about it, he would have to hear it no matter what. It was going to ruin him, but right now he had to be strong for her.

The next morning, Ailese found herself in the hospital. Her head was pounding once again. She looked around panicked for a minute until she saw Mikell on the other side of the room asleep in the chair. There was no Andrew in sight. She wasn't chained to the bed. She was relieved to see her husband in the chair. It was the most beautiful thing she had seen in a long time. She cherished this moment and would never forget it.

"Hi, beautiful. How are you feeling, baby?" "My head ... hurts ... But I'll be fine. I have some tough skin under this hideous night gown." They both smiled. "Baby, I am so happy to have you back. I am the happiest man alive," Mikell whispered as he walked over to his true love and gave her a kiss gently on her forehead. He kissed her gently on her face and told her how much he loved her. He hated that he had to tell her that an officer would be there shortly to ask her some questions, but Mikell wasn't going to let the officer take advantage of Ailese, and besides, the doctor told Mikell that she needed to rest and to avoid too much stress. "Baby, in a few minutes, a police officer will be here. He needs to ask you some questions. Okay. I will be right here." "Okay," she said as she coughed. Her throat was very dry. "Let me get you some water. I will be right back. The water machine is right outside this door. There you go." Mikell put a straw in her cup and held it up to her mouth until she was finished. There was a knock on the door.

"Hello, I am Officer Dewitt. I do apologize for interrupting your rest, but I am here to close this case regarding Mr. Andrew Mc Gee II. I will not keep you from your rest, Mrs. LaShae, right?" "Yes," she said as she sat up as best she could. "Now you have known Mr. Mc Gee for a few years, correct? Ailese cleared her throat before speaking. She hated hearing his name, but she knew that the officer was only doing his job. We have been told that he kidnapped you against your will while on vacation, correct? Ailese shook her head. I have to ask you this. Is it true that Andrew McGee's real name is Rico? Um, sorry, give me a minute. Oh, here it is, Rico. Well I don't have a last name, but I am told that he was someone from your past? Ailese shook her head, yes.

He was out to get revenge on something that happened a long, long time ago. Is that right?" "Yes, that's right. Is that all you need, sir? My head is pounding. Can we take this up later?" "Okay, but I just needed to ask you a very important question. You had no indication that he was this Rico character at all?" "No, because he changed everything about him, down to his name. We had no idea. No idea that he would do this to me."

"Wake up, wake up, baby, it's me, Mikell. We need to talk about Andrew. Mikell hesitated on bringing his name up, but she had to hear this. I don't know if you remember this, but remember when Andrew passed out? "Yes, I am still trying to get that out of my head, among other things." "I just got off the phone with Jacob, and he told me that Andrew is in a coma. It doesn't look good. His sickness has gotten the best of him. I know that you don't care about that crazy bastard, but I just thought that you should know. They don't think that he'll ever wake up from his coma." Ailese didn't say much, and he was right- she didn't care about what happened to Andrew; she knew it was wrong to feel this way, but she had every right to feel the way she was feeling.

Jacob had visited Ailese a few times while she was in the hospital. They had become really close. He told her stories about his life, and how he became an officer, and how much Mikell meant to him and how honored he was to help her family find her. The kids were happy to hear that their mom was okay and would be home soon when she was better; the whole family was happy. They wanted to meet Jacob. He was their angel. He was responsible for saving her life. They all were so grateful to him.

When Jacob had got word that Andrew's goons were caught and booked, he was happy; everyone was happy. Officer Brown ended up turning himself in and spilling all his guts and then some. They were going to spend the rest of their natural lives in jail. This pleased Ailese as well. Ell and Melinda were going to pay for what they did to her while she was held against her will. They both befriended her, pretending to be her friend, but she had the last laugh in the end. She didn't care if she never saw Elle again. She put so much trust and faith in Ell, only to discover she was one deceptive bitch!

Maybe she was unhappy with herself and unhappy with her life; maybe these were the reasons why she betrayed Ailese.

"I just wanted to tell you how proud I am of you. You're doing good, baby, given that you've been through so much. I thought that I lost you for good. I can't live without you. I'm so, so, so sorry, baby. I should have put two and two together sooner, when you weren't at the airport. That wasn't like you, but I thought that you mixed up the dates, baby. Please forgive me."

"I don't blame you for any of this. Please know that, Mikell. No one had anything to do with what happened but Andrew, okay? Don't forget that. I am just glad that I am alive. I will be forever grateful for you, for Jacob, Chris, and my brother. You all were determined to find me, and you did, and that is all that matters." Tears rolled down her face, Mikell wiped them off her face and held her until they both went to sleep.

"So now that's all settled. I will see you guys in a bit." Allen and Chris were on their way to the hospital to see Ailese. They couldn't wait to see her; they had missed her so much. "Baby, could you help me into the restroom? I'm getting a massive cramp in my leg." Mikell helped her to the restroom. "Slowly, okay, you need to go slow. Do you want me to stay in here with you?"

"Could you please, just in case my legs give out." When Mikell focused on her wrists, he could see that there were scars on both her wrists; he decided not to mention it or ask Ailese what happened, not just yet. She was under so much stress, and she didn't need any more. "Okay, I am done. Could you please help me up?"

"Sure, baby, I'll help you back into bed. Do you need any more water, baby?"

"Actually, I do."

SHELBY LIES

"Hello, we're here, sis. Where are you?"

"We will be right there, guys."

"Oh my God, I missed you so much." Allen gave his sister a hug. He wanted to hug her so tight, but he knew that she was in some pain. He was so happy to see her all in one piece. He thanked God that he had her back.

"How are you feeling?" Chris asked as he hugged her as well. "I can say that I hope I get better soon. I need my strength so I can go home to my babies and my nieces. How are they doing?"

"They're growing and doing well."

Allen didn't want to leave his sister's side. He laid down with her in her bed. He told her how much he loved her and how happy he was that she was safe and that they could bring her home soon, back to Shelby.

She took a deep breath before speaking. "I know that this has been a scary, scary time for our family. I thank God every day. I thank him every day for watching over me, and my family. I love all of you. It goes to show how we came together as one. I really do thank all of you. You didn't give up. You kept your faith, and if it weren't for that, I may not be here, even though I'd rather have my own bed." Everyone smiled at her. Hearing her voice was a blessing.

"Today's the big day, baby. We get to take you home. Are you feeling good about that?"

"Yes, I am. I am indeed." After the doctor examined Ailese and discharged her, Jacob, Allen, and Chris waited outside for her. They had flowers, balloons, and gifts waiting for her. As Mikell wheeled Ailese out of her room, the nurse stopped him. She said that someone left him a message, and it was urgent. She handed him the message. The message was from Officer Dewitt. When he read it, he couldn't believe his eyes. Should he tell Ailese about Andrew? Did she really want to know this? Where should he start?

"Baby, what's wrong? You look like you've seen a ghost or something. Baby, what's wrong?"

"Um, we'll talk about it later, okay? We need to get you home. we don't want to miss our plane, baby."

"Mikell, tell me what's wrong. You're scaring me. Please tell me, please!"

"Baby, you don't need the stress."

Ailese interrupted him. "Let me see the note, please. I know that you're looking after my best interests, but I need to know." She took the note from Mikell and read it. She went cold. Her heart went cold. She didn't have words to say. Andrew was dead!

He couldn't hurt her anymore. He was out of her life forever, but why didn't she shed a tear for him? She didn't want hatred in her heart, but in due time, one day, her heart will heal and all her hatred for him will someday disappear.

Andrew's sickness got the best of him; he was sick inside and out.

"Let's go home, Mikell. The guys are waiting for us." Mikell didn't ask her how she felt about Andrew; he decided not to. He knew that when she was ready to talk about Andrew and what happened when he kidnapped her, Mikell would be all ears. He knew that when that day came, he had to be really strong. He knew that it was going to be a long, long road ahead. Nothing will ever be the same. He knew that it would take some time for Ailese to get back to who she used to be, but he could still see her heart; it was still huge. He could still see that strong, beautiful woman that he would always love and move heaven and earth for.

Ailese slept most of the time on the plane because the doctor had given her some medications that made her sleepy and groggy. "I love you so much," Mikell whispered as he kissed her softly on the cheek. "I don't know what I would do without you." He closed his eyes and thought about the first time that he saw her smile. She was so beautiful then, and she is even more beautiful now. He just watched her sleep the whole time.

He would always remember Andrew took a lot from her, but she would get it all back and more in due time. "I got you covered, baby. Here you are." He had given her some ice water and helped her sit up so she could drink it. She took a few long sips, handed it back to Mikell, and looked at him. "I'm so sorry," she sobbed. "Sorry for what, baby?"

"For everything I put everyone through, I'm so sorry."

"Baby. Mikell touched her face. Please don't say that. You have nothing to apologize for. You hear me. Nothing. You understand?" Mikell kissed her on the cheek. Shh, don't cry. I'm here for you. It's going to be okay, baby. No one's going to hurt you anymore. You're safe now, baby. You're safe. I love you."

About the Author

Angela S. Moore is an author and mother, this is her first novel. She resides in California with her family. She enjoys writing, since it is very calming, so she writes every day. Her instructors gave her courage to finish what she started and that is what she is doing now.

Thanks to everyone who will go on the journey with her when you read her novel.